The FIRES *of* PRIDE

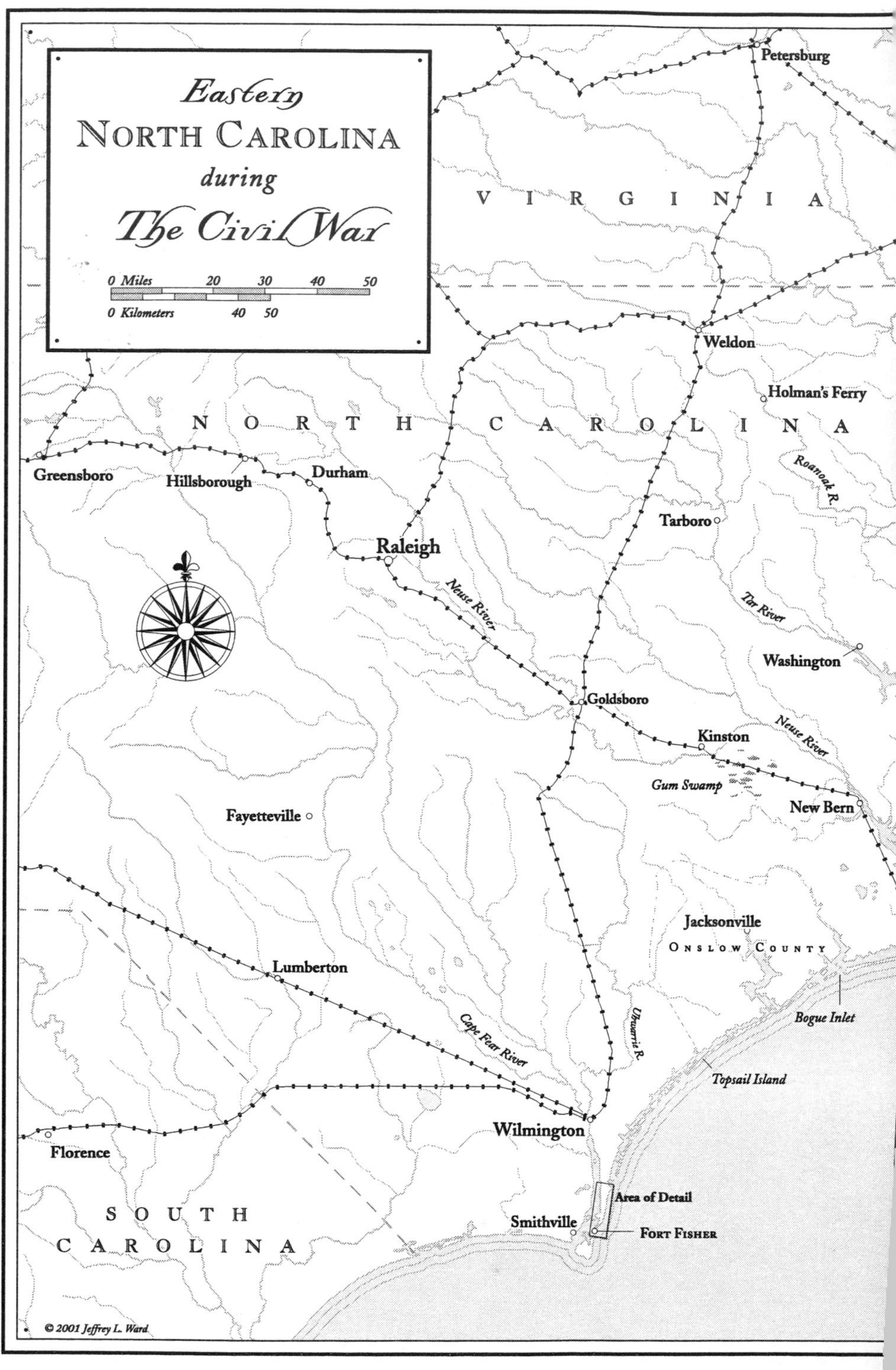
Eastern
NORTH CAROLINA
during
The Civil War
0 Miles 20 30 40 50
0 Kilometers 40 50
Petersburg
VIRGINIA
Weldon
Holman's Ferry
NORTH CAROLINA
Roanoak R.
Greensboro
Hillsborough
Durham
Tarboro
Raleigh
Neuse River
Tar River
Washington
Goldsboro
Kinston
Neuse River
Gum Swamp
New Bern
Fayetteville
Jacksonville
Onslow County
Lumberton
Bogue Inlet
Cape Fear River
Uwarrie R.
Topsail Island
Wilmington
Florence
Area of Detail
SOUTH
CAROLINA
Smithville
Fort Fisher
© 2001 Jeffrey L. Ward

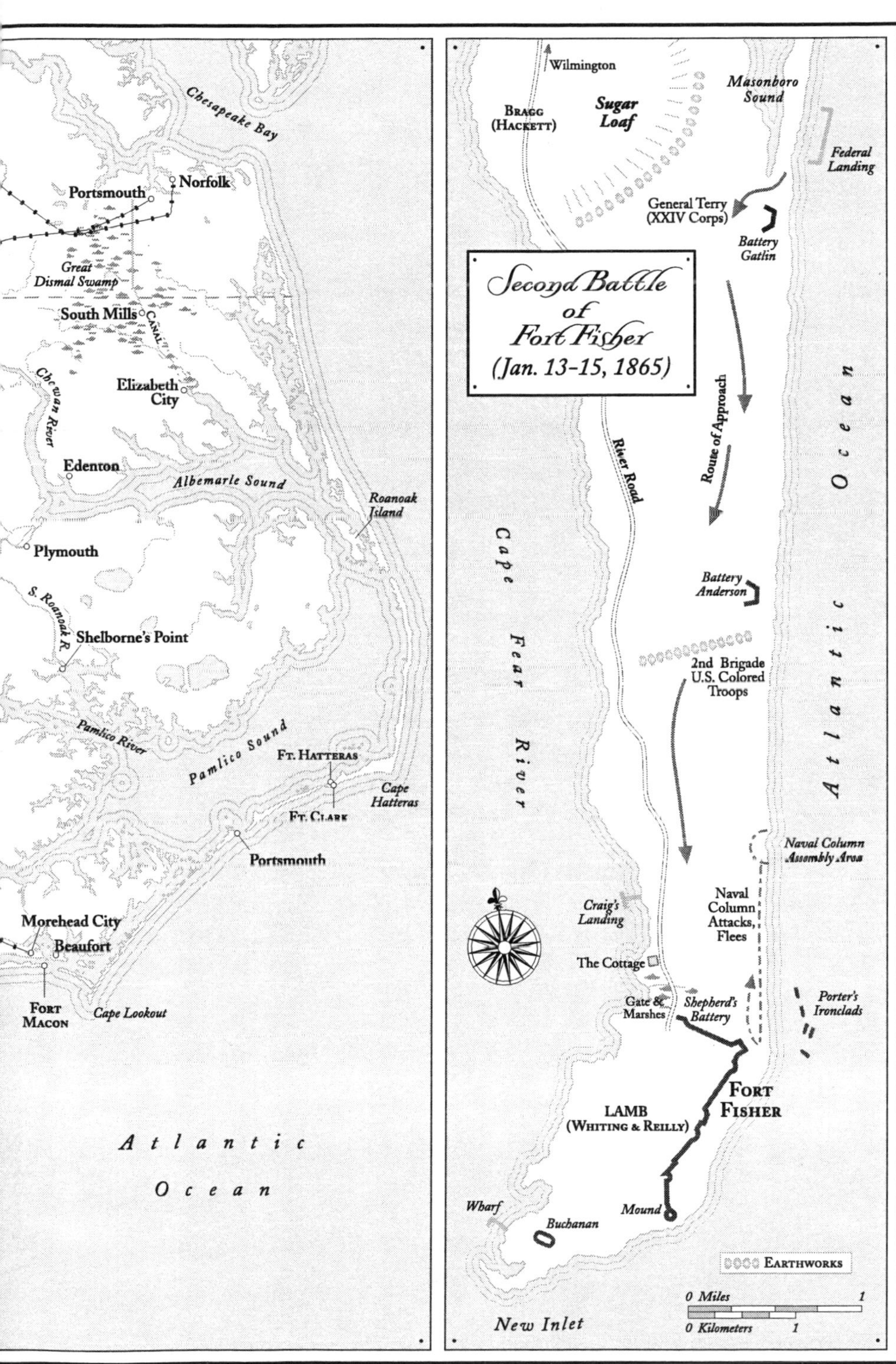

Chesapeake Bay
Portsmouth
Norfolk
Great Dismal Swamp
South Mills
Canal
Chowan River
Elizabeth City
Edenton
Albemarle Sound
Roanoak Island
Plymouth
S. Roanoak R.
Shelborne's Point
Pamlico River
Pamlico Sound
Ft. Hatteras
Ft. Clark
Cape Hatteras
Portsmouth
Morehead City
Beaufort
Fort Macon
Cape Lookout
Atlantic Ocean
Second Battle of Fort Fisher (Jan. 13–15, 1865)
Wilmington
Bragg (Hackett)
Sugar Loaf
Masonboro Sound
Federal Landing
General Terry (XXIV Corps)
Battery Gatlin
Route of Approach
River Road
Cape Fear River
Battery Anderson
2nd Brigade U.S. Colored Troops
Atlantic Ocean
Naval Column Assembly Area
Naval Column Attacks, Flees
Craig's Landing
The Cottage
Gate & Marshes
Shepherd's Battery
Porter's Ironclads
Fort Fisher
Lamb (Whiting & Reilly)
Wharf
Buchanan
Mound
Earthworks
0 Miles 1
0 Kilometers 1
New Inlet

Also by William R. Trotter

Fiction

Winter Fire
Honeysuckle
The Sands of Pride

Nonfiction

Life Begins at Forte: Stokowski as Musical Hobo (1942–1960)
Deadly Kin: A True Story of Mass Family Murder
Silk Flags and Cold Steel, The Civil War in North Carolina, volume 1
Bushwhackers!, The Civil War in North Carolina, volume 2
Ironclads and Columbiads, The Civil War in North Carolina, volume 3
A Frozen Hell: The Russo-Finnish War of 1939–1940
(Awarded the Finlandia Foundation Arts and Letters Prize)
Priest of Music: The Life of Dimitri Mitropoulos
Close Combat: Normandy Campaign
Close Combat: A Bridge Too Far

The FIRES *of* PRIDE

A Novel of the Civil War

WILLIAM R. TROTTER

CARROLL & GRAF PUBLISHERS
NEW YORK

The Fires of Pride
A Novel of the Civil War

Carroll & Graf Publishers
An Imprint of Avalon Publishing Group Inc.
245 West 17th Street
11th Floor
New York, NY 10011

First Carroll & Graf edition 2003
First Carroll & Graf trade paperback edition 2005

Library of Congress Cataloging-in-Publication Data is available.

ISBN: 0-7867-1448-4

9 8 7 6 5 4 3 2 1

Book design and flag illustration by Michael Walters
Printed in the United States of America
Distributed by Publishers Group West

How lov'd, how valu'd once, avails thee not;
To whom related or by whom begot.
A lump of Dust alone, remains of thee.
'Tis all thou art, and all the Proud shall be.

—From a tombstone in the graveyard
of St. James Episcopal Church,
Wilmington, North Carolina

Though I would take comfort against sorrow,
My heart is faint within me . . .
The harvest is past, the summer is ended.
And we are not saved.

—Jeremiah, 8:20

Contents

Synopsis of *The Sands of Pride*

North Carolina was the last Southern state to secede from the Union, and did so, very reluctantly, only on May 20, 1861—a full month after the fall of Fort Sumter.

The state was ill-prepared for war, but its long, rugged, easily defensible coastline made it an ideal location for privateers, who would dash out into the Atlantic, seize Northern merchant ships, and scamper back to safety behind the Outer Banks (which were pierced only by five inlets deep enough to admit seagoing ships). It was largely to end this pin-prick annoyance that the Union mounted the first amphibious operation of the war in August, 1861, under the capable leadership of General Ambrose Burnside (who displayed brilliance in this campaign that he would seldom equal again).

The Federal armada easily swept aside the feeble fortifications on the Outer Banks, overcame considerably stiffer but still ineffectual resistance on Roanoke Island, and captured by siege Fort Macon, which opened up to Union control the useful small ports of Morehead City and Beaufort—later developed into a major naval base.

To oppose Burnsides 149-gun armada, local Confederates could send forth nothing more formidable than a collection of hastily armed coastal craft collectively known as the Mosquito Fleet. This pathetically ill-suited gaggle of ships fought heroically in the one big naval engagement of Burnside's campaign—the Battle of Elizabeth City (February 2, 1862)—but was overwhelmed in less than twenty minutes.

After the capture of New Bern (March 14, 1862), Burnside's conquest of coastal North Carolina was complete—with one very critical exception.

The old colonial port of Wilmington was well protected; it lay far up the Cape Fear River and was screened by so many hastily emplaced batteries that Burnside did not dare attack it. By the summer of 1862, Wilmington had become one of the most important ports in the Confederacy, for it was ideally positioned to offer sanctuary to the increasing numbers of blockade-runners who dashed out of New Inlet on moonless nights and traded valuable Southern cotton for military supplies (primarily of British origin) which the South was unable to manufacture in large quantities . . . or at all.

By the start of 1863, Wilmington was experiencing a boom comparable only to San Francisco during the days of the Gold Rush. Scores of new ships entered the runner trade, for the profits of a single successful voyage could make a skipper rich for life. The U.S. Navy, of course, tried to blockade the Cape Fear coast, but not until the start of 1864 were there enough ships, and smart enough tactics, to make a dent in the runner traffic. Nine out of ten blockade-runners got through.

One reason they enjoyed safe passage into the sheltered waters of the river was the existence of Fort Fisher, a stupendous earthwork, built almost wholly out of sand and mounting thirty-eight big coast artillery pieces.

Astonishingly enough, the concept for the fort was the inspiration of a relatively junior officer, a Virginia native, Colonel William Lamb, who had never formally studied military engineering, but who had a brilliant eye for terrain and who was quick to capitalize on the fact that even the heaviest contemporary naval ordnance simply could not do significant damage to ramparts made of *sand.*

By July, 1863, Fort Fisher had assumed its final configuration: a "Sea Face" 800 yards long, and a "Land Face" 600 yards wide, shaped like an inverted "L." Its walls were 20 feet thick and up to 27 feet high, and the huge mounds ("traverses") between its gun batteries were honeycombed with magazines, bombproof shelters for the gun crews, and a very well equipped field hospital. Over a quarter-million cubic tons of sand were moved and shaped, mostly by hand, to construct this "Confederate Gibraltar." Blockade-runners had only to slip through the porous Federal patrol lines, steer for the surf, turn south, and by the time any pursuing Yankee warships were within range of them, they were protected by an umbrella of heavy shellfire from the fort.

The Fires of Pride picks up the story at the moment when the dreadful news of Lee's defeat at Gettysburg heralds the permanent decline of Confederate fortunes. But not the end of Richmond's defiance! As long as Fort Fisher remained unconquered, the Rebel armies would continue to receive large quantities of strategic metals, raw materials, ammunition, and weapons through the blockade.

That the North did not get around to attacking the fort until December, 1864, was and still is a mystery. By that time, Wilmington was the only significant port still in Confederate hands, and its strategic value was simply incalculable.

Major and Supporting Characters

Actual historical characters are marked with an asterisk (*). All others are made up by the author, although they may in fact be conflations of real historical persons with imaginative embellishments.

The Confederacy

Bragg, Braxton, General (*): Without question, the most despised and controversial Confederate commander. Bragg had strong abilities in the areas of logistics and organization, but proved a bafflingly inert field commander. He won just a single major battle, on the first day of the Chickamauga campaign, and then failed to follow it up with an aggressive pursuit of his broken opponent, Union general Rosecrans. As a result, the Confederacy lost Chattanooga—a position so naturally strong that a troop of Boy Scouts armed with slingshots could have held it, if properly led, in 48 hours. My account of Bragg's inexplicable behavior at Wilmington is largely accurate; my hypothesis that Bragg was a closet opium addict is speculative, but provides at least a plausible explanation for what would otherwise seem like almost treasonable negligence.

Branch, William, Flag Officer (equivalent to the modern rank of Rear Admiral): In the war's early days, Branch led the improvised Mosquito Fleet with great audacity, but after it was destroyed, he became an admiral-without-a-fleet, succumbing to ennui and frustration, as well as a deepening opium addiction (the real stuff, not laudanum tincture, which he obtained from blockade-runner captains), which rendered him an ineffectual leader of Wilmington's minuscule naval forces. He rallied at the end, however, and fought bravely in the defense of Fort Fisher.

Bright, Fitz-John: Overseer of Pine Haven plantation who became navigator/pilot of the blockade-runner *Banshee.*

Burgwyn, Harry, General (*): Zebulon Vance's executive officer in the Twenty-sixth North Carolina regiment, then its commander after Vance retired to run for Governor. Burgwyn was a strict disciplinarian who turned the 26th N.C. into a crack unit. He was killed on the first day of Gettysburg, after leading a heroic and essentially hopeless assault on McPherson's Ridge, during which four-fifths of the regiment were killed or wounded.

Conver, Ezekial Jeremiah Prosper-for-Me de Vonell, Corporal (*): Purportedly the smallest soldier in the Confederate Army (just over four feet tall), Corporal Conver had the heart of a lion and proved it during the battle of Fort Fisher. His mythical apotheosis in this tale is, of course, fictional, but entirely deserved; as Major Reilly

astutely observes, "Any battle this big deserves at least one good ghost!"
Hackett. Donald, General: One of the few North Carolina division commanders in Lee's army, a resourceful and well-liked commander and an expert tactician. He was called upon twice to redeem Confederate fortunes on the Carolina coast: once, when Lee permitted the first serious counterattack against the Federal enclaves, in conjunction with the first sortie of the *Hatteras*, and then again as the major strategic reserve for Fort Fisher. In the latter capacity, Hackett strained at the leash, but was never allowed to take significant action, due to the caution of Bragg.
Harper, Stepney: Father of Mary Harper Sloane, and the richest rice planter in South Carolina; owner and master of Limerick Plantation.
Fulton, John (*)**:** Bombastic, cheerfully bigoted editor of the *Wilmington Journal* and a zealous hardcore Rebel, Fulton's actual editorials furnished a historical armature for the chapter-headers in *The Sands of Pride*. Paper shortages forced the *Journal* to publish only sporadically during the last two years of the conflict, so for better or worse, the chapter-headers in this volume are a congeries of actual quotes, made-up but plausible extracts, and blends of the two.
Lamb, Daisy (*)**:** Wife of Col. William Lamb, originally from Rhode Island, but as staunch a Confederate as any lady of the time. She was a stunning beauty, and contemporary photos reveal a vivacious, darkly sexy woman who bears an uncanny resemblance to the great silent movie actress Theda Barra.
Lamb, William, Colonel (*)**:** A lawyer and journalist by training, Lamb was an innate genius as a military engineer; his brilliant design for Fort Fisher—part-Gibraltar, partly a gigantic bluff—kept Wilmington open as a haven for the blockade-runners until January, 1865.
Landau, Jacob: Bavarian Jewish immigrant and prominent Wilmington merchant, his mission in life (accomplished posthumously by his daughter) was to build the city's first Jewish house of worship. An ardent Confederate patriot, despite the enormous ambiguities of that stance, Jacob was one of the original three founders of the longest-lived and most successful blockade-running consortium, the Anglo-Confederate Trading Company, and part-owner of the first and most successful runner ship, the *Banshee*.
Landau, Largo: Jacob's free-spirited daughter, Largo saw the war as a means of liberating herself from the stifling existence society demanded of middle-class women during the mid-Victorian period. Her at-first scandalously open love affair with the dashing **Hobart-Hampton** served as a model for other young women of her class, and by the war's end, she was hailed as a precocious example of women's liberation. After the terrible Yellow Jack plague of 1862, Largo organized relief charities for the downtrodden inhabitants of Paddy's Hollow, an activity which turned dangerous in the final two years of the war.
Murphy, Leota: Founder and owner of the "Residence for Ladies," Wilmington's classiest and most beloved whorehouse. Leota's customers always came first, but she had a heart of gold for her employees.
Parker, Samuel, Commander: After valiant early service in the Mosquito Fleet, Parker masterminded the construction of the formidable ironclad ram the CSS *Hatteras*. Parker took his crew and manned the heavy guns atop Battery Buchanan at Fort Fisher.
Reilly, Frederick, Major: An expert gunner and the designer of the *Hatteras*,

Reilly commanded the Sea Face artillery at Fort Fisher.

Sloane, Mary Harper: The daughter of baronial South Carolina rice planter Stepney Harper, she assumed control of Pine Haven plantation when her husband **Matthew Sloane** scampered off to enjoy the adventurous life of a bold blockade-runner. She proved to be a true Steel Magnolia lady, however, and not only kept Pine Haven running peacefully under conditions of enormous stress, but transcended the roots of her upbringing and by the end of the war, was working to achieve a visionary financial and political future in the New South.

Sloane, Matthew: Master of Pine Haven and first captain of the legendary *Banshee*, Matthew's one mistake—if one can call it that—was to become sexually obsessed with the famous Rebel lady spy, Belle O'Neal. In saving her from a high-seas abduction by the ruthless second-in-command of the Secret Service, Lafayette Baker, Matthew ended up in jail at Fortress Monroe. His ultimate loyalty, however, was to his wife. Although he vowed, after a Presidential pardon, never to return to sea, the Confederate authorities more or less forced him to assume command of the last-gasp commerce raider, the CSS *Chickamauga*, in which role he had the time of his live tearing holes in the Yankee merchant fleet during the closing months of the war.

Swain, Edward (*): Asheville's only resident doctor during the period, Swain was a lifelong friend of Zeb Vance and a thoroughly decent gentleman.

Smith, Peter (*): A legless mechanical genius and owner of the shipyard-in-a-cornfield at Holman's Ferry, Peter's ingenuity helped **Samuel Parker** enormously in the construction of the *Hatteras*. His son, **Charlie Smith**, devised an ingenious means of fortifying the topside casemate of the ironclad.

Vance, Zebulon Baird (*): A fiery orator from the mountains around Asheville, Vance was one of the greatest governors in North Carolina history and a staunch defender of civil liberties. He clashed frequently with Jefferson Davis with regard to Richmond's increasingly draconian policies of conscription and economic confiscation. It was said that the mere sight of a new telegram from Vance, landing on his desk, gave President Davis heartburn. Indeed, the correspondence between the two men so often exceeded the usual circumspection of the day that it ought to have been conducted on asbestos paper.

Whiting, William Chase, General (*): Vigorous organizer of the coastal defenses of the Cape Fear District, and a firm supporter of Lamb's efforts at Fort Fisher, Whiting's two attempts to make a name for himself as a field commander were compromised by terrible bad luck and his reputation suffered from his notorious fondness for a glass or ten of good bourdon. Although he might literally have saved Jefferson Davis from death or capture by preventing the Confederate President from riding into Union lines on the night after the Battle of Malvern Hill, Davis held a deep grudge against Whiting. In the end, however, Whiting showed himself to be a man of honor and remarkable courage; although he did not have to, he threw in with Lamb and fought as a company commander during the final horrific struggle for Fort Fisher. In the end, Whiting was remembered as a hero, and Bragg as a fool. Photos of Chase Whiting, incidentally, show a remarkable resemblance to another legendary tippler, author Edgar Allen Poe.

The Union

Ames, Adelbert, General (*): Commanded the Second Division of General Terry's XXIV Corps during the Fort Fisher expeditions.
Butler, Benjamin F., General (*): A notoriously ugly and vicious political infighter, Butler was a terrible field commander, but a powerful political figure behind the scenes. He established a bogus blockade-runner scheme at Shelbourne's Point in *The Sands of Pride*.
Curtis, Martin, General (*): Commander of the First Brigade of Ames' Second Division, in both attacks on Fort Fisher. His unit attempted to breach the walls of the fort.
Cushing, William Barker, Commander, USN (*): The most decorated naval hero of the war, on either side, his exploits were many and colorful. He often led his men in operations that might reasonably have been described as "suicidal." Cushing reminds one of Patton: he had a psychopathic love of being in battle, and was happiest when men were shooting at him. An inspiring figure . . . up to a point.
DeWitt, Edmund, General: A zealous abolitionist, DeWitt suffered from what doctors of the period liked to call "neurasthenic" disorders—he was excitable, paranoid, sadistic toward civilians, and conducted his part of Foster's Goldsboro offensive as though it were a personal crusade. He instigated the mass hangings and rapes at Faison's Groves, and was for that atrocity cashiered from the Army and confined in a lunatic asylum.
Elliott, "Big Red," Captain: A big, bruising ruffian who found his true métier as commander of one of the Buffalo companies. After Rush Hawkins abandoned the Buffs to their fate, during the evacuation of Shelborne's Point, Elliott swore he would track Hawkins down and kill him.
Fairless, Jack, Colonel: A gangly hillbilly, Jack enlisted in the Confederate Army mainly to obtain a bounty that would help his mountaineer kin through a hard winter. He had no comprehension of what the war was about, scant loyalty to his own army, and when his new friend Cyrus Bone urged him to desert, Jack followed. Bone became the first leader of the Buffaloes, and Jack was his second-in-command—until the night Jack murdered Cyrus to put a stop to Bone's homosexual abuse of him. As the new commander of the Buffaloes, Jack finds he has a natural gift for command; with the help of his new black friend, Bonaparte Reubens, Jack turns the Buffaloes into a disciplined, reliable fighting unit; under Reubens' tutelage, Jack also develops a keen appreciation for music, literature, and all the other "finer things" that were not available to him back home in Spillcorn Creek.
Flusser, Charles, Commodore (*): Flusser commanded the "brown water" navy in North Carolina's sounds and rivers, and did so with great aggressiveness. He was an inspiration for Will Cushing, and the two officers were close friends.
Foster, John G., General (*): Foster replaced Burnside as commander of all Union ground forces in eastern North Carolina. For two years, he carried out this unglamorous duty with exemplary professionalism. His most ambitious military operation was a two-pronged invasion toward the critical railroad nexus

at Goldsboro, in the autumn of 1863, which was at least partly successful and skillfully handled (at least, Foster's part of it). Not long after the withdrawal of his Goldsboro columns, Foster was replaced as commander in chief of North Carolina by Ben Butler. He left his old command with mixed feelings, and his subsequent Civil War record was solid if unspectacular. His insistence that his garrisons behave with the utmost civility to civilians did much to engender peaceful relations between occupation troops and those caught behind Federal lines.

Hawkins, Rush C., General (*): A native New Yorker with a vainglorious streak in his character, Hawkins had immodest political ambitions and was easily swayed to join Ben Butler's corrupt cabal by setting up an inconspicuous base at Shelborne's Point, where bogus blockade-runners—commanded by men suborned by Ben Butler—put in from the Atlantic, were disguised as ordinary merchant ships, and delivered their valuable cotton to Northern industrialists, who then repacked their holds with worthless junk (muskets that would blow up, infected blankets, spoiled food, etc.). Once these vessels had again been repainted to look like authentic runners, they returned to Wilmington and sold their defective goods to Richmond's purchasing agents. Butler and his cronies grew rich at both ends of the deal, and Rush Hawkins, as the main facilitator, did not do badly for himself either. Hawkins was courageous enough on the battlefield, but like any sane man, preferred to avoid combat whenever possible. A morally ambiguous character, to be sure, but not without some likeable qualities.

Manchester, Adolphus, Major: A fed-up Confederate deserter who joined the Buffaloes after his final disillusionment with Richmond. He served first as Jack's artillery commander, and alternatively as commander of an infantry company. Some questioned his loyalty, but his final act proved that he was an honest and trustworthy man.

Porter, Benjamin (*): A handsome, widely beloved young naval officer who chanced to find himself in command of **Admiral David Porter's** flagship, the USS *Malvern*. I confess to taking one extreme liberty in this volume: Ben Porter was not, in fact, related to the admiral. The last-name business was sheer coincidence. Ben Porter did, however, die as described during the block-headed "boarding party" assault on the Northeast Bastion. I trust the reader will forgive this bit of literary license: it was just too good to pass up.

Porter, David, Admiral (*): The last commander of the North Atlantic Fleet, Porter not only tightened the blockade effectively, but led the naval element of the Fort Fisher attacks with great professional skill. A crusty, cantankerous man, he was the very picture of the "Old Salt."

Reubens, Bonaparte: In *The Sands of Pride*, Reubens appeared as a half-mad vagabond who ended up commanding the Negro company of the Buffaloes. In this volume, we learn that he was, in fact, a French aristocrat buffeted by the post-revolutionary winds of Paris into a state of exile. Reubens believed himself a man of Destiny, and his utopian vision for a "New South" in which blacks and whites could work side by side for the mutual benefit of all was a mixture of Thoreau, Karl Marx, and John D. Rockefeller. Like so many other utopian movements of the late nineteenth century, it was rooted in an unquestioning faith in the power of science and education to better the lot of all people.

Sloane, Elias: The first successful runaway slave in Pine Haven's history, Elias ended up enlisting in Reubens' colored company of the Buffaloes, and proved his courage and innate intelligence during the Tar River campaign.

Valentine, James J. (Lieutenant-Commander, USN): A career old navy man who fell under the charismatic spell of Will Cushing and served him, at great personal risk and considerable cost to his own career.

Weitzel, Godfrey, General (*)**:** Commanded the ground forces in the first Fort Fisher expedition, and made the mistake of allowing Ben Butler to bamboozle him. Stolid and capable, but somewhat dense and slow.

Welles, Gideon (*)**:** Lincoln's Secretary of the Navy; known as "Old Neptune" because of his gruff manners and trademark Biblical whiskers.

The British

Hobart-Hampton, Augustus (*)**:** A Royal Navy officer on extended leave (and also a kind of Victorian James Bond character who was always conducting mysterious "missions" for HM Government) he came to Wilmington both to provide intelligence to London on the Confederacy, *and* to make a personal fortune as a blockade runner. His recreational use of hashish is speculative, but was not uncommon among Englishmen who "went native" when posted to the wilder extremities of the Empire. He had many and powerful connections, including at least indirect access to the Queen. A law unto himself, H-H (as his friends called him) remained enigmatic. We never see inside his head as we do the other characters in this novel; but it became obvious, as the tide turned against the Confederacy, that he also shared another common trait with British adventurers of his day: a powerful but suppressed streak of Romanticism.

Pendleton, Standish, Captain (*)**:** A composite of several real English adventurers, young "Standie" served first as Largo Landau's bodyguard, then as the last captain of the fabled *Banshee.* A gallant, if somewhat foppish young man, he also married one of Leota Murphy's daughters.

The FIRES of PRIDE

Part One

July–December 31, 1863

Shadows of Gettysburg

THE WOUNDS WERE, are, and always will be not alone for those who fell upon that ghastly field. You and I understand: there is a kind of suffering greater than the dying know—the prolonged anguish of those left behind to mourn them.

—Lieutenant Commander William B. Cushing
to his mother, August 3, 1863

In a letter dated June 30, 1863, Alonzo Cushing conveyed exciting news to his brother, Lieutenant Commander Will Cushing: Alonzo and his unit, Battery A of the 4th New York Artillery, were breaking camp and preparing to march for Pennsylvania, as part of the mighty host General Meade was gathering to repulse Lee's audacious invasion of the North. Alonzo was fearlessly eager: *"It may well prove so that this campaign shall be the most decisive of the War. You will understand that I have prayed fervently to God that I be given an important part to play in winning the most important victory yet achieved by Northern arms! When next I have a chance to write, I hope I can describe to you, in every vivid detail, the circumstances of a triumph!"*

Alonzo's six-gun battery had been attached to Hancock's Second Division and deployed on Cemetery Ridge, at the most critical position in the whole Union line—the focal point of Lee's grand assault on July 3. Using every available cannon, Lee commenced his preparatory bombardment at precisely one o'clock. No man on the Federal side had ever experienced such a barrage. Battery A was hit hard: four guns dismounted, half its ammunition caisson blown up. Alonzo was struggling to replace a shattered wheel when, at 1:30, a shell exploded five feet behind him, and fragments lacerated both of his thighs. He paused long enough to bind the wounds, wrapping the cuts with strips of cloth cut from the relatively clean shirt of a decapitated mule-skinner, then resumed his labors, lurching with every step, his face twisted in pain. When his regimental commander urged him to leave the battery and seek medical aid, Alonzo Cushing refused. "I'm only scratched up a bit, sir. It'll take more than that to knock me out of this scrap! I must stay here and fight it out with my men!"

The bombardment seemed endless, but it only lasted an hour—the Rebels needed to conserve some ammo to support their infantry. When their fire slackened, the choking, rotten-egg stink of shell smoke began slowly to dissipate over Cemetery Ridge, then Alonzo saw them, emerging from the tree line, a mile and a half distant. Every soldier on Cemetery Ridge sensed the truth of the moment: Lee was rolling the dice of history, by launching against their position the largest attack ever made by the Army of Northern Virginia.

Alonzo watched them come, rank after rank, steady and determined: the finest infantry in the world, and every honest Yankee soldier knew it. He made Battery A as prepared as it could be, what there was left of it. He and his men were staggering under the heat, their eyes streaming from the irritants in the smoke, their throats raw and sore, their canteens long since emptied. He had but two cannon left in firing condition, but he tried to make them fire like six. Orders came from General Hancock: the Union artillery should not fire until the Rebel brigades reached a rail fence bordering the Emmitsburg Road, where they would be forced to break formation and bunch up, to climb over the obstacle or to pull it down.

When that time came, Battery A commenced fire with explosive shells, but rapidly exhausted the supply. Hundreds of Rebels died crossing that fence, but they never faltered, despite the holes torn in their ranks. When they closed to three hundred yards, Alonzo reopened with double canister. Whatever ammunition Lee's gunners had been holding in reserve, they now expended, in a largely futile attempt to support their infantry before the two armies became intermingled. One of the last Confederate shots—a 24-pounder ball—scored a direct hit on the gun next to Alonzo's, smashing the carriage killing or wounding the whole crew. Now he commanded but a single gun, surrounded by dismounted barrels, shattered wheels, large fly-covered chunks of dismembered horses, and dying gunners.

An instant later, Alonzo's left shoulder was drilled clean through by a Rebel skirmisher's minié ball. The impact threw him over the barrel of his one remaining gun. It was like flopping against a roaring stove, and the searing heat flung him back onto his feet.

"Come on, men, let's reload!" he shouted. "Triple canister, that's the ticket!" But there was only one other man standing with him now, a sergeant who had miraculously escaped injury. Together they managed to cram three loads of canister into the scorching muzzle. Alonzo, his face now a filthy mask of berserk fury, primed the gun and reached for the firing lanyard. Sighting along the heat-shimmering barrel, he could see nothing but Rebel faces, still coming on furiously, mouths agape with Rebel yells that could not possibly be heard above the stupefying roar. Alonzo knew that a triple charge of canister, delivered at such intimate range, would simply obliterate those faces, turning them into an angry red mist, and that was exactly his murderous intention. But before he could fire, another bullet punched into his stomach and drove all the air from his lungs.

"Mister Cushing, sir, you must go to the rear! They'll overrun us any second!"

"I must give them one more shot," Alonzo managed to say as his fingers closed around the greasy cord. Somehow he mustered enough strength to stand fully erect, almost as though he wanted to make certain that *his* face was the last thing the attackers saw before they died.

"One more shot, by Almighty God!"

Then a third ball entered his open mouth and shattered his skull. But as he fell dying, he fired that "one more shot," and it was later estimated that the blast killed about twenty-five men. On both sides of Alonzo's gun, the Rebel tide surged but the great charge faltered and died in a chaotic welter of hand-to-hand savagery on the crest of Cemetery Ridge, where Alonzo Cushing's body and the wreckage of his shattered guns marked the highest tide of Confederate gallantry.

Vicksburg surrendered on July 9, 1863. From New Orleans to St. Louis, the Mississippi River had become a great sword stroke across the belly of the South. The Confederacy was sundered in two. News of the capitulation spread swiftly, for there were good telegraph communications between the western front and Richmond; in only twenty-four hours, confirmation of the catastrophe howled from the black-bordered front pages of every newspaper in the Confederacy. *Yield not to despair*, urged the more patriotic editorials. *Remember that General Lee and his legions are loose in Pennsylvania, perhaps even drawing near the gates of Washington, and they will surely trounce the Yankees so badly that Vicksburg's fall will seem like a minor setback in comparison. If you have heard rumors to the contrary, disregard them as contemptible Yankee lies!*

Indeed, so far the news from Lee's theater of operations was sparse, late, and contradictory. True, some Northern newspapers were already trumpeting, like bronze-clad heralds, the claim that Meade had won a stunning victory at a place called Gettysburg, but for several days the details were so sketchy that most Confederate newspaper editors saw no reason to pass them on to their readers. But on the stagnant front lines along the Rappahanock, where the soldiers on both sides routinely fraternized to swap rumors, tobacco, and souvenirs, lowly Confederate privates learned the truth about Gettysburg much sooner than the politicians in Richmond. The Davis administration, of course, routinely got copies of all the major northern papers, usually within twenty-four hours of their publication, but for several anxious days, Davis and his cabinet simply refused to believe what they read—the import was just too dire. Had not similarly boastful exaggerations been rushed into print after the shattering Yankee defeats at Fredericksburg and Chancellorsville? Besides, there was as yet no official report from Lee . . . perhaps it was *Meade* who had taken a drubbing in Pennsylvania!

But denial was no longer possible after the night of July 13–14, when Lee managed to slip his battered and shrunken army back across the Potomac, and telegraphed to Richmond a grim dispatch confirming everything the Northern papers had claimed. Marse Robert's audacious grand invasion had failed utterly. The Army of Northern Virginia had pitted its matchless courage against the low stone walls of rural Pennsylvania and learned that courage and élan were no longer enough; had marked in blood the absolute limit of what valor alone could achieve. Lee had lost twenty-eight thousand men, the cream of his veteran brigades—men who could never be replaced. In its numbing, near-biblical magnitude, the truth about Gettysburg—coming hard upon the fall of Vicksburg—staggered the Confederacy. Something unprecedented and ominous had occurred: at the South's moment of greatest strategic advantage, Lee's vision had been clouded, his energy fitful and guttering, his tactical grip uncertain, even fumbling. And so, through the enervating scorch of summer, there passed through every Southern heart a chill of foreboding.

Will Cushing could never quite decide whether his assignment to command the U.S.S. *Barney* was a sneaky form of reprimand or a simple matter of bad luck. Her last angry broadside had been fired at the forts of Vera Cruz in 1847, her engines were more fit for a museum display than for active duty off Cape Lookout, and in rough seas she wallowed like a cow. Too slow to chase a blockade runner, the *Barney* served no military purpose other than to plug another hole in the porous offshore patrol line; a tour of duty aboard her was, to Cushing's way of thinking, little more than a dull, floating version of purgatory. The only break in the monotony was the rare visit of a mail boat and the increasingly lethargic games of chess and rummy he played with his executive officer, Lieutenant James J. Valentine—the only other survivor of the *Foxglove*'s crew unlucky enough to draw the same assignment. Fortunately, that shared experience deepened the bond of friendship between the two officers. Valentine was a true "old salt" who, at age forty-three, seemed mired indefinitely in the prewar navy's glacial system of promotion, despite his unblemished service record and well-rounded competence in every realm of shipboard expertise.

Valentine showed no bitterness at being passed over, however. He retained a phlegmatic faith in the old navy's tortoise-slow promotion process and took it as an article of faith that eventually he, too, would exchange his lieutenant's bars for the bronze oak leaves of lieutenant commander, the next rung up the professional ladder. And if he resented the fact that Will Cushing, only half his age, already wore those insignia, he gave no sign of it.

Valentine was a realist. He knew that by accepting the post of Cushing's second-in-command, he was probably delaying his own promotion to a desk job; too many old-fashioned officers found Cushing's zest for reckless adventuring to be distasteful—the self promoting stunts of a glory-hungry prima donna who had been indecently elevated beyond his proper hierarchical station mainly because the Northern public adored reading about his swashbuckling exploits, and their prejudice extended to those older officers, such as Valentine, who chose voluntarily to serve with the boyish hero. Valentine knew perfectly well how the system worked, and fully understood that by allying himself with Will Cushing, he was also relegating his personnel file to the lower tiers of the advancement process, somewhere between the ranks of known alcoholics and the navy's bottomless pool of uniformed mediocrities. A few years ago, that knowledge would have caused him great distress; now he did not give a ten-cent damn. He had joined the navy, twenty-two years ago, for the same romantic ideals that had motivated Cushing, and he was much happier serving as an overage executive officer under a much younger man who thirsted for action and went looking for battle on the slightest pretext, than he could possibly have been serving under a dutiful but conservative captain whose main concern was counting the years until his retirement and pension.

More to the point: after they had shared the hardships and dangers of fighting for survival in the swamps of Onslow County, after the *Foxglove* had been shot to pieces under their feet, the two men had become a complementary, well-balanced command team. Cushing did some things with incomparable flare and dash, and foremost among them was his innate genius for leading men on the most hazardous sort of missions, then inspiring them to fight their way out again when things got hot; James Valentine was brave enough when the situation called for bravery, but ninety-five percent of a wartime sailor's time was filled with routine chores. Valentine somehow conveyed, as Cushing never could, that those who polished brass fittings and holystoned teak decks, who mended torn canvas and spliced frayed rigging, who made constant war on mildew and rust, were doing something vital in the service of their country.

Such a well-meshed blend of command styles was especially important in the confines of an old, slow, third-rate vessel such as the *Barney*. Aboard one of the big, modern, blue-water cruisers, with their 350-man crews, the boredom of blockade patrols nourished discontent the way swamp mud fertilized mushrooms. But on a ship as unglamorous as the *Barney*, the skipper and his exec *were* the engine that powered morale, for good or ill. Cushing's restless bravado and high-strung nerves would have made everyone jittery, but when combined with Valentine's calm, Ancient Mariner authority, and mastery of every nautical skill from sail mending to navigation through a dense-as-milk fog, the two men melded into a single authority figure. The *Barney*'s crew was efficient but apathetic. Among themselves, they spoke seriously of how much more exciting it would have been to serve with Cushing on a small, fast gunboat like the *Foxglove*, even if it entailed the risk of being killed. Although it had almost cost them their lives, Valentine and Cushing often reminisced about that action-packed tour of duty.

It had been great fun, until the day Will Cushing pushed his luck just a little too far. As they always had before, the crew followed him with unquestioning confidence—and many of them paid for that loyalty with their lives. But the little gunboat's final battle, in the words of the secretary of the navy, had been a "gallant episode, in the finest traditions of our service!" The court of inquiry had been perfunctory, and Cushing's vindication complete. Even the mothers and widows of some of the men he had led to their deaths came forward to testify about how proud their men had been to serve with the "great and legendary William B. Cushing." Lieutenant Valentine was never asked to testify at all. The Northern papers told the *Foxglove*'s heroic saga as though it had been the equal of Trafalgar, instead of an obscure backwater skirmish of no lasting importance.

But even after Cushing's exoneration, it was clear to Valentine that there was still a powerful clique in the Navy Department who thought Cushing was getting too big for his britches and who wanted to take him down a peg or two. So to teach Cushing a little humility, they gave him command of the slow, leaky, obsolete *Barney.* Lieutenant James Valentine could have requested a new assignment on any number of bigger, more modern warships, and many old friends advised him to, lest he become too closely identified with Cushing and the young navy "progressives" who idolized him. But Valentine had found the ideal captain to serve with, and faithfully followed Cushing into exile. "Exile," in their case, was an oblong of Atlantic Ocean about five miles wide and sixty miles long, an empty loop that the *Barney* and its wretchedly bored crew scoured night and day, without seeing anything more interesting than the occasional porpoise.

Deliverance came on June 30, 1863, when a mail-and-supply boat brought an order for Cushing to nurse the tired, old *Barney* back to Hampton Roads, for final decommissioning. Once the vessel was docked there, and her gleeful crew dismissed for a week of well-earned liberty, Cushing put in a formal request for the continued services of Lieutenant Valentine. Nobody in the Navy Department objected, but nobody had any new orders for them, either. After much searching, and the calling-in of a few old favors, they did manage to secure a cramped two-room suite in a requisitioned boardinghouse. And there they waited . . . and waited, until the novelty of being on dry land wore off and they began to grow restless once more.

To pass their idle hours, they took long walks together, paid social calls—alone or separately—to every relative and former colleague they could locate, ate in dingy cafés, and even splurged on a pair of tickets to a popular show at Ford's Theater. But Washington was in the lowest ebb of its social and cultural cycle, baking under a humid sky tinted a perpetual ocher by clouds of traffic dust that made everyone cough and wheeze, and stuffed beyond toleration by far more people than the city could hold. Within a week, the two beached sailors had run out of places to visit and, inevitably, were growing rather tired of one another's company. Cushing dealt with it by retiring to his bed early; he had a knack of being able to fall asleep almost instantly. Valentine, however, was a man who liked to stay up late, and he found Cushing's habit a source of growing irritation. Valentine required the sedation of copious whiskey and the distraction of stacks of old newspapers. He was, therefore, only half relaxed when someone knocked on their door at ten o'clock on the night of July 7. The visitor was an elderly telegraph messenger who grumbled sourly at the size of his tip and who slammed the door on his way out. The message was from the Navy Department, so Valentine made the logical assumption: someone had found a new job for them. He shook Cushing vigorously.

"Wake up, Mister Cushing, wake up! We've received new orders at last!" Cushing popped up like a jack-in-the-box and suffered a paper cut for his impatience in ripping open the flimsy envelope. But when he read the message Cushing's face turned chalk white. He folded the document and slipped it under his pillow. Without a word of explanation, he climbed out of bed and donned his uniform.

"Well, what does it say, man? Have they demoted us to a garbage scow?"

"Read it yourself when I'm gone, Lieutenant."

"Gone? Gone where? Why on earth are you leaving at this hour?"

"Out for a walk, just a walk. Because a ship captain should never lose control of his emotions in the presence of his executive officer."

Then he was gone, and Valentine was able to read the news for himself. Alonzo Cushing was dead.

Cushing did not return that night, although he did send Valentine a note, explaining that he had gone to the Navy Department as soon as it opened for business, to request an emergency leave of absence, a week's furlough so that he might attend Alonzo's funeral and go home to be with their mother. His intention was to depart immediately for Gettysburg, where he hoped to take charge of his brother's remains and escort them to Fredonia, in upstate New York, where Alonzo could be laid to rest in the rich, brown soil of home.

But by the time Will reached the battlefield, Alonzo's body had been placed on a train, along with the remains of several other Union heroes, and the only thing Will could do was follow the coffin back East. Alonzo was buried, on July 12, at West Point, with full military honors. Mary Cushing had been invited, *implored,* to attend, but had flatly refused. Will stayed only long enough to honor his brother with a graveside prayer, to acknowledge the somber condolences of the many officers, cadets, and midlevel politicians in attendance. As soon as he could slip away discreetly, Will made his way to the old fortifications overlooking the noble Hudson, and gave way in solitude to the grief he could not display in public. Then he went home to be with his mother.

He was met at the train station by Sampson White, a longtime friend of the Cushing family and editor of the town newspaper, the *Fredonia Censor*. Ever since the awful news, he said, Mary Cushing had been in seclusion, refusing to open her door to pastor, physician, or neighbor. All Fredonia was in mourning for its fallen son, said Mister White, a fact Will had already verified from seeing the abundance of half-masted flags and coiling wreaths of black crepe. White offered Will a seat in his buggy, and on the ride out to the Cushing house, after repeatedly expressing his deepest sympathies, he made a determined conversational effort to secure from Will a first-person account of his daring exploits in Carolina waters.

"They say you've become a one-man invasion force, Mister Cushing—that you've made the Carolina coast too hot for the Rebs any time and any place you take a mind to strike them!"

"That is a considerable exaggeration, Mister White. It's just that I grow bored very quickly with routine patrols, and I am fortunate enough to have a commanding officer, Charles Flusser, who shares my aggressive tendencies and sometimes lets me off the navy's leash."

"They say you're like Blackbeard come back to life, Will! Tell me: Where do you plan to strike 'em next? Surely you must be planning some spectacular act of retaliation for your brother's death! If you could just give me a hint, I swear I won't publish a word that might compromise the mission!"

Cushing turned slowly to face the man, and his usually mild blue gaze had turned hard as a murderer's glare just before he deals the lethal thrust.

"At the moment, sir, my greatest need is for privacy. It's not within my power to strike the Rebels a blow commensurate with my brother's worth, or bloody enough to fill the depth of my loss. Nothing I have done—nothing I am *reputed to have done*—remotely compares to my brother's heroism and sacrifice. For me to crow like a boastful cock, while the earth above his grave is but freshly turned, would be a dishonor to his memory."

"Of course, Commander Cushing, of course. I meant no disrespect! But you must be burning to tell your saga to someone . . . perhaps on your next visit to Fredonia?"

"Perhaps. If I live to *make* another visit."

By the time Will Cushing embraced his mother and closed her door on the outside world, neither had any tears left to shed. Mary Cushing rejoiced to see her surviving son once more, but grimaced angrily at the news that he could stay for only three days. "What if it cost Abe Lincoln the war to share you with me for a whole week?"

At first their reunion was awkward, and on that first day, especially, the passing hours were heavy, shrouded, and brightened only by the exchange of small, quiet reminiscences. Every hour, it seemed, people knocked on Mary's door, bringing baskets of food and heaps of flowers and sentimental prayers and poems written by local schoolchildren in honor of Alonzo's memory. Will intercepted them all at the threshold and received their tributes with courtesy and good grace, but he did not invite anyone into the house.

Slowly, mother and son came to terms with their loss. On their final evening together, they even managed to summon a few tentative smiles. Life would go on, and so would the war. Of what account was their private grief, when sixty thousand other sons, fathers, and brothers had died or been forever maimed on the soft summer meadows and rocky hilltops of Pennsylvania? What healed them the most, finally, was the sheer scale of that collective loss relative to their own. The Cushings were a family of people who took life as it came. If you allowed despair to pull you into its abyss, then death had already stamped a claim upon you. Since death always won its victory in the end, the steadfast response to that verity lay in quiet defiance—one mourned and honored the fallen—and then, one morning, one simply got out of bed with no more lamentations and got on with one's life. Therein lay the dignity of human existence, the small, cumulative victories to be won by starting a task and finishing it to the fullest measure of your skill and your stength.

At his mother's urging, Will spent the last day of his furlough by paying brief visits to those neighbors whom he remembered, with special fondness, from the happier days of his youth. When he returned at twilight, he opened the front door and was immediately comforted by the evocative, mouth-watering smell of his favorite meal: roasted turkey, mashed potatoes, and rich, stovetop gravy. Mary had set a festive table for this farewell dinner, bringing out the gay red tablecloth reserved for birthdays and holidays, the best china and silverware, and such an abundance of candles that the dining room seemed touched with sunlight. After the cooking and gravy-simmering were done, she had also changed into the shamrock-green satin dress he had bought for her on the day he left Annapolis, after being thrown out of the Naval Academy, in 1860, for rambunctious youthful pranks that now seemed laughably trivial compared to the events that followed so soon after his expulsion. Mary Cushing was now fifty-seven, and for many of her years she had struggled hard to keep the family from slipping into genteel poverty. The last three years, in particular, had taken a visible toll. Of her quiet, solemn beauty, which Will had sought to honor with his gift of fancy satin, only traces now remained—in the warmth of her eyes, the enduring grace of her profile, and the elegance of her hands. But her face was lined, her skin without luster, and her hair coarse and gray.

But in her satin dress, flattered by the candlelight, she still seemed beautiful to Will, and he told her so, as she had hoped he might. After supper, Mary served tea and placed in front of Will a platter of her "extra-special, family-secret" sugar cookies, which proved to be the finest treat he had eaten since his last visit, in 1862. Finally, thanks to the homely ritual of simple homebaked sugar cookies, they were able to talk to each other without Alonzo's death casting a shadow over every word.

"Did you visit the Greenleaf house, Will?"

"No, Mother. My time was limited, and I don't seem to remember them as clearly as some of the others. Is there any reason why I should have?"

"Have you really forgotten?"

" 'Forgotten'? Obviously I must have! Please remind me. . . ."

"Their oldest daughter, Julia, took quite a shine to you when you were both about fifteen—the first female to do so, I believe, and for all I know, the last, since you never mentioned any women, not once in all your letters."

Will blushed and shook his head. "Mother, I spend most of my time at sea, surrounded by men whose conversation, when it comes to the fair sex, is rarely of a gentlemanly nature. Don't be in such a hurry—I am only twenty-two, and there is no point in fretting about courtships when my circumstances make it a very impractical activity. Don't worry, though—in due time I will meet the right woman, marry her, and give you lots of grandchildren to coddle and spoil!"

The very mention of "grandchildren" produced a smile that melted years from her face. She even felt at liberty to tease him, by wagging a schoolmarm's finger above the cookie platter: "I only assumed that a dashing young naval hero, one whose exploits have been written about so flamboyantly in the newspapers of *both sides*, might have the traditional 'girl in every port.' "

Cushing's cheeks reddened. He lowered his eyes, stirred a bit more cream into his tea, and nibbled deliberately on his fourth cookie.

"You know, Mother, oddly enough, I *did* meet a woman who struck me as the sort of lady I might pay court to. Alas, there were several very practical obstacles. For one thing, she was already married—to a famous blockade runner! And she was the mistress of a big Rebel plantation, the life-or-death ruler of almost a hundred slaves."

"Forgive me for laughing, Will, but that is so wonderfully typical of you! After all these years of masculine independence, you develop an interest in a rich, *married*, Confederate slaveowner! But now, since you've broached the subject with such tantalizing remarks, you absolutely must tell me the whole story, especially the spicy bits of your flirtation!"

"Mother! There was a lot more to it than that!" So Will told her about his desperate trek across North Carolina's coastal wilderness, after the destruction of the gallant gunboat *Foxglove*, and how he and his starving crew were discovered, nursed back to health, and ultimately helped to escape captivity, by Mark Harper Sloane, the mistress of Pine Haven plantation. Mary Cushing leaned forward eagerly, soaking up every word.

"What a captivating saga! There are so many questions I would like to ask a lady of her background and obvious intelligence. But since she isn't here, you must answer them for her. For example, is secessionist zeal as passionately held on that plantation as we are told it is on every big plantation? And most of all, I should very much like to know where *Mister Sloane* was while his wife and my son were chatting so amicably!"

"That would be 'Captain' Sloane, skipper of the *Banshee*, the first and still one of the most successful of all the blockade runners. And given the phase of the moon during my visit to Pine Haven, I suspect he was either loading a cargo of rifles and gunpowder in Nassau, or leading our blockade ships on a merry chase as he made the dangerous return trip to Wilmington. Captain Sloane leads a charmed life, and he has outwitted our patrols time and time again."

Mary wagged her hand excitedly. "Now I recall the name! It was in all the papers! Wasn't he the one who got captured trying to save some notoriously wanton Rebel spy?"

"The very man. He even fought a pitched battle, in international waters, with the ruthless Federal agent, Lafayette Baker. One cannot help but admire his pluck, and I almost regret that he got caught. At the time I befriended his wife, Captain Sloane was languishing in the prison at Fortress Monroe, and remains there to this day, as far as I know. But to get back to my sojourn at Pine Haven . . ."

From the fullness and coloration of her son's narrative, Mary Cushing sensed that Will had found much to admire in this older woman's character. Indeed, she suspected that he might have felt something more ardent than "admiration," although if he had begun to develop a crush on Mrs. Sloane, he would never have allowed things to go beyond the level of casual tea-party conversation. Or would he, if Mrs. Sloane had given a sign of willingness? No, Mary Cushing thought, sighing. Will might be one of America's most widely admired naval heroes, but his naïveté about women remained astonishing.

"There was one thing she said, Mother, that I feel obligated to bring up with you. Promise me that if I do, you'll give me a totally honest reply."

"Will Cushing, I am amazed you would even think that I might respond in any other way!" She was teasing, of course, but for just an instant Will saw a flash of irritation.

"Forgive me, Mother—I didn't mean for that to sound like I was doubting your honesty!"

"Oh, Will, stop blathering and just tell me what Missuz Sloane, what *Mary Harper,* said that made you so flustered."

"It's about my letters . . ."

"What about them?"

"Well, she said . . . *Mary Harper* said, that it might cause you distress when I describe some of my riskier adventures. I promise—you are the only person in the world to whom I can, or would, boast about such things."

Mary Cushing sighed.

"I have known, since both you and Alonzo were small boys, that boasting about your exploits was something you both *must* do, or the pressure that built up inside you from *not* bragging about them would sooner or later cause your eyeballs to burst from their sockets. That's just the sort of personality God gave you at birth, and not a pompous affectation as it is with some men, most especially the generals and politicians. If you were a hero of ancient times, you would employ a bard to sing about your deeds. Indeed, if *someone* didn't compose ballads in praise of your adventures, I think you might choke on the memory of them, but Homer, alas, retired quite a long time ago, and though you're the captain of a warship, you can hardly expect the crew to listen to your stories. Therefore, recount them to *me!* Every time I get a long letter from you, recounting your adventures and hairbreadth escapes, it makes me so proud of you I could burst, and it also reassures me that, *because you're writing about those battles,* it means that you survived them. What would really freeze my blood would be the arrival of a long letter written in some other officer's hand. . . . And for another thing, I know you will tell me the plain truth of what you saw with your own eyes, which is not always the case with our newspaper accounts. Why do so many Northern journalists assume they're writing for an audience of simpletons who cannot distinguish between wild hyperbole and objective reportage?"

"Probably because wild hyperbole sells more newspapers," said Will with a laugh.

"But when I read your accounts, Will, I can visualize the maneuvers, hear the shells, and almost smell the powder smoke. And the Will Cushing I visualize in those battles is my own flesh-and-blood Will—not the idealized, saintly paladin of the newspaper accounts, but just a very young man to whom God gave the gift of leadership. I know, of course, that you spare me the worst of the horrors, but you honor me by not trying to *sanitize* the whole hideous business. You know, of course, that Alonzo was in many skirmishes and battles before Gettysburg, but in every letter he wrote to me, there is not one mention of blood or pain or sacrifice—and precisely because he tried so hard to spare me the realities of war, it had an effect quite different from the one he intended: it caused me to visualize him always at the point of greatest danger, made me fill in the details with my own imagination, so that I always thought of him being surrounded by things more horrible and more dangerous than was probably the case! Do you recall what you wrote me after you witnessed the attack on Roanoke Island? In one sentence, you managed to put many things in their proper perspective: 'A naval officer might spend twenty years on active duty, yet in all of that time, experience only a few hours of mortal danger and the excitement that are the price, and the reward, of his chosen profession. . . .' "

Will made a deprecating little gesture. "I suspect that in the army, the ratio between boredom and mortal peril might be somewhat different. But you caught the meaning of what I was trying to convey. So, then, Mary Harper was wrong? You really don't mind if I sometimes become a bit too *graphic*, when I write those letters to you? You honestly don't mind if I continue to write in the same vein as before?"

Of course she minded—she was his *mother,* for God's sake—especially when he described, with the same bemused and clinical fascination an ornithologist might employ when trying to describe the migratory habits of hummingbirds, the wide variety of curious sounds made by minié balls and shell fragments passing within inches of his own skull. But she evaded the truth gracefully by replying:

"Of course not, Will. If they were written in any other way, I would suspect they were forgeries concocted by someone who was jealous of your fame."

His relief was so palpable it was almost comic. Mary Cushing hurriedly changed the subject. "Do you know what ship you'll be commanding next?"

"Not yet. And I might not get another command at all! I was cleared of any culpability in the sinking of the *Foxglove*, but that doesn't mean the navy is in a hurry to trust me with another ship! The powers-that-be may decide it would do me good to cool my backside at a desk job for a while, or they may place me in a junior capacity, on a much larger vessel, under a captain who is much less prone to having his ship blown up."

"But your independent spirit is your greatest asset, Will! You don't just go charging blindly after glory—well, not *all* the time—but you take calculated risks that more cautious officers would see as foolhardy. It seems to me that in a war of this magnitude, the navy needs both kinds of leaders. And I suspect that Secretary Welles knows this as well as I do. Why, just a few weeks ago, I read a newspaper interview with General

Grant, old 'Unconditional Surrender' himself, in which he mentioned you by name. 'I like that young fool's style,' he said, 'because he knows the quickest way to win the war is to take the fight to the Rebels, wherever and whenever he can do it! I'd like to have him leading a division in *my army!*' "

"General Grant said that about me?'

"Indeed he did. It was reprinted in the *Fredonia Censor!*"

"At least I know where to apply for a new job if the navy ever boots me out!"

Both mother and son had negotiated some heavy emotional seas on this day, and it was no small private triumph that the evening concluded with genuine, not forced, laughter. When Will Cushing left home the next morning, he was almost jaunty. And for her part, Mary Cushing performed no small act of heroism by completely hiding from him her desperate fear that she might never see him again.

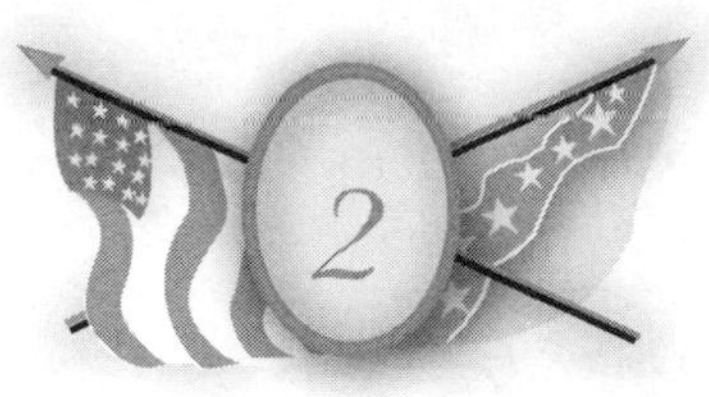

So Many Ways it Could Have Gone . . .

BACK IN THE early months, before most Confederate regiments had seen any fighting, the men elected their commanders, *a practice which may seem quaint today, but since we all figured one red-blooded Rebel man could route a company of Yankees, professional military training, while desirable, was a secondary consideration. We elected Zeb Vance because he was a great storyteller, a back-slapping good old boy, and a born politician. He was, however, a mediocre colonel. He read his manuals diligently, but for the life of him he couldn't see any earthly reason why "Right Shoulder Arms!" HAD to be preceded by "Port Arms!" As for camp discipline, about the only thing Zeb insisted on was that we always put the shit-house downstream from the drinking water.*

When Harry Burgwyn came along, fresh from V.M.I., and became our second-in-command, we all hated him at first. I mean, what difference does it make in a battle whether your buttons are polished or not? But there was a point *to all that petty discipline, and when we went into that misbegotten bloodbath called Malvern Hill, we learned what it was: Of all the Rebel regiments who charged into that storm of lead, the 26th N.C. was the only one that held its ground all day—because Harry had taught us how to load and fire prone, and find cover where less-trained men saw empty ground.*

The smartest thing Zeb ever did, was to resign and turn command over to Harry. Vance was as brave as any man, but he was not a natural-born soldier and Harry was. By the time we went into battle on the first day of Gettysburg, he had whipped the 26th N.C. into one of Lee's best regiments. And Zeb Vance, of course, went to Raleigh and became one of the greatest governors in our history.

It was Harry who saw, at one glance, that the key to defeating Meade was for Lee to seize the high ridges around the town before the Yankees did. But we were serving then in Harry Heth's division, and Heth had never commanded a division before. He wouldn't let us attack those ridges until he got Lee's permission, which took six hours to obtain, and by that time, Meade's boys had beat us to the top. So instead of an easy skirmish, we fought a battle that effectively destroyed the regiment. On the morning of July 1, roll call was answered by 804 men . . . when the sun went down, there were 168 of us still alive. We fought like wild men, and it was Harry Burgwyn who finally pushed us to the top—he'd been shot at a thousand times on the slopes of McPherson's Ridge and not a bullet touched him. But at the moment of victory, a whole fresh Yankee regiment counterattacked and we broke. We were used up; nothing left. And Harry took four Minié balls in less time than it takes to write it. He lived long enough to say: "Tell my boys how proud I am for what they did today—I have no regrets that I was struck down in the company of such brave men. God's will be done . . ."

With that, he breathed his last, and every damned one of us cried like babies.

—Major Jerome Winkler, *Sketches of a Tar Heel at War*; Unpublished manuscript, c. 1882; State Archives, Raleigh.

Zebulon Vance knew that his old regiment, the 26th N.C., had gone to Gettysburg, and that Lee's casualties were reportedly very heavy. The fact that Richmond was very slow releasing the official tolls, and released them only in small regional packets of information, suggested a calculated plan to lessen the public's shock. Lee's total losses must have been so catastrophic that the Davis government was afraid to let the truth come out except in small, measured doses. One week into August, and losses had been published for only half the North Carolina units that had taken part. About the 26th, the newspaper remained mute. Every morning, Governor Vance waited anxiously to learn the truth, and on the morning of August 9, he finally did—not from a black-bordered list on the front page of the *Raleigh Standard*, but in a personal letter written from a hospital by Major Godfrey Jones (who had been a sergeant when Vance resigned his commission. Actually, the letter was *dictated* by Major Jones, for a brief postscript by the person who had transcribed his words informed the Governor that the Major's injuries were too severe for him to hold a pen. Transcribed or not, the power of Jones' emotions came through:

Harry Burgwyn was dead, from multiple wounds sustained on July 1, the first day of Gettysburg. In what turned out to be a prelude to the main drama, the 26th N.C. had played a pivotal role when part of Henry Heth's division stormed McPherson's Ridge, in an ill-fated attempt to seize the high ground before Meade's main force arrived. Had the attack been launched at ten in the morning, when the first Union cavalry patrols were spotted reconnoitering the heights above Gettysburg village, it would have succeeded and Meade would have lost the best ground on the map, along with the initiative, in the battle's first hours.

But Lee had passed word to his division commanders that he was not interested in bringing on a "general engagement" in rural Pennsylvania, his aim was to interpose his whole army between Meade and Washington, and thereby compel Meade to come after him on ground of Lee's choosing. Though inexperienced, General Heth had already learned that leading an entire division was a much more complex task than commanding a brigade. He was too insecure to follow his own good intuition by capturing the high ridges first and telling Lee about it afterward.

By contrast, Meade had told *his* subordinates to use their own judgment, so while Harry Burgwyn and his men waited impatiently for five and a half hours, Meade's forward commanders were pushing every man and gun they had toward those ridges. By the time Lee's written approval finally took the leash off Heth's division, there were as many Yankees throwing up breastworks atop McPherson's Ridge as there were in the five Confederate regiments assigned to capture it. Major Jones described what happened in vivid language:

> *On the crests of McPherson's Ridge and Cemetery Ridge behind it, are some very pretty scenic overlooks, and the local families often enjoy picnics there in the spring and autumn. Walking paths lead from the meadows below to the overlooks, and I have been told that in times of peace, a man in good health can climb to the summit in fifteen minutes of easy hiking. It took us two and a half hours to cover that same distance and so thick were the Minié balls flying that trees were stripped of their bark. I have been in every major campaign since Malvern Hill, but as God is my witness, Colonel Vance, that was the hottest and most bitterly fought battle I ever saw. If General Burgwyn had not tirelessly inspired us to push on, we would have reached the limit of what flesh and mind can endure after the first hour of fighting. Harry seemed invulnerable, though—he made no effort to hide himself, and the Yankees must have fired a thousand bullets at him from as close as twenty feet and did not hit him until after we finally reached the summit and driven off the men who had defended it so stubbornly.*

The Confederates retained control of that ridge for less than twenty minutes before fresh Union forces counterattacked and swept aside the feeble resistance put up by those who had survived the attack. Harry Burgwyn was hit by four rifle balls almost simultaneously. As they retreated, the remnants of the 26th N.C. carried their young general's body, almost certain that he was dead.

Astonishingly, Harry Burgwyn was not only alive when he was carried off that dreadful slope, he became calm and lucid for about ten minutes before his final breath. Major Jones was nearby when Harry asked if someone would please unbuckle his sword belt and take care to preserve it.

It was the very blade you handed to him, Col. Vance, on the night you relinquished command and elevated Harry to be your successor. I was the man who unfastened the scabbard and Harry said to me, 'Please see that Governor Vance gets his sword back. He gave me the honor of commanding some of the finest infantry in the world. Tell him how much I have missed his bawdy jokes, and tell him how frequently I thank God that each of us ended up in the place we were destined for.

Major Jones hoped that Vance could find the time to pick up Harry's sword in person, for he did not want to risk losing it or having it stolen by trying to ship it to Raleigh. He closed with a heartrending plea: all the hospitals in Richmond are full to overflowing, and even the small field hospital at Rapidan Station, where he was convalescing, was jammed with 500 men even though its "official" capacity was 150. Basic medical supplies were running low or had been used up completely. Chloroform had become so scarce, that only men undergoing major or multiple amputations were being put to sleep—for someone who was "merely" losing a finger or two, there was nothing but whiskey and a leather strap to bite on. The Richmond authorities were trying to hide the true scope of the crisis, so there was nothing in the newspapers about these shortages. But if "Colonel Vance" had any spare medical supplies, Jones implored him in the name of human compassion to send them to Richmond as soon as possible, for there was "an ocean of human suffering, and the doctors are reduced to coping with it on the same primitive level as the surgeons in George Washington's army."

Major Jones's dictation ended abruptly at that point, and the transcriber had added, on a separate sheet of paper: "This patient succumbed to his wounds only one hour ago. The chief surgeon has put General Burgwyn's sword in a secure place and will follow your wishes as soon as you apprise him of them. Jones was a brave and decent man, and too many brave, decent men are dying here every day for lack of medicines. I can best honor his memory by adding my own pleas to his—if North Carolina has even a case of clean bandages to spare, there are men here from every state in the Confederacy who will bless you in their prayers for any help you can provide. That the government in Richmond will not issue a public appeal for fear of the effect it might have on civilian morale, is not merely a bad policy, it is a ghastly scandal. Yrs faithfully, S. Ledbetter, Volunteer Nurse."

Zebulon Vance locked the door to his office and wept. Then he ordered his staff to bring him every document they could find about the stocks of medical supplies in storage or in the holds of blockade runners due to arrive in the next three to five days. By twilight, August 6, Vance had learned that his own state was better stocked with medical supplies than the Confederate government: Case after case of first-quality prerolled linen bandages from France and Holland, more than 200 fine English surgical kits whose instruments were made from Sheffield steel, prosthetic devices, 200 gallon jars of ether, and 600 quart bottles of chloroform, and newly arrived in Wilmington, 100,000 tablets of the powerful new painkiller, morphine. Altogether, he was prepared to send two tons of assorted medicines and supplies, starting as soon as a freight car could be attached to the next train bound for Richmond. He had a complete list of these items drawn up and appended to an urgent telegram to Robert E. Lee, imploring the commander-in-chief to make sure the medical authorities in Richmond were prepared to distribute the shipments to the places where they were most needed.

Lee's response, expressing the profoundest gratitude to the the governor and people of North Carolina, arrived the very next morning. Governor Vance could be certain that this magnanimous donation would be distributed promptly and efficiently, adding pointedly "Trusted members of my own staff will take charge of each shipment and if any other agency tries to lay claim on the supplies, they will have to answer to me personally." Vance thanked the general and casually mentioned that he would be visiting Rapidan Station in the next day or two, on a personal errand of great importance. Would it be possible for him to schedule an appointment with General Lee, to discuss important "strategic matters"? Yes, Lee replied; "Would you honor me by accepting an *ironclad* invitation to dinner, here at my pleasantly rural headquarters near Culpepper?"

Vance could not remember ever mentioning the *Hatteras* project to Lee—after all, he did not often have occasion to wire the general directly. But somehow, Lee knew. And with just a touch of sly humor, the general had freed Vance from any need to be coy about the subject. How much did Lee know and how had he learned it? Vance might never learn the answers to those questions. But whether by design or coincidence, the auguries were beginning to seem favorable, with regard to the super-ironclad.

At the very least, Vance now had an invitation to dine with Robert E. Lee, simultaneously with the satisfaction he felt at being able to send to the hospitals flooded with the Gettysburg wounded enough medical supplies to ease the suffering of thousands of brave men. He could not, however, resist the temptation to have each box and crate stenciled with the legend: "A gift from the people of North Carolina."

Just so the doctors in Virginia would know who to thank.

The dinner engagement with Lee was scheduled for the evening of August 10. The hospital at Rapidan Station was only twenty miles south of Lee's headquarters near Culpepper. By happy coincidence, Vance arrived to pick up Harry Burgwyn's sword only six hours after some of Lee's men had delivered a wagon full of medical supplies from North Carolina. The chief surgeon, who looked like he had not slept in five days, welcomed Vance with almost tearful gratitude—that single wagonload would probably save the lives of a hundred men and ease the terminal suffering of another hundred who were beyond medical repair. Vance had left an extra day in his schedule, even though Lee was only an hour's train ride away, so that he could meet the North Carolina wounded and spend some time with them.

He also met the volunteer transcriber, "S. Ledbetter," a sorrowful thin woman, widowed now for fourteen months, who spent five hours a day writing letters for patients who could not manage the task on their own. She proved to be a gentle, melancholy person who might once have been a beauty. Childlessness and the death of her husband made her seem older than her thirty-nine years, but she had deep black eyes and a voice like crushed velvet, and when she invited the governor to dinner in her small frame house within walking distance of the hospital, they both knew they would end up spending the night together before either came within rifle-range of saying anything suggestive. The encounter turned out to be surprisingly intense for both participants, and wholly out of character for Vance. Yet when he woke beside her the next morning, he felt buoyantly free of guilt or regret, and Mrs. Ledbetter had a smile for him that knocked about five years off the both of them,

Naturally, because Vance had allowed plenty of time to travel the twenty-two miles to Culpepper, the train broke down twice in that distance. Since the heat inside the coach was so oppressive, Vance waited out the second unscheduled stop under a shade tree beside the tracks. On his way out, he spotted a newspaper someone had left under the seat behind his. Since no one was there to claim it, Vance sat down on a patch of shady grass and sought distraction in the August 8 edition of the *Richmond Enquirer*.

His attention was immediately drawn to an "eyewitness account," by an unnamed correspondent, of the climactic and disastrous Rebel attack of July 3, which was already, and inaccurately, being called "Pickett's Charge" despite the fact that only half of the troops involved were under that gentleman's command. Despite his intention to be as respectful and even-tempered with Lee as he was frequently cantankerous in his dealings with President Davis and Secretary of War Seddon, what he read made him boil with anger.

According to this Virginia reporter, the attack had failed primarily because the five North Carolina regiments supporting Pickett on the left had failed, in cowardly fashion, to perform their duty. After absurdly describing these units as "raw troops", the correspondent averred: *"I saw by the wavering of this line as they entered the conflict that they lacked the firmness of nerve and steadiness of tread which so characterized Pickett's command, and I felt that these men would not, could not, stand the tremendous ordeal to which they would soon be subjected. And so it proved to be, for they faltered badly and failed to support their Virginia comrades, who were thereby compelled to face the Yankee hordes alone."*

This account, as Vance knew from the testimony of several men who had witnessed the event, was nothing less than an egregious slander—a perfect example of the haughty disdain so many Virginians felt toward their Tar Heel neighbors. Dear God, the injustice of it! Provisions from North Carolina accounted for one-third of the rations consumed by Lee's whole army, arms and accoutrements funneled through Wilmington had enabled the Davis government to equip dozens of new regiments, and Robert Lee himself had personally commended Vance's former, now worse-than-decimated, regiment on its valor! What was even worse, this was one of the first "eyewitness accounts" to appear in any Southern newspaper, and as such, it was sure to be reprinted in many other journals throughout the Confederacy. As a politician, Vance knew that "first impressions" had a way of sticking in peoples' minds like a burr. No matter how many other, more accurate accounts might be published in the future, many thousands of readers were going to remember *this one*, which asserted that Lee's defeat could be explained away, not by his own flawed judgement, but because at the moment of crux, Pickett's noble Virginians had been let down by a bunch of cowardly North Carolinians!

Vance tucked the newspaper into his map case. Now, he hoped the train would be delayed, at least long enough for him to regain his composure. As if to mock him personally, the train made excellent time, and he arrived at Culpeper Court House with three hours to spare before his six o'clock appointment with Lee. Upon learning that the general headquarters was only a half-hour walk from the railroad stop, Vance decided to spend that time inspecting several of the big supply depots clustered around the once-insignificant village. In his pocket was an all-purpose safe-conduct pass signed by Lee himself, so he had no trouble from the sentries and officious quartermaster sergeants who would otherwise have barred his way. As he went from one warehouse to another, two things quickly became obvious. One was that the recent offensive had drained Lee's stockpiles to a dangerously low level, and the other was that wagon loads of resupply were arriving hourly, and from the markings on their containers, it was clear that more than half of these vital shipments—tinned rations, uniform cloth, powder, leather, and medical supplies—had come to Virginia from the blockade-runners of Wilmington.

This cursory inspection strengthened Vance's confidence in the proposal he intended to make to Lee. There was no doubt in his mind that Lee would take the offensive again, after his army had recovered and his supply situation had improved. But it was also clear that, however unquenchable Lee's appetite for taking the fight to the enemy, the Army of Northern Virginia would never again have the capacity to launch another offensive on the scale of the one that led to Gettysburg. Vance's plan had the merit of offering Lee a chance to win a resounding strategic victory, at little risk, without committing more than a modest part of his resources.

And his case would be strengthened by the fact that the Union Army showed no sign of preparing to follow up on their recent victory by launching an aggressive push toward Richmond. George Meade might well be the hero of the hour to Lincoln and the Northern populace, but his pursuit of Lee after Gettysburg had been exceedingly cautious, which showed, if nothing else, that the enemy's high command still feared Lee's tactical genius for unexpected maneuvers and his willingness to take calculated risks. In his heart, Meade must have known that simple good luck had played no small part in his recent triumph. It was one thing to pursue Lee when his forces were battered and depleted, but it was quite another and far more dangerous thing to attack him on his home ground. On the Virginia front, the situation was one of stalemate, and might remain so until the spring of 1864.

By February, March at the latest, surely the *Hatteras* would be finished and ready to sail. Vance was convinced the ironclad was powerful enough—or *would* be, if the long-frustrated Sam Parker ever received the armor and weaponry Richmond had promised him—that it might by itself give the Confederacy at least temporary naval dominance along the North Carolina coast. Without their gunboats to protect them, or their transports to resupply them, the isolated Federal enclaves could be overwhelmed, one by one. If Vance could persuade Lee to loan him just one elite division, augmented by some heavy guns and a small force of cavalry, that expeditionary force, acting in concert with the *Hatteras*, should be strong enough to purge the state of every invader. Surely, a commander of Lee's temperament, who thrived on hitting the enemy with surprise jabs where he least expected them, would be receptive to a plan that could easily win a major strategic victory on-the-cheap.

Like the canny country lawyer he had been before succumbing to the lure of politics, Vance had prepared his brief with plenty of supporting documents: inside his dispatch case were carefully marked maps, schematic drawings of the ironclad, and endorsements of the plan by prominent generals, including Chase Whiting, D.H. Hill, and Pierre Beauregard, who were familiar with the topography and the Union fortifications in the region.

Vance did not expect, nor would he seek to obtain, a formal, written commitment from Lee; God knew what developments might intervene between now and the spring day when the *Hatteras* was finally ready for action—but if he could coax from the general an understanding, an agreement-in-principle, Vance had no doubt Lee would honor his commitment when the time came.

Vance also knew he must never forget that Robert E. Lee was a Virginian, afflicted by the same myopia that exerted such a basilisk-pull on the mind of Jefferson Davis. If, when the time came for the *Hatteras* to fight, Richmond should again be seriously threatened, Vance's counterattack plan would be shelved without a second thought.

Lee had established his headquarters in a plain white wooden farmhouse, pleasantly situated atop a sloping meadow, bounded by the willow-lined banks of the tranquil little river. By the time Vance presented himself there, the day's worst heat had drained away, and in the surrounding thickets, clouds of fireflies pursued their luminous courting rituals, weaving complex and mysterious sarabandes of light. This was the beautiful Virginia countryside Lee had sworn to defend, and Vance could understand the general's love for the land; had the enemy threatened his own beloved mountains, Vance too would have found it hard to maintain a broadly objective viewpoint.

A very sharp-looking young aide-de-camp met Vance on the front steps, greeted him with the utmost courtesy, saw to it that the governor's horse was tended to, then ushered him inside. Vance had expected Lee's headquarters to resemble a bee hive, with messengers and orderlies rushing in and out, and staff officers in every room, scribbling or transcribing telegrams, attending to important things. But, except for the young aide, and a pair of sentries flanking the front door, the place was remarkably quiet, almost serene. A somnolent, wasp-colored glow suffused the hallway as twilight deepened, and there was an unexpected scent of fresh-cut flowers.

"General Lee is looking forward to the pleasure of your company, Governor Vance. Right this way, please."

Vance suddenly put a restraining hand on the officer's shoulder and asked: "If I may ask, Major, how many other officers and guests will be present? Politician that I am, I would feel more properly prepared if I had some foreknowledge of the rank and status of the other guests."

The young captain smiled affably, arching his brows ever so slightly.

"Why, Governor Vance, you are the general's only guest tonight. If General Lee wished to surround himself, at every meal, with politicians and fellow officers, he would have chosen a headquarters closer to Richmond. I believe, in light of the recent events in Pennsylvania, that he's in something of a solitary and reflective mood these days."

"I am indeed a privileged man, in that case," said Vance. *And a lucky one—after reading that pack of Goddamned lies in the Richmond paper this morning, I'm still scratchy as a polecat. Lee's the only Virginian I could stand being in a room with.*

Zebulon Vance was not easily awed by any man, and at the moment, his regard for Lee's legendary military "genius" was at rather a low ebb; but his political success derived, in no small part, from his ability to take the measure of strangers quickly. The man in gray who rose to meet him was neither demigod, nor royalty, but he had a *presence* that made it easier for Vance to understand why his men loved him and followed him, even if by doing so they risked the kind of slaughter Lee had exposed them to on July 3.

"My dear Governor Vance," Lee said, clasping his hand firmly and meeting his gaze with disarming frankness. "I bid you welcome and I am sincerely gratified to meet you at last. Would you care for a glass of sherry before dinner?"

"Thank you, General, that would be most agreeable."

Lee decanted the wine himself, took a seat across the table from Vance, and smiled rather slyly at his guest.

"I am sure you would prefer something stronger, but I think it is best to avoid strong spirits altogether—otherwise, the daily struggle for temperate use would prove too distracting. In any case, may I propose a toast to the great state of North Carolina?"

"On behalf of my state, I am honored to accept."

Vance judged Lee, now well into middle age and with hair and beard almost entirely gray, to be about five-eleven in height, trimly built, perhaps 165 pounds, many of them compacted in a rather massive chest. *Such a man must look splendid on a good horse*. Beneath their rough thatchy brows, Lee's eyes were a clear, penetrating brown, his nose elegantly proportioned, and his mouth wide with thin but finely arched lips. His voice was pure Virginia gentry, the very timbre of *noblesse oblige,* the vowels more rounded, the weight of inflections slightly more orotund, than one would hear in the speech of a Carolina gentleman of comparable status. Vance had known such men in his time, *serious* men, and most of them displayed a certain gravitas of spirit, which in Lee's case seemed darker than usual. So much was to be expected, Vance thought. It was well known that, only days after giving Meade the slip and returning to the Virginia side of the Potomac, Lee had offered Jefferson Davis his resignation. He accepted full responsibility for the carnage at Gettysburg, and his offer of resignation was no mere gesture. This was not a man who made "gestures." Vance was prepared to believe that, had the offer been accepted, Lee would have retired with dignity and served, with selfless grace, in any subordinate post the Confederacy offered him. But of course, Davis refused even to consider the matter.

While they ate, the general and the governor conversed amiably about the state of affairs in North Carolina—a subject about which, Vance was happy to learn, the commander in chief was reasonably well informed. Every now and then, Lee favored his guest with a glimpse of his slightly impish sense of humor, as when he playfully poked at a slab of cornbread with his knife.

"I fear the cornbread is somewhat burned and the chicken overcooked, but we ought not to mind—they'll only stick with us longer that way."

When the plates were cleared and coffee served, Lee briefly consulted his pocket watch.

"I apologize for any appearance of rudeness, sir, but we have only one more hour to enjoy each other's company—after that, I fear, there is a military conference over which I must preside. There always is, even if there's nothing really important to be discussed . . . So perhaps we ought to devote our attention now to the strategic matters you mentioned in your telegram."

"Indeed so, General Lee. I have some things in my case which will, I hope, engage your interest." But when Vance opened the case, his hand—performing its own act of secession—closed around the *Richmond Enquirer* and held it up so that Lee could see the front page. At first, Lee just squinted blankly, then sighed and put on his spectacles. When he saw what Vance was pointing to, his brow knitted with concern and he said: "Oh, that."

"General Lee, this article is infamous, blatantly false, and an egregious slander on the North Carolina soldiers who shed their blood so copiously for you at Gettysburg. Without wishing to seem impertinent, I must remind you that I have repeatedly asked that you bestow official credentials on a newspaper correspondent from North Carolina. There are several men of experience, probity, and impeccable honesty whom I can recommend. As it is now, our people learn about the actions of their sons and fathers only from cold, formal, belated official reports reprinted in our papers, or from letters written home, or from so-called 'eyewitness accounts' such as this one."

Betraying just a touch of pique, Lee rose from his chair and paced the room, hands clasped behind him, giving his shaggy head a few disapproving shakes.

"Governor Vance, I have read that account, and I know it to be greatly exaggerated in tone and downright wrong in many particulars. I understand your resentment—there are times, it seems, when the Confederate government treats North Carolina as though it were a *province* instead of a coequal, sovereign state. Whence comes this prejudice, I cannot say, other than the fact that your state *was* the last to go out . . ."

Now Lee turned and wagged a stern finger at Vance.

"These correspondents from the *Enquirer*—they are all accredited by the Davis administration, under which I *do* serve, and there is nothing I can do to restrict their movements or censor their dispatches. But my policy with regard to the Army of Northern Virginia remains the same, sir: If I issue credentials to correspondents from *one* state, I must do so for all of them. And then, sir, every move my army makes would be accompanied by a plague of scribblers, who would get in our way, distract anyone they chose to pester with their endless and sometimes asinine questions, and even then, *even then*, sir, they would write whatever they pleased, truthful or not! It is also my policy to release, as soon as they are available, all of the official reports compiled by participating officers. I believe those reports to be fair, accurate, and timely. Except for what I have seen with my own eyes, these are the documents I must also rely on to fill out my understanding of what happened and why. Of course editors are free to interpret them differently—I don't think I've had anyone hanged for doing so . . . yet. With all due respect, and with full understanding of the resentment you and your constituents must feel when you read this kind of tripe, my policy with regard to state-sponsored journalists remains the same: they are not welcome and will not be issued credentials. If it were up to me, that rule would apply to the writers from Richmond as well, but in that matter I am outflanked. And, to speak frankly, I have far more important things on my mind."

Chastened, Vance could only nod, mumble an apology, and shove the offending newspaper back into his case. But when he looked up, Lee was still pacing, a distant and mournful expression in his eyes. When he resumed speaking, it took Vance a few seconds to realize that Lee had moved beyond the issue of war correspondents and was meditating out loud, in a quiet and almost confessional tone, about the recent campaign.

"After our victory at Chancellorsville, the army was larger, better armed, and more confident than it had ever been; it possessed a tremendous sense of momentum, like the force in a great coiled spring. My confidence in the troops and their commanders was absolute, as was theirs, I think, in me. It was not arrogance, you understand, not hubris . . . and until General Meade's legions reminded me of it, I had forgotten than an excess of pride can be the undoing of an army, just as it can for a state or an emperor. And so there came a terrible day when I ordered the cream of my army to do a thing that was simply impossible. The failure was mine, not theirs.

"If future events develop in a manner favorable to our cause—and I pray every night to the Most High that they will—the recent campaign may come to be seen in a more favorable light, for it did show the world that we had the power to invade the enemy's heartland. But it was not a great victory, although I believed at the time that such a triumph was within our reach. I still think that if all the elements had come together as I envisioned, we would have accomplished something remarkable. But with the knowledge I then had, and in the unique circumstances which I felt vibrant in the air around me—the crucial balance of world opinion, the uncertain commitment of large segments of the Northern polity to the continued effusion of so much blood and treasure, the palpable and incredible *elan* of our troops—I do not know what better course I could have pursued.

"I truly believed, sir, that our successes on the first two days, and the grievous losses we inflicted on both flanks of Meade's front, made it a certainty that if we smote his center with all the concentrated power at our disposal, we would shatter them, drive them down from those heights, and send them reeling in disorder the way Hooker's troops had crumbled at Chacellorsville. If I had not truly believed so, I would not have ordered that assault! You must believe that, sir!"

"I do, General Lee," Vance whispered, his voice suddenly thick.

"I would have done . . . something else . . . perhaps feinted a retreat so that Meade would advance on our guns and been decimated by them as we were by his . . . Pete Longstreet pleaded with me relentlessly to adopt that scheme, but I was in no mood for a defensive stand when I felt with all my heart and soul that an attack would beat them faster and more decisively . . . so many ways it could have gone differently—my mind ties itself in knots when I dwell on it . . ."

Vance walked around the table and touched Lee's arm very diffidently.

"General Lee, take no counsel of what might have been. The South is not licked yet, not by any measure of God or man. Let us talk now about how we might achieve a significant victory in North Carolina, one whose strategic and political impact would be far out of proportion to the modest commitment of military resources by which it can be won."

Lee blinked a few times, adjusted his spectacles, and responded in a businesslike tone: "Yes. Yes, that is what we are here to discuss, after all. Show me what you have in that case, Governor Vance, and tell me all about this formidable new type of ironclad you are said to be constructing . . . in a *cornfield*, or so the story goes."

Encouraged, but also mindful that a quarter of his allotted hour had been usurped by the general's unexpected soliloquy—not to mention his own angry speech about Richmond's newspapers—Vance spread his documents across the table and summarized the situation succinctly, as many hours of rehearsal had prepared him to do.

"As you may recall, North Carolina had the distinction of being the site of General Ambrose Burnside's one great victory—I give him credit for vigorous leadership, but if the Outer Banks had been properly fortified, he would never have been able to conquer virtually our entire coastline, in less than six months, bringing under Federal control thirteen of the state's most productive counties—that equates to about three million bushels of corn, a half-million bales of cotton, and several hundred tons of naval stores which should be flowing into your supply depots, not those of the enemy!

"Having achieved so much, and having suffered only modest losses in the bargain, Burnside asked Washington for enough reinforcements to invade the Piedmont region and capture Raleigh. He could have done it, too, for there were very few troops standing in his way, Providentially for my state and the Confederate cause as a whole, McClellan ordered Burnside, along with eight thousand of his best troops, to leave North Carolina and join him in the Peninsula campaign. This left his successor, General John Foster, with only nine thousand men to garrison all the towns Burnside had captured.

"As you can see, some of those localities are widely separated. If there were anything to be gained by doing so, we could already have recaptured the smaller enclaves, such as Edenton and Elizabeth City, but the cost in blood was not worth such minuscule victories. John Foster is a fine engineer, and he had multiplied the strength of his forces by surrounding every Union outpost with elaborate fortifications. Moreover, he has absolute control of the sounds and rivers, thanks to an armada of powerfully armed, shallow-draft gunboats. He can rush reinforcements, or bring up devastating firepower, to any threatened location, thanks to his gunboat and transport flotillas. And his naval counterpart, Commander Charles Flusser, is a very aggressive, very bold fellow . . ."

Lee raised a hand to interrupt. "There's another young firebrand in that fleet, too, I believe. Bold as brass, much given to risky raids and reckless adventures, usually without bothering to ask permission from his superiors. Even the Richmond papers have made him out to be a hero, the veritable reincarnation of John Paul Jones . . . or is it Blackbeard?"

"That would be Lieutenant Commander William Cushing, sir. He sticks pins in us whenever he can, up and down the coast. I understand he even took a boat right up the Cape Fear River and tried to kidnap General Whiting from his own bedroom! Thankfully, Whiting was not at home."

Lee laughed—the first true laugh Vance had heard, and it was a surprisingly warm and rumbling sound.

"I'll bet that drove old Chase back to his bottle!"

Vance stiffened a bit. "General Whiting has been both sober and diligent, on every occasion I have met with him. And he has wrought a tremendous improvement in the strength of Wilmington's defenses."

"Yes, yes, of course. Chase Whiting is a fine engineer, none better. If he has pledged an oath of temperance for the duration, I am happy to hear it. But, please, get on with your presentation."

"Foster's headquarters is in New Bern, and he has fortified the place like Gibraltar, but New Bern is a special case because the topography lends itself to extensive engineering. However, none of Foster's other outposts are nearly as formidable. If we attack the weaker ones first, Foster must either suffer the disgrace of sacrificing their garrisons, or he must weaken his own reserves by sending reinforcements from New Bern.

"Notice, too, that each of these Yankee enclaves is wide-open to naval gunfire from the sounds and rivers. Why should Foster waste time and resources fortifying the shorelines, when there isn't a single Confederate warship left in North Carolina waters? But there *will be* a mighty vessel in these waters come next February at the latest. The *Hatteras* will be able to anchor at point-blank range, and shell the defenses from behind! New Bern is not as impregnable as it looks, not if the ironclad gives us the capability of landing troops right down here, on the docks!"

No doubt about it: General Lee was scrutinizing the map with the eye of a military engineer, and his professional interest was stimulated by the possibilities he was seeing. "I see, I see, yes . . . Hmmmm. It would be feasible . . ."

Vance sensed that now was the moment to describe the more visionary part of this strategy, the aspects that might change Lee's attitude from one of detached, almost academic interest, into a rush of genuine excitement.

"There is much more at stake here than just throwing all the Yankees out of North Carolina. Once we have done that, we must *keep them out.* Observe how the Outer Banks resemble a castle wall, and the waters of the sounds, a gigantic moat. General Lee, there are only *five* channels along this whole expanse of barrier-islands that are deep enough to permit large vessels a safe transition from the open sea to the sheltered sounds. Only five!

"The Yankees never bothered to repair those pathetic forts we had back in Sixty-One—all Foster has done is build some observation towers out there, connected to New Bern by a submarine cable. If there's any sign of small-boat smuggling, the watchmen can telegraph New Bern and some gunboats will be on the scene very quickly. Otherwise, there is not a single cannon anywhere along that 'outer wall.' Now, if we succeed in ejecting Foster from the mainland, we stand to inherit a number of very powerful and easily repairable guns—we can seal those five inlets with proper fortifications, just as Fort Fisher seals off the New Inlet below Wilmington, and suddenly, the blockade-runners have three ports they can run for instead of only one. The shipping and storage facilities at both Morehead City and Beaufort have been greatly expanded by the enemy. If we open two more ports to the runners, that gives the blockade patrols another two hundred miles of ocean to worry about. In one stroke, we force the U.S. Navy to weaken the blockade around Wilmington, we increase the odds of any given ship making a successful run, and that in turn will attract a new surge of interest by European shipowners in the blockade-running business. Their profits will still be huge, but their risks will be reduced! The end result, sir, will be more and better equipment reaching your army."

"Perhaps, Governor, you missed your real calling, for you would make an excellent salesman!" Lee was actually enjoying Vance's presentation. "Are there any other long-range benefits to be derived from this scheme?"

"Oh yes, indeed, General Lee! Those thirteen productive counties now under Union control? Once they are back under Confederate control, they'll produce significant amounts of cotton, tobacco, naval stores, and probably several thousand fresh recruits as well. Secondly, this victory, or this chain of victories, ought to rekindle patriotic zeal among the common folk—fewer deserters, more enthusiasm in the ranks! So you see, to sum it all up, the ramifications of a military victory could be profoundly more important than the victory itself!"

Lee listened very intently to this expanded strategic prognosis. He began to pace around the table restlessly, hands clasped behind his back.

"I am very much impressed by the breadth of your strategic vision, Governor. You have thought this thing out to its farthest reverberations! Your logic is undeniable, and yet, in the end, it all hinges on one very big question: Will the *Hatteras* truly be the kind of supership needed to do all the things you've planned for her to do? According to my information, there are at least thirty-five gunboats under Foster's control, and another two or three dozen armed auxiliary vessels—tugs and mortar barges, that sort of thing. Can one lone ship, however formidable its design, really triumph over odds of fifty-to-one? If you can convince me of that . . ."

Now was the time for Vance to pull out the schematic drawings of the ironclad, and to explain to Lee why that lone ship *could* turn the tide.

"The man who designed the *Hatteras*, Major Frederick Reilly, has never formally studied naval architecture. But he is very learned about modern technologies, and he has an innate genius for innovations. For example—the gun-mountings are radically different from those you would find in a conventional ironclad. These rails, pivots, and gear mechanisms, make it possible for a gun to fire straight ahead, then be repositioned to shoot port or starboard, in an average time of sixty-seven seconds! In the simplest terms, the *Hatteras*'s two big guns can do the same work as six weapons on conventional mountings. This saves a tremendous amount of weight, and increases the space available for ammunition and fuel storage.

"And the armor itself, that is Major Reilly's true stroke of genius. He calls it 'composite protection,' a sort of laminated, layer cake configuration. Layers of rolled iron plate alternating with layers of oak and pine; horizontal layers alternating with vertical, and the whole outward carapace slanted at the optimal angle needed to deflect, or minimize the power, of any shells that strike the casemate. Unlike simple iron-plate armor, this stuff actually bends a little when it takes a hit, which further dissipates the kinetic energy of both shells and solid shot.

"Even when she's fully armored, the *Hatteras* should be nimble enough to match the maneuvering capabilities of Foster's gunboats. If we can procure engines strong enough to give her a speed of eight knots, in a quarter-mile run, she can work up enough momentum for that great iron-shod ram to break a gunboat in half."

Lee seemed genuinely fascinated by Reilly's design. "If everything works as it should, this ironclad will be able to do things no other ironclad has ever done. The first Federal gunboats that come out to engage her, should be in for a nasty surprise! Have you got enough iron to finish installing the armor?"

"Um, most of it, sir. There is a bottleneck at the Tredegar works, however, and it sometimes takes months before the raw iron is shipped back to the construction site in the form of rolled plate. Even so, the plates arrive in ones and twos, and the machinery available to accomplish their fitting is barely equal to the job."

"I can do nothing about that, Governor, but I will send a memorandum to the Tredegar administration, recommending that they give a higher priority to rolling the armor plates. Whether that will light a fire under them or not, only God and Jeff Davis can say. As the largest foundry in the Confederacy, the place has acquired its own bureacracy-within-a-bureacracy and I have no power to order them, merely to urge them in one direction or another. Still, my wishes carry *some* weight. Now, as to the ship's battery . . ."

"She was designed with a pair of six-point-four Parrotts in mind, but despite numerous assurances, they have not materialized."

"But she could carry heavier ordnance, without compromising her design?"

"Yes, General, up to a certain point."

"What I have in mind is some of the new double-banded nine-point-five-inch Brooke rifles. They are powerful and reliable—they don't blow up after sustained firing the way so many Parrott guns do. There is a small stockpile of them in Richmond. Our intent was to use them to strengthen the works at Vicksburg, but obviously that purpose has been rendered moot. I will most forcefully remonstrate with the Ordnance Department to have a pair of them allocated for the *Hatteras*. Telegraph me when the ship is ready to receive them, and I will personally see to it that their movement is expedited.

"As for diverting a full veteran division to support this counterattack you have outlined, I cannot of course predict when, or if, that will be practicable. As you say, there is a lot to be gained on your coastline for a very modest investment of resources. Communicate the vessel's progress to me at regular intervals, and when she is ready to challenge the Yankee navy, I will see what can be spared.

"And now, Governor Vance, I must bid you farewell and attend to my other commitments. This has been a most stimulating discussion. Thank you for coming to see me and for being so well prepared as to waste none of my time—not all of my visitors are so considerate."

Vance shook Lee's hand and gathered up his papers, satisfied that things had gone as well, or better, than he had hoped. As he was leaving, Lee called to him once more.

"Governor Vance, I understand the resentment you and your people feel about the condescension with which you are treated by the Richmond press, and by some members of the Richmond administration. Please be assured that I know, and my men know as well, how great has been the effort and sacrifice of North Carolina's soldiers. Without those regiments, and without the supplies and weapons coming through Wilmington, this army could not long stay in the field."

"May I quote you, General Lee?"

"Not in the public press," Lee snapped. Then, more warmly: "But you may spread the word informally, if it will help assuage the ill-feeling that seems so prevalent among the people of your state. Feel free to paraphrase."

The Curious Discontent of Matthew Sloane

OF ALL THE "nonviolent" inmates I dealt with, few captured my interest more than Captain Matthew Sloane, skipper of the intrepid and hugely successful blockade-runner Banshee. *He was the only "runner" we ever had at The Fed (most runner captains simply went out of business when their ships were captured, so the Government seldom bothered jailing them). Sloane, however, was not captured* in the act *of blockade-busting, but because he had taken as passenger the notorious (in every sense of the word) Rebel Spy, Belle O'Neal. Somehow, the Secret Service learned of her departure from Nassau, and her intent to return to Dixie, and mounted a rather dastardly attack on the* Banshee *in midocean. This heavy-handed seizure was led by the widely feared Mr. Lafayette Baker, second in command to Mr. Pinkerton—when rough-stuff was called for, Baker handled the job. Only he didn't handle this job very well. Sloane very cunningly gave him the slip, and delivered Miss O'Neale to the shores of North Carolina, where she was drowned trying to escape capture, and Sloane was arrested as her accomplice.*

The case had interesting repercussions, because the Banshee *was in British waters when Baker waylaid her, and was, legally, a British ship, being registered out of Liverpool. The Governor of Nassau lodged a strong protest with the Lincoln Administration, calling Baker "a scoundrel and a pirate," then the British Consulate weighed in, and finally, Old Abe got an indignant letter from Queen Victoria herself. Had Sloane engaged a vigorous attorney—and there were many eager to take the case!—he would have walked out of my jail after only a few weeks. The odd thing was, he seemed not only indifferent about staying in prison, but actually seemed quite comfortable about remaining there indefinitely! That was fine with me, because I found him a most enjoyable companion, albeit a man much given to brooding introspection.*

—*Recollections of a Happy Jailor*, by Major G. K. Fellows,
The Union Veteran, June, 1880

After an absence of only seven days, Will Cushing returned to the shabby rented rooms he shared with Lieutenant Valentine. One look at Cushing's slumped shoulders and dejected face evoked a fatherly concern from the older officer. Naval regulations be damned: this was a bereaved young lad who needed a hug. So Valentine opened his arms and embraced his commanding officer, who was not in the least offended.

"Let me stow your luggage, Will, while you pour a drink for yourself. And one for me as well."

Cushing was grateful to be rid of the baggage, to be slumped in one of the shabby but comfortable lounge chairs, and to have a fresh drink with a trusted companion near at hand. Since leaving Fredonia, Cushing had been tight as a drumhead.

"How did it go, Will? As much of it as you care to tell me about, that is."

Cushing shrugged, as if to say, "A funeral is a funeral." But he decided to be more forthcoming than that. "All the needful things were done and all the eulogies were fulsome, especially the one at West Point—and all the requisite sentiments were expressed. President Lincoln sent flowers. When I reached Fredonia, it looked like the whole town was draped in widows' black—rather overdone, if you ask me, considering how eager Alonzo was to *leave* the place at the earliest opportunity. And my mother, God bless her, is holding up like a rock. But having lost one son, I fear she may now become unhealthily obsessed with *me*. I must remember to tone down the bloodthirsty details in my letters." Cushing actually voiced that final remark with a tiny, self-deprecating chuckle. Valentine was greatly relieved when he heard it; the healing process had begun.

"I spent four days and five nights with my mother, James, and I don't recall any other time when we felt so close to one another, despite our grief—or maybe because of it. What a strong, proud, admirable woman she is."

"Yes, and you inherited some of her best qualities."

Again, Cushing's mouth bent into a sly, boyish grin. "Except for the one virtue that has sustained her more than any other: *patience!* That trait, as so many superior officers keep reminding me, was not passed along to me, I fear."

Valentine refilled their glasses. "You sound like a man in dire need of a new ship. I wish I could tell you that, during your absence, another telegram had come from the Navy Department, but so far there's been nothing."

"More likely, there is some cabal of older, more orthodox officers who think I got off far too lightly in the *Foxglove* inquiry. And who also think that my penchant for taking independent action is setting a bad example to other young officers. The department is a bureaucracy so vast there could even be multiple conspirators plotting to reign in that 'shameless glory hunter, Will Cushing.' Well, I have made up my mind: if another week goes by and I have not been given a new and suitable posting, I will simply march straight into Secretary of the Navy Welles's office and deliver an ultimatum—a new ship or my resignation, followed by an uproar in the newspapers. I'm sure the army could find a suitable place for me!"

Valentine could never tell how *serious* Cushing was when he delivered one of these intemperate rants, but Valentine thought it would not be amiss to offer some fatherly advice.

"If you do that, Will Cushing, you'll only be proving yourself to be exactly the kind of headstrong young fool your enemies have painted you out to be. Secretary Welles has many times expressed his gratitude for the interest your exploits have generated in the navy, and for all the enthusiastic newspaper coverage, too, but he is responsible for running the entire war effort at sea, and I doubt that his goodwill runs deep enough to let you barge in like that, and threaten, like a spoiled brat, to take your toys out of the sandbox and go skulking off unless your wounded pride was immediately soothed. In Welles's place I would probably say, 'Well, resign and be damned, sir, as you have finally become more trouble than you're worth!' "

Valentine's impersonation of "Old Neptune's" foghorn voice and pompous hand gestures was so pitch-perfect that Cushing had to laugh, in spite of himself. Seeing a chance to further brighten his roommate's mood, Valentine asked, "Are you hungry, Will?"

"Now that you mention it, I surely am."

"Excellent, because I have discovered a marvelous new restaurant on the fringe of the brothel district. It serves authentic Chink food, and as long as you don't ask what all the ingredients are, much of the fare is really tasty. You can get a nine-course meal for pocket change!"

"Let me change into a fresh uniform and we shall embark on a 'reckless and insubordinate' culinary adventure."

At eight-thirty the following morning, a messenger from the Navy Department knocked on the door with a telegram for "Lieutenant Commander W. B. Cushing and his chosen executive officer."

Valentine was shaving when Cushing opened the envelope and read the message. His yelp of joy was so exuberant that Valentine instinctively jumped and cut himself rather badly on the chin.

"Listen to this! *'In recognition of the outstanding services he has rendered to the nation and to the service, Lieutenant Commander William B. Cushing is hereby promoted to the rank of full commander and is appointed to take command of the U.S.S.* Monticello.*'* Secondary paragraphs confirmed the appointment of James J. Valentine as the new executive officer, with at least the brevet rank of lieutenant commander, and informed both officers that their ship was presently undergoing a complete overhaul at the Hampton Roads maintenance yard.

"By God," cried Cushing, so enlivened now that he could barely match the proper foot with the appropriate trouser leg, "she's a real warship!"

"Aye, sir, and one of the prettiest vessels in the fleet. We seem to have done all right for ourselves, after all."

"Well, don't just sit there, man—start packing your bag! Let's go take a look at her!"

"But Will, we have already seen the *Monticello* a hundred times, both at sea and in port. She won't look any different in dry-dock."

"Yes, Mister Valentine, she *will* look different, because for the first time we will be seeing her as *our* ship!"

"A week, at least, before she's ready for sea," replied the dockyard foreman to Will's impatient question. Cushing groaned at the prospect of more enforced idleness, but when he learned that the delay was caused by the need to install new boilers, he changed his mind. New boilers meant high speeds for the *Monticello,* and higher speeds meant a better chance to bag a runner. In the meantime, however, he and Valentine were forced to find temporary lodgings again—no easy task, given the number of other stranded officers whose ships were also being repaired or overhauled. Finally they located a cramped little apartment that the landlord was willing to rent at a very low price. "Most people don't like the view," he said, throwing open the curtains covering the room's two dingy windows. After taking a quick peek, Valentine muttered: "I can certainly understand why."

Little sunlight could enter this room; the view was almost completely obstructed by the great, hulking, sooty brick facade of the Federal prison at Fortress Monroe. Cushing agreed that he had seen more picturesque views, but as they were only renting for a short while, and the price was so low, he told the landlord they would take it.

"I'm curious to know why the windows on the first two stories are barred, but not the ones on the stories above. In fact, where their occupants had left curtains drawn, the upper-level cells looked more like comfortable dormitories than dungeons of woe. Exactly what kinds of prisoners are housed in that facility?"

"Well, obviously it ain't your average prisoner-of-war camp. Men incarcerated in that particular prison are gentlemen whose 'crimes' usually revolve around diplomatic or political causes, Some of them, the would-be assassins and thugs, are kept down in the barred cells, but the prisoners up above are often well-connected gentlemen, and very often representatives of foreign governments, which always means a long, complicated trial. I guess President Lincoln doesn't want those fellows to complain about what a barbaric place the United States is, so he makes their imprisonment about as light and pleasant as the basic experience allows. Those high-class prisoners have sofas and writing desks, all the books they want to read, fairly decent grub, and are exempt from all manual labor. Hell, I've stayed in hotels that weren't half as cozy as some of those cells. I know of at least two published novels that were written inside those walls, and one successful German opera! No, sir, those men imprisoned on the upper stories are not common criminals!

"Tell you what: if you're really interested, you can get a brilliant guided tour from the warden, a somewhat portly but very affable gent named Major Fellows. He lost a leg at Chickamauga. He loves his job, really does, and often plays chess or discusses art and politics with his guests. He told me one day, 'This is the most interesting place a student of human nature could ask to spend his days.' Ol' Fellows, he'll talk your ears off, but you'll enjoy the tour enormously, I promise."

"That is all very interesting, and I think I'll just do that, early tomorrow." Cushing put a generous tip in the landlord's hand as he ushered him out the door. Then he returned to a windowsill and peered at the ugly pile of masonry blocking the view.

"By God, James, do you know who's in there? Captain Matthew Sloane, the daring blockade runner whose wife saved our lives at Pine Haven plantation. The same man, also, who outwitted the Federal spy service in a running battle on the high seas, the same man who was finally captured only because he was trying to save the beautiful Rebel spy Belle O'Neal. I confess, I am most curious to meet this gentleman."

"What better time and setting to find out a man's true nature than in his prison cell, eh? Go pay him a visit, Will, find out what kind of a man he really is."

"A damned lucky one, in the wife department," muttered Cushing, a touch wistfully.

The next morning, after breakfast, Cushing sent his *carte de visite,* along with a brief note, to the commandant of the prison facility requesting permission to visit Mr. Sloane to communicate messages of a personal nature from his wife. Major Fellows replied in the affirmative within hours, setting up an appointment for nine o'clock the following morning and rather cheekily adding that he would be delighted to meet the famous young naval hero and most especially looked forward "to learning the circumstances under which you obtained information of a 'personal nature' from Captain Sloane's wife."

A bizarre, tenuous web already connected Cushing and Matthew Sloane, despite the fact that they had never met. The fact that Cushing was *here,* preparing to advance his career by taking command of a fine blue-water cruiser—rather than languishing in a Confederate prisoner-of-war camp—was due almost entirely to the compassion of Mary Harper Sloane and the recuperative effects of his sojourn in lovely Pine Haven. When Mrs. Sloane and her tiny multiethnic private army had discovered them, Cushing and the other *Foxglove* survivors were emaciated, at the end of their strength, and vulnerably asleep. But instead of turning them over to the Confederate authorities in Wilmington, Mrs. Sloane had taken pity on these unlikely wayfarers; indeed—after a brief period of mutual wariness—she treated Cushing and his men more like guests than captured enemies. Her slaves and her curious little militia were courteous, the wounded and sick were tended with surprising skill, and their hunger put to rout by ample servings of the tastiest vittles any of them had eaten in months. Ultimately, Mrs. Sloane had helped the party to escape down the Cape Fear River and return to active duty—an act that many of her compatriots might reasonably have defined as "treason."

Mary Harper Sloane had certainly not conformed to Cushing's stereotypical idea of a "Southern belle." She had grit and intelligence to spare, and if there had ever been anything flighty or frivolous in her character, the grindstone of wartime responsibility had abraded those girlish qualities utterly. By the end of his stay at Pine Haven, Will Cushing felt not only a strong obligation to Mrs. Sloane, he also felt disturbingly attracted to her. He had, of course, offered to carry a letter from Mary Harper to her imprisoned husband, but she declined to write one—a most curious decision, and one she made no effort to explain. Yes, indeed, Will Cushing had a fund of curiosity about Matthew Sloane, and since fate had placed them, so to speak, in the same neighborhood, he decided to meet Sloane face-to-face and take his measure.

The commandant, Major Fellows, was very much as the landlord had described him: portly, affable, and radiantly content to serve out the rest of his enlistment right where he was. After listening raptly to Cushing's account of his sojourn at Pine Haven, the jailer brought Cushing up to date on the unusual case of Matthew Sloane.

"We know he was captain of the blockade runner *Banshee,* a very saucy and successful ship, but he wasn't captured *on* that vessel, so technically there is no proof. The wording of the indictment that keeps him locked up here goes something like: 'aiding and abetting a known spy and agent provocateur in the commission of seditious acts against the United States.' "

"That would have been the notorious Belle O'Neal," mused Cushing.

The major grinned lasciviously. "Aye, it was, and our friend Captain Sloane had a tumble with her, I suspect. Lucky bastard if he did."

"Has he told you that?"

"No, no, quite the opposite—he refuses even to discuss her, even though he's entertained us with many other stories about his adventures.

"When does he go on trial?"

"I don't think the Secret Service is in any hurry to have a trial. And the reason for that, I think, is because the Pinkertons hope that he might have gotten information from Miss O'Neal about other Rebel agents in Washington–they figure an open-ended jail sentence might help to refresh his memory. Personally, I doubt he spent much of his time with her discussing military secrets, and even if he did, all the Rebel spy networks would have changed their modus operandi as soon as they learned the Secret Service gents were hot on Belle's trail."

Fellows waxed philosophical for a moment. "I am a student of human nature, Commander Cushing, and this place is a veritable zoo of strange, interesting men. But Sloane is unique. He seems not just indifferent to the prospect of remaining in prison, he actually seems comfortable here, which makes him an unusual prisoner indeed. Well, you will see for yourself. Come, I'll walk you to his cell."

The word "cell" conjured images of chains, straw pallets, and dank walls crawling with vermin, but Matthew Sloane's quarters were more commodious than many a cheap hotel room Cushing had slept in: reasonably spacious and well ventilated by a window that afforded a picturesque view of Chesapeake Bay. The furnishings were comfortable, too: a decent bed, a writing desk, some chairs, and a well-stocked bookcase.

During his stay at Pine Haven, Cushing had studied a daguerreotype portrait of Matthew Sloane as he had appeared just prior to his wedding: he kept looking for some glint of rebelliousness in the young Sloane's features, some foreshadowing of his decision to leave behind a prosperous plantation *and* a beautiful wife to pursue the dangers and uncertainties of the blockade runners' trade. But that portrait was a study in *propriety.* Cushing saw no roguish spark of discontent in Sloane's gaze; this was a portrait of a young man who seemed completely satisfied with the way of life he had inherited. Why, then, other than sheer lust for profit, had this complacent gentleman farmer turned into a high-seas adventurer?

Now, as Cushing shook Sloane's hand, he tried to match his memory of that portrait to the actual man, and the differences were striking. Sloane had grown a salt-and-pepper beard, and his hair was streaked with gray. His eyes seemed deeper than they appeared in that old daguerreotype, and beginning to show the weather lines of a veteran seaman. There was also a furtiveness in Sloane's gaze, but that might be ascribed to the most unusual nature of this visit. After introducing the two men, Warden Fellows bid them enjoy their conversation and left the cell. The fact that he did not bother to lock the door struck Cushing as both odd and significant. Perhaps Sloane really did feel at home in this relatively comfortable jail.

"Are you being treated well, Captain Sloane?"

"The food is monotonous, but that's to be expected. I have access to books; an hour's daily exercise in the courtyard, weather permitting; and I play a lot of cards with the commandant, who is a jolly companion. The guards are decent young chaps, too, and keep me supplied with daily newspapers, in exchange for my colorful accounts of the *Banshee*'s adventures. All things considered, my days pass agreeably enough. Now, sir, what brings you here? When the commandant told me that the famous Will Cushing wanted to visit me, I envisioned an older officer. You seem much too young to have performed the daring exploits for which you've been lionized in the press."

"Is there an age limit to courage, Mister Sloane? By the same token, I would judge you to be too mature a man to relinquish the comforts of Pine Haven and the company of a lovely wife in favor of a dangerous career as a blockade-runner."

Matthew favored Cushing with a tiny smile.

"Touché, sir! Now that we've had our little verbal fencing match, please tell me how you came to be at Pine Haven and what you found there. In the note you wrote to Major Fellows, requesting a visit with me, you mentioned that you had news of home and family. So how did you come to be *there,* of all places?"

Cushing summarized his tale: the exhausting days wandering through the wilderness of Onslow County; the desperate crossing of the Uhwarrie River while being attacked by a huge rogue alligator; and finally ending up dead asleep on the grounds of the Sloane plantation, then waking up to see Mary Harper pointing a shotgun at his head, attended by a trio of exotic foreigners whom she referred to as the "Pine Haven Militia."

"Ah, so the Chinaman, the Pole, and that morose Portugee all stayed on? And Fitz-John Bright is in good health?"

"Yes to all three questions."

"And the children ? . . ."

"They are staying with your father-in-law, I believe, and at last reports, were all doing fine."

"That is a comfort."

A mantle of silence settled over Matthew Sloane. He seemed determined not to ask the one question that most imprisoned husbands would have asked right away. So when the silence attenuated to the point of embarrassment, Cushing asked it for him.

"And how is your dear wife? I shall tell you, even if you will not broach the subject yourself."

Sloane looked up, and Cushing was startled to see the pain in his eyes.

"I am not worthy of her, Commander Cushing. If she knew *how* unworthy, she would not wish to see me again."

"Your pardon, sir, but that is outright humbug! Missuz Sloane is a woman with great strength of character, and she has done all within her power to maintain Pine Haven as it was when you left it, but she is overburdened and she needs you by her side. I must speak frankly: if Lincoln does grant you a pardon, it is your duty *as a man* to put aside this mood of self-reproach and go back to your home and family, where you belong."

Matthew's shoulders slumped, and he bent his head like a chastened schoolboy. Then, staring up at Cushing with a spark of defiance, he snapped back: "Would you be so eager to send me home if you knew I was planning to return to the blockade-running business?"

"Could you really be so foolish? You've barely escaped the gallows, thanks to your friends in Great Britain; why stick your head right back in the same noose? Surely you have already made enough money from your previous voyages."

"Obscene amounts of it, yes. So if I *were* to return to the runner business, it would not be for the additional profit."

"Ah! You are motivated by Confederate patriotism, then! How admirable!"

"Don't be so quick to mock me, Cushing! The North has no monopoly on love of country. I do not know if secession was a wise decision or a stupid, prideful mistake, but I do know that the passions that engendered it were deep and very real. In my case, however, I find that too much stiff-necked 'patriotism' can be the foundation of petty tyranny. I do love my state and wish to see the South victorious, but I would never make an important decision simply because Jefferson Davis might approve! Men who spout off constantly about how patriotic they are, tend to be quite vulgar. There is a lot of truth in Samuel Johnson's remark that 'patriotism is the last refuge of a scoundrel.' "

"Well, then, what *does* motivate you?"

Sloane rose and clasped his hands behind him, pacing restlessly as he spoke. "You of all men should understand. Until that first day when I stood on the bridge of my ship and steered her into dangerous waters, I did not know what *real* freedom was! I felt uplifted, as though a great eagle were bearing me aloft, and I felt surging through me an intoxicating vigor! My blood seemed to run as hot as that of a strong, much younger man! Every moment of the *Banshee*'s voyages, I experienced with a startling vividness—even the times when we were under fire. At sea, on the bridge of my own ship, I felt such magnified and total exhilaration that everything else I had ever done seemed to pale in comparison. Mind you, I had never before even thought about seafaring, but once I tasted salt air and felt the wind on my face, it was as if I had suddenly found my true destiny! I became Poseidon's child, and the sea revealed to me many sights that were awesome, majestic, beyond the ken of landlubbers! And you, Cushing, you have dedicated your life to the sea—do not tell me you haven't felt those same emotions."

"Yes, of course I have. But—"

"Hear me out, please! My very nature changed over time and many voyages; is it possible for a man to become *addicted* to the sea? To crave that galvanic quickening of the senses that comes when you are under fire, or fighting to keep your ship afloat during a great storm? I experienced such enormous zest at such moments that I began to have an exaggerated notion of my seamanship and courage—how I disdained the toilsome, sleepy, unvarying routine of the rice farmer I had been! If I had not been under such a spell, I do not think I would have left my emotions so unguarded, my vows of fidelity so trivial when viewed from the overweening pride of my new identity. If I had been able to blend Sloane the rice planter with Sloane the adventurer, perhaps I would never have fallen in love, like, like some lust-besotted innocent, with Belle O'Neal. There, I have said it openly at last! Consider yourself an honored confidant . . . ."

"People speak of her as if she were Helen of Troy combined with the Whore of Babylon . . . . What was the secret of her appeal?"

"It was not sheer physical beauty, I can tell you that—I have known prettier women, and many who were much more elegant and graceful than Belle. Before I became engaged to Mary Harper, I flirted with dozens of them. They fanned themselves to cool the vicarious passions that absorbed from romantic novels; they twittered like birds about finding a duke, a knight, a dashing prince to sweep them away to a gilded but ever-so-chaste-sounding domestic Paradise. Even at the time, I thought of them as shallow, ridiculous creatures. They longed for adventures, yes, including the erotic kind, but would have died from embarrassment rather than admit to such fantasies.

"But by the time Belle set foot on the *Banshee,* had come to believe that in order to have *real* and powerful adventures, you must be willing to take concomitant risks! A shorter life in trade for a more intense one! I had known danger, taken my share of risks by that time, and I would gladly have traded the tranquility of ripe old age for another three or four years of a life in which every sight, sound, and sensation was a hundred times more intense and vivid than it had been before I went to sea.

"A few minutes in Belle O'Neal's presence, and I knew that here was a woman who lived by that very creed, and courted far more danger than I ever had. For her, the role of the courtesan-spy was a *calling.* She could coax secrets from generals with acts of volcanic passion, and yet the core of her intellect remained calm, analytical, soaking up, like a sponge, any information of possible military use to the Confederacy—a cause she believed in passionately and ultimately gave her life for.

"I realize that she had the reputation of a high-priced whore, but I swear to you, Cushing, that there was something truly heroic about her. She had slept with some of the most powerful men in Washington, and created a network of couriers to pass information across the Potomac. By the time the Secret Service caught on to her, the fact that she was a woman would not save her from the hangman. How she regretted having to flee Washington when Pinkerton and Baker closed in on her! It did not take long for me to become infatuated with her, you may be sure; but I was far too timid in her presence to make any attempt at . . . . further intimacy. All I had done, after all, was dodge a few badly aimed cannon balls and ride out a few squalls. Compared to Belle's adventures, my own were trifles.

"But each man has in him, I think, one occasion, one day, one challenge, that calls him out to be . . . *superb!* And my day came when Lafayette Baker and his thugs tried to seize Belle from my ship. These were ruthless men, hired for their willingness to kill, and when the *Banshee* came abreast of their ship, which had been painted and altered to appear storm-damaged, a fake deckhouse collapsed, revealing a howitzer, and from belowdecks swarmed two dozen armed deputies. I had a vision of the coarse hangman's rope tightening around Belle's alabaster neck, and . . . I don't know any other word for it, Cushing, but I was *transformed—I became superb,* and on the instant, I conceived of a desperate plan. While Baker and his brutes were rowing across, under cover of their howitzer and many rifles, I whispered orders to my crew, and they acted! When Baker's boarding party climbed onto the *Banshee*'s deck, we pretended that a dangerous fire had broken out in the forward hold—it was actually nothing but a coal scuttle filed with turpentine-soaked rags—and went through the motions of a fire-fighting drill. But the hose we dragged on deck was not connected to a water pump, but to the main bleeder valve of the steam engine. We scalded the hell out of that boarding party, then went at them with fists, belaying pins and sidearms. Two of them, we killed—my first time for that, incidentally—and the rest, many of them badly blistered from the steam, we simply tossed overboard like a bunch of fish too small to take home for dinner. I had already ordered full steam raised, so we turned quickly away and showed Baker a clean pair of heels, despite all the grapeshot he fired at us.

"And that battle, that improvised but inspired plan, was the high point of my career at sea. One moment, I was meek and cautious—the next, I was fearless and bold, eager to draw blood, quite willing to shed it! And I, who had not even been in a barroom brawl since I was twenty-two, had broken the skull of a hulking brute twice my size."

"You enjoyed the killing?" asked Cushing quietly.

"Not the killing per se, but the context in which I did the act. When we sailed away under fire, I could scarcely believe it: an unarmed blockade runner, commanded by an amateur sailor, had gotten the drop on Lincoln's most elite gunmen and agents! I, Matthew Sloane, gentleman and rice farmer, had taken on the toughest bunch in Yankeedom and beaten them smartly!"

"And, of course, also saved the fair lady from a cruel abduction and almost certain death," said Cushing with a smile. "In that moment of triumph, you exceeded your own fantasy and became, in fact, the hero you longed to be. I am impressed, Sloane! If my ship is ever under threat of a boarding attack, I shall remember your brilliant little trick. So, now that you were victorious and ten feet tall, I think I can guess what happened next. . . ."

"It was as natural and uncontrollable as the tide, I swear it. I made love like a savage and a voluptuary rolled into one—and as for Miss O'Neal, it did not take me long to understand why men had divulged state secrets to her. We made love every night, and sometimes in the day, all the way back to North Carolina, where the vengeful Mr. Baker ambushed us, and Belle drowned herself rather than face capture, and I was knocked out with a rifle butt and ended up, well, *here!* Don't you see, Cushing? If I returned to the life of a genteel planter, and to the arms of my wife, would I not find that existence insufferable? Would my wife's embrace no longer satisfy me? What if I made the effort, with all my heart, and still I longed so much for the open sea that I ended up leaving her for a second time? God help me, I have tasted forbidden fruit and found it unbearably sweet. I am afraid now that I cannot ever return to my former way of life, and I would spare Mary Harper the indignity of knowing she had reclaimed a liar and a hypocrite."

Cushing chose his next words carefully—his feelings toward this man were more complicated than he would have believed possible after such a brief acquaintance.

"I have two things to say, Captain Sloane. First: it is likely that no one of your class will ever again enjoy that 'old way of life.' Whichever side wins, most of the things we all took for granted before this war *will be changed*, and changed profoundly. Your future may still hold surprises, and you may still face challenges that will test your wisdom as well as your courage. The other thing is that your wife, Mary Harper, is not the same woman she was when you last saw her—even as you are not the same man. She commands respect from the slaves, and loyalty from that strange little army of vagabonds—they are all quite prepared to give their lives in her defense. Pine Haven is isolated, and if my men and I could sneak up on the place, so could a band of bushwhackers. Your wife, sir, has courage and determination, and she works from dawn until well into the night, just to keep things running. My point is this: compared to the responsibilities she has taken on, and the dangers that could descend on her in the future, your single indiscretion—while it may have been earth-shattering to you—might very well seem small potatoes to her, a minor irritant, but certainly not a thing that would wreck your marriage, not compared to the relief she would feel at seeing you again. You do not have to confess your sins in every detail, man! You keep replaying that incident in your mind, like a man who keeps sucking on a bad tooth because he has a compulsion to verify the pain. Ever since you entered this prison cell, you've been wallowing in guilt, and when I entered this room, you practically exploded at the chance to make confession, to lance the boil, as it were. I am not your priest, Sloane, but if you feel cleansed and less burdened after blurting it out to me, then I'm happy I could be of service. But as for confessing to your *wife,* there is no damned need for you to do it, sir! Mary Harper is no bubble-headed debutante—the circumstances of your capture have already tied you and Belle O'Neal together in the public's imagination, and Mister Bright *does* bring back the newspapers when he makes those supply runs to Wilmington. I'd bet my last dollar that Mary Harper has already figured things out for herself, and almost certainly she has resolved never to bring up the matter. You should resolve to do the same. Go home if you can. Help her and protect her."

Matthew sighed, but it was a normal sigh, not that theatrically heavy moaning-of-the-damned sound he had periodically emoted since Cushing's arrival.

"Perhaps you are right. But tell me, since you, too, have acted the hero on occasion: Was that rush of emotion, that elevation of the spirit, a genuine thing, or was it a delusion?"

"It *is* a genuine thing, for I have felt it and I am as addicted to it as you are, if not more so. The difference is that when I charge into enemy fire, I am also doing *my duty* as a naval officer, and being paid for it, whereas your duty is *not* to keep on chasing that treacherous harlot we call 'glory.' If it were possible to live each moment in that heightened state, we would both be consumed by it very quickly, and be forced to live out the rest of our lives as burned-out husks. Each time it happens, that berserker battle lust, the very fire that animates us to acts of bravery, also devours some portion of our nerves and spirit. Each man had a fund of courage, and no man knows in advance just how many times he may draw upon that fund, not until the day he makes one demand too many and discovers he has nothing left. If the enemy doesn't kill me first, even I will reach the limit someday. No, Matthew, chasing after glory is a form of madness—allow yourself to become obsessed with it, and it will either get you killed, or desert you at the very moment of danger when you need it the most."

Cushing rose to take his leave. He had said his piece and satisfied some of his curiosity about Matthew Sloane. They shook hands, aware that if they had not exactly become friends, they had at least forged a curious bond. As Cushing opened the door, Matthew called out his name.

"Yes?"

"I just wanted to wish you good luck. I think you will need it. And . . . well, to thank you for coming. Talking to you helped me see things more coolly, and in their proper perspective. I have avoided the hard decisions for too long. But now, assuming they ever let me out of this place, I will do as you suggest, and go back home."

"By God, sir, if I had a wife like yours, I would move heaven and earth to get back to her." Cushing blurted these words unintentionally, and his face turned a sunburn pink as he hastened down the corridor outside Matthew's cell. Perhaps Mary Harper had changed far more than her husband had given her credit for—and this made him curious about his wife again. After all, the most popular and dashing young naval hero of the war had just revealed how big a crush he had on Mary Harper Sloane.

I wonder if they did it. That thought, too, was strangely exciting, but for all his valor with a cutlass and a Colt, Matthew got the distinct impression that Will Cushing would retreat in panic from an overt seduction by any woman.

A Brief Kaddish and An Expeditious Funeral

ALTHOUGH THE SUMMER of 1863 marked the start of the Confederacy's irreversible decline, it also marked the apex of profit and prestige for the Anglo-Confederate Trading Company. Of the three original investors—Jacob Landau, Matthew Sloane, and the British adventurer Augustus Hobart-Hampden—Jacob was dead, Matthew in jail, and Hobart-Hampden was so frequently absent from Wilmington, on enigmatic "missions" for the Queen and Zebulon Vance, that day-to-day management of the corporation devolved upon Jacob's daughter, Largo.

She proved to have as good a head for business as her father, along with a much bolder entrepreneurial spirit. Under her management, the A-ATC thrived and expanded. The founding triumvirate now owned four ships outright—the legendary Banshee *and three progressively more modern iron-hulled, twin-screw British steamers; Largo had also acquired part-ownership, ranging from one-tenth to one-third, in twelve other successful blockade-runners. Such diversified ownerships helped to amortize individual risks, because the Federal blockade was finally getting its act together, with more ships, better tactics, and the cumulative experience of its officers and crews.*

—Rich Smith, *The Gentlemen Smugglers: Wilmington and the Golden Age of the Blockade-Runners*; Bastinado Press, 1998 edition

The morning of August 7, 1863, was cloudless and still, and the sun ripped away the night's brief respite so swiftly that Largo Landau could feel the temperature rise and the humidity thicken, in stair-step increments of one degree for every quarter-hour tick of the clock. A pitiless coppery glare covered the Cape Fear delta like the lid on a giant pot.

Taking advantage of the last cool hour of morning, Largo Landau had decided to pay one of her irregular visits to Jacob Landau's grave, in the "Hebrew Half Acre" of Oakfield Cemetery, the ever-so-politely segregated corner reserved for deceased members of Wilmington's small Jewish community. When she selected the plot and commissioned the headstone, Largo had chosen something different from the small forest of six-pointed stars, all faded now to a dingy uniform gray. No matter how bright their marble or milk-veined granite might once have been, they struck her as oppressively weary. For all the moral ambiguities he wrestled with as a Confederate Jew, a profiteer made rich by his early decision to invest in the risky business of blockade-running, and as a dutiful husband whose entire married life was compromised by the knowledge that his wife's secret heart had long ago been given to an Austrian musician, Jacob had been a vital man: gregarious, open-hearted, honest in his business dealings, fond of a good party, and quick to bring out his fiddle when the occasion called for a lively tune . . . until he died a vile, lingering death during the Yellow Jack epidemic, almost exactly one year ago.

So Largo had chosen to adorn his tombstone with a replica of his treasured *shofar* and a bas-relief likeness of Solomon's Temple—or at least some artist's idea of that half-mythical monument, which she had found in one of Jacob's books. To reinforce the symbolism of the motif, she had told the sculptor to incise, below her father's name and dates, this legend: "Founder of Wilmington's first Jewish house of Worship."

How distant Largo felt from their old life together. . . . Something had been wrenched apart on the night she witnessed his terrifying death from the yellow fever, a final sundering of the ethnic identity that had already grown tenuous during the first years of her womanhood. But she had made a solemn vow to Jacob that she would carry out his dream and see to it that a suitably imposing House of God was built with his money and in his name. Now the plans for Temple Emmanuel had been completed, and Largo had come to her father's gravesite to tell him.

She had commissioned from a prominent English architect a design both "ornate and dignified," but not one inch taller than the Protestant churches, or more grandiose inside than they were—she did not want to exceed their pretensions, merely to equal them.

When the plans were completed, Largo had shown them to the handful of prominent Jews still residing in Wilmington, and declared that it was up to them to come up with the interior details, provided those plans included a prominent plaque honoring her father's contribution to the building and to the Jewish community as a whole. She showed them documents attesting to the more-than-ample trust fund set aside for construction, now safely ensconced in the Royal Bank of Nassau. When they were ready to start building, she would release the money and she would attend the ceremony of laying the cornerstone. When that time came, she told them, she might or might not still be in Wilmington, but she would return to perform that final act of homage to Jacob, and then she would depart without a backward glance. She knew the local Jewish elders disapproved of her, probably regarded her as a whore and an apostate; but on *that* occasion—knowing full well the extraordinary value of the bequest she now controlled—they had been most respectful.

"So, Poppa, there you have it. I have tried to carry out your wishes, to fulfill your great dream, and I have channeled much of our fortune into good, charitable works. In these things, if not in many other ways, I have remained your faithful, loving, and obedient daughter. But for now, I must say farewell, for I do not like coming to this place. It's nothing personal; *all* cemeteries oppress my spirit. And besides, if your soul does hear my voice, why am I standing here talking to a big, cold slab of stone? Be glad for me, Poppa, for I have become strong and free and somewhat wise in the ways of this world. But even so, it won't hurt if you put in a good word for me with the Lord. I am not sure I believe in Him any longer—and I will never forgive Him for allowing you to die so hideous a death—but I am willing to keep an open mind about the subject. May you know eternal peace, even if I do not, for my present character has been shaped by the exigencies of war as surely as any soldier's, and I have developed a most immodest desire to see the wilder places of the world and have so many memories of great adventures stored away, that in my old age I will never have to gaze into my teacup and say: 'Oh, how I wish I had seen India, or Singapore, or the deserts of Arabia, but I was too timid and now I'm too old.' If God disapproves of me, I'm sure He'll arrange for me to be eaten by a South Seas crocodile. If not, I intend to have a simply wonderful time. Enjoy your rest, Poppa. You were a good and gentle man."

Rising, she placed a stone on the grave. Then she strode briskly back to her carriage and drove away from the genteel gloom of the cemetery. The shortest route back to the Landau store would have taken her through the heart of Paddy's Hollow, Wilmington's traditional enclave of vice, but Largo no longer rode those streets, not even in daylight, without an armed escort.

Mary Harper Sloane's mother, Rosalee, died of an apparent heart attack on the night of July 31. As was their long-time custom, Stepney and Rosalee Harper had retreated to Limerick Plantation, up-river from Charleston, to their mountain home, "Sparkling Rock," near Asheville, before the start of the brutal, unhealthy Low Country summer, taking Mary Harper's two children with them. Customarily, they would remain in the cool blue hills until late September, when the peak malaria season had passed and the Low Country weather turned less infernal. To judge from the two children's occasional letters, their summer was passing in rustic tranquility. Their last notes had arrived only one week before the telegram announcing their grandmother's death.

The news threw Mary Harper into a dilemma as well as the conventional throes of grief. She had become unalterably convinced that her children would be safer at Limerick, the Sloane's vast rice plantation on the Asheley River, or at Sparkling Rock, than at Pine Haven. But her reasoning was complex and not altogether free of self-recriminations. No mother lightly consigns her children to exile, no matter how luxurious, and Mary Harper felt guilty almost as soon as she had done so. But her reasons were more complicated than a simple wish to be free of the distractions that come with two small children. Her energy and emotional resources were not infinite; her husband was in prison and his fate undecided; Pine Haven was remote and isolated; and in the rough, swampy counties a hundred miles north there were numerous and growing bands of deserters, guerrillas, and outright brigands who were growing bolder as Confederate authority grew feebler. In June, a plantation in northern Onslow County, not more than two days' ride from Pine Haven, had been plundered by an outlier gang, and eight people killed, including three children. That was too close for comfort.

Mary Harper Sloane could either spend her energies being a proper mother, or maintaining and protecting Pine Haven—she could not do both, and there was no Solomonic compromise available to her, not as long as Matthew was in jail. She had made her choices, kissed her children goodbye, and not looked back. But the news of her mother's death shattered her equilibrium and along with her natural grief came a sudden and passionate desire to be with her children again.

Her mother's will clearly stated her desire to be buried at Limerick, in her favorite corner of the garden. Because of transportation problems, the funeral could not be held before August 11.

All of this Largo learned in a rambling, tear-stained letter Fitz-John Bright had brought to town on August 7. Immediately, she had written back: "I will go with you to the funeral, dearest friend. You must not make this journey alone, and my staff can run the store just as well without me. I have missed your company a lot lately, and although this is not the sort of reunion either of us would have chosen, let us make the best of it together. And then, when we return, by God, let's let down our hair and have some fun! You remember what 'fun' is, don't you? I seem to remember we shared a lot of it, but that was much too long ago…"

Mary Harper was much too well bred to boast about her father, but Stepney Harper's wealth, accomplishments, prankish good humor, and phenomenal business acumen had made the grand old squire a regional legend, and Largo had heard plenty of family stories. She had formed a larger-than-life image of the patriarch long before she actually met him. If allowing for some exaggeration, she imagined Limerick plantation to be roughly the size of Luxembourg; its annual rice crop was abundant enough to relieve a Chinese famine; and to cultivate that abundance, Stepney Harper owned more slaves than any other planter in South Carolina.

Limerick was more than just a very big and very successful rice plantation, it was a Low Country landmark, and Charlestonians spoke of it with the same awed timbre they might have used when talking about the Pyramids or the Parthenon. So it was that the city's elite mobilized en masse to honor Rosalee's passing with the kind of ceremonial pomp more commonly associated with death of royalty. So many people wanted to attend the funeral they chartered a steamboat for the trip up the Ashley River. Largo squeezed aboard along with almost two-hundred other passengers.

There was no mistaking the moment when the steamboat crossed the borders of the Kingdom of Limerick. One moment the boat was surrounded by a seemingly impenetrable jungle full of spiky underbrush and dangerous-looking bogs the color of tannic acid. Then suddenly the wilderness simply stopped, replaced by watery lines of demarcation so sharp and ruler-straight that Largo could not imagine how they had been made. Beyond these perfectly groomed irrigation canals, the ship curved away from the main river channel and entered a lush lagoon, beyond whose sloping embankments Largo glimpsed enormous formal gardens, and avenues of majestic live oaks bearded with long skeins of Spanish moss. When the bow passed a navigation marker trimmed in bright yellow stripes, the captain rang "full stop," the paddle wheels obeyed, and the boat made contact with the passenger dock so gently that everyone applauded.

At the point where the passengers disembarked, a miniature city of threshing mills and warehouses cut off all traces of the breeze that had made the voyage surprisingly bearable. The first dry-land breath that Largo inhaled was so dense with humidity that for an instant her lungs interpreted it as a liquid. Like most of the other passengers, she coughed and sputtered until her body sorted things out and acknowledged the fact that, yes, this *was* "air," after all. As accustomed as Largo was to August in Wilmington, the Low Country equivalent was an altogether more hellish climate. Every motion, every spoken word, required an act of will; the muggy heat pressed down like a strangler's glove, and everyone, including the servants gathered to welcome the mourners from Charleston, was glazed with perspiration—a fact that everyone pretended not to notice.

The Sloane mansion came fully into view only after a ten-minute processional carriage ride up a winding driveway paved with a blindingly white surface of crushed shells, hard ivory sand, and a binding compound made from lime-and-water cement. The roadway was flanked on both sides by elaborate gardens that must have been rapturously beautiful in the spring but were now predominantly the color of burned toast.

The Big House proved to be a classic example of grandest plantation style, a giant edifice rooted into the earth by columns of titanic height and girth. It was stately, to be sure, but it was *too* immense, too defiantly, impractically, grand. And its hundred-year-old splendor had begun to fray around the edges. Here and there the paint was flaking, shutters drooped, and the once-handsome wicker furniture sprinkled around the broad verandas was sagging and worn-out-looking. A first-time visitor's impression was still that of imposing, ostentatious grandeur, but beneath that facade was a pervasive hint of neglect, perhaps even the first slow encroachments of decay. Mary Harper had told Largo that for all his inherited wealth, Stepney Harper had not turned a decent profit from his rice crop since the autumn of 1861. The supply of new slaves had dried up, and the poor white laborers who formerly supplemented the black workforce, especially at harvest time, were now in the army, as were the carpenters, blacksmiths, overseers, and other craftsmen so essential to the upkeep of such a vast estate. It seemed to Largo that Limerick might be passing into the shadows of history, and to her perceptions, the place gave off a palpable air of sadness.

When the long parade of guests filed inside, they found food and drink in abundance, and plenty of room for everyone to sit, stroll, continue (or escape from) the conversations begun on the riverboat. Before Mary Harper had a chance to ask anyone where she might find her father, an elderly Negro butler, sliding effortlessly through the throng, greeted her with both respect and familiarity, and said that her father wanted a few words in private, out in the gazebo overlooking the scenic lagoon that had been his and Rosalee's favorite place of refuge. Mary Harper gestured for Largo to follow, implying that this was as good a moment for friend and father to meet as the occasion was likely to present.

As the two women drew closer, they saw two other men besides Stepney. One was obviously the clergyman hired to preside over the funeral service; the other—a fussy little man with a goatee and pince-nez spectacles—was just as clearly the physician who had been summoned to look after Stepney Harper's well-being. When Mary Harper opened the screened door and motioned for Largo to follow her inside, the doctor and the cleric turned to glare at the interlopers, making gestures that asserted their authority to command silence and reverence.

"Father?"

"Please, ladies," grumbled the doctor. "Mister Harper's nerves are in a delicate state. Unless you have some urgent reason to be here, I must request that you depart in silence and allow me and the good reverend to continue our ministrations."

Sitting upright from the chaise lounge where he had been dozing, Stepney Harper spoke in the voice of a man not accustomed to having lesser men speak for him. His voice was raw and gravelly but hardly frail.

"She's my daughter, you jackasses! I'm perfectly fine, so get the hell out of here and go mix with the rest of those vultures. And you, preacher, however much you might be tempted, I want the service to be short and plain. If you add as much as one extra Bible verse, I shall knock a dollar off your fee for each word! Now leave us."

Bowing to the women with the absolute minimum display of courtesy, the doctor and the preacher stalked out, obviously resentful at being banished from the cool, privileged sanctuary of the gazebo and back into the tropical glare where the common herd was forced to mill around.

"Father, can I help you to stand?"

"No, you cannot. Never needed any man's help to stand on my own two feet, and I sure ain't going to ask for a woman's help now . . . even though I am heartily glad to see you again, girl."

However mentally prepared Mary Harper was for her father's appearance, it was plain to Largo that the moment was worse than anticipated. Mary Harper had always described her father as a robust man, much in love with riding and hunting, hale and sharp-witted even on the verge of his sixty-seventh birthday, which was the last occasion she had seen him. The white-haired gentleman in a baggy old mourning suit who shambled forward to embrace his daughter seemed older and much frailer. His eyes were clouded with sorrow, his step faltering, his once-rugged features now deeply lined, and his mouth was slack and seemingly unconnected with the muscles intended to control it. He spoke his daughter's name in a halting, almost incredulous voice—as though he could not quite believe she was really before him in the flesh—and embraced her tightly with his long, bony arms, his shoulders quaking with quiet sobs. Largo was standing just behind Mary Harper and could see the convulsion of emotion pass through her body at her father's touch. The old man's hands were large, long-fingered, and raw-boned, and they seemed to cover most of Mary Harper's shoulders, their wrists astonishingly thin and skeletal, age-spotted, rough with sparse white hairs.

But the old man seemed to draw strength from this embrace, for when he pulled back, hands resting on Mary Harper's shoulders, his gaze was clear and his expression transformed into one of stoic resolution.

"How long has it been, Mary, my darling—two years? Ah, God, this war distorts the flow of time itself, as it has so many other things. But the very sight of you does me more good than the fool preacher's homilies or that quack sawbones, trying to make me drink 'patented elixirs' that taste like dog piss. I said to him, 'Never mind the patented nonsense, just hand me the one that's got the most opium and alcohol in it, and when I finish one bottle, hand me another one.' Just imagine: the only doctor left in Charleston and he's such a notorious drunk not even the damned army will take him! Oh, what a lucky man am I!" His no-longer-sleepy eyes rose above his daughter's shoulders and focused with sharp approval on the face and figure of Largo Landau.

"And this enchanting beauty must be your friend Largo. Mary has written of you with great affection, but she grossly underpraised your beauty. I bid you welcome to Limerick, lass, and hope you won't be offended by an old man's hug—'tis a family custom around here."

" 'Tis the custom of an old lecher! Father, be ashamed—remember the reason why we are here, and behave yourself."

"In my family," said Largo, "we are firm believers in the therapeutic value of a good, warm hug, sir!" Ignoring Mary Harper's half-amused, half-irritated glare, Largo stepped forward and gave Stepney Harper a bit more of an embrace than he had been expecting. The old man lit up with pleasure, and seemed to shed some measure of age and sadness.

"You see, daughter? Your mother, God rest her soul, knew I was an incorrigible flirt, but she also knew I was faithful to her from the day we met. At my age, you don't get many chances to hug a beautiful lady—don't begrudge me. Now, tell me if there is any news of Matthew."

"Nothing has changed. He is still in prison, but the Lincolnites don't seem inclined to hang him just yet. I still have hope."

"Ah, do not worry, lass! Any man who has a wife like you waiting at home would tunnel his way through solid granite, just like . . . what's his name? The count of Monte Carlo?"

Stepney seemed to draw energy from the women's presence. Abruptly, he stood ramrod straight and seemed to don his dignity like a garment.

"Let's get on with it. Now that you're here, I see no reason to delay. It won't be any cooler, and if the guests keep drinking my liquor for another hour, half of the rascals will be drunk by the time the preacher clears his throat. Take my arms, girls, and help me back to the Big House."

Stepney Harper's abrupt appearance, and his commanding announcement that the funeral service was going to start in ten minutes, caught many of the guests by surprise, many with hors d'oeuvres in transit to their mouths, or standing in line at the punch bowls, waiting for a refill. Most of them reacted with a shrug and began forming up for the processional to the graveyard. Stepney walked into the big, central hallway and commanded the Negro majordomo, "Go tell the boys they can bring her out of the icehouse now, and be quick about it!"

Returning to the parlor, he instructed another house slave, "Go and fetch the children." From inside an adjacent room, their expressions both expectant and somewhat timorous, came Mary Harper's two children. For an instant they froze and simply stared at Mary Harper, who, for her part, seemed equally paralyzed by the confrontation.

Largo had seen portraits of the Sloane children at Pine Haven, as infants and as toddlers, but she had never met them in person. Francis Marion, the firstborn, was dressed in a diminutive Confederate officer's uniform, complete with general's stars and epaulettes that appeared to have been fashioned from the heavy fringe of a bedspread or a curtain, and a wooden sword almost as long as his legs. He had his father's close-set dark blue eyes and the same contemplative, slightly downturned mouth, which, along with the uniform and the let's-play-soldier dignity of his posture, lent to his gait and demeanor an endearing but slightly ridiculous swagger. I have seen that same stride in his father, Largo thought, and she felt a spontaneous surge of affection for the lad.

Henrietta, now eight, entered the room more hesitantly and only after being gently prodded forward by the Negro maid who had obviously been appointed temporary nanny. Henrietta had round and rosy cheeks, a rosebud mouth, and shy but keenly observant hazel eyes. These were crowned by long ringlets much lighter in color than her mother's chestnut-brown tresses, almost a shade of tawny bronze, which seemed to float above the floor from her buoyancy. Her hesitant entrance elicited a chorus of crooning sounds from many of the ladies in the room. "You could eat her with a spoon!" whispered one elderly relative standing nearby. It was obvious that the child had no real comprehension of the reason why so many grown-ups were assembled. Something serious was going on, and her grandmother had suddenly and mysteriously disappeared from the scene, but whatever sadness that might have caused earlier, the excitement of the hurried trip from the mountains, and her joy at being back in Limerick, had caused that shadow to recede. In her glorious and fragile innocence she took each day as it came, untroubled by the past and unconcerned by the future.

After Mary Harper and her children had regarded each other in frozen assessment, Francis Marion grabbed his sister by the hand and together they ran into their mother's arms. Largo had only to see the intensity of her friend's emotion, the sudden flood of tears, to know that all of Mary Harper's reasons for sending them away from Pine Haven had just turned to dust. A long moment passed before Mary Harper looked up and realized that everyone else in the room was waiting. To the children she said, "We will have a lot of time to talk later, but right now, we must go with your grandfather."

Ten minutes later, the assembled guests were arrayed in a silent semicircle beneath the brawny limbs of a majestic moss-draped oak. Stepney held Mary Harper's right hand and Largo took her left, and as she did so, she felt the small right hand of Francis Marion burrowing into her free hand, then settling there, inside the warmth of her palm, like a frightened bird curling up in the deepest part of its nest. Stepney waited until the mourners were finished clearing their throats and rustling their hoop skirts, then made a let's-get-on-with-it downbeat in the pastor's direction.

Like so many members of his profession, the pastor relished any chance to strut his rhetoric before a large, distinguished, and captive audience. He clutched a sheaf of papers—no doubt a compendium of suitable hymns, homilies, and scriptural glosses intended to illuminate every facet of Rosalee Harper's virtuous character. But every time he took a deep, preparatory breath and glanced at one of his papers, Stepney Harper shot him a stern premonitory glance, reinforced by a sharp, negative twist of his head: *I warned you, preacher: keep it short, keep it moving—do not force my guests to endure this purgatorial heat one second longer than is absolutely necessary!* Despite the preacher's pained expression, the service was condensed to the bare essentials, moving along at such a clipped, expeditious pace that some of the older and more conservative mourners actually gasped in surprise—and many others in relief—when it reached the "ashes to ashes" coda, and the coffin-bearers unspooled their burden with audible sighs of relief. When the coffin touched bottom, Stepney Harper leaned forward and threw into the pit, not a handful of earth, but a pattering shower of long-grained rice. Then he turned and faced the crowd, dry-eyed, and announced in a clear, unfaltering voice: "It is done, and done according to her wishes. No point in lingering out in this satanic heat. I for one intend to go inside and get drunk, and I invite all of you to join me, or to partake of the food and sugared punch, according to your tastes. This mourning has been artificially prolonged, due to the distance we had to travel to bring my wife's remains back to her home, and in the Harper family, we rend our hearts, not our garments." After raking all of them with a ferocious scowl, he turned around and set off for the Big House with a firm, almost military, stride. Mary Harper drew Largo and the children around her.

"My father wants to speak with me privately—after he's had a few drinks, of course—and so I cannot be with you until later, even though I want to with all my heart. Perhaps your 'Aunt Largo' would be interested in seeing the nursery, if you will be kind enough to lead her there." She glanced at Largo to see if that was agreeable, and Largo nodded emphatically that it was. So Mary Harper kissed her offspring and walked briskly away. Largo knelt before the children and spoke to them with an earnest voice, and tried to convey her goodwill with an openhearted smile.

"Is that all right with you, children?"

Evidently it was, because they each took one of her hands and steered her through a maze of hallways and up a veritable ziggurat of stairs.

"Are you really our aunt?" asked Francis Marion.

"I suppose you could call me an 'honorary aunt,' Francis Marion, because your mother and I are as close as sisters. But I would really prefer it if you just thought of me as your good friend, Miss Largo."

"All right," said the boy. "You seem like a very nice lady. We'll let you be our friend."

"By the way, do you prefer to be called by both first names, or is there some less formal name, or maybe a nickname. 'Francis Marion' seems awfully formal, and most boys do just fine with only one name."

"I've never given it much thought, Miss Largo. Grandpa Stepney always calls me by both, because I was named after a great hero, but when mother was impatient or cross, she called me "F-M," for short. I don't know what she will call me now. My father sometimes called me 'Frank,' because it sounded more like a grown-up man's name."

Largo laughed. "Now I am really confused! Maybe, in view of that uniform you wear so proudly, I should call you 'Colonel Sloane.' "

"Oh, yes! Please do, Aunt Largo! I think that's a capital idea!"

After the children showed her to the nursery—a large, bright room with many windows, strewn with toys, including a matching pair of finely wrought rocking horses—Largo told them to wait for her while she went upstairs, because she had brought some presents for them. When she returned with the packages, the children were still standing in the same spots, faces aglow with anticipation.

Before departing Wilmington with Mary Harper, Largo had returned briefly to the store and searched through the merchandise to find suitable gifts. She wanted them to like her, because if they did not—if they resented Largo's closeness to the mother, who had not hesitated to banish them from Pine Haven—they would surely generate friction, perhaps even spoil what had hitherto been a wonderfully uncomplicated friendship. A straightforward, generous bribe might win their loyalty, if not their affection. So, with a Santa Claus–like flourish, Largo presented to Henrietta a beautiful porcelain doll imported from France, complete with its own wardrobe full of fancy clothes; to the boy, she gave a collapsing telescope of polished brass, and a box of handpainted lead soldiers, dressed in scarlet uniforms and crowned with towering bearskin shakos, identified on the box label as "Guardians of the Queen."

When the children ripped off the wrapping papers and beheld Largo's tributary offerings, their spontaneous squeals of delight proved that her instinct had been dead-on. Instead of seeing Largo as a rival for their mother's affections, they now identified her as the-nice-lady-who-owns a toy-shop, and no sane child would want to alienate so valuable a friend.

While the children played with their gifts, Largo asked them to tell her about life in the mountains. Henrietta demurred to her brother, who was not just older and more worldly, but who also was obviously the more loquacious and self-confident by several orders of magnitude.

"It is wonderfully cool in the summer, and right before Thanksgiving, we had *snow*—and it was *seven inches deep!* It was the first snow we had ever seen, and it was much more beautiful than it ever looks in a storybook! Have you ever seen real snow, Miss Largo?"

"A few times, but never as deep as that. I wish I could have been there."

"Maybe someday you will be. . . ." Francis Marion sidled close to Largo's ear, first glancing around to make certain that Henrietta was totally focused on her new doll. Then he whispered to Largo, in the sort of voice a child uses when he decides to run the risk of taking you into his confidence.

"Aunt Largo . . . will Mother take us back to Pine Haven with her?"

Be careful, girl—a very innocent trap was just laid for you, and if you make the wrong assumptions, everyone could be hurt.

"I'm sure that depends on many things, most especially your grandfather's wishes, during a very difficult and painful time in his life. Wouldn't you rather go back to the mountains, where it's so nice and cool?"

"We certainly want to go back at Christmas, so we can play in the snow again," said Francis Marion. "But I heard Grandfather say that he needed to stay at Limerick for a while, to 'settle his affairs' and try to 'straighten some things out,' whatever that means. So if we're going to be stuck in hot weather for a time in any case, why not spend it with Mother, back at Pine Haven? That is our home, after all. Can you persuade her, Aunt Largo?"

Largo hesitated before replying; it would be wrong for her to give even the appearance of taking sides in this matter.

"Besides," Henrietta insisted, "it will be Francis Marion's birthday in three weeks."

"Indeed? And which birthday will it be?"

Francis Marion stood up proudly and tried his best to fill every inch of his small uniform. "I will be *eleven!* And when I turn fifteen, I can join the army."

Largo suppressed a shudder. Chronically short of manpower, the Confederate army accepted volunteers as young as sixteen, provided they had written permission from their nearest relative, and sometimes if they did not.

"Don't you want the war to be over as quickly as possible?"

"No! Not until I kill my share of Yankees!" To prove his zeal, the boy brandished his wooden sword and pretended to hack the heads and limbs off several invisible enemy soldiers.

At this point, the Negro nanny reappeared. She would take over in the nursery, she said, because Missuz Sloane wanted a private chat with Miss Landau. "Here, miss—Ah made you a map so you won't get lost. Lots of folks do, their first visit here." Largo hugged the children, who displayed their good manners by once more thanking her for their presents.

Mary Harper embraced her when she entered, then closed the door and bolted it, insuring their privacy. On the end-table beside Mary Harper's chair stood half-empty decanter of sherry and from the fidgety was Mary Harper twirled an empty long-stemmed goblet, it was obvious who had consumed it.

"It is only three o'clock," sighed Mary Harper, "but I feel as though it were midnight."

"The trip was long and you were under a lot of strain before we even left Wilmington. I'm surprised you can still stand . . . especially after drinking half a bottle of sherry. . . ."

"Damn it, I refuse to lie down until my father does. And if you don't want to help me polish off the rest of the bottle, that's fine—just don't give me a temperance lecture. I'm sorry, I didn't mean to snap at you." Her voice lost its brittle edge, modulating to a not-quite-convincing casualness. "So, how are you getting along with the children?"

"Wonderfully well, I think. They have accepted me as 'Aunt Largo', especially after they unwrapped the presents I brought. But it is you they really want to spend time with…"

"Yes, of course, and as soon as I can, I will give them my undivided attention. In fact, that is what I wanted to talk about."

"You know I will do whatever I can to help you, but any advice I might give you also comes from a childless woman who never had brothers or sisters."

"That's exactly why I trust your advice so much. My father is putting up a brave front, but his grief is crushing the life out of him. He needs to focus on some big, external, distraction, and he knows it. He's drawn up this huge list of repairs that need doing—told me the place was 'going to seed', which is true, of course. He swears he can get everything fixed before October, which is his favorite time of the year at Sparkling Rock. And he *does* want the children to join him for the holidays—he tells me they had a wonderful time there last winter—especially when it snowed."

"They did indeed—just ask them."

"If my father's determined to refurbish Limerick—though God knows where he's going to find enough skilled labor these days—the children simply cannot stay here. In his current state of mind, they would drive him to distraction."

Largo patted her hand. "Then it all becomes simple, doesn't it?" The only thing you *can* do is to take them home to Pine Haven. They want desperately to return with you, and Francis Marion has his heart set on celebrating his birthday at Pine Haven."

Mary Harper looked stricken. "God forgive me, I had entirely forgotten about that! Tell me truly, Largo: have I become such a bad mother that I've been fabricating reasons why my children would be better off somewhere other than with me? At the time, my reasons for sending them away all seemed logical. And after all, I did spare them from that malaria outbreak…"

"Yes, but now you have plenty of quinine."

"And what about the danger from those bushwhackers and partisans?"

"You have four good loyal men standing guard and H-H has supplied you with an arsenal of the best weapons money can buy. Bandits prey on the helpless—point a few Spencers at them and they'll tip their hats and bid you a good morning as they ride away. Let them see that Pine Haven can't be violated without pitched battle, and they'll move on until they find easier pickings. If most of them weren't cowards and bullies to begin with, they would still be in uniform. I'm not saying that Pine Haven is always going to be safe and peaceful, but from everything I've read, there's a lot more of such violence up in the mountain counties than there is here on the coast."

"So much for the two most important excuses I had for sending my children away…I suppose I already knew as much, but it helps to hear the truth from someone else whom I trust, before making up my mind. There's really only one choice I *can* make, isn't there? And maybe *that* is what I resent the most! I know that children are supposed to be the greatest joy in every woman's life, and who could not love them when they're adorable, helpless infants? But when they stop being so adorable, they can make everything complicated, and they put you in confinement. Every woman who is not completely a simpleton knows that, somewhere deep in her heart, but that truth is never spoken aloud! If women really knew how brief the *joys of motherhood* really are, and how much thankless aggravation they are signing up for, they would not leap so eagerly into this form of bondage. I know that I love my children, yes, but I also know how fulfilling it has been to succeed in managing Pine Haven *all by myself.* If I had been forced to divide my energies running the plantation and minding my brood, I would have done a poor job of coping with both responsibilities."

"That may have been true a couple of years ago, but you are stronger now, and they are older. They are bright and capable—you may be surprised at how much they can help."

"I hope you're right. But in any case, that matter is settled. I have 'decided', even though we both know there was no other decision I could make. We will pack up the children's things and we will take the steamer back with all the hung-over 'mourners'. At least motherhood is something I was trained to do, while running a plantation is something I had to master simply by *doing it.* I'm proud of what I've accomplished, Largo, but sweet Jesus, I am also heartily sick of it!"

5

The Children at Pine Haven

WELL, OF COURSE, everybody wants to be "free," but my grandmother told me the black folks at Pine Haven were more concerned about the Yankees burning down the place than they were about being "liberated." It was the only home they knew—they could not conceive of where they might go, or how they might live, if it was destroyed. I believe she told me that they only had one Negro flee during the whole war, and everybody figured he never made it through the alligator country between Pine Haven and the nearest Yankee outpost. Some of the Negroes admired him, but most of them thought he was a fool!"

—Transcribed interview with Sally Robinson Sloane,
WPA Cultural Project File S-263, Library of Congress.

When the train pulled in from Charleston, Fitz-John Bright was waiting, with a rented wagon, to transfer the travelers' belongings into the Pine Haven launch. To assist, he had brough along Fernando, the Portuguese vagabond who had signed up in the "Pine Haven Militia" for the duration, and who had proven to be as reliable as he was reluctant to explain his reasons for doing so. Bright's homely, perpetually sunburned face was a welcome sight to the children, who had not seen him for almost a year. They swarmed over him, all but knocking him over with the force of their hugs. Fernando, rather to Mary Harper's surprise, stepped forward, bent toward the children with one of his rare, diffident little smiles, and timidly asked, "I get hug, too?" Henrietta did not really know who he was, but she was happy to oblige any friend of Mr. Bright's; Francis Marion chose to proffer a dignified handshake. Bright turned to Fernando with a quizzical expression, and Fernando responded by shrugging his shoulders and saying, "Children, I like . . ."

It was dark by the time the two men had transferred all the baggage from the train to the boat. While waiting for the wagon return, Mary

Harper took the children to a nearby hotel and bought them a light supper; Largo walked to her house, and picked up some additional gifts for the children: a few sparkling bits of costume jewelry for Henrietta, and an old purple ostrich feature that would add a Jeb Stuart flourish to Francis Marion's collection of Confederate hats. Largo cried a little when she waved goodbye from the shore.

Pine Haven was peaceful and dark when they finally docked. Fitz-John Bright carried Francis Marion from the boat landing to his bedroom, surprised at how much bigger the boy had grown in just one year; Francis Marion opened his eyes briefly, at the instant his body made contact with his old goose-down mattress. His mouth curled into a cherubic smile and he whispered, "This feels like home." He was already asleep again when Bright responded, "It is, my fine young boy-o, and always will be, the good Lord willing."

Before retiring, Mary Harper met briefly with Mr. Bright in the library, anxious to hear what had transpired during her absence. Nothing much, thank God: three mild cases of malaria—the quinine had done its job well this season; the birth of a new calf; the slaves were content; and the "militia" diligently watchful. Mary Harper thanked him, then poured herself a good, stiff whiskey, enjoying the privacy and quiet and the now-familiar comfort of Matthew's favorite reading chair. She fell asleep after two sips, and did not wake until the housekeeper Aurelia rang the breakfast bell for the field hands.

With that familiar sound, life at Pine Haven resumed its usual rhythms. Taking coffee and rolls at her work desk, she jotted down a list of chores, hurriedly changed into her work clothes, and spent the morning making sure the inventory of staples, medical stores, and ammunition was exactly as it should be. By ten-thirty she was pulling weeds from a melon patch, working side by side with two slaves. When Francis Marion appeared, wearing yet another of his beloved Confederate costumes, he saw his mother, working *in the dirt,* with two slaves. So unprecedented was this sight that he gaped incredulously and blurted out: "Mother! What are you doing?"

With a trace of snap in her voice, Mary Harper replied, "What need to be done, Francis—weeding this garden. If you care to lend a hand, there's an extra trowel and a bucket over by the trellis."

"But Mother," he piped, his voice turning squeaky, "that is *niggers' work!*"

Brittle silence fell over the little tableau, and the two slaves stiffened for a moment before studiously resuming their labors. Mary Harper sighed, put down her garden tools, brushed the soil from her knees, and stared hard at her son. *How could she make him understand?* Down at Limerick, everything but Stepney Harper's morning bowel movements was considered "niggers' work."

"You need to understand some things, Francis. In the past year, we have lost about a dozen people from our . . . workforce. Some died of old age, some died of malaria last summer, and two young men ran away, presumably to join the Yankees up at New Bern. Ever since your father was captured, I have assumed all the duties and responsibilities of running Pine Haven, and it is my policy that *everyone* pitches in, because we are on our own out here, black and white alike, and I want every person living here to feel that this is their *home*. We do not use the word 'nigger' any longer, not even in jest, and I want to make it clear to you that as long as you're living here, you will treat the Negroes respectfully and behave toward them with civility. By the time you stand to inherit this land, I doubt very much that there will be any *slaves* at all, anywhere in the South, and if you want to keep enough experienced hands to make a go of it, you'd better get used to the idea that someday you will be paying these people wages and not just ordering them around."

Francis Marion gaped in disbelief. Had his mother become one of those dreadful "abolishers," or whatever the word was, that Grandfather was always raging about?

"It's not complicated, Francis Marion—just behave like a gentleman to everyone you meet. You will be surprised how quickly it becomes a natural habit. Why don't you spend the rest of the morning helping your sister with her writing and spelling exercises? After lunch I will drill you both, and if you've been properly diligent, I may allow you to accompany Mister Bright and Mister Chiang when they go hunting this afternoon."

Now the boy's face broke into a huge grin. "Oh, yes, the Chinaman! I want to see how he fights with a sword—Aurelia told me it's quite a spectacle!" He bounded back into the house. Mary Harper returned to her gardening and noticed, with wry amusement, how fixedly the two Negroes had pretended not to notice the tense exchange with her son.

Of course, Mary Harper's words had been directed at them as much as to the boy, but the slaves' reaction to her little speech remained, as usual, inscrutable. Logic told her that if the war continued to go badly for the South, there might come a day when men in blue uniforms rode up the carriage path or disembarked from boats on the Uhwarrie, and from that moment on, Pine Haven would cease to have "slaves." *Then what*? Without sufficient laborers, the plantation would fall apart. Perhaps, by showing her willingness to share the grubbier tasks, and by treating everyone who worked for her with a mixture of firmness and decency, she was storing up some fund of goodwill against that day of forced abolition. But sometimes, in the most pessimistic of her fluctuating moods, she wondered if the prospect of imminent freedom might unleash such long-simmering anger that some of these apparently docile blacks would suddenly run amok, burn down the house, steal the valuables, and commit violence against her and the children. There was not the slightest discernible sign that they would—she and Matthew had been the kindest of masters—but she also knew that there were other plantations, run by cruel and brutal slaveowners, where such atrocities were bound to happen. And she shared the same heritage that bred such monsters; no matter how different from them she felt herself to be, she shared the common denominator: she *was* a slaveowner; when the day of reckoning came, her skin was as white as the skin of the cruelest master, and her blood would be as red. Not all her gestures of kindness and liberality could change that fact, and on the nights when her sleep was light and troubled, she had become prey to nightmares in which she saw herself running in terror from packs of howling black demons.

Francis Marion was puzzled by his mother's changed attitude and briefly angry at her for humiliating him in front of those two nig . . . *black people,* he corrected himself. But Mother's word was law, and he tried to act according to her wishes, mainly by avoiding contact with any Negroes other than Aurelia and Agrippa, who had been an intimate part of his life for so many years that he felt genuine affection for them. But how could he possibly extend the ambit of that friendship to incorporate all those sweaty, sullen, utterly anonymous field hands, whose names he had never learned, and who all looked alike in any case.

Otherwise, the children seemed to have settled in quite easily. Mary Harper found them less of a distraction than she had feared they would be, and their presence more of a pleasure than she remembered. Four-fifths of the Sloane family, at least, were functioning as a family again, that was something, at least.

Henrietta, with the guileless instincts of a child, had somehow befriended Fernando, who was normally the least conversational of men. Perhaps, when she hugged him at the train station, she had broken the seal of his silence, for now she followed the Portuguese sailor like a faithful mascot, both of them engaged in long, earnest conversations—about what, exactly, no one could imagine.

Francis Marion soon gravitated to Sunny Chiang, the diminutive, affable Chinese whose mastery of occult fighting styles quickly turned the boy into a worshipful acolyte. When Chaing was not on patrol duty, and Francis Marion had finished his studies, the two could be seen practicing the martial arts—Chiang performing seemingly impossible acrobatic maneuvers, making the air hum with the big Sheffield cutlass Hobart-Hampton had given him, twirling it as though it were a twig, and Francis Marion earnestly rehearsing some basic cut-and-thrust exercises with his wooden cavalry saber, striving earnestly to imitate Chiang's repertory of ferocious grunts and piercing shouts. Mary Harbor thought it all a bit too bloodthirsty until she overheard Chiang sternly admonishing his pupil, "Do not try so hard to kill, young warrior! The true master subdues his enemy by making clear he *could* kill the foe, but chooses only to prove to him the futility of his violent ways."

Thanks to an ample supply of quinine, and Mary Harper's insistence that everyone, black or white, young or old, choke down a proper dose of the stuff every morning, the peak of the malaria season brought only three mildly debilitating cases. And when the second week of September brought cool, dry weather that spread over the region like an unexpected benediction, Mary Harper decreed an early First Fire celebration. Once again there was abundant food, and singing, and joy, and it occurred to her that this blessed interlude might be magically connected with the return of her children. Everyone agreed that a mantle of peace had descended over Pine Haven. Perhaps the war would pass them by after all.

Fitz-John Bright had no special affection for Negroes, but neither did he despise them. He was widely known as a successful overseer in this corner of the state, but there was nothing esoteric about the reason why he was so good at his job—which was, basically, to make Pine Haven as productive and profitable as he could. You needed a lot of hardworking hands to run a rice plantation. It seemed too obvious for other overseers to grasp, but Bright figured that you did not turn unpaid, unmotivated workers—brought under your authority because you had bought them at a market just the same as you would buy a bucket of fish, and had no more legal rights than a pig—into an efficient workforce by beating them into sulky compliance. During his almost twenty years as Pine Haven's overseer, there had never been any use of the lash, the branding iron, or the leg shackles that broke a man's pride if they did not break his ankles first. When Bright observed a slave who was habitually lax or laggard in his duties, he usually could effect an attitude adjustment by turning upon that individual a blue eyed stare as hard as steel and saying to him in a dead level tone of voice: "I know what you're up to, boy, and I'll give you exactly one week to mend your ways, or I will have you trussed like a turkey, take you back to the Wilmington slave market, and sell you dirt-cheap to the meanest-looking white bastard I can find. If you don't like workin' for me, I'm sure you'll *love* workin' for that other boss-man." Usually one such tongue-whuppin' was enough, because the miscreant would ask the other slaves in private and learn that, while Mister Bright was a humane and tolerant man, he had on several occasions "fired" unruly slaves by doing exactly what he said he would do.

Matthew Sloane approved of Mr. Bright's nonviolent methods, which dovetailed perfectly with Matthew's "progressive" style of plantation management. Working in harmony, the two men had reduced to a simple equation the whole complex interdependency between slaves and masters and the Southern economy as a whole: if you put in a full day's conscientious work, then at the end of that day, your life was your own. Pine Haven's slaves were expected to work hard and maintain a respectful attitude, but in return they enjoyed decent living quarters, adequate food, medical attention when they were injured or sick, and the blessed knowledge that no one would arbitrarily break up their families or burn "P.H." into their flesh with a red-hot iron. Mister Bright may have "fired" a few slaves, but not a single Negro had ever turned violent, stolen, or run away, not within the memory of an entire generation.

Mary Harper had become wary, sensitive as never before to any sign, however subtle, of discontent. And now, with Matthew gone, she relied more than ever on Fitz-John Bright to be her eyes and ears. No portents of conspiracy were too faint to escape his notice. But even he could not read minds, and there had been no signs of impending trouble from the handsome, ebony-skinned young buck named Elias. One of Agrippa's several nephews, Elias had been born and raised at Pine Haven. He seemed intelligent, polite, hard-working, and was very popular with the ladies. Outwardly he was just the kind of field hand Matthew's enlightened policies were intended to produce.

But one day in mid-October, after returning from a routine mail-and-supply trip to Wilmington, Fitz-John Bright requested an audience with Mary Harper to discuss "a serious matter." He came into her office with a troubled expression on his freckled face, and even before he started speaking, she noticed the way he kept nervously twisting the brim of his big, floppy straw hat. That little gesture, she knew, was a bad sign.

"You seem troubled, Mister Bright. Please tell me why, without trying to spare my feelings. I am no stranger, now, to bad news."

"It's the young buck Elias."

"I thought you regarded him as a first-rate worker."

"That I did, ma'am, until the night of the First Fire celebration. I had a bladder full of punch and did not want to make a long walk to the proper facilities, if you get my drift."

"You mean you went into the bushes to take a pee?" Mary Harper was teasing him, just to see his face turn red, but he was not amused.

"Yes'm, exactly. And when I came around the corner of one of the slave cabins, I saw Elias having a very earnest, secretive-looking conversation—one that came to an abrupt end the instant they saw me. Oh, they made a great fuss of hailing me and bantering about what a great party it was, and I went along with it, just so they wouldn't know I was suspicious of anything. I decided to take Elias on the next run down to Wilmington, just so I could keep an eye on him, try to see any change in his manner.

"But a bunch of runners had just come in, and the docks were crowded, and somehow he gave me the slip for a while. Not long, mind you, and when it came time to load the launch with supplies, he was back, and working as hard as anybody could ask. But when he lost his footing loading a heavy sack of feed, his jacket flapped open and I saw what appeared to be a rolled-up newspaper stuck in his waistband. Now, *this* is odd, I said to myself. But I said nothing, for after all, it's not a crime for a man to read a newspaper.

"However, when he went out to do field work yesterday morning, I snuck into his cabin, poked around some, and found a loose floorboard. Hidden inside, I found these."

He handed Mary Harper a sheaf of newspaper clippings, all of them featuring reports about Confederate reverses and heavy casualties. Elias had been one of the brightest pupils in her twice-a-week reading classes, and apparently he had used his newly acquired skills to collect information about every Confederate defeat since Vicksburg.

"If you ask me, the boy's caught a real bad case of 'abolition fever,' and since he ain't been able to read about any sensational Rebel victories, he probably thinks the war's as good as lost, and he's cheering the Yanks as hard as he can."

Mary Harper's spirits sank. She knew exactly what Bright was thinking, even if he was much too respectful to say it aloud.

"I do remember, Mister Bright, that when I first broached the idea of teaching the slaves to read and write, you warned me that it might have unforeseen consequences. But I believed then, and I still believe, that it is morally wrong to willfully keep them ignorant. But I see now that I was also naive because I used to hand out newspaper pages, and give a small prize at the next class for the student who gave the best reading of some article of their own choice. It never occurred to me to censor anything. All right, then, we have a problem. I hope you can advise me on how to deal with it."

"I do not recommend an open confrontation about the matter. I'll return these papers to Elias's hiding place, but the next trip to town, I'm going to tell my black helpers that nobody is allowed to bring a newspaper onboard, period, unless he shows it to me first. That will send a signal to anybody's who's been smuggling papers to Elias—lets 'em know we're aware that something fishy's been going on, but gives them the notion that we're just being bossy, not that we're actually *afraid.*"

"Should we be?"

"Missuz Sloane, I may know a lot of things about Negroes, but I've never had reason to speculate about what effect it might have on them to read a newspaper. I just want to put a little hesitation in their minds. But you may be sure I'm going to keep a close eye on Elias, and I'll make sure he knows it. That may be enough to put a chill on his enthusiasm. It also might tip me off if he plans to do anything rash. We can only watch and wait."

But the second half of September was so remarkably pleasant, and

Pine Haven's harvest gave promise of being so bountiful, that the prevailing mood of all its inhabitants was one of seeming contentment. The storehouses were full of canned and dried fruit, the corn crop was as good as any in memory, and the hog population had been unusually prolific, so the smokehouse was full of hams, and there would be plenty of good bacon for all. The slave families' garden plots replicated on a smaller scale the splendid yield of the plantation's much larger fields; no one would go hungry at Pine Haven this winter. And Mary Harper's one-third interest in the Anglo-Confederate Trading Company entitled her to a considerable share of the luxury goods brought in by the company's ships. Pine Haven's launch returned from every trip to Wilmington with bags of coffee and sugar, bolts of good-quality cloth, cans of imported sweets and tea biscuits, and varying amounts of other luxuries. Mary Harper personally distributed small bags of assorted delicacies to every slave family, inaugurating a new and very popular Sunday ritual. She also requisitioned enough fine woolen cloth to provide new winter shirts for all who requested them. It was a not so subtle way of reminding her Negroes that, because they lived at Pine Haven and belonged to a generous mistress, they were eating better fare and wearing much finer clothes than most of the white people in the whole beleaguered, impoverished Confederacy. Whether this gesture was interpreted by the recipients as sincere generosity or as a transparent form of bribery designed to firm up their loyalty, the overall effect was the same. As September mellowed toward true autumn, the sense of community that Mary Harper had worked so hard to create seemed to be sturdier than ever. As her misgivings faded, she was able to enjoy her children's company wholeheartedly, and she knew she would be very sad when the time came to send them back to Limerick.

So when trouble suddenly flared on October 9, Mary Harper was bushwhacked by surprise; that lulling sense of normalcy was shattered like broken glass.

Like his father and grandfather, Francis Marion was a born horseman. His greatest pleasure, weather permitting, was to dress up in his "Jeb Stuart" regalia and ride around the grounds, brandishing his wooden saber against imaginary Union columns. That October morning was a perfect day for such a ride—mellow sunshine, vividly colored leaves, and brisk invigorating air. Fitz-John Bright accompanied the boy to the stable, for this also was his day to ride morning patrol around the plantation's circumference. For that reason, Bright had a Colt strapped to his waist and a Spencer carbine strapped across his back.

Also in the stable that morning was the slave Elias; it was his turn to clean up the previous night's droppings, collect them in a big handcart so they could be used as fertilizer, and put down fresh straw for all the horses. These were not the most popular tasks, but since every male slave got the job only once every two weeks, by impartial rotation, there was no stigma attached to those who performed these malodorous but necessary services.

When Bright escorted Francis Marion into the shadowy building, he took note of the big black man's presence, then promptly got distracted, while saddling the boy's favorite horse, when Francis Marion started begging for Bright to let him shoot the Spencer. Despite the momentary confusion caused by Francis Marion's yammering and the mare's reluctance to accept the bridle, some long-honed instinct awoke in Bright a vague sense of unease. Most of the other stable hands would have greeted the two whites with something formulaic but appropriate *("Maw'nin', Mistah Bright! Good day fo' a ride, young master Sloane!")*, but Elias had welcomed them with a perfunctory nod and a rather surly grunt. Now he resumed stabbing his pitchfork into a mound of manure-caked straw with a vehemence that bordered on anger. Bright had seen this kind of behavior before: a cranky slave tasked with a chore he disliked expressed his resentment by performing that task in a manner that went right up to the edge of insolence without crossing the line. Elias's attitude was too rude and sullen to ignore. A sharp rebuke was hot on Bright's tongue, but he decided against delivering it because he did not want to spoil Francis Marion's happiness. So he turned away from Elias and hoisted the saddle onto the mare's back, while the boy patted the animal's muzzle, murmured endearments to her, and offered her a lump of sugar. While Bright was adjusting the stirrups to accommodate an eleven-year-old's legs, he heard Elias move to the stall directly opposite theirs and begin once more to stab his pitchfork into muck and straw, each thrust made with such unnecessarily grating noise that it amounted to a challenge. Well, thought Bright, that settles it: as soon as the young master leaves for his ride, I shall have strong words with this man.

"Oh! That hurt!" cried Francis Marion. "Now I'm all dirty! And look at my hat!"

Bright whirled around and saw instantly what had happened. In a gesture that *could* be interpreted as a clumsy accident, but in this case most certainly was not, Elias had flung a full load of manure with such force and carelessness that the stuff had sailed right over the compost cart and struck Francis Marion full in the face, spattering him liberally with dollops of shit and almost poking out one of his eyes with a long spear of straw. Worse, and much more alarming, one of the pitchfork tines had come so close to the boy's face that it had snagged the plume of his cavalier's hat and ripped it off. Elias tried to look shocked and regretful, but he was not fast enough, and for just a knife-flick of time, Bright saw murder in the Negro's eyes and knew beyond any doubt that the man was perfectly capable of driving that pitchfork into Francis Marion's belly—indeed, that he *wanted to* so badly that he was restrained only by the certainty that if he did, Bright would kill him on the spot.

Now Elias made a great display of contrition and regret, wailing out abject apologies for having ruined the young master's fine uniform. It was a wildly exaggerated performance, and the hypocrisy of it kindled a cold fury in Bright that he had to suppress because of the boy's presence.

"Go back to the house and change your clothes, Francis Marion. Aurelia will clean your uniform and fix your hat—by tomorrow, it will be good as new. You'll just have to take your ride in hunting clothes today. I'll mind the horse until you return."

By now, the boy was on the verge of tears, but he took the slave's display of remorse at face value, and in a gesture that embodied the very essence of good breeding, he paused long enough to say: "It was an accident, Elias, and I am not hurt. Please don't feel so badly," and then, to Bright's astonishment, the boy had the grace to reach out and pat the Negro reassuringly on the shoulder.

As soon as Francis Marion was out of earshot, Elias stopped performing and just stood his ground, his powerful hands resting on the pitchfork's handle, trading stares with Bright like two warships firing broadsides.

"It was a accident, boss. Tha's all it was."

"No, Elias. We both know it was much more than that. And if you ever again cause harm to that boy, or to any other white person on this plantation, or if I ever have cause to suspect that you are even planning such, you will see a side of me that few men have ever seen, black or white. I have never lashed a Negro in my life, but I can handle a bullwhip well enough to slice your ears off, and after I do that, I will take you down to Wilmington in chains and sell you to the meanest-looking white man I can find who wants to buy an earless nigger real cheap. Now you get back to work, and when I return, this stable had better be clean enough to eat off the floor."

Bright pretended to ride off on patrol, then doubled back and went immediately to report the incident to Mary Harper. There could be no doubt that Elias had "turned"—the first of Pine Haven's blacks to do so in many years. The first crack had appeared, the first sign had been given, and Mary Harper knew that her world had just shifted by one crucial inch.

"He was crafty, I'll admit. An 'accident' that was also a very dangerous gesture. I knew that at once, and he knew that I saw right through him. I do not think his purpose was to harm the boy, so much as to provoke me into a violent response, to inflict the sort of physical punishment I have always taken great pride in *not* employing. Then he could sneak around afterward and say to the others: 'You see? When times get hard, *these* white folks ain't no better than the rest!' And that is precisely why I did not punish him as he deserved."

"But Mister Bright, will he not try to provoke you again? Perhaps commit some act so heinous that it *does* warrant punishment? If the man hates us so much, and finds his life here so intolerable, why doesn't he run away?"

"Because, unlike those men, Elias knows there is no place he can hide where our hunting dogs won't find him. He can't run fast enough or far enough."

"But this is intolerable—even if he does nothing, his very presence is like an infection. God be my witness, but we have never done anything to deserve such spite, such hatred."

"No, Missuz Sloane, we have not—not as individuals. And I do not think Elias's hate is directed at us personally, but toward the society we represent."

"Oh, please, I refuse to bear the guilt of Southern history! But what in heaven's name can we do, Mister Bright?"

"I will handle it, ma'am, in my own way. I know you would not countenance cruelty, even as I deplore the use of it, but I promise you: the problem will be solved."

Two nights later, when Elias made his usual prebedtime visit to one of the slave outhouses, Bright made his move. Carrying a shotgun and accompanied by Stepan and Fernando, both armed with drawn Colts, Bright waited outside while the rebellious young buck did his business. When Elias emerged and closed the creaking outhouse door behind him, Bright lunged forward and dropped a burlap sack over the black man's head. Elias immediately started to struggle and curse, so Bright stepped close and clouted him on the shoulder with the butt of his shotgun, not hard enough to break bone, but certainly hard enough to get the man's attention. Then he pressed the twin barrels against Elias's forehead so he could feel the unmistakable sideways "eight" shape of its muzzle, and the Negro's cursing ended in midvowel; in that abrupt silence, the sound of cocking hammers was as loud as church bells. Elias's breathing became hoarse; fear and anger conjoined to form a sound like the growl of an asthmatic old lion.

"No cussin', now, boy," said Bright. "One more outcry from you and you'll spend the next hour spittin' out teeth. Nod if you understand. Okay, good lad. Now, Mister Stepan here is going to tie your hands and put a rope around your neck, and then you will march along behind us quietly."

They prodded him over rough ground, detouring through a patch of woods so nobody in the slave cabins could glimpse their business. Then they angled back until they reached the smooth wagon track leading to the Pine Haven docks. When Elias realized that they were forcing him into the steam launch, he began to tremble and moan, certain that his abductors planned to carry him to some remote cove and lynch him. He gasped in surprise when Fitz-John Bright reached forward and patted him reassuringly on the shoulder.

"Relax, boy. If my intention was to kill you, you'd be shakin' hands with Jesus already. What I *am* going to do, though, is to liberate you from the dangerous temptation, not to mention the opportunity, to commit violence against any of Pine Haven's white folks. You came right up to the edge the other day, when you threw that load of horse shit at the little master—don't bother denying it, because I saw it in your eyes: that rage to strike out. I understand it more than you might believe, for I have worked all my life with black people, and many members of my race have treated your people barbarously. Now you think freedom is so close you can almost taste its sweetness. Problem is the Yankees ain't here yet! But you, Elias, you're a bombshell just waiting to go off, and the next time you try to hurt one of the Sloanes, I'd just plain have to kill you, and that might have a very bad effect on every black person who saw it. Get 'em riled up, to no useful purpose."

Bright glanced around at the snaky course of the Uhwarrie. They had steamed three miles north of Pine Haven and had reached the place where the river began to lose its identity and fade into an unmapped wilderness of blackwater creeks and cypress-dotted swamps.

"Stop the engine, Fernando. We've come far enough, I think."

The bow crunched softly into a bank of slimy mud. Bright reached out and yanked the sack from Elias's head, thrusting a lantern so close to the Negro's face that he was blinded and disoriented, staring around wildly with wide, rolling eyes, gasping for air. His three captors looked at him coldly over the barrels of their weapons. Fitz-John Bright poked a sliver of firewood into the tiny boiler, lit a cigar with the flame, and studied the bound black man as though he were some kind of previously undiscovered animal.

"You were born at Pine Haven, Elias, and grew up surrounded by your family, which is more than many slaves can say, and treated better than most white sharecroppers. Until you got a case of abolition fever, you were a damn good field hand. Think back on it, now: Did you ever go hungry?"

Elias met Bright's gaze without flinching. "No."

"Were you ever beaten? Were you ever asked to do more work than a man of your years and vitality could perform in the time allotted?"

"No."

"Do you honestly think that if the Yankees occupied Pine Haven tomorrow, your life would suddenly improve?"

"Maybe not, but it would make me a free man."

" 'Freedom' *is* a noble word, son, but you would still be a field hand—that's all you know how to do. If the Yankees do win, the South will be crawling with discharged veterans, all of them looking for work.

And they will get the jobs, such as there will be, long before any 'emancipated' Negroes. Bet your big black balls on it, boy, you'll live lower and meaner as a freed man than you have as a slave on my plantation."

"That don't matter. I can already read and write—I could live anywhere I pleased. Go to school and learn a trade. Become something *better* than a field hand. I hear that the colored soldiers on the Yankee side will get a bonus when the war's over, enough to get started on a new life. And they'll have something else that I want and can't ever have at Pine Haven."

"What might that be, Elias?"

"Respect."

Bright mulled it over, then nodded—rather sympathetically, for a man pointing a shotgun at a Negro over whom he held the legal power of life and death.

"Cut him loose, Stepan." Warily, the muscular little Pole sawed through the ropes binding Elias's hands. For a moment everything was silent except for the rough, fleshy rasp of Elias trying to massage some feeling back into his wrists. His eyes flicked from one captor's face to the other as he waited to learn what might happen next. Far off in the distance, something big splashed into the water, and Fitz-John Bright suddenly smiled.

"Glory be, if that's don't sound like old Beauregard, tryin' to get the jump on some dumb log turtle. If I was you, boy, I'd stay clear of that ornery gator. Mister Cushing lopped off one of his paws when old Beau was chasin' his sailors, so he's liable to be a foul-tempered alligator as well as a hungry one."

Into the astonished Negro's lap Bright now dropped another burlap sack, this one bulging and heavy.

"Now here's the deal, Elias. You want to go enlist in one a those Yankee colored regiments, you are free to do so. I'd say that a man as robust and determined as yourself has a fifty-fifty chance of makin' it through the swamps. Inside that sack is some food, and a full canteen of drinkin' water, also a small-game snare and enough stout fishin' line to set it up properly. The nearest Yankee outpost, I reckon, is somewhere between New Bern and Kinston—travel north until you hit the first railroad tracks, then turn right and follow the rails toward the coast. And just as I would not turn any man loose in this wilderness without provisions, nor would I feel right about leavin' him defenseless, so here's a big ol' Bowie knife. Won't do you much good if you run into Beauregard or one of his cousins, but it might give you an edge over the average black bear, and a means to skin any game you're lucky enough to catch."

"Why you doin' this, Mistah Bright?"

"So you won't make no more trouble at Pine Haven, Elias. If I read your character right, you *would,* sooner or later. And then I would have to kill you. The simplest way, of course, would be just to kill you, but if word got back to the black folks—say, if some coon dog was to dig up a recognizable chunk of your anatomy—well, then we'd still have a problem. This way, I wash my hands of you, and do so with a clean conscience. If Cushing and his half-starved sailors could make it through this wilderness, so can you. I'm givin' you a fair chance, boy, and you'd best believe that's a testament of respect for your manhood. You understand, Elias? *You're a free man.* And as long as you never set foot on the Sloanes' property again, I wish you well. If you *do,* you can expect no mercy under my hand. Well, that's the whole of it, so you'd best git before I change my mind."

Bright cocked the hammer of his shotgun. Bewildered, his face rippling with conflicting emotions, Elias grasped his sack of provisions, put the knife in his teeth, and dropped over the bow, staggering for purchase on the slippery bank. Without looking back, he squared his shoulders and marched off into the wilderness.

After the launch had gone back downstream for about a mile, Bright heard Elias's voice from deep inside the tangled forest: "If'n you see me again, Mistah Bright, I'll be wearin' a blue uniform! And I'll be ridin' with five hundred colored boys just like me! That day is comin'! You make ready for it, 'cause when that day comes, your world's gonna wash away like Pharaoh's army into the sea!"

Battle of the Birds

Topsail Island is a nesting ground for the endangered loggerhead sea turtle. These giants of the sea, who can weigh as much as 500 lbs., typically nest from mid-May through mid-August, with the females coming ashore between sunset and sunrise, depositing at least 150 eggs in each nest. Visitors are urged to report sightings of flipper tracks to the Topsail Turtle Project. Nest sites must be left undisturbed to incubate fifty-five sixty-five days before the hatchlings emerge to begin their perilous journey to the sea.

Loggersheads are fighting for survival and are protected by the Endangered Species Act. It is a violation of Federal Law to interfere in any way with nesting or hatching turtles. *There are stiff fines and penalties for infractions of these laws.*

—*Visitors' Guide to Topsail Beach,* 2002 Edition

Aunt Charity could mass-produce the world's finest flapjacks with the steady efficiency of a steam press minting coins. Every time she finished piling up a fragrant hillock on her serving platter, she passed it to her niece, Fanny, who scurried into the dining room and exchanged it for the empty platter. Pancakes with real maple syrup, side-meat bacon, and a jug of blockade-run orange juice from the Indies—the favorite morning meal of children and parents alike, it was not only delicious, it also was the kind of meal that stuck to your ribs through a long, busy day. The Lamb family was in vigorous appetite this morning, and it was not until after the fourth platter had been swept clean that Daisy Lamb called: "Enough!"

Little Dick—not so "little" now that he was close to his twelfth birthday—rubbed his bulging tummy. "Can't I have just two more?"

"No, Richard. The school boat will be here in ten minutes, and you barely have time to brush your teeth, and remember to pack your lessons *neatly* in your schoolbag. I don't want any more notes from your teachers about wrinkled or torn assignments."

"Look, Mother," chirped Maria Lamb, three years younger than Dick, "I'm a member of the Clean-Plate Club!"

"So you are, my love, and how I wish I had never planted that term in your brain. Now you run upstairs and brush your teeth, too."

"I don't have any homework," 'Ria said with a smirk at her brother, poking out her tongue saucily.

"That's 'cause you're still a *baby! Baby, baby, baby!*"

"Mother, make him stop!" 'Ria's complaint was as bogus as the phony tears she was trying to squeeze out to match her pout.

"Maria," Colonel William Lamb spoke in his no-more-nonsense voice, "You know that Dick will only tease you more if you rise to his bait. Just ignore him. Your mother and I find that perfectly easy to do, and so should you."

"*Some* of the time, anyway," muttered Daisy.

When Daisy and the children arrived at the cottage, in the autumn of '62, Daisy had tried home schooling the siblings. The charm of that routine had completely worn off by the start of the new year, and when she learned that several retired or invalid teachers had opened a private academy in Smithville—catering to the families of Confederate officers scattered throughout the Cape Fear district—she had been among the first of many parents to gratefully subscribe. Chase Whiting had donated a slow but relatively safe old cargo barge to serve as a pupil collector. It left Smithville at five-thirty every weekday morning, and gathered children from the garrisons of Forts Anderson, Holmes, Caswell, and, in the Lamb's case, Confederate Point. From the time the school boat's jolly whistle tooted at the end of their dock until approximately five thirty-five in the afternoon, Daisy Lamb had the entire day, luxuriously, to herself, and she liked this new arrangement very much.

Daisy had found many agreeable things to fill up her liberated days: long, meditative rides on the beach; an ambitious diary that was growing to the proportions of a Dickens novel; and a newfound passion for collecting, pressing, wildflowers. Last month she had found a specimen so exotic-looking that she had arranged to send a blossom, along with detailed notes of her observations, to the head of Harvard's Botany Department—by way of a blockade-runner's mail pouch to Nassau and thence to New England. She was anxiously waiting to learn if she had discovered a new species. . . . Meanwhile, after an entire year had passed without the Yankees attacking Fort Fisher, she was much more relaxed about William's duties as the Bastion's commander. Every morning she kissed him good-bye as he mounted his horse and rode off "to work," a ritual identical to the one performed by millions of other couples in hundreds of towns and cities, but with one significant difference: her husband's "business suit" included a sword and a pistol.

Weee-eeep! Hweee-yooo!

"Hurry, children—school boat's at the landing! Aunt Charity, make sure they grab their lunch bags as they run past you!"

" 'Bye, Mother! 'Bye, Father! 'Bye, Auntie C!"

"Well, that certainly beats walking three miles through the Rhode Island snow every morning," said Daisy with a sigh.

"I thought it was only two miles," teased her husband.

"The older I get, the longer the heroic trek seems in my memory. And by the time I have grandchildren to tell the story to, my daily walk to school will rival the journey of Lewis and Clark! Have we time for another cup of coffee?"

Lamb was already fidgeting. "No, no, 'fraid not! It's getting too close to hatching time. I'd never forgive myself if I missed the great event." He went over to the wall calendar, as he did at least four times a day, and toted up the days.

"Honestly, William, you weren't *this* anxious when I was in labor with Dick! They're just *reptiles,* for heaven's sake!"

"Amphibians," he corrected.

"Whatever! They are cold-blooded, scaly little brutes. If it was a litter of puppies, I might be more sympathetic—at least puppies show affection . . . ."

"How do you know Cleopatra's little wigglers won't wag their tails and cover me with little turtle licks?"

"Oh, now, there's a heartwarming thought! I must be the only wife in America whose rival is a five-hundred-pound turtle!"

"It was just a casual fling, my dear—one night of stolen bliss! Besides, I assure you, you're much more exciting in bed!" He ducked out the door before she could hurl a teacup at him.

Chuckling merrily, Colonel William Lamb mounted his horse and cantered briskly down the road to Fort Fisher, eager to learn if the turtle watch had anything new to report.

When Corporal Ezekiel Jeremiah Prosper-for-Me de Vonell Conver saw William Lamb returning to the fort on the morning of July 10, the molten silver of dawn blazing off the pewter-gray horizon giving him the haloed penumbra of a mad but saintly prophet lacquered in Byzantine gold in the foreground of a giant fresco, Conver sensed at once that the sandy wastes had rendered unto Lamb some manner of revelation—how else to account for that altarpiece radiance burning 'round his head? This impression grew stronger when Lamb got close enough for Conver to see his eyes, which had the look of a skeptical man who rises from a grudging baptism, astonished to find himself suffused by unexpected grace. He still seemed half entranced when he climbed the steps to his observation post, where the proud, rank-conscious commander and the shortest corporal in the Rebel army leaned against the parapet, side by side, and Lamb began to relate, in confessional tones the details of his encounter with a giant sea turtle: The primal grandeur of her patience as she carefully deposited hundreds of fragile, glistening, encapsulated offspring into the cool, deep cave of sand she had spent all night excavating for them; how carefully and painstakingly she had covered and camouflaged their hiding place; how, when the monumental task was done, she had seemed to heave a vast sigh and how, despite her exhaustion, she had resolutely begun her inch-by-inch crawl back toward the sheltering surf, pitting her failing strength against the rising sun and the slow-death effects of soaring heat; goaded pitilessly by instinct to reach cool, deep water before her strength failed utterly and the sun baked her skin to leather even as its light revealed her presence to Confederate Point's myriad predators, awaking in them another, crueler instinct—their dormant lust for the sweet and salty delicacies of amphibian meat. Her steady but agonizingly slow progress—so urgent in its drives, so glacial in its pace—had compelled Lamb to interpret her as a sentient ironclad, and made him want to cheer her on. If she did not make it to deep water before the snapping, slashing, rending swarms descended on her, she was quite prepared to sacrifice herself for the nestlings. Lamb heard the first raucous squawk of a seagull scout, and when he turned toward the high white swelling dunes leading up to Sugarloaf Ridge, he spied a rising cyclone spiral of ravenous gulls—*so swiftly they rose, thickening like clotted cream, until they formed a leprous blotch upon the sunrise!* Cleopatra still chugged forward, but a whole night's labor had drained her; the gulls, he feared, would reach the obsidian meat of her eyes before she could possibly reach the surf. So William Lamb, somehow and forever after bonded with this prehistoric voyager, had gone down on all fours, bracing his knees and toes in cold grit, and intervened with human hands and human perceptions, daring to interpose his own need for a successful completion to a process anciently ordained by God, presuming that His design required the turtle to survive and the scavengers to go hungry, else why had Lamb been allowed to witness this ataristic contest at all?! Galvanic first contact with Cleopatra's body changed forever his perceptions of what was meant by the word "turtle"—Great God, she was massive, inert as granite, her chitinous carapace matted with greasy seaweed and rough coral-hard encrustations, five hundred pounds of primordial amphibian! Until his boots and knees gouged out a mighty purchase on the sand, he might as well have been trying to move the Armstrong Gun. But, inspired either by his understanding of mechanics or the whisper of God's advice gleaned from the booming waves, he found that if he timed his shoulder-to-the-wheel heave to coincide with the turtle's own push, he added force and momentum, an extra precious increment of progress beyond the most she could achieve unaided. When her flippers felt the first soothing kiss of a wavelet, she lifted her inscrutable face, and Lamb fancied he saw in her eyes fresh glints of vitality—a quickening that, in the eyes of a human being, could reasonably be defined as hope. Suddenly Cleopatra heaved with all her strength and drove that galleon's prow of a head straight into the next and stronger wave. Soaked now to his waist, Lamb braced for the next rolling swell, and put all of his strength behind the push—her hind flippers roiled up volcanic eruptions of bottom sand, and—she had made it, she was fully buoyant! Liberated from a mountain of weariness and inertia, she seemed suddenly to slide forward as light and lithe as a dolphin. Angry, thwarted, *hungry*, shrieking congeries of gulls swooped down and raked open the air bubbles left in Cleopatra's wake, so many hundreds of swirling, agitated birds that they formed a cold, shuddering shadow above Lamb's head and shoulders, but she was beyond their distempered protests, and almost beyond his sight, as she sped deeper and deeper into another realm, and nothing more of her could he see but a vast, mysterious shadow sliding deeper into a translucent olivine canyon, heading down and down and down, for a well-deserved slumber on a bed in noble, drowned Atlantis. How the seas of the earth must have beckoned to her, now that she had completed her ultimate mission: delivered and sheltered her offspring, and all traces of her path from the hidden nest to the verge of the sea were swiftly being wiped clean by the tide; now the predators could find no trace. Of course, the giant turtle could not hear him, but Lamb spoke his pledge to her aloud, so that the waves and clouds could hear it, at least: "I will protect your babies, Cleopatra!" Exhausted and elated at the same time, Lamb dragged his heavy legs through the surf, the clammy bottom sucking at his boot soles like glue. He staggered more than walked back to the fort, gasping and bruised as a boxer after the most punishing round of his career. As the sun warmed him, he was so filled with wonder and joy that he wanted to sing, but failed to think of any Christian hymn suitable for what had been essentially a pagan mystery. As his trousers dried and the heavy crust of sand fell away in slabs, his step became lighter, and his chest expanded with a strange but weirdly sanctified elation and he began to sing the first happy tune that came to mind:

She's the sweetest rose of color this darkie ever knew,
Her eyes are bright as diamonds; they sparkle like the dew;
You may talk about your Clementine and sing of Rosalie,
But the Yellow Rose of Texas beats the belles of Tennessee!

It was that sudden burst of carefree song that made Corporal Conver swing his head in a northward direction, and so it was that the diminutive sentry first beheld his dutiful, ever-pragmatic commanding officer striding o'er the dawn-gilt dunes, his hair wildly tousled and his uniform frosted with salt and clumps of mud-pie sand, serenading the whole beach with his church-choir baritone. *Well now, bless my blue-eyed soul, but here comes a wonder, indeed!* The courtly Southern knight, the pious but fiercely belligerent Young Soldier of the Lord, loping toward the fortress all wild-eyed and filled to overflowing with the Holy Spirit; emerging from some distant landscape and from some private state of rapture like Elijah staggering back from the desert. The colonel was still humming when he passed the bemused sentries guarding the sally port. Pausing at the mess tent long enough to grab a mug of coffee, Lamb strode briskly up to the Pulpit and there held conclave with the smallest of his heroes, as excited as a little boy because he had glimpsed a rare and genuine wonder of the deep.

"You have witnessed a rare and wondrous thing, all right, Colonel. I've lived on these shores all my life and only met a few men who had seen the great turtles perform their birth ritual, and every man who witnessed it, well, they spoke of it in the same tones of awe as you have."

"How long until they hatch?"

"I doubt you can set your watch by it, sir. Seven or eight weeks seems to be the consensus. Probably varies, too, according to the weather, the tides, all kinds of factors. I wouldn't get too fond of them little wigglers, sir. The minute one of 'em pokes his tasty little head aboveground, there'll be gulls and gannets and sand crabs swarming in hordes all around that nest. That's why God makes the litters so numerous, you see—not one in ten will survive to reach the surf, just enough to propagate the species."

"One in ten? By God, I've sworn to protect those helpless infants, and I shall give them better odds than that! If we're ready to take on the whole Yankee fleet, we can surely figure out how to thwart a mob of scavenging gulls and sand crabs! Since the men are always griping about how bored they are, let them turn their imaginations to this tactical problem!"

Indeed, except for gun drills, the occasional barrage to discourage pursuit of a runner making its final desperate lunge for the safety of New Inlet, and a rare three-day pass to visit the fleshpots of Paddy's Hollow, the Fort Fisher garrison endured a daily routine of numbing tedium. *Any* diversion was welcomed. As word spread about Lamb's early-morning adventure, the garrison adopted the colonel's passion as their own, and the ensuing mass obsession became known as Turtle Fever. It began on the first day after Cleopatra had dug and filled her nest. Lamb led a work party out to the site and surrounded it with high wooden stakes topped with brightly colored rags so that no nighttime beach patrol might inadvertently crush the nest beneath their horses' hooves. Five hundred cooped-up soldiers with nowhere to spend their monthly pay will always find something new and diverting on which wagers might be made, and the fate of turtle eggs was such a novel subject for a betting man that it engendered new and sometimes eccentric variations. The major division was between two factions Corporal Conver named the "Six-Week

Adventists" and the "True Believers in the Eight-Week Incubation." Calendars, tide tables, and almanacs were consulted as tools of divination. Across the spectrum defined by those two polarities were those who used weather prognostication, astrological and lunar geometries or biblical references; others made pilgrimages to the handful of old-time fisherman who still dwelled on Confederate Point to collect their personal funds of giant-turtle lore, and all these gleanings were used to handicap the betting, which primarily focused on the date and time when nature would call the little wigglers forth to write their collective birth certificates, with scrabbling little claws, upon the sand.

Despite the intense and increasingly esoteric debates between those who put their money on one date and those who invested in another, there was complete unanimity of interest when the talk turned to the best tactics, weapons, and formations the nest watchers would employ to repel the anticipated hordes of predators. The overarching purpose, of course, was to give the maximum number of turtlettes the best possible chance of reaching the water. Much creativity was focused on this, privates and lieutenants working side by side, scratching diagrams in the sand, arguing the possible effects of temperature, wind velocity, and atmospheric conditions. As soon as a prototype of each new device was cobbled together, it was field-tested on a broad expanse of dunes about a hundred yards north of the nest's actual location. Confederate Point was home to an enormous population of seagulls, most of which lived fairly close to the fort because, after all, that was where the best and largest accumulations of garbage could be found. These "ordnance trials" followed a systematic procedure. Since the gulls were especially fond of stale hardtack and petrified bread crusts, the baiting team loaded a wagon with barrels full of crumbs and breadcrust scraps and threw clouds of the stuff into the air. Invariably, this human largesse attracted hundreds, possibly thousands, of vicious, ravenous birds who resembled, from a distance, a white-and-gray tornado funnel. Once the birds had reached maximum feeding frenzy, the nets, shotgun loads, and bird-scaring devices went into action, while impartial observers took notes on the efficacy of each.

These noisy demonstrations, four or five each week, soon attracted the curiosity of the blockade ships stationed around New Inlet. Why on earth were those Rebels waging an apparent war of extermination against the local bird population (a project doomed to failure anyhow, since the supply of birds along the Carolina coast was, to all intents and purposes, infinite)? Finally, about one week before the date of the earliest possible emergence, a sleek Federal cruiser hoisted a big white flag and came close enough to the fort to begin a signal-light dialogue:

Ahoy, Fort Fisher! Intense curiosity compels us to ask about the purpose of these curious drills you are conducting. I assume no military secrets would be violated by an explanation—extensive wagers have been made!

Major Frederick Reilly happened to be on signals duty atop the Mound Battery. He responded: *Please identify ship and identity of spokesman.*

U.S.S. Monticello, *Lieutenant Commander William B. Cushing in command.*

Not THE Cushing? Sincerely honored to meet you, sir. Large nest of sea turtle eggs laid some weeks ago on beach quarter mile north of fort. Garrison has adopted them. Conducting tests now on how best to protect hatchlings from predators during their perilous trek to the sea.

A novel way to pass the time. Have we permission to watch this epic contest from close range? Provided, of course, that hatching occurs in daylight. Truce will be scrupulously honored. My word is my bond.

So we have heard. If Colonel Lamb and majority of garrison have no objection, I see no reason why you cannot attend the party. Let me consult. Return tomorrow for our answer.

Fair enough. One suggestion from my gunnery officer: a salvo of grape, fired high enough to cause no injury to your men, might serve as an excellent deterrent to bird reinforcements orbiting at higher altitudes.

Capital suggestion. Lamb and soldiers might not agree, but I can ask.

When Reilly approached Lamb and recounted this curious dialogue, Lamb's eyebrows rose. "The legendary Will Cushing? A distinguished audience indeed. Such an audience might well inspire our men to prodigies of effort. Conduct a straw poll at dinner, and if the majority of the men have no objection, inform the *Monticello* that she is welcomed to observe and lend support with her guns. This surely adds an extra frisson to the whole enterprise. If she runs aground, however, we will consider her fair game, once the turtles have made good their escape. When the action appears imminent, we'll fire a red rocket from the Mound Battery. Remind Cushing that our sea-face guns will be loaded, however, and tracking his every move."

Reilly and his gunners rolled the Whitworths into sand-and-timber revetments after sunset on September 24, the last Thursday of the month. In fact, all the sea-face batteries were on full alert. The big new runner *Phoebe* was considerably overdue on her return from Nassau by a mild but persistent mid-ocean hurricane, and this was the last night of suitable darkness—just a fingernail paring of a crescent moon, rising at 3:00 AM. If the *Phoebe* did not make it home tonight, she would not likely try it again until the next cycle of optimum darkness. The blockade captains knew this, too, and all night long they patrolled with fussy alertness, hovering around Fort Fisher like a pack of anxious nannies. When the first predawn light made it possible for the fort's observers to identify individual Union ships instead of ghostly blacked-out silhouettes, a weary pall of disappointment settled over the parapets. The tension of vigilance and eyestrain gave way to yawns and a collective heaviness of eyelid. At four-fifty, Lamb was ready to order a stand-down. Whatever had caused the runner's delay—hurricane or capture—she was certainly not going to run the blockade in full daylight.

Reilly told his Whitworth crew to secure the piece for transport, whistled for the teamsters to bring up the mules and caissons, then strolled off to the top of a nearby dune, smushed a ruglike mat of sea oats to keep his bottom from getting sandy, sat down and lit a meditative cigar. He watched the nearest blockade ships secure their own guns, heard the bo'suns pipe their mates to breakfast, and watched the helmsmen set new courses for the horizon. If it were possible for warships to look sulky, these did. Then a sleek, familiar-looking cruiser pulled up parallel to Reilly's dune, dangerously close to the big sandbar that ran parallel to the beach from New Inlet up to Masonboro Sound. Ah, yes, it was the *Monticello* again, and that blue dot waving at him from the bridge was assuredly the famous Mr. Cushing. The cruiser's starboard signal light began to blink.

Oh, where has my darling Phoebe *gone?*

Reilly did not feel in a bantering mood, so he responded to Cushing's message with an upraised middle finger. Unfazed, Cushing blinkered back: *Expectant stepfathers should not use bad language!* Reilly made elaborate shrugs and head shakes to indicate he had no idea what the hell Cushing was talking, or Morseing, about.

Allow me to be the first to congratulate. Our big telescope reveals signs of disturbance at turtle nest. Remember Lamb said could we watch?

Bosh! thought Reilly. The Six-Weekers didn't plan to start counting until Saturday. On the other hand, six weeks was just a guess, and so was eight. And recent nights had been unusually cool—wasn't temperature one of the factors that supposedly influenced incubation time? The stakes were only a hundred yards from where he sat, and from an elevated bridge, with a good telescope, Cushing could see that part of the beach much better than he. *What the hell? Might as well go take a closer look.*

There was already a full roster of volunteers for the Egg Patrol, two-hour shifts, day and night, just somebody standing around with a lantern, or sitting on a camp chair and reading, occasionally peering closely at the drifts covering the nest. All seven hundred to eight hundred eggs would not hatch simultaneously, of course—regional turtle lore described a gradual "slow boil" of undulations and tiny humps that might go on for hours, or even days, before the bravest and most curious hatchling would actually poke his tiny, almost-blind head through the last millimeter of sand (and probably have it bitten off instantly by a sand crab). The others would emerge by twos and threes until, at some point, the herd instinct flared in all of them and a veritable flood of tiny turtles would gush forth and run the gauntlet of predators who wanted to devour them as passionately as the turtles wanted to reach the sea.

When Reilly peered through the encircling stakes, it was clear that the "slow boil" had indeed begun: grains of sand shifted, shadows dappled the surface as the bolder hatchlings explored their dark, overpopulated surroundings. Evidently Colonel Lamb had observed Cushing's signals to Reilly and had leaped into the saddle to see if the climactic moment was at hand.

"It's started, Colonel! Commander Cushing could see it with the big telescope on his bridge! Signal the Turtle Brigade to assemble!"

"I shall, although we've been taken by surprise by the timing. If any of the beasties emerge before we can deploy the whole force, I'm relying on you and your gunners to hold off the predators' initial attacks."

"Like the legions of Caesar, sir. We have aiming stakes, ramrods, and our sidearms, if it comes to that. Not to mention our 'naval support,' courtesy of the enemy blockade fleet. I do hope Cushing remembers to fire over our heads."

"Yes, sir, he has a 24-pounder howitzer loaded with musket balls and plans to use only half the regulation powder charge, so as to better concentrate his fire. I must say, he's every bit as keen about this as we are!"

"I certainly hope so," said Lamb. "Because we have enough heavy guns trained on his ship to blow her to matchsticks." Looking every inch the Southern knight, Lamb made his horse rear in dramatic Napoleonic style, then galloped full tilt toward the fort, war-whooping all the way.

Some mysterious influence seemed to be accelerating the emergence, for during the brief time it had taken Reilly to have his conversation with Lamb, the deeply buried nest had begun to acquire a domelike elevation, as though a balloon were inflating under the beach. Striations and small oscillating humps came and went. *This is all happening rather too quickly.* He loped back to the Whitworth revetments, where the crews were lazing about and speculating on the *Phoebe;* both field pieces were hitched up, and the mules looked exceedingly bored.

"They're hatching!" Reilly shouted, reaching for a ramrod fastened to the side of the gun carriage. "Grab anything that looks like it might scare off a starving seagull—we have to hold off the predators until Lamb gets back with the Turtle Brigade."

"What about this?" asked a teamster, brandishing a snaky, braided whip.

"Hell, yes! If I were a sand crab, I'd run away from getting hit with that, especially if some vicious-looking ape like you were wielding it!"

"MAJOR REILLY?" Reilly started and looked around in alarm. Whence came that booming, godlike voice? "OVER HERE, MAN! IT'S ME, CUSHING, WITH A BIG MEGAPHONE."

Well, Reilly could hear *him* plain enough, but would scarcely be audible from the *Monticello*'s bridge due to wind, surf, and the rumble of idling steam engines. So Reilly just nodded: *I can hear you fine.*

"WE CAN OBSERVE SEAGULLS FORMING TO THE NORTHWEST. I THINK THE CAT, AS IT WERE, IS OUT OF THE BAG."

Reilly and the huffing gunners took up stations around the nest just in time to see it happen: a small rift of sand and a tiny, slime- and grit-encrusted gray-green head popped out into a world it could scarcely have dreamed about until that second. Its mucus-filmed eyes darted around, incredulous, but with the unerring instincts of millennia, the tiny head stopped spinning when it saw (or smelled, or felt some compelling magnetic tug from within) the sea, and its tiny flippers, no bigger than fly wings, began wiggling frantically, trying to gain some purchase on sand that was growing more agitated by the second. *Poit! Poit!* Two more inquisitive heads broke through, one of them covered by a fragment of eggshell that looked exactly like a helmet. *That one's got the right idea!*

"MAJOR REILLY, THERE'S AN IRRESISTIBLE CLOUD OF GULLS BEARING DOWN ON YOU, SO PLEASE DON'T JUMP WHEN WE COMMENCE FIRING."

Reilly did, of course, and so did the other turtle guards; it was impossible not to when a large-bore howitzer discharged along roughly the same axis as your eardrums. It was indeed an "irresistible" target: a roiling wedge of gulls dense enough to block a big piece of the sky, and all of them so hungry for marinated amphibian that the bullies in the flock were already pecking at the eyes of lesser birds that got in their way. "Two hundred of 'em, at least," muttered the man on Reilly's right. Then the flock encountered a double charge of grapeshot, both birds and lead colliding at maximum velocity, generating an ugly loud *crunch* and a deranged chorus of gull shrieks. Approximately half of the flock was reduced to a plunging, spiraling, lazily drifting mélange of meat, bone kites, and shredded feathers. "Great shot!" Reilly called up to the *Monticello*'s stern gun platform, where the howitzer crew, enormously pleased with themselves, was reloading.

But the remaining half of the flock was not distracted for one second by the apocalyptic obliteration of their fellow gulls. As soon as the lead gull spotted a straggling parade of appetizing slime dots wiggling toward the surfline, it squawked the seagulls' equivalent of "Tallyho!" and a hundred gluttonous scavengers dived on their pathetically vulnerable prey, swerving aside to avoid the frantic swings, blows, and roundhouse swipes the gunners on land dealt out in defense of their squirming wards. Reilly bashed in one bird's skull with the hard end of a ramrod, broke the wings of two others, and dispatched with a shot from his revolver one particularly leprous-looking brute who had seized a hatchling in his beak and was methodically gnawing its innards while perching comfortably atop one of the stakes. Meanwhile, oblivious to the slaughter of their nestmates, more and more baby turtles boiled up from their subterranean shelter and joined the suicidal parade toward the ocean. In contrast to the filthy-sounding racket of the gulls, stealthy sand crabs rushed out of their holes, picked off stragglers, and began unraveling their flesh with dainty precision. With astounding telepathic speed, news of the great breakfast buffet had evidently spread to every barrier island between Confederate Point and Cape Hatteras—in every direction he looked, Reilly could see wave after wave of gulls, gannets, sandpipers, and solitary hawks converging on his location. Again, the howitzer roared, and swept clean one portion of the sky. Some of the *Monticello*'s crew were now banging away with shotguns, and Reilly, spotting a flank attack by a phalanx of crabs, waded into them furiously, swinging his ramrod like a croquet mallet, but the population of predators was inexhaustible, and their primitive minds seemed unable to register fear. No doubt the humans' spirited defense *was* making a difference; instead of the gloomy prediction of 90 percent killed before they reached the sea, it seemed to him that 20 percent were actually reaching water—he could see their heads bobbing up and down, apparently in the throes of primitive joy, like fields of gray-green corks.

But why were Cushing and his sailors cheering so lustily? Reilly glanced southward just in time to see William Lamb, his saber in one hand and some sort of heavy-duty scooping device in the other, lead the Turtle Brigade on its first charge. On horseback and on foot, crammed into wagons and towing pine-board sleds filled with implements for stabbing, slicing, or ensnarement, the full formation of volunteers swept like a gray tempest across the intervening dunes and formed a bristling human shield on either side of the little wigglers. They thrust with flounder-gigging tridents, they snared angry knots of birds and stomped them flat, they stabbed multiple targets with custom-made bayonet racks. Others tried to repel the predators with braying, roaring noisemakers and hurled small short-fused bags of gunpowder into the air. No man waded into this merciless gladiatorial arena with more bloodthirsty, berserk fury than William Lamb, whose sword was a vibrating blur; and when one huge, fearless bull of a gull, his feathers and breast splotched with turtle gore, singled out the colonel for a personal attack, Lamb reeled from the impact of the bird against his chest. Ignoring the crawling sweetbreads of amphibian delicacies, this bird wanted *human* blood. Its claws raked Lamb's uniform to sheds, its wicked dagger-sharp beak punctured his forehead, scalp, and ears as it tried to get at his eyes. With no room to swing his sword, and no chance to grope for his pistol, lest his flailing hands uncovered an eye, Lamb finally immobilized the murderous bird by the brute strength of his arms, working his grip higher and higher. Then, breaking free, bellowing a cry of triumph, he seized the bird's wiry neck in a death grip and swung it full force against the hard-packed sand at water's edge, raising the screeching, flapping, clawing assassin like a living club and swinging it, in a powerful overhead arc that went from the small of his back to the level of his sword belt, dashing it against the barrel of a Whitworth again and again until he had shattered every bone in its body, tenderized every muscle into jelly, and left no part recognizable save for its ugly head, which continued to flail at him with its beak even after the eyes went glassy and the primitive brain stopped working. Lamb did not cease hammering the giant bird against the finest English gunmetal until he sensed an eerie silence all around him. Only then did his fevered brain comprehend that the Battle of the Birds was over and the gasping human combatants had been frozen in place as spectators, watching their dignified young commander howl like a drunken Viking and continue to pulverize his long-dead assailant until there was nothing left to break, no more blood to spill, until every part of it save for its flopping head and vacant, glass-bead eyes had ceased to resemble any living thing at all. As his mind cleared of battle lust and his vision expanded, he realized that he still had both hands clamped around the throat of a sodden, inert bag of organic mush, crusted with a foul mixture of blood, sand and the copious fling of his own sweat. Half mortified, half astonished at the depth of his own savagery, Lamb finally signified his restored sanity by mounting a bright, sheepish, naughty-boy grin, raising aloft one more time the grisly, shapeless mass of offal dangling from his fists, and called out to the captain of the U.S.S. *Monticello:*

"You see, Commander Cushing? This is how I've trained my boys to fight anyone who attacks Fort Fisher!"

And Cushing, who had seen the battle madness blaze in Lamb's eyes and recognized it for what it was, inclined his head respectfully to a man whom he now acknowledged as a brother warrior. "In that case, Colonel, I hope I can be present on the day the Union tries to storm your magnificent fort. That is one battle I should very much like to witness."

Lamb tossed his grisly burden into the waves, submerged his hands and arms into the purifying brine, and called back: "I shall send you an engraved invitation, by way of thanking you for your valiant assistance in today's engagement. I was too preoccupied there at the climax of the engagement. Did we save most of the hatchlings?"

"Not 'most,' sir, the odds against them were overwhelming. But a great many survived to reach the sea who would surely have perished otherwise. I believe you have honored your vow to Cleopatra in full, and I would not have missed this spectacle for all the tea in China. But now, I fear, we must return to the tedium of blockade duty. Officers and crewmen of the U.S.S. *Monticello,* three cheers for Colonel Lamb and his gallant soldiers!"

The Tale of Bonaparte Reubens

AS A JEST, the gods created a messenger in the form of a mongrel dog, and gave him powers of speech, so that he might tell mankind that the gods had granted immortality to all men. But the village people laughed at him and said, "Who cares if you can talk? You smell like shit and are covered with fleas!" Furious, the dog replied with a snarl, "The will of the gods is that man shall live but the moon shall be destroyed! Does such good news not merit a tasty bone and some cool water?" Again, the villagers laughed at the dog, and one man filled a bowl with cow dung and straw, setting it before the hungry dog. Furious, the dog growled and told them, "Now the gods have changed their minds! The moon will be reborn over and over, eternally, but all men will die!" Then he hiked up his leg and urinated on the bowl, then ran off into the fields, laughing like a hyena.

—Creation myth of the Nandi tribe, Uganda

Major General John G. Foster, commander in chief of all Federal forces in coastal North Carolina, had one thing in common with Zeb Vance, the state's outspoken governor: both men saw major strategic opportunities for their respective sides based on the stalemate on the coast—but neither Vance nor Foster could make a dent in their respective leaders' mesmeric fixation on Richmond.

For more than a year, Foster had submitted memo after memo, trying to convince someone in authority of the strategic importance of the railroad nexus at Goldsboro. *All* of the blockade-runners' cargoes were sent to General Lee along that supply line. Given adequate reinforcements, Foster thought he had an excellent chance of catching the local Rebel forces by surprise, sweeping them aside and destroying their vital railroad bridge before the Confederates knew what had hit them.

More recently, Foster had bolstered his arguments by forwarding numerous "eyewitness" reports confirming the rumors that the enemy was building two extremely powerful ironclads, so far up the Neuse and Tar Rivers that they were impossible to attack with the forces he had on hand. Foster did not realize that many of these vivid "eyewitness" accounts were delivered by agents on Zeb Vance's payroll, and they were very successful in focusing the Yankees' attention on the Neuse and the Tar rather than the Roanoke River, where the *real* ironclad was under construction.

Foster's latest information about these superships indicated that both were nearing completion; and if both ironclads went operational at the same time, they could drive the U.S. Navy back into the Atlantic. When General Meade realized the full strategic implications of such a dramatic Confederate victory, he suddenly developed a strong interest in John Foster's plans.

Meade authorized Foster to plan a two-pronged "reconnaissance in force" as soon as the necessary troops could be assembled—probably in late September—and promised to send a convoy of reinforcements, including a crack regiment of veteran cavalry. The Confederates understood very well the importance of Goldsboro, and could be expected to defend it vigorously; the ironclads' construction sites would doubtless be well protected, too. Therefore, the Neuse River column would be far stronger than the northern force advancing along the Tar: 9,600 infantry, 670 cavalry, and 32 guns. Foster's first objective, of course, was to locate and destroy the ironclad there. If he deemed it feasible, Foster was authorized to push on to Goldsboro and destroy the big trestle bridge across the Neuse, along with whatever supply dumps, repair shops, and other such facilities he could reach without actually storming the town. When Lee learned that Goldsboro was threatened, he was certain to react quickly, probably detaching a whole division and rushing it south by train, in hopes of striking Foster on his northern flank before Foster's men had time to finish burning the warehouses and repair shops. Meade cautioned Foster: "Go in fast, raise all the hell possible in twenty-four hours, then scoot back to New Bern; otherwise you may be cut off and wiped out."

The northern arm of Foster's raid was primarily intended to prevent Lee from doing that by blocking egress from the smaller but equally vital bridge northwest of Tarboro. On their way up that river, the Tar River expedition also was expected to locate and destroy the other ironclad. Their route of march was through much rougher terrain than the route Foster's column would follow, and the Tar River bridge was thought to be strongly fortified, but the tracks south of it were not. Tearing up a few hundred feet of rails ought to delay any troops from Virginia long enough for Foster to complete his destruction and escape the potential trap. The reinforcements Meade sent to augment the Tar River force were not large, nor were they drawn from the cream of his army. Meade told

Foster bluntly, "Nothing more is required of those troops than to sink the ironclad and to tear up some track. If they manage to extricate themselves afterward, fine; if not, they are expendable."

Foster had ordered General Rush Hawkins to bring three-quarters of the 6th Massachusetts, about 760 men, and a pair of 12-pounders, down from Shelborne's Point. For flank protection and scouting, Foster would perforce have to rely on the mounted riflemen of the "Buffaloes." General Hawkins had assured Foster that the former bushwhackers' new commander had worked hard to turn them into *real* soldiers, and they were eager to prove themselves in the coming campaign. Foster would give them one chance, but if the "Buffs" did not perform up to snuff, he would disband the unit—assuming any of them made it back to Shelborne's Point. To reinforce the Tar River expedition, Meade had dispatched a newly formed brigade of all-Negro infantry and several batteries of field artillery, commanded by Major General Edmund DeWitt. It was General Meade's desire that DeWitt be given tactical command of the Tar River force for the duration of the operation. "Rank and seniority," Foster said with a snort when he read the words, had less to do with it than "political influence," and Rush Hawkins was not going to like playing second fiddle to a bombastic jackass such as Ed DeWitt, but *c'est la guerre*.

On the eve of their first real campaign, the "Buffaloes," still carried on the Union pay list under their formal designation as the "1st North Carolina Unionist Volunteers," were a larger and more disciplined unit than ever before. After learning that Jack Fairless had killed their original commander, the charismatic but increasingly cruel Cyrus Bone, men who had deserted to escape his brutal tyranny began trickling back into the regiment's fortified camp at Edgefield plantation. Since the twin disasters of Vicksburg and Gettysburg, a number of fed-up Confederate deserters had gone to General Foster's headquarters at New Bern and sworn renewed allegiance to the Union. Foster's policy was to assign these renegades to a variety of units, where they could more easily be watched during a period of "probationary service"; their performance in the impending campaign would reveal just how serious these men were about changing sides. Foster thought that several of the turncoats might really be spies, so he assigned them to the Buffaloes, which he believed to be an outfit of the most dubious military value; a real spy would learn nothing of value to Richmond from serving with *that* raggedy-assed collection of misfits. But Jack Fairless welcomed them without prejudice—hell, his own military career was successful only because he, too, had deserted the Confederate army. He interviewed each man in private, and although their stories differed in some detail, they all shared the same basic motives: they had lost faith in General Lee, and they had nothing but contempt for the politicians in

Richmond. They believed, as one veteran colorfully put it, that the Confederacy "was a treed coon" and that Jeff Davis should negotiate peace to avoid prolonged and pointless slaughter. Jack believed they were sincere, and each man was a seasoned veteran, so he spread the word to his company commanders: treat these converts with respect, for they are valuable additions.

There also had been a significant influx of Negro volunteers, runaway slaves from all over the eastern half of North Carolina. What these men lacked in education they made up for in zeal. Bonaparte Reubens, newly promoted to captain, welcomed them into the ranks of his all-Negro Company B, which now numbered 189 men. Reubens drilled his men hard, but instilled in them both pride and confidence. The Negro troopers still lived separately from the white soldiers, but otherwise Jack Fairless maintained a policy of absolute racial equality. The enemy's bullets, he told the troopers, were color-blind, and in combat you had to trust the man fighting by your side—the color of his skin was irrelevant. On the whole, there was very little racial friction. The soldiers saw how deep was the bond that had formed between Colonel Fairless and Captain Reubens, and tried, with varying degrees of success, to follow their example.

The Buffaloes now comprised 572 mounted rifles, organized in three companies—two white, one colored—and a battery of three 12-pounders. To command his guns Jack had chosen one of the newly attached ex-Confederates, Major Adolfus Manchester, for he brought to the job two years' worth of experience with General Longstreet's artillery. Manchester's decision to change sides had been made quickly. Granted convalescent leave after Gettysburg, where he was cut up badly by shell fragments, Manchester was thoroughly disillusioned about the Confederate cause long before that battle: he had not been paid in five months, and he suffered from chronic stomachaches caused by bad rations. After witnessing the one-sided carnage of "Pickett's Charge," he had lost all faith in the generalship of Robert E. Lee. After an exhausting four-day trip, he reached his home, a modest farmhouse in Buncombe County, and was devastated by what he found there. Both his middle-aged father and his sixteen-year-old brother had been conscripted. His mother, crippled by arthritis, could not run the farm by herself, and had put the place up for sale before moving in with a charitable cousin who lived in Salisbury. Sometime between her departure and Adolfus Manchester's "homecoming," a band of Unionist guerrillas had used the house as their temporary headquarters, then burned it to the ground when they moved on. So when at last Major Manchester came home, for the first time in two years, he found nothing but charred ruins, untended fields covered in weeds, and the ghosts of memory. That very night he stole a horse, rode to the nearest railroad depot, bought a ticket to

Goldsboro, and walked from there all the way to the Federal lines around New Bern.

Nobody who had known Jack Fairless before the war would have recognized him now. Back in March 1862 Jack was a gangling, pig-ignorant hillbilly. He deserted the Confederate army primarily because his new friend Cyrus Bone asked him to. And at that stage of their friendship, Jack would have followed Cyrus anywhere. But a taste of power turned Cyrus into a drunken despot, and most of the men in his command were delighted when Jack killed him. So were Generals Hawkins and Foster, who gave Jack command of the Buffaloes with one proviso: "Turn this riffraff into real soldiers, and do it fast." With Bonaparte's help, he had done just that. Now, when Jack looked into the big dressing mirror that dominated one wall of Edgefield's master bedroom, he saw a young man transformed.

Back when he enlisted, his skin was pale, and his lank, straw-colored hair made the blue of his eyes seem weak and watery. Now he was tanned by the coastal sun, his hair had taken on a striking bronze color, and his eyes seemed darker, harder—he could deliver a truly "commanding gaze" when the situation called for it. From the start, he had no trouble asserting his authority—the Buffaloes welcomed his command, having grown tired of Cyrus Bone's casual I'll-fight-when-it-damn-well-pleases-me attitude. They wanted respect, and Jack seemed the man who could give it to them. And Jack soon realized that he loved being in command; both the privileges and the responsibilities of leadership seemed to fit him like a tailor-made suit. No doubt about it: the Buffaloes were now sharp-looking, disciplined, and anxious to prove themselves in battle. They had been given an important role to play in Foster's upcoming campaign; this would be the first real test of their new professionalism and of Jack's ability to lead men in *real* combat, not skulking bushwhacker ambushes. The moment when he vowed that he would be no man's catamite and decided to kill Cyrus Bone was the day he had "crossed the Rubicon" and never looked back. And yes, he knew what "crossing the Rubicon" meant. His intellectual horizons had expanded along with his self-confidence.

Give Cyrus his due, thought Jack, as he strapped on his sword and pistol belt; at least he taught me how to read and write, awakened in me a thirst for learning. But Bone's intellectual pretensions were based on scattershot exposure to life's finer things, and his attempts to sound sophisticated were mostly bluff. The man who had really nurtured Jack's latent intelligence was Bonaparte Reubens.

What made Reubens so interesting was the fact that Reubens and Bone shared a certain quality that made men want to follow them. There was a ten-dollar word for that quality, one that Reubens had once used when discussing Bone . . . *"car-sis-matic?"* No, not quite. Jack knew that if he kept shuffling syllables, it would come to him; when he was trying to master new vocabulary, Jack would worry the words like a dog gnawing a bone until suddenly he "got it." *"Carry-se-mantic?"* No, damn it, but that was close!

Charismatic! Yes, that was it! Some kind of inner glow that drew followers the way an open flame draws moths. In his gross, primitive way, Cyrus had been a *charismatic* leader. Having seen both men in action, Fairless knew that Bonaparte Reubens could strike with every bit as much savagery as Cyrus Bone—and with much more precision, if only because he was not reeling drunk most of the time. Yet Reubens was also, by a very large measure, the most *cultured* man Jack had ever known. How could one man contain such extremes and contradictions yet still project such an aura of inner harmony? Not once, since the start of their unlikely friendship, had Reubens made fun of Jack's peasant origins or showed irritation at Jack's near-total ignorance of life's finer things; rather, Reubens seemed to take real pleasure in gently lifting the veil between his world of books, poetry, and deep ideas, and the obstinate backwoods narrow-mindedness of the world Jack had grown up in.

Jack was eager to learn; Reubens was happy to teach; that equation was the simple fulcrum on which their comradeship was balanced. And solely as *men*—both thrown together by the exigencies of the soldier's life—that comradeship flourished. On the afternoon of September 29, after leaving the officers' meeting in which General Hawkins had revealed the Buffaloes' role in their first *real* military campaign, both men had returned to Edgefield plantation with the same notion in mind: What better way to mark the occasion than by heading over to the brothel and getting their ashes hauled?

Usually, when the two officers made a trip to the colored brothel, they dallied a while after concluding their primary business, playing cards or "talking trash" with the girls, but on this occasion both men were so tightly wound by the prospect of the looming campaign that their encounters were cavalry-charge affairs, and neither felt much like the sexual company of women when they donned their uniforms again. Instead, they gravitated to their favorite refuge: the late Dr. Edgecomb's library, which had been furnished in the relaxed masculine style of an English gentlemen's club. The mere act of closing the walnut doors and adjusting the lighting to their favorite mellow shade had a soothing effect. In this room Bonaparte Reubens had gently but effectively opened the mind of Jack Fairless to the world of international culture. After opening a bottle of the best whiskey Rush Hawkins kept in stock—shipped down from Washington, courtesy of Ben Butler—each man settled back in his favorite overstuffed chair. They lifted their glasses in a toast.

"To victory and glory!" offered Jack.

"I will settle for 'victory,' Jack. Let glory take care of itself."

They drank lustily, wanting to take the sharpness off their nerves as quickly as possible.

"Tell me the truth, Bonaparte: Are the Buffaloes ready for a real, proper battle?"

"As ready as any troops can be. But many things can go wrong, and certainly will. Our part of Foster's offensive is pretty weak for the tasks we've been given, which means we will have to fight intelligently as well as bravely. And believe me, there is a *big* difference . . . ."

"Bonaparte? Could you play that piece for me? The Beethoven? That would do more to calm me down than anything else."

"You're not tired of hearing it?"

"Remember: all that stuff is brand new to me."

"That's why such music is called 'classical'—it never really wears out its welcome!"

After removing his coat and rolling up his sleeves, Reubens sat down at the late Dr. Edgecomb's grand piano and began to summon from its keys the stoic melancholy of "Für Elise." As he always did when Reubens played the piece, Jack leaned forward, frozen by its sad beauty, hearing new subtleties, receptive to overtones and harmonies, and the assured poetry of Reubens' phrasing, and as he had done the very first time Reubens had played it for him, his eyes filled with tears. Reubens remained motionless at the keyboard for several minutes, then took his seat again, gratified and surprised, as always, at the way Jack Fairless soaked up every note, straight into his heart. When Jack came out of his reverie and brusquely slugged down another ounce of whiskey, Reubens quietly asked:

"Describe in your own words what you feel when you hear that piece."

Jack took a deep breath. "It makes me feel . . . like I was deeply in love, but with a woman I haven't actually met. If I ever see a woman who brings that music spontaneously into my heart, I will know she is the one true love of my destiny, even before I say a single word to her. . . ."

"Upon my soul, Jack, the wellspring of poetry in you grows deeper all the time. Is there much music-making in that remote, curiously named village where you came from?"

"Spillcorn Creek? Oh, yes. No grand pye-annas, of course, just a fiddle, a banjo, a mouth organ. Sometimes, in the autumn, when the air is clear as crystal and the woodsmoke snakes through the valleys, you might hear some old fella playin' a ballad on his porch, and the lonesomeness of it stops you in your tracks, fills you with a nameless ache, a longin' for . . . somethin' that I guess has no name."

"But no Beethoven."

"No," Jack laughed. "Leastwise, no tunes I ever heard identified with him!"

"When the war is over, I must take you to hear his Fifth Symphony, played by a full orchestra. I promise, you'll be so excited afterward you'll forget where you put your hat when you leave the hall."

"Probably not anyplace in the South where we could do that. . . ."

"I think I can confidently say there is not. We would probably have to travel to Boston or New York, but as I have never seen either city, it would be an equal adventure for the both of us."

"But you have seen lots of other big cities—in Europe, I mean. London, Paris . . ."

"Rome, Vienna, Berlin, Amsterdam . . . when I was young and rich, I made the whole Grand Tour. Young men of my class were expected to do that, or forfeit the right to call themselves 'civilized,' and it was very important to me that people regard me as civilized. In fact, as the product of a racially mixed marriage, I had to be *more* civilized than my white contemporaries." Reubens suddenly clammed up, for he could tell by Jack's expression that he had just conveyed more information about his past than he had ever vouchsafed before. The mood between them grew slightly brittle.

In the gentlest, most encouraging voice Reubens had ever heard from his lips, Jack Fairless turned the full beauty of his blue eyes against Bonaparte's slightly hooded ebony stare and said: "It occurs to me that you know just about everything there is to know about Jack Fairless, which admittedly ain't a lot, but nobody, not even me, knows much about you. You just kind of *showed up* one day. We're friends now. You've opened the doors for me to all these beautiful realms, but never told me, until just now, how you came to be a man of culture. Now, add to that the fact that you also are a crack shot with rifle or pistol, a man as well versed in infantry tactics as any West Pointer I ever saw, and you sit a horse like a prince.

"Bonaparte, just who the hell *are you,* and how did you end up here? I know that you don't like to brag about yourself, but if you get killed on this campaign and I do not, God forbid, there will be no one who knows your story. Do you want me to carve on your gravestone: 'Here lies Bonaparte Reubens, date of birth unknown, who lived and died a complete enema'?"

Reubens guffawed so hard part of his drink came bubbling out his nose.

"That's ENIGMA, you dumb peckerwood! *Mon Dieu,* and I thought you were making such progress!"

"Not that dumb a peckerwood—I had to say something to unlock your jaw. I do know what the two words mean, maestro."

Still wheezing with laughter, Reubens mopped himself with his handkerchief.

"Well, why not reward such a clever ploy? Truth to tell, I've had in my head for a long time that I would talk about my private life only with another black man, but as bizarre as it seems, you're the only man I know who would appreciate it—a white hillbilly who couldn't write his own name two years ago! The irony is so droll, I can almost think Koka-Ghita had a vision of this moment."

"Co-Co who?"

"I'll get to him in time. Let me start at the beginning. . . .

"My father's name was Willem Caspar Reubens, and he was recognized at an early age as a brilliant scientist. He graduated from the University of The Hague with highest honors, and two years later, published a treatise on the agriculture of ancient Greece and Rome that was universally hailed as the most important work ever written about this admittedly arcane subject. It was translated into several languages, and the French edition brought him an invitation to lecture at the Académie Française in Paris. Stimulated by the city and patronized by the Bourbon aristocracy, he soon published books on medicinal botany, animal husbandry, and a biography of Aristotle.

"The Dutch are a freedom-loving people, and when the French Revolution broke out, he traded the chalk of a pedagogue for the musket of a rebel. But the chaos and violence of the Terror repulsed him, and he went into seclusion until a leader emerged who brought order and stability: Napoleon Bonaparte, for whom I am named.

"Napoleon is today thought of as a tyrant and a despot, but in the early years of his rule he did many extraordinary things unrelated to war. He created a code of law that is still considered one of the most enlightened in the history of Europe. He wanted Paris to be the capital of learning, science, and the arts. My father not only returned to the Académie, as the head of its Department of Natural History, he also became a trusted adviser to Napoleon.

"When the emperor invaded Egypt in 1798, he brought with his army a corps of scholars, cartographers, linguists, antiquarians—he wanted them to unravel natural and historical mysteries that had never been penetrated before. Ancient treasures, manuscripts, statues, exotic plants and animals—anything that was novel or previously obscure was to be plundered and shipped back to France, to enhance the glory of Napoleon's prestige, to turn Paris into the Athens of its day. My father must have thought he was in heaven. His most important contribution to the scientific expedition was to be part of the team that discovered the famous Rosetta stone. What was that? Well, it's complicated, but in essence it was the object that made it possible, for the first time, for Europeans to decipher the strange hieroglyphic language of ancient Egypt. Not long after that discovery, the emperor sent for him and entrusted him with a secret mission.

"Throughout ancient literature, starting with Ptolemy and Virgil and continuing to the esoteric writings of Heinrick of Veldeck, a fourteenth-century alchemist and mystic, men had written of a mysterious peak known as the Magnetic Mountain or the Great Lodestone. Its location was thought to be somewhere in eastern Africa, and all the accounts mentioned the fact that it radiated such a powerful magnetic field that if a ship sailed within ten miles of it, all of the nails in its hull would be wrenched out and drawn through the air toward the great Lodestone Peak. At that point in his career, Napoleon's chief worry was the British navy. It occurred to him that if boulders of this powerful magnetite could be extracted, they might be used as a devastating weapon against Nelson's fleet. In theory they would be mounted on French ships inside a massive wooden container, and when an English ship drew near, one end of that container would be lifted, the wooden box turned to point at the man-o'-war, and its rays would rip out the iron nails holding the ship together. *Voilà!* The English ship would simply fall apart without a shot fired.

"Mind you, the emperor was a man of reason and pragmatism, so he was not swallowing this legend whole. Nevertheless, he told Willem Reubens, on the off chance that such a powerful anomaly did exist, that it was worth searching for. He commissioned my father to lead an expedition down the Nile—escorted by two thousand infantry, sixteen guns, and a brigade of cavalry. Even if the Lodestone Mountain proved to be a myth, my father would surely discover many wondrous things, spread the 'glory of France' among many exotic and previously unknown peoples, and bring back the first detailed maps of the most strategically important river in Africa. For a scientist whose range of interests was as wide as my father's, it was the opportunity of a lifetime.

"His expedition was gone for two years. He heard many rumors about the Lodestone Mountain, but it was always 'just a bit farther south' or 'beyond the next range of mountains.' It never was, of course, but after a few months, that hardly mattered. The expedition gathered a vast amount of cultural, geographical, and historical information. When my father's notes were finally published, they filled four volumes.

"He got as far as the mud-walled city of Jinga, near present-day Lake Victoria, almost to the source of the White Nile. For weeks he had been traveling among tribes who had never heard of the Lodestone Mountain, and his column had been so reduced by diseases and skirmishes that he saw no point in continuing. He camped in Jinga for one month, to let the surviving troops regain their strength and to gather supplies from the fertile plains in that region. The chieftain who ruled there was quite hospitable—he had never seen white men before, and he believed, in spite of all my father's protests to the contrary, that the Frenchmen were emissaries of the Supreme Deity, whoever he was. Most of all, the chieftain was astonished by gunpowder and was willing to trade anything he owned for a twelve-pounder and a cart of ammunition. This, he believed, would make him invulnerable to tribal enemies and bandits alike. What would my father take in trade for one of those iron thunder logs?

"My father, you must understand, had been living an ascetic, scholarly life and had never spared much time for dalliance with the ladies. But all that changed the moment he set eyes on the girl who was to become my mother. Her name was Shenaika. She was about sixteen, and had been living in Jinga for four years, as one of the chieftain's servants. She had escaped from a Bedouin slave caravan and somehow ended up here, at least two thousand miles from her homeland. She was born in one of the many Tuareg tribes, desert nomads noted for their ferocity and pride.

"The Tuareg are not black-skinned, nor do they have particularly Negroid features. Shenaika's complexion was a satiny bronze; her enormous almond-shaped eyes were a captivating smoky gray; her nose was Roman, or perhaps, given the region she came from, Carthaginian; and her mouth—ah, if you could see a portrait, you would gain a whole new appreciation of simple kissing. When my father first saw her, his heart was struck by lightning. The chieftain was reluctant at first, for he had planned to incorporate Shenaika into his harem as soon as her breasts got a little bigger, but he could always get more women and this was his only chance to obtain a cannon and the ammunition for it. The bargain was struck, and the girl moved into my father's tent that very night. He made it clear, by sign language and the few words of local dialect he had picked up, that he intended no harm, and would not molest her. She understood his meaning, but looked at him as though he had been deranged by sun fever and in halting French asked, 'Is my new master not a man?' Then she slipped gracefully out of her robe and hopped upon him like a tigress. By the time the expedition straggled back into Alexandria, in January 1800, they were utterly and forever after in love.

"Napoleon was already planning to withdraw from Egypt and had long since forgotten that harebrained idea of developing a magnetic ray to sink British ships. He was, however, delighted with the enormous amount of data and specimens my father had collected, and in honor of the luster this material would add to French scholarship, he elevated my father, on the spot, to be the count of Ablantes, an honorific that came with a five-hundred-acre estate and château, an elegant town house in Paris, and an annual stipend of one million francs.

"As far as I know, they were completely, rapturously happy, except for one thing: Shenaika was unable to bear a child to term—until the year 1818, when for some mysterious reason I emerged into this world, bawling my lungs out. Mother regarded me as a gift from God; Willem believed that I must have been born for some great destiny, to have defied the biological odds so remarkably.

"They spoiled me rotten, of course, but they also gave me the finest education money can buy—including the Grand Tour, which commenced on my sixteenth birthday and gave me the chance to travel in luxury to every place I wanted to see. My father's letters were invariably cheerful, so I had no idea how precarious their situation had become, under the Bourbon Restoration, until I was suddenly summoned home in early 1837. My mother was dying. She had been run over by a carriage as they were leaving the opera house, and sustained critical internal injuries. I reached the Paris residence in time to see her die.

"In fact, the family's situation had deteriorated rapidly during the years I was wandering from Rome to Vienna to London and so on. Paris was seething with intrigue, and the weak-willed new monarch, Louis-Philippe, was trying to consolidate his power by exposing 'Bonapartist' conspiracies, even if he had to make them up. He was also, as it happened, an unabashed racist, who viewed my parents' marriage as an abomination. He referred to my mother as 'that nigger witch,' and there were persistent rumors that her accident was, in fact, a bungled assassination. As for my father being a Bonapartist conspirator, well, the man was seventy years old and nearly blind. He also had made some very bad investments in his old age, and had been forced to sell the château to cover his losses and the staggering, punitive taxes levied against it by the new regime.

"Shenaika's death broke his spirit, and soon after, his health. She had been his greatest joy, his exotically beautiful jewel of Africa, and without her to share it with, life turned to ashes for him. When a man decides he has nothing to live for, his body eventually gets the message. In the winter of 1839, he took to his bed and waited calmly for death, believing that he would soon be reunited with his wife in some sphere vastly more beautiful and peaceful than Paris. Just before the end, he called me to his bedside and handed me a folded scrap of antelope hide, on the reverse side of which was a crude map of some utterly unexplored part of central Africa.

" 'Your mother wanted you to have this, saying that it was insurance against hard times. As my estate is virtually exhausted, I fear hard times will be your lot. She made this map during her journey after she escaped from the slave caravan. Here is the village of Jinga, where we met, and if you backtrack about eight hundred miles, to this range of mountains, you will find, or so she swore, a hidden fortress, which guards a great complex of diamond mines. If not the fabled mines of Solomon, then some other king's—I cannot remember his name. The tribe living there has guarded the diamonds for a thousand years, she said, and because they treated her cruelly, she wanted to expose the location by means of this map. "Tell Bonaparte they have no knowledge of firearms. A few bold men should be able to capture their stronghold and take away, in only their pockets, enough flawless gems to make them rich for life." I tended to think this was a fantasy, born in the brain of a frightened young girl, but who can say? In any case, it is your inheritance.'

"He died on New Year's Day 1840. Because a sign had been hung on the palace saying 'No Niggers Need Apply,' I could not find employment. It was plain that I would have to sell the town house and . . . well, I knew not what would become of me, but I could not long live in Paris. So I did what thousands of disenfranchised young men have done: I enlisted in the French Foreign Legion.

"Now, Jack, I want to show my two most precious possessions, which I wear on this chain around my neck. First, this medal. It is the Croix de Guerre. In all the history of France, only seven men of color have won this decoration. Five years in the French Foreign Legion, Jack—there is no better school for war. I won this medal for an action in Algeria, during the savage Bedouin uprising of 1844. I commanded two companies of legion infantry, in a small stone fort guarding an oasis, during a siege that lasted nine days. We were surrounded by thousands of desert tribesmen. The food ran out after four days, the water after five. Men went mad from thirst, died of sun poisoning; a few gave up all hope and shot themselves rather than be taken prisoner by nomads who had refined torture to an art form. When we were finally relieved, by a regiment of Zouaves, only forty-eight of us were still alive, and nine of those were stark, barking mad. But there were five hundred and ninety-eight Berber corpses strewn around our barricades. I would have stayed in the legion, I think, had I not contracted a fever that nearly took my life. I was in a coma for months, and barely able to walk for many months after I regained consciousness.

"Well, I regained my health, I had a medal and a tiny pension, plus a tidy sum on deposit in Paris from the sale of the town house. But I was adrift in Marseilles at age twenty-eight. I had a fabulous education, but because of Louis-Philippe's hatred of Negroes, I could not even find work as a village schoolteacher. I felt very sorry for myself and began to drift into alcoholism, slowly eating into my money, living in cheap rooms, and developing a robust opium habit. There were hundreds of ex-legionnaires just like me in Marseilles, men for whom the legion had been a family but who had been discharged for wounds or illness.

"Often we would drink together and swap legion stories. One night in 1850—I cannot recall how the topic came up—we were talking about African legends, a truly inexhaustible subject, and I pulled out my mother's map to the hidden diamond mines. When he saw it, one of my companions gasped. 'I have heard of this place, too!' 'And I,' said another. 'The nomads speak of it, but claim that its location is a closely guarded secret. Supposedly many adventurers have gone in search of it, but none has ever come back. None ever had a map, though!'

"I suppose you can guess what happened next. I recruited an expedition of thirty-four ex-legionnaires and bought arms, provisions, and camels. My life had come to such a dead end that I figured: Why not risk everything on one last adventure? At least you will feel alive again!

"We retraced my father's route down the Nile and, once again, the village of Jinga welcomed us. My father's bronze twelve-pounder had become a venerated object, and some old men, who were children at the time, could remember my mother. But when we asked for a guide to lead us west, to backtrack the route shown on the map, the natives warned us that the place we sought was sacred, ancient, and fanatically guarded. Of course, all we heard was a further confirmation that it really existed, so we set out in high spirits, each man heavily armed.

"Nine exhausting weeks later we found the Valley of Diamonds, the home of the Guruz, for that was the name of the tribe, or sect, or cult, that had guarded the diamond mines for more than ten centuries. They were not intimidated by our firearms. We never got to use them. As we rode down a narrow defile toward our goal, the Gurus—who had been tracking us for days—unleashed a cloud of arrows, each one tipped with a poison that brought instant paralysis.

"Aside from being chained by one leg to stone walls, we were surprisingly well treated, given three huge meals a day and all the wine we could drink. Nor were we the only Europeans—there was an elderly Belgian Jesuit, Father D'Albert, who had been in the hidden city for twenty-six years. He had persuaded the Gurus that he was truly a holy man, so that they hadn't killed him. Of course, they would not release him either, so he had become a kind of mascot. Thanks to his translations, we learned a bit about this otherworldly place.

"He believed these actually *were* the fabled mines of Solomon, but in the centuries since caravans last visited regularly, the guardians had evolved a cosmological belief that they guarded the diamonds because if any of the diamonds were stolen, the world would end.

" 'Many explorers have stumbled into this place,' he said, 'but none is allowed to leave. If they have swallowed even a single gem, and that gem leaves the valley, the sun goes black, the stars wink out, and all life dies.'

" 'If we are doomed,' I asked, 'why are we being fed so lavishly?'

" 'Oh, that's to fatten you up for the crocodiles,' Father D'Albert said with a cackle. 'In a week or two, when they think you're appropriately succulent, they'll take you out, one by one, and throw you into the croc pool. They think the crocs are gods, or demigods—their theology is complex and always changing. But it does leave a loophole if you're incredibly lucky. According to their legends, the first man who discovered this place was a poor nomad searching for a lost sheep. He was standing right over there, when the God of Creation, Koka-Ghita, smote his mind and heart and he knew, instantly, that upon this ground he must fulfill his destiny. If he left without discovering what that destiny was, he would never find peace and would die the most wretched of men. This vision, or seizure, was powerful enough to convince him, and after poking around aimlessly for a few days, he found the first deposit of diamonds.'

" 'So what's the loophole?' I asked.

" 'Before each man is led off to the croc pit, the high priest daubs his forehead with a potion of some kind and rests his palm upon that spot. If he senses that this man, too, is destined to receive a vision from Koka-Ghita, a command that he accomplish some great deed on a particular patch of earth, then it would be blasphemous to feed him to the crocs, for the deity has a plan for that man and will be very angry if any harm comes to him. The chosen man is given a cup of a potion that will make it impossible for him to ever find this place again, and then he is given a powerful personal fetish to take with him into the world—so the God of Creation can locate him when it is time for his revelation.'

" 'How many prisoners have escaped by this means?' I asked.

" 'Oh, since I've been here, only three. Out of perhaps four hundred who were sacrificed.'

"Well, I resigned myself to death by crocodile, for those were not good odds, and why would any god single out *me* to receive His vision? I did not tell my legion comrades why we were being fed so well. For two and a half weeks we were confined in cells but otherwise not mistreated. Aside from all the food and wine, comely women were sent to us every night. Then one day we were all taken outside and lined up. One by one the high priest examined each man closely, smeared his forehead with pungent salve, and rested his palm on that spot. After a moment he stepped back and shook his head, whereupon guards seized that man and carried him off to a subterranean pool. Thank God I could not hear the screams.

"When he came to me, however, he kept his palm pressed against my forehead for a long time. His touch, or the unguent he had painted me with, conveyed a tingling heat, and before long my head began to swim. When he stepped back, his expression had changed—he looked on me with curiosity and great respect. He motioned for Father D'Albert to come forward and translate.

" 'The God of Creation has chosen you to perform a great deed. It cannot be foretold when or where this will happen, but it will be unmistakable, like being struck by lightning. Wherever you are when that happens, it is upon that ground that your work must be started and nowhere else. So that the God of Creation can find you, you must wear this.'

"And he placed around my neck this little wooden fetish—my second precious possession, Jack. The power of suggestion is great, of course, but I distinctly felt . . . something. A blessing, an anointing, a power melting into my flesh. But this blessing came with a danger as well. Whoever the God of Creation selects for his works, that person is also watched closely by the God of Chaos, and the same amulet that protects me also can summon the God of Chaos, for these two deities are perpetually at war, the one seeking to build and the other seeking to destroy. Once the summoning strikes you, the amulet becomes a beacon for the God of Chaos, and both deities, depending on which one is the stronger from one day to the next, can channel their power through the fetish, thereby influencing other people who are near, and causing them to aid you or try to thwart you.

"That was all the high priest could or would tell me. He bowed, and ordered some guards to bring forth my camel, which was fully provisioned. My firearms were returned, and I was given a compass bearing that would, eventually, lead me to the Portuguese colony of Angola, on the eastern coast of Africa. From there I should take passage to the Indies—beyond that, the high priest could not descry what path I should take. And finally, for me to live and travel, until the summoning struck me, I was given a purse full of gold and gems—not diamonds, of course. Then I was sent on my way, to do . . . what?

"As the old Jesuit had foretold, I lost all memory of where the Valley of Diamonds was located. Of the events that took place there, however, I had perfect recollection. I am still, sometimes, haunted by the fate I brought on my old legion comrades, but *c'est la guerre*.

"From that day until the day I ended up in Wilmington, drawn there like so many others by the perfume of profit, I wandered the Caribbean. I did whatever came to hand: smuggling, gun-running, even hired myself out as a mercenary, sometimes to rebels, sometimes to the dictators they were trying to overthrow—whoever paid the better wages. I was, as the British say, 'knocking about,' drifting from place to place, when I heard about the Civil War in America and about the great profits that were being made in Wilmington. It was not easy for a black man, even one with cash in his pocket and proof of French citizenship, to make his way through the blockade, and by the time I reached Wilmington, the days of easy opportunity were over, I was low on funds, and my spirits were at their lowest ebb. All I had was my natural gift for leading men, and I gradually recruited a small band of stranded souls who were even more penniless and adrift than I was, men who accepted me as their employer simply because I could negotiate work contracts for us that they could not have obtained on their own. What a band of gypsies we were! A bankrupt prince; a Polish soldier of fortune who could barely speak a word of English; a Portuguese drunk so far gone in melancholy silence that he communicated only through grunts, shrugs, and hand gestures but who could play the guitar like a fallen angel; and, God help us, a *Chinaman* who had been expelled from some esoteric order of warlike monks. I never did learn the full story behind *him*. . . .

"Rejected and downcast men, all of us, the flotsam of the mechanical age, thrown up on these shores like shipwrecked mariners and barely able to feed ourselves. They submitted to my leadership out of necessity, and I regret to say I was not the kindliest boss in Wilmington. I looked down on them, but in reality I was no better than they.

"I picked up information that a big rice plantation needed extra hands to bring in the harvest, and somehow persuaded the master to hire us. Not that any of us knew a thing about rice except how to eat it, but I learned about the necessary skills from talking to some freed Negroes who had done that sort of work before the war, but who loathed it and were earning much better wages on the docks. All it took, apparently, was a strong back and a few harvesting techniques you could train a monkey to perform. I applied for the contract, and we were hired, although I took an instant dislike—unfairly, it turned out—to the master, a very successful blockade-runner captain named Sloane. He struck me as typical of his class: arrogant, smug, self-righteous. I did not learn until later that he was, in fact, one of the kinder and more humane masters and that most of his slaves felt some measure of genuine respect, even affection, for him.

"But after I signed the contract, I felt I had reached the absolute bottom. From rich aristocrat to common field hand! My mood grew uglier every day. I woke each morning with bile on my tongue and anger gnawing at my heart, consumed by rage at the circumstances that had brought me down into the gutter. I took notes about rice farming and shoved the knowledge down the throats of my men, so that by the time we traveled upriver to Pine Haven, we had soaked up a certain amount of competence, like sponges. I was in a balky, 'uppity' mood, and insisted on unreasonable treatment from my employer—sleeping quarters in the Big House, a place at their dining table, a little stage where I could show off my erudition, let them know I was not just another nigger for hire.

"I drank far too much at dinner and became rude, so rude that one of the house slaves insulted me! It was all I could do not to rise up from my chair and strike the old man! Unpardonable. Before things got totally out of hand, I had the good sense to excuse myself and retire, in a great sulk, to my room—and on the way, to steal a bottle of good imported whiskey from Mister Sloane's pantry. I drank myself into a stupor and woke the next morning with a savage headache.

"Nevertheless, a job was a job, so I reported to the rice fields with my men at the appointed time, and we worked as hard and as efficiently as any of the blacks who had been harvesting rice all their adult lives. But my mood grew foul in all that heat and itchy muck. Word had gotten around to the Pine Haven slave community about my insulting behavior to the head house nigger the night before, and they managed, by glances and subtle signs—the secret communication of all slaves in the history of human bondage—to convey their utter contempt for me, and that, you may be sure, made my blood boil. On that day, in those steaming fields, the most abject, ignorant field hand felt superior to *me!*

"As the day wore on, my condition worsened. My head throbbed, I was dehydrated, I was pouring rivers of sweat. At some point in the day I realized that because of all that sweat, and all the bending you have to do to harvest rice plants, my amulet had fallen off. I scrabbled madly through the mire, desperate to find it. It was only a few feet away, but when I slipped it around my neck and stood up, I was like a man suddenly gone blind. I could *feel it* coming, Jack: the summons! When it struck, it was indeed like a bolt of lightning! I had some kind of dreadful seizure, foamed at the mouth, became violent, struck out wildly at whoever was in reach—black or white, it made no difference—and I was, quite properly, beaten unconscious.

"I was awakened later that night by someone throwing water on my head. The madness had ebbed, and someone had located my pouch and retied it around my neck. 'Whoever you are,' I said, 'I thank you with all my heart, for you have saved both my life and my soul—if I still have one.' Then I raised my head, and was astonished to see that same old darkie, the house slave who had borne without complaint the silly and patronizing name of 'Agrippa.' His face was an ebony mask. All he said to me was: 'The fetish you wear—it is a thing of immense power. You must be free to pursue the task that is your destiny.' But the voice was not that of old Agrippa, Jack, it was the voice of the high priest from the Valley of Diamonds, either that or . . . well, let us not stray too far into the supernatural. 'I am setting you free,' the not-Agrippa said, sawing through the ropes that bound me. 'You are charged with creating something good and noble *here,* in the South, by using your powers of leadership to unite men of goodwill, *both blacks and whites* working together, to create a prosperous New South, for this is fallow ground, or soon will be, when the old ways are smashed forever by the Northern conquerors. You can show men a new way, give them a vision of what can be done by the power of brotherhood. There is an old fishing boat hidden in the weeds north of the dock. Go to the Yankees' base at New Bern and become a liberator once again, form a black legion to fight for freedom, and welcome as your brothers the white soldiers who ride with you. Once that victory has been achieved, forsake the cruel pleasures of revenge, and show by your *deeds* that black men and white men can build a new South together. This I charge you, in return for your life and freedom! But be always on your guard, for the God of Chaos will try to destroy you, and I cannot always be with you. As your soon to be good friend Jack Fairless will say, 'Some days you eat the bear, some days the bear eats you.' "

Reubens said this with such perfect deadpan seriousness that Jack almost bought it. Then he realized how mightily his leg had been pulled, and he groaned.

"Sorry—I couldn't resist. Ever since that day, my sense of humor has improved markedly. Otherwise, everything I have told you is God's truth—well, some God's truth, at any rate. As for the rest, you know it. I ended up here, and being here felt right. Cyrus Bone, alas, did not feel right. I think the God of Chaos was using him. The earth is cleaner without him."

"God Amighty DAMN, that is one hell of a yarn. If any other man had told me that story, I would call him a liar. Have you got a plan for achieving your 'good and noble' work?"

"Well, I've made a good start, Jack. In the Buffaloes we have proven that black soldiers and white can live and train side by side, as brothers in arms. The campaign we're about to embark on should prove conclusively whether that brotherhood can survive the shock of battle—real battle, not just the penny-ante skirmishes we've fought until now. The Confederacy may be in decline, but the Rebels have a lot of fight left in them, and some of us will surely die in this campaign. But when the South does break, it will break utterly. The vast plantations will be sold off and broken up, the towns and cities will need goods and services, and a lot of Yankee vultures will flock down here to pick at the bones. We—and by that I mean myself and the men who choose to stay with me after the fighting stops—we can provide an alternative to the scoundrels; a disciplined, orderly movement for progress, for a new South, and I promise that our ranks will be open to white men who have divested themselves of prejudice and black men who have larger things in mind than revenge. Right now the concept is still new and unformed, but as the war goes on, it will acquire focus and a systematic plan. For a few years, at least, a unique window will open in history, and we must act swiftly to plant the seeds of a progressive future, to create a society that may become a shining beacon of hope, a place where the old hatreds are cast aside, where men of all colors can have what *all* reasonable men ask for: a fair chance to reach their full potential."

"I wish I knew more about history, Bonaparte, but it seems to me that this sort of thing must have been tried before. Your grandfather tried it, for one, and like you said, he ran into a brick wall called human nature. . . ."

Reubens looked tired now. "We have to keep trying, Jack! If we assume we will fail before we even begin, what is the point of struggling? Even if something fails, it still may leave lessons that later generations can learn from. Of course, there never will be a perfect society, or perfect equality! Still, someone must keep trying!"

Jack Fairless was now about as drunk as he cared to be, considering the responsibilities he would soon face as a commander. He recorked his bottle and held out his hand. Reubens shook it.

"It's been a privilege to hear your story, Captain Reubens. You've honored me. And given me a lot to think about, more than a poor ol' mountain boy can digest in one night. Let's get some shut-eye now, so we'll be ready to tear the Rebs a bunch of new assholes! Like you said, first there has to be victory, right?"

"True enough, Colonel Jack. First there has to be victory. But *then* things must happen that give victory a deeper meaning. Otherwise it simply means a stronger army has beaten a weaker one—and there is nothing special about that. And don't forget: sometimes, it is the beaten army that leaves the stronger legends!"

Buffaloes on Campaign

BECAUSE CYRUS BONE had coerced the naïve Fairless into the practice of Sodom, Jack's sense of sexual identity was precarious. The way Capt. Reubens saw it, if Jack was to become a respected and effective replacement of Bone, it was imperative that he be purged of sexual ambiguity. History proves that homosexuals could be great generals—Alexander the Great comes most readily to mind—but the Buffaloes were not Greek hoplites, and their performance on the battlefield would be greatly enhanced if they knew their commanding officer had the balls to match his rank.

Before Jack's first visit to the Negro brothel, Reubens prepared the women for exceptional performances by handing out a bonus and explaining to them that he wanted Col. Fairless to sample each woman's charms and skills in peak performance, so that one of them would become known to his soldiers as "the Colonel's lusty wench". At first, the prostitutes thought this was a ludicrous and faintly insulting scheme. "Calm down, ladies!" Reubens admonished them. "Just think of it as a friendly competition. Whoever throws Jack Fairless the best fuck, wins the prize—this fifty-dollar gold piece—and she only has to service one man, not a multitude." These remarks helped greatly to put the women in a proper frame of mind; each was resolved to give Jack Fairless her best. Their communal attitude changed after Jack's first visit, when the word got around that this white cracker was blessed with a male standard of prodigious size and a tireless tongue to match. Suddenly, the competition grew fierce, but Jack picked his partner after only five visits. The coveted title of "The Colonel's Lady" went to a voluptuous light-skinned young woman named Hattie Smalls . . .

—"Adventures of a Black 'Buffalo,'" Sgt. Washington Pierce,
unpublished manuscript, State Archives, Raleigh, N.C.

By the morning of Thursday, October 1, 1863, the transformation of Jack Fairless had reached its high point. In the span of little more than a year, he had gone from Rebel private to regimental commander, an illiterate hick private to avid student of literature, from sexual novice to one hell of a cocksman. No one had the slightest doubt of Jack's virility, particularly Jack himself. He was as primed for heroism as a man could be.

"Jack, baby, you looks good enough to eat," crooned Hattie Smalls his voluptuous new black mistress from her side of the late Dr. Edgecomb's enormous bed.

"Well, when I get back from this campaign, you'll have to show me how strong an appetite you've developed in my absence."

"My handsome white colonel, you take care some Rebel don't shoot off that big pecker, you hear?"

"Don't fret, girl. It's made out of iron, or so you told me last night."

"I tol' you it was hard as iron, not *made* out of it. I'm gonna worry about you, Jack."

"We'll cut the Rebels to pieces, Hattie. The Buffaloes are fired up and ready to show the generals just how much we've learned about *real* soldiering. If we falter, fail, or break, General Foster will disband the unit. Therefore we are determined to fight better, harder, and smarter than any other regiment."

Outside, a bugle blared assembly. Jack straightened the lines of his uniform, adjusted his wide-brimmed hat to a rakish angle, blew a kiss at Hattie Smalls, then strode confidently from the room.

His day of destiny had arrived, and God had blessed the occasion with mild temperatures, a cloudless sky of achingly pure blue, and a lavish outpouring of honey-colored sunlight. An orderly flung open the front door for him, and there they were: *his* soldiers, arrayed with the steady-eyed sharpness of veterans. Jack returned the salutes of each company commander with the snap and precision of a West Pointer. He held up both hands to let the men know he was ready to give the obligatory inspirational speech—and make it all very plain:

"Men, the time has finally come to make the Rebs feel the sharp end of a Buffalo's horns! There are some mean-spirited Union officers who would love to see us fail, to be disgraced. We shall not give them that dastardly satisfaction! Make the enemy howl and General Foster proud. The transports are waiting at the docks, so let's ride!"

General Rush Hawkins was somewhat less confident of the Buffaloes' military prowess than was their strutting commander. It was true that Fairless had cleaned up their pig wallow of an encampment and drilled them hard, so that at the very least they *looked* like regular soldiers instead of Corsican brigands, but neither Colonel Fairless nor 99 percent of his men had ever been involved in a real battle. General Foster would like nothing better than a legitimate military reason to disband the Buffaloes. Worse, Foster had shown a worrisome interest in Shelborne's Point, and a dismal showing by the Buffs might give him the leverage to pry more deeply into Hawkins' operation. The small, remote river port had no real strategic value; it had not been one of General Burnside's objectives; and Rush Hawkins was known to be chummy with Ben Butler, whom Foster loathed. There was some kind of unsavory connection linking these facts, and Foster wanted to dig a little deeper, turn over some rocks, and see what might be wriggling underneath them. Only yesterday Foster had sent Hawkins an updated operational plan, and appended a scolding reminder:

> *In closing, I wish to remind you that you are, at least ostensibly, in command of the largest mounted infantry unit at my disposal. You have repeatedly assured me that the "Buffaloes" are now prepared to carry their own weight in a major campaign—to march and fight like real soldiers. I expect them to perform accordingly. If they do not, if they prove to be an embarrassment instead of an asset, I will not hesitate to launch an inquiry, at the highest levels of authority, into all of the activities over which you have presided at Shelborne's Point.*

Inquiries! Investigations! Reprimands! Exposure! Damn Foster, anyway! How was Hawkins supposed to concentrate on his own part of the campaign while being distracted by visions of his grand political career crumbling into dust . . . before it had even started?! But his patron had not deserted him, for just a few hours after Hawkins had read Foster's sour-apples addendum, a picket boat chugged up to the dock and delivered an "urgent" dispatch from General Benjamin F. Butler. Butler had gotten wind of Foster's unhealthy interest in their business—was there *anything* that escaped Butler's eye?—and had sent Hawkins another of his avuncular letters of reassurance:

> *Cooperate fully with Gnl. Foster, but do not fear him. He is a bit of a dullard, but he has done a capable job of sustaining the Union presence in eastern North Carolina—a job nobody else wants. Naturally, Foster does not want it either, and has been incessantly petitioning the War Dept. for a field command. If he sticks his nose too deep into our private business, I shall arrange for him to get one. Therefore, be bold and scrupulous in carrying out your duties, and everything will turn out in your favor. But do try not to get yourself killed! Willy-nilly, barring some unlikely major Rebel offensive in your part of the country, things will continue to go well for us. Of that you have my utmost assurance, as well as my warmest affection.*

A straightforward, reassuring message . . . yet with Butler, you never knew. When Hawkins read it a second time, he found subtle hints that Butler was laying the ground for a major comeback; indeed, he had probably been doing so since the army took him off the active-duty list—the public outcry over Butler's scandalous behavior as the de facto emperor of New Orleans compelled the army to administer some kind of rebuke, and sending him back home to Lowell, Massachusetts, on indefinite leave had defused the crisis. It also had given Butler plenty of free time to plot his next move. When he made it, Hawkins predicted, it would be dramatic and swifter than the thrust of Brutus's dagger. If Butler said that Hawkins had nothing to fear from John Foster, you could take that to the bank. Liberated from a host of worries, Rush Hawkins was ready to go campaigning.

Hawkins' men moved by barge and tugboat down to "Little" Washington, escorted by three gunboats: Lieutenant Stonechiper's *Trenton* and two of the new "Riverine Class" gunboats, the U.S.S. *Allison* and *Sentinel.* General DeWitt's transports were scheduled to rendezvous there on the afternoon of October 2. But they were delayed by uncharted sandbars in Hatteras Inlet, no one knew for how long. Hawkins called his officers together and told them to make their men as comfortable as possible while they waited. And no, he could not tell them how long that might be.

The Buffaloes pitched their tents on a field just north of the village, where an ample supply of dry corn shucks made for comfortable mattresses. Bonaparte Reubens retired early, and was extremely vexed when a sentry woke him at midnight, bringing the news that Company B had just gained four new recruits. A quartet of runaways, all of them fit men of fighting age, had presented themselves at the picket line and announced their intention to enlist with "Bonaparte's Colored Heroes." Reubens said with a chuckle: "I did not know our fame had spread so far or that our victories were so stunning as to render us 'heroes,' but any recruits who are *that* eager are welcome to join us. Is there any man who seems to be their leader, or who speaks for them?"

"Yes, sir. Good-looking fella, 'bout twenty-five, talks like he's had a smidgen of education."

"Send him in."

After bending to get through the tent flap, the tall Negro volunteer snapped to a reasonable semblance of attention.

"At ease, son. What's your name?"

"Elias, Your Honor."

" 'Captain Reubens' is the correct form of address. Any last name, or didn't your former masters bother to acknowledge your humanity with even that minimal courtesy?"

Elias scratched his cheek, ruminating, then broke into a smile that was tinged with irony.

"Elias *Sloane,* Cap'n Reubens, tha's my rightful name."

Reubens slapped his thigh in amusement. "*Quelle surpris!* I thought you looked vaguely familiar. How are things back at dear old Pine Haven, and how come you here from that idyllic spot?"

"I got tired of waitin' for 'the Jubilee,' Cap'n, wanted to li'brate *myself.* Got cross with that ol' overseer, Mistah Bright. We had angry words, and Ah thought for sure he was gonna shoot me and leave me for rot in the swamps, but instead he *let me go*. 'The Yankees are *that* way, boy! If'n you can't wait for them to come to you, you go to them!' 'Course, he probably warn't expectin' me to survive the trip."

Again Reubens laughed, truly savoring the runaway's tale. "Expelled from Eden, by God . . . . And my former employers, the Sloanes, how are they faring these days, with the South crumbing on every side?"

"Everybody all tensed up an' waitin'. Mistah Sloane, he got caught runnin' the blockade and he got tossed into this special kind of Yankee jail; most folks say he'll be there till the war's over. Missuz Sloane, she tryin' her best to pretend nothing' has changed, but every livin' soul on the place knows they have, and Ah might be the first nigger *born* at Pine Haven to run away, but Ah won't be the last. I heard 'bout your colored cavalry and made my way here. Picked up three more recruits along the way."

Reubens poked his head out of the tent and bellowed for his adjutant, who appeared quickly, still clad in his red woolen long johns.

"Mister Sloane—I mean, Private Sloane—you and your friends follow this gentleman. He will administer the oath; issue the uniforms; and, if you're hungry, scrounge up some rations for you."

Elias grinned and bowed, then turned his head around to the three shadowy Negroes outside the tent: "See, boys? Couldn't ask for a better deal than that!" They nodded vigorously.

"What about guns, Cap'n, sir?" Elias's voice took on a hungry edge.

"Are you trained in the loading, firing, and cleaning of the Springfield rifled musket?"

"No, suh, of course we ain't. But if somebody shows us that stuff, and we get a couple hours to practice tomorrow, I reckon we'll be right smart shooters by sundown."

"Your eagerness is commendable, but I'm afraid there's a bit more to basic training than that. You four new men will ride with the supply wagons at the rear of the column. Pay close attention to the soldiers around you, ask questions, and if we are fired upon, do as they tell you without hesitating. If we take casualties, your first job will be to carry the wounded back to the ambulance wagons. Do not, however, pick up a rifle and start shooting without my express orders. I'm not belittling your intelligence or your courage, Elias, it's just that things always get very confusing in combat and, until you develop a sense for it, it's often hard to tell friend from foe in all that smoke. Don't worry—we'll train you as we march. Any idiot can learn how to load and fire a rifle, and a baboon can master close-order drill. You'll learn fast, and when I think you're ready, I'll bring you forward and put you in the firing line, same as the veterans. They won't let you down, and you'd best not let them down—that's how it works, that's what enables frightened men to stand under fire and not flinch. I guess that's my welcoming speech. Now off with you. After the formalities, find a piece of straw and get whatever sleep you can, because we march at dawn, day after tomorrow." Then, under his breath, Reubens muttered: "Assuming all those other niggers ever show up."

Rush Hawkins knew, of course, that the Union army was raising and training dozens of Negro regiments, but it was a revelation to actually see so many colored men under arms. When he saw DeWitt's two colored regiments march off their transports, on the morning of October 3, and form up for inspection, they certainly *looked* eager, drilling with the strut and outthrust chests of newly minted soldiers—well trained, but a little too smug and cocky. Well, thought Hawkins, they all look like that until they get their first close look at a grapeshot casualty! DeWitt's troops, combined with the force Hawkins had brought down from Shelborne's Point, gave Foster's northern column a total strength of 4,200 infantry, 11 pieces of field artillery, and Jack Fairless's 572 mounted riflemen, who would have to do the best they could to function as regular cavalry.

Hawkins was not nearly as upset about being made subordinate to DeWitt as General Foster had expected him to be. Given DeWitt's limited field experience and the untested fighting quality of his troops, this operation might quickly and seriously turn into a first-class debacle, and DeWitt, not Hawkins, would have to shoulder the blame. What Hawkins did resent was the smug little scowl on DeWitt's face as he made a perfunctory inspection of the troops from Shelborne's Point. He was inordinately proud of "his boys," and his expression clearly showed that he had a lesser opinion of Hawkins' Massachusetts troops, and an attitude verging on open contempt for the Buffaloes.

Given his background, such spontaneous, dismissive prejudices came easily to Edmund DeWitt. He had grown up spoiled by inherited—not *earned*—wealth. Motivated by some vague compulsion to atone for his good luck, he became a passionate abolitionist, using his fortune to buy scholarships for worthy black students; contributing heavily to political candidates who shared his views; subsidizing publication of the collected speeches of Frederick Douglass; and, when the war broke out, buying himself a colonel's rank and command of the 10th New Jersey. He had briefly seen action during the Peninsula campaign, but when a shell fragment penetrated his skull, traced a path around the side of his head, and came to rest only a hairbreadth from his spinal cord, he was forced into early retirement. No surgeon would risk extraction—one slip of the knife would leave DeWitt paralyzed for life. His recuperation was slow—periodic swellings and inflammation affected his nervous system, giving rise to "spells" of erratic behavior and uncontrollable spastic motions of his limbs. But when he learned that Congress had authorized the raising of all-Negro regiments, he traveled to Philadelphia, sought out a famous specialist in "nervous disorders," and offered him twenty thousand dollars to remove the piece of shrapnel his colleagues had refused to touch. Apparently the operation was a success, because when DeWitt applied for command of his own black regiment, the army doctors pronounced him "miraculously" cured.

This much Hawkins had been able to learn about DeWitt—an inquiry about him, wired to Butler, had produced quick results. The man had shown courage, true, but what concerned Hawkins was the general's *current* state of mind. He soon got a chance to make that appraisal, for DeWitt summoned all officers to a strategy conference, to commence promptly at 6:30 P.M., in the commandeered dining room of the town's only hotel. Along with his own staff, Hawkins brought Jack Fairless and Bonaparte Reubens. DeWitt provided something rather more colorful than a routine staff conference.

He was a portly man of early middle age whose prim, rather pinched mouth hid behind a thick, drooping mustache. His close-set, restless blue eyes and broad, academic-looking forehead were framed by a luxurious quaff of gleaming, pomaded hair that smelled faintly of beeswax and more strongly of floral-scented cologne. *Too much cologne,* thought Hawkins. *DeWitt smells like an ambulatory orchid.* His wound had left him with a stiff right leg, and, as if to compensate for the limp, his movements were disconcertingly brisk. He had a propensity to whirl about suddenly, for no apparent reason, which made him look like a spinning top. He spoke in a loud voice, in grating, staccato cadences, accompanied by jack-in-the-box gestures; in some respects he reminded Hawkins of a barking seal he had once seen in a traveling circus.

DeWitt's plan for organizing the march was textbook-orthodox, though overstuffed with fussy details of the sort generals usually left to their underlings. These he adumbrated in a jittery, rapid-fire manner that had everyone scribbling furiously in their notebooks. Then, quite abruptly, DeWitt stopped speaking. His captive audience looked up from their notes, pencils poised, and waited. DeWitt was glassy-eyed, his expression quite inscrutable. The silence attenuated for an uncomfortably long time. Had he suddenly gone mute? Fallen into a trance? DeWitt waited impassively until the silence became truly oppressive, then he made a barking sound and suddenly jabbed his forefinger on a wall map, striking every hamlet, bridge, and crossroads along their axis of advance.

"Heathen lands!" he cried. *"Dwelling places of evil! And we, gentlemen, are the sword of Gideon, the strong right arm of righteousness, the cleansing torch of fire!"*

Up to that moment, DeWitt's manner had been merely eccentric. Now he spoke with raw, evangelical fervor, unabashedly imitating the cadences of Negro preachers.

He pounded the tabletop like a trip-hammer, paraphrasing from Scripture, evoking the rhythms of prophetic incantation:

"Thus saith the Lord unto Pharaoh: How long wilt thou refuse to humble thyself before Me? If thou refuseth to let my people go, then on tomorrow morning I will bring upon the land of Egypt a plague of *locusts,* and they shall be so numerous as to blot out the sun and bring a darkness more fearful than that of the eternal night of the grave! . . . And of your fertile lands, not one green thing will remain. [A transitional pause—he's going somewhere new with this, thought Hawkins, and his officers were starting to grin, anticipating the effect their general's soliloquy was going to have on a new audience . . . and, yes, was that a tentative, baiting little chuckle?] Not a single stalk of wheat, not an ear of corn, neither fruit upon thy vines, nor the healing herbs within thy gardens! Not a lamb! Neither will I spare thy pigs, thy great smoked hams! [Every soldier in the room chortling now.] Thy cows shall be turned into steaks and stew meat! Thy honeycombs shall sweeten our coffee! Of all thy livestock, nothing shall escape our consumption! Nay, not so much as a chicken—even unto the scrawniest bird that can provide a pair of roasted drumsticks!"

It was a virtuoso performance, Hawkins thought, as Fairless and Reubens joined him in applauding DeWitt. *Campaigning with this righteous old loon might turn out to be downright fun!* But DeWitt cut off the applause and cheers with a quick chop of fist into palm, and when the room fell silent once more, he made it clear that there would be nothing amusing about his treatment of the enemy.

"Gentlemen, you have your orders, relayed to you, through the instrument of my presentation, from our commander in chief, General John G. Foster. We shall, of course, follow those orders. But in addition, it is my intention to prosecute this campaign with much greater stringency than John Foster, who is a man of mild temperament, might consider necessary or proper. General Hawkins, have your fearsome 'Bisons' utterly scourged this part of the state, or did they leave some gleanings for us?"

"We never had any reason to come so far from our base, General, so whatever you may find along our route of march has not been touched by any previous Union soldiers."

"Excellent. Every officer in this room should impress upon his men the fact that no Union soldiers have ever penetrated North Carolina as deeply as we are about to. Therefore I intend to make our expedition into an unforgettable event. Our columns will shatter the peace and complacency of these counties, and the severity I intend to impose along the way will be such that none of these Rebels will ever enjoy a peaceful sleep again.

"In combat against uniformed Confederate regulars, we will, of course, observe all the conventions of civilized warfare—a term that I personally have always believed to be an oxymoron!" DeWitt chuckled at his own cleverness, and Hawkins, in turn, was amused when he saw Jack Fairless bend toward Captain Reubens and mouth silently the words *What kind of 'moron*? and Reubens roll his eyes and whisper "I'll tell you later!"

"But against bushwhackers or armed civilians," DeWitt continued, "should any of them be bold enough or foolish enough to oppose us, we are not obligated to show either restraint or mercy. If you are in doubt as to the status of any prisoner, bring him to me and I will judge him on the spot! Harden your hearts, gentlemen, for I intend to use the noose or the torch as circumstances warrant. If I deem it necessary to *make examples*, then examples shall be made—and made with a clear conscience.

"Do not carry into battle the useless weight of sentiment or ambiguity. These people must learn just how utterly impotent the Richmond government is when it comes to protecting their lives and property. Most of these Rebels probably believe that just because the front lines are three hundred miles away, they are safe from the ravages of war. We shall bring those 'ravages' right into their parlors, their kitchens, their barns, and, hell, maybe even their outhouses, too! And as for any slaveowners we encounter, it will be worth every mile of the march just to imagine their feelings when they look down the road and behold, marching toward them, *three thousand Negro soldiers with outthrust bayonets!*"

After DeWitt's "revival meeting," Rush Hawkins called a separate staff conference, aboard the *Trenton.* Under no circumstances, he admonished, were the men of the 6th Massachusetts or the Buffaloes to rob, molest, or injure the peaceful civilians they encountered. If General DeWitt gave them orders to commit dishonorable acts, they were to refuse, and DeWitt could bring his complaints to Hawkins. "This man is bloodthirsty and mentally unstable—if General Foster had known these facts, he would never have let Meade dump DeWitt's brigade in our laps. Pass the word to your men."

After the *Trenton* conference broke up, Captain Adolphus Manchester, the Confederate veteran who had resworn his allegiance to the Union after Gettysburg, took Jack Fairless aside for a private conversation.

"Colonel Fairless, I donned the blue uniform precisely because the

Richmond government could not protect my family from the sort of uncivilized mayhem this fanatic DeWitt seems determined to inflict on a lot of equally innocent people. I will fight for the Union, sir, but I cannot condone atrocities nor will I order my soldiers to commit them."

"My opinion, Adolphus, is that General DeWitt is mostly putting on a show, spouting off a lot of abolitionist horseshit. I no more intend to let my boys start raping and pillaging than you do. Even so, you can't be squeamish about hanging a few bushwhackers or stealing a few Rebel chickens . . . ."

"No, sir, not if it *stops* there. But to burn out some poor farmer simply because he happens to be in our line of advance . . . that is not what I changed sides for."

"No, of course not. You strike me as . . . what was the term Bonaparte used? Yeah: 'a disillusioned idealist,' not a zealot. But I need your expertise with those twelve-pounders, man—you're my only trained artillerist. And to prove my confidence in you, I'm also giving you temporary command of Company C, since their regular captain has been felled by what seems to be dysentery, but which I suspect may be a case of sudden cowardice. The men in that company *will* obey your orders or answer to me. That gives you some control over what happens. You will not be required, at least not by me, to commit any 'atrocities.' Just shoot your guns when and where you're ordered to, and lead your infantry like the veteran you are."

The ex-Confederate nodded, but did not salute or leave. Clearly he was still uneasy. Jack tried another tack.

"Look, Manchester, General Foster's made it clear that he expects every man involved in this operation to behave in a manner that reflects credit on his leadership, and General Hawkins ain't about to do anything that'd piss off John Foster. That happened once before, and it almost resulted in the shutting down of Shelborne's Point."

"Yes, sir, I realize that. But General Hawkins is not in command of this particular dog-and-pony show, so if any finger-pointing needs to be done later, it can be done at General DeWitt's expense. As I see it, this phase of Foster's operation will be taking place in a moral vacuum, under circumstances that virtually guarantee all manner of mischief. I will serve my guns and lead my company in a professional manner, but if somewhere along the march things do get out of hand, I cannot just shut my eyes and look the other way."

Fairless was losing patience. In the kind of war the Buffaloes had been fighting, moral niceties were abstractions.

"Goddamn it, Manchester, don't go all saintly on me! And don't even think about switchin' sides again, just because you don't have the stomach for hard war. You cross me in the heat of battle and I'll shoot you myself!"

Manchester saluted coldly, regarding the blue cloth on his arm as though it had suddenly become scratchy and uncomfortable.

"With all due respect, Colonel Fairless, I led a regiment through the Seven Days' Battle, Fredericksburg, Chancellorsville, and Gettysburg, where I lost three-fourths of the men I had left. I have seen more 'hard war' than any man in this outfit."

Without another word, the ex-Confederate spun on his heel and stalked away toward the field where his three guns stood ranked with the eleven cannons DeWitt had brought down from Norfolk.

7:18 A.M., OCTOBER 4, 1863

If sketched on a map, General Edmund DeWitt's order of march would have resembled a long, thin arm preceded by a spread of severed "fingers" about three miles ahead of the "wrist." These were composed of Buffalo detachments: eighty to one hundred mounted riflemen spread out in an arc approximately two miles wide. Their job was to scout the land ahead of the slower-moving main column as it crossed into eastern Pitt County—a landscape of rolling sandhills and boggy pine forests whose primeval conditions were interrupted only by an unmapped network of narrow wagon lanes connecting isolated farms and tiny hamlets.

Fairless's orders were to give advance warning of any Rebel ambush—a possibility Jack considered most unlikely at this early stage of things, and, more importantly, to locate the hiding place of the ironclad and send that information back to DeWitt. They were strictly enjoined from attacking the vessel, even if it was weakly guarded; DeWitt had reserved that honor for his own units.

DeWitt's main force marched on a towpath and market road that clung to the Tar's southern shore. DeWitt and his staff rode in front, at the head of his premier Negro unit, the 29th Rhode Island (which he had christened the "Frederick Douglass Regiment"); next in line, after an interval of a hundred yards, tramped the 30th Rhode Island ("John Brown's Avengers"); and behind them, almost like an afterthought, came Rush Hawkins and eight-hundred-odd men of the 6th Massachusetts.

More or less in the middle of this ungainly formation steamed the gunboats Commodore Flusser had assigned to support DeWitt's infantry with heavy, long-range fire, at least until the river got too shallow for safe passage. Where that point might be was anyone's guess, for the Tar could rise and fall by as much as two feet in as many days, depending on the amount of upstream rainfall.

At sunrise on October 4, the gunboats set off first. Lieutenant Stonecipher, who had served Rush Hawkins faithfully since the earliest days of the Shelborne's Point enterprise, had begged for permission to lead the gunboat flotilla with the U.S.S. *Trenton,* which was only logical, since that ship drew less water than the newer and heavier *Sentinel* and *Allison*. Thus permission was granted. After two years of drinking and whoring at Shelborne's Point, Stonecipher suddenly had a yen for action. Hawkins thought this was commendable (it also would add luster to his otherwise totally blank service record), so he made a point of being there when the gunboats started upriver. Stonecipher was aglow with naval heritage, standing proudly on the bridge, leading his crew in many *huzzahs,* and mouthing the words *Thank you!* as the *Trenton* passed the spot where Hawkins sat ramrod-straight in his saddle. Hawkins waved and mouthed back, *Don't fuck up!*

To Hawkins, the gunboats' passage was a stirring prelude to the operation about to unfold. Over his right shoulder rose an early-autumn sun the color of a waxed tangerine. Far off to Hawkins' left, the fading crescent of a quarter moon hung yet in the topmost spires of a pine grove, like the snared remnant of a fallen kite. The river was so thickly carpeted with fog that the iron-sheathed gunboats seemed to be moving on clouds, their fittings and gun barrels bejeweled with dew, the quarter-speed heartbeat of their engines lending them the spectral aura of mythological beasts.

From his place in the column, Hawkins heard General DeWitt's booming, pulpit-pounding voice ordering a general advance, and his words bounced back down the road from one black sergeant major to the next, each black company dressing its ranks briskly. DeWitt evidently suggested to the commander of the Frederick Douglass Regiment that a rousing song might be in order, and the black soldiers complied with zest and exceptionally good harmony—apparently DeWitt had made choir practice a part of their training regimen. Hawkins liked the singing but thought it was rather imprudent. Now any Rebel lurking within a mile of the river could hear the Negroes coming, and make what he would of their intention to "hang Jeff Davis from a sour apple tree!"

Rush Hawkins doubted that General Foster's column, which was currently marching more or less parallel to theirs about sixty-five miles to the south, was pouring forth "The Battle Hymn of the Republic" as they tramped up the road from New Bern, not with Foster so determined to achieve some degree of "surprise." But DeWitt damned well *wanted* the Confederates to know his "boys" were coming, and any slaves in their path would, of course, recognize the sound of *black* voices and know that in this part of the state at least, the Jubilee was drawing nigh.

12:14 P.M., October 4, 1863

Bonaparte Reubens and his men spent the first half of the day riding cautiously through an almost equatorial wilderness, following dry land when possible, but mostly splashing through shallow tarns covered with rinds of greenish pond scum. By midday the horsemen slumped in the somnolence induced by humidity, their heads bobbing and their hands constantly, listlessly swatting at clouds of insects whose variety, density, and numbers increased along with the temperature. At noon Jack passed the word to each of his "fingers": a fifteen-minute halt for food and water. One by one, the Buffalo detachments dismounted, scraped some of the bog muck from their boots, joylessly gnawed some hardtack, and refilled their canteens with the cleanest-looking water in sight. Nobody talked much. Five minutes into the halt, the heavy, wet-rag silence was broken by a single dull "*boom*" that sounded too slow and rounded-off to be a cannon blast. Then, after a distended silence during which every man in the clearing strained his ears in the same direction, came a rapid crescendo of louder, sharper detonations, powerful enough to slap vibrations against the soles of Jack's boots.

"By God, that's gunboat fire, Colonel Jack!"

But after a few minutes the cannonade sputtered out, leaving only the same oppressive, bug-buzzing ambience as before.

Jack figured things out as best he could from the sounds. If it was a skirmish or an ambush, it was obviously nothing serious, or the firing would not have petered out so soon. If the main column *was* in trouble, then the Buffaloes' duty was to ride to its aid, no doubt about that; but if the disturbance was trifling, it was their duty to continue sweeping through the wilderness. Well, then, unless he heard a helluva lot more ruction, or some dispatch rider caught up with orders from DeWitt to do otherwise, the Buffalo detachments would keep on going west.

12:23 P.M., OCTOBER 4, 1863

General DeWitt was so energized by the possibilities of waving the "terrible swift sword" of abolitionist wrath at every Confederate in his path that he was visibly irritated by the fact that, so far, the only locals they had seen were two raggedy colored boys fishing with cane poles, who ran off in pop-eyed terror at the sight of their liberators.

For the first few hours of the march, the infantry had maintained a lively chatter, but as the miles and minutes crawled by without any letup they grew too tired to do much more than grumble. For the present, Hawkins did not mind the pace—the sooner they reached their objectives, the sooner they could turn around and head back to the relative luxury of Shelborne's Point—but he was watching his men closely, and if they started faltering, he was going to respectfully suggest to DeWitt that a ten-minute break was in order. Maybe that was DeWitt's very notion: to have the *white* soldiers plead for a rest before their colored comrades.

As it happened, everybody got a long recess anyhow, but that was an incidental benefit from an otherwise tragic and pointless chain of events. From his place in the rear of the column, Hawkins had caught only a few glimpses of the escorting gunboats, since they had steamed ahead through the morning fog, but now they were clearly visible and close enough for the Massachusetts men to hold cupped-hand conversations with their sailor friends aboard the *Trenton.* All three gunboats had reduced speed to "dead slow," for they had reached a stretch of river that was strewn with rocks, and the navigable channels were very narrow. For a while the infantry moved faster than their naval escorts. At about twelve-forty, however, the channel widened enough for the gunboats to increased speed; their crews waved good-bye as the vessels surged ahead and vanished around a bend.

Ten minutes later, Hawkins' part of the column caught up with them again, all three stopped and their skippers holding an earnest conclave, pointing ahead at a belt of trees and knotted brush that blocked the northern two-thirds of the river. There was something suspiciously man-made about the appearance of those mounds of flotsam, so the gunboat captains had decided to go no farther until men in small boats could row up to the barrier and take a closer look.

General DeWitt was steaming at the delay. Stamping his feet and bellowing, he told the gunboat captains to waste no time, but to "bull their way through." To open the way, he ordered the heaviest ship, the *Sentinel,* to back up, ring on "full speed," and ram her way through. "That's just flood debris!" he shouted. "Open up your throttle and shove that rubbish out of the way! Time's a-wastin'!"

Reluctantly, the *Sentinel*'s skipper complied, aiming for a low, squishy-looking mass of vegetation. As the bow knifed in, however, it cut a cluster of submerged wires, releasing a set of air-filled barrels that popped to the surface, carrying with them a thick wad of fishing nets. Drawn in by the natural suction of full-speed turbulence, the nets wrapped themselves around the paddle blades and caused the gunboat to shudder, spin wildly on her axis, and come to a sudden stop. Observing how badly fouled the propulsion system was, Hawkins estimated it would take two or three hours for the sailors to cut the snaring nets free with knives and saws. You had to admire the Rebel engineers' cleverness—lacking shore batteries to oppose a waterborne incursion, they had designed a cheap, effective way to delay the Union advance: a gunboat-snare that probably had cost a hundred dollars to build but that had stopped the *Sentinel* as effectively as a heavy battery.

Realizing he had been gulled thanks to his own rash impetuosity, DeWitt was furious. He pointed to a shallow open space, close to the southern bank, and ordered the lighter-draft *Trenton* to pull around the *Sentinel* and press on upriver. He would rather have one gunboat escort *now*, he fumed, than three gunboats in the morning.

Stonecipher respectfully demurred. "General, that channel looks a bit too inviting, almost like the Rebs wanted us to go through it. I have a qualified diver aboard. Can we halt for just ten minutes, so he can make sure that passage is safe?"

"I don't have the goddamn time, Lieutenant! I can see from here—that water is clear and easily passable. Now take your ship through it so my column can get moving again."

"General, I really advise caution—whatever you may be able to see, from my perspective up here on the bridge that water looks awfully murky. Perhaps if you came aboard and examined it from my vantage point—"

"Damn your vantage point! We are losing valuable time, sir. Now do as I order you!"

Stonecipher glued his eyes to binoculars and grumpily complied: "Ahead slow, stay at least four feet from the bank, helmsman."

All of DeWitt's infantry, having heard the general's choleric outburst, came to the river's edge, rested on their muskets, and watched intently as the *Trenton* swung her bow to port and nosed into the open channel. Inch by inch, the gunboat reluctantly threaded her way forward. Bow . . . midships . . ." "Looks like she's gonna make it, boys!" A few more yards and she would once more be in broad, clear river.

Instead, there was a great sodden *whump!*, a spurt of yellow flame, and a huge knuckle of boiling water that lifted the gunboat's bow several feet into the air and then obliterated all sight of it with a cascade that drove the bow back under the surface and washed over the deck all the way to the smokestack. The shock wave knocked down clumps of flailing, half-drowned sailors and hurled several into the river before it subsided. The *Trenton* stopped as though it had run into a stone wall, and as the water receded and her crew struggled to regain their footing, the watchers on the south bank could see tons of water pouring into a ragged hole in her bow. Only the river's shallow depth prevented her from sinking.

"Friction-fired torpedo!" cried Hawkins. "You, you, you, and you! Get in there and drag those boys to safety!"

All but three of the *Trenton*'s crew were rescued. Unfortunately, Lieutenant Stonecipher had been standing directly over the torpedo's explosion. Stunned by the impact, he was thrown into the water headfirst and landed on a submerged rock. When the rescuers dragged his body out, his wobbling head left a long red slick that swirled away in the current. On the dead officer's face was an almost comical look that seemed to say, *I told you so!*

Hawkins lost his temper. He ran up to the gaping DeWitt and spun him around by the epaulets.

"Are you satisfied now, DeWitt? The whole river's blocked, one gunboat sunk, and my good friend is dead, all because you couldn't spare ten minutes to check that water for Rebel mines? You just handed the enemy a very cheap victory, and they didn't have to fire a single shot!"

The sole operational gunboat, the *Allison*, her anxious crew having mistaken the torpedo explosion for a Rebel cannon shot, was lustily throwing shells at every clump of brush they could see.

"General Hawkins, you forget yourself! I am in command of this expedition, and if you cannot accept that, I will send you to the rear and place you under arrest for insubordination! Now get back to your troops and never, ever, publicly question my authority again!"

Trembling with anger and frustration, Hawkins ordered the 6th Massachusetts to fall out and brew coffee. They were going to be stuck here for quite a spell.

1:48 P.M., OCTOBER 4, 1863

About an hour after hearing the last detonations from the river, the Buffalo detachments rode out of the swampy wilderness and began to encounter rough wagon tracks that seemed gradually to converge, like wheel spokes, toward some as yet unglimpsed centrality. All around them now were evenly spaced pines, each one bearing the scars of old slash marks and the amber beads of resin that denoted turpentine collection. Such open, flat terrain was totally unsuited for an ambush, so the riders felt secure in following the tracks, and made good time by doing so. Eventually each "finger" of scouts came within sight of the others. Fairless had only to shout, and his company commanders quickly assembled.

"Damn, I never did see that pesky ironclad!" joked Big Red Elliot.

Bonaparte Reubens deadpanned: "I did. Water mocassin ate the sumbitch. Send a dispatch to General DeWitless."

"Okay, gentlemen, gather round. I'm glad you're all in high spirits, but now we should pause and discuss our choices. We seem to be entering a large turpentine plantation, and since converging roads always meet *somewhere,* I suspect there're factory buildings, maybe a village, up in that direction. Red, didn't you used to work at one of these places?"

"Sure did, Colonel Jack. All these feeder paths, they'll come together into a big central thoroughfare, the main transportation road, and that eventually will take us . . . somewhere."

"Perhaps," mused Fairless, "if we approach this 'somewhere' in an unthreatening manner, we can glean some useful information from the inhabitants . . . if any. So let's just get to that main road and ride on to where it takes us. We've seen no sign of Confederate activity, so I think we're in no real danger. Anybody disagree?"

No one did. They all felt the same: the mood and innocence of this landscape were so pure that the war seemed never to have touched it.

A mile farther on, they came to a well-laid corduroy road, wide enough for two wagons to pass abreast, and only lightly reclaimed by weeds. Maybe no one was working these trees now, but they had been until recently.

At a Y-shaped intersection the corduroy road forked left, toward a cluster of docks and commercial structures; on the right was a wide avenue, paved with crushed gravel and lined with poplars and willows. Fairless led his column in that direction and halted at the foot of a stout, handsomely carved bridge that arched high enough over a wide, deep creek to allow the passage of sizable boats. A weather-beaten sign beside the bridge greeted the Buffaloes heartily:

Welcome to Faison's Groves (white population, 213),
The turpentine and naval stores capital of Pitt County.

"I sure as hell wish we could see to the other side of this bridge. There might be a whole Rebel brigade waitin' to bushwhack us," muttered Jack.

Captain Manchester gave one of his rare smiles. "If that's so, they must be the best-fed brigade in Lee's army. I don't smell rifle oil or campfires, but I sure do smell some mighty fine home cooking!"

"Now that you mention it, my stomach just reminded me of what fried chicken used to smell like, and it's growlin' like a mad dog. Gentlemen, form up as if you were on parade. Maybe if we can convince them people we're proper and polite regulars they'll offer us a bite."

"And if not, we can shoot 'em and eat their share," said Elliot with a chuckle.

Jack glared at him. "Let's try it my way, first, Captain Elliot."

Fairless wanted to make a picturesque as well as dramatic entrance. He ordered the flag uncased and brought to the officers' vanguard. "Captain Reubens, I give you the honor of being the first black soldier to bear the Union flag this deep inside enemy territory. The rest of you, sabers at port, try to look cool as ice." He swept his own sword high so it would flash the sun into the eyes of whoever might be watching from the far shore. "First North Carolina Unionist Volunteers, form on the colors, by companies—form a column of four . . . . *Forwarrrd HO!*"

Like the rattle of military drums, the horses' hooves beat an impressively loud tattoo on the planks. As each rank of horsemen came over the bridge they beheld, some with suspicion but most with openmouthed surprise, the citizens of Faison's Groves, a small gathering of whites, drawn up on the far side of a pleasant, well-tended village square. A statue of George Washington gazed at the visitors with impassive bronze eyes from beneath the shade of three noble elms. For a long moment both parties merely stared at one another. Then a florid, white-haired gentleman—overdressed in a formal cutaway, string tie, and a top hat that would have been stylish if Andrew Jackson were still in the White House—hoisted a makeshift white flag and advanced diffidently toward the Buffaloes' officers.

"Good afternoon, gentlemen. My name is Joshua Simpkins, and I am the mayor of this here little town. To whom have I the honor of speaking?"

"Colonel Jack Fairless, First North Carolina Unionist Volunteers . . . um . . . at your service."

"Not quite," said Simpkins with a chuckle. "Be that as it may, sir, I wish to proclaim Faison's Groves an open city—well, an open hamlet. No harm will come to you here, and we wish no harm done to our poor but peaceful community. These good folks behind me represent all that are left from the population of what was once a very prosperous center of the turpentine industry."

Jack surveyed the sixty-odd whites: the elderly, the very young, about twenty careworn women—*I'll bet they hid all the pretty ones!*—some cripples, and a handful of bitter-faced veterans, men who had done their service and returned minus an extremity, or, in the case of one poor soul who sat alone on a cabin porch, rocking nervously back and forth and carrying on unintelligible conversations with comrades who were invisible to everyone else, their very sanity. It was hard to judge how many slaves there were, for the darkies kept in the background, peeping furtively around corners or through window shades.

"As long as I perceive no hostility," said Jack, "we'll gladly leave you be, but we would like to water our horses and rest up a bit before continuing."

Simpkins beamed. "Oh, we'll do you better than that, sir. We've taken the liberty of preparing some vittles, enough to give you all a fair-to-middling repast. Nothing fancy: cornbread, sweet potato pie, fresh melons, smoked bacon, fried chicken, and either lemonade or apple cider, as each man prefers. We've known you were coming for at least two days, you see."

"So much for the fucking element of surprise!" growled Elliot from the side of his mouth.

Simpkins called out, and, like a well-rehearsed scene from an opera, some fifty or sixty smiling Negroes suddenly moved into the commons, carrying picnic tables and benches and armfuls of food and drink. Most of the Buffaloes whistled and cheered.

Bonaparte Reubens alone maintained his reserve. He dismounted and confronted Simpkins at very close range, enjoying the mayor's discomfort as he struggled to hide his innate distaste for stern black officers.

"Tell me, Mister Mayor, do you still produce naval stores in any quantity?"

Simpkins became uneasy. An affirmative answer would automatically make this village a legitimate target.

"Well, now, that's our cause of woe. Until recently, we did, in fact, producing at near-capacity, selling our goods to Confederate purchasing agents up in Tarboro, and in exchange, the Richmond government agreed not to conscript our young men, although some did volunteer, of course. All of that suddenly changed about three weeks ago, when a big, well-armed conscription party swept into town and took away every healthy man between the ages of fifteen and fifty. Cannon-fodder is needed more than our excellent products, apparently."

Simpkins spat in the dust. His anger was very real as he continued:

"Those men were arrogant swine, sir! Already they have dragged off every healthy farmer in the county, leaving women and children to cope with all the work or face destitution. Now they have done the same to us. If your men behave toward us in a civilized fashion, sir, we will certainly do the same, for no man in a blue uniform has ever harmed us worse than those conscription vultures in gray ones!"

Reubens turned to Fairless and Elliot, eyebrows raised in a question. The two officers gave slight nods, but qualified them with shrugs. A good feed was a good feed.

"Very well, sir. I'll order my men to fall out and enjoy this repast, but only one company at a time. And I'm going to bring two Napoleons over the bridge, load them with canister, and if there's any sign of trouble, they *will* fire on you. I admit we're grateful for the food, but you know as well as I do that you want something in return for it. If you put your cards on the table, face up, that'll go a long way toward earning my trust."

Simpkins wiped his forehead with a bandanna. "Well, sir, it is simple enough: It is our hope that by sharing with you the best that we have, you will be less likely to take *all* that we have. We're not simpletons—when we heard you were coming, we buried all the silverware in places you would never find and herded all our good livestock to far-off shelter. There is nothing valuable here for your men to steal; only our good food, and in return for that, I implore you not to burn down any of our buildings or take away our Negroes. They are decently treated here, and would only be an encumbrance to you on the march."

"Fair enough, but not far enough. My added condition is this: Your commercial facilities are a fair target, and they would already be in flames if our commanding general, a fire-and-brimstone abolitionist named DeWitt, had gotten here before we did. I need some information about what lies ahead. Cooperate, and I'll send a message back to him saying there is nothing of interest in this neck of the woods, so he will march right by you, for he is eager to keep his appointment with glory at the Tarboro bridge. First you must tell me where to find that notorious ironclad."

"I'm an old soldier, sir. Do not ask me about military secrets."

"You're also an old humbug. DeWitt won't leave until he finds the damned thing, so the sooner it's destroyed, the sooner you'll be rid of him. Either you give me some idea of where that damned ironclad is, or I will send a dispatch to DeWitt, who will turn his black soldiers loose on this place until *somebody* tells him where it is. Believe me, I would not want to see that happen. Now, if you tell *me,* DeWitt will march on by, and not even know this lovely town exists."

Frightened murmurs from the townspeople finally forced the mayor's hand.

"Very well, then. Have you got a map?"

The ship had been moved a while ago, but at the moment it could be found in a deep tributary called Gum Branch, on the south bank of the river, about twelve miles below Tarboro—passersby had reported much hammering and clanging from that place, at any rate. And the vessel was not far up the branch, either, because some clever Rebel engineers had fashioned a screen from underbrush and painted cloth so that no one passing the mouth of Gum Branch could see what might be anchored there. As to how much of it was complete, Simpkins could not say—the site was guarded, and curiosity-seekers were kept away. A landward approach might be difficult, too, but you would know you had reached Gum Branch when you crossed the second bridge north of here.

The riverbank road was sometimes patrolled by Rebel cavalry, but as far as he knew, there were no permanent defenses. As for Tarboro itself, the garrison was relatively weak—all the really strong defenses were massed at either end of the railroad bridge.

"If your General DeWitt does not move faster that the news of his coming, he might find the bridge heavily reinforced. And that, sir, is all that I can tell you and all I would tell you, even if I knew more. Are these negotiations concluded? Fine. Then tell your men to dig in."

While Jack ate with gusto, Bonaparte Reubens took a canteen full of lemonade and a mess plate piled with chicken, greens, and cornbread and went off to find a private place to dine. This had been a good day. Pleasant weather, no fighting, and a feast provided by the enemy. He found a wide, dry stump overlooking the creek and shoveled food into his mouth. It was the best meal he had eaten in ages, and when it was consumed to the last crumb, he stretched out languidly in the syrupy light of an autumn afternoon, dozing in the righteousness of his mood.

He snapped awake, pistol halfway drawn, when he felt a shadow blocking the sun. But it was no sneaky Rebel bushwhacker, only that last-minute recruit from Pine Haven, Elias—who stood at attention and saluted with enough precision to show that he had been keeping his eyes open.

"At ease, Private Elias Sloane. What is on your mind?"

"Here, Cap'n—dis here's a message from General DeWitt. I'se supposed to deliver it to Colonel Fairless, but Ah can't find him no place, so I brung it to you."

"Well done. We'll make a real soldier of you yet."

Elias remained standing while Reubens unfolded the dispatch.

"You may go now, Elias—you're blocking my light."

"Kin I hear what it says? I want to keep everythin' straight in my mind, this bein' my first . . . um . . . campin'?"

" 'Campaign,' " muttered Reubens. The message was terse and grumpy—DeWitt must be beside himself with frustration. "It says that one of the gunboats has been sunk by . . . well, a big explosion . . . and it will be nightfall before the river is clear enough for the other two to proceed. General DeWitt regretfully orders us to bivouac where we are, so that we can maintain our planned distance from the main column. Unless we hear otherwise, we are to resume operations at dawn." Reubens refolded the paper and stood up. "Well, that at least explains all that racket we heard earlier. And there could be worse places to spend the night. We'll have to double the guard, of course. I'm not as convinced by the mayor's festive welcome as Colonel Fairless seems to be, though I'm not exactly sure why. Keep your eyes peeled, Elias. If you see anything that just doesn't look right—not matter how small a thing it might be—come and tell me."

3:12 A.M., OCTOBER 5, 1863

Mayor Simpkins was not overjoyed to learn that the Buffaloes would be staying overnight, but accepted the news stoically. Fairless assigned a quarter of the whole unit to picket duty, with orders to let no one in or out, and positioned the 12-pounders to cover both the bridge and the westbound road out of town. Satisfied with these arrangements, he promptly fell asleep on a bed in one of the abandoned houses.

Bonaparte Reubens had elected to sleep outdoors in a cozy rope hammock. His wariness took some time to ebb away, but when it finally did, he sank into his favorite kind of oblivion, one untroubled by dreams of Africa.

He was therefore grumpy and slow when Elias shook him insistently on the shoulder and whispered urgently into his ear: "Boss! Wake up, suh!"

Reubens groaned and hoisted himself on one elbow. The new recruit's eagerness to serve was commendable, but Reubens thought he was overdoing it. *This had better be good. . . .*

"What the blue blazes is it?"

Elias knelt conspiratorially, as though Rebel spies lurked nearby.

"You tol' me to keep my eyes skinned for anythin' that don't look right?"

"Yes, yes. So what is it that 'don't look right'?"

"Well, suh, I snuck out around midnight, just to have a look around."

"You idiot! You're lucky you didn't get shot by the pickets."

Elias ducked his head and grinned, mischievously. "Boss, Elias know how to move quiet as a snake when he wants to. I passed by two of them 'pickers' close as the length of yo' arm and not one of 'em seen or heard me."

"All right, I'm suitably impressed. Now what is it you wanted to tell me?"

"It's a shower, Cap'n, not a teller. Grab a shutter lantern and follow me."

Intrigued now, Reubens armed himself with an extra revolver, and ordered the corporal of the guard to inform all the sentries that Captain Reubens was going out on reconnaissance and would use the password "diamondback" upon his return. Then he followed Elias into the turpentine forest. The boy moved like a shadow, never hesitating, sure of his course. Silent as a jungle cat, he led Reubens about a mile before he even paused. That boy's stamina is amazing, Reubens thought; he's already made this journey twice and he's still breathing through his nose!

"It'll be dawn in a couple of hours, Elias. How much farther?"

"Not far now, suh. But we'd best move slower now, 'cause somewhere in this here turpey-tine woods they's a big bunch of horses."

Sure enough, as they moved forward again, Reubens thought he heard a muffled whinny off to the west, but sound traveled strangely in these woods, and he could not guess how far away the sound had come from. He was still walking forward, straining to hear any additional sounds, when he almost bumped into Elias, who was standing very still and pointing down. They had reached another one of those radiating sandy tracks formerly used by the tree tappers. Faint as chalk dust, it ran arrow-straight in the direction of the same creek that flowed under the bridge at Faison's Groves.

"Open the shuttuh just a bit, Boss, and take a look."

"Hell and damnation!" Even the narrowest beam of light revealed the hoofprints of many horses, some pointed toward the creek, some pointed away. Fresh hoofprints. *What the hell is going on*? Reubens wanted a closer look, but Elias was already tugging him toward the big creek. Thirty yards more, and the sandy path dipped, fanned out, and merged into a wide beach. The hoofprints ended where the sand was rutted and deeply scored, the sort of indentations that could only have been made by fairly large, heavily laden boats.

Of course! Even if Faison's Groves was temporarily out of business, the barges and tugs used to haul its produce up to Tarboro *should* have been in evidence. Simpkins had not said anything about the Rebs confiscating his boats, a rather curious omission considering how wrought up he was about having his young men dragged off to war. And that rather well-rehearsed al fresco banquet had been nothing more than an elaborate diversion while the village's boats were off . . . doing what? From the look of things, loading a fairly large number of men and transporting them downstream in the direction of the Tar. But to what purpose?

"Cap'n? Over here, quick."

Elias had been poking around in the thick brush bordering the beach and had discovered an old, waterlogged fishing pirogue. Together they lifted it far enough to drain the standing water, then inspected it closely. There was a small crack near the waterline, but otherwise the bottom was sound. Elias pulled a ragged bandanna from his overalls and stuffed it in the opening.

"It's almost a mile to the river," mused Reubens. "The current will carry us down, but how do we get back?"

"Already thought 'bout that, too, Cap'n, my first trip here." Elias leaned into the bushes and pulled out a couple of flood-washed limbs that made serviceable barge poles. "Current's real gentle tonight—these'll speed our trip down, and two strong men, we oughta be able to pole our way back."

"Back from where?"

"I ain't got that far yet, but it bound ta be worth findin' out, right?"

Helped by the current, they made good time and very little noise. When Reubens felt the current start to strengthen and saw the creek spreading out, he knew they were close to its confluence with the Tar. They turned the pirogue toward the north bank and ran it aground. It was impossible not to splash when they went into the water and heaved it up far enough to keep the creek from pulling it back in, but Reubens hoped no one was close enough to hear. When Reubens finally stood upright, there was just enough ambient light to make out the river, a hundred yards from their location. Just above them, beyond the brushy overhang of thick red clay and thorny vines, rose an overgrown knoll. It was just high enough, Reubens figured, to offer a view of what might lie between here and the creekmouth.

"Stay here and keep the boat from drifting off," Reubens said. "I'm going to crawl up there for a look-see."

Elias whispered back, somewhat indignantly: "Boat ain't goin' nowhere. I got us this far, so I deserve to see the reason why."

Reubens shrugged and began ascending the knoll, using every stealthy movement he had learned in the Legion. Dawn was gathering behind the Atlantic's sharp gray verge, far to the east, but by now his eyes were so accustomed to darkness that he could make out individual spikes of grass. A few more stealthy wiggles, and they were on top with a panoramic view all the way to the river.

Christ in the craphouse, what a setup! Thirty yards from Reuben's knoll, extending from there all the way to the river, was a superbly built and expertly laid out earthen bastion, and the Rebel troops occupying it had an absolute wet dream of a target. Beyond the south bank of the creekmouth, at least fifty feet wide where it rumbled and gurgled into the Tar, the riverbank road was pinched by the terrain into a narrow funnel, just barely passable by a single wagon. It changed into a long, ascending causeway, squeezed on its right by the river, and on its left by a square-mile morass of mushy, bramble-choked bog. Infantry *could* crawl through that terrain, but their progress would be slower than winter molasses, and they would be fully exposed to sharpshooters on the higher ground across the creek. Sitting ducks? No, more helpless than that. Ducks could waddle and flap their way across much faster than men could crawl, one dismal inch after another.

To cross the creekmouth, from the first incline of the causeway to the dry, elevated land on the western side, DeWitt's men would be forced to bunch up and march carefully across a shaky-looking wooden bridge whose guardrails had been carefully sawed down. Halfway over, the bridge was blocked by a dense abatis of interlocking pine logs, their branches sharpened to needle points. Even unopposed, it would take hours for DeWitt to thread his whole ungainly column through that needle. And they would *not* be unopposed.

Into this perfect bottleneck the defenders of the Rebel earthwork could pour heavy fire straight across the bridge, and even deadlier enfilade fire against the column's jammed-up, almost helpless left flank. There was absolutely no room for DeWitt to deploy his artillery, and the ambushers were protected from gunboat fire by a massive six-foot-thick earth-and-timber wall across their own left flank. *Whoever thought this up was good!* So good that the Rebel defenders—at least 150 men, Reubens estimated—seemed to feel utterly secure. They were noisily breaking camp, cooking breakfast, and ambling into the woods to answer nature's call. As for their armament, Reubens saw an awful lot of shotguns, which would sweep the bridge like iron brooms, a lightweight 6-pounder smoothbore, and a stubby 12-pounder howitzer.

From the look of it, the redoubt probably had been constructed months ago; those cannons, long ago emplaced, were covered with tarps against the rain; the Rebs probably had stored ample ammunition, too. Then, when a Union force was spotted ascending the river, all they had to do was bring up the men. And how had they done that? In a gaggle of cargo barges pulled by three brawny little steam launches. Every barge and boat bore the words "Property of Faison's Groves."

Given lots of time and a prodigious expenditure of ammunition, DeWitt's gunboats could eventually chew down that protective dike. When things got too hot for them, the defenders could spike the guns and scramble away to those sequestered horses. But until then they would slaughter the head of DeWitt's column with near impunity. And DeWitt's "terrible swift sword" would become a "not-so-terrible, very slow sword," for it would take him the rest of the day to reorganize, another day for the enemy to strengthen the defenses at the railroad bridge, another day for Lee to send a trainload of crack troops down from Virginia.

The only thing these bushwhackers had not counted on was the presence in their rear of the Buffaloes riflemen presently snoring away the last hours of sleep back at Faison's Groves. Bonaparte Reubens made a fast decision. He dragged Elias down from the rise and handed him a Colt.

"You know how to use this thing, son?"

"Seen it done a lots of times, suh. Don't reckon I could hit nobody, 'less he was standin' close to me as you is."

"I don't *want* you to shoot anybody. What I want you to do is to fire this pistol into the air as soon as you see the first sign of General DeWitt's column on that road. That will at least give them a warning. After you do that, Elias, turn around and get your black ass back to the village as fast as you can haul it, because if those good ol' boys down there catch a nigger with a pistol, especially one trying to spoil their fun, you're a dead coon."

"Think Ah don't know that already?"

"You've done well, Elias, and maybe saved a lot of lives. I won't forget this exploit, and neither will the U.S. Army. Now I'd better see how much stamina I still have in this old body. Good luck!"

Poling upstream, single-handed, was a lot harder than two men poling with the current, and by the time Reubens ran the old pirogue aground near the place Elias had found it, he was gasping. He also could see a little better, and on the assumption that DeWitt had marched early and was pushing fast, Reubens also knew he was in a race against time. Even the short climb uphill to the terminus of the sandy track was a struggle that left him gasping. He simply *had* to get his wind back if he were going to double-time it back to the village before the clock ran out. Some water would definitely help. He found a trace of three-day-old rainwater that was stagnant but at least appeared to be potable. Just a few sips, he thought, and if it gave him the squitters, he would worry about that later. But the stuff was vile and thick, more like spoiled soup than water, and he had to fight to keep down even a swallow. His stomach, by now empty again, tried to reject the liquid by cramping, and Reubens had to curl into a knot until the spasm passed. That was his salvation.

A lone Rebel rider, quite unaware of Reubens' presence, was pounding down the sandy path, bound, presumably, for the boats, a dispatch case slapping the rump of his horse. With the speed of desperation, Reubens clutched a spindly pine branch, jumped up in front of the man, and struck him flush in the face. Surprise more than force knocked the man halfway out of his seat, and the branch shattered into useless lumps.

While the Rebel was still off-balance, Reubens grabbed his pistol belt and jacket and drove him to the ground. Bloody-nosed, the rider stared in horror at this sudden apparition: a massively built half-naked leaf-spattered Negro with burning eyes and a savage grimace of sharp white teeth—a demon from abolitionist hell. Reubens wasted no more time—he drove his fist into the man's mouth twice, his brawny arms like steam pistons, and felt flesh and teeth crack. The horse, almost as startled as its rider, was about to bolt, so Reubens grabbed the loose reins while simultaneously kicking the fallen rider in the stomach and ribs. Half conscious now, the Confederate corporal, for that was his rank, could only gaze imploring at his assailant and croak a single plea: "I never hurt any of you people. . . ."

"Maybe you didn't," wheezed Reubens as he drove his Bowie knife into the man's throat and sawed a half-moon smile across his windpipe, "but you damn sure didn't try to stop the people who did."

Once he had gentled the horse, Reubens felt a surge of renewed vigor and purpose; this fortuitous encounter had changed the whole equation. With a fresh mount under him, he dashed through the rest of the pine forest, and by the time the first snakes of mist were being conjured aloft by the promise of sunbeams, he was within hailing distance of the sentries around Faison's Groves.

"Corporal of the Guard! Captain Reubens coming in! Password is diamondback! Wake up Colonel Fairless, and do it quickly!"

Home is the Sailor

FIVE YEARS AGO, when hooped skirts were first introduced, everyone predicted for them a speedy decline; but after encountering the shafts of ridicule and opposition in every conceivable form, they still remain not only a fixed fact, but have become a permanent institution, which no caprice of fashion will be likely wholly to destroy.

—*Peterson's Magazine,* October, 1861

October was Daisy Lamb's favorite month, and while she missed the golden opulence of the New England autumns she had grown up with, she had learned that the season-change here on Confederate Point was not without its own charms. Over the broad sweep of the Cape Fear delta, October sunsets were elegiac and tender. The brass-ball sun and hard-baked blue glaze of summer's skies turned more humane, its colors diluted with a spoonful of cream—pastels instead of primal oils. This year the heat and glare of Dog-Day summer had lasted well into September, but October brought a gentling of Nature. Clouds evolved each afternoon into wide, blurry streamers, sometimes trailing long mysterious filaments, like wind-borne wisps of spiderweb. The greater incline of sunlight brought out, in the dense tangles of maritime forest, a myriad of quieter colors: pale limes, honeydew oranges, ashes-of-roses.

On her daily rides from the Cottage to the beach far north of the Fort, Daisy saw new and wondrous seasonal spectacles: migrating herds of dolphins, spouting joyously in graceful arcs, and every day for two weeks, until they vanished as suddenly as they appeared, miles-long columns of small, lively fish, so dense that when the light caught them just-so inside the translucent tube of a great rolling comber, they turned into walls of living silver darts.

Most glorious of all, was the ten-day invasion of monarch butterflies, exquisite living clouds of delicate gold, they orbited her head fearlessly, fanned her with the faerie-faint breeze of their wings, and sometimes landed on her sleeves or on the pleats of her white riding dress, as though cheerfully hitching a ride or pausing to bestow on her the blessing of their peerless beauty. They were the jolliest of companions and she never tired of riding amongst their riotous golden whorls, ensorcelled by their intricate aerial ballets and gentle visitations. She was sad when they moved on, for they were autumn's finest glory.

On the afternoon of October 2, she cut short her afternoon ride, for it was clear to her after only an hour that the landscape had lost its brief poetry and everything seemed weighed down by the tilt of seasons toward the dismal Winter, with its long misery of gray cold surf and bitter winds—a world that would be leeched all colors save the most somber and funereal. Already, some of William's soldiers were bringing wagonloads of firewood to the Cottage. Time to unpack the blankets; time, Daisy Lamb sighed, for Dick and his Negro friend Cassius to haul the pirate-raft ashore, cover it with tarpaulins and lash it down with ropes to keep it safe from the elements. Time, Daisy Lamb sighed, to catch up on my reading and figure out ways to cope with two bored children whose world had suddenly grown very small. Then she smiled again, as she turned the horse back toward home, for even that depressing thought had a positive twist to it. She and William would have the Cottage to themselves for a week, and she could catch up on more than just her reading. At the owners' gracious invitation, both Maria and Dick, chaperoned by the ever-reliable Aunt Charity and the diligent young Cassius, were spending a week visiting Orton Plantation. Such light housework as remained to be done in their absence, Daisy agreeably shared with Aunt Charity's shy but energetic niece Fanny, who was so gravely silent in the performance of her duties that her sudden appearance from the kitchen or the laundry could be as startling as the manifestation of a ghost.

But on this particular afternoon, instead of Fanny waiting to help her dismount, Daisy saw a uniformed rider waiting on the front porch, a Navy lieutenant whom she recognized as an aide-de-camp to Flag Officer Branch. This was unusual and therefore caused her some apprehension. But the young man was wonderfully polite when he greeted her. He had an important dispatch for Colonel Lamb, from Flag Officer Branch, which he was ordered to deliver into the colonel's hand personally. Daisy assured him that she would do that, and after enjoying a glass of lemonade, the naval officer departed. Daisy examined the sealed packet. It was not marked "secret" and her curiosity was intense, but she would have to let William open it when he came home.

At 5:40 Daisy heard the front door open and close, followed by the clump of William's boots as he went upstairs to exchange them for a pair of slippers. When he came back down, she kissed him and handed him a tall glass of fine Scotch.

"You have some interesting mail, William—a lengthy missive from Flag Officer Branch. I was very tempted to open it, but . . ." She handed him the dispatch.

"Most unusual. Let's adjourn to the back porch and see what our friend, the admiral-without-a-fleet, has to say."

In another week or two it would be too chilly to enjoy the rocking chairs and river-view, but today was ideal. Daisy settled into her favorite chair and waited for William to wade through Branch's tome. Evidently, the contents were not dire, for Lamb was nodding agreeably.

"Why, this is good news indeed! Our friend, Matthew Sloane, has been 'sprung,' as the lawyers would say, and is coming back to Wilmington on the fourth. Here, read the particulars while I replenish my drink."

Branch's spidery hand did convey an interesting story: The fate of Matthew Sloane had finally been decided, by none other than President Lincoln himself, who had evidently grown so weary of the legal and diplomatic complications surrounding Matthew's case that he had waved his presidential pen and made them vanish. By handwritten order of the president, Matthew Sloane had been pardoned and released. He would arrive off Fort Fisher, aboard the Federal frigate *Miskatonic,* on Sunday, October 4. Arrangements for transferring him to shore were complicated by the need to keep prying Union eyes away from the fort, or so Branch averred, although Daisy could not imagine what the U. S. Navy might see that it had not already studied to the point of boredom. Colonel Lamb was directed to plant a large flag of truce on a suitable landing spot at least three miles north of the fort and to have a wagon available for Mister Sloane and his belongings. Sloane's wife and business associates, Branch continued, had already been notified of his imminent return, but Mr. Sloane had expressly asked for a few days' time to mentally prepare for the reunion. Would the Lambs mind accommodating him in the Cottage until he was ready to move on to Wilmington? That would be no problem—Daisy had grown so tired of passed-out runner captains snoring on her sofas that she had insisted on adding a guest bedroom to the north side of the Cottage.

"Very good news, indeed. I would love to throw a party for him, but who knows what kind of ordeal he endured in that dungeon at Fortress Monroe?"

"According to Hobart-Hampden, who gets his information straight from the British Consulate in Washington, by way of the Governor of Nassau, our friend Sloane has not been languishing in some medieval pit, but in a rather commodious apartment, complete with a library—the sort of 'cell' reserved for prisoners with lofty connections. I hardly think we will find him marked by cruel tortures or gaunt with starvation. Melancholy, perhaps, if the rumors about him are true."

Daisy made a face of mock severity. "And what rumors might those be, sir?"

"You know very well what I'm referring to: that it was not patriotism alone which motivated his desperate efforts to save the beautiful Belle O'Neal. Hobart-Hampden told me, admittedly while deep in his cups, that Sloane had enjoyed a rather torrid liaison with Miss O'Neal during the last days of that fateful voyage."

"Hmph! If even half the rumors about that woman are true, so did Generals Meade, Hancock, and most of the War Department. I daresay, William, that if *you* had been alone on a ship with her, you too might have been tempted by her famous charms."

"Daisy Lamb, how could you even say such a thing?"

"Because, my dear, for all your noble qualities, you are still a man with healthy physical appetites. Even Sir Lancelot succumbed in time to Guinivere's charms. Oh, wipe that indignation from your lovely face—I'm teasing you. If anything, it would have been Miss O'Neal who fell for *you,* for you are a truly beautiful man, while Matthew Sloane is merely . . ."

" *'Merely'* . . . what?"

"Handsome, rugged, and far more dashing on the bridge of his ship than he must ever have looked as a mudstained rice farmer. But we can banter about illicit love at the dining table! Fanny has prepared a good meal and we should dig in while it's still warm. Afterward . . . Well, it's not often that we have the Cottage to ourselves, is it?"

"But," he ruffled the dispatch as though a galvanic current were running through the papers, "I must get telegrams off immediately! To Whiting, to . . . to . . ."

She plopped her teacup on the armrest of her chair; *why were men so thick at times like this?* Then she realized that he, too, was merely teasing. She wagged a stern finger at him.

"The telegrams can wait, Young Soldier of the Lord. I cannot. Not much longer than it takes to eat dinner, at any rate. Do I have to grab your sleeve like a streetwalker down in Paddy's Hollow?"

"Hmmm. Why don't you try it and see what happens?"

When Matthew Sloane learned that Lincoln had decided to release him, he took it as a sign from God, an affirmation that it was time for him to stop wallowing in guilt and get on with his life. It was time to go home, time to reconcile with Mary Harper. Once he was actually standing again on Carolina sand, he felt surprisingly invigorated. When Lamb asked if Sloane was "up for a homecoming party," Matthew decided that he was.

The Lambs' pantry was filled to overflowing, so the additional guests suffered no want of food or drink. The night before Sloane's clandestine arrival, the long-delayed *Phoebe* finally showed up, almost exactly one month late, due, her captain said, to "last-minute installation of a powerful new type of engine." Evidently, the delay had been well worth it, for when the *Phoebe* made her run for New Inlet she wasted no time with evasive maneuvers, but charged arrow-straight through both rings of the blockade, making fourteen knots with no strain. By the time the blockaders managed to get within range of her, they were also within range of Fort Fisher's guns, which scored at least three good hits before the *Phoebe* dashed triumphantly past the Mound Battery, blowing her whistle to wake the dead. In gratitude, her captain had dispatched to the Cottage a large wagon filled with Cuban cigars, Jamaican rum, cases of potted ham, ten-pound sacks of coffee and sugar, a huge orange wheel of Dutch gouda, sesame-seed tea biscuits, and case after case of champagne, cognac, and Bristol sherry. Centerpiece of the banquet was a sixteen-pound smoked turkey, courtesy of Orton Plantation.

Though Lamb had tried to keep the guest list small and select, there were some who had more or less invited themselves and could hardly be turned away—Flag Officer Branch, foremost among them. Branch did indeed look ruddier and more self-confident than Matthew could remember him ever looking before; either he had cut back on his opium habit, or he had finally been assigned some military task that he was actually capable of achieving with the pathetic resources at his command.

Also present were Major Reilly, the fort's chief surgeon, Dr. Reece, a pair of musicians from the garrison (fiddle and button-accordion), Chase Whiting and his plump, vivacious wife Katie, and *definitely* self-invited, the editor of the *Wilmington Journal*, James Fulton, who intended to run an interview with Matthew on the front page of his next edition.

They took their food in buffet style, each guest retiring with glass and plate to the back porch, where folding tables had been set up. The evening was unseasonably mild, and a brief early frost, two days before, had dramatically reduced the insect population. Matthew chose a rocking chair overlooking the river and soon found himself flanked on one side by Fulton and on the other by Branch.

". . . but you see, the situation *has* stabilized!" Fulton was bringing Matthew up-to-date on matters of strategy, having already covered several pages of his reporter's notepad with shorthand transcriptions of Matthew's account of his capture and incarceration. Matthew had covered the topic of Belle O'Neal's death briefly and dispassionately: when her vicious sworn enemy, the Secret Service agent Lafayette Baker, had closed in to capture her, she had flung herself into the sea, knowing that if she fell into his merciless hands, those same hands would soon drape a noose around her neck. Of his own involvement with the beautiful spy, he said nothing, and the cold look in his eyes deflected Fulton's fumbling attempts to steer the interview in a sensational direction. Sensing that Sloane had said all he was going to say, Fulton launched into a discourse on how much the Confederacy's overall situation had improved since the low point of July.

"Bragg has the Yankees bottled up in Chattanooga and their situation grows daily more desperate. They are receiving few supplies, and Bragg occupies such unassailable high ground that the enemy will never be able to break through with relief forces."

" 'Never' is a long time," observed Matthew, who had been acutely uncomfortable during the interview and was correspondingly voluble now that it was over.

"And let us not forget," rumbled Branch, who knew more about the South's long-term weaknesses than Fulton and who sometimes took an undisguised pleasure from taking the opposite side of whatever argument Fulton was advancing, "that if a more energetic general than Bragg had been in command on September Twentieth, General Rosecran's entire army would have been bagged like a dead cat. Any fool could see that Rosecrans was *finished* by midafternoon, but Bragg once more succumbed to his bizarre lethargies and allowed the enemy to get back across the river and entrench in Chattanooga. I'm afraid, Mister Fulton, that I must concur with the opinion of General Forrest, who, when he heard about Bragg's stunning early victory and his equally stunning refusal to press ahead and finish-off 'Old Rosie,' is said to have remarked: 'What the hell does he fight battles *for*?' "

Fulton was undismayed. "But, surely, sir, if Bragg can lure the Yankees into attacking his prepared defenses, which are all on *mountaintops* after all, he can do wicked slaughter to them at little cost to himself!"

"Grant . . ." muttered Matthew Sloane.

"Beg pardon, Sloane?" said Fulton. " 'Grant' what and to whom?"

"*General* Grant, Mister Fulton. Lincoln has ordered him to establish a unified command structure in the west. He will send Rosecrans packing and then he will use the same tactics he used at Fort Donelson and Vicksburg to unhinge Bragg's line. He will send troops over the river to get behind Bragg; he will attack in one place, then in another and another, relentlessly. He will not be bothered in the slightest by high casualties. He knows that in the end, Bragg is too inflexible, too stuffy, and too despised by his own subordinates to take full advantage of the good terrain he presently occupies."

"Hmph. I did not know you were so well versed in the strategy of land warfare, Mister Sloane."

"While imprisoned at Fortress Monroe, sir, I had full access to the northern papers, along with endless hours to converse with experienced Yankee veterans. I suspect that by now, my expertise is at least equal to your own."

Branch chortled quietly into his glass. Fulton was nonplussed. Although he knew Sloane had just tweaked him smartly, it would be bad form to get into an intemperate argument with the guest of honor. So he just excused himself on the pretext of getting another drink. His absence removed a sense of prickliness from the air, and the others—who were beguiled by a resplendent autumn sunset—seemed palpably to relax in his absence. Suddenly, Chase Whiting turned and spoke to Matthew: "What now for you, Captain Sloane? You are still part-owner of a fleet of blockade-runners, and your friend Hobart-Hampden, that remarkable Englishman-of-all-trades, will surely want you back on the bridge of one ship or another."

"I have retired from the runner business, General, although I will keep my hand in when it comes to the business end of things. And yourself, sir? Are you still angling for a new field command?"

"Yes. Now that Bragg is out of favor, *again,* and my champion, General Beauregard, has done such a good job of fending the Yankees off from Charleston, I may be able to achieve that goal by the time the spring campaigning season rolls around again."

Just to be polite, Matthew turned to Branch and asked: "How are things in town these days?"

"Dismal and deteriorating. The waterfront is bursting at the seams; on Water Street these days, one sees more ruffians and vagabonds than gentlemen. Paddy's Hollow grows larger and more crowded week by week, like a swelling tumor, and conditions there, especially on the weekends, verge on anarchy. The city police either cannot control the spread of crime, or look the other way when the perpetrators sidle up to them and slip a roll of greenbacks into their greedy hands. Increasingly, my Marines are having to act as deputy sheriffs, which displeases me and them."

"Does Miss Landau still minister to the poor and needy down there?" asked Matthew.

"Indeed she does, sir, but she no longer ventures into the Hollow after dark or on the weekends. And when she does, she is always accompanied by two heavily armed bodyguards, courtesy of the ubiquitous Hobart-Hampden. You will be somewhat shocked, I fear, by how seedy the waterfront has become in your absence. Except, of course, for the shipyards of Mister Beery and Mister Cassidey, which have now come under my control after Richmond made them subject to martial law. And that reminds me, Mister Sloane: I understand that you're to be reunited with your wife Tuesday evening, at a party being given at the Yellow House. Would you please make room on your schedule for an official visit to my headquarters? There are things we need to discuss, and this is not the place for it."

Puzzled, Matthew tried to read Branch's expression, but the naval officer had drawn a mask over his features, except for his eyes, which strove to hold Matthew in place with a clear, powerful look of authority.

"I've already declared my intentions *not* to resume blockade-running, sir. I fail to see what interest the Navy would have in me, now that I am once again a rice farmer with a plantation to run."

"All the same, Sloane, do favor me with the courtesy of a visit to my headquarters. Shall we say one o'clock in the afternoon, day after tomorrow? I'm told that your wife will be arriving at three, on the Pine Haven steam launch, so you will still have plenty of time to get prepared for your reunion."

Matthew suddenly felt ill-at-ease—back less than twenty-four hours and already people *wanted* him for their own purposes. He needed another drink.

"Are you issuing a command, Flag Officer Branch?"

"I can make it one, if you like. I *do* have the authority."

"Indeed, sir, you seem to wield more of that than was once the case."

"The Confederate Navy itself is more than was 'once the case.' And in these waters, all the way up to the Virginia line, I *am* the Confederate Navy."

There was a degree of confidence in Branch's voice that Matthew had never heard before. The man had a better grip on his private daemons, that was obvious. Matthew would gain nothing by generating animosity.

"Very well, then. One o'clock it shall be."

Matthew Sloane returned to Wilmington on the morning of October 4, to keep his appointment with Flag Officer Branch and to give himself a whole day to prepare for his reunion with Mary Harper. After hiring a dockside lackey to take his suitcase to the Yellow House, Matthew walked south of Second Street toward the former hotel that was now the headquarters of the Confederate Navy.

Branch had been right about one thing: the waterfront had changed considerably while Matthew was away. It was the difference, he reflected, between "busy" and "clogged." Pyramids of cotton filled most available flat surfaces, and the necessary lanes between them were so cluttered with ropes and bits of rigging that he did not see how a man might make his way from one dock to the next without breaking an ankle.

Flag Officer Branch greeted him heartily, rounded up an escort of two armed Marines, then steered Matthew on a course for Cassidey's Shipyard, at the foot of Church Street. The last time Matthew had seen Cassidey's yard, it was a wide-open complex of sheds, slip-ways, steam powered cranes, chugging little donkey engines—swarming with ship-fitters, engineers, stevedores, and some anxious investors in one-ship runner companies, who prowled the yard daily, nagging the owners and foremen, imploring them to speed up the repairs of their ships, so they could get back to *making money*. The last time Matthew had seen Cassidey's, the shipyard had trebled in size and was feverishly busy seven days a week. Now, however, the place was greatly altered once again. Runner repairs were handled by Beery's yard on Eagles Island, while Cassidey's had taken on the mood and appearance of a *military* base. Where before it had been open to the public eye, it was now surrounded by a tall wooden palisade—horseshoe shaped—with both ends anchored on the river, manned by Marine sentries in crude watchtowers. Nor could anyone traveling by on the river see what was within this fortified expanse, for the yard was hidden in that direction by large canvas panels and curiosity was discouraged by a pair of sandbagged howitzers and large signs proclaiming: DANGER! DO NOT APPROACH WITHOUT PERMISSION OF CONFEDERATE NAVY. GUN CREWS AUTHORIZED TO FIRE!

"This place is greatly changed," said Matthew, as Branch ushered him past the sentry box at the main entrance.

"Aye, Captain Sloane, and so has the status of the Confederate Navy in Wilmington!" There was such boyish pride in Branch's voice that Matthew had to suppress a smirk. No wonder the man seemed reinvigorated. Richmond had finally given him some real ships to play with. And when Branch led him to an observation point overlooking the yard's two biggest slipways, he whistled in admiration.

"Behold, sir, the armored ram *CSS Raleigh* and the brand-new commerce raider, *CSS Chickamauga*!"

"By God, that's a runner, not a cruiser, and a brand new one, at that."

It was, explained Branch, the newly arrived *Phoebe*, straight from Liverpool, and designed from the keel up so that she could easily be converted to a commerce raider. She had brought some of her own armament on her maiden voyage: a 100-pounder Armstrong shell gun which was being mounted as the bow-chaser. When completely refitted, Branch explained, the raider would have for its broadside armament a quartet of 7-inch double-banded Brookes, port and starboard, and a swivel-mounted 100-pounder Blakely on the fantail.

"She can outrun any ship powerful enough to engage her, and destroy any ship she chooses to engage. She's large enough to store provisions for four months at sea, and will carry enough gold to insure replenishment at any neutral port. She can range as far as the Indian Ocean, or cross the Pacific if need be, to pick off any Union merchant ships with ease. She can also carry many tons of confiscated cargo, and the laws governing cruiser warfare will enable her to use captured vessels as transports, colliers, and prison ships for captured enemy crews. She has twice the hitting-power of the *Alabama* and three times the horsepower—a real terror of the seas!

"But the other ship you see *will* significantly improve our local defensive strength. She's an armored ram, the *CSS Raleigh,* one-hundred-fifty-two feet long, and when fully outfitted she'll be almost as potent as the

Hatteras. I plan to use the *Raleigh* as a floating version of Fort Fisher, to strike at the blockade lines on moonless nights, pick off a ship or two, and dart back through one of the inlets before sunrise. Think of the consternation it will cause if the U.S. Navy starts losing three or four blockade ships every month! You understand now, the reason for my excitement? At last, I have command of a warship that can take on anything the enemy has afloat!"

"Revenge for the Mosquito Fleet?" murmured Matthew. Branch's eyes flashed—at least Matthew Sloane remembered the gallant but hopeless sacrifice of that pathetic collection of armed tugs and mail boats!

"Aye, Sloane! I have at last been granted a chance to avenge my poor brave lads who died in Sixty-One. Now, as for the commerce raider . . . I need someone special to command her, someone who's got the requisite dash and seamanship to make the most of her striking power and range; someone with imagination and flair. You, sir, could be just the man!"

"But I have no training as a naval officer!"

"Your commission as a *real* captain is a formality. I shall appoint experienced Navy men as your subordinates—they can handle any professional tasks you've not been trained for. This ship will wage *unconventional* naval war, Sloane, and unless I completely misread your character, I think you're a 'natural'—your record as skipper of the *Banshee* proves it! You have pluck, and that splendid strategy you devised to repulse those Secret Service thugs proves you can improvise brilliantly in a tight spot. Plus, you have an indefinable quality that will make sailors eager to serve with you: you are known to bring *good luck.* Now look me in the eyes and tell me that the idea does not strike a chord in your heart!"

Oh it did, by God! The very thought of it made Matthew's skin prickle. Branch had baited an irresistible hook. What greater adventure could he hope to have than to lead such a swift, powerful ship against the enemy's lines of commerce? Oh, the temptation that swelled within him—and the oppressive weight of conscience that crushed it down again!

"Mister Branch, I have foresworn the sea. For too long, have I neglected my home and family. I must decline your offer, although it holds a great allure for me."

Branch clapped him on the shoulder, a gesture of sympathy, to some degree, but not without a certain sternness.

"Well, you do not have to decide right now. The *Chickamauga* is far from ready to be commissioned, and by the time she is, you may have a strong incentive to be commissioned along with her. The hard, straight truth of your situation is this: now that you are free again, and no longer engaged in a strategic service to the Confederacy, you have become a prime candidate for the draft. There is nothing, beyond my personal intervention of course, to prevent a conscription party from showing up at Pine

Haven next week and hauling you away for service in the Army. Of course, with your prestige, you could easily arrange for a colonel's rank and command of a regiment. But do you have any idea what the life expectancy of a new colonel is these days? It is far shorter than the time it would take for you to become proficient in tactics and leadership. Now, while it is also true that you have no formal training as a naval officer, you've acquired a great fund of seamanship, not in a classroom, but on the sea itself—the greatest teacher there is. And what you still need to learn, your subordinates will teach you, or handle the problems for you. On the bridge of that ship, you stand a very good chance of surviving this war and performing splendid service to the Confederacy; you will return as a greater hero than ever. As long as I can tell Richmond that you're my handpicked choice for that job, the conscription agents cannot touch you. But if you turn that commission down, when the ship is ready to sail, they will grab you and send you into what may well be the last, longest, and most murderous campaign of the land war. Your chances of returning to Pine Haven would then be small indeed, compared to the alternative. . . . But for the time being, enjoy your homecoming, renew acquaintances, so to speak, with your lovely wife. Some months from now, when the raider is ready to enter service, you'll get a message from me saying that the time has come. Return to Wilmington and be sworn in as a naval officer, or be dragged off to die as cannon-fodder; there will be no third choice, and your wife will certainly understand the life-or-death urgency motivating your decision." Branch consulted his pocket watch. "Ah, I've kept you too long. I understand there's to be a lively party tonight for you and Missus Sloane, at the notorious Yellow House, or as I like to think of it, Queen Victoria's smallest colony. So then, my good fellow, off you go for what is sure to be a memorable evening. My compliments to your lovely wife, to Miss Landau, and to the mysterious but formidable Hobart-Hampden, who, I am sure, has pulled out all the stops for this affair."

When Hobart-Hampden informed her of Matthew Sloane's imminent return to Wilmington, Largo realized that fate had put her in a unique position to stage-manage Mary Harper's reunion with her husband. Indeed, she instantly perceived that to be her *mission*; she contemplated the nuances of strategy with all the solemn earnestness of an imperial minister who has just been made responsible for the smooth conjoining of two partly estranged branches of a royal family. One of the challenges was that she had to cultivate neutrality, which was not at first so easily done. She knew much more about Mary Harper's emotional needs—and about the trials and burdens she had faced since Matthew's imprisonment—than anyone else, and for that very reason, she made an exceptional effort to analyze the situation objectively. To start with the basics: both of these people were wary, vulnerable, and as emotionally taut as a pair of overwound watch springs. The more Largo pondered the character of her two friends, the more certain she became that altogether *too much* depended on the crucial first moments of their reunion, that great mischief could be wrought upon their future by a misinterpreted glance, a chance inflection of the voice, any perceived hesitancy felt in that first, all-important, embrace.

The wild card was Matthew Sloane's lustful, much-gossiped-about "fling" with Belle O'Neal. Of course, neither Largo nor Hobart-Hampden had been so tactless as to mention that, but the beautiful spy's death had been front-page news on both sides, and Matthew's role in thwarting her would-be abductors on the high seas had been far too colorful a yarn, witnessed by far too many tattling sailors, to be glossed-over easily. Yes, Matthew had been brave and gallant, but how much of his derring-do had been inspired by a desire to save Belle's neck from the hangman's noose and how much by the desire to be invited into her bed?

And Matthew had acted very stupidly by not availing himself of the chance to send his wife some reassuring, affectionate, letters. His silence was not enforced by cruel, unfeeling jailers; he had pen and paper and plenty of time to compose masterpieces of reconciliation. That he had not done so might reasonably be interpreted as a sign of profound guilt. Out at Pine Haven, Mary Harper was spared much of the lurid gossip, but she did read newspapers, and she must have known that *something* tormented Matthew to the point of rendering him mute. That "something," most likely, was a guilty conscience. Equally disturbing was the fact that not once had he acted, alone or in concert with an attorney, to expedite his own release—all the machinations that eventually procured his pardon had been initiated by Hobart-Hampden.

Perhaps Matthew had only developed a fleeting crush on Miss O'Neal, the way some married men swoon inwardly over an actress or an operatic diva. No, that was untenably naïve; according to the crew, the action in Belle's stateroom had been wild enough to give new meaning to the nautical cliché "shiver me timbers!" All right then, we must assume that some really torrid action took place in that room. But how to deal with it in the present context—this was a matter both subtle and rife with pitfalls.

As a starting point, Largo posited the fact that Mary Harper was no longer—if she ever really *had* been—a sheltered, sentimental belle. At the moment, by God, she was the *Boss* of Pine Haven, and strong men obeyed her wishes as if they were a general's commands. She could not possibly be so naïve as to believe that her dashing husband had never, ever, succumbed to the temptations of the flesh during his trips abroad. But was she truly liberal-minded enough to regard those presumed carnal adventures as harmless escapades—recreational frolics quite detached from his deeper commitments to marriage and family? Was not a blockade-runner of legendary prowess, a hero of the Confederacy, entitled to a bit of manly fun? Well, that point was endlessly debatable. But at least he had never sneaked out to the slaves' quarters to boff some dusky rice-picking wench, a common enough peccadillo among gentlemen of his class. And he had certainly been a good *provider*; he had made the Sloane family very rich indeed, and had done so at the risk of life and limb. For that kind of prestige and security, many wives would happily overlook a few casual romps with dockside trollops. But, ruminated Largo, there was no small distinction between that kind of behavior and a heedless, wild-fire passion for a notorious courtesan who reputedly numbered her conquests in the hundreds and who might be conversant with rare, little-known erotic techniques so enslaving, so refined, so powerful that—*let's face it!*—the renewed *obligations* of the marriage bed might now seem, in comparison, like a mug of flat beer. Yes! All of Largo's feminine instincts told her: it was *that* aspect of the matter that troubled Mary Harper most deeply.

Yet domestic satisfaction did not exclude real passion—and Mary Harper had told Largo, many times, that she believed as much with all her heart. There were other powerful attractions to an enduring union, however, which could never be found in a brief, volcanic, affair: comfort, the easy intimacy of conversation, the strength to confront the drab miseries of old age—so many adversities were easier to bear with a beloved spouse at your side. These were the things that nourished love over the whole span of our years, and Largo thought it was essential for both husband and wife to be reminded of *partnership* when they faced each other across this temporary chasm. Neither must enter that first embrace with their minds, bodies, and souls distracted by *comparisons*. It must be self-referential, that first hug; it must be an affirmation of their future-to-be-shared, that first kiss. It was going to be a terribly fragile moment, and the most likely scenario—unless Largo intervened by concocting a better one—was not auspicious. She could visualize every tense moment . . . *Matthew pacing nervously on the dock—Mary Harper gripping white-knuckled the gunwales of the Pine Haven launch—each first perceiving the other as a remote speck—the slow enlargement of speck into human being as the boat draws closer—What looks different about him/her?—Was that a frown/scowl or the shadow of a passing cloud? Is his/her facial expression "tense" or "excited"*?

No, no! That would not do! By the time Mary Harper actually climbed out of the boat they would have been eyeing each other for half-an-hour like two unflagged warships waiting for either a hearty wave or a hostile broadside. Too much time for both parties to become confused by old memories, to scan each other for the signs of freshly healed wounds, to overspeculate, for each to become so anxious about how the other would react to the otherwise very uncomplicated act of reunion, that their moods might be murderously *wrong* before it could even take place.

Far better, Largo thought, that the very moment of first contact should be quick and spontaneous, unencumbered by a heavy ceremonial build-up; it should be gentle, almost casual, reconnecting these two people so quickly, so matter-of-factly, that there would be no time for doubts and hesitations to get in the way of simply *touching each other*! She gradually devised a tactical plan, her pen scratching furiously, and when she had refined it to her satisfaction, she took it to Hobart-Hampden—who had loyally rearranged his own schedule to help orchestrate the reunion in any way he could. He studied it thoughtfully, and then smiled approvingly at her. "This is quite good," he said, giving her a congratulatory pat on the bottom. "My word, yes—subtle, but very sensible. Those two people bloody well *belong* together, and you've come up with a damn good plan to make them realize as much. So, sit down at my writing desk, and start composing this letter you've identified as 'Step Number One.' "

"Should I use the vellum stationery?"

"Definitely. Ummm, with or without the Queen's portrait?"

> *"I have thought this thing through very carefully, my dear friend, and have devised genuine 'strategies' which should maximize the chances of success and mutual happiness. My home is yours, for the duration of this 'campaign.' Do not bother to pack all your finery—I have new and suitably flattering clothes picked out for you, freshly brought-in from Paris, by way of London and Nassau. Just come, without delay! We will hide your boat and find appropriate lodgings for dear old Fitz-Bright!"*

Hobart-Hampden hired a boatman to take the letter upriver to Pine Haven, and to Largo's immense satisfaction, Mary Harper arrived the very next morning. She was, she frankly confessed, in a state, and so wrought-up were her nerves that she was grateful to put herself in Largo's hands and eternally grateful that Largo was trying to orchestrate this momentous event, rather than allowing it blindly to *just happen*.

The centerpiece of Largo's "battle plan" was a jolly "gentlemen only" party at the Yellow House, complete with a buffet table spread with simple, robust, "manly" fare (but nothing so heavy as to induce torpor!), and high-quality but small-caliber alcoholic refreshments. Matthew was allowed, as H-H delicately put it, to get "lightly greased" but not drunk. The Yellow House lads were rehearsed for their role, which was to put Sloane at ease with witty, slightly bawdy "manly talk," and to encourage him to boast a bit about his exploits on the bridge, but not in the bedroom. Around three-fifteen, he would be led to a comfortable upstairs suite for a massage, a shave whilst soaking in a hot tub, and some expert advice about his wardrobe. Then, about forty minutes before the Pine Haven boat was scheduled to dock, he would be escorted to the landing site by Hobart-Hampden, Captain Standish Pendelton, and a small honor guard of Yellow House bravos.

Mary Harper, for her part, would already have been in town for two days, going through a slightly more elaborate ritual of preparation. Largo had solicited the help of Kate and Winona Murphy to instruct her guest in some of the more esoteric refinements of their profession—had, in fact, told the girls to purge Mrs. Sloane of the last vestiges of reticence she might have with regard to the full spectrum of erotic arts and practices. These rather giddy master classes were lubricated with plenty of good wine. It had not taken long before Mary Harper's feigned displays of shock had given way to bawdy exuberance. "My God," she gasped at one point, "I had no idea there was still so much to learn!"

Both principal parties would be on the same dock at the same time, but Mary Harper would be hidden behind a convenient mound of cotton bales. Sloane, of course, would station himself close to the designated mooring place, and all his attention would be focused upstream. The other men in his escort would discreetly fall back an appropriate number of paces. After a certain amount of suspenseful build-up, Mary Harper would quietly approach her anxious and preoccupied husband and wrap him in her arms with some quiet phrases of welcome and endearment. The all-important moment of first contact would thus be made spontaneously, and all the potential barriers of doubt, anxiety, hesitation, and—on Matthew's part—residual guilt, would be outflanked; defenses breached before they could be manned. The effect, Largo fervently hoped, would be to strip away all extraneous considerations and turn a hugely complicated transition into . . . a simple hug.

Their friends and witnesses would allow this spontaneous embrace—Largo thought of it as a "surprise attack" by Cupid—only a moment or two to work its effect, then they would descend, with hearty and ostentatious displays of welcome, and whisk the Sloanes off to the Yellow House party as though they were hapless newlyweds before there was time for lingering doubts and hesitations to resurface. After a few hours of celebrating with good companions, the evening would reach its natural conclusion, with the Sloanes retiring to privacy—not all the way up to Pine Haven, of course—but straightway to the Landau house, which would be theirs for the next forty-eight hours, lavishly stocked with refreshments. As the crowning touch, Largo had redecorated the master bedroom in a style that evoked the essence of the word "boudoir." Largo wanted the couple to feel as though they were stepping into a warm, inviting, utterly *private* world.

While Matthew was enjoying his bath and being sagely counseled about men's fashion, Hobart-Hampden and Largo retired to the Englishman's luxurious private suite and shared a few bowls of hashish. Things were going well, so far.

"I thought it was a masterful psychological touch to give them the run of your house, rather than renting a hotel room. That all-important First Fuck *should* take place on neutral ground. Especially if Mrs. Sloane wants to show off all the new and interesting things she learned from the Daughters Murphy!"

"Lord, does she ever! Of course, at first she made a show of blushing and stammering. No wife likes to admit that her sexual repertoire might benefit from the expert coaching of 'professionals,' but just think of how many marriages would be saved if more of them did. The last time I peeked in, they were just beginning to explore the girls' collection of interesting toys and novelties, and can you guess what Mary Harper said as I was leaving?"

"She probably said, 'Oh, my, which holes does *that* apply to?' "

"No, you awful bugger! What she said was: 'By God, I'll make him regret that he dallied so long in that Yankee prison!' "

"By which she also means, I'm sure, that she intends to do her damndest to exorcise the memory of Belle O'Neal! Oh, happy is the man whose wife is willing to take lessons from a bevy of skilled and shameless harlots!"

Largo swatted him playfully. "I can also teach her a trick or two, you rogue!"

"Indeed you can, my exquisite daughter of Zion, and when tonight's party is over, I shall drag you into our cork-lined room, ply you with aphrodisiac drugs, and encourage you to show me all your 'tricks.'"

They kissed again, long and lavishly. "I have been away too much on business, I know, but the tempo of the war is picking up, the blockade tightens, and sooner or later, we will lose a ship. So one of the things I investigated was the state of your personal investments, deposits, and so on. I'm happy to report that your private fortune steadily increases, even as the fortunes of Richmond seem headed for the shitter. I give the whole Confederate farce a year, at the most."

For an instant, Hobart-Hampden's gaze lost its customary blade-flick of worldly irony—that characteristic expression, which Largo had come to love, which seemed to say to everyone who conversed with him: *Don't try to gull me, my good fellow, for I have seen it all and done things you cannot imagine, in places you have never heard of*—and he looked straight into Largo's eyes with such frank affection that she actually recoiled from the impact.

"And you, my dear Largo, what will you do and where will you go, after the curtain comes down on the drama? Will you be content to settle down in postwar Wilmington, as the city returns to the dull but respectable rituals of peacetime commerce? You will surely be one of the wealthiest single women in the town, if not the entire state—and one of the most comely. Your Jewishness will not deter the onslaught of many handsome Presbyterians."

Largo knitted her brows; one reason why she stayed so perpetually busy was just so she would not have to think too much about *her* post-war existence. Abruptly, and thanks in no small part to the pipes they had smoked, she saw a bright-light possibility beyond the bleakness of a defeated South and a melancholy Wilmington that would never again be as exciting as it had been during the conflict.

"If you find the prospect agreeable, Augustus, I should like to join you and share in the new adventures that will no doubt come your way when your time in the Confederacy is over. No *commitment* is necessary, nor will I insist on trapping you within the cage of marriage vows. Dear God," she chuckled merrily, "I can think of nothing that would more quickly cause us to loathe one another than to become 'Lord and Lady H-H'!"

He scrutinized her as though seeing her exotic beauty and feeling the aura of her independent spirit for the first time.

"Nor can I," he said quietly.

"I want to see the wild, untamed parts of the world, before your Empire makes all of their inhabitants into Church-of-England dullards. I don't care a damn for the drawing rooms of polite society, and as for the Louvre and the Tower of London or the antiquities of Rome, there will be plenty of time to visit them when I am a crabby old woman. I would rather feel the magic of far and desolate places, and I am certain that your duties to the Queen, whatever they may be, will send you to those places. I realize fully that there will come a time when we will grow weary of each other's company, and when that happens, we shall part as friends; no recriminations, no regrets, no sense of betrayal! I ask of you no promise of fidelity or eternal devotion—and you dare not ask them of me! The past three years have awakened in me wanderlust, an appetite for wonders that would be stifled if I remained here one day longer than it takes to lay the cornerstone for my father's temple. We are extraordinarily compatible as lovers and I will not be an anchor, weighing down your lovely independence of spirit. Do not answer quickly—just give my offer some consideration and I think you will realize that while you can certainly find women who please you as much in bed as I, you will not find another so well suited to share your adventures."

Hobart-Hampden shook his head in surprise and genuine perplexity: she had issued a challenge no less serious than a summons to a duel. Finally, he grasped her hands and drew her close in a warm, ardent, familiar embrace.

"It will not be a life of easy comfort," he whispered.

"If I wanted that kind of life, I would stay here."

"It could, sometimes, be very dangerous."

"I should damned well hope so!"

"And I am not yet ready to father a child; I might never be."

"And I have always regarded the so-called rewards of parenthood to be few, fleeting, and greatly exaggerated by those who are enslaved by them."

"Well, then . . ."

He had only to speak a few more words, and the pact between them would have been sealed. But at that very moment, someone knocked loudly on the door of Hobart-Hampden's suite. He disengaged himself from their embrace with an expression of commingled relief and irritation.

"Oh, sod it! Who can that be?"

Largo laughed teasingly and brushed the wrinkles from her gown. "That, I suspect, will be our nervous but exceedingly well-turned-out guest of honor, Captain Sloane."

"Come in, come in!" barked Hobart-Hampden, a little gruffly.

"My apologies if I am interrupting a private conversation . . ." said Matthew Sloane in a tone of uncharacteristic meekness. "But it is time for us to head for the dock, and I don't want to be late . . . or . . . or . . ."

Hopart-Hampen clapped him heartily on the shoulders. "My God, Sloane, you're as nervous as a virgin bridegroom!"

"And as handsome a bridegroom as I have ever seen," said Largo, impulsively stepping forward to hug Matthew, who did indeed look very sharp: a Prince Albert frock coat, delicately checked, tone-on-tone, in sable black and dark charcoal; striped waistcoat, rust and dark gold; contrasting cravat of dark maroon; shirt of snow-white linen; a tastefully rich stickpin mounting two small but exquisite rubies. He was also clean-shaven, a tonsorial concession to the Yellow House dandies, who agreed that "gaunt" was better than "ursine." His "new look" was ceremoniously topped off by a soft, understated, silk hat, broad-brimmed and rounded at the crown—all the latest rage in London, they assured him, if worn at a slightly rakish angle. When Matthew was at last permitted to examine himself in a full-length mirror, he was rather pleased. He *looked* like a new man; a man of wealth and station, determined to impress the woman dearest to his heart. *I take nothing for granted,* his appearance seemed to proclaim, *and if I must court you anew to earn your love and respect, then I am ready to do so, with even more determination than I did when first you captured my heart.*

"Well, Largo . . . H-H . . . do I pass inspection?"

"Indeed you do, my dear Matthew," said Hobart-Hampden. "I declare, I even feel a touch of jealousy!"

"Gentlemen, we must away!" said Largo, offering her arm to Matthew. "We want you to be properly displayed when Mary Harper sails into view!"

Between Largo's taste in clothes, and the Murphy girls' expertise in cosmetics, Mary Harper was also confident that she looked her best. After much experimentation and sisterly debate she had finally chosen a simple, figure-flattering dress of emerald green, cut daringly low to show off the mature, gravity-defying fullness of her breasts and a silver necklace with turquoise filigree. The alluring whiteness of her shoulders was both enhanced and teasingly obscured by a light-as-air shawl of Irish wool. Her ladies-in-waiting applied cosmetics with a much lighter hand than she had feared: some powder to smooth her work-roughened complexion, a faint wash of rouge to bring out the fullness of her lips. After a brief internal debate, she allowed the plucking of some gray hairs—just the most visible ones—then tied her hair in a casual but rather voluptuous chignon. A few dabs of lilac cologne provided the finishing touch. "Not one thing more," whispered Kate Murphy. "May God grant me half such looks when I'm your age!"

And now, she was hiding behind the cotton bales, thankful that the Murphy girls were far enough away so that Matthew could not hear their stifled giggles.

The welcoming committee of gentlemen arrived, dismounted, and took up watch. Matthew was naturally in front, and as casually as possible, the other men slowly drew back, leaving enough space so that, when Mary Harper did make her presence known, the surprise would not topple Matthew into the river. It was a colorful tableau: Matthew in front, straining for that first glimpse of the Pine Haven launch, Largo and Hobart-Hampden holding hands a few feet behind him, eyes glittering mischievously, and a gaudily uniformed contingent of the Yellow House lads, clanking in dress swords, bits of imperial uniforms and tuning their varied assortment of musical instruments, under the honorary conductorship of Captain Pendelton, who was turned out in full Royal Navy splendor, wielding a bandmaster's baton as though it were the Queen's own scepter.

All the players in this well-rehearsed drama were in position, and as the anxious moments passed, curious onlookers gathered at a discreet distance, eagerly speculating on the significance of this colorful assemblage. Obviously, some important personage was about to make landfall from the northern channel of the Cape Fear, and speculation was rife. Who was coming this time, Jeff Davis or the King of Siam? Those whose business kept them close to the teeming waterfront had seen many strange and colorful visitors since the full blooming of the blockade-running enterprise: foreign diplomats, mysterious but exotic soldiers-of-fortune, military observers in the full-dress finery of France, Italy, Spain, and the comic-opera republics of South and Central America, and furtive, darkly preoccupied men who *must* have been couriers, spies, and secret agents.

But the minutes ticked slowly by and no sleek foreign warships or gilded barges appeared, just the grimy routine parade of tugs and packet boats. Matthew Sloane, brows furrowed and eyes staring with near-feverish intensity at the long, cold, olive-colored river, began to fidget, clasping and unclasping his hands behind his waist, shifting his weight from one glossy boot to the other. He was obviously trying to conjure the sight of Pine Haven's launch by sheer willpower, and so fierce was his concentration that he did not hear the muted gasp of the assembled crowd when a strikingly attractive woman of mature years, displaying her charms most dramatically in a form-flattering and boldly revealing dress of emerald green, suddenly came into view from behind a fluffy pyramid of cotton bales, followed by two giddily smiling young women who seemed to be her maids—but who were instantly recognized by some of the male spectators, as daughters of the legendary Leota Murphy. Had Matthew Sloane not been so oblivious to everything but the river and the hammering of his own heart, he would surely have sensed the sudden puzzled, expectant hush behind him.

Mary Harper paused briefly when she reached a spot just inches from her husband's tautly braced back and knotted hands. She took a deep breath, leaned forward, and brushed her lips against Matthew's neck, speaking in a throaty whisper that only he could hear:

"Welcome home, my dearest . . ."

Matthew Sloane's eyes widened in amazement, and the expression on his face, had it not been so instantly flooded with powerful emotion, would have been comical—the shock of recognition was so great that he looked like a man who has just been struck from behind with a hammer. He struggled for composure, inhaling deeply, recognizing instantly, from the subtle sweet whisper of lilacs, the inimitable scent of his wife's warm flesh. He took a halting, half-stunned step forward, then turned slowly, fascinated anew by the familiar yet once-more-novel warmth of her gaze. Their mutual friends had stage-managed the moment to perfection. Husband and wife regarded each other with such intensity that every other person, indeed ever object, in the vicinity ceased to exist for them. He had half-expected, and greatly dreaded, that she would greet him with a wary, reserved, perhaps even bitter expression, but all he saw was the wide bright welcome of her smile and the joy that filled her eyes. He tried to speak, but could only stammer a chaotic assortment of grunts and solitary, quivering vowels.

Then Hobart-Hampden broke the stasis of Matthew's astonishment by gruffly muttering: "Kiss her, you fool, because if you don't, by God I *will!*" Even the onlookers who did not know the Sloanes now understood the sense of the moment, and when Matthew Sloane enfolded his wife in his arms and joined his lips to hers—finding in the tender generous ardor of her kiss no trace of hesitation, no reserve, no withholding borne of resentment or suspicion—he felt like a man redeemed by a wondrous gift of grace. The spectators broke into spontaneous cheers. The kiss went on and on, their embrace gave off such a palpable heat that two of the Yellow House lads struck up a fiery jig with fiddle and pennywhistle, soon joined by two harmonicas, another violin, a flute, and the lusty patter of an Irish dancing drum. Someone ran into a nearby store and bought out the vendor's stock of artificial flowers, passing them out to any open hand. An old blind Negro, who eked out his living by playing banjo tunes for anyone who dropped a penny in his out-thrust hat, leaped up from his stool and joined in, picking up the tune effortlessly and playing with such contagious gusto that several other nearby Negroes ceased their dockside labors and began joyfully to buck-dance and clap in time.

Her eyes full with tears of relief, Largo wrapped Hobart-Hampden in a crushing hug and gestured at the dozens of people, black and white and brown-skinned sailors from God-knew what tropic lands, who had been swept up in the moment and were now joyously capering, clapping, and vocalizing in a Babel of tongues and exotic accents. "Augustus, this is wonderful! How on earth did you organize such a fiesta?"

Bowing and tipping his hat, he grasped her hands and swirled her around in a giddy improvised gallop.

"It's not my doing, lass! It's the spirit of *old* Wilmington, flaming up in defiance of gloom, defeat, and plague! Only the great god Eros and the wild intoxication of Irish music could have sparked this outburst! My God, how long has it been since most of these people enjoyed a good careless fling? And, mark you, the Sloanes have not yet come up for air! Fuck the war, let's *all* dance!"

Everyone who took part in what came to be known as the Great Waterfront Party had a different theory about why it started—only the relative handful who witnessed the reunion of Matthew and Mary Harper Sloane knew that, through some strange and wonderful human alchemy, the passionate embrace of a long-separated husband and wife had sparked what could only be regarded as a very benign kind of riot. As more and more people heard the music and left their routine labors to join the revel, it was as though, for the space of a few hours in the burnished air of the coastal autumn, the people of Wilmington and the transient visitors who wafted to her shores by the harsh tides of war, whatever the color of their skins or the lonely displaced strangeness of their accents, had declared their own ceasefire.

Nowhere in all the city did the pulse of this bedizened interlude beat hotter or more lustily than inside the shuddering walls of the Yellow House, where (it was later calculated) an entire month's worth of blockade-smuggled liquors and tea-party delicacies, from Dutch chocolates to fruit-filled Belgian eclairs, disappeared so swiftly that a Biblical swarm of locusts could not have done a better job. All who had witnessed the Sloanes' first embrace, hot and urgent and numinous as a star gone nova amid the teeming squalor of the docks, later swore that it was the spontaneous ignition of their love which had, in some faerie-magicked way, ignited the citywide explosion of revelry. Every dashing young officer and blockade-running freebooter beseeched Mary Harper for a dance, as though she were Venus incarnate and the privilege of a brief, perspiring whirl with her around the crowded ballroom floor was a balm to their masculinity roughly equivalent to a night with Helen of Troy; and it was the same with Matthew, who found himself besieged by every pretty woman at the party—married, single, precocious adolescent or camp-following, free-spirited adventuress who had come to Wilmington because it was a good place, she had been told, to find a newly rich husband. Both Matthew and Mary Harper basked in this extraordinary blast of adoration, and when they chanced to swirl close to each other on the dance floor, they shared a sweetly intimate glance, for no matter who they danced with or dallied with around the punch bowls, an invisible tether connected them at all times. No matter how many handsome young sailors flattered Mary Harper with compliments ranging from drunken unction to boldly straightforward propositions, and no matter how many flighty young belles flattered the gauntly handsome and famously daring Captain Sloane with doe-eyed, bosom-thrusting gestures of seduction and coarser, more indecorous hints of availability, both of them knew that, at some point in this out-of-control Saturnalia, they would quietly join hands and leave together. Matthew had been put on notice that the Landaus' house was reserved for them alone on this night, and the guest bedroom was already stocked with iced-down champagne, a wicker basket filled with imported fruits and chocolates, and—should they be in the mood for a bit of daring enhancement—a petite Egyptian hookah and a small fragrant pat of Hobart-Hampden's finest Afghan hashish. What Matthew did *not* know was that the room was also well stocked with erotic playthings and novelties, and that his wife was bursting to share with him her newly acquired fund of esoteric knowledge concerning the manifold ways these curious devices and unguents might be employed by a pair of imaginative and uninhibited lovers.

By two o'clock in the morning, the Yellow House party had become a drunken sprawl just a few degrees short of an unrestrained orgy. No one noticed when the Sloanes slipped out, hand in hand, and amidst many outbursts of tipsy laughter, managed to seat themselves in the carriage reserved for their private use. By now, the rest of the city had fallen silent—the revelers who had filled the streets earlier had by now dispersed, and the spell that had spontaneously dazzled the inhabitants had worn off, leaving only the crisp clear air of an autumn night and the arctic-white crescent of a waning moon burning above the dark slow ribbon of the river. At first, as they rattled south in the direction of the Landau house, Matthew drove with inebriated recklessness, but as they neared their destination, he slowed the horses and his expression became once more grave and somewhat brooding. Mary Harper felt the mood-change instantly and was resolved not to put up with it for a single minute. Seizing the reins from him with surprising vigor, she halted the coach and turned toward him with a look of concentrated resolve such as he had never seen on her face before. And when she spoke, she did so in carefully measured words that seemed girded with armor plate.

"It has been a grand afternoon, Matthew—the most joyous and carefree time we've ever enjoyed together—and I warn you: I *will not allow* you to spoil the climax of it, so to speak, by squeezing out of your conscience some little puss-spurt of a confession. Do you hear me, sir? *I will not stand for it!* Not one of us who lives through this war, man or woman, will ever be free of memories we would rather not carry in our hearts. That is what *happens* to people in war! I can see it in your face: now that we are alone and undistracted by revelry, this festering boil of guilt has begun to ache once more and because you were raised to be a certain kind of gentleman, you feel compelled to exorcise it by heaving it out like a drunk man heaves his breakfast. I will have none of it, Matthew! I will not have the rest of this fantastic evening soiled by its stench. Hear me well, for I will only say this once: *I do not give the slightest damn about what sort of 'sins' you committed in your days as a wild sea-rover!* I do *not* feel betrayed or diminished, not as a wife, not as the mistress of your plantation, not as the mother of your children, and not as a woman.

"Swallow it down, Matthew, this ridiculous compulsion to confess! Your confession is neither required nor welcomed. There, I absolve you—simple as that. Swallow it down and drop it in the chamber pot tomorrow morning along with all the other shit."

Intimidated—when had this streak of iron come into her will?—Matthew shook his head, gulped deeply of the chill night air, and turned to his furiously insistent wife, a shy, hesitant smile slowly warming his lips. The sharpness of her words, and their raw sincerity, had indeed lanced the boil upon his conscience.

"You are very beautiful," he finally said. "And you have grown very wise while I was gone. I am your servant, madam, and if you will have me, your true and devoted husband for the rest of our days."

"I'm glad to hear it, Matthew. Now: let us never speak of this again. Let tonight be our *real* wedding night. And I hope you still have a full head of steam, sir, because I intend to fuck your eyes out and I will not settle for a fainthearted performance in return!"

She spurred the horses onward, rattling at reckless speed, and after a moment of shocked silence, Matthew Sloane began to quake with bawdy laughter, for it was a lucky man indeed who could still feel such a sword-stroke of lust for his wife of fourteen years.

The Unpleasantness at Faison's Groves

LESSON XI: THE AFRICAN OR "NEGRO" RACE
The African Negroes are slothful and vicious, but possess little cunning. The climate in Africa is so unhealthy that white men can scarcely go there to preach to them, so they know nothing of Jesus . . . These people are the descendents of Ham, and the Bible tells us that God ordained them to be servants of their betters forever. That would seem a hard sentence, but it was done to punish their ancient wickedness and serve as an example. We do not know how they came to be black and to have wool on their heads . . .

—Miranda Branson Moore, *Geographical Reader for the Dixie Children.* Raleigh, Branson and Farrar, *1864*

6:28 A.M., OCTOBER 5, 1863:

The Buffaloes rode out of Faison's Groves without pausing for breakfast, but also without any signs of undue haste. Jack Fairless wanted things to appear normal, so Mayor Simpkins and his fellow conspirators would not try to alert the Rebel ambush down by the Tar. For the same reason, he did not share Reuben's intelligence with anyone except his company commanders, so there would be no sign of anger or tension among the troopers.

As soon as Jack thought it was safe, he halted the column long enough to spread the tale to all ranks and to hide his artillery, which would slow them down too much. Major Manchester therefore assumed his alternate role as commander of Company C's infantry. The Buffaloes dismounted *en masse* about five hundred yards from the Rebel position, leaving the horses heavily guarded. Then they advanced on foot, using the stealth they had learned during their own bushwhacking days. It was full morning by that time, and DeWitt's column had to be approaching the deadly trap so cunningly laid for it. Just as the Buffaloes began their final approach to the knoll overlooking the Confederate redoubt, Red Elliott scuttled over to Jack and said: "My men want to know—are we takin' any prisoners? Any quarter for the wounded?"

Jack's face was cold as stone. "All prisoners will be shot 'while trying to escape,' and they won't *be* no wounded when we get through with them bastards!"

6:59 A.M., October 5, 1863

Rush Hawkins and the Sixth Massachusetts were too far back in the column to see the deadly bridge, but he started feeling apprehensive when he realized that the riverbank road was getting narrower, steeper, and causing the John Brown Regiment to lose formation and scrunch up tighter. His sense of foreboding increased when the growing light revealed, on his left, a square mile of glutinous, briar-tangled mud. Any formation trying to extend a flank in that direction would find the going slow and exhausting. Suddenly, he heard a distant *pop-pop-pop* of pistol shots—was someone trying to warn DeWitt? Seconds later, all hell broke loose at the front of the column. A sheet of rifle fire blazed on the far bank, grapeshot, too! A hideous crimson convulsion lashed the John Brown men, and the air was rent with a cacophony of oaths, screams and confused, contradictory orders. Hawkins felt disgusted. *It's an ambush, and what a great spot to pull one, too. Leave it to DeWitt to fuck things up twice in two days.*

General Edmund DeWitt had started the day full of piss and vinegar, determined to make such rapid forward progress that the misfortunes of yesterday would be forgotten. Marching proudly between his two regiments, he set a blistering pace, but gradually fell farther behind, pausing more and more to wipe his brow and sneak a little nip from his canteen. He waved and joked as the foremost company marched to the top of that annoyingly narrow causeway and started across an even more annoyingly skinny bridge with no guard rails. Just like Southerners, he thought, too lazy to finish a job properly. Then things went awry very quickly and very badly. Evidently, there was some kind of obstacle blocking the middle of the bridge. Company A was stymied, stopped in its tracks, but Company B just kept marching, unable to see the blockade, and Company C, whose men did see the human log-jam, tried to stop, but were pushed forward irritably by the officers of Company D, until the whole bridge was so hopelessly congested that men started losing balance and toppling into the creek, yelling in vain for rescue as their heavy packs pulled them into the deep, swift, currents of the Tar.

Even those men who recognized Elias's warning when they heard it were so immobilized by the crush in midspan they could do nothing but shout warnings that went mostly unheard. But just before the hidden

Rebels unleashed their first devastating volley, the entangled black soldiers clearly heard one of them sing out: "Hail Colombia, happy land! If I don't shoot ten niggers, I'll be damned!" Then a typhoon of lead engulfed the mass of blue on the bridge. Until the falling dead thinned out the congestion, all DeWitt could see were rippling geysers of wood chips, shreds of Yankee-blue cloth, tobacco-spits and fountain-spurts of blood, gobbets of ruined flesh, and the broken-eggshell fragments of shattered skulls, trailing the moist gray yolk of brain matter.

Verging on a seizure, DeWitt screamed orders that were either totally unexecutable ("Climb over that barricade and keep going!"), completely obsolete ("Don't bunch up, you men! Spread out!"), highly unlikely to produce any significant improvement ("Goddamn it, return their fire! Shoot at those men!"), or just impossible to carry out ("Bring up the artillery, fast!"). After the southern half of the bridge was choked with scores of casualties, DeWitt finally managed to scream out a single command that some of his companies, at least, might be able to execute: "Extend the left flank and charge across that creek!"

"Guess that means us, General Hawkins," croaked a terrified lieutenant nearby.

"Not a bit of it, sir. We're under orders to bring up the rear, so that command was plainly directed at our dusky comrades in line ahead of us. Until we receive *specific orders* from General DeWitt, I suggest you all lie prone on the slope of this embankment and make yourselves very small."

Eyes rolling in fear, but commendably determined, the John Brown troops scrabbled down the south slope of the causeway and tried to form a skirmish line in the morass, moving like men trying to walk on flypaper. The farther they extended their line, the more attention they received from Rebel snipers on the far shore, who could not have prayed for more helpless targets.

"Shouldn't we shoot, too, General Hawkins? Might help those poor darkies a little bit, anyhow."

"Good idea, son. You see a Rebel target, blaze away. Oh, hell, everybody shoot at least once. If DeWitt comes down this way, I don't want him to find us with cold rifle barrels."

By this time, nobody was even trying to storm the barricade on the bridge. Despite DeWitt's exhortations to valor, threats of summary punishment, and appeals to their manhood, not one more black soldier moved forward. The bravest did try to return fire, but they were just throwing lead blindly. The Rebels' fire never slackened in the least.

Then, astonishingly, it *did*. Or at least, it suddenly changed direction, apparently to meet a sudden, fierce, and completely unexpected assault from behind. The combat seemed furious and close—Hawkins thought it sounded like the wildest, meanest, barroom brawl imaginable. Nor was it a long engagement: seven minutes at most, followed by a swift diminuendo to silence. Finally, there was a stark little coda: wild pleas for mercy or cries of surrender, followed by the particular kind of throttled-back pistol report that only occurs when the muzzle is close enough to set fire to the victim's overcoat.

Well, I'll be dipped in shit! chuckled Hawkins. The Rebels had been assailed, and obviously quite savagely, by Fairless and his Buffaloes! After the sad sound of the last *coup-de-grace* faded away, Hawkins heard the unmistakable mountaineer twang of Jack Fairless's voice:

"Hallo, General DeWitt and all you fine black soldiers! You may now cross the bridge without any more perturbance or delay, courtesy of the Battling Buffaloes. Glad we could be of service to y'all!"

8:00 A.M., October 5 until 2:00 A.M., October 6, 1863

Rush Hawkins had made his way forward about fifteen minutes after the shooting stopped. One look at the sickening human gumbo clogging the bridge, and he decided to avoid that route. Just north of the bridge, however, he found a line of flat rocks that enabled him to cross the creek with relative ease. The interior of the Confederate redoubt, when Hawkins finally reached it, was an abattoir, a slaughterpen. He stopped counting bodies after he reached sixty. The Buffaloes, faces black with powder, eyes still glazed with a combat fever that would be slow to ebb, were methodically looting the Rebel dead and eating their rations. Hawkins found Reubens, Fairless, Elliott, and Manchester sitting together on the sandbagged revetment near the Rebels' howitzer, where they could catch a river breeze. All three white officers still had the adrenaline-shakes, but Reubens looked as composed as he usually did—an inscrutable *café-au-lait* totem—calmly puffing on a cigar. It took Fairless a minute or two to realize his commanding officer was standing in front of him. When he did, he saluted haltingly, as though he was still amazed at the carnage he had wrought in so brief a battle.

"Jesus Christ, Fairless, you boys really tore up the henhouse!"

"Yessir, General Hawkins. I reckon we did. It ain't like I haven't killed men before, but this was different. They hardly had time to fire a shot."

Hawkins patted him reassuringly. "Neither did the black soldiers they ambushed, Colonel! Your attack saved hundreds of Union soldiers—maybe saved this entire expedition. By the way, which one of your men fired those warning shots?"

Reubens snapped upright like a jack-in-the-box. "God-almighty, Elias! I clean forgot about him! I must go find him. That boy had never even fired a pistol before in his life—I hope he had enough sense to run away after he did."

Elias had, in fact, been smart enough to do just that, but he had only gotten as far as the edge of the nearest turpentine grove. Reubens found him sitting calmly on a sap-crusted pine stump, chomping on a shag of tobacco he had lifted from the pocket of the dead Confederate private sprawled nearby. There was a big ragged exit wound in the center of the Rebel's back, and Elias, when he spotted Reubens coming through the pines, jauntily lifted the Colt and grinned wickedly.

"Guess what, Boss? Ah guess ah *can* hit somebody with this thing! I saved one shot, just in case they was about to take me alive, you know, but I spotted that cracker running like the Debil was after his ass, and when he was about to run right over me, I figured: Elias Sloane, you jes' point that thing and squeeze. Boom! Down he went—don't think he ever even seen me."

"Just as a matter of curiosity, Private Sloane, what did you feel when you killed your first man?"

Elias shrugged. "Nothin' but glad that it was him instead o' me!"

"You will indeed make a good soldier, Elias."

Once his casualties had been cleared off the causeway and his disorganized companies had regrouped, General DeWitt sent word to the rear of the column to have a "special supply wagon" brought forward, with all possible haste, to the survivors of the John Brown Regiment—who almost tore the vehicle to pieces in their eagerness to grab some of its contents.

"What the hell is DeWitt up to now?" muttered Jack. Hawkins pulled out his field glasses and took a long close look at the mob scene on the causeway. "Jesus, I don't believe that man! DeWitt's passing out whiskey to those boys, a whole bottle per man! He is flagrantly violating at least three Army regulations, not to mention setting an appalling example for his other officers! Does he *want* that whole regiment stinking drunk when they resume their march?"

Jack Fairless sighed and shook his head wearily. "Matter of fact, sir, that's exactly what he wants. DeWitt came through here about ten minutes before you showed up, and when he saw all those boats with 'Faison's Groves' painted on 'em, he asked some questions, and I told him how we'd found this little turpentine village by that name, and how the people at Faison's Groves kept us diverted so the Rebs could use their factory boats to bring up the garrison for this little fort. This morning, when I learned about their deception, I was angry as hell, too, but DeWitt—he's in a whole other world of angry. Now that I've had time to think about it, I wish I hadn't told him about Faison's Groves."

Hawkins was confused. "Is DeWitt going to bring his 'Terrible Swift Sword' to that village? If civilians took an active role in setting up that ambush, then DeWitt has the right to hang a few of them in reprisal."

Fairless squirmed, trying to reconcile a lot of powerful ambiguities.

"I know that. And the village mayor knew what kind of risk he was takin'. Mind you, I hate being tricked as much as any man, but I kind of admire the old guy's balls. See, General Hawkins, DeWitt doesn't plan to just hang a few conspirators—he plans to get the John Browns likkered up, then turn 'em loose on the whole town. I think something really *ugly* is going to happen, and I think DeWitt wants to take part personally. When he said 'I shall make *an example* that will leave a scar on this land for generations,' well everyone of us who heard him felt sick to our stomachs. And his eyes, sir—they were like thc eyes of a mad dog!"

Hawkins kicked at the dirt in frustration. "Until today, I had thought that God put limits on one man's folly, but I see He allowed some exceptions. We're already a day behind schedule, but if DeWitt pushed on vigorously, he could still capture Tarboro by nightfall. Hell, there's two thousand men and eleven guns sitting idly beside the river—not to mention two extremely bored gunboat crews—we can capture Tarboro by ourselves, then DeWitt can catch up in the morning, after he's had his 'fun.'"

"Sorry, General," Fairless said, "but he's going to order you and his other black regiment to bivouac right where you are. See, if the rest of the column pushes on, then DeWitt misses his chance to knock off that ironclad, and he really wants the credit for that."

"He can *have* the credit, goddamn it! But if we don't reach that railroad bridge by day after tomorrow at the latest, we'll find half the Army of Northern Virginia waiting for us!"

"I tell you, sir, his mind is set on vengeance and that's all there is to it. You might as well tell the Massachusetts boys to take their packs off and go fishin' in the river, because DeWitt ain't going one step farther up that road until he's brought the 'Wrath of God' down on Faison's Groves."

"How do the Buffaloes feel about it, Fairless? After all, you boys uncovered the plot. Don't you want a little revenge, too?"

"Problem is, General Hawkins, this ain't a 'little' revenge. DeWitt's intentionally getting his men drunk before they even get to Faison's Groves, so by midafternoon, there won't be any stoppin' them. He wants blood and fire, and he's whipping his men into a frenzy. It won't be vengeance, it'll be a massacre. Me and the other officers, we don't want any part of it. If it's all the same to you, we'll sit this one out. We've already butchered every Rebel in this fort, and that's as much as we want on our consciences for one day."

"Oh no, Fairless, you don't get that luxury. You set this in motion by telling DeWitt about that village, and now you're going to march back up there and watch what happens. He may act with more restraint if there are witnesses, but if he does go hog wild, I want you there to see it, take careful notes, and be prepared to testify at the court martial that fanatic is setting himself up for. You *will* do this, Colonel Fairless, and that's an order!"

By the time the Buffaloes rode back into Faison's Groves, the John Brown survivors had already rounded up the white population, crowding them together in the town square, fencing them in with a ring of bayonets. When DeWitt and the last barge-load of Negro troopers arrived, along with enough whiskey barrels to stupefy a small city, a dining-room table had been moved outdoors to provide him with a suitable podium. Some of the Buffaloes asked for permission to retire, not wanting to see what was probably going to happen, but Jack refused. So the whole unit was spread out as an audience—a very subdued, ambiguous audience. Jack settled into a rocking chair. Red Elliott and Bonaparte Reubens pulled their chairs up beside his.

Before DeWitt started his oration, he ordered every one of his soldiers to line up at the whiskey barrels and draw a full canteen of liquor. None was allowed back in ranks until he had consumed at least half of the contents. While this ritual played out, Reubens leaned to his two companions and made a dispassionate observation: "Observe the men who are only pretending to drink. They are the ones who find this business morally repugnant, but mark my words, a half-hour after the killing starts, they too will be swilling whiskey, and not one of them will break ranks or utter a word of protest. Eventually, they too will shed blood, and once they cross that line, they may show even more ferocity than the obvious brutes who are eager to get started. DeWitt is shrewd enough to know their psychology. Most men go into combat not because they are brave so much as because they don't want to be seen letting down their comrades. In this case, no one wants to be thought of as being soft or squeamish. When this is over, all of those men will be bonded by guilt and shame. And the next time DeWitt calls on them to commit an atrocity, even the most compassionate among them will find it much easier."

Once his men were suitably numbed by drink, DeWitt rose to his podium and began to harangue the captive whites. He was already half-potted, and as he continued to drink, his rhetoric grew rambling and his features more bestial: *Base treachery . . . cruel oppressors of the Colored Race . . . Israelites in bondage . . . more "terrible swift swords" than twenty men could have wielded . . . God, not I, is the instrument of retribution . . . An example must be made . . . object lessons must be taught . . . every slaveowner will one day face a just and terrible retribution . . . Bzzzzz . . . Frummmm . . . Sput!* The sermon went on for so long that even a few of the terrified whites began to yawn. Finally, a gaunt one-legged veteran in the center of the crowd shouted: "If you're gonna kill us, you drunken old windbag, go ahead and do it before I die of old age!"

"I apologize for trying your patience, sir! It is indeed time to get things started. As a reward for your forthrightness, I'm going to save you for last and provide you with a novel method of avoiding the miseries of old age!"

There was only one noose and DeWitt used a short rope, so none of his victims would die quickly of a broken neck. Instead, they were drawn up just far enough to give their feet some elusive scrabbling contact with the ground, but not enough to rest upon it; the hanged men gyrated wildly, slowly strangling, sucking in just enough air to prolong the ordeal, while mucous streamed from their noses and their bowels voided in helpless spasms. The first victim took eighteen minutes to die, and when the time was called out DeWitt boasted: "I do believe that's a new record, boys!" After the first corpse was carried off and a second man dragged from the crowd, screaming words of love to his family, Red Elliott began to growl deep in his throat.

"At ease, Red. We've been ordered to bear witness to these events, and not to interfere."

"God-a-mighty, Jack, you and me did some hateful things back when we rode with Cyrus Bone, and I'll answer to God for killing two men just to settle old scores, not for being Rebel sympathizers. But even Cyrus Bone never tortured a man in front of his family! Those women and children, they'll wake up screamin' from nightmares for the rest of their lives."

Reubens leaned over, a sardonic half-smile twisting his lips. "But don't you see, Captain Elliott? That's exactly General DeWitt's intention—to spread the horror across as many generations as he can. A quick, ordinary hanging? *Phsaw!* Even your wife would get over that memory after a while. But not the memories implanted on this day. Every time one of those widows and orphans bolts up in bed, dreaming about what happened to these men, the soul of Edmund DeWitt will be laughing down in Hell."

By late afternoon, all the white men were dead except for Mayor Simpkins and the one-legged veteran who had taunted DeWitt earlier. The old man showed admirable grit right to the end, though, for when two drunken brutes came to get him, he whipped a straight-razor out of his boot and slashed one man's throat before he was cut down by scores of minié balls.

The amputee veteran had been taken away after the third hanging, and tied to a chair with a hood pulled over his face, so that he could not see the preparations being made for his own "novel" execution. A special detail of very drunk soldiers had constructed a closed circle of vertical bayonets, sharpened stakes, shards of broken glass and heaps of highly flammable oil-soaked rubbish. In the center of this cruel arena, they left a clear bulls-eye of bare dirt, and in the very center of that, they placed a tall spindly three-legged stool affixed to a ten-foot length of rope, which could be yanked across the barrier quickly. DeWitt waddled over to inspect the preparations and nodded his satisfaction.

"Okay, boys, strike up the band!"

Even stone-cold sober, the regimental band would have been a trial on sensitive ears. Lurching drunk, they struggled to approximate the notes. After a raucous demonstration of their ineptitude, DeWitt called for silence.

"Bring forth the Rebel heckler!"

Still hooded, hands bound, the one-legged man was carried to a place where the circle of bayonets and stakes was overhung by a strong tree limb. After passing a rope around his chest and under his arms, his captors hoisted him up, yanked him forward until he dangled above the stool. DeWitt drew things out, step by step.

"Now, sir, a man with a long sword is going to cut the ropes from your hands. Just beneath your rear end is a stool. When you are comfortably seated, just give a tug on the slip-knot and the other rope will be pulled free from your upper body. Good, good! Comfortable, isn't it?" DeWitt gestured imperiously, and men with torches ran up to ignite the heaps of oil-soaked rubbish.

"Even a cozy fire to warm your bones! Now then, we come to the moment when I make you a proposition. My musicians will strike up a tune that generally lasts for five minutes, but it might last longer today, on account of their inebriated condition. When you hear them start to play, stand up as best you can and remove your hood. Then, start dancing—or hopping, in your case. If you can keep dancing and manage to stay upright for the duration of that tune, I will grant you a quick death by rifle fire. If you should lose your balance and fall, well, I've made a wager with the sergeant-major over there that it'll take you at least five minutes to die. He says you look like an agile fellow, and so has bet on seven minutes. I'm looking at my watch, and when I say 'Begin,' the stool will be pulled away, the music will start, and so forth . . . Everybody ready? Five . . . four . . . three . . ."

So fiendish was the brave veteran's predicament that many of the drunken colored soldiers were shocked into silence. DeWitt cried "Begin!" and the band commenced to play. The one-legged Rebel ripped the hood from his eyes, saw where he was, and gamely attempted to make some kind of hopping motions without losing his balance. His eyes were squeezed shut for better concentration, the muscles in his arms knotted as he tried to use them as balancing poles. DeWitt and his staff were clapping and shouting.

One second, Bonaparte Reubens was sitting very still in his chair, the next, in one fluid leap, he covered half the distance to the flaming barrier, whipped out his Colt, and shot the one-legged man in the heart. As he fell, he raised a hand toward Reubens and gasped "God bless you, sir!" Before the onlookers could grasp what was happening, Reubens spun a half-circle and pointed his pistol at Edmund DeWitt's face. The click of its drawn-back hammer was very loud. So was the sound of scraping chairs as dozens of Buffaloes, black and white, rose from their seats and gripped their own weapons.

"Damn your eyes, Reubens! You're a traitor to your race! Is your skin really black, or is that just minstrels' makeup."

"My skin is nowhere near as black as your heart, DeWitt, and if one of your men so much as cocks a weapon, I'm going to put a third eye in the middle of your greasy forehead."

"Do you mean to start an open battle between my regiment and your rag-tag bushwhackers!"

"If that's how far you want this insanity to go, just give the order. But if your pickled brain can still think, consider that most of your men are so drunk they can scarcely hold a weapon, much less aim one, while my 'rag-tag bushwhackers' have already got about three hundred rifles aimed at them—including a dozen Spencers. So let's you and I negotiate a bargain, DeWitt. I promise not to blow your ugly head off, if you'll swear that no harm will come to any of the white civilians, or to their homes."

"I must lock them up, Reubens, lest they escape and raise the alarm!"

"You may confine them in a barn or some other suitable place, but with ample food and water for several days. When this military campaign is finished—if that is still the word for what we're doing—my men will leave messages telling the Confederates where to find them."

DeWitt looked all around and instantly became more conciliatory; his soldiers were confused, dithering, and in a number of cases, barely able to stand upright. The Buffaloes aiming at them, however, were steady and cold-eyed.

"All right, calm down! We are all on the same side, aren't we? Let's lock up the women and kids and dig into some food! Then we'll dance and drink some more, and shout 'Hoorah!' for the Union!"

After exchanging a curt nod with Jack Fairless, Reubens reholstered his piece, yanked a half-full bottle of whiskey from the nearest colored soldier, and stalked off to sit by the creek alone.

Just after sundown, while most of DeWitt's troopers were still gorging themselves into a stupor, a shambling, thick-tongued group of engineers crossed the bridge and started burning down the turpentine facilities. Reubens watched the rising flames glimmer on the dark velvet creek. They were more beautiful in reflection than they were when he looked at them directly. When he heard someone approaching quietly, he was neither alarmed nor surprised.

"Evening, Corporal Sloane."

"How'd you know it was me, Boss?"

"I'm tired of telling you, but now that you are a corporal, my first name is 'Captain,' not 'Boss.'"

"Yessuh, I forgot. I gots a lot to learn, but I'm quick."

"That you are, son. Sit with me a minute. I'm curious as to what you think of this . . . spectacle. And of General DeWitt's proud colored regiment."

"It be a lot more complicated than I ever thought it could be. Them colored soldiers, I thought they looked mighty sharp in their uniforms, and marched like proud, free men. But back there at the bridge, they acted all confused and panicky, didn't hardly even shoot back, just stomped all over each other tryin' to run away. Fact is, they ain't killed a single Rebel soldier yet—just a bunch of old men and a cripple! And they had to get stinkin' drunk to work up enough guts to do *that*."

"They would be good soldiers, Elias, if they did not have a buffoon for a commander."

"Oh, I don't doubt that! But the way they was actin' today . . . don't seem like they 'complished anything except to do the kind of horrible things every nigger-hatin' white man's always *said* they would do, if they had a chance. 'Nother thing, Bo—Captain, Ah been talkin' to some of the local coloreds. They be mighty upset. One lady said to me, 'If this is what 'freedom' looks like, I been a fool for wantin' it so long!' "

"I spoke to some of them, too. They all told me they had been treated decently here. And they had good jobs waiting for them after the war, too. Turp-tapping isn't like pulling cotton, Elias. It's work that demands a lot of skill. Takes years to become experts at it. Those bonfires raging over yonder? That's their future going up in smoke. If we hadn't come along, the war would have passed this place by. This was a very happy village. Nobody ever went hungry, or cold, or had to cringe beneath a whip. They had a *skill*, a trade, and a good market for the things they produced. Tomorrow morning, all that will be ashes and memories. Where will they go? Who will hire them?"

Both men jerked upright at the sound of screaming women, whose shrieks and pleas for mercy just went on and on. Reubens buried his head in his hands.

"Wha . . . what's happenin' over there?"

"Those arsonists seem to have discovered where the people of Faison's Groves had hidden away all the young and pretty women. Soon as those boys get finished, they'll send word to the others. In thirty minutes, you'll see a parade of drunk, horny, troopers lined up to get their poke."

"Poke? You mean, them boys are forcin' themselves on white women?"

"Elias, your innocence will be the death of you. What they're doing is holding down a bunch of terrified white girls and raping them, over and over again. Dear God, I thought it couldn't get any worse, but when word about this gets out—and it will, son, it will—every white man in eastern North Carolina is going to come after us. If you think DeWitt can find interesting new ways to torture his victims, well, he's an amateur compared to a mob of white vigilantes bent on avenging the honor of Southern womanhood. If it looks like they're about to capture you, you'd better put a gun to your head before they do. DeWitt's going to rouse the beast in every white man's heart, and hundreds of Negroes will suffer for it, not even knowing the reason why. You had it right, Elias—'freedom' and 'slavery' only *sound* like simple things. Don't ever forget what you saw and heard here today. Now go back, please, and tell Colonel Fairless what's happening over there. Too late to stop it, but if he puts a strong guard on that bridge, he can at least prevent it from getting worse."

7:31 A.M., October 6, 1863

DeWitt had passed out before remembering to post sentries, so when the Buffaloes rode out of town, no one challenged them. No one even saw them except for a moon-faced Negro wet nurse who was suckling a newborn white infant, smoking a corncob pipe, and gently swaying in a rocking chair. Perceiving no hostility in her eyes, Jack halted and tipped his hat. "Good day, ma'am. Looks like you're the only citizen of Faison's Groves still left in town."

"Good mornin' to you, too, Buffalo Man. You'se right—me and this baby, we the only ones left here—everybody else, black and white, ran off soon as the soldiers got too drunk to notice. I can't run away on account I got the rheumatiz real bad, and the child's mother . . . well, she was one of the purty ladies those bucks had their way with last night, so she cut open her wrists with a piece of broken glass and bled herself to death."

"My men took no part in that madness, and those who did will be punished by their own army. You have my promise on that."

"I'll come haunt yo' ass if you don't keep that promise! Meanwhile, you want some friendly advice, Buffalo Man?"

"From a wise lady like you? I'd be a fool to turn it down."

"Yeah, you would be. Whatever yo' bizness is here in Pitt County, you'd best finish it quick and high-tail it back down the river. Telegraph wires in Tarboro been hummin' since dawn, and by ten o'clock this mornin', every man east of Raleigh's gon' be headin' this way to kill you. Don't matter if you innocent or guilty—if they see a blue coat and a black face, they goin' to string you up . . . or worse. So go do what you been ordered to, then git back to where you belong, 'cause that jackass DeWitt has poked his pecker into a hornets' nest."

Gum Branch was right where it was supposed to be, and the much-feared ironclad was exactly where Simpkins had speculated it might be: in a big inland cove, hidden from the view of anyone passing on the riverside road by a camouflaged screen of painted canvas and tacked-on brush. The vessel proved to be less than formidable, however: cheap-grade pine boards for hull and casemate, some ordinary shingles painted to look like armor plates, painted tree trunks for guns, no engine, and dangling from the phony oil-cloth smokestack was a sassy placard: *Howdy, Billy Yank! Sorry you came all this way for nothing!*

There was nothing to do but laugh. "I must admit," chuckled Bonaparte Reubens, "I admire their cheekiness."

"What now? Ride back and tell DeWitt his glorious quest for the ironclad has been a farce from the beginning?"

"Oh, why spoil his fun? Besides, Jack, we need to start writing affidavits about what we saw last night, while things are fresh in our minds. If we get crackin' on that, by the time DeWitt tells his version, Hawkins will already have a stack of *consistent* testimony he can lay before General Foster. Captains Manchester and Elliott, what say you?"

"What says I, is that I want to tarry long enough to put up another sign, one DeWitt and his boys can't possibly miss. One of you men, ride back to the bridge and yank down that Gum Branch sign, while I mix up some paint from this red clay and a little water.

So when the Buffaloes reformed on the riverside road and rode east, they left behind, impaled on a high branch so it could be seen by as many of DeWitt's men as possible, a helpful bit of information:

> *This Way to the Secret Rebel Ironclad!*

4:35 P.M., October 6, 1863

Urgent Dispatch taken by courier down to Little Washington:

> *From Major General Edmund DeWitt, Headquarters of the Tar River Expedition*
> *To General John Foster, Commander in Chief, Department of N. Carolina, New Bern*
>
> *I have this afternoon located the Rebel Ironclad, the destruction or capture of which was a prime Objective of this expedition. Our swift and successful ascent of the river had caused the enemy to abandon the warship and scuttle her without a fight. She is deep in the water and badly damaged, so that the enemy will not be able to salvage even her armament. The vessel is no longer a threat to our Cause in any way, and is in fact in such a ruinous state that no portion of her can be repaired. This part of our mission has been an unqualified success.*
>
> *Wishing you much glory and success in your campaign, the details of which I am most eager to learn upon my return.*
>
> *Yours & c.,*
> *Major-General Edmund DeWitt*

6:30 P.M., OCTOBER 6, 1863

After making a cursory and apoplectic inspection of the sham ironclad and tearing Red Elliot's mocking sign to pieces, DeWitt pushed his men toward Tarboro as hard as he could. Near sundown, he was forced to adopt a more cautious pace when the gunboat captains signaled that the river was too shallow for them to proceed any further.

When Tarboro came in sight, its defenses certainly did not seem formidable: some trenches and modest earthworks, manned by scared-looking teenage conscripts and a leavening of gray-haired Home Guard. DeWitt allowed the Frederick Douglass boys to have the honor of making the assault, after he wasted still more time bringing up his artillery and firing a ten-minute barrage. To their credit, the defenders stood their ground long enough to fire three disciplined volleys, and then withdrew in good order into the town itself. DeWitt was forced to regroup again before trying another attack; his men were exhausted, cranky, and had never made a night attack before. DeWitt tried to motivate them with a shrill but rather incoherent harangue: *Now is not the time to rest—push on now, and by sunrise, we'll be at our objective! Time is short and there is GLOW-REE up ahead!*

As darkness closed over Tarboro, Jack Fairless thought its narrow streets looked like an ambush waiting to happen. He sent some scouts on a wide patrol around the village, and they came back within the hour, confirming Jack's suspicions. Scores of armed men were pouring in from the west, fortifying the houses and setting up roadblocks. Many of them were excitedly waving a poster of some kind. A Buffalo scout had found one beside the road and when Jack read it, the ink was still tacky. After he read it, he hurried off to show it to Rush Hawkins.

A CALL TO ARMS!!

MEN OF NORTH CAROLINA! AVENGE THE SHAME OF YOUR VIOLATED WOMEN AND THE BRUTAL MURDERS OF YOUR FELLOW CITIZENS!!

Like wildfire before the hurricane, word has spread across the Eastern Counties of the unspeakable murders of innocent civilians and, most horrible of all, the savage wanton violation of helpless White Women in the village of FAISON'S GROVES on the night of October 5th, by drunken and depraved NEGRO soldiers, commanded by the mad Abolitionist General Edmund DeWitt! Draw sword, load musket, and to horse! These Black Devils are reported to be marching on the Tar River Bridge, and must be repulsed as Gnl. Foster was repulsed at Goldsboro.

But unlike General Foster and his troops, this Tar River expedition has conducted itself without a shred of Manly Honor, intent only on spreading

Terror, on inciting every docile Colored Man in their path to rise up against his lawful Masters, to slay poor farmers in their beds, to pitch their sobbing infants on their pitiless Bayonets, and to leave only smoking Ruins where once dwelt peaceful honest Christians!

A General Call to Arms is therefore in effect until these black fiends have been exterminated or driven from our soil. Their deeds are so barbaric as to place the perpetrators beyond protection of the Covenants of Civilized Warfare!

Strike them down, and show no mercy to any black man wearing blue who comes under your hand.

The lamentations of the Violated Innocents of Faison's Groves call out to every Man of Honor and Courage: AVENGE US!

This declaration of a General Emergency has been issued under my legally granted Powers as the Governor of this sovereign State, on the morning of October 6th, in the Year of Our Lord, 1863.

ZEBULON BAIRD VANCE, GOVERNOR

Hawkins felt his stomach lurch. DeWitt was still whipping up his darkies to charge straight through Tarboro, while every able-bodied man in Eastern North Carolina was loading his shotgun and forming a posse with his neighbors. As if matters needed to slide even closer to the abyss, dozens of Negro troopers had already sneaked into the presumably undefended town to pick up the odd gold watch, silver teapot, or whatever struck their fancy. Now a few of them were fleeing in wide-eyed terror, pursued by a growing volume of fire from the upper windows of darkened buildings, and by cries of "Faison's Groves!," "Remember Faison's Groves!"

Jack Fairless crouched beside Hawkins; he was shaken, angry, and scared.

"Has General DeWitt gone completely insane?"

"If not, he's just a cock-hair away from it. But he's also afraid of turning back now without being able to prove it was impossible to take that bridge for military reasons, on account of overwhelming Rebel superiority—he can't tell Foster he was chased out by the biggest lynch mob in Carolina history."

Just then, another officer joined them, saying: "Beg pardon, General Hawkins, but I have a suggestion."

"Who the hell are you?"

Jack Fairless introduced Adolphus Manchester. "Captain Manchester had come up with a pretty clever scheme, sir. It might be just the thing to bring DeWitt to his senses."

"If you've figured out a way to do *that,* Manchester, I am all ears . . ."

"You said DeWitt wants proof that he turned back because he faced impossible odds, not because of his own incompetence. If I were in his position, the one thing I would welcome more than any other is documented proof that the Rebels between here and that damn bridge now enjoy a truly overwhelming numerical superiority. Evidence, not just panicky impressions, that he can drop on Foster's desk.

"Well, I noticed a telegraph wire leading into town from the west. Tarboro must be in the same command district as the garrison at the bridge, so any messages concerning redeployments and reinforcements would automatically be copied to the telegraph station here. If I can sneak into town and follow that wire, it won't take long for me to locate that relay station and collect enough message copies to *prove* how badly outnumbered we are. There are so many armed civilians drifting around in the streets, all I need is a change of clothing, and I can blend right in. Colonel Fairless will put some of his best marksmen as close to the town as they can go, so if I have to make a run for it on my way back, I'll at least have covering fire. With a little luck, I can be in and out, with a case full of telegrams, in two hours."

"It sounds risky as hell, Manchester, but it might be our ticket out of this trap. By all means, give it a try. And may God go with you."

With or without God's help, Manchester found the telegraph office with little difficulty. In nondescript civilian clothes, he looked like any other armed vigilante who had come to Tarboro in response to the Governor's summons. His southern accent was authentic, so the few men who did speak to him had no reason to be suspicious. He did have to knock out the telegraphist, but he found plenty of suitable messages and was scrambling back into Union lines only ninety minutes after leaving them. By that time, however, the firing from Tarboro *("Faison's Groves!" Ka-blam!)* had grown so hot that DeWitt's and Hawkins' men had been forced to take cover in the abandoned Rebel trenches. Jack Fairless welcomed him back, then hurriedly escorted him to an old storage shed, where he could spread out the captured documents, and Hawkins could study them, in privacy and with plenty of lantern light.

These electronic gleanings proved to be substantial; they detailed the mobilization, routes of march, and estimated arrival times of Home Guard units, companies of regulars on their way to or from Virginia, training camp cadres, and ad hoc companies of clerks, signalmen, and supply sergeants. Most significant of all, there was up-to-date information about Foster's operations around Goldsboro. As predicted, Lee had dispatched General Donald Hackett's veteran division from Virginia, and because DeWitt's forces were unable to sabotage the railroad tracks, Foster had been forced to pull back toward New Bern before Hackett could outflank and possibly surround him. With Goldsboro once more secure, Hackett's division had turned around and was even now disembarking from its boxcars, up at the Tarboro bridge, and preparing to attack DeWitt.

"What can you tell me about this man Hackett and his division?" asked Hawkins.

"One of Lee's best men, and his troops are first-rate. At least seven thousand men and a regiment of cavalry. If they get here before we can retreat, DeWitt's darkies won't last twenty minutes. When you add Hackett's division to the gathering hordes of vigilantes, it seems we are outnumbered by at least seven-to-one at the moment, and by morning it'll be more like ten-to-one. Surely, this documentation ought to give DeWitt the excuse he's praying for."

"One would think so, Manchester, but the last time I saw DeWitt, he was mired in a total funk. It has finally dawned on him just how deep a shit-hole he's dug us into. He can't advance, he's scared to retreat without some kind of excuse that will convince Foster how hard he really, really, tried to carry out his orders, and he's beginning to see that his little Atilla-the-Hun performance at Faison's Groves has inflamed the entire state of North Carolina. You did a fine job, Manchester, and I won't forget it. Now, help yourself to this flask while I go show this information to DeWitt."

DeWitt studied the Confederate troop numbers with trembling hands, practically whimpering with gratitude.

"Well, obviously, we cannot be blamed for trying to take on a force ten times greater than our own, can we? I'll form my boys up right away, so we can reach the gunboats before daybreak. General Hawkins, your troops have suffered far less, so it is only correct for your men to act as the rearguard. Besides, your Buffaloes are experienced in setting ambushes, are they not?"

"Not against entire Confederate divisions, sir."

"Don't get snippy with me, Hawkins! All those snipers firing from Tarboro? It isn't your white soldiers they're shooting at!"

"This proclamation may have something to do with it, sir." Hawkins handed him Governor Vance's inflammatory "Call to Arms!" "By now, these have been distributed to every city, town, and farm in eastern North Carolina."

"I have no time to read advertisements, sir. The Sixth Massachusetts' will provide rear guard protection for my withdrawal, and the Buffaloes will provide flank security for everyone. Those are my orders! Your men occupy the former enemy entrenchments, so you should be able to fend off any attacks by the civilian bands in town. This General Hackett and his division can't possibly go into action before midmorning, so you have my permission to withdraw at any time after eight o'clock tomorrow."

October 7–10, 1863

Rush Hawkins had no intention of waiting until eight o'clock to start pulling his men back from Tarboro. He coordinated plans with Jack Fairless, who had worked out a sound fire-and-fall-back strategy for screening the slow-moving infantry. As soon as DeWitt was no longer watching him, Hawkins planned to begin leapfrogging the Massachusetts regulars back down the river road, one company at a time. His intention was to reach the vicinity of the becalmed gunboats before full daylight revealed empty trenches to the Rebels occupying Tarboro. Luckily, those men had not come out to fight during the night—they were waiting for Hackett's division.

At dawn, Hawkins was enormously relieved to find the U.S.S. *Sentinel,* faithfully waiting, the big Parrott on her bow slowly traversing. He hailed the captain from the riverbank.

"I am very relieved to see you! I was afraid DeWitt would simply commandeer both gunboats and leave us, as my sainted grandmother used to say, fucked-and-far-from-home!"

"DeWitt tried, sir, but we had a mysterious case of engine trouble. It's fixed now, fortunately. The 'Great Liberator' and his staff commandeered the *Allison* instead and took off downriver at high speed. That man's so yellow, he must glow in the dark. He tried to tell his infantry that he was going to bring more boats to pull 'em out, but some of them just threw rocks at him."

"How far ahead of us is the Negro column?"

"It isn't a 'column' anymore, General. It's a mob of scared men running for their lives. And they have good reason to be scared, too—about an hour ago, two companies of Rebel cavalry and a battery of guns passed by us on the north bank, hardly even glanced at us, riding so hard we didn't even have time to train a gun on 'em. They were goin' after the coloreds *only,* and from the firing we heard later, I guess they caught up with 'em. But don't worry—we will stick by you all the way, and my gunners are just itching to drop a Parrott shell on some Reb cavalry!"

"We are indebted to you, lieutenant. Could you please send a boat over—we have a few men seriously wounded."

"It's on the way, General Hawkins. I'm curious about one thing, though. How in the world did General DeWitt expect your two regiments to fend off a whole Rebel division?"

"He didn't. He wants us to be wiped out, because some of my men saw what happened at Faison's Groves."

"Just what *did* happen there, sir? Supply barge came up last night with some food and ammo for us, and they said they counted sixteen dead niggers hanging from trees on the other shore, and all of them had a sign hung around their necks that said: 'Faison's Groves.'"

"What happened there? Possibly the worst atrocity in the history of this state, which is why there's about ten thousand vigilantes on our tail along with Hackett's division. Well, we'd better get to marching before we encounter that gentleman in the flesh. Thanks for watching our backs, lieutenant!"

All morning, Buffalo patrols had seen small bands of armed men heading east. It would have been easy enough to wipe out most of them, but also a waste of time, for these impromptu Avengers of Southern Womanhood were not exactly elite soldiers—old men and young boys, discharged veterans with missing limbs, lung cases so far gone you could hear them hacking up blood from a hundred yards away—but they were numerous and fiercely determined to smite the invaders. They came on bony, half-starved horses, worn out mules, crammed into buckboards, hay wagons, drays, and phaetons, armed with a motley array of heirloom flintlocks, fowling pieces, varmint guns, and pitchforks. But they knew the countryside, and they were taking paths and game-trails Fairless and his men had not yet scouted. By noon, it became obvious where they were all heading: Faison's Groves. When they had collected the largest force available, they would cross the village bridge and attack the flank of DeWitt's column. At least, Jack surmised that to be their plan. But his scouts had told him that most of the colored soldiers, running as fast as they could still move, were already past this point on the map. Which meant the attack would hit Hawkins and his Massachusetts boys instead, and the Buffaloes felt duty-bound to protect their New England comrades.

Jack conferred with Reubens, Elliott, and Manchester; they all agreed Faison's Groves would have to be taken by storm at once. A methodical, dismounted attack would take too long, and cost too many casualties.

"Well, then, gentlemen, it appears that the Buffaloes are going to mount the first honest-to-God cavalry charge in our history. Swords and pistols only, don't stop for anything, just ride 'em down."

"I lost my sword!" griped somebody in Company A. Red Elliott leaped from his horse, picked up a long straight tree branch, and chopped a point on one end of it with his Bowie knife. He handed it up to the disgruntled trooper.

"Now you got a fuckin' *lance,* Sir Galahad."

With practiced stealth, the three companies fanned out, Jack and his color-bearer out in front. As he drew his saber, Jack looked at it in childish wonder and muttered: "You know, I've always wanted to yell this . . . CHAAARRGE!!"

The next two minutes were the most exciting Jack Fairless had ever experienced in combat. Screaming like demons, the horsemen covered the distance to the village so fast the defenders only had time to squeeze off a few rounds before the riders were leaping over their cowering backs, firing Colts at pointblank range, hacking and slashing with their sabers. Even the token "lancer" managed to skewer two men before his tree branch snapped. The defenders saw what was bearing down on them and took to their heels in all directions. It was all over in minutes.

Elias Sloane thought it was all a grand adventure, for this time, he *had* been armed, and he had killed at least two foemen. He was cantering up to Bonaparte Reubens, beaming with pride, but just as he drew near, one white-haired old Rebel, who had been hiding under a wagon, suddenly popped up, carrying a huge old bell-mouth blunderbuss, shouted: "This is for the women you raped, you filthy nigger!" and fired, just as he was all but shredded by minié balls. Elias went down hard.

Reubens was at his side quickly, rolled him over to examine the wound. It looked very bad—the blunderbuss must have been loaded with a brickbat, for it had torn a hole five inches wide in Elias's shoulder. But the wound was wider than it was deep, and not a major artery was severed. Reubens stuffed bandages into the hole, forced some whiskey between Elias's trembling lips, and slung him over a pack-mule's saddle.

"How bad?" asked Fairless.

"It's messy, but not deep. If we can get him to a surgeon in the next hour or two, he ought to make it."

When General John Foster realized how grave the situation had become along the Tar River, he sent gunboats and transports as fast as they could be refueled and turned around. Despite his standing orders from Meade, Foster told the ships' captains to ignore DeWitt's chaotic mob and head straight for the Sixth Mass. While four gunboats laid down a furious barrage that stopped the pursuing cavalry in its tracks, Hawkins' led an orderly evacuation. The Buffaloes emerged from the pine forest just in time to hitch a ride on the last two transports.

Cradling Elias in his massive arms, Bonaparte Reubens strode up and down the riverbank, bawling for a surgeon. Finally, a doctor in a blood-smeared leather apron responded, waving him toward a transport filled with groaning, bandaged men. Reubens did not wait for a boat—he waded into the river, holding Elias's head above water as though the young man weighed no more than a child. Elias was hauled aboard, and Reubens, shivering and matted with river-slime, followed the surgeon down into the stink and misery of his makeshift operating theater. After one of the surgeon's assistants sloshed a bucket of water over the operating table, the doctor rolled Elias over and held a lantern over his gaping wound. Probing with a blood-soaked forefinger, he voiced a hopeful diagnosis.

"The ball's a big un, but it's not deep. Didn't even break any bones. This boy's lucky. Hand me those forceps, and we'll just pull that rascal out while he's still groggy."

The projectile slid out with just a tug, followed by a welling of blood that was easily stanched.

"He's going to be all right, isn't he, doc? My friend just has a flesh wound, right?"

But when he cleaned the blood off the ball, the surgeon groaned. "Those savages!

"A dum-dum bullet, by Christ, and the first one I ever extracted."

"Is that bad?" asked Reubens.

"Look here—whoever fashioned this thing took a lot of time and trouble. See those grooves carved into the lead? Each one's been tightly wrapped in copper wire, covered with verdigris—the stuff that turns copper green. It's highly toxic if it gets in the bloodstream. These things have been outlawed by every civilized army. Not only do they cause massive tissue damage, but they're guaranteed to induce blood poisoning. If this man had been hit in the arm, I might have saved him by a quick amputation. As it is, the infection's already moving toward his heart. I'm powerless to help him."

"You mean, he's going to die?"

"Depending on how strong a constitution he has, it may take two hours or ten. But all I can do is make him as comfortable as possible, keep him dosed with opiates when the pain and fever start to peak. Eventually, he'll just close his eyes and drift away. Take some comfort from the fact that there are a thousand worse ways to die. You can stay with him if you like, Captain. And write down the next-of-kin information, where his family will want the body sent, that sort of thing."

"I guess I'm his next-of-kin, and Company B was his family. We'll take him to our headquarters and bury him with full military honors. He has earned them."

For the first time in his long, dark memory, Bonaparte Reubens began to weep.

General John G. Foster's raid on Goldsboro was the most aggressive action launched by the occupying Union forces on coastal North Carolina since Burnside's invasion in 1861. In the main, it was judged a success. Foster had fought and won a sharp little battle at Kinston, torn down two hundred miles of telegraph wire, burned a number of supply wagons and rolling stock, captured and burned an entire train full of supplies at Mt. Olive, and moderately damaged, though he never had a prayer of totally destroying, the vital railroad bridge near Goldsboro. His men had also located the elusive Neuse River ironclad, only to discover that it, too, was a hollow sham, an even cruder fake than the one deployed on the Tar.

On the last day of his orderly retreat, Foster began hearing vague rumors about some horrific actions committed by DeWitt's Negroes at an obscure place named Faison's Groves. Not until he reached his headquarters and confronted a mountain of telegrams, did he realize what a catastrophe DeWitt had spawned. Newspapers on *both* sides of the Potomac, scenting a sensational story and not content to wait for the actual facts, were printing lurid, wildly inaccurate accounts of a mass holocaust worthy to be ranked just below the Sack of Constantinople. All of the politicians who had pressured Meade to make Foster accept DeWitt's colored troops, and who had demanded DeWitt be given operational command, suddenly vanished into the bureaucratic woodwork. All Foster knew for certain was that DeWitt's Negro regiments had disintegrated into a terror-stricken mob, and the only thing preventing their wholesale massacre was a very skillful delaying action being waged by the once-maligned Buffaloes on the southern flank and the steady discipline shown by the Sixth Massachusetts in a succession of roadblocks on the main road. Foster acted quickly, sending additional barges, transports, and two field hospital units from New Bern to the Tar, hoping that sufficient ships would get there before the entire expedition was annihilated. With this catch-as-catch-can flotilla, he also dispatched his Adjutant General, along with a staff of pit-bull attorneys, to compile the facts, take depositions, and collect sworn affidavits. Their preliminary findings were enough to convince Foster that the Tar River campaign was more than a military disaster—it was a stain on the honor of the Union Army.

As soon as Foster arrived in Little Washington, the court-martial of Edmund DeWitt was swiftly convened, and after two days of stomach-turning eyewitness testimony, merciless in its verdict. The charges were as numerous as they were damning: inciting the wanton murder and rape of civilians, looting and destruction of private property, rank incompetence, severe intoxication while on active duty, cowardice under fire, and—the final nail in any officer's coffin—desertion of his command when said command was under imminent threat of attack by an overwhelmingly superior enemy force. The unanimous verdict of the court: Dishonorable discharge, forfeiture of rank and pension, and one year's enforced confinement in a lunatic asylum. DeWitt was dragged from the courtroom in restraints, sobbing and babbling. Both the Sixth Massachusetts and the First North Carolina Unionist Volunteers—whose performance during the campaign was universally praised—were recommended for a Presidential Citation. Rush Hawkins and Jack Fairless were recommended for decorations.

Fairless and Hawkins jubilantly congratulated each other as they left the courtroom.

"Imagine that, General! Jack Fairless, hillbilly bushwhacker, coming home with a shiny medal! My Pappy's gonna bust, he'll be so proud."

"Be careful who you show it to, Jack. After all, it's a *Yankee* medal. Some of your kinfolk might find that a bit unsettling."

"Shee-it, General, my clan don't have the slightest idea what this war's about or which side I fought it on. I can tell 'em it's from the King of Prussia, and they won't know any better."

General Foster broke out the whiskey as soon as the courtroom was cleared and locked. The testimony had been wrenching, but the man responsible had been fairly tried and properly punished. The U. S. Army had salvaged its honor. All in all, Foster thought, it had been a good end to a nasty episode. After unwinding with a few drinks, he left the courtroom and returned to his temporary headquarters in a relaxed and genial mood.

Which lasted just long enough for him to read the telegram handed to him by an orderly as he climbed the front steps.

Effective immediately, John Foster was relieved of command and ordered back to Washington for a new assignment.

The new Commander of the Department of North Carolina was General Benjamin F. Butler.

The Governor of North Carolina Sends his Condolences

DURING OUR WHOLE journey we encountered only one house inhabited by white Unionists which had never been plundered by the Home Guard or Rebel guerrillas . . . We were told so frequently—"My father was killed in those woods," or "The guerrillas shot my brother in that ravine"—that finally, these tragedies made little impression on us.

—Albert D. Richardson, correspondent for the *New York Tribune*

December brought soft, hazy mists up the river, veiling the woods and rice fields in a dreamy light that suited the contentment of Matthew and Mary Harper Sloane. The reclaimed happiness affected everyone. Outside of Pine Haven—somewhere—there raged a terrible war; but here the river flowed as it always had and the fields were tranquil at the start of their winter slumber. When Matthew returned, he brought with him a sense of normalcy. It might be an illusion; it was almost certainly a fragile temporary state, but everyone, black or white, welcomed it. Not long now, people began to say, until it was time for the great Christmas feast!

On Sunday, December 20, the holiday rituals began. A suitable Christmas tree had already been scouted, and on that frosty morning Mister Bright and a team of workmen chopped it down, loaded it into a big wagon, and brought it into the parlor. Aurelia and two of her house-girls climbed into the attic and brought down a trunk filled with the Christmas decorations collected by three generations. Energized by spiced punch and warm gingerbread, the house slaves passed ornaments to the Sloanes, who made a great fuss over finding just the right spot to hang each one. Slowly the tree began to sparkle and glow and chime with tiny bells.

By eleven o'clock that night, all the ornaments and decorations were in their customary places, the floors swept clean of bark chips and spruce needles, and everyone had gone to bed except for Mister and Missus Sloane. They lit pinecone candles, sipped champagne, and revived cherished memories that neither had been able to spare much time for on the past two Christmases. Their mood should have been harmonious, yet neither could ignore a sense of this tranquility being, somehow, *illicit.* Matthew broached the subject first: "Here we are, in a parlor that smells of Christmas, with a toasty fire and good champagne, and yet both of us are feeling—well, *guilty* isn't quite the right word, but it's close. It's the children, isn't it? Or rather, their absence."

"I was reluctant to bring it up, but now that we can afford the luxury of being sentimental again, I'm starting to miss them dreadfully. Of course, when they *were* here, I was often exasperated by them. I wish the pendulum of my maternal feelings did not swing to such extremes."

Matthew nodded. "This kind of setting has been known to bring on attacks of serious nostalgia. But at this date it would be impractical, if not impossible, to retrieve them from Sparkling Rock in time for Christmas. Besides, they might not *want* to come! Up there at Stepney's manor house, it's a different world. They can build *snowmen.*"

"But that's just it," said Mary Harper. "*This* world, this way of life, even this very house, might be gone by next Christmas. And whether history judges Pine Haven kindly or condemns everything we stood for, the children's roots to this land need to be stronger or else the future may blow them about like dandelion puffs."

"I agree, but the children have their hearts set on spending Christmas with Grandpa in the mountains. They surely won't have the chance to build a snowman down here! But I've given it a lot of thought, and perhaps there is a way we can 'have our candy-cane and eat it, too.' Why don't I leave the morning after Christmas and fetch them all back here for New Year's Eve? We could leave the tree and decorations just as they are, and have a second Christmas after they arrive. *Two Christmases!* What child could resist that offer?"

Mary Harper snapped her fingers. "I've just had an excellent idea. We must remind Stepney how much fun he used to have by dressing up as Santa Claus and passing out the presents from his 'magical toy bag.' " We still have that costume, in a cedar chest in the attic. Father could play Santa Claus again, and this time Henrietta and Francis Marion will be old enough to engrave that special moment on their memories."

Matthew rose to refill their champagne glasses. "All right, it's settled! I shall leave the day after Christmas. Meanwhile, this very night, you draft a telegram to your father, letting him know I'm coming. I wouldn't dare disturb the old badger by showing up unannounced. And be forceful—don't invite him, just *tell him* to pack his bags because he *will* be spending New Year's with us. After you've drafted it, Mister Bright and I will go to Wilmington, put it on the wire, and load up on presents. Everything falls into place!" They clinked glasses, kissed, and snuggled together.

There was a soft, sputtering music in the pine-log flames, and their resinous perfume evoked bittersweet memories of Christmases past, when the big house vibrated to dancing feet and guests sang carols with inebriated gusto—laughter, music, the joyous shrieks of children opening their presents, and Stepney with a pillow under his St. Nicolas costume, bellowing "*HO-HO-HO*" This had been a *good* place. Let the future bring what it would! If this were Pine Haven's last Christmas before the end of the world its inhabitants had always known, at least it would be a memorable finale.

But the future intruded sooner than anyone could have expected. Mary Harper spent the morning in the library, drafting her telegram to Stepney; Matthew made lists; Agrippa organized Mister Sloane's warmest clothes, so that Aurelia would have time to mend and clean them. After lunch, Matthew and Mister Bright climbed aboard the launch for their trip to Wilmington. They were about to cast off when a loud steam whistle made them jump and look down the Uhwarrie, where they saw one of the Navy's fast patrol cutters churning toward them at flank speed.

"What the hell d'you suppose that signifies?" said Fitz-John Bright.

Matthew thought back nervously to his last conversation with Branch. No; it could not be *that*—nothing short of divine intervention could have made that commerce raider ready so soon. Nevertheless, his stomach fluttered tensely—whatever this portended, it could not be good. When the cutter came to rest at Pine Haven's wharf, a smart-looking Confederate officer clambered ashore and introduced himself as Major Alton Bennett, aide-de-camp to Governor Zebulon Vance.

"Welcome to Pine Haven, Major. Clearly, you're on urgent business, but so am I. Whatever it is, can we deal with it as swiftly as possible?"

"It may be, sir, that reflection is called for rather than brevity. I have here a personal letter to you from Governor Vance, and my orders are to wait for a reply. I *am* sorry for the inconvenience."

Matthew took the envelope. It even *felt* like bad, or at least *serious,* news. Logic told him that only a matter of some gravity could have motivated the Governor of North Carolina to dictate a personal letter to Matthew Sloane, *retired* blockade-runner.

The Governor's Mansion, Raleigh
December 20, 1863

> *My Dear Captain Sloane:*
>
> *Please accept my heartiest congratulations on your recent release from enemy incarceration and permit me to add my portion of joy to that of your family, friends, and countless admirers upon the occasion of your return to North Carolina soil!*

But now, I regret to say, I must relate to you some very grave news, intelligence of which reached me only yesterday afternoon. Preamble cannot soften the message, so I lay it before you bluntly: your father-in-law, the honorable Mr. Stepney Harper, is dead.

Because of your long sojourn as Mr. Lincoln's guest at Fortress Monroe, you may not be aware of how badly the situation has deteriorated in our mountain counties. The peaks have become a haven for ever-growing numbers of deserters, conscription-dodgers, and partisan guerrillas fighting on both sides—but seldom acting under any officer's formal command, they are therefore beyond the constraints of military discipline, and, with increasing frequency, disdainful of the merciful customs of simple human decency.

On the afternoon of December 17th, one such band of barbarous men descended on Mr. Harper's beautiful estate, roughly demanding to be fed. Without stint, Mr. Harper laid before them an ample meal, and when the brigands had eaten their fill, their leader drew his pistol and shot Mr. Harper. What motivated this cold-blooded assassination no one can say. The grudges nurtured in these remote places sometimes last for generations, and are often as gnarled and deep as the roots of the very oaks.

According to the preliminary account I received, dispatched by my old and trusted friend Dr. Edward Swain of Asheville, the attackers were slain or driven off in large part because of the fierce resistance put up by your son, Francis Marion, who is credited with killing at least two, including the brute who shot his grandfather. I cannot provide more details at this time, but Dr. Swain is compiling the testimonies of all who witnessed these dreadful deeds. He and his lovely wife are at present caring for your children, neither of whom was injured in the fracas.

I have sent this sorrowful report to you by the hand of my trusted aide, Major Bennett. If you cannot detach yourself from your home at this time of the year, Bennett will faithfully transmit your wishes to me. But if it is possible for you to journey to Asheville and attend to the sad but necessary formalities, I would be honored to provide transportation for you in one of the Governor's private cars, which are very comfortably appointed. If you must make so sad a journey, at least make it in luxury! It is the least I can do to show my appreciation for your signal efforts on behalf of the Confederacy, and the honor that your bold achievements have brought upon this State.

Major Bennett is also a mountain man, from Ashe County, and he will serve as guide and bodyguard, for he knows the terrain and keeps up-to-date, as best anyone can, with the fluctuating loyalties in the mountain counties. As you probably know, the western railroad terminates at Morganton, so you will have to ride the rest of the way to Asheville. I have arranged for a very colorful military escort to meet you in Morganton, and accompany you to and from Asheville. I will say no more, as I want you to be memorably surprised! Permit me to close this heavy-hearted communication by stating that, although I did not know Stepney Harper well, I did several times have the pleasure of visiting his estate during the years immediately preceding the outbreak of war. The beauty of its natural setting was equaled only by the vigor, zest, and impish good humor of the man who built it. Convey to your dear wife my deepest sympathy for her loss.

Major Bennett will, presumably, hand you this document on the morning of December 22nd; the last train from Wilmington to Raleigh departs—assuming the tracks are not broken again!—at ten o'clock in the evening. Pack lightly, but for God's sake do not go unarmed!

If I can be of service in any other way, please do not hesitate to contact me.

With deepest condolences,
Zebulon Baird Vance

Matthew refolded the letter. Fitz-John Bright, ever discreet, had returned from escorting Major Bennett to the kitchen and was standing by.

"Mister Bright?"

"Aye, sir?"

"I shall not be shopping for presents in Wilmington after all. Please have Agrippa pack my three-day traveling bag with my warmest clothes. I'll be leaving with Major Bennett within the hour. It seems my trip to Asheville will take place sooner than I had planned."

To the amazement of everyone who had purchased a ticket, the train was only twenty minutes late departing Wilmington. By blustering, pulling rank, and vigorously waving a fancy-looking travel authorization signed by Governor Vance, Major Bennett managed to commandeer a semiprivate compartment. Matthew stayed up late, first talking Raleigh politics with the affable Bennett, until he dozed off, and then sitting in on a poker game, trying to hold his own despite the numerous complimentary drinks from well-wishers who were honored to meet "the legendary Captain of the *Banshee*."

When Major Bennett shook him awake, the train was crawling into the Raleigh depot. Groggily, Matthew pulled out his watch and saw that it was almost nine o'clock in the morning. He bolted upright.

"Did we miss our train?"

"Captain Sloane, if Zeb Vance wants to hold up a train until his guest of honor arrives, he will do it. In fact, that's his private car on the track next to us. Let's go aboard and make ourselves comfortable."

• • •

About ten miles east of Salisbury, the train squealed to an unscheduled stop. A few moments later, someone rapped briskly on the door. Matthew, being closer to it, opened the sliding panel and admitted a uniformed man in a stovepipe hat decorated with swirls of gold piping. He was the station-master, and he bore news that, due to a breakage in the track between Salisbury and the end of the line near Morganton, there would be a delay of "several hours" before the governor's car could proceed.

"Exactly how long, sir, is 'several hours?' " growled Bennett testily.

Uncomfortably, the man shrugged. "To judge from past experience, I would be deceiving you if I said there was any chance whatever of resuming your journey before dawn. Would you like for me to find accommodations for you and your friend in the town?"

"No, goddamn it! I've been to Salisbury before, sir, and I seriously doubt there are any rooms available that are more comfortable than this coach. Captain Sloane and I will bed down here. Please be so good as to inform the workmen that we are on official business for Governor Vance and that the governor would appreciate their maximum efforts."

"I will inform their foreman, sir. It's very cold out tonight, so perhaps your admonition will warm them to their task." So saying, the fellow doffed his ridiculous hat and withdrew, making sure to slam the carriage door as he stepped back on to the station platform.

"Am I mistaken, Sloane, or did that fellow just twit me with insolence?"

"I believe he did, yes."

"Damned railroad men! I'll wager that jackass makes more money a year than Governor Vance!"

After a few more drinks, both men decided to turn in, as they were not going to get much rest tomorrow. Matthew's sofa bed, once he figured out how to extend it, was covered with crisp clean sheets, and there were several layers of blankets. Warm and secure, just drunk enough to feel calm and resigned, he soon fell into a numb, dreamless sleep.

CRUNK!! SK-REEEE!!

Spine-bending jolts . . . steam whistle like buggy whip on raw brain meat . . . Matthew Sloane, *AWAKE!!* Four-forty-five, train in lurching motion . . . coach windows whited with frost . . . Major Bennett fixing coffee and biscuits in the little galley . . . *Where the hell am I*? Orientation came slowly. Matthew pressed his face against the nearest window and saw a livid streak of dawn, fragmented like a broken rose-window by the ice crystals on the coach window. Morning had come to western Burke County, where the rail line ended, and he could see the iron-hard domes of the Appalachians stenciled against a pale brittle sky. Sharp-tipped evergreens rose thickly on either hand. Just as the train began to slow for its final stop, the sun detonated over the long ebony hump of a summit, flooding the woods with frosty jade-green light, grainy as pollen, throwing into sharp relief every maculation of bark, every fleck of sparkling mica in the boulder clumps dotting the open meadows like the bones of prehistoric titans. A cluster of big, rough, pine-board sheds rolled past, one of them attended by a sentry who looked miserably cold and whose fixed bayonet glowed like an icicle.

"Well, this is it, Matthew, the literal end of the line. From here on, we ride . . . hopefully in some form of covered conveyance." Before donning his heavy coat, scarf, gloves and hat, Bennett strapped on a Colt and took down from an overhead compartment, a brand-new Henry repeater and an over-the-shoulder bandolier stuffed with fifty rounds. He turned toward Matthew and sharply asked: "You did bring a firearm, I presume."

Matthew patted his valise. "I am never unarmed when I venture outdoors, sir. Not even on my own porch."

Bennett nodded approvingly. While Matthew was strapping on his gun belt and struggling to push his sleeves through a heavy Royal Navy watch jacket, he said: "In his letter, Governor Vance said something about a 'colorful' military escort. Could you enlighten me?"

Bennett chuckled. "I could, but that would spoil the surprise."

Outside their coach, the evergreen-spiced air was crystalline, achingly pure, sharp as a slap on the cheek. Matthew was unused to such cold, or to the sight of deep snow drifts piled in places not touched by the sun's direct rays. He felt incongruously like an explorer about to enter a harsh, exotic land, not a North Carolinian setting foot on native soil. He blinked against the dazzle of winter sunlight striking ice. At first, the only sound he heard was the ticking of the locomotive cooling down. A moment later, he discerned a restless chiming that he did not, for a few seconds, recognize as the hoofbeats of numerous horses, rising in volume, then suddenly drowned by a wild and savage outcry: *"Yip! Yip! Yah-EEE!"* He was astonished to see approximately twenty Indians, obsidian eyes flaring, their long pigtails decorated with tatty clumps of feathers, come charging out of the forest in his direction.

"My God, we're attacked by redskins! Draw your weapon!"

Bennett guffawed and slapped his hip in satisfaction.

"Did the Governor not promise you a 'colorful escort'? Relax, Sloane, they are on our side."

As the Indians wheeled their lean ponies in a circle just inches from him, Matthew realized that they were indeed clad in Confederate uniforms, or at least in such pieces of uniform as suited their fancy. Now, too, he observed a white man, tall and lantern-jawed, who was obviously their commander. The man rode forward and exchanged salutes with Major Bennett.

"Colonel William Stringfield, assistant commander of Thomas's Legion, at your service, gentlemen. I've managed to locate a stagecoach in fair condition. Though our road be exceedingly rough, it will have to do."

Both travelers shrugged. The coach had clearly seen better days, but at least it would dull the wind's sharp edge. Resigned, they climbed aboard and wrapped themselves in some rather fragrant bearskin robes the Indians provided. When the two white men were tucked in, a tall Cherokee sergeant, much tattooed and decorated with ritual scars on his cheeks, saluted and climbed into the driver's seat. He nodded with great solemnity at his passengers and showed them his sawed-off shotgun. Then he stabbed a finger at his chest and proclaimed: "Sergeant Unaguski. Man-who-guards-your bodies! Yankee bushwhacking mule fuckers attack, I fight, maybe die, to save you." The Indian was pointing at Major Bennett, presumable because he wore a uniform and Matthew did not. After the Indian gave Matthew a more thoughtful second look, he added: "You, too, mister—if there is time."

With that, the Indian snapped the reins and barked a few words in his native tongue, which sufficed to set the mules in motion. Although the way was rocky and steep, they made fair time. Matthew was fascinated by the Indian troopers, and as they bounced westward, Bennett filled him in on their story.

"White speculators wanted the Cherokee lands and when the tribe refused to oblige them, Andrew Jackson brought in the Army, broke their attempt to mount armed resistance, and imprisoned all the militant chieftains and their followers. Then he evicted three-quarters of the tribe to a squalid puke-hole of a reservation way out in Oklahoma. Eighty percent of the Cherokee who started on that senseless and punitive trek died along the way—the ones who survived called that march 'The Trail of Tears'. After that, only a couple of thousand Cherokee were left in these mountains, peaceful but poor as dirt. The land speculators kept nibbling away at their territories, until one white real-estate baron 'got religion' and started fighting for them in court. He was Will Thomas, the colonel in command of these troopers, and the only white man I ever heard of who was made an honorary Indian chief!

"When the war broke out, Thomas traveled to Richmond. He offered to equip and organize the Cherokee braves into a Confederate 'legion,' and to do it at his own expense, in exchange for Davis's promise to pass laws after the war that would protect the tribe and all the land it still inhabited. Best deal Jeff Davis ever got! There are three small battalions of the Legion, but each one of them is worth a regiment of regulars in this terrain. Nobody can match those braves when it comes to tracking, long-range scouting, and safeguarding the Tennessee border from here down to Georgia. Wasn't for Thomas's Legion, the Unionists across the state line could come and go as they pleased."

"Do they really understand what the Confederacy is fighting for?" asked Matthew.

"No more than a skunk can read Homer," chortled Bennett. "The

Cherokee went to war more or less because Will Thomas *asked them to.* But it's my personal opinion that their main reason for taking the oath was because of all the old scores they had against white men in uniforms. Now, by putting on a *gray* uniform, they have the legal right to kill anybody in a blue one! You might say, being Rebel soldiers gives them a chance to do something the whole tribe's been itching to do ever since Andy Jackson stomped all over 'em. One thing's for sure: the white Unionists in Tennessee are scared shitless of these boys."

Matthew was about to ask for more particulars, but he did not have to; the reason for the Unionists' fears was quickly demonstrated when one of the Cherokee troopers from the advance guard, having evidently spotted something suspicious up ahead, turned his horse around and rode back to report to Colonel Stringfield, passing very close to the side of the coach where Matthew was sitting. As the warrior rode by, Matthew observed two curious objects dangling on leather thongs from his saddle horn: shriveled clumps of fur encrusted with faint dark maroon streaks that looked very much like spots of old dried blood. At first he thought the brave was carrying the mummified corpses of two small rodents. This struck him as a curious sort of trophy for a warrior to keep; the bearskin robes bespoke of mighty hunting indeed, whereas a couple of dead squirrels were hardly the stuff of tribal legends. But after a moment's reflection, another thought struck him and made him shiver. He tapped Bennett's shoulder and pointed to the "trophies" before the rider passed beyond sight.

"Good God, Major, were those . . . could those possibly be . . . I mean . . ."

Bennett nodded sagely. "Human scalps? Yep, that's what they are all right. Now you see why these boys are such a caution to the Yankee troops across the state line."

"But that's barbaric! Not to mention being completely against the rules of war!"

Major Bennett gave him a look of withering indifference. "In the first place, *nothing* that goes on in these mountains is governed by 'the rules of war' or by any damned rules at all, for that matter. In the second place, these Indians have been taking scalps for the past two thousand years or so and aren't going to change their ways just because some white officers' rule book says it's not 'civilized' to do that kind of thing. If it soothes your sensibilities, Matthew, the practice is for the most part performed only on enemies who are already dead. I've heard tell that sometimes the Legion warriors bend that custom a little, but I suspect that's just Yankee propaganda, don't you?"

Sunset brought swiftly falling temperatures and to low-land farmer Matthew Sloane, a new definition of the word "cold." The old road grew rougher and rockier as it followed the ebony turbulence of the French Broad River into higher ranges. Matthew was grateful when Bennett opened his valise and produced a bottle of whiskey, or as he described it, "a liquid campfire." By the time the two men had consumed all but the bottom inch, they were drawing close to Asheville. Matthew had fallen into a doze, lulled by alcohol and the rumble of the coach wheels on a better-graded stretch of road, when Major Bennett jostled him awake for his first glimpse of the town: a scribble of lamp light in a broad, dark valley. Ahead was a sturdy plank bridge spanning a foaming tributary of the French Broad River and on its other side, standing around a huge campfire beneath a wind-whipped Confederate flag, stood a small group of armed men.

"Yonder is our welcoming committee—Doctor Swain and a few of the local Home Guard. While you were asleep, one of the Injuns rode ahead and told 'em we were coming. I hope they haven't been standing out there too long—we might have to use an ice pick to get 'em moving again."

"When can I speak to my children?"

"That'll be up to Doctor Swain. There's no telegraph out of Asheville, so he is the only man who knows what really happened at the Harper estate. I suspect you will want to learn more about it before talking to your children. After we thaw out, I reckon me and the Indians will do some hunting, maybe check a few of the local caves for outliers, that sort of thing. But we'll be close by, so when you're ready to go home with the young-uns, just give a holler."

As soon as the coach stopped, it was surrounded by men who smelled well-fortified against the cold and who welcomed them with bear hugs and hearty back slaps. Matthew stomped around to restore circulation in his legs, until all the boisterous how-de-do quieted down. Bennett spoke softly to one member of the welcoming committee and peeled him away from the group, leading him to Matthew.

"Matthew Sloane, may I present one of Zeb Vance's oldest and dearest friends, Doctor Edward Swain. Doc, this here is the famous blockade-running buccaneer Captain Matthew Sloane, of whose bold exploits you may have read."

"Indeed I have, sir! Welcome to Asheville, although I wish your visit were occasioned by happier circumstances. Come, please, my office is not far and it's warm inside. We can talk there in privacy and comfort."

Inside the doctor's office, a small potbellied stove glowed a dull cherry-red, filing the room with delicious warmth. Matthew stripped off his layers of winter clothing, toasted his hands by the stove, then accepted a big mug of coffee and sat down in what he assumed was the patient's chair, while Swain reached into a compartment of his big roll-top desk and retrieved an inch-thick stack of foolscap. With an expression of great solemnity, he handed these papers to Matthew.

"These are the affidavits of everyone who was present on that ghastly day, including the black folks; all are honest people, and their accounts are consistent. You're welcome to read every word, but there's a lot of repetition, so for now it might be best if I just summarize the story, since I know it by heart now and I'm sure you're anxious to see your children." Swain opened a drawer and placed a bottle of whiskey on the desk between them. "It is not an edifying tale, Mister Sloane, and if you want the advice of this old country doctor, you will find it less painful to hear if you sweeten your coffee with some of this Ashe County mountain dew."

Matthew held out his cup and Swain poured a healthy dollop of suspiciously clear liquid into the coffee. "This stuff will make the dead jump up and square-dance. Now, let me start by setting the scene for you . . ."

"Things had grown quiet around here by mid-December. The outlier bands had gone into winter quarters, deep in their hidey-holes. It's been this cold since the day after Thanksgiving, so only the most urgent need or the most desperate errand would cause a man to venture far from his hearth. Winter storms boiling over the Blue Ridge, some of 'em gathering strength all the way from the Great Plains. Up on the heights, the winds can reach hurricane force, and on the day preceding the events of December seventeenth, the whole county was hammered by the worst blizzard in years. Not many folks were out and about.

"In the mansion at that time, along with Stepney and the two children, were two guests from Duskin, over in Hamilton County: Mister and Missus Randolph Clark, staunch Confederates and wealthy landowners. Not bad people, but like most rich town dwellers, they felt vastly superior to their poor, rural neighbors.

"Because the weather had been so vile, Stepney was startled when six unknown men knocked on his door, requesting food and shelter—no matter where they came from, they were a long way from any traveled road. He recognized none of the men, and was instantly suspicious, for they were a rough-looking bunch, hard-eyed and well-armed. Five of them spoke no word of greeting but just watched impassively while their leader did the talking, all five of them with hats pulled low and mouths wrapped in scarves, they might have been carved from stone but for the jets of steam coming from their nostrils. But their leader, a rangy man with close-set blue eyes and a bristling beard streaked with ice, was well-spoken and courteous. He apologized for the intrusion, explained that he and his men were on Confederate business. He hinted that they were carrying information about an impending raid by the notorious Unionist guerrilla chieftain George Kirk, whose usual headquarters were in Tennessee and who had launched a number of daring raids between April and October, terrorizing Confederate sympathizers, stealing livestock, and even ambushing a Rebel pay wagon up near West Jefferson. 'Ol'

Kirk,' the leader explained, 'is planning to strike again, in the dead of January, when no one expects it, and we have knowledge of his plans.' If Mister Harper—and how did this fellow know Stepney's name?—would permit him and his men to enjoy some food and warmth for an hour or two, they would be on their way again and mightily grateful for his Christian charity. The man politely doffed his hat and, despite his wild, travel-stained appearance, his manner and speech were those of an educated man. Granted, the gentlemen with him were disreputable-looking, but so would anybody compelled to travel in such weather. Stepney was by nature a hospitable man, and would not have turned any wayfarer from his door in such brutal weather. But here were *six* men, and doubtless he figured that a blunt refusal was the one thing guaranteed to anger them. Before inviting them in, however, he tried to learn the leader's name, but the man refused to divulge it, saying that if Unionist partisans later appeared, asking about him, Mister Harper would be able to claim ignorance without lying. 'You may call me Mister Brown,' he said, 'if you really need a name. 'Tis as good as any other.'

"It was two-thirty in the afternoon, and the white folks had long since finished eating. But there were still plenty of leftovers in the kitchen, and Stepney ordered out a generous sampling of everything for his mysterious guests. The men behaved correctly, cleaning the snow from their boots and removing their hats before entering the parlor, bowing to the ladies and finding seats on the periphery of the family gathering. Their leader shook hands with Mister Clark and made a special point of jollying up to your son, Francis Marion, calling him a 'fine-looking young Rebel soldier,' perhaps because he saw how the boy went stiff with apprehension the moment the strangers filed through the front door. Francis Marion did not respond to these overtures. Without actually being rude, he made it plain that he had no wish to banter with these interlopers.

"Strange to tell, but the atmosphere in the parlor became rather festive after a time, while the visitors waited for their food to be warmed up. The leader asked permission to entertain everyone at the upright piano and proved to be a surprisingly accomplished player. One of his men produced a mouth-organ and joined in with a spirited accompaniment. Then, much to her husband's discomfiture, Missus Clark was persuaded to join the leader in a couple of sprightly duets. By the time the food was laid out, the mood had become much more relaxed.

"When the meal was ready, the strangers dug in, and while they wolfed down everything in reach, their leader engaged Stepney and Mister Clark in spirited conversation—mostly generalities about the weather and the lamentable state of disorder in the region, nothing overtly partisan. But if the adults were starting to take the strangers at face value, Francis Marion felt his skin prickle each time he glanced at them. He simply knew that these men were acting a charade, even though, for the moment, their behavior was quite civil. He feigned a yawn, excused himself for a nap, coaxing Henrietta to follow him by promising to read her a story. By doing that, he may have saved her life. Once the children were alone, he told Henrietta to take a letter to Mister Coggins, the overseer, who lived in a cabin next to the barn and who had been caretaker at Sparkling Rock for many years. Henrietta thought this was some new kind of game, so she readily agreed. However, the note actually said—well, here, read it for yourself:

> *Help Mister Coggings, there are six strangers in parlor—I think maybe bushwhackers out to rob Grandpa! Pls arm yourself & any other man you trust & stay close but don't let them smell a rat! Put Henry-etta somewhere safe, too. I am fetching Grandpa's pistols just in case. Pls hurry! Francis M. Sloane.*

"While Henrietta ran off to deliver the note, Francis Marion quietly went into Stepney's bedroom, where the old man always kept a loaded brace of Colts in a bedside drawer. He hid them in recessed sconces just outside the door from the parlor to the main hall, out of sight but within easy reach. Alerted, Mister Coggins took Henrietta to one of the Negroes' cabins, placing her in the care of Tom Plunkett's wife. Taking this trusted old retainer with him, Coggins went to the closet where Stepney stored his hunting gear. There he loaded Stepney's 'bear killer,' an Austrian Mannlicher chambered for an enormous sixty-two caliber ball and charged with a powder cartridge the size of a bread loaf. He handed Mister Plunkett a double-barreled shotgun, which Plunkett loaded with double-ought buck. Finally, Coggins stuck his own pistol in his belt, a slim, handy thirty-two caliber 'stagecoach pistol.' Thus armed, the two men snuck into the hallway by detouring through the kitchen, where they cautioned the cook and maids to do nothing that might alarm the strangers. Then they took positions just to the side of the parlor door, near the place where Francis Marion had secreted the Colts. They waited and listened.

"After half-an-hour of gorging, the strangers had picked the platters clean, and were smiling and patting their full bellies. Their period of welcome was at an end, however, and Stepney made a point of glancing at his watch, then saying: 'If you gents would like, I can have some leftover chicken and cornbread wrapped for your saddlebags. I do not know your ultimate destination, but you should start riding if you want to reach it before dark.'

"The leader favored him with a big vulpine smile.

" 'Mister Harper, we thank you most kindly for that grand repast. But honesty compels me to say that this house, in fact, is our "ultimate destination" and we aim to stay on a while yet. I figure a rich old bastard like you must have a lot of valuables in this grand place, and we intend to relieve you of some of them before we move on.'

"Frigid silence fell upon the room. It was clear from Stepney Harper's expression that he understood the gravity of the mistake he had made in offering hospitality to these men. But he was proud! He cast a glare of such withering scorn at the bandits' leader that, had he been capable of feeling shame, he would have withered on the spot.

" 'Have you no sense of gratitude or decency?'

"The leader shook his head rather tiredly. 'Not a shred, your honor. We've been on the run and fighting for our lives for almost two years, and while we did not start out as bad men, we have become hard merely to survive.'

" 'I beg of you not to bring your troubles into this house!'

"The leader rose and glared like a hawk diving on a chipmunk.

" 'Well, you pompous old Rebel windbag, you got more trouble now than you can say grace over.' He glanced left and right at his henchmen. 'Ready, boys? Then draw!'

"From beneath their coats and inside their boots, the riders pulled out revolvers, and fired a wild fusillade. The leader and two others shot first at Stepney, striking him in the abdomen, the rib cage, and the left shoulder. He fell across the dining table, howling in agony, his blood pulsing into the empty plates. Two other outliers fired at Mister Clark and his wife. With admirable courage, she flung herself in front of her husband and caught a ball square in her face, which collapsed like a rotted melon. Clark had learned never to travel unarmed, so as his wife's disfigured body fell away, he came up shooting with a Remington and managed to wing one of the gunmen before collapsing, riddled by four bullets. The brigands roared terrible oaths and feverishly began reloading.

"Lunging to grab his two secreted pistols, Francis Marion cried: 'Now, Mister Coggins, before they can reload!' And so help me God, Francis Marion came out with both guns blazing. Coggins testified that the boy showed unbelievable coolness and presence of mind, for he did not shoot wildly, but advanced a few paces until he was pointblank from the cursing, frantically reloading gunmen. Methodically, alternating a shot from one gun and a shot from the other, he pumped two balls into one bandit's pelvis and three into another's chest. Plunkett charged in behind the boy and emptied both shotgun barrels at the leader, who was already running for the front door. The man's heavy coat absorbed some of the charge, but he was knocked by the impact clean through the front door glass, gashing himself all over. Ignoring his cries for help, the three uninjured scoundrels high-tailed it for the woods. Coggins went after them with that big-game rifle, after first tossing the unfired stagecoach-pistol to Francis Marion, whose own guns were now empty. When Coggins fired that Mannlicher, the blast from it dropped all the icicles from the gutters! The man he was aiming for caught that massive slug in the center of his back, the force of it lifting him off the ground and spinning him around in midair like a screaming acrobat. Francis Marion aimed carefully with both hands and fired all six shots at the other two fugitives. One, he struck in the buttocks, knocking him ass-over-nosey, but the range to the remaining fugitive was long, so the boy only nicked him before he disappeared into the trees. Mister Plunkett had by now reloaded one barrel of his shotgun, and then he calmly walked over to the man whom your son had plugged in the nether cheeks, rolled him face up, and when the man opened his mouth to plead for mercy, Plunkett thrust the muzzle against his tonsils and fired.

"All the outlaws were down or fleeing. Their leader, the back of his coat peppered with buckshot holes, kept pulling his head up from the snow, gasping for air. Coggins straddled his back, clouted him on the head with an ornamental rock from the garden, then used both hands to push his face deeper into the snow until he drowned.

"Nothing could be done for the Clarks: both lay dead, the husband slumped over his wife's ruined face as though trying to comfort her. Stepney Harper clutched at the gash torn in his bowels, exploring the wound with his fingers. All color drained from his face when he understood: he was badly gut-shot, and would surely die. To keep from screaming, he clamped his jaws on the wooden handle of a carving knife. Mister Coggins, ashen and trembling, ordered two of the slaves to carry Mister Harper to his bed. Everyone could see that his death would be slow and painful. The finest surgeon in the world could do nothing more than give him laudanum for the pain. In lieu of that, Coggins brought a bottle of the strongest whiskey in the house, and Stepney drank it down with gusto, even though he knew most of it was just running out onto his bedsheets.

"Coggins tried to push Francis Marion out of the room, hoping to spare him this awful sight, but the boy, though trembling and weeping, responded bravely: 'I will not leave my grandfather while yet he lives. I wish I had shot all of them while they were eating!'

"Game to the last, Stepney managed to smile. 'So do I, boy, so do I . . .'

"By twilight, a merciful delirium had set in, and Stepney Harper held long, rambling, intimate conversations with his dead wife. At least Mister Harper was thereby distracted from his agony. Gradually, the muttering ceased and it seemed certain he had lapsed into final unconsciousness. But just before the end, he opened his eyes and spoke in a calm, utterly lucid voice. He asked for Francis Marion to grasp his hand, and the boy, bravely immersing himself in the stench and horror of the old man's wounds, complied and even managed a loving smile. 'I am here, grandfather,' he said. Then Stepney Harper smiled gently at the boy and said: 'You fought like a lion today, lad. I die more peacefully knowing my blood flows in your veins.' And with that, he closed his eyes and went to meet God."

• • •

"What happened to the last bandit," whispered Matthew, "the one who was only nicked?"

"Well, as soon as the news reached town, we formed a posse and brought out the dogs, followed the blood drops to a creek, and there we lost his trail. He must have waded in that creek for a long time. If there's any justice, he also contracted frostbite! Of course, he may have found shelter among the local Unionists and survived, so we're keeping our eyes peeled."

"Any idea who they were, where they came from . . . or why in God's name they chose to plunder Stepney Harper's house?"

"Because they thought they could, is why. Also, maybe, some old grudge—the leader knew Stepney well enough to call him by name, remember? It doesn't take much of a motive to kill someone these days, Mister Sloane, not in the kind of war we've got up here in the mountains. Most likely, we'll never know for sure. They came out of the fog like evil wraiths, and died the deaths of rabid dogs. If not for the foresight and courage of your son, they would have looted or destroyed or taken control of the estate for their own nefarious purposes. They would have killed your children, too, I believe—why should they have even that one scruple left?"

"Tell me—can this man Coggins and the remaining staff, white and black, be trusted to stay on at the estate, not help themselves to the silverware?"

"I'd stake my life on it. Stepney liked to sound grumpy, but it was mostly just bluster. He was fair and square with anyone who gave him an honest day's work. Many of the Negroes wept, too, when they learned he was dead, and their grief was real, I can assure you."

"And none of the blacks have run away since that day?"

"My dear Sloane, it is the middle of winter in the Appalachian Mountains! Where in God's name would they go? They don't exactly blend into the scenery . . ."

"Do you think Coggins is willing to stay and manage the place?"

"He may want to move a few of his relatives on to the property—safety in numbers, and all that—but, yes, that family is poor but honest as the sunrise. He has been there since the foundation stones were laid. He also risked his life to defend the place; I would say his qualifications are excellent."

Matthew was pacing now, trying to prevent himself from going into shock by concentrating on small, practical details.

"Sparkling Rock now belongs to my wife, and I want it well-defended, so no desperadoes can ever set foot on its floors again. I mean to set up a small but permanent garrison there. Excluding those already serving in the Home Guard, are there some other trustworthy men? Older, perhaps, or discharged veterans who can shoot one-handed, or one-legged for that matter?"

"I can think of a half-dozen such men without trying. But they'll need provisions, ammunition, and better weapons than the Home Guard has."

"I can arrange that easily enough. Although it may take a while, I can send a crate of Spencer repeaters—I'll even throw in a few for the Home Guard. Understand, sir, I don't mean this to be undertaken as an act of civic virtue . . ." Matthew bent over his baggage, rummaged for a moment, and then extracted a small but very heavy leather bag. He opened it with a flourish, and spilled some of the contents on to Swain's examination table.

"My God, that's—"

"—*Gold,* my friend, the real stuff. British sovereigns, to be exact. Each one worth more than a trainload of Confederate shin-plasters. Here's two hundred and fifty, which should be more than enough to get things started. Naturally, if you agree to handle the arrangements, you'll be well compensated, too."

"No, sir, I'm comfortable enough and my needs are minimal. However, since you have the connections to get your hands on some Spencers, the town is awfully short of medical supplies . . ."

"Make a list of what you need; I'll have everything shipped to you as soon as it can be brought in aboard one of my runners. I owe you a great deal for compiling these affidavits, and even more for looking after my children."

"Speaking of which, why don't you go have a look at them? We can settle all this business tomorrow."

Edward Swain and his wife, Matty, had wanted a son, but the Lord, displaying His persistent love of irony, had sent them three girls, all of whom had married early and well and were now dispersed in Atlanta, Salisbury, and Charlotte. Their husbands, to a man, were in Confederate service and, so far as the Swains knew, all were still whole and in good health. Not for three years had any of their grandchildren been able to visit Asheville, but the Swains maintained a children's room, complete with toys and stuffed animals. No better sanctuary could have been found for the Sloane children, who had made themselves perfectly at home. Indeed, they had already taken to calling Missus Swain "Aunt Matty." Dr. Swain had kept a close eye on Francis Marion. In the past three years, he had counseled dozens of discharged veterans, and he had learned that not all combat wounds could be seen on the flesh. But so far, he explained to Matthew as they mounted the front steps of the Swains' home, Francis Marion had displayed no signs of delayed nervous hysteria or morbid melancholy. As far as Swain could tell, Francis Marion was just a normal twelve-year-old boy—who happened to have bested three hardened desperadoes in a close-range gunfight. Of all the things that might have troubled him, he seemed most concerned about the well-being of his little sister. Fortunately, Henrietta had not seen any of the butchery in the parlor; all she knew was that Grandpa "had gone to heaven."

When Swain finally brought Matthew Sloane into the presence of his children, they were profoundly, cherubically, asleep, the girl snuggling a doll, the boy—with what Matthew regarded as grim appropriateness—tightly clutching a wooden soldier.

"There's a trundle bed, Mister Sloane, over near the wardrobe," whispered Matty Swain as she ushered him into the nursery. "It might be a little snug for a man your size, but I figured you would want to sleep with the wee ones, so they can see you when they first awaken. When I told them you were coming to fetch them home, they were so overjoyed that I had a hard time getting them to sleep. Rest as long as you wish, and stay as long as you like, until they're ready to leave. I serve a bodacious breakfast, and I'll keep it warm until you're all ready to eat. God bless the tykes—it breaks my heart to think of what they've been through. And I've grown exceedingly fond of them. I'll miss them when they go."

Snuffling quietly at the thought of parting with her newly adopted fosterlings, Mrs. Swain lit a candle on the wardrobe and bade Matthew goodnight, closing the door softly as she left.

At first, Matthew simply went from one bed to the other, bending close to his children, inhaling the sweet fragrance of their tender flesh, gently touching their hair, his emotions boiling. Finally, sheer exhaustion overcame him and he curled up on the narrow trundle bed, fully dressed, covering himself with a patchwork quilt. Within seconds he fell into a deep, black, dreamless sleep.

He was awakened just as dawn was tinting the surrounding hills. Francis Marion was thrashing in the grip of a nightmare, uttering sharp little cries of distress. *Dear God,* prayed Matthew Sloane, *please spare my son the memories of what he has seen and done!*

He remembered, with a pang of grotesque irony, how much Francis Marion had enjoyed dressing up in his little Confederate uniform and strutting around with his wooden sword, skewering hundreds of imaginary Yankees; how often and how passionately the boy had declared his hope that the war would not end until he was old enough to be a "real soldier." Well, now he was. He had unhesitatingly defended his grandfather against men who were little more than cold-blooded brutes, gotten the drop on them, and killed three of them with such cool presence of mind and unflinching bravery that no veteran infantryman could have planned smarter, faced death more fearlessly, or shot straighter. My God, Matthew thought, how could this *child* have even lifted two loaded Colts, much less aimed and fired them with such deadly precision, even as the air around him was full of flying lead and his grandfather lay screaming nearby with his guts blown open? As the boy's nightmare reached a crescendo, causing him to twist and writhe in his blankets, waving the wooden soldier like a club, Matthew debated whether to waken him.

But suddenly Francis Marion grew peaceful once again, and as the first gentle saffron wash of dawn stole into the room, Matthew saw that his eyes were open and he was indeed awake, transfixed by the silhouette of his father, who had now lifted his legs from the trundle bed and was bending toward him.

"Father? It that really you?"

"Yes, my darling boy. It's not a dream—I'm really here. No one can harm you now. I have come to take you and Henrietta home to Pine Haven."

"Can Missus Swain come with us? I am very fond of her."

"Well, she must stay here with the good doctor until the war is over, because he's needed to tend the wounded, but as soon as things grow peaceful again, we will invite them to Pine Haven for a long visit."

"I would like that very much." The boy's features were now beatific and his wiry preadolescent body had relaxed again. He began to breathe deeply, utterly at peace once more. But he had one more thing to say before surrendering to the healing magic of sleep.

"Father?"

"Yes, son?"

"Promise me you will never tell Henrietta how Grandpa died. It was not something a little girl should even know about, and if she had seen all the blood, it would give her terrible dreams."

All the blood . . .

"I promise. There is no need ever to speak of it again."

Apparently satisfied, Francis Marion Sloane gave a profound sigh, then began gently to snore.

Matthew Sloane bent over and kissed his son, and he could feel with his lips as the feverish heat engendered by the nightmare drained away like a dank mist swept clean by sunlight, and the boy's skin became cool and silken once again.

When he was sure the boy was fast sleep once more, Matthew went to the window and watched as encroaching daylight began to pick out the dark emerald green of the forests on the distant mountains, and the highest streaks of snow began to burn like rivulets of white diamonds. Somewhere far away, in a distant peaceful valley, a cock crowed. It was, perhaps, the simple earthiness of that immortal sound, but for whatever reason, Matthew Sloane put his hands to his face and began, finally, to weep.

Part Two

January–December 11, 1864

Blow-up in Paddy's Hollow

BY THE START of 1864, the frivolity of the early days was gone, replaced by a crueler lifestyle. The city had developed a worn, neglected look. Paint peeled from formerly well-kept homes and businesses, missing shingles were left unreplaced, streets were dotted with potholes, garbage lined the avenues, and municipal government had virtually ceased to function. Most local citizens, like the city's numerous soldiers and sailors, had become seedy-looking, dressed in worn, patched clothing . . . Feral half-starved dogs roamed the streets, and troops had to patrol the docks around the clock to prevent deserters from stowing away on outbound ships.

—Anthony Howell, *The Book of Wilmington. Privately printed, c. 1930*

Paddy's Hollow exploded—as Leota Murphy had prophesied it would—on the night of Saturday, February 20, 1864. She had stuck it out for as long as she could, and longer than was prudent, because until recently, she had believed that the war was winding down, that the combination of Confederate defeats and the growing political power of the "negotiated peace" movement in the war-weary North would force both sides to the bargaining table before the start of another spring campaign. When the war ended, the greedy horde of opportunistic criminals and low-life scoundrels would slither out of Paddy's Hollow much faster than they had arrived. Life in Wilmington would return to normal, and Madam Murphy's Residence for Ladies would once again regain its lustrous reputation as North Carolina's cleanest and most genteel whorehouse, an oasis for horny sailors from Madagascar to San Francisco. Last summer, when Rebel prospects went into such a precipitous decline that conditions in the Hollow looked to be verging on chaos, she had packed "get away" bags for her and her daughters, tucked away in the strong room, and conducted some drills, in case of a riot so dangerous that flight became the only prudent response. Those bags remained packed, but during the waning months of 1863, when Leota still clung to the notion of a peace treaty, she put aside her plans to close down the Residence for Ladies. Business was booming, and her private army, the Provost Guard, was composed of tough, well-armed, and fiercely loyal men—she paid them good wages, and on their off-duty days they could enjoy deep discounts at the bar and a free tumble with the ladies. Nobody made trouble for Missus Murphy—not more than *once* at any rate. Envious small-time rivals watched the crowds line up each weekend and marveled at how much money the Ladies' Residence took in and how little violence occurred within its walls, no matter how much mayhem took place inside the eight square blocks that surrounded it.

When Leota ventured out of doors, always attended by a phalanx of sharp-eyed Provost Guardsmen toting shotguns and repeaters, she walked past the establishments of her opportunist, not too successful competitors with an expression of open disdain. They resented her for it and for the high falutin "tone" she maintained inside the walls of her brothel. *Thinks too much of herself, that one! Just another Mick madam, but look how she carries on, would ya, like the fuckin' Queen of England!*

They might casually fantasize about wanting to take Leota down a peg or two; they might wish and pray for a bolt of lightning to set the Residence for Ladies on fire one night, but none of them had the wit, the guts, or the resources to *organize* against her. Back in '62 a few newcomers had tried, and they were no longer in business. Two, at least, were no longer among the living. Leota Murphy was an institution, and had been such long before these common ruffians moved to town. The sheriff was a regular customer, and so was the mayor; the fire chief; the harbor master, who controlled all commercial river traffic; and just about every local Confederate official, from the head of railroad security to the chief customs inspector. Runner captains and their mates, the commandants of all the local training camps, and virtually every politician—on the local, state, or Richmond level—who passed through Wilmington, lent their patronage to and spent their money in, Madam Murphy's Residence for Ladies. Any spiteful crook who dared to harm her or her establishment would almost certainly be found floating facedown in the river soon afterward, with a necklace of crabs nibbling at the ragged edges of his slashed throat.

Now it was almost the end of February, and Leota had no more illusions about "peace movements." When the ground dried out, the spring campaigns would start all over again, both armies tearing into each other with undiminished fury. If the South could no longer prevail, it could certainly defend itself to some sort of apocalyptic bitter end that would turn "losers" into "legends." As Leota stood on the veranda, waiting for one of the

Provost lads to bring her carriage around, she basked in the sparkling sunlight and quaffed the tangy ocean breeze, which was sharp enough on this day to awaken bittersweet memories, for the sea-wind smelled the same in North Carolina as it did on the coast of County Cork. Leota had been dreaming lately about going back to Ireland.

She was exactly as old as the century, the youngest of seven scabby-kneed kids in a dirt-poor family of potato farmers. After the landlord evicted them in 1811, her parents had indentured themselves to a life of sweatshop labor in New York, in order to pay for steerage tickets to the New World, where at least some of their children might one day enjoy a decent life. Leota had overcome every kind of adversity the city could throw at its lowliest and most despised immigrants. Now, she was independently wealthy; she had raised three fine strapping daughters—one of whom was about to marry an absolute dream of a young man, and he was a bloody Royal Navy officer in the bargain—and what better time for her to retire? She was a mature but still vital lady, and she could afford to buy the outhouse seat out from under their old landlord's heirs. It would be most enjoyable to return to the faerie-green hills of home.

And it was also the right time to leave Paddy's Hollow. All her instincts told her it was time to move on, and her sense of the street had been prodding her with increasing urgency since September. If this blessedly beautiful day reminded her of all the good times she had enjoyed in Wilmington, every nuance she picked up just from looking at the Old Kentucky Home, where two of the new owner's henchmen, built like gorillas and probably far less intelligent, periodically threw her the sort of glances a timid woman might find unsettling.

The Old Kentucky Home had been Leota's only respectable competition—a smaller, less pretentious, working man's bordello half a block south, on the opposite side of the street. Its owner, a burly fellow hailing from St. Louis who called himself "Black Jack" Saunders, had set up shop in 1855, and although he, too, had a variety of ladies for hire ("A tart for every taste," he used to say!), he ran the second-story whorehouse almost as a sideline, preferring to invest more heavily in the saloon and gambling rooms. The two establishments complemented one another more than competed, and the two entrepreneurs became good friends. Many nights they had stayed up playing cards or shooting billiards, lamenting the Hollow's decline. Until one Saturday night in September, when Saunders tried to reconcile two quarreling Portuguese sailors, both of whom suddenly turned around and stabbed him to death.

Saunders was barely cold in his grave before the property was bought by another Irish refugee, a gang leader named Liam Mulligan, who had ended up in Wilmington by God-knew-what circuitous route after fleeing New York with a large price on his head. During the draft riots in June 1863, Mulligan boasted, he had shot a police detective, and the long memories of New York coppers had driven him south. Leota had grown-up among his type, and from the moment he crossed the street to introduce himself as the new owner of Old Kentucky—practically blinding her with the flash of gold teeth and half smothering her with the mingled scents of hair pomade and a cologne he insisted on identifying as "Oh De Roses"—she knew he was the genuine article. She also knew he was bad news. None of the other scoundrels and third-rate pimps who had set up shop in the Hollow over the past two years had enough charisma, money, or imagination to recruit, never mind profitably manage, a real "gang"—the more successful operators might have two or three ruffians working for them as touts and bouncers, nothing more. But Mulligan had brought four pug-faced henchmen with him, and a sizeable bankroll. He thought the war might last another three years—a logical enough assumption, given the ferocity of the antidraft riots he had seen in Manhattan—and after the shooting stopped, there would be a large garrison of occupying Yankee soldiers whose recreational needs he wanted to provide for.

If Mrs. Murphy should ever be interested in selling the Residence for Ladies, he said, the first time he had dropped in for a neighborly chat, perhaps they could come to an amicable business arrangement. Mrs. Murphy did not think that was in the cards, but she would bear it in mind. During the weeks since that conversation, Mulligan had demonstrated what might happen to entrepreneurs who spurned his business propositions. After a rash of "accidents" to their property, and minor but painful injuries to their persons, about half the "businessmen" in Paddy's Hollow had signed up for Mr. Mulligan's "protection service" and some of the more timid operators had simply folded their tents and left town. The ones who fancied themselves tough as nails had, at first, told him to go fuck himself, but their attitude began to waver after the owner of a cockfight pit roasted alive when his tent caught on fire and collapsed on top of his head.

Leota began to fidget. Ten minutes had passed; Mulligan's simian henchmen continued to whittle sticks and perfect their glaring technique, and *Where the hell is my carriage?*

From within the swinging doors of the Old Kentucky, Mr. Mulligan now appeared, nattily dressed, nibbling daintily on a toothpick. *Oh God, he's not coming over here to talk to me? . . .* Yes, he was.

"Missus Murphy, you look especially lovely in such flattering light! A splendid day, is it not?"

"Indeed, sir, it is. You'll excuse me if I don't spend much more of it in conversation—I have a very important guest arriving on the four o'clock train."

"Oh, now, what are the chances of that train arriving on the dot? Spare me but a moment, please. I'd like to take our business relationship to the next level, as expeditiously as possible."

"Mister Mulligan, we *have* no relationship, business or otherwise."

"We soon will, provided you accept this generous offer." He handed her a three-page legal document, florid with phraseology and witnessed by a notary public. On the last page, there was a space reserved for two names. His own was already inscribed on the right-hand side; the blank space on the left was obviously reserved for her signature.

"What the hell is this?"

"A simple and completely legal bill of sale, already duly notarized, which states, in essence, that I will hand you ten thousand dollars in cash, and you will hand me the deed to the Residence for Ladies. A very tidy sum, and absolutely my final offer."

"Are you barking mad? We take in more than that in a single good month! Why in God's name should I want to sell this place to a . . . to you?"

"Because, as I said, it's my best and my last offer. I'm building a wee commercial empire here in the Hollow, y'see, and the Ladies' Residence will be the jewel in its crown, so to speak." With the quickness of a striking rattler—for he could tell from her expression that she was about to tear the so-called deed to shreds—he yanked the document from her hands.

"I'm a patient man, Missus Murphy. I'll give you a couple of weeks to think it over."

"Or *what*? My customers are very loyal; the Residence has been their refuge and fount of pleasure for twenty years. This is not New York, Mulligan—you can't do business here just by paying-off the local coppers. Some of my friends are much too rich to bribe and far too powerful to fuck with, if you get my drift."

"No need for such language, madam. I'm merely a businessman, making an offer. In time, you may find that offer more attractive. Well, I shan't detain you from meeting your guest . . ."

Mulligan tipped his hat, ostentatiously thrust the bogus deed into his coat pocket, and sauntered back across the street. The two Whittling Henchmen stood respectfully for him, then followed him inside through the swinging doors.

"Uh, Missus Murphy, ma'am?"

"Christ, Willoughby, you startled me! Where is the carriage? You've been gone long enough to fetch it from Dublin."

"I'm afraid it's one of the horses, ma'am . . . well, at first I thought he was ill, but on closer inspection, he turned out to be dead. I examined the animal thoroughly, but there's not a mark on him. I can't imagine what happened."

I can, by the Virgin Mary: poison.

"Well, whatever it was, it's not your fault. Is the *other* horse still ambulatory?"

"Yes'm, she's just fine, a mite skittish from . . . what happened to her stall-mate."

"Throw a saddle on her and ride up to the Yellow House! Hobart-Hampton will loan us a carriage, I'm sure. Get back here as quickly as you can—I don't want to keep Mister Ethridge waiting on an empty platform. I've made dinner reservations in one of the private rooms at the Stars-'n'-Bars, and you know how hard those are to come by!"

"So it was in Nassau that you met my dear friend Augustus, Mister Ethridge?"

"Yes ma'am. As he no doubt told you, I have been employed for some years as the assistant manager of one of the port's oldest and most reputable brothels. H-H knew you were thinking of retirement, and thought I might have suitable qualifications."

"Not something you can advertise in the papers for, is it?"

"Precisely so, madam. I suppose to the low-minded citizen, a brothel manager must equate roughly with a slave overseer, but in a high-class establishment, it's not at all similar. One must keep peace amongst the ladies, make sure the customer always leaves with a smile on his face, maintain the highest standards of cleanliness . . . well, what am I telling you these things for? The Residence for Ladies has a reputation that spans the seven seas!"

"You can make a tidy living for as long as the war lasts—in fact, we make as much in one busy weekend as we used to make in a month, provided there are a lot of troops passing through town, and the runners are laying up—if you'll pardon my little play on words!—until the next dark of the moon. And even after the war ends, assuming the South cannot negotiate a settlement, you will still have a large Yankee occupation force to take up the slack. But eventually they will go home, too. What will you do if you can't turn a profit after they leave?"

Mr. Ethridge, as it happened, did have an alternate plan—for he fully expected American society to turn in a puritanical direction for a while, in reaction to all the excesses of wartime. "I grew up on a large and successful dairy farm in the Midlands. Should the white-stockings shut us down, I will at least have saved enough to pursue my ultimate dream: to become a rich cattle baron in the West!"

Leota rather liked him for that notion. "Look at it this way, Tony: even if you go bust as a cattle rancher, you'll always have a valuable skill to fall back on! There will always be a great demand, in the western territories, for two things: reliable six-guns and good, cheap pussy! Now finish up your dessert, and let's get back to the place. I want you to meet everyone, get familiar with the layout, and unload your baggage in one of the spare rooms. After tomorrow, of course, you can move into my quarters, which I'm sure you will find amply comfortable. There are some . . . *issues* I need to discuss with you, but we should do that in the company of my sergeant at arms. Hobart-Hampden *did* explain about the Provost Guard, I trust?"

"Indeed he did, madam. He advised me to keep them 'well paid and well laid.' It seems your neighborhood can get a little rough on the weekends."

"As always, a master of understatement . . . Anyway, you'll be spending the night, and certainly not alone, so you'll have plenty of time to learn all about 'the neighborhood.' My oldest daughter, Kate, is getting married tomorrow, to a divinely handsome Royal Navy captain named Pendelton, and I'll be leaving shortly after eleven to attend the engagement party—which ought to be just about the time when things start to get lively in the Hollow. I have to stay until my youngest daughter, Winona, finishes her last performance—an exceedingly popular interpretive pantomime entitled 'The Beheading Dance of the Wicked Princess Salome.' It always draws a standing-room-only crowd on Saturday nights!"

Mr. Mulligan's henchmen, who had been in his employ for more than a decade and whom he fondly referred to as "the Four Horsemen," each had a specialty. One, a forger who could duplicate anything from passports to customs vouchers, had created the note-perfect "deed" using his big kit of pens, inks, document-style papers, changeable seals and stamps, and fine engraving tools. Another Horseman had been known, back in New York, by the honorific "Mister Match." He could set fire to an ice cube or turn a two-story building into ashes so fast it would not matter if the neighborhood firehouse was on the other side of the street.

Mulligan would have preferred buying the Residence for Ladies to incinerating it, but once the old barn was a pile of charcoal, he could buy the land it stood on for a pittance. He could then build a more up-to-date, gaudier version of Mrs. Murphy's establishment. Of course, the change of ownership would go much more smoothly if Mrs. Murphy were *inside* the place when it burned down, but *getting to her* would not be easy.

Both her person and her building were well guarded by loyal, sharp-eyed men who were every bit as tough as any New York gang and better armed by far. "Mister Match" was very efficient at his work, but this torch-job had to appear *completely accidental*—if Mrs. Murphy's influential friends even suspected Mulligan of arson, he would be turned into crab bait before the ashes were cool.

Success depended on the right context, preferably a convincing nearby fire or fires. But Mister Match could hardly apply his skills to a whole square block. Paddy's Hollow comprised the most flammable real estate he had ever seen—any conflagration big enough to disguise arson might also be too big to control. A fickle shift in the wind, and the Old Kentucky Home might go up too. All Mulligan could do was stock the supplies Mister Match would need and then pray that sooner or later, some drunken fool would drop a lantern in just the right spot.

On the night of February 20, someone did.

• • •

The Great Fire of Sixty-Four was caused by a convergence of random circumstances, and Mr. Mulligan could not have asked for a more suitable "diversion."

Firstly, the Hollow began to fill up early, and for that he could thank the remarkably balmy weather. Not even the dullest brute was insensitive to the lulling effect of a February day so unseasonably mild that it lured outside a great many people who would otherwise not have stirred from the warmth of their hearths. By twilight, the other random ingredients were in play. The railroad line between Wilmington and Goldsboro had broken down—again!—and two trainloads of Confederate troops were stranded side by side at the depot just two blocks north of Paddy's Hollow. One train was full of former deserters who had grown tired of life on-the-run and had taken advantage of Richmond's latest amnesty offer and who were on their way back to the frontlines in Virginia. Jammed like sardines in the other stranded train were approximately 250 new replacements, who had just finished their basic training at Camp Whiting, on the outskirts of town. The deserters were well guarded, to be sure, but they had rolled into town from Charlotte at one o'clock on Friday morning and they had not moved all day. The raw replacements, most of them beardless teenagers swept up in the latest conscription drive, filed aboard their train at ten o'clock Saturday morning, serenaded by catcalls and bloodthirsty taunts from the embittered veterans, separated from them by about ten feet of gravel and a thin line of cranky, increasingly bored sentries. Forbidden to exit the train except to visit the depot's reeking latrines in the company of a disgruntled guard, the veterans entertained themselves by regaling the jittery recruits with the most gruesome war stories in their repertoire. By midafternoon everyone aboard either train was hungry and irritable. Finally, a pair of wagons pulled up bearing kettles of lukewarm stew and hardtack, the same monotonous slop the trainees had been subsisting on for weeks, and the conscripts each received just enough food to remind them of how hungry they were but not enough to fill them up. The reclaimed deserters received nothing but hardtack, and by twilight the water supply on both trains had run out.

But refreshment was soon at hand, for word had spread around the Hollow that two trainloads of soldiers were stuck at the depot, and a swarm of pimps and saloon keepers descended on the place. Free samples of whiskey were dispensed, along with vividly exaggerated descriptions of the variety and quality of nearby entertainments. At dusk, a platoon of Confederate Marines cleared the riffraff out of the area, but only long enough for the lieutenant in charge to announce that the trains would be stuck until at least midday Sunday. This intelligence was received with loud groans and curses from everyone attached to both trains, including the guards, who had grown less and less keen about performing their duty as the hours creaked by. Having minimally performed *their* duty, the Marines marched away and the emissaries from Paddy's Hollow once more emerged from the shadows, to cajole and entice, and this time they dragged along a wheelbarrow loaded with pints of rotgut whiskey, which they sold to the guards at such a cut-rate price that the motive behind their generosity was transparent to all: once the sentries got a snoot-full, they would probably wander off to the Hollow in search of more. Which was, in fact, what happened.

Now the older veterans began to taunt the nervous and somewhat confused recruits. Boys, they called out, this might be your best, and last, chance to cast off your virginity before your pecker gets shot off in Virginia! And the boys were wondering: Why not? They had already been told that the trains weren't going anywhere until tomorrow. As long as they were back onboard before departure, they were not, technically speaking, deserters. And the former deserters, who had picked up a ten-dollar bonus as a reward for voluntarily turning themselves in, magnanimously offered their services as protection against any would-be robbers and swore that, from their own vast fund of experience, they could point out to the boys which ladies were diseased and which were worth the asking price. Once the first daring souls climbed off and headed toward the enticing bustle of Paddy's Hollow, the exodus became general; by eight-thirty there was hardly a corporal's guard left on either train.

But the Hollow was already crowded with sailors from the blockade-runners and off-duty regulars from the training camps and river forts. After two trainloads of soldiers managed to squeeze into the streets, there were a thousand men milling around in spaces that were adequate for half that number. Tempers flared as rivers of cheap whiskey eroded both good manners and common sense. The sailors—who felt they were entitled to be first in line for everything—grew exceedingly testy.

After they reached a certain stage of inebriation, many of the former deserters began to wonder what sort of temporary derangement had prompted them to return. Many of the young conscripts, heads spinning from strong cheap spirits, became loud and obnoxious as they rhapsodized about the brief perfunctory thrusts that had given the *coup de grace* to their virginity; others slunk back toward the train in shame and sometimes fear. Now, when the deed could not be undone, they began to recall their drill instructors' stern and gruesome lectures on the subject of venereal disease. One of those ex-virgins, a seventeen-year-old private from Alamance County, concluded—after a process of cogitation made serpentine by immoderate alcohol consumption—that he *must* inspect his member carefully before passing out on the train, just to see if there were any visible signs of infection. He hesitated at the demarcation between the railroad tracks and the jumbled rows of warehouses, repair shops, and multipurpose sheds that marked the boundary between the rail yard and Paddy's Hollow. He searched for a private place, but also one sufficiently well lit to carry out a thorough hygienic examination.

Finally, near the riverbank, he spotted a brakeman's lantern leaning against a nondescript wooden shed. Here was light; now to find privacy. He fumbled in his tunic pocket and found there a cigar, which one of the deserters had given him while they were both inching forward in the line outside the Riding Academy, and also a box of wooden matches the man had loaned him. The young soldier from Alamance County ducked out of the choppy fitful wind, and on his fourth try managed to light the lantern. Wandering through the deserted facilities like the gravedigger from *Hamlet,* he tried each door he came to until he found a small warehouse that was unlocked—a temporary holding shed where goods were kept out of the elements until they could be transferred from one train to another. Above the entrance, a sign admonished NOT FOR STORAGE OF AMMUNITION OR FLAMMABLES!, but in his confused state of mind the soldier did not see it.

After closing the door, he lit the lantern and unbuttoned his fly. His penis was slippery and elusive—it was like trying to grasp a minnow just taken off the hook—but when he finally clamped it and pulled it forth, it looked . . . perfectly normal. How many hours did the sergeant say it took? Before you could see the first signs of syphilitic rot? Hard to recall! Still, he was hugely relieved to see that his organ had not yet erupted in loathsome cankers. Satisfied, he rebuttoned and decided to celebrate by smoking the deserter's cigar—another manly thing he had not yet accomplished. But the first few puffs made his head reel, and when he inadvertently sucked a big dollop of smoke into his lungs, he began coughing so hard he almost fainted. No sir, smoking was not the vice for him! Fornication, on the other hand, seemed worthy of further experiment, should the opportunity ever present itself.

Upon that instant came epiphany: he was young and reasonably healthy, and since he could not yet conceive of how randomly death selected its victims in battle, he felt sure that the Lord would spare him. Yes, by the Almighty, he was going to survive this war, and might be destined to perform a heroic deed or two before it was over. With his mood now brightened and the optimism of youth once more bearing him aloft on the comforting wings of illusion, he flipped the cigar butt away and left the shed. Before climbing back into the train and falling instantly asleep, he was careful to replace the borrowed lantern.

Meanwhile, the cigar butt had come to rest on a small pile of wood shavings, igniting a sullen smoldering glow, which finally burst into flame when an errant wind slid through a crack in the walls. Ordinarily, nothing flammable *was* stored here, but on this night, someone had thrown a tarpaulin over a stack of crates just unloaded from one of the runners, without noticing that behind those crates packed with bolts of uniform cloth, saddle blankets, and blacksmiths' tools, someone had negligently stacked eighteen kegs of fine English gunpowder.

The storage shed blew up like the crack of doom, hurling flaming debris all over Paddy's Hollow.

Just as Largo approached the back door to the Yellow House, it flew open from within, propelled by such manly vigor that she was not surprised to see the groom, Captain Standish Pendleton, R. N., flushed with excitement and wine, on the other side.

"Standie, you rogue!"

"Largo, my pet! The fleet's in and the Queen is coming to tea!"

"And you are leaving already? What does your bride-to-be think of this?"

"The bride-to-be is surrounded by my envious mates, so that I can barely see the top of her head. Meanwhile, the lines at the water closets are very long and my need is pressing. So . . ."

"Unlimber, close your eyes, and think of England, Standie! We'll chat later."

As soon as she closed the door, Largo was blasted by shouts, cheers, laughter, and a rich gumbo of music produced by every instrument stored in the place—a sonic tour of the British Empire, from bagpipes to a didgeridoo. The Yellow House lads had vowed to pull out all the stops for this one, and given their customary standard of party-throwing, that was no small achievement.

When Largo entered the ballroom, a wave of applause spread before her and a score of women rushed over to inundate her with hugs and sisterly kisses. Some of these women, she remembered from the awkward cotillions of prewar days, albeit dimly. Now, apparently, she was a dear old friend. For Largo, it was as if Wilmington's social world had tilted on its very axis. Two years ago, most of these women would not have spoken to her in public, at least not within sight of their parents or their parents' friends. In those days Largo was a shameless apostate, just one step above harlotry, because of her open, scandalous relationship with that British cad, Nay-bob Netherton or whatever his name was. Now the belles of Old Wilmington were greeting her with unfeigned affection, even diffidence. In this vignette, the cataclysm of war was encapsulated, writ small but vivid.

They were not here simply because the very walls vibrated with ruddy English virility, nor—entirely—because the once-deep pool of desirable bachelors had shrunk to a mud puddle, but because they had undergone a metamorphosis similar to her own and they were paying homage to Largo the Bold, Largo the Trail Blazer. If the parents knew where their daughters were, they would be clutching each other in aggrieved despair. These young women had flown the coop. Largo knew she was seeing the cumulative effects of a devastating plague and three years of grinding war. Taken together, these two shattering experiences had engendered a new outlook on life, one which occupied the shifty terrain between a philosophy and an attitude. However circumscribed and trivial their prewar expectations may have been, they had all learned the same hard truths: death wields his sword without discrimination and far more often he bestows a brutally unfair termination rather than the mellow old age these ladies had been taught to expect. Pride was just another sort of cosmetic, dignity might be rewarded with scorn; a stack of love letters in your sweetheart's knapsack was not going to stop a minié ball. A long and prosperous life was *not* guaranteed by Christian virtue or ancestral pedigree; the plague, no less than the cannonballs, had cut down the poor and the rich without distinction, and no one who had lived through that ghastly event had been spared the sight of some friend or relative dying in agonized putrefaction. A hard thing to witness: someone whom you have embraced and revered, being transformed into an object of unspeakable disgust. And how many handsome, seemingly immortal young beaux had died in equal agony upon battlefields no one could find upon a map? Too many! Assumptions and verities burned away; a quarter-million prayers unanswered.

So those who had been wed were single again, and those who had never known a man's touch were now avid for all the caresses they could hoard! Why not taste the honey and drink the wine while you still could? There were never as many tomorrows as you deserved!

Largo smiled at the thought: *I may well have been the first Wilmington belle to lose her virginity in this repository of manhood, but I certainly was not the last!*

And then she caught sight of Augustus, and it was almost like the first time, when their eyes had locked across a typically vapid soiree, and she had been drawn toward him as irresistibly as the western horizon draws down the sun. He was resplendently turned-out, and she felt envious eyes following her as she threaded through the crowd and tilted her face into an openly lascivious kiss. *My God, some of those ninnies are actually applauding! Go find one for yourselves, girls—on this night, there are plenty to go around.*

When they both came up for air, they were joined by Maggie Murphy, who shed suitors like falling leaves as she crossed the room to greet them. The youngest of the daughters Murphy was already tipsy, a condition that had the effect of making her look at least five years younger than the twenty-three she could legitimately claim.

"Augustus, can I ask you something in all frankness?"

"Yes, dear Maggie, of course you can, just as soon as we get there."

She swatted him with her fan.

"Stop teasing me, you limey rascal! What I want to know is, what will

Captain Pendleton's family think when he introduces his new bride as a former . . . um . . . as someone who used to be . . . err . . ."

"A whore?"

"You make it sound so indelicate!"

"I dare say the subject will never, ever, come up. I know young Standie's parents quite well, and they will automatically assume that Katie *must* be a princess of the fabled plantation aristocracy."

"But what if one of *these* fellows tells them?"

Hobart-Hampden's brows wrinkled as though that question was quite the most preposterous he had ever heard.

"My dear young woman, these are *gentlemen!* And if the truth be known, the British aristocracy is positively littered with the offspring of similar unions."

Largo had to chime in. "Oh, Lord, now you've done it—here comes a long conversational detour down the quaint byways of English history! Augustus, I came here to dance and be gay, not to hear about the legitimization of Lord Upshot-on-the-Downswing's favorite strumpet, so please spare both me and Maggie from . . ."

Hobart-Hampton never learned exactly what he was supposed to spare them from, for at that moment all the music and all the laughter went silent, in response to a distant but powerful roar that rattled the windows and caused plaster to sift down from the ceiling.

"My God, what was that?" Largo exclaimed.

"By Jove," piped someone with a distinct Yorkshire accent, "I think we're experiencing an earthquake!"

Hobart-Hampden shot him a withering glare. "We are in *North Carolina,* you dolt. Mister Lancaster," he instructed a young crewman who was serving drinks and hors d'oeuvres, "would you be so good as to dash up to the widows' walk and see if anything unusual is visible from the cupola?"

After young Lancaster dutifully trotted upstairs, conversation fell to the level of a confessional booth.

"Yankee raiders shelling the docks from the river?"

"Not likely—nothing larger than a rowboat could sneak past Fort Fisher."

"Maybe one of the runners blew a boiler . . ."

"Sabotage!" declared Hobart-Hampden loudly. "I'll wager with any man here that some Yankee infiltrators have managed to blow up a warehouse or an ammunition bunker. Any takers?"

No one proffered a bet; whatever had happened, the collective mood had plunged from gaiety to foreboding, and the erstwhile revelers remained frozen in place, waiting to hear whatever intelligence their designated observer might gather from the observation deck atop the house.

Mister Lancaster's descent was rapid and his eyes were wide.

"There's a bloody great fire over toward Paddy's Hollow! The sky's all aglow!"

Largo looked at Hobart-Hampden and so did everyone else.

"Augustus, what should we do?"

"Whether it's a Yankee raid or that big riot everyone's been predicting, most of us have friends and others whom we care about down there. Perhaps we can help out, but we must stick together, and everyone must be armed! Not to mention organized. We should take blankets, brandy, the medical kit, and about sixty rounds per man. Let's meet back here, ready to go, in fifteen minutes."

"Getting organized" took more than fifteen minutes, but eventually that goal was more or less achieved. Just as Hobart-Hampden was about to give marching orders, however, Winona Murphy came bursting through the back door, her face twisted in panic and her hair dotted with airborne ash. Kate and Maggie ran to her and Captain Pendleton gallantly swooped to her side with brandy in hand. Largo waded in, gesturing for quiet and speaking to the frightened girl in the calmest voice she could muster.

"Is the Residence safe? Is Leota all right? Take a deep breath and tell us, very calmly, what happened."

"There was a big explosion in the rail yard and Mother sent the Provost Guard and all the customers out to fight the fires. When I left, she was fine and the Residence in no danger, and then, a few blocks from here, I remembered something that makes me think Mother might need escorting out of there. Maggie, do you remember what mother told us earlier today? About that brute, Mulligan?"

"What about the bastard?" snapped Hobart-Hampden. "A deep-dyed rotter if I ever saw one . . ."

"He . . . he tried to get Mother to sell the Residence to him. Showed her this phony-looking deed and offered her ten thousand if she would sign on the spot. Of course, she told him to go stuff it, but he became rather threatening. Said she had better change her mind or . . . well, he didn't say, but the implication was 'or else.' Mother didn't take him seriously, seeing as how we were all leaving tomorrow anyway. But there's a lot of confusion down there now, and only a couple of guards in the house . . ."

"That settles it," said Largo. "Let's not waste another minute."

Hobart-Hampden turned to Captain Pendleton. "Standie, I'm leaving you in charge of the Murphy sisters' safety. Pick a half-dozen good men and don't drink all the liquor while we're gone. The rest of you: Largo and I will lead in her carriage, those of you who have horses should saddle them, and those who do not . . . well, grab some of the mules and drag them around the neighborhood—see if you can't find some sort of conveyance to hitch them to! We may need room for casualties and for some of Leota's private things."

"Beg pardon, H-H, but those of us 'dragging' the mules—if we see a wagon or something, do we just hitch up the beasts and take it or leave a note or ? . . ."

"If the owner of said conveyance tries to stop you, just tell him he will receive fair compensation from the Queen of England if anything happens to his property."

"Oh yes, indeed," giggled one of the tipsier seamen in the back. "Sometime in the year Nineteen-Twelve, I should imagine!"

Hobart-Hampden glared at the man. "Stoker's Mate Fletcher, are you too drunk to accompany us?"

"Oh, no, sir—just too drunk to aim a pistol."

"Fine. Then you can hold the horses of those who can. All right, everyone, let's move smartly!"

Taking Largo aside, he spoke to her privately: "Do you still have that fancy Frog pistol I gave you, the pin-fire . . . *de la Roquefort* or whatever it is?"

"LeFaucheux—right here in my handbag, with two reloads."

He nodded and shouldered his way through the lesser ranks, confidently projecting the authority of a born aristocrat. Cheering and brandishing weapons, the Yellow House lads scurried behind.

Considering how drunk most of them were, Largo thought they were "beating to quarters" in a manner reflecting credit on the Royal Navy. Some were mounted on their personal horses, and the less affluent sailors were dragging a small herd of recalcitrant mules up to people's houses, down nearby alleys, and around corners, searching for any kind of vehicle they could "borrow." Up and down Market Street, the rattle of carriage wheels was followed by the outraged squawks of the vehicles' owners, who were treated to a combination of threats, entreaties, and the occasional brandishing of firearms. "We are on urgent official business for the Crown, you rancorous old sow!" she heard one sailor bark, "and your little runabout may help to save the lives of some noble southern ladies. You'll get it back in the morning, and if there's any damage, why, all you need do is send a claim to Buckingham-fucking-Palace. I'm a personal chum of Prince Albert, so you have nothing whatever to be concerned about!"

Hobart-Hampden climbed in the driver's seat of Largo's carriage and took the reins and whip from Largo's hands. Three more knights-errant squeezed into the cargo space, bristling with swords; revolvers; Enfield rifles; and even a pike, which had been filched from some citizen's ornamental statue of Ivanoe.

By now most of Wilmington had been roused by the clanging of fire bells, the smell of burning railroad depot, and the rattletrap racket made by the Yellow House column as it swept down Market Street. A colorful spectacle this proved to be, and when William Fulton's account of it appeared in the next day's edition of the *Journal,* he described dashing heroes who "rode like princes"—in fact, many of them could barely hang on to the saddle. Behind the riders came a gaggle of freight wagons, buckboards, fiacres, and lastly a moth-eaten conveyance that had long ago served as a hearse. Not until the column turned north on Third Street did they obtain a good view of the fires and when they did, it was enough to silence all banter. Ahead lay anarchy in the streets, and behind that loomed a very angry-looking fire.

"I don't think it's spread to the Residence yet!" shouted Largo, squinting down the half-obscured road and brushing the first of several cinders from her hair.

One useful purpose was served by the titanic explosion and resulting fire: if it had not happened, there almost certainly *would* have been a riot in Paddy's Hollow, because the place was bursting at the seams and the mood was getting uglier by the minute. Crewmen from eleven runners, the trainload of disgruntled ex-deserters, and the 250-odd jittery replacements were all jostling for their share of the local "entertainment." Bartenders were pouring as fast as possible; the whores were fucking and sucking like locomotive pistons, but still there was a lot of pushing and shoving. There simply was not enough physical space for the number of men trying to occupy it. But the explosion and subsequent blaze united them in common cause: obviously the Yankees had raided up the river and tried to destroy a vital strategic railroad yard.

It was also obvious that the fires were gaining ground, as building after building heated up and blisters of old dry paint exploded. Equally alarming were the smaller scattered fires in Paddy's Hollow itself, ignited by flaming debris thrown out by the gunpowder blast. For the time being, the wind was subdued, but a few sudden gusts would turn embers into torches and about the only structures in sight that would not catch fire were the watering troughs.

Dragging the somewhat shaken Mr. Ethridge with her, Leota Murphy ran up to the cupola atop the Residence for Ladies. She was relieved to see no smoldering embers on her roof. She watched in fascination as the habitués of Paddy's Hollow, once they had recovered from their initial shock, began to organize their own firefighting tactics. Property owners whose buildings were in danger put employees and customers to work saving the establishments. But as soon as the drifting firebrands were doused or buried with sand, they sent the firefighters north to join the main bucket brigade near the rail yards. Leota did the same, moving down the halls and banging on doors, telling the customers to pull up their pants and lend a hand. She had planned a sentimental farewell at midnight, during which she would pass out a cash bonus to the cooks, bartenders, sentries, and waiters as well as the whores, but there was no time for that. She rounded everyone up and told them to march to the safety of the park near the slave market, four blocks south, and as each employee filed out the door she gave that person an envelope and a hug.

She retained two of the Provost Guards, one at each entrance, to discourage looters, then ordered the rest of them to stow their weapons in the armory and go join the firefighters. She ordered her one remaining horse saddled and brought around to the kitchen entrance. Winona had already resigned herself to the idea that there would be no "Grand Final Performance" of Salome's Dance, so she had already changed into street clothes by the time the horse was ready. But she was reluctant to leave; something kept nagging at her mind and although everything seemed to be under control, she could not shake off the notion that her mother was in danger.

"I'll be along directly, luv. Mister Ethridge has rented a nice fiacre and he'll escort me to the party after I show him around the office and lock up the place one last time. Now go on and start celebrating—I won't be long."

Leota really did intend to shut things down quickly, but while she was showing Mister Ethridge where the essentials were kept in her office, she was overcome by sentiment and could not resist showing him some of her memorabilia and photographs. Mister Ethridge, who had spent a thoroughly pleasant evening soaking up the ambience—and taking a complimentary spin with one of the ladies—was only too happy to oblige. Leota found him an appreciative audience, and they were reliving the past glories of the Residence for Ladies, Leota proudly showing him some of the autographed testimonials in her scrapbook ("Best wishes always to Leota and her peerless ladies, and thanks for a grand old time—Senator Zebulon B. Vance, 1858") . . .

After ten minutes passed, she became aware of a renewed commotion on the streets outside. She had already shuttered and locked all the downstairs windows, so she trudged back upstairs into Maggie's room, and threw open the window so she could see what the hubbub was about.

Just when it looked like the bucket brigade was gaining the upper hand, a diabolical wind swept up from the river, scooping up great handfuls of glowing cinders, wrapping them into whirlwinds—like thousands of crimson-orange fireflies—and dropping them all across the northern half of Paddy's Hollow. In moments, dozens of new fires sprang up on rooftops and in the trash-strewn alleys. The sight did not alarm her so much as make her cross.

"Oh dear, I guess it really is time to go," she muttered.

Halfway down the stairs, she smelled something new and sharp above the general char hanging over the Hollow: the greasy scent of highly inflammable coal oil. Down in the poolroom there was a grunt of pain, followed by the sound of a falling body . . . furtive shuffling footsteps . . . the *clang!* of an empty fuel can . . . serpents of fresh, thick, choking smoke writhed up the steps and wound about her legs. She reached inside her gown for the .32 caliber she always wore in a shoulder holster. "Mulligan, you son of a Belfast whore," she snarled. More loudly, she called a warning: "Mister Ethridge, be on guard! Theives and arsonists! Leave the place at once!"

But Mr. Ethridge, in a theological sense, had already left, for someone had pierced his liver with a footlong shiv and he lay across her bed, bleeding copiously across her scrapbook.

Leota could hear the flames *inside* now, as they hissed along cunningly laid trails of coal oil and rose incredibly fast along the building's structural supports. Professional work, so much was clear—just like the quick, economical thrust that killed poor Ethridge.

By the time she made it down the stairs, half-blinded but waving the pistol in a steady arc, the perpetrators were gone and both of the guards were dead. Also—clever touch!—the front door had been padlocked on the inside and a pair of heavy billiard tables were upended to block the two barred windows that could be raised from within—as emergency fire escapes! She already knew there was no point in trying to lift them by herself.

Coughing steadily, dodging a piece of flaming roof beam, she staggered to the kitchen door, but she was not surprised to find that a big freight wagon was jammed hard against it.

Right behind her, skillfully placed under the stove flue, was a fused ten-gallon drum of coal oil. When it blew up, the Residence for Ladies shuddered like a living thing and a furious pillar of fire shot up to the second floor.

By the time the Yellow House expedition careened on to Front Street, the second outbreak of small fires had been extinguished and a large, mournful crowd had gathered to watch, helplessly, the death of a beloved institution. So great was the heat inside that inferno that the second-story windows exploded, one by one, like cannon shells. Largo stared openmouthed at the cyclonic firestorm devouring the Residence for Ladies, and when she could bear it no more, she buried her head against Hobart-Hampden's shoulder and sobbed: "Maybe she got out in time, Augustus . . ."

But Hobart-Hampden did not think so. He knew the work of a good professional arsonist when he saw it. Whoever did this would have made certain that no one got out, least of all Leota Murphy.

But just before the roof collapsed in a roaring welter of blazing shingles and red-hot nails, Leota Murphy did get out. Largo heard someone in the crowd shout: "Jesus, there she is!" and Largo automatically raised her head to look, and wished forever after that she had not.

Like a living ball of pitch, Leota Murphy crashed through an attic window. She was almost certainly dead before she hit the glass, or so everyone prayed who saw her. As she fell, globules of melted fat peeled away, so that she resembled a meteor of liquefying flesh. Perhaps, in her final seconds of agonized consciousness, she had tried to aim for a water trough in the street below, but when burning flesh made contact with open air, the flames consuming her boiled up furiously, her internal organs exploded, and what landed on the street, in five or six large and splattering pieces, no longer resembled a human body.

When Hobart-Hampden regained his wits, he chambered a round in his Spencer and ran over to the front door of the Old Kentucky Home. The place was dark and locked up tighter than a mint, but there was a neatly lettered sign hanging on the door:

Closed in order that we may fight the fire!
Be a good citizen and join us, so that Paddy's
Hollow will be here tomorrow!

L. Mulligan, Prop

Neither Liam Mulligan nor his Four Horsemen were ever seen again on the streets of Paddy's Hollow, but some clue as to their fate was revealed eleven days after the Great Fire, when the blockade-runner *Wild Rover* got her anchor fowled as she was trying to back away from the Dock Street wharf.

When the anchor was finally winched aboard, one prong was found to be snagged on a heavy, shapeless canvas bag. The badly decomposed body inside was thought to be that of Mr. Mulligan, even though the only identifiable parts were a pair of gold teeth. Before stuffing him into the burial-at-sea bag, someone had sewed his lips together with a sail-mender's awl and filled the bottom of the sack with eight 32-pounder cannonballs. Across the corpse's chest, someone had used a hot iron to brand the words:

"Rule Britannia!"

A routine report was filed by the police, but no formal investigation was ever conducted. Every Sunday morning, there were two or three bodies floating in the river near Paddy's Hollow, and seldom did anyone claim knowledge of their identity.

Dinner Guests

"I HAVE NEVER READ the damned Army Regulations and what's more I shan't. That way, I shall never know if I do anything against them."
—Butler, Benjamin F. *Daybook Entry, Feb. 21, 1864* (Papers & Manuscripts. Library of Congress.)

MARCH 25, 1864

Major Frederick Reilly missed the last ferry to Smithville by about twelve minutes, which would have signified remarkable punctuality by the Wilmington and Weldon Railroad except for the fact that the train he had boarded in Weldon was officially scheduled to arrive in Wilmington at 3:00 P.M., two hours before the ferry departed. Everybody knew the railroads were falling apart, so Reilly accepted the delay with a stoic shrug. If he could find a horse and/or a buggy for rent, he could still make it to the Lambs' in time to participate in his own homecoming dinner.

For a time he stood on the passenger platform, hoping to spot a driver who seemed to be looking for a paying customer. Since the platform was ten inches higher than the surrounding ground, he did not at first see the Confederate soldier standing nearby. Only when the man cleared his throat to attract Reilly's attention did he glance to the right, where a corporal who was either a large dwarf or a very small man was throwing a salute in the direction of Reilly's belt buckle.

"As I live and breathe, Corporal Conver!" said Reilly, returning the salute. "It's good to see you again and that's the gospel truth. Are you my welcoming committee?"

"Manner o' speakin', Major Reilly; manner o' speakin'. It were my time to enjoy a weekend pass in town, and I was in the midst of fleecing a young French sailor—who had never before learned the estimable game of stud poker and was willing to lose a considerable share of his pay from the last successful voyage of the *Queen Charlotte* in return for the privilege of learning the game from a legendarily successful practitioner such as myself."

"Please *do* get to the point, Corporal."

"Yes sir!" snapped Ezekial Jeremiah Prosper-For-Me de Vonell Conver, the shortest soldier in the whole Confederate army (four feet, one inch) and an acknowledged master of the game of poker. "Anyway, this smartly turned out Marine comes over to our table and hands me a telegram from Colonel Lamb, ordering me to find and rent the best available horse and have it here when your train finally arrived. I'm instructed to tell you that the pleasure of your company is still expected and that Daisy—I mean, Missus Lamb—has obtained a prime ham from Orton plantation and roasted it in a glaze of orange marmalade! From the manner in which the major is licking his chops, I'd wager that dish to be one of his favorites."

Reilly clapped the diminutive soldier on the back, his mouth indeed filled with anticipatory juices.

"Corporal Conver, I would ride to the mountains of Tibet for one of Daisy Lamb's glazed hams! Now, where is that horse?"

"Livery stable, corner of Water and Grace Streets. They'll store your bags and send 'em to the fort on the morning ferry, or they'll rent you a pack mule."

"The morning ferry will be fine. I think I'll just put my toothbrush and a few clothes in the saddlebag and travel light—I am not much of a horseman, but the weather is mild and it might be . . . fun, just riding across the dunes alone, so a mule would just be an encumbrance."

"Then I'll be glad to take your bags, sir, on my way uptown."

"Thank you, Corporal. And now that your official duties are completed, how do you plan to spend your free time 'uptown'?"

"I have a ticket for the revival of *Macbeth* at the Thalian—one of my favorites. And quite timely, don't you think? I find more than a passing resemblance between the politics of ancient Scotland and those of the modern world . . ."

"*Macbeth*? No offense intended, Corporal Conver, but I never would have figured you for a devotee of classical literature."

"Well, Major, I have my pappy to thank for that. He always told me: 'A man of such small stature will be better armed against the cruelties of the tall-men's world if he develops a large and muscular intellect.' He force-fed me Shakespeare and Homer and such from the time I was old enough to walk, and damned if it didn't stick with me!"

"I shall expect a full and exact review of the production when you get back to the fort!"

Conver flashed one of his disarming smiles and went his way with a jaunty wave instead of a regulation salute. Reilly chuckled—you might command 150 artillerists for two years and think you know each man's strengths and weaknesses and general character, but you still can be knocked over with surprise by a casual remark! He wished good luck to all his gunners, but he would say a special prayer, on the inevitable day when the Federal fleet at last came down to pit its cannon against those of Fort Fisher, for the safety of the miniature corporal. *My God, the teasing he must have endured when he was growing up!*

Fortunately, the horse proved docile and sound of limb—about as much horse as Reilly could handle, really. As soon as Reilly entered the sandy wilderness south of Wilmington, he knew his decision to take a solitary ride was the right one. Winter's harsh rains were over and the air today was as cool and soft as silk. He urged the horse on, following the coarse, puddle-splotched track of the River Road into a stretch of undulating gullies which led gradually upward to the long windswept snowy escarpment of Sugar Loaf Ridge. As though it shared Reilly's appreciation of the solitude, the horse picked up his pace, until Reilly leaned forward and patted the animal's neck, murmuring: "This will do, old fellow—no need for undue haste. Let us both enjoy this fine afternoon, and don't mind me if I seem to ignore you. I have much to think about . . ."

Reilly had taken leave of Fort Fisher in late September, when the long-awaited telegram came from Captain Parker: *"Armor plate problems solved. First shipment arrives Tredegar on or about October 28. Your presence requested. Indefinite leave approved Gen. Whiting, orders copied Col. Lamb. All regard your design as brilliant. Now come help us put it together without screwing anything up."*

True to his word, Captain Samuel Parker had kept Reilly informed of the progress—or, more often, the *lack* of it—attending his efforts to build the *Hatteras.* The work progressed in spurts throughout the summer of 1863, as one problem was overcome and three new ones arose.

From the start, the project had been energized by Peter Smith, a legless veteran of Fredericksburg, who owned Holman's Ferry and all the surrounding land. Apparently, Smith was either related to, or good friends with, every Confederate sympathizer living on or near the banks of the Roanoke River, and his efforts brought to the construction site the sort of men Sam Parker needed, but would never have been able to recruit on his own: craftsmen arrived who understood the arcana and specialized lexicon of shipwrights, men who could fashion oak and iron into the myriad specialized shapes required to build a great man-o-war, men who were no more intimidated by the weight and mass of huge, ten-inch-thick frame members than a journeyman carpenter would be when confronted with a pile of ordinary roof shingles. These artisans brought with them some of the exotic tools and fittings that Samuel Parker had not even known he would need, and if some rare piece of hardware were suddenly needed, Peter Smith sent forth men who knew where it might be found, and if those things could not be found, they were, after varying degrees of trial and error, forged on the spot.

Everyone who actually knew what was going on at Holman's Ferry maintained absolute secrecy about it, but of course the burgeoning shipyard could not be rendered invisible, and any traveler who glimpsed the rising keel and framework knew instantly that a very large ship was under construction in a place where no ship had ever been built before. But thanks to a scheme hatched by Parker and Peter Smith, and carried out by agents of Governor Vance, the Union high command in New Bern had been duped by two sham ironclads planted far up the Neuse and Tar Rivers. General Foster had uncovered the deception during his probe along both rivers, but the truth availed him little, for he was transferred out of North Carolina shortly after he learned it. If Foster's successor, General Benjamin F. Butler, was the least bit perturbed about the potential threat represented by the *Hatteras*—and John Foster had certainly *tried* to make him so—he did not show it. No Union forces ever disturbed Holman's Ferry, which was Samuel Parker's biggest piece of good luck.

Strategically, the time was ripe for the *Hatteras* to come down the river and fight. But until recently she had remained only the skeleton of a warship. Samuel Parker had been thwarted from completing the vessel by the same intractable problem he had grappled with since the day he had set up shop on Peter Smith's farm: The Richmond bureaucracy's refusal to make the ironclad project a top priority.

Whether it was the shock of defeat at Gettysburg, or the suave diplomacy of Zebulon Vance, Robert E. Lee had suddenly become a passionate advocate of the *Hatteras*. All it took was a nudge from Marse Robert, and the logjam was broken. That's when Parker wired Reilly: Come on up and help us launch this ship!

Easier said than done! Even without armor, engines, and a pair of 14,000-pound Brooke rifles, the hull weighed one hundred tons. If it became unbalanced, during that brief journey from meadow to river, the torque might split the keel and the *Hatteras* would sink without ever having been, technically speaking, a *ship*.

Four hundred men and eighty-six mules were required to move the massive keel far enough down the heavily greased ramps for gravity to kick in and power the final slide from cornfield cradle to open water. Men and beasts together, all straining until their tendons bulged, could barely move the frame more than a quarter inch with each collective "Heave-ho!," but that was as Parker had foreseen and even planned. He wanted both bow and stern to strike the river simultaneously, or else the enormous weight might become unbalanced, causing timbers to go out of plumb or even break from the strain and the tremendous, brick-wall impact as the ship crashed into the river. So it was best to do the thing by tiny increments, regardless of how long it took. Reilly fluttered like an anxious hen from one side of the scaffolding to the other, and by his frequently consulted watch it required seventy-five minutes' worth of *Heave-Ho* to move the hull to the point where the force of resisting gravity began to equal the force of overcoming it. The whole mass of the unfinished ship now trembled on that precarious verge. Fifty additional men ran forward to keep the ironclad balanced, while the animals were unhitched. Now was the critical moment. If she hit the water with equal force all down the centerline, she ought to be fine. If she landed in a state of torque, she might break her spine. When all the animals had been led to safety, and the straining men who had taken their places looked like they could stand no more, Frederick Reilly fired a pistol shot into the air, all hands let go at the same time and dove flat or sprinted quickly away from the vicious snapping whips of towropes suddenly released from tremendous strain. Ponderous at first, and then with what seemed like sentient eagerness, the CSS *Hatteras* crashed into the river, throwing up two huge fans of spray, and . . . actually *floated!* Never had Reilly heard a cheer to equal the one raised now by the shipbuilders of Holman's Ferry.

Weeks of additional work followed, of course. One engine turned out to be bigger than the other: *Structural modifications!* The gunners complained that Reilly's traversing system was too complicated: *Simplifications!* The racket caused by the blacksmiths fitting armor plate drove everyone working or drilling beneath them half-crazy: *Frustrations!* Sixty-two men came down with dysentery: *Defecations!*

But at 1:45 P.M., March 20, the C.S.S. *Hatteras* was complete. That evening, Reilly and Parker sat together as the sun went down, sipping some of Peter Smith's excellent scuppernong wine. They shared similar thoughts: How long before the order came to take the ram downstream and challenge, with a single ship, the Federal armada that had ruled North Carolina waters unchallenged, since it had slaughtered the gallant but hopelessly outgunned sailors of the Mosquito Fleet, back in the autumn of 1861?

A partial answer arrived at sundown, when a dispatch rider came galloping down from Weldon, bearing a telegram from Zebulon Vance:

Heartiest congratulations on completion of your great work! Hercules himself would be envious. My confidence in ship and crew absolute. Communication this A.M. from General Lee suggests you be prepared for action soon and on shortest notice. Specific orders will come directly from him, and I think will arrive fairly soon. Kick those bastards out of North Carolina! Prayers and pride of the entire State go with you.

"Well, Frederick, there it is. Lee has committed. Are you sure you can't sail with us?"

"I design ships as a hobby, Sam, but I'm not a sailor and I would only get in your way. You and your crew will fight her splendidly, I know. Besides, I have my own command to look after, down at the fort—a lot of fine lads who've drilled and practiced and eaten a peck of sand with their meals, all so they could save many a bold blockade-runner, but never with a chance to prove their mettle in a real fight! Yet all that time, they've known that one morning they would have to fight the whole U. S. Navy. Who knows when that day will come? But when it does, I must be there beside them."

Reilly had reached the summit of Sugar Loaf. Far off to the south, across an undulating plane of lesser dunes, tidal ponds, and gnarled patches of maritime forest he could discern a hazy disturbance, a form that was not sculpted by wind and tide. Like a desert mirage, Fort Fisher was both there and not-there, an illusion formed of twilight glints and shimmers, a man-made thing, amidst a huge natural desolation. But if Reilly felt touched by the mystical, his horse was of a more practical mind—the animal suddenly strained forward, apparently bored with his rider's immobility.

"You're right, old fellow—time for me to pay my respects to a glazed ham."

Reilly packed away four slices, while trying to answer Lamb's many questionns about the ironclad. After Aunt Charity cleared away the dishes, Daisy Lamb excused herself, saying that she would rejoin the men for coffee after they had finished "all the soldiers' talk."

" 'Soldiers' talk,' Colonel? That sounds somewhat ominous."

"Well, first of all, there is a good chance that General Whiting may be leaving us. His old friend General Beauregard has been transferred from Charleston to Petersburg, and he may be able to arrange a new field command for Whiting."

"Why, that's splendid! I guess President Davis has forgiven Whiting for upchucking at his inauguration."

Lamb snorted, half-laughing. "Davis may forget a man's foibles, but he never *forgives* anyone. I think it's a matter of brutal arithmetic—Lee lost so many officers this summer that there is actually a shortage of generals." Lamb paused awkwardly.

"Come on, Colonel—there's something you hesitate to tell me."

"It's just that there have been some changes at the fort, Major. Some good, some not. I wanted to mention them to you in advance of your return tonight."

"Why don't you start with the good news?"

"Yes," Lamb sighed. "That would be best. Do you remember how we discussed the idea of building one final bastion inside the walls, a sort of castle keep that could be defended for some time even if the enemy breached the main walls? You will see it under construction when you wake up tomorrow. It is already named Battery Buchanan and to my astonishment, Richmond has sent us some powerful guns: eleven-inch Brooke smoothbores and ten-inch columbiads, newly rifled at Tredegar—a pair of each. When finished, the new work will not be as high as the Mound Battery, but it will be much larger in circumference—there will be a hospital bombproof inside the base, and entrenchments around the base for two hundred men. If, God forbid, we are *not* reinforced before the enemy attacks, then surely, surely, Richmond will dispatch a relief force and Battery Buchanan might enable us to hang on to the fort long enough for that force to arrive."

"That sounds good—like the keep of a castle. Now tell me the not-so-good news, please."

"Two things, Frederick. First, we have not received any reinforcements, not so much as a company! I need at least two thousand men to defend this place adequately, and I at present, discounting the gun crews, I have barely five hundred. That is one problem that was *not* solved during your absence. The other one, I'm afraid, is the loss of your Flying Battery."

"Merciful God, did the enemy capture my Whitworths?"

"No, sir; that is the irony and the bitterness of it. The Whitworths were taken away by Richmond—the ordnance bureau wanted to study their efficacy as field guns, so they ordered me to send *both* weapons and their ammunition to the capital. I appealed, I protested, but my arguments were ignored."

"What imbecile gave that order? Those guns are too delicate for hard field service, and what earthly use will just two of them be, unless Richmond intends to purchase a hundred more Whitworths from Great Britain? This smacks of ignorance bordering on the absurd. Those two guns will add nothing to the defensive power of the capital, while they have done brilliant service right here!"

"I understand your anger, Major. I was equally outraged when the order came down. As for the 'imbecile' responsible, who can say? The order was signed by some obscure lieutenant in the Ordnance Department, but my own sources tell me that the idea originated with General Bragg. He may be disgraced in the public's eye after his signal failures in Tennessee, but he still commands the ear of President Davis. Blame me, too, if it will make you feel better, for I decided not to protest too strongly. I sacrificed the Whitworths in the hope of gaining some favor in Richmond, so that the next time I beg the War Department to send us reinforcements, perhaps we will get them. We need soldiers more than we needed the Flying Battery, Major Reilly. I'm sorry about the loss of those guns, for I know how attached you were to them, but my chief responsibility now is to the fort as a whole. We have our full complement of heavy guns, but a large, determined attack by land would wash over us like waves melting a sand castle."

"I understand, Colonel. You did what you had to do. At least the enemy fleet still *thinks* we have the Whitworths."

But on the ride back to the fort, after bidding goodnight to the Lambs, Frederick Reilly was so disturbed by the loss of his beautiful Flying Battery that he barely responded when the other two officers tried to engage him in conversation. No, it was not Lamb's fault—if the order had originated with Bragg, however, it was an insult to every better soldier in the army. Reilly had once visited Chattanooga, a two-day layover on his way to his new posting on the Cape Fear. He had studied Lookout Mountain with a professional eye, and it seemed to him a virtually impregnable spot. Five hundred determined men could hold that summit against ten thousand, hold it until hell froze over. They wouldn't even need rifles—they could repulse the attackers by rolling boulders down on their heads! But General Bragg had put more than two thousand men on top of that mountain, and somehow contrived to demoralize them so greatly that the enemy scaled sheer cliffs, and overran them between breakfast and lunch. If sacrificing the Whitworths meant keeping Braxton Bragg far away from Wilmington, it was a trade worth making.

April 2, 1864

General Butler's jaunty little steamer hove into sight around the northward bend of the South Roanoke and vented three loud toots from its whistle. Rush Hawkins had been forewarned by a fairly jovial telegram that Butler intended to visit Shelborne's Point, for a "warm reunion" with his protegee, now that Butler was settled in at Fortress Monroe as the new commander of the Army of the James and of all Union forces in North Carolina. Hawkins had spent the past two days scurrying from one end of his perimeter to the other, making sure every piece of trash was picked up, every spot of flaking paint refurbished, and every man in the garrison—save for a skeletal force on picket duty—was turned out in freshly laundered uniforms, sparkling buttons, and icicle-bright bayonets. Hawkins and his staff stood on the main wharf while the companies of the 6th Massachusetts, veterans now of some real honest-to-God fighting, were smartly formed in ranks on the parade ground, and the Buffaloes, whom General Foster had singled out for conspicuous valor during his half-successful march on Goldsboro, were assembled behind the infantry.

And yes, there was Butler, waving from the bridge. Two years had passed since Hawkins had met face-to-face with his ungainly, controversial, and shamelessly self-promoting patron. Time and distance had softened

Hawkins' recollection of just how ugly Butler was, but the scheme Butler had proposed, the bogus blockade-runner swindle Hawkins had agreed to with a handshake, had made Hawkins a rich man and a part of Butler's inner circle. The political career Hawkins yearned to embark on, once the fighting was over, was now within reach. Butler might well be a scoundrel, a crook, and a hopelessly incompetent field commander, but Hawkins had a warm spot in his heart for the man anyway.

When Butler disembarked, he crushed Hawkins in a bear hug that nearly smothered him with the combined odors of hair pomade, sweet cologne, cigar smoke, and perspiration.

"Hawkins, my boy! You look fit as a fiddle! Marvelous to see you again!"

"And you, too, General. Congratulations on your new command!"

"The people insisted on it, sir! And the newspapers! Halleck and Meade both advised against it—wanted to send me to a desk job in New England—but Lincoln ignored them and Grant signed the orders, then sent along two of his best corps commanders to make sure I didn't botch things up when the new campaign begins. And that, by the way, is one of the things we need to discuss. But first I want to review your troops! Good work in that Goldsboro affair, by the way! You have always justified my confidence in you, and now you have as fine a combat record as any brigadier in the Union army!"

Butler's "review" of the Massachusetts infantry was cursory, but he lingered a bit more when he inspected the more colorful and racially mixed ranks of the Buffaloes. He paused in front of Jack Fairless.

"I've heard of you, Colonel! Good things! There are black units in my army, and white ones, but none that are black *and* white. How is that working out?"

"All of us serve the Union, sir. We ride together, we fight together, and we look out for each other—we are color-blind and proud to be so."

Hawkins, slightly behind Butler's slumping shoulder, nodded approvingly. *Good answer, Jack!*

"Well said! Good luck to you all in the future. And now, General Hawkins, let us retire so these men can fall out and change back into comfortable clothes."

After giving orders for the men to fall out, Hawkins showed Butler to a waiting carriage. "I have the dining table set for eight, General Butler, out at my headquarters. Shall we round up a full complement of hungry officers or shall we dine privately?"

"Privately would be best. But I *do* look forward to sampling the culinary skills of your cook, the Negress you mentioned several times . . . 'Harmonica' or something like that . . ."

"Calliope, Calliope Keene. General Butler, when you taste one of her ham biscuits, you'll think you've arrived in Heaven!"

Hawkins waved away the assigned driver and took the reins himself. The carriage springs groaned as Butler settled beside him and lit a cigar. Neither man spoke again until they reached the outskirts of the village, following the road to the handsome columned house of the late Judge Murdock, but now the luxurious headquarters of General Rush C. Hawkins.

"Relations are still cordial with the local civilians?"

"Cordial enough for two marriages and three engagements between my men and some local girls. There was some hostility toward us at first—we were ambushed on the river, as I reported to you, and I reacted rather hotly."

"Most men do, I find," mumbled Butler.

"But since then, all has been peaceful. The regimental brothel helps, of course . . ."

"Which I intend to visit this evening, if that's all right."

"Arrangements have already been made, General Butler. But, to continue, these villagers are not fools. Their lives have been peaceful and prosperous since we set up shop here. For them, the war is a distant rumble, nothing more. I dare say most of them now regard us as their protectors, not as an occupying foe."

"Look, Hawkins, we may as well have our discussion now, rather than spoil the feast you've promised me by talking business. What I chiefly came down here to tell you, aside from congratulating you on a job well done, is that our, um, business arrangement will be winding down much sooner than either of us would like."

"Well, General, I have noticed a slow but steady decrease in the number of bogus blockade-runners in recent months. Come to think of it, there has only been one arrival in the past month."

Butler gestured philosophically. "Business arrangements such as ours, well, they have a cycle of life that's fairly predictable: a fumbling start until all the pieces are in place, a period of maximum efficiency, and then a gradual decline. Some of the contractors I used to deal with got too greedy, and started selling inferior supplies to our own troops along with sending their junk to the Rebs. Hostile newspapers got wind of it, there were inquiries, the occasional scandal or two—political enemies tried to link me with the scheme. As usual, they found no tangible proof, just innuendoes and gossip. But the increased number and efficiency of the blockade squadrons gradually drove up the risks for those skippers who were on the payroll of the original consortium, even as that consortium grew smaller, due to the scandals and to some of the original investors pulling out before they, too, could be implicated. In short, we have too few captains willing to take the risk, and the risk itself has multiplied many times over."

Butler sighed, almost sad. "Oh, but it was a beautiful operation while it lasted, was it not?"

"Positively elegant, General! I shall retire from military service with more than enough funds to launch my political career in fine style. But, of course, much depends on your approval and continued patronage, sir." Butler gave him an avuncular pat of reassurance.

"I can be a loyal friend to those who are loyal to me—of that, there is plenty of evidence. I am sure our postwar friendship will continue to be mutually rewarding. However, for that to happen, we must both finish the war with as much glory as we can accumulate. This brings me to the second topic of our discussion: Grant intends to go after Bobbie Lee from all sides, with everything he has, and if he can't break him in one huge blow, he plans to grind the Army of Northern Virginia until it crumbles. And he does not give a good goddamn how many Federal soldiers have to die in the process. He has such a superiority of numbers that he can lose three men to every one of Lee's and still he will prevail. There is nothing subtle about his strategy; it is pure brute attrition, but in time it will do the job. My Army of the James is to be ready for movement anytime after the first of May."

"That's splendid news. But what does it have to do with my small command?"

"I do not, personally, think that Grant can get so huge a force in motion until several more weeks have passed. In the meantime, Grant has taken great pains to give General Lee the impression that the Potomac front is quiet and will remain so indefinitely. I have heard reports—too many to ignore—that Lee means to use this period of inaction to detach one of his veteran divisions, and combine forces with this supposedly formidable new ironclad, the *Halibut* or something like that. He thinks there's a chance that, if the ship can sweep Commander Flusser's gunboats from the local waters, he might be able to pick off the isolated Union enclaves along the coast, one by one, very quickly, and still bring the expeditionary force back to Virginia in time to redeploy it against Grant. What do you know about this chimerical vessel?"

"The *Hatteras*? Oh, she's real enough, all right, and many miles away up the Roanoke. But she can't possibly be ready to sail yet—I had information only last month that she has neither engines nor guns nor a full coat of armor."

"Is that so? Well, I received information only last *week* that she's already launched, armed, sheathed in iron, and ready to sail as soon as Lee makes his move. The counterattack on this coast could begin approximately one week from now. I came down here to warn you personally."

"Good Lord, General, I don't have the forces here to stand up to an ironclad *and* a first-class division of Rebel infantry!"

"Of course you don't, my boy. You'd be an idiot even to try. But the first place they will attack is Plymouth, north of you. If Flusser's ships can't stand up to the ironclad, that place will fall quickly, and all the lesser garrisons will topple like dominoes, until the only place we still hold is New Bern. I am trying my damnedest to convince Grant to send a division of reinforcements to this theater, but he's as obsessed by Richmond as every commander before him, and to speak candidly, Ulysses Grant and I have never enjoyed what you might call warm personal relations. I shall, of course, keep trying, but I can't make any promises at this stage of the game.

"As far as you are concerned, Hawkins, that's mostly beside the point anyway. What matters to Shelborne's Point is the fact that the whole Rebel campaign would be speeded up considerably by sending the ironclad down *your* branch of the Roanoke, rather than out into the deeper waters of the sound. You're a minor outpost, to be sure, but after they deal with Plymouth, they *will* clean you out. You're in their path, you could threaten their line of supply, and they can probably overrun you in a single day."

Hawkins felt his stomach tighten. Everything Butler said made perfect sense, assuming that the half-mythical *Hatteras* really was finished and ready for action.

"What would you have me do, General, if things develop as you seem to think they will?"

"As soon as I learn that Plymouth has been invested, I'll dispatch a fleet of transports and pull you and your regiment out of harm's way. You'll come back to Fortress Monroe and serve on my staff. Or I may be ordered to reinforce New Bern. It all depends on how this vaunted Rebel supership performs."

"You mentioned 'me and my regiment' . . . Does that include the Buffaloes?"

"Of course not. What the hell use would they be in a conventional campaign? They'll guard the rear while the Massachusetts boys file aboard the transports."

"They are to be sacrificed, then?"

"They will serve a valuable purpose by delaying the enemy for a few hours. Then they can scatter into the brush. You need not tell them in advance, of course, that there won't be any boats waiting for them should they fall back to the river."

"The Negroes in Captain Reubens' company—they'll be butchered if they're caught."

"That, I suspect, is something they have always known and accepted as a possible fate."

"But . . . I would be betraying my own men!"

Butler turned that cold cuttlefish eye toward him, all the warmth gone from his demeanor in an instant.

"Sentiment, Hawkins? That is a luxury no successful commander can afford . . . nor any successful politician, for that matter. If by some chance you ever run into the survivors, just tell them that you tried to wait for them, but the transports had to flee from the ironclad or be sunk. There is nothing implausible in that. A bit weaselly, perhaps, but not implausible at all!" Butler pointed ahead as the former Merdock residence, in all its white-columned graciousness, came into view.

"It seems we have arrived! And smell that fried chicken, would you? Come, introduce me to your '*cordon noire*' cook, so that I can flatter some extra-large helpings out of her!"

Battle Plans

THE ONLY KNOWN civilian witness to the Hatteras' *first sortie down the Roanoke was a Bertie County farmer named Galusha Cooke. Although he had been hearing rumors about this fearsome dreadnought for two years, Mr. Cooke was decidedly unimpressed when he glanced toward the river at 2:30 A.M., after a visit to the outhouse, and got his first glimpse of the actual vessel: "I never conceived of anything more perfectly ridiculous than the appearance of that critter as she slowly passed my landing."*

—Still, William. *Iron Afloat—the Story of the Confederate Ironclads. Vanderbilt University Press. 1971*

April 3, 1864

After taking command of the *Monticello* in early September, Will Cushing had once again been assigned to the blockade squadron off Cape Fear. There were some exciting moments, for the constant increase in the number of blockade ships inevitably resulted in more frequent contact with the elusive runners, but on the whole, Cushing found blockade duty as stultifying as ever.

In late March, he had written to his friend and mentor, Commodore Charles Flusser, asking if he could "trade" the blue-water *Monticello* for one of Flusser's brown-water gunboats. Cushing knew this would be a retrograde career move, but it would also afford a much better chance of seeing action. Flusser's reply was good-natured, but scolding: ". . . much as I would enjoy working with you again, I simply cannot endorse such an unorthodox request. Reflect for a moment: You are the youngest officer in our history to be given command of a *Monticello*-class warship—the summit of every Annapolis man's ambition—yet you whimsically ask to trade her for a much lesser vessel?? The Navy Dept. will think you mad! This, surely, will not be the last war fought by our service! In ten years, or twenty, when battleships are all made of steel and mount turreted guns more powerful than we can imagine, you might well command a high-seas squadron in a great battle against . . . well, who knows? The French, perhaps, or even the Nipponese! Play by the Navy's rules and your star will rise along with your rank. Rock the boat now, and you will never get the chance to take part in the next Trafalgar!"

So Cushing endured and maintained both the morale and efficiency of his crew to a high professional standard. Lord, he wished *something* would happen!

When Flusser, on April 2, requested his presence "for a good meal and some stimulating conversation," Cushing's spirits rose, for that phrase was a private code between the two men. Flusser was telling him that something exciting was in the wind.

The bustling atmosphere of New Bern, when Cushing arrived there two days after Flusser's invitation, communicated an undercurrent of tension. Something, by God, *was* going to happen. Another telltale sign was the gleam in Flusser's eye and the jauntiness in his step.

"Welcome to New Bern, Commander Cushing!"

"My most sublime pleasure to be here, Commodore Flusser!" Then, dropping his voice: "Anything to get away from blockade duty, Charles, even for a few days!"

"Most men would be perfectly content to spend the whole war in such a tranquil berth, but not you, Will! The only time you are truly happy, I think, is when people are shooting at you."

"My mother is of the same opinion. Is it some kind of mental pathology, Charles? I sometimes do wonder."

"Not for heroes, it isn't. Come into my cabin—we have much to discuss and time is pressing. And don't worry about being summoned back to the blockade line for a while—you are nominally under my command, on a mission of the utmost secrecy."

"Is it? Really?"

"Considering that approximately half the officers on both sides have some inkling of it, yes."

Flusser's flagship, the steam frigate *Miami*, was of recent construction and design—the largest and most powerfully armed warship that was considered practicable for the sounds and rivers of North Carolina. Moored alongside her was the only other ship of this class, the U.S.S. *Smithfield.* The commodore's cabin was comfortable and well stocked with good liquors. Without further banter, Flusser tossed his cap aside and spread a chart on the dining table. Will Cushing's heart quickened, for he recognized instantly the snaky course of the Roanoke River and the fortifications surrounding the town of Plymouth.

"The *Hatteras* is coming out," whispered Cushing.

Flusser nodded. "Aye, Will, and not alone. Lee has detached one of his best divisions, General Hackett's, to operate with her. When Hackett encircles Plymouth, the ironclad will come down and pound it from behind. The Union commander there, Brigadier General Wessells, will fight, but he's burdened by a town full of women and children, and his garrison includes two companies of local Unionist volunteers, who may not be allowed the option of surrender. I've already sent four transports, early this morning, to take off the civilians. I'll be going there tomorrow morning with two supply ships, to bring Wessells more ammunition and to evacuate the Unionists. I believe I can beat the *Hatteras* to Plymouth, but the race will be close. Once the transports are clear, I plan to entrap and destroy that ship. With your help, of course, unless you'd rather go back to the blockade line . . ."

"You will have to chloroform me to keep me from being there!"

"I thought you might enjoy it, Will. I might even let you fire a cannon or two."

Cushing's schoolboy grin slowly diminished, replaced by a more somber expression. "Do you really think we can take her with just two ships, Charles? They say she's three times the size of the *Merrimac* and carries much bigger guns. And her captain, Samuel Parker, is a first-rate sailor."

"In point of fact, Will, the *Hatteras* is only half again as big as the *Merrimac* and not nearly so formidable as the enemy would have us believe. After General Foster discovered that the ironclads on the Neuse and Tar were fakes, I sent my own spy up the Roanoke River to get some information on the real one. I sent him *downstream* of course, from Weldon, because that's the last direction the men guarding the ironclad would expect. He was also a Negro, fitted out as an itinerant knife and scissors grinder, a white haired old darkie who impressed everyone he met as being happy-go-lucky and a little bit feeble minded. In reality, he's an experienced actor from Boston, who had been crossing the Potomac for two years, working for Mr. Pinkerton's network. Turned out that the crew at . . . what is the name, now? Yes, 'Holman's Ferry' . . . had a lot of work for the old sharpener—kept him around for three days, in fact. At night he made notes about everything he saw and heard, and when nobody was paying attention, he paced off some measurements. Parker's men treated him kindly, and when he had finished sharpening their pocketknives and swords, they tipped him two dollars and wished him good luck, telling him to keep heading downstream, that he would find lots more work at Scotland Neck and all the way down to Plymouth. Hell, he was so good he convinced the *captain* of the ironclad to write a letter of recommendation—which of course my fellow pretended he could not read. As soon as he was far enough away to hole up for a while in an old barn, he unpacked the drawing paper we had hidden in the false bottom of his grindstone cart and made several sketches of the vessel, while it was fresh in his mind."

With a flourish, Flusser unrolled those drawings on top of the map. The draftsmanship was quite good, and depicted the *Hatteras* from several angles, along with various perspectives on the terrain and buildings surrounding the ship.

"Unfortunately, he left before the ship's guns arrived, so all he could draw was the keel, the superstructure, and this great brute of a ram—*that* is what worries me, Will."

Flusser tapped various parts of the sketches. "I estimate her length to be a minimum of one hundred fifty feet, not counting the ram, which unfortunately was covered with tarps and scaffolding when these drawings were made, so I can only guess at its dimensions. Whatever they are, it's a damned *big* weapon! Here in the aft section there is ample space for two rather large engines, so whatever the armor weighs, it won't take but a few extra knots of speed and a mile or so of open water to work up enough momentum for the *Hatteras* to peel open the *Smithfield*'s hull like it was a tin of beans. Also, even though my estimates may be off by a few inches here and there, I don't see how the Rebs could possibly cram anything heavier than thirty-two-pounders into the space available for their port and starboard guns. They might be able to beef up the bow and stern positions to accommodate, perhaps, a pair of six-inch Brookes—dangerous weapons, to be sure, but even so, my two frigates carry more than twice the broadside weight. And unless they've discovered some brilliant new formula for rolled iron, our hundred-pounders *will* put some pretty deep dents in her plates, pop a ton of rivets, and chip away at her until sooner or later we breach the casemate. Then we can knock the stuffing out of her. No, my friend, the thing we have to fear most is that ram! If we can immobilize the *Hatteras* or restrict Parker's ability to maneuver her, I think we can pound her to pieces, or at least to the point of surrender!

"The river stays fairly narrow between Plymouth and Albemarle Sound, and we must engage her in confined waters, so she won't be able to make any sharp, high-speed turns without the risk of running aground. Parker will expect us to 'cross his T,' turn broadside to his course, so we can fire full broadsides at him while he can only reply with his bow guns. That is what he *wants* us to do, of course, to present the best possible target for his ram. But when he reaches the river's mouth, instead of seeing our two ships at right angles to his, Parker will be surprised to see us advancing straight for him, one on his port side, one on his starboard. What he will *not* see, however, is the boom of interlocking chains we'll be dragging below the surface, tethering our ships together and leaving just enough room in the center for him to pass between us."

Cushing leaped in: ". . . but not enough room for him to sail around us!"

"Exactly! If Parker had time to study things, he might figure out we were trying to snare him, but he won't *have* time because all three ships are closing so fast, there will be only one tactic he can take: ring on full speed and dash between us, hoping to reach the sound, where he has room to maneuver. But when *he* goes to full speed, *we* will stop engines."

"Yes, yes!" Cushing was almost dancing with joy. "So the ironclad's own momentum pushes it deeper into our snare! All three ships come to a grinding halt, with us at close range and the *Hatteras* unable to back up! By God, we might be able to capture her with a boarding attack!"

"I rather thought it would appeal to you, Will."

April 16, 1864

Captain Samuel Parker inducted young Charlie Smith into the Confederate Navy, with the rating of Gunners Mate, Second Class, one week after the Richmond government lowered the age of conscription to sixteen. After investing so much sweat and energy in the *Hatteras*, it was unthinkable to Charlie that the ironclad might sail into battle without him.

During the great upsurge of activity which followed the arrival of the Brooke guns, everyone realized that combat orders would follow soon. Abstractly, Charlie Smith understood that there was only one reason to be packing powder bags and shells into the ram's magazine, but he did not see the connection between that strenuous chore and the unusual gravity that darkened his father's face whenever Peter Smith looked at his only son. Charlie's older shipmates, particularly those who had actually been under fire before, said nothing to discourage him—like every other sailor sent in harm's way, he would either pass the test of battle or he would not. The enormity of what was about to happen did not sink into Charlie's mind until the afternoon of April 16, when a launch from Weldon pulled alongside the supply dock and disgorged half-a-dozen Confederate army officers, one of whom wore the stars of a major-general. Charlie thought the officer was very young for his rank, but he had the unmistakable bearing of a born leader. While Charlie was studying the young general, he heard the familiar rasp of his father's wheelchair and was only mildly surprised when the elder Smith took his hand.

"Now, boy, you have seen your first real hero. That is General Donald Hackett, born in Fayetteville, first in his class at the state university when the South left the Union, rose in the space of a single year from lieutenant to colonel, and my commanding officer when I served with the Thirty-first North Carolina—all the way from the battle at Seven Pines until the day I got my legs shot off at Fredericksburg. You will never see a finer officer—or another major-general who's only twenty-six, I reckon."

Oh, yes, Charlie Smith had heard of Don Hackett; he had heard all of these facts about the "boy general" many times before, from Peter Smith's lips; but it was an altogether different matter to see the man up close, in the flesh, and to know that he was counting on you and your ship to destroy the Yankee gunboats so that his division could throw the enemy off the soil of North Carolina—for good!

And then General Hackett glanced in their direction, just as Sam Parker was unfolding the written orders Hackett had come here to deliver, and he heard the general beg Captain Parker's pardon, for he had just spotted an old comrade and wanted to pay his respects.

Hackett strode purposefully down the gangway and advanced toward Peter Smith, his hand extended in comradeship. Peter Smith tried to come to attention in the seat of his wheelchair.

"I was told that a farmer named 'Smith' had conjured this great ship from a barren cornfield, but until now I did not know they were talking about my former color sergeant! The last time I saw you, our surgeons had despaired of your life, but I declare that except for that wheelchair, you look fitter than I do!" Hackett offered his hand, and Peter Smith grasped it so hard the general winced.

"It is evident, sir, that all the power of your legs has been transferred to your arms! Do not break my sword-hand, I beg you!"

"General Hackett, may I introduce my son, Charles? He will be serving as a sharpshooter on the ironclad's fighting top during the coming engagement."

When Hackett turned the full force of his smile on Charlie, the general's youth became much more apparent.

"Well, Charles Smith, I'm especially glad to meet you because the same people who said your dad was a miracle-worker, also told me he had a son who was seven feet tall and braver than a lion. I thought they were liars, but now I see that they were only reporting the truth. Would you care to join us while we discuss our battle plans? I'm sure that between you and Peter, you'll spot any flaws I may have overlooked."

Charlie Smith had never attended a "strategy conference" before, but when all the officers had assembled in his father's dining room, gathered around a map spread on the table, the chambered solemnity of the occasion reminded him that men would live or die, be victorious or defeated, because of what was said in this room. All eyes turned toward General Hackett, who would naturally speak first. As he outlined his thoughts, Hackett illustrated his main points by placing black poker chips upon the map; Captain Parker anxiously clutched a few blue chips, to represent naval units when his turn came to speak.

Hackett's advance elements—cavalry, engineers, and signalers—had arrived in Tarboro the night before. After detraining, they had marched northeast, guided by local scouts, and made camp at the narrow confluence of the Roanoke and the South Roanoke. At twilight, armed tugs pulling strings of wallowing barges had started downstream from

Weldon, intending to rendezvous with the advance party some time around 3:00 A.M. This convoy was carrying the materials for a pontoon bridge, along with Hackett's artillery, his gunners, and the heavy tools needed by the engineers already in position. As soon as they unloaded these implements, those engineers would start throwing a bridge across the South Roanoke.

His infantry was detraining at Tarboro in unpredictable batches, as large or small as the number of available boxcars from one hour to another. With luck, the entire division would be reunited by noon, April 17, at which time the pontoon bridge should be ready to support their crossing.

"Wessell is a very cautious general, so I don't expect he will try to ambush us. He is also said to be very frightened of the *Hatteras.* He will pull all his troops behind the town's fortifications and try to hold out until he is either heavily reinforced from New Bern or given permission to withdraw aboard transports protected by Flusser's gunboats. But Flusser will certainly not send transports into the river until he has neutralized the ironclad—if he can."

Hackett intended to probe Plymouth's defenses, looking for weak spots and conducting a leisurely but thorough bombardment during the remaining daylight hours of April 17. If the *Hatteras* defeated Flusser's gunboats, Parker would bring her back upriver and start lobbing shells into Wessell's fortifications from the rear. When Hackett judged those works to be sufficiently "softened up," he would commence an all-out assault on whatever portion of Wessell's line seemed most vulnerable.

"Captain Parker, if the *Hatteras* cannot drive Flusser's gunboats away or destroy them, then it will be the enemy who enjoys naval gunfire support instead of my division, and I will not order an attack if that is the case. So, I suppose it's time for you to give us your appreciation of the naval aspect and tell us what you propose to do."

Parker leaned over the map and dropped two blue poker chips on the Roanoke, a mile or so below the town. "Here is what we know for certain. Flusser has stationed his two most powerful ships, the *Miami* and the *Smithfield,* approximately here, just before the river widens out into Albemarle Sound." He scattered a few more chips on the open waters of the sound. "His transports are way out here, screened by a half-dozen small gunboats. If he can stop the ironclad or drive her back upstream with heavy damage, he is free either to reinforce Plymouth *and* add dozens of naval guns to its defense, or to withdraw the garrison under the protection of those guns, depending on his orders."

Parker took two pencil stubs and laid them across the river, about five hundred yards upstream from the first of Plymouth's shore batteries. "The Yankee engineers at Plymouth have sunk two rows of pilings, here and here, hoping to block the *Hatteras* or to entangle her propeller, making her an easy target for a big hundred-pounder Parrott, which they have emplaced here, at the edge of town—its sole purpose is to engage the ironclad. I will have to move very slowly to thread a path through these obstacles. What I'm counting on, though, is the effect of all those heavy rains that fell around here during the past week. The Roanoke was already high from the normal spring run off. The ironclad does not draw as much water as her appearance suggests—one of the many unique aspects of her design. Gentlemen, any naval officer would conclude, from looking at the ironclad, that she *must* have a draft of at least eight or nine feet. In fact, she draws only five and a half feet. These pilings are uneven in height and some of them look very unstable. We may well be able to scrape through, or simply push them aside with the ram. If not, we might have to put our lifeboat down and deal with them by hand. So what I propose to do is sail her down tonight to a point about here—blue chip an inch upstream from the first line of obstacles—and drop anchor, then simply take a close-up look at the condition of these obstructions. But I promise you, General Hackett, that the *Hatteras will* get through those obstacles before sunrise tomorrow. You will know we've made it when you hear that big Parrott gun open fire."

"Can that weapon hurt the vessel?"

Parker, Loyall, and every other member of the ironclad's crew lit up the room with their smiles.

"Let me put it this way—those two big Brooke rifles she's carrying have twice the muzzle velocity of that Parrott. We test-fired them at a typical section of casemate armor, and they only left a dimple the size of my thumbnail. I am so confident that the shore batteries cannot harm us that I won't waste ammunition replying to their fire."

Hackett rubbed his chin thoughtfully.

"You are an experienced naval officer, Parker, and you know your ship's capability better than anyone, but on the face of it, the odds would seem daunting. You'll be engaging at least two dozen heavy guns with only a pair of Brookes."

"Don't forget the ram, general. It's the ram that's the real ship-killer. The Brooke guns will only clear a path for the ram. If we strike those ships at a favorable angle, even at a speed of only five knots, the whole ironclad in effect turns into one gigantic projectile weighing approximately four hundred tons, a self-propelled mountain. We can stove in their hulls as easily as you would crack a walnut."

Hackett nodded, looked inquiringly at his staff. They nodded back. The earlier somber mood had yielded to a palpable confidence. "I guess the only thing left to say is 'good luck.' I shall be listening for the first bang from that Parrott gun," said Hackett as he opened the door.

At 12:25 AM, the CSS *Hatteras* cast off and slowly drifted into the river current's silken embrace. Sam Parker climbed into the small armored cupola that was his battle station. A long thin slit allowed him to observe what lay ahead of the ram, through an arc of forty degrees, and should the enemy's fire get dangerously hot, he could drop an armored flap across the slit and still be able to see through several holes bored through it. For now, he could steer the ship alone, with a small helm or by shouting orders to the engine crew through a voice pipe; in battle, he would be joined in the cupola by his trusted helmsman, Able Seaman Joshua Steeley. This command cupola was encased in six inches of plate and should protect him from anything smaller than a falling meteor. Close at hand was a small pouch full of cotton wads that he could stuff in his ears when the firing started.

Once the ironclad had reached the main channel Parker ordered "All ahead, slow" and felt the engines vibrate to life. There was a half-moon rising in the west, so he could easily discern the channel, but he knew this stretch of river so well he could have navigated it blindfolded. Two days ago, he had sent a patrol downstream, to within five hundred yards of the Yankee pilings. Their job was to locate any new hazards, such as drifting logs or sandbars, and to mark them with lanterns: one if the problem lay to starboard, two if it were on his port side. When he saw three lanterns, he would know he was as close to the first line of pilings as he should go; at that point, he would cut the engines and quietly lower the anchor.

Constant drill had perfected the gun crews' timing and confidence, but Parker was glad to hear them drilling again, over and over, so that when the noise and confusion of battle enshrouded the ship, they could perform their tasks like automatons: *"Shift gun to port side! . . . Drive in spike! . . . On nut below and screw up! . . . Vent and load with shell! . . . Set fuses for contact! . . . Prime! . . ."*

More faintly, he could here the ship's riflemen rehearsing their own drill, clattering up the ladder behind the smokestack and taking positions behind the waist-high breastworks of oak beams and sandbags that would give them reasonable protection when they popped up to snipe at officers and gunners aboard the enemy ships. The breastworks had been Charlie Smith's idea—inspired, the young man claimed, by the crenellations on the walls of medieval castles—and the carpenters had only finished bracing them yesterday with leftover iron clamps. All the sharpshooters chosen for this task were men with combat experience, but not one of them had proven to be a better marksman than Charlie. A few days ago, one of the older, more grizzled snipers had come to Parker and asked if he would grant Charlie Smith the "honorary" role of commanding them in the coming engagement. Yes, he was young and he had never smelled angry powder before, but he was not only a crack shot, but he was also on fire with a desire to wreak personal revenge on the enemy for blowing off his father's legs and condemning him to life in a wheelchair. They would follow Charlie's orders willingly, but would not hesitate to override them in an emergency—the peculiarities of the situation had already been explained to young Mister Smith and he understood clearly where the line was drawn. As unorthodox as this arrangement sounded, Parker gave his approval, much to Charlie's joy and his father's anxious pride. There were three rifles for each marksman, so that when a fired weapon was handed down through the hatch, a freshly loaded one could be handed back by one of the sailors assigned to the job. Parker did not think a boarding attack stood much of a chance—the armored casement was too steep to walk on—but just in case, there were loaded pistols and cutlasses braced in wooden racks throughout the ship.

He spotted the triple lanterns at 3:50 A.M. and immediately ordered the engines stopped, the anchor slipped over the side as quietly as possible, and the longboat lowered. Lieutenant Loyall and three muscular volunteers loaded the boat with tow ropes, chain collars, saws, and shielded lanterns, then set off to investigate the current condition of the obstacles. Sentries were posted, the gun ports were closed so that no light could escape and betray the ship's presence. Parker hung his cap, sword belt, and binoculars on a peg, then curled up on a narrow mattress he had brought into the command cupola. There was nothing more anyone could do except wait, so he scrunched up as comfortably as he could and, much to his subsequent surprise, fell asleep.

Loyall's party returned half-an-hour before dawn. Parker came to full alertness at the first sound of the longboat being hoisted aboard and returned to its protective sunken well on the stern. He climbed down into the fighting deck, tip-toed over several lines of rails and gun-handling tackle, then climbed up the iron rungs leading to the ship's fantail. Loyall was soaking wet and sprinkled with bits of vegetation, but the wide grin on his face indicated good news, and Parker felt the first rush of adrenaline rising in his body.

"We can clear them, Captain. Doesn't look like Wessells has sent anybody out to make repairs. About a third of the pilings are so wobbly you can move them by hand, and another third are at least a foot below the current water level. Either the enemy had no chains suitable for lashing them together, or else lacked the wit to use them, just ordinary one-inch hemp, and most of it water logged and loose. We saw no sign of any submerged booms or torpedo-mines. Just point her straight down the main channel, and we can slide over or push aside everything in our way!"

Parker clapped his executive officer on the back and thanked his crew, ordering them to go below and change into dry clothes. Then he returned to the gun deck, ordered the cook to heat up coffee and cornbread for breakfast, and shook awake those few men who had managed to find sleep beneath their excitement. Charlie Smith was curled up next to a stand of loaded rifles, snoring gently. Parker knelt down and shook the young man awake, while all around them men stirred and spoke softly, spreading the news.

"Wake up, Mister Smith. We'll be sailing into action very soon. The enemy's river blockades turned out to be nothing but an inconvenience, so as soon as we have all enjoyed a little breakfast, it's full speed ahead and we'll bash right through them."

"Cap'n Parker? Can me and the riflemen take a crack at that Parrott gun's crew when we run past her?"

"A commendable thought, Gunner's Mate, but save your bullets for the crews of those two steam frigates."

"Aye, sir. And that's where I will keep the promise I made to my father: that I would kill at least two Yankee officers, one for each of the legs they blew off of him at Fredericksburg!"

Fleetingly, Parker wondered if a sixteen-year-old boy who had never heard an angry shot before would find it an easy thing to shoot a man at such close range you could see the color of his eyes. That was no small, uncomplicated act, even if you had done it before. But at that moment, Charlie's eyes looked a great deal older than his chronological age, and Parker felt radiating from him such a firmness of intent that he knew the youth spoke in earnest and would not hesitate one heartbeat to pull the trigger when the moment came. He nodded approvingly.

"Well spoken, lad. But for God's sake, do not stop at only two!"

Parker rose to his feet and addressed the whole crew, struggling to keep his voice down and to maintain a dignified composure.

"Men, the enemy's river blockade has been thoroughly inspected and I am reliably informed that we can sail right through it! The day we have all worked for and dreamed about is at hand! When we close with the enemy's ships, remember the brave men who suffered defeat and humiliation at Fort Hatteras, not through any fault of their own, but from a lack of proper guns and from the ignorance and neglect of the new government in Richmond. We *have* the power that they did not, and so today we shall avenge them. *From this day forth, the enemy's navy will no longer roam the waters of North Carolina with impunity! With God's help, and the strength of this ship, we shall take back what is rightfully ours!*"

Stirred, the men opened their mouths to shout three cheers, but were stopped by Parker's fierce glare and chopping gestures.

"Save the cheering for later, goddamn it! Do you want the bastards to know we're coming?"

15

Thunder on the River

"LADIES, I HAVE waited two long years to get that Rebel ironclad in my sights. Have no fear! The Navy will do its duty. We will sink, destroy, or capture it, or find our watery graves in the Roanoke."

—Commodore Charles Flusser, speaking to a "Ladies Committee" in New Bern, regarding the hysteria gripping the town with regard to the imminent appearance of the fearsome *Hatteras*

April 17, 1864

High above a sandbag rampart hung the limp, dew-drenched flag of the 42nd Pennsylvania Artillery, upon whose lemon-yellow field a young Plymouth seamstress had woven an optimistic motto "The Ironclad Killers." Flag and staff were stenciled clearly against the fading stars, but everything below was wrapped in coils of thick, clinging fog. From the regimental cookhouse in Plymouth, five hundred yards downstream, came the faint but tormenting aroma of coffee and bacon.

Corporal of the Guard Matkinson, a big-shouldered man who had worked as a railroad brakeman before the war—and who found military service, on the whole, to be a less dangerous occupation than his former one—palmed back a vast yawn and consulted his pocket watch for the fifth time in twenty minutes.

"It's three forty-five, Corporal," muttered the private on the opposite side of the Parrott emplacement.

"How the blazes do you know that, Jenkins?"

"Because every night at about this time, you start checking your watch at five-minute intervals and this is the third time you've checked it since you grumbled 'three-thirty.' "

Matkinson checked his watch anyhow, and the fact that it was indeed three forty-five only served to make him grumpier. General Wessells had doubled the number of sentries for three nights in a row—in response to the supposedly imminent appearance of the near-mythic *Hatteras*—but the logic of that order was not apparent to the men charged with executing it. There was *always* a heavy predawn fog, so if the ironclad sailed by between one A.M. and first light, there was no better chance of spotting it with one hundred pairs of eyeballs than with fifty. Still, the fog was unpredictable stuff and responded capriciously to the winds and tides—now and then, the sentries did catch a glimpse of river, slick and oily beneath the swirling vapors, and several times already jumpy pickets had sounded the alarm after fleeting glimpses of sodden logs or other harmless detritus.

They were, thought Corporal Matkinson, like sailors who had been told, by their captain, that there was a fearsome sea monster nearby, and that some unspecified honor would crown the brow of the first man who actually set eyes on it.

Aye, aye, Cap'n! Eyes peeled it is, sir! Only . . . what, exactly, does this sea monster look like?

I could not tell you, Corporal—it looks just like a sea monster is supposed to look, I presume.

And how will I know for certain when I've spotted it, sir?

Because, you idiot, it will be a sea monster!

And it might even look just like that.

"Jesus, Mary, and Joseph," whispered the corporal.

"It's three fifty-five, no need to look," grumbled Private Jenkins.

As the aperture in the fog expanded, Corporal Matkinson loped across the Parrott gun's enormous pedestal, spun Private Jenkins around, and tilted his head down over the parapet.

"That, by Christ, is not a floating log!"

"Well, tickle my ass with a feather," responded Jenkins.

Jenkins was closest to the alarm bell, so he grabbed the tug-rope and began ringing it frantically, while Matkinson ran downstairs to the gunners' barracks, shouting like a mule-skinner: "Man the Parrott! It's the Rebel ram, come down at last, and heading right into our sights!"

"What does she look like, Corporal?" piped a sponge-and-bucket, struggling into his boots.

"She's big as a fucking mountain, so even you jackasses might be able to hit her!"

Outside, across the length of Plymouth's fortified waterfront, boots pounded up the ladders of gun emplacements, and men shouted excitedly to each other, as the prospect of action flushed away their long suppressed tensions.

Below and to the left of the high, dominating Parrott emplacement, crewmen buzzed frantically around a trio of supporting six-inch colombiads. "Solid shot, load and prime!" The gunners' strategy was to try a massed salvo of solid shot for their initial challenge, followed by one of shells. Whichever projectile had the most visible effect, all four guns would switch to that type and commence rapid independent fire.

The fog lifted just as the ironclad's full length came into view, the sharp low wedge of its prow nosing past the first white aiming stake, driven into the river at 600 yards. No need to calculate angle and deflection: the guns were all synchronized to fire at that stake, aligned so their projectiles would land in a tight zigzag line, each point of impact ten feet from the next. All guns primed, all four lanyards taut, the lieutenant commanding the battery waited until the lozenge-shape of the ironclad's casemate came abreast of the aiming stake, then slashed the air with his signal flag.

The Parrott's report was deep and heavy; the Columbiads' sharp as the crack of a teamster's whip; the four synchronized muzzle flashes ripped like comets through the fog. Impatiently, the gunners leaned forward, eager to hear the mighty impact of their hits . . . and were shocked to hear nothing but four dull, puny clangs. All four guns had made solid hits, yet the Rebel warship steamed serenely on.

Frantically, the crews reloaded with shells and fired their second salvo just as the *Hatteras* cleared the 500-yard aiming stake.

Fuse-settings had been calculated to a nicety and this time the gunners could see exactly where their shots made contact. Again, they scored four direct hits, but relative to the target's looming bulk the shell-explosions seemed dinky as firecrackers. As though responding more to a nuisance than to a deadly threat, the ironclad gained a little speed, generating a saucy little bow-wave, but remained maddeningly undisturbed by the hits scored against her. The Pennsylvania gunners looked at each other, consternation and anger on their faces. With a monumental grace that belied her crushing weight, the *Hatteras* sailed past the 300-yard aiming stake like a dinosaur on a steeplechase. Now it was pointblank range and a ninety-degree angle—if they were ever going to damage her, they had about two minutes to do it, so the battery commander shouted: "Independent, rapid fire!"

He suddenly had a very good thought and was about to add: "Aim at the damned smokestack!" but no one heard him above the now-continuous roar of all four guns firing as fast and steady as well-drilled crews could make them fire.

"Steady as she goes, Mister Steeley," said Samuel Parker to his helmsman. The speed and discipline of the Yankee gunners elicited his professional admiration, for they were maintaining a blistering fire as the *Hatteras* went by, scoring hit after hit, but Frederick Reilly's laminate armor was not only absorbing the rounds' impact, but also had the welcome effect of deadening their sound. Each cannonball, which ordinarily would have made a deafening crash, struck instead with the chime of a flabby gong. The effect was more comic than frightening, and the force of the hits—which he had expected to be bone-cracking—was so dissipated by the armor's slope and layered composition that he felt no greater vibration than that conveyed by a jogging pony to its rider's buttocks. Then the *Hatteras* passed out of the shore batteries' arc into sudden silence.

Parker flipped up the iron lid on his observation slit and noticed that General Wessells had not ignored the possibility of an amphibious attack, for the *Hatteras* was now taking fire from a score of well-entrenched field guns. Their projectiles, too, made no more sound—and inflicted no more damage—than brickbats thrown by schoolboys. *Go ahead and waste your powder, gents—after we take care of Flusser's gunboats, you'll not be receiving any new supplies!*

Parker's crew was jubilant: the enemy had taken his best crack at the ironclad, but the *Hatteras* had shaken off the barrage like so many raindrops. He checked his watch: 4:12 A.M. According to the almanac, morning twilight on this date would officially being in sixteen minutes. Now, Hackett's batteries opened fire. Thump! Bang! Whoosh! Shells traced sparkling arcs from his cannon, spattering the Union earthworks with dingy flashes. Parker refused to be distracted by the spectacle and turned his gaze resolutely eastward. Soon, the *Hatteras* and her crew would face the U. S. Navy's best. He owed a victory to the memory of the Mosquito Fleet, and if revenge was best "served cold," he felt appropriately cool.

Dear Lord, let me redeem their sacrifice today, with this mighty ram! Scatter their burning wreckage across these tranquil waters!

"Cap'n Parker?"

"Yes, Mister Steeley?"

"Dead ahead, sir, about a thousand yards: a pair of enemy frigates."

Parker shouted: "Battle stations!" into the voice pipe. Then he put on his cap, lit a cigar, and smiled grimly.

With an executive officer named "Loyall" and a helmsman named "Steeley," how can he possibly fail?

Charles Flusser and Will Cushing had a five-dollar bet laid on as to which man would spot the Rebel ironclad first. Both were braced against the Miami's bridge railing, eyes clamped to binoculars, and both had been staring up the Roanoke so intently their eyeballs ached. When the Parrott gun above Plymouth opened fire, both men jumped, but neither allowed his eye to waver from his glasses, for fear of losing the last remnant of their night vision. For the next past ten minutes the wall of fog shrouding Plymouth had been disturbed by faint powdery muzzle-flashes—and the drum rolls from a far-off stage band, heralding the start of a great drama. When the last timpani-stroke faded into silence, Flusser muttered: "Won't be long now, Will—she's passed through their arc." Without taking his gaze from the eyepieces, Flusser raised his voice to command volume and gave the first order of battle: "Signal the *Smithfield*: both ships engage engines, course straight ahead, speed two knots. Helmsman, make sure that you and your counterpart keep these two ships absolutely parallel to each other. Tell the engine room to stand by for more speed. Officer of the deck, are all guns manned and loaded?"

"Aye-aye, sir! Solid shot in the Parrotts and shell in the Dahlgrens!"

"And what is your aiming point?"

"The front of her casemate and the smokestack, sir!"

"Two weeks' shore leave to the first crew who damages that stack! If we can trim a couple of knots off her speed, so much the better!"

Neither officer won the wager, for they both spotted the *Hatteras* simultaneously. Through their glasses, the fog bank seemed close enough to touch, and its cottony texture was by now a familiar and much-foreshortened field of gray shadowy whorls. When that texture suddenly changed, a single patch of it acquiring mass and definition and dark solidity, they knew the ironclad was about to make its entrance centerstage. Both men cried: "Here she comes!" at exactly the same instant.

So at last, the *Hatteras* came fully into view, her great bulk shouldering aside the mist, the broad slope of her casemate now clearly defined, small scarves of fog wrapping around the forward gunports. Sparks belched from her stack as it played out a ribbon of gritty black taffeta. Cushing focused as tight as he could, thinking: Where are all her guns?

"I make her speed to be six knots, Charles, and picking up slowly. Heading straight for us. Range: one thousand yards."

"Signal the *Smithfield*: Increase speed to three knots. Engine room: increase speed to three knots. Helm: keep us absolutely even with the *Smithfield*."

Beneath his feet, Cushing felt the deck vibrate more urgently. So far, neither side had fired a shot, but through his glasses Cushing could see the shutters go up, like eyelids heavy with sleep, above the ram's forward gunports. Her guncrews would be running out their weapons, surely nothing heavier than 6.5-inch Brookes. If he were Captain Parker, he would not fire just yet. And when he does, he will surely aim for our bridge. On that thought, Cushing instinctively tensed his upper body, presenting a smaller target. The ambient light had now increased, but it was all coming from the sea, behind the frigates; he doubted that the enemy gunners could make out any details on the Union ships. But they could see the masts, which pointed like arrows at the bridge's location. He and Flusser must have been thinking the same thing, for they automatically put more distance between each other. No point in the same shell killing both!

"Range: nine hundred yards and closing," said the *Miami*'s lookout, secured by safety lines on a narrow platform ten feet above the wheelhouse.

Very calmly, Flusser replaced his telescope in the brass mount that secured it to the bridge railing. From here on, binoculars would be sufficient . . . and in another few minutes, even they would be superfluous.

"Range: eight hundred yards, estimated speed: seven knots," called the lookout, a bit more anxiously than before.

There was a hint of concern now on Flusser's face as well. They had expected the *Hatteras* to be a large warship, but not quite so monumental as she was starting to appear. And still, she had not fired! Captain Parker must have been very confident, and that alone was something Flusser had to take into consideration. "Lieutenant-commander Cushing—do you agree with me that it is time to open fire?"

"I absolutely concur."

Flusser picked up a megaphone and shouted: "All guns: rapid, independent fire! If you see a clean shot, take it!"

"Range: seven hundred yards, speed unchanged!" called the lookout.

The big sleek Dahlgren and the forward broadside Parrott roared in keel-shaking unison. The guncrews were as worked up for this encounter as Cushing and Flusser; they ran through their drill with snap and dispatch, getting shots off steadily and finding the range quickly. Shell-strikes flared brightly on the ram's forward casemate wall, in sooty yellow-red boils; solid-shot heaved up so many towering water-plumes that the ironclad vanished behind them. But the *Hatteras* took no evasive action. Straight and steady, she plowed ahead.

"Range: six hundred yards; speed unchanged!" called the look-out, his voice now dry and raspy.

"Why the hell doesn't he fire?" snarled Flusser, all professional instincts prickling, eyes searching, mind racing. The one-sidedness of the gunnery was bizarre, ratcheting-up the tension. "Will Cushing," said Flusser, "you're about to jump out of your skin." "That may be so, Charles, but I'll bet those poor Rebel bastards are hysterical!" Yet still the great ram came on, without deviating a single degree from its ruler-straight angle of attack.

"Give Parker his due," said Cushing. "That's one hell of a disciplined crew."

At approximately 520 yards, the *Hatteras*'s two forward gun ports flew open and a pair of very large muzzles rolled out. With a shock wave so violent it blew off Flusser's hat, both Brooke rifles fired as one. The size of muzzle-blast and density of smoke were unpleasantly surprising.

"Those are not six-inchers, Will," said Flusser.

"So I see. I guess our information was faulty . . ."

No Federal sailor had ever been a target for a nine-point-five-inch Brooke shell, so Cushing had the unpleasant distinction of being the first naval officer to observe empirical proof of the weapon's power. Cushing knew instantly that the projectile hurtling toward the *Miami* was the largest ever fired at him by a Confederate cannon. Not only was the muzzle-flash distinctive, but the big warhead—which was serrated by deep grooves in a "pineapple" pattern, so it would fragment into unusually big hunks of shrapnel—vibrated visibly as it cleaved the air, producing a low sinister wail very different from the "ripping silk" sound of smaller, more elongated shells. When the approaching missile merely grew in diameter instead of assuming the shape of a blurred lozenge, Cushing realized it was coming straight at the mast above his head. Either it was going to skim by, only inches from the mast, or it was going to score a direct hit on the lookout's platform.

Cushing dropped to his knees, crouching into the smallest possible knot of flesh, but could not take his eyes off the shell as it scorched past, shaking the air like a bumble-bee from hell. In the last millisecond before it scored a direct hit on the platform, he clenched his arms on top of his head and pressed his face flat to the deck. But even with his eyelids tightly sealed, he was half-blinded by an enormous, saw-toothed yellow-white flash and stunned by the sheer loudness of the explosion. He gasped as super-heated powder fumes seared his windpipe, and then a two-foot piece of supporting beam crashed into his buttocks, followed, a second later, by a large portion of the lookout's torso. Other anatomical sectionings, large and small, splashed the bridge with gummy scarlet oysters. When Cushing struggled back to his feet, he saw that nothing remained of the armored lookout-post except a smoldering wooden stump. Everything else was just gone.

Even Charles Flusser was shaken. The *Hatteras* was less than 400 yards away and still steaming on a line that would take her between his two frigates, and therefore straight into the trap set to ensnare her. On both Federal ships, every man not otherwise occupied had taken a rifle and was banging away at the ironclad, lashing the water with such a deluge of lead that the ironclad appeared to be sailing through a hailstorm. Lead smacked flat against iron: the casemate rippled with sparks. Flusser's guns could hardly miss, yet for all the banging and flashing, the only discernable signs of impact was a tartan pattern of scorch marks from the shells; solid shot was useless—most of the rounds shattered like melons.

"Goddamn it!" Flusser stamped his feet in anger and frustration. "We might as well be throwing spitballs at her!" Impatient to do something, Flusser threw off his cap and uniform jacket, told his exec to take the con, then climbed down to the main deck and went to take charge of a giant Dahlgren on the bow.

"What can I do to help, Charles?" yelled Cushing above the deafening clangor.

"Organize a boarding party, Will! Use grappling hooks, after she's caught in the boom! And tell the sharpshooters to concentrate on that big pimple-thing. That's where Parker is, I'd stake my life on it!"

Aware that his friend might already be staking his life, Cushing went below to round up a boarding party.

At the range of 300 yards, Sam Parker tried to ignore his hammering pulse as he studied methodically the warships firing at him. The *Hatteras* was taking one hell of a beating, but so far as he could tell, she had suffered no damage. In his armored cupola, saved from deafness by the cotton plugs stuffed in his ears, he still felt in control. Below him, however, the gun deck was an inferno of shock waves, blinding flashes, and choking powder-stink. Reilly's design, he thought, was now thoroughly vindicated—the ironclad had absorbed enough punishment to sink ten ordinary ships. Now Parker was ready to demonstrate her full offensive power.

He had expected his opponent to form a battle line at right angles to the ironclad's bow; to his surprise, Commodore Flusser seemed intent on maintaining a parallel course that would allow both his ships to pass the *Hatteras*, port and starboard, at very close range. Given the combined closing-speed of all three ships, Flusser would have time to rake the iron-clad with one good broadside at most; conversely, Parker would have a very poor angle for ramming either opponent. Was Flusser planning a boarding attack? Parker hoped he would try—Charlie Smith and his riflemen were itching to go topside and start killing Yankee sailors. The roof of the iron-clad's casemate would be about three feet lower than the decks from which a boarding party would have to descend, but the casemate walls were so steep, so barren of hand- or footholds, that the only place boarders could land and not fall off was in the middle of Charlie's fighting-top.

As for his own tactics, Parker knew that logically, he should already have moved the Brookes to their port and starboard positions. But like Flusser, he would only be able to get off one shot before the *Hatteras* passed through the 'tween-ships gap. Some instinct told him to leave the guns pointing straight ahead. This tactical situation was unique in his experience: an 18th-century duel fought with modern weapons and steam propulsion. History offered no reference points, so both captains were trying to read each other's minds. Flusser would not shrink from boarding, but only as a last resort. He could do no damage with one broadside. Therefore, he must have something else up his sleeve. At a range of 120 yards, at right-angles, neither side could land more than a glancing blow, so both ceased fire for a moment. With greater ambient light and no smoke in the way, Parker carefully scrutinized the frigates' bows. Something was not right. The frigates' bow-waves were rumpled and knotted, where they should have been smooth and symmetrical. There! When the *Miami*'s big Dahlgren fired, the flash cast a stark and vivid light on the water below. There again! A long, liquid hump pushing up the surface from beneath! When Parker swept his glasses to the right, he could see that same rounded, uniform disturbance stretching from the port bow of one ship to the starboard bow of the other. Now that he had noticed this phenomenon, he realized that the bows of both ships were riding low, as though . . . they were weighed down heavily by something.

My God, why didn't I see it before? They're dragging some sort of massive boom between them!

"Helmsman, left full rudder and hold that course until I order right full rudder!"

Puzzled, Steely did as he was ordered, and the *Hatteras* swung in a slow, ponderous arc to the left. As she did so, the gunners on the *Smithfield* were, for the first time, able to fire all their starboard guns at the ironclad. Pile-drover blows rattled and quaked, causing the men inside the casemate to hunker down. The chief gunner's mate poked his head into Parker's cupola, his face a mask of sweaty powder-grime.

"Shall I shift both guns to their side positions, sir?"

That was the logical thing to do but . . . Damn! I've got them now! "Keep them in the bow and load solid-shot! In about thirty seconds, I'm going to execute a hard right turn, and when I do, I want you to blast a hole in that damned ship's side—I intend to stab the ram as deep into her guts as it will go! Don't wait for my order, just fire both guns at the same spot as soon as you have a good angle—rip open a barn door for me, man!"

Parker's sudden change of course looked, at first, like a retreat, and through his glasses he could see the enemy sailors cheering and taunting. There was not much maneuvering room—Parker had to come about facing the *Smithfield* from only 150 yards away or run aground. When the horizon stopped spinning, he had the *Hatteras* lined up perfectly, her bow pointed directly as the center-frame of the *Smithfield*'s starboard hull. "All ahead full, both engines!" he shouted into the voice pipe. "Brace for ramming!"

He could have used more distance. From here, the highest speed he could hope for was a shade over five knots. Not ideal, but enough—especially if the Brooke rifles blasted a hole in the *Smithfield*'s hull before the ram struck.

When they opened fire, Parker's gunners threw a one-two punch: a cast-iron bolt weighing 138 pounds struck first, gouging deep into the frigate's hull, throwing out a corona of shattered planking and splintered chine, leaving a saw-edged hole two feet wide just above the waterline. With superb marksmanship, the second Brooke crew hurled a shell right through that aperture, and when it detonated, Parker saw a blinding flash deep inside the ship. A spear-point of flame spurted out through the hole, coughing up a big wad of flaming debris. In the stunned silence following the explosion, he heard shouts of alarm, for the enemy crew now understood what the captain of the *Hatteras* intended to do next.

Not a shot was fired at her as the ironclad bore down on her target at five-and-a-half knots, the tip of her ram cutting the water like the fin of a gigantic shark. Some of the *Smithfield*'s crew panicked and leaped overboard; most stood frozen on the deck, spellbound by the sight: Leviathan, all clad in mail, was about to smite their ship. Helmsman Steeley, as reassuringly calm as his name, gripped the wheel-spokes with white-knuckled concentration, his eyes narrowed to predatory slits and his teeth bared. At the last second before contact, Steeley threw back his head and gave his very first Rebel yell.

"Yeeee-HAH!!"

Parker was braced for a sledgehammer impact, but the actual moment of penetration was amazingly smooth, producing instead a long moan of violation. Even at five knots, the momentum of 400 tons drove the *Hatteras* deep into the frigate's vitals like a titanic railroad spike. Parker watched in amazement as the ram plowed through a wooden bulkhead and crashed into the *Smithfield*'s main storage compartment, crushing crates and barrels and big pillowy sacks of cornmeal, throwing up a great flurry of barrel staves, tinned food, and so much flour-dust that when the bow finally came to rest, the ironclad's front half looked like a gigantic pastry rolled in powdered sugar. Just for the hell of it, one of the Brooke crews fired another cast-iron bolt, which ripped through the crew's sleeping compartment, a barrel of drinking water, and the ship's laundry, before exiting out the portside hull. By the time the *Hatteras* came fully to a stop, she had penetrated the gunboat's innards to a depth of sixteen feet.

There was no time for self-congratulation. Parker heard a sound every sailor's dreads: the surge of in-rushing seawater. The ironclad's enormous weight was pushing the gunboat's right side deep under water. With every passing second, another half-ton of Albemarle Sound flooded in, and the ram's entry hole was about to go under. Parker raised his hatch and observed, with real panic, that not only was the *Smithfield* sinking fast, the ironclad's retreat was blocked by a great tangle of fallen timbers, rigging, spars, and thick hemp lines wrapped around every part of his ship aft of the smokestack. Without doubt, he had dealt the *Smithfield* a mortal blow, but now the two ships were locked in a deadly embrace and it seemed entirely possible that both vessels would go down together.

"Reverse engines, full power!"

Even as the twin screws gathered power—whup . . . whup . . . whup . . . whup-whup-whup—the Union ship lurched drunkenly to starboard, her list now so steep that every loose thing aboard her was tumbling in that direction. Both engines straining toward full power, the *Hatteras* shuddered and retreated a few inches, then halted again, her keel groaning with stress. Bow-first, the *Smithfield* was sinking like a brick and seemed determined to take her assailant to the bottom with her. But on this fateful morning, the very waters of North Carolina seemed to take sides, for Albemarle Sound was shallow at best and heavy run-offs from the Roanoke had rucked-up the bottom, raising some large but temporary sandbars. As she gathered speed for her final plunge, the *Smithfield*'s bow crashed into one of these underwater hills. All the while, the ironclad's engines poured so much power into her propeller shafts that the pressure gauge trembled above the red line—at any second, one or both boilers would surely explode. At the last second, with a rusty-nail shriek, the ironclad popped free of her victim, riding a volcanic eruption of foam. When the screws finally bit into deep water, the strain on her engines eased off and she floated free, still trailing garlands of rope and rigging, and pulled away from the stricken *Smithfield*. Parker ordered the engineers to throttle down and began planning how to maneuver the *Hatteras* to gain a favorable ramming angle against the *Miami*.

• • •

But the *Miami* was already coming for her, with a bone in her teeth, and Charles Flusser at full boil. For a time, he too believed that the ironclad was doomed to sink with its first victim. Working feverishly, men used axes and heavy bars to detach the bolts and winches fastening the heavy, now-useless chain boom to the *Miami*'s bow. When the last of the boom's attachments were cut free, Flusser felt as though his ship had been taken off a leash. He saw the *Smithfield* crunch into the sandbar and watched in despair as the once-proud vessel slowly turned turtle, rolling over and digging into the bottom until all he could see of her was part of her keel, scabbed with barnacles and oily green thickets of seaweed. Ordinarily, he would have felt pity for the crew of the Rebel ram, for surely they were doomed to drown, while virtually all of the *Smithfield*'s crew had been able to jump clear or find a place in the lifeboats, but such honorable professional emotions were numbed by the shocking suddenness with which the *Hatteras* had killed her opponent; he was also seething because the Rebel captain had sniffed out the trap so laboriously set for him. Then he heard an almost incoherent shout from Will Cushing, who had a much wider view of things from his position on the bridge.

"Charles! Charles! The damned ironclad is loose again! I can see her from here, about a hundred feet from the *Smithfield*. She's still moving in reverse, and dead slow, too. We can catch her, Charles! The boarding party's rarin' to go!"

"By God, we'll do for the bastards yet!" Flusser pointed at his executive officer: "Lieutenant Welles, you have temporary command of the bridge. This is one battle I intend to fight personally! Tell the engine room to give me maneuvering speed and to be prepared to come to a full stop at an instant's notice. Will, bring your band of cutthroats down to the starboard side and round up some ladders and planks—you'll have to climb to reach the top of their casemate. Every sailor not manning the guns or join the boarding party, grab a musket and make 'em keep those gun ports closed!' "

"Three cheers for Commander Flusser!" shouted someone amidships, and the cheers went ringing out across the silken waters of the sound, out toward the windswept ruins of Forts Hatteras and Clark, out to the first bronze gong-stroke of rising sun inching over the sea's cut-glass horizon.

"And three more cheers for Mister Cushing!" shouted one of the Dahlgren gunners. These tributes were rendered with equal volume and passion, for every man aboard the Miami knew in his heart that whatever happened in the next half-hour would inevitably become a chapter in the history of the United States Navy: In all the Eastern Theater of Operations, there were two genuine naval heroes, and both of them were present at this historic battle.

As soon as Samuel Parker saw the *Miami* come into view around the *Smithfield*'s upturned hull, he knew there was neither room nor momentum to try another ramming attack. Flusser would be furious: How DARE the Rebels challenge him with a superior warship? "Commodore Charles," Parker thought, wanted to take this fight back to the days of John Paul Jones. He would grapple, and when the ships were locked together, he would bludgeon, burn, bash, and probably board one another until there was some sort of decisive "historic" outcome. Did the *Hatteras* possess superior technology? Very well, then Flusser would take her on in an alley-fight.

Parker was reasonably sure that his Brooke guns, in time, could have taken the Miami apart, but he could not outrun her, and since Flusser's crew outnumbered his by four-to-one, a barroom-brawl type of fight might go against him. Thank God Charlie Smith had thought about fortifying the casemate roof—otherwise, the *Hatteras* might be overwhelmed by sheer numbers. Both Brookes had been moved to their starboard mounts by the time Parker descended to the gun deck, which was ankle-deep in cold filthy seawater. He called for the gunners to gather around.

"We shall engage her with the same gunnery tactics we used on the *Smithfield*, gentlemen: a solid shot to puncture the hull, followed by a shell to go through the holes and burst deep in her guts. Set fuses for four seconds, maintain a steady fire, and do not be distracted by the many hits we are sure to take. They may have three times more guns than we do, but ours are more deadly."

The gunners nodded, grim-faced but reasonably calm. Parker then moved aft, where Charlie Smith and his skirmishers stood beside their arsenal of preloaded rifles, shotguns, and crudely fashioned hand grenades. Parker had no great confidence in the grenades—tin cans and small wooden boxes, containing a core of tightly packed powder, encrusted with shotgun pellets, nails, pistol balls, bits of iron filing, sharp-edged pebbles, and broken oyster shells—each one sprouting a fuse ostensibly calculated to burn for three-and-a-half seconds. Dozens of these bomblets lay stacked in ration boxes, like a harvest of giant prunes. Charlie's plan was to pin down the Yankee boarders with continuous fire, then when they were crouching and bunched up, bring down upon their heads a sizzling rain of bomblets.

"Sharpshooters!" called Parker. "Time for you to do your stuff! The enemy means to lay alongside us and fight it out pointblank. No doubt, at this moment, there is a large group of bluejackets, armed much as you are, who intend to come swarming over the railing and try to capture this ship with a boarding attack. I am prepared to blow her up and go down with her, before I let that happen. So unless you want to swim home, the order of the day is 'Repel Boarders!' We will work the Brooke guns coolly down here, and in time we shall sink that frigate or drive it away. But I need you to buy us that time. If a single determined Blue-jacket gets through that hatch with a full revolver or a sack of grenades, he can wipe out everyone on this gun deck. Make sure that does not happen!"

"Don't worry, sir," piped Charlie Smith, about an octave higher than usual. "The only way a Yankee can get down that ladder is by climbing over our dead bodies!"

"That's the spirit, Gunners Mate Smith! Gentlemen, to your posts! Um, except for you, Able Seaman Plunkett! A word with you, if I may."

Plunkett, a broad-shouldered man with biceps the size of twelve-pounder balls, nodded tightly. "Aye, Cap'n?"

"Please repeat the order I gave you last night."

"If a boarding party does get into the fightin'-top, I'm supposed to grab Mister Smith and chuck him through the hatchway, no matter how much he kicks and yells and protests. And if he becomes too wild to handle, I have your permission to knock him out."

"Good. I won't deny young Charlie a chance to prove his valor, but if it is humanly possible, I want to bring him back to his father with a full compliment of limbs and eyeballs. Peter has already given enough to the South without donating his only son as well. And the rest of the, um, 'Musketeers' are all right with that?"

"Absolutely, sir. He's got balls the size of honeydews, that kid, but he don't know how bad it's liable to get up there. We can't stop a minié ball, but we can prevent some tar from lopping his head off with a cutlass."

They traded salutes and Parker made his way carefully across the cluttered rails, ropes, and ammunition pyramids on the gundeck and climbed the ladder back to his command post. He ordered the engineers to maintain just enough pressure for steerageway, took one final glance at the *Miami*'s looming approach, then occupied himself by laying out several preloaded pistol cylinders within easy reach. Mr. Steeley was filing down the points of a fishing trident, which he intended to thrust into the shins of any Yankee who tried clambering on top of the command cupola.

"Any minute, now, Cap'n Parker," muttered the grizzled helmsman.

As if on cue, the *Miami* unleashed its first broadside.

From Cushing's viewpoint on the *Miami*'s starboard side, the *Hatteras* seemed to be enduring more punishment than any ship could possibly survive. At times, the ironclad all but vanished behind water-spouts and clouds of smoke from exploding shells, but a sunrise breeze had picked up, carrying off the smoke as soon as it formed, and every time the ironclad became visible again, he could see no vital damage. Her dingy was blown away, her flagstaff shot in half, her armored carapace was mottled with scorch-marks, but despite at least one hundred heavy-caliber hits, not a single iron plate had been dislodged. The Rebel captain understood the futility of trying to escape, so he was turning the *Hatteras* broadside, seeming to accept Flusser's challenge. Cushing figured its broadside guns were probably 32-pounders. Thank God there wasn't enough room inside that casemate for more than two of those monstrous bow-guns!

He was most unpleasantly surprised when the two starboard gunports swung open and revealed the menacing black stare of two muzzles just as wide as those of the forward guns. How did they do that? Up in the *Miami*'s rigging, scores of riflemen immediately threw a concentrated cone of lead at the open ports, hoping to tag some of the gunners within. Unflustered by the hailstone of minié balls, the Confederate gunners took their time aiming and when they were ready. both gun ports belched huge spears of flame and doughtnut-rings of soupy brown smoke. The muzzle blasts were so potent that the shock wave knocked off one of the lifeboat davits, and the meteoric suck of their solid bolts, skimming mere inches above the water, left a liquid trough in their wake as the draft from their passing blistered the hitherto placid surface. At this range, neither side could possibly miss, and the Miami's entire frame shuddered from the impact, both rounds punching through her hull like giant awls. From below deck, he heard ominous crashing and splintering noises as the solid-shot rounds tunneled halfway through the hull, crushing everything in their path. *They'll fire shells, next, straight into those holes, or at least that's what I would do!*

Flusser sensed what Sam Parker was trying to achieve with his guns: the same kind of one-two combination that had wrecked the *Smithfield*—a solid round to puncture the hull, followed by a shell along the same trajectory, which would detonate deep inside the ship. If the Rebels could score enough such hits, his flagship would be blown to pieces from the inside out. To counter this tactic, he ordered another course-change and reduction in speed, so that until the very last moment, the *Miami* would offer the smallest possible target: nothing but the steeply raked angles of her bow.

At the last possible instant, Flusser rang "full stop" to the *Miami*'s engine room and the helmsman threw her into the sharpest possible portside turn. Ironclad and frigate came together with an anticlimactic thump, then recoiled from each other until not more than six feet of open water separated their hulls, forming a narrow canyon which immediately crackled with the lightning bolts of pointblank broadsides. The range was so close that when the guns were run out to firing position, the opposing muzzles almost kissed. The roar and snarl of this alley-fight, vastly amplified by confinement in such a small sliver of space, stupefied the senses.

Through the volcanic boil of smoke, Will Cushing could no longer see Charles Flusser, even though he was less than thirty feet away, but he did hear fragments of his friend's shouted commands, and the blast of his Dahlgren rifle, now depressed as low as it could go, was as huge and terrifying as a comet. Cushing could barely discern the top of the *Hatteras*'s casemate, and even though he knew that the boarding party's objective was only a few feet higher than the deck on which he stood, it seemed a monstrously huge cliff-face—a bad landing could snap a man's ankle. Between cannon shots, he heard the unmistakable clang of a hatch thrown open. Risking a quick peek over the railing, he saw phantoms lurching up from inside the casemate, then taking up firing positions behind some kind of curiously medieval-looking breastwork, flickering smoke-shrouded man-shapes, making themselves as small as possible, slapping their rifle barrels through narrow embrasures and taking very purposeful aim at the railing behind which Cushing's increasingly apprehensive sailors were tightly crouched. A carpenter's mate, jammed hard against Cushing's left hip but suddenly seized by a compulsion to be valorous, rose up, rested his forearms on the railing, and began methodically to empty his revolver at the murky figures beneath. A few others followed his example, bolstered by the confidence of knowing they held the "high ground"—if only by a matter of three or four feet—and therefore enjoyed all the traditional advantages of men shooting from a greater elevation than the men shooting back at them. Then Cushing had a revelation: the curdling smoke between the two ships was thick all the way up to that fortified casemate roof, but beyond that height, the breeze thinned it out rapidly.

They can see us much better than we can see them!

"I think I got one of them!" yelled the carpenter's mate, his face forever frozen in triumph as a minié ball drilled a hole into the jutting pride of his jaw, tunneled an expanding mineshaft through his mouth, and finally exited at the top of his forehead.

From behind the Rebels' breastworks, a high-pitched youthful voice cried out: "That's one, Poppa!"

At that moment, a large work-party of sailors arrived, carrying grappling hooks, coiled 3.5-inch manila rope, and an assortment of planks and ladder-sections, which could be assembled, like pontoon bridge segments, into any desired length. The ensign in charge gave Cushing a quick salute, then dropped on one knee while Charlie Smith's riflemen gouged splinters from the railing, shattered portholes, and very occasionally, swatted a Marine sniper out of the rigging.

"Commodore Flusser's compliments, sir! He said 'Now's the time to board that bastard before he turns this ship into a Swiss cheese.' I presume you know how all this stuff works, Mister Cushing?"

"We run the same drills on my ship as you do on this one, Ensign. Care to join us for the fun?"

"Ordinarily, nothing would excite me more, however I have . . ."

"Say no more, sir. Go do . . . whatever it is, and tell Flusser we're about to conduct the first boarding attack in these waters since the days of Blackbeard."

Grimly, still trying to stay as hidden as possible, Cushing's men tied ropes to hooks, assembled ladders, and made ready for their desperate attempt. As they worked, Cushing gave them a pep talk:

"Are you going to just sit here until that ironclad blows the decks out from under us, or will you follow me on to that damned Rebel ship and take her for the honor of the Navy? When I give the signal, heave those grappling hooks! Put those ladders over the side! There can't be more than a dozen men down there and there are twenty-five of us! When we close on them with cold steel, they'll scatter like rabbits!"

Will Cushing figured that he probably had about twenty seconds to live, but he stood up, swept out his cutlass, and cried: "Boarding Party away!"

Another minute and the whole detachment would have been too paralyzed by fear to take action. But there stood the indestructible, the legendary, Cushing, bullets zooming around him like angry wasps, slashing his blade toward the armored giant below, and it was true what his men said about him: Will Cushing seemed to glow with a supernatural aura of invincibility. His melodramatic pose and unflinching determination conveyed an inspiring fantasy: the bullet has not been cast that can kill me! And sure enough, when he was not instantly cut to pieces by the hail of lead directed at him, the others took heart and joined him in a furious assault. A half-dozen grappling hooks, knotted to lines of stout hawser rope, arced upward and out, some of them looping completely over the casemate roof, and most of them hooked firmly on something or other—a ladder rung, a stanchion, a mooring cleat—lashing the two vessels even more closely together than before. Like medieval storming parties, small groups of Union sailors upended ladders and pushed out planks until their forward ends landed on something stable enough to support a man's weight. Cushing's cutlass swung like a windmill blade and his men went forward. Some boarders chose to sling their Springfields on their backs and climb across on the grappling lines, hand over hand, like monkeys; others clenched their teeth, hunched their shoulders, thrust out their bayonets as though they were shields, and took the first shaky steps across the wobbly catwalks.

Charlie Smith handed his empty rifle to someone behind his back; it was seized and a loaded weapon slapped into his impatient grasp. The Yankees were coming! And from their shouts he realized, with a thrill of awe, that they were commanded by none other than the legendary Will Cushing. My first fight, he thought, grinning with a high private excitement, and I have the honor to face the modern-day Achilles! Where was he? Which of those reckless bluejackets was Cushing?

But now that the enemy sailors were committed to their assault, they swarmed so thickly that Charlie no longer had the time to choose a particular target. He swung his rifle; it moved and quivered like a predator sniffing out prey, and the front blade sight steadied itself on a frightened-looking but determined bluejacket who was bobbling up and down on a rope line, rifle slung across his back, a dagger in his teeth, almost close enough for Charlie Smith to reach out and touch his chest with the muzzle of his Enfield. I'm sorry, sailor, and whoever you are, may God receive your soul in Heaven! Charlie thumbed back the hammer, steadied his aim, and fired. The Enfield's recoil delivered a smooth rolling punch to his shoulder, and the brave man in his sights saw the muzzle flash and braced himself, had time to take one last deep breath, and then the blue cloth over his chest puffed out like a paper flower, followed by a scarlet bubbling fountain, and his mouth opened, his expression melted into a strange mixture of sadness and resignation, the piratical dagger falling out of his teeth, his left hand loosening its grip and curving down to clutch at the mangled rosette of sodden blue cloth through which his heart's blood was pumping into the sea. And then he dropped, heavy and limp as a sack of potatoes, vanishing into the seething curds of smoke boiling in the hellish crevice between two dueling warships.

"That's two, Poppa!"

After seeing five men shot down in as many seconds, Cushing could feel the resolve start to drain from the boarding party. However brave or strong or sure-footed, no man had yet been able to reach the *Hatteras*. Cushing crouched beneath the railing, aware that everyone else was looking at him with an expression that seemed to say: Okay, hero, what now? Well, there had to be another way of getting on to that ship.

Then a nearby tar nudged his shoulder and pointed to their right. "Lookee there, Mister Cushing, it's Carpenter's Mate Jones!"

Cushing took a careful peek. "Now, that's using your noodle!"

An intrepid carpenter's mate, one Hezekiah Jones by name, had donned a pair of fireman's gloves, wrapped himself around a long dangling shroud line, tucked a pair of pistols through his belt, and had begun to work up momentum—like a boy on a rope swing—until he had enough of an arc going to carry him across to the *Hatteras*. He dropped quite neatly on to the space between the forward edge of the casemate and the front of Sam Parker's armored cupola.

"Way to go, Jonesy!" shouted a comrade.

Other Union sailors cheered and shouted encouragement. Jones heard them, over a brief pause in the cannonade, and coolly paused to make a theatrical bow before scampering toward the observation slits, both guns drawn. His intention, clearly, was to pump the cupola so full of lead that anyone inside was certain to be hit. But as he leaned over to shoot, something long, green, and pointed—to Cushing, it seemed like the forked tongue of a viper—stabbed out through the slit and deeply impaled Jones's right shin. Immediately it was withdrawn, the iron shutter slammed down, leaving Jones hopping almost comically on one foot and glancing desperately around, wondering how he was going to extricate himself before word of his presence was passed to the skirmishers and someone climbed up to finish him off. Observing his predicament, someone on the *Miami* threw him another line. Jones grabbed hold, his right leg now sopping in blood, and jumped. With no momentum behind him, he dropped dangerously low, between the two ships, and when he realized he was dangling only two feet from the muzzle of Number Three Starboard Parrott gun, he began scrabbling like a chimpanzee, clawing his way higher before that gun fired. He almost made it.

But Number Three Parrott gun did what Parrott guns were famous for doing: it blew up. Not disastrously for the gunners, for this malfunction was a slow cook-off, and did not explode so much as burp, generating enough force to dismount the gun from one of its trunions. That same amount of force was sufficient to shove the already loaded shell out the muzzle with only a fraction of its normal velocity. The pointed projectile exited the gun so slowly Cushing could easily track its path, and it smote the hapless Jones squarely in the stomach. It penetrated halfway through his body, a massive dull-black cylinder, hot as a stove-top. Steam spat and boiled around its circumference: iron melting human tissues and turning every fluid in Jones's body cavity into scalding pasty soup. Jones looked down, saw the great iron shaft protruding from his torso, and was so thunderstruck with amazement that he literally forgot to scream. Another second or two, and the shell's weight would have pulled him down, but Jones only had a half-second to contemplate the outlandish nature of his impending death before the fuse timed-out and he was blown to pieces. When the smoke cleared, one of his hands, severed at the wrist, still clung to the burning rope. As his shipmates watched in horror, the flames spread upward and roasted that extremity like a pig's knuckle on a spit. Cushing averted his eyes and groaned. The crews of both ships were so stunned by the sight that a brief lull silenced their guns.

But Charlie Smith's "Musketeers" recovered first, and since they knew perfectly well where Cushing and his thwarted boarders were gathered, they decided that this was as good a time as any to use up their motley collection of hand grenades.

At first, Cushing and his followers did not understand the nature or purpose of the sparkling, multifarious objects that suddenly began to rain on them. In the U.S. Navy, hand grenades were not standard-issue. But the pinned down boarding party quickly learned what hand-thrown missiles could do at close quarters, for when that shower of cans, boxes, whiskey bottles, and crockery began to explode over their heads, against their midriffs, and in the hands that instinctively reached up to catch these curious objects, they inflicted, if not mortal wounds, then an endless variety of gashes, lacerations, partial scalpings, digital amputations, and at least four cases of whole or partial blindness. Cushing had ducked and scrunched himself into the smallest possible target, so he was luckier than most, sustaining only a long shallow cut across the top of his forehead. It was an inconvenient injury—like all cranial cuts, it bled like a stuck pig—and not particularly painful, but the sudden torrent of blood effectively blinded him until he could crawl off and locate a strip of cloth suitable for making an improvised bandage. By the time he had stanched the flow and regained most of his vision, what remained of his boarding party had melted away. A few stalwarts were still gathered by the railing, lethargically trading shots with the Confederate riflemen, and when Cushing rejoined them, they saluted and told him they were ready to make another try. He thanked them for their gesture of faith, but he could tell from the wariness in their voices that they no longer had the nerve for an assault, even if one had been practicable. A quick peek over the rail told him that all the boarding ladders had been dislodged or chopped loose by the enemy. A few sagging ropes still connected the two ships, but after seeing the death of Carpenter's Mate Jones, few sailors would be inclined to use them.

"Thank you, gentlemen, but I think we've lost our chance at boarding her. Assuming we ever had a chance. This boarding party is officially dismissed. Look after your injured mates, while I go ask Commander Flusser if he has anything else for me to do."

Not long after helmsman Steeley had gleefully stabbed that impudent boarder with his fishing trident, Samuel Parker received word from below that the *Hatteras* had fired off sixty percent of her ammunition. The rest of it would be needed to support General Hackett's assault on Plymouth. Reluctantly, he passed the word for Charlie Smith's riflemen to retire, for the engines to give him one-third power, and for the Brooke crews to secure their weapons. As his propellers began to bite water again, Parker took a long last look at his adversary.

By all rights, the *Miami* should already have sunk. Smoke was pouring from her in a half-dozen places, indicating that fires still burned deep inside her hull, and her starboard side was mangled, a veritable Swiss cheese, with so many holes he stopped counting after twenty. What had saved her was the close range of the action, for the Brookes could not be depressed low enough to target the waterline. Nevertheless, Parker was satisfied: even if Flusser's flagship made it back to New Bern, it would take months of repairs to make her seaworthy again. To stop the *Hatteras*, the enemy had sent his best captain and his two most powerful ships, and had failed utterly even to damage her.

Flusser was stripped to the waste and tiger-striped by a crust of powder grime and sweat. He was still standing behind the big Dahlgren, whose exhausted and hollow-eyed crew was moving like sleepwalkers. The sponge-man had dug up a flask and was passing it around, a flagrant violation of regulations which Flusser chose to ignore in exchange for a captain's share of the whiskey when the flask came his way. After returning the flask, he once more bent over the sights and called out, in a frustrated and snappy voice, a series of fussy adjustments that changed the weapon's aim only by microscopic increments.

"Goddamn it, crank this piece one more degree to the left!"

"It's a hundred-pounder, sir, not a sniper's rifle," grumbled one of the straining gunners.

"Don't be too harsh on them, Charles," Cushing announced himself. "It's been a frustrating day for members of the gunnery trade."

"Hello, Will," replied Flusser, not taking his eye off the target he was apparently obsessed with. "No luck with the boarding party, I gather."

"It was suicide to try. But I do have some interesting stories about our experiences . . . when you have the leisure, that is. And by the way, I think the ironclad's preparing to disengage—she's working up steam, at any rate."

"I have time for one more shot, Will."

"I suppose you do, but what difference will it make? We've already hammered her with more than at least a hundred hits and done nothing more serious than ventilate her smokestack."

"I've been trying to put a shell right into her captain's little turret-thing. Only missed it by a hair just a few seconds before you arrived. If I can throw a shot right on to one of those shutters, I believe it will penetrate—I've been studying them. They're just half-inch iron panels, obviously worked by pulleys or hinges, which means they can be knocked off or punched-through if I hit them at just the right spot."

"How long on the fuse, sir?"

"Four seconds. If the shell does punch its way inside, whoever is in that compartment won't have time to blink."

"Do you really want to kill such a gallant opponent?"

Cushing had never heard his friend speak so coldly, as though he were working out an equation, not scheming to kill a fellow naval officer—indeed, a man who had demonstrated courage, bold enterprise, and exceptional skill.

"You're goddamned right I mean to kill the son of a bitch," growled Flusser, wrapping his fist around the firing lanyard. Then he adopted a more reasonable tone of voice. "It's nothing personal, Will, but it is unthinkable for the United States Navy to lose a battle without inflicting a single casualty on the enemy! And I will not be the first captain in the history of our service to claim that distinction. If I can pick off Captain Parker, that will salvage the Navy's honor, at least . . . not to mention my own self-esteem. Now cover your ears and stand back while I send that man to his Maker!"

Flusser took one final squint to make sure the big Dahlgren was lined up to his absolute satisfaction, then stepped back until the lanyard was taut and gave it a smooth pull. Even though Cushing had covered both ears, the big cannon's discharge was prodigiously loud and the back-blast felt strong enough to peel the skin off his cheeks. At this range, a mere thirty-five feet, the shell-hit would be almost instantaneous. But in the thinly shaved second when the projectile was traveling down the cannon barrel, two things happened that, conjoined in their effect, deflected the missile from its intended path. First, the *Hatteras* put on a small burst of speed as pent-up pressure finally drove the shafts and delivered some spin to her propellers, and second, the battered *Miami* suddenly lurched hard to starboard, dropping the Dahlgren's muzzle by a couple of inches.

That was all it took, however, to cause the shell to strike the top of the heavily armored casemate instead of the vulnerable observation slit. Had the range been long enough for the shell to achieve maximum velocity, it probably would have cracked apart like so many of the *Miami*'s shells had done earlier. But when it banged into the casemate, it had only worked up a third of that speed, and so instead of shattering, the big round bounced hard and high—Cushing could follow its almost lazy ascent and much more rapid fall—and returned whence it had come, embedding itself in the *Miami*'s deck about three feet in front of the flabbergasted Charles Flusser. He stared, wide-eyed with horror, at the sizzling bomb and had time to say: "Not like this!" before the shell detonated.

Will Cushing had time to throw a protective arm across his face and partly turn him away before the blaring yellow flash temporarily blinded him and, riding the shockwave that knocked him flat, Charles Flusser's right arm struck him on the temple so hard that Cushing lost consciousness just as his brain shrieked out the message: Will Cushing, we are dead!

Cushing regained consciousness in the *Miami*'s surgery. At first, he could not see Charles Flusser, but when he struggled to one elbow, he realized that all the medical personnel were bending over the operating table, examining his best friend's wounds. Fighting off waves of nausea and dizziness, Cushing struggled to his feet, and almost fell again, because the blood was so thick on the floor that he could have sledded on it.

One of the surgeons saw him staggering over and tried to restrain him.

"Mister Cushing, no need for you to see this! No need!"

"I will see my friend, by God!" Cushing shoved the doctor away and gasped at the sight of Flusser's wounds. Not any two square inches were intact. The right foot was gone, as was the left leg below the knee; of the one intact hand, just two fingers remained; while one surgeon tried to force morphine tablets into the pulpy slit that had been Charles Flusser's lips, another was trying to repack his intestines—staring at the glistening loops and tubes in his hands as though trying to figure out a complicated mariner's knot. Surely, Flusser was already dead! But not only was he alive, he was conscious, for when he heard Will's voice, he opened his one remaining eye and held out that two-fingered hand, motioning for Cushing to come closer.

Cushing took his friend's mangled hand and stroked his forehead—the only comfort in his power to give.

"How is it, Charles?"

Flusser's voice was small and clogged with fluids, but perfectly audible. He even tried to smile.

"Why is it that people always say things like that to someone who's in this condition? Frankly, even if there were words for it, I would not even try to tell you 'how it is' . . . Stop poking those damn pills into my mouth! I'll be dead long before they take effect! Will, as you love me, swear to me one thing."

"I do love you, Charles and whatever you ask, I will swear it."

"Destroy the *Hatteras* for me! Not one ship in these waters can stand up to her, but you . . . you might figure out a way."

"I do swear it, my friend," said Cushing as his tears began to pour freely.

"It's a great beast, that ship, a dragon! Only a great hero can slay her!"

Then a torrent of blood and tissue welled up in Flusser's throat and, mercifully, he coughed once and died.

The surgeon who was fiddling with Flusser's ropy bowels muttered: "Damn! I almost had this figured out . . ."

"I'm Sorry, but You're On Your Own Now!"

GENERAL HACKETT'S ARTILLERY had been pounding my earthworks since 4:00 A.M., with moderate effect, and his brigades were skillfully deployed to the west, south, and east of Plymouth, so that I could not determine from which direction his main effort might come. The entire garrison, of course, had heard the heavy firing when the Hatteras *passed the town, and by sunrise, every man knew that our heaviest weapons had scored many direct hits on the ironclad, but inflected* no visible damage. *Naval shelling is especially demoralizing to infantry; doubly so when they perceive they cannot harm the ships conducting it! Thus my troops were very anxious by the time the* Hatteras *returned to Plymouth, at 9:30 A.M., for its appearance signified not only that the Navy had been impotent to harm the ironclad, but also that they could expect no reinforcements nor any transports to evacuate them.*

Indifferent to my shore batteries' feeble replies, the ironclad began systematically to destroy every battery, bastion, and entrenchment on my left flank. When Hackett ordered Ransom's brigade to assault that weakened sector of my line, at approximate 11:45, the defenders broke in disorder after firing a few perfunctory volleys, spreading panic as they ran through the streets.

Our position was thus no longer tenable; to avoid the useless effusion of blood, I ordered a white flag to be run up the church steeple at 12:40 P.M. General Hackett took my surrender graciously, remarking, "This is the happiest day of my life."

Gravely, I replied, "Yes, but it is the saddest of mine."

—General Godfrey Wessells. "A Pretty Southern Town: Two Years of Peaceful Fraternization in Plymouth, N.C." *The Union Veteran,* March, 1873.

After his men spent the afternoon securing twenty-six hundred prisoners, General Hackett's quartermasters collected significant and very useful military bounty from warehouses in Plymouth, including two tons of supplies and munitions, six field guns in perfect working order, fourteen supply wagons, and enough well-fed mules to pull them. In a strategy conference he convened at six o'clock, Hackett could not resist gloating. "General Wessells has inadvertently supplied us with many needful things, including twenty percent more artillery than we had this morning! Now, let us figure out how to take advantage of this unexpectedly swift victory by deciding what our next move should be and when we should make it."

Attention was focused on the two Union strongholds between Plymouth and New Bern. Both were small coastal towns like Plymouth, and therefore vulnerable to the ironclad's punishing bombardments: The nearest town, Washington, on the Pamlico River, was known to be weakly garrisoned and Hackett thought it likely that the enemy would evacuate the troops stationed there in order to beef up his strength at Wilmington. If the Yankees chose to make a stand there, Hackett was confident he could overrun the place in a matter of hours.

Shelborne's Point was a strategic question mark. Some of Hackett's staff were in favor of bypassing it altogether; its landward fortifications were fairly strong, but at last reports there was not a single battery covering the South Roanoke—the ironclad could run past the place with impunity. Apparently the tiny port was the site of some maintenance and repair facilities, but it was guarded only by a single infantry regiment and some mounted bushwhackers of marginal military value. After returning from Foster's expedition, the troops in Shelborne's Point had remained docile. In Hackett's opinion, the town could safely be left undisturbed. "I'll detach a small cavalry screen, so we'll have plenty of warning if the troops there do try something, but although their commander, a New Yorker named Hawkins, demonstrated competence in Foster's recent campaign, he has otherwise shown no aggressive tendencies whatever.

"Why waste time and energy laying siege to the place when we should press on to New Bern as quickly as possible, before it can be further reinforced? Once New Bern falls, the remaining Federal enclaves can be picked off at our leisure. I therefore propose that we ignore Shelborne's Point and press on to Washington, assuming we do not receive intelligence that the garrison there has already been evacuated. With our communications to Plymouth thus secured, we can lay siege to New Bern in three or four days. Does everyone agree with this proposal?"

Samuel Parker respectfully cleared his throat and raised a hand. Hackett made an encouraging gesture. "Share your thoughts with us, Captain Parker. After all, you know this neighborhood much better than we do."

Parker pointed to the map. "With regard to those 'mounted bushwhackers' at Shelborne's Point—who call themselves 'the Buffaloes' by the way, though I have no idea why—their recent inactivity has nothing to do with a docile temperament. They've been quiet simply because there is nothing left to plunder and no one left to intimidate within a thirty-mile radius of Shelborne's Point. The Buffaloes drove off or killed every Confederate sympathizer in three or four counties. They are not likely to challenge your troops in open battle, that's true, but it would be a mistake to underestimate their skills as guerrillas or as mounted riflemen. You can screen the road from Shelborne's Point with as many cavalry as you like, but those boys know every deer path and hunting trail in the woods and can almost certainly evade detection if they choose. They are hard men, and their commander seems to like a good fight—if they decide to attack your supply line back to Plymouth, they can cause a lot of trouble. My advice is for you to seize Shelborne's Point and eliminate that potential threat. I do not expect General Hawkins to mount a stubborn defense—except for their reluctant participation in Foster's expedition, his Massachusetts regulars have enjoyed a soft life for the past two years. You won't have to fight very long or very hard to seize the town, so my counsel would be to take the place, if only to put the Buffaloes out of business. A small nest of vipers is still a nest of vipers."

Parker knew he was making no small presumption by giving strategic advice to veteran infantry commanders, but his convictions were strong and, as Hackett himself had observed, he "knew the neighborhood" better than they did.

"It will take us one day to get reorganized and one day of hard marching to reach Shelborne's Point . . ." mused Hackett. "Is there a chance the *Hatteras* can be fully operational in two days?"

"There's a blacksmith's shop here in Plymouth," said Parker, "so we may be able to reattach the loose armor plates rather than install new ones. If we can find some sheets of tin, we can patch the smokestack. If you can spare a good rider, I'll send a message to Holman's Ferry, requesting ammunition be loaded on the first barges they send down, rather than ironmongery . . . Yes, General, the *Hatteras* will be ready to support you at Shelborne's Point in forty-eight hours. But after we've taken the place we will have to pause and make proper repairs before heading to New Bern. I expect the U.S. Navy to fight like blazes there, with every ship they can muster. I do not want to hazard such a one-sided encounter unless the *Hatteras* is in top-notch condition."

Hackett nodded, then addressed his staff: "Gentlemen, we will do as Captain Parker suggests. Prepare your men to march on Shelborne's Point. And tell them that the *Hatteras* will once again support them."

To reach Rush Hawkins' headquarters, Jack Fairless first had to ride through the dockside area of Shelborne's Point, then pick up the carriage road leading north to the stately white-columned mansion Hawkins had appropriated after Cyrus Bone murdered its former owner, a pompous judge named Murdock. Fairless noticed that there were more lights burning than usual and more uniforms bustling about the waterfront than he expected to see eleven o'clock on a Monday night. Something was up, and Jack hoped that meant the Buffaloes would see more action; life had been a little dull since the outfit got back from the Tar River adventure.

Lights blazed in Hawkins' headquarters, too, and security was tight. Despite his rank, Jack was stopped twice by sentries and required to show them Hawkins' note—requesting his presence to discuss "important developments"—before he was allowed into the general's office. Hawkins greeted him warmly, but wasted no time on pleasantries.

"Well, Jack, you've been telling me the Buffaloes are hankering to see some more action—it looks like they'll have the chance, and a lot sooner than I would like. I've just learned that the *Hatteras* has finally come down the Roanoke. At dawn this morning, she sank one of Flusser's big new frigates and mauled another so badly it had to be towed back to New Bern. I regret to say that the gallant Commodore Flusser was killed in the battle. In conjunction with the ironclad's sortie, General Lee has sent a crack infantry division to attack every Federal position on this coast. Plymouth surrendered at noon. You know enough about strategy to see what the Rebs' ultimate objective is: to retake New Bern. And we, alas, are smack in their path. It will take them a while to get organized for the march, but we can expect them to attack Shelborne's Point sometime around midday, on Monday, the twentieth.

"The ironclad, too, General Hawkins?"

"Almost certainly. We cannot hope to defend the town against such overwhelming odds, and besides, about one third of the civilians are Unionists now. Six of the Massachusetts regulars have married local girls and some of them have babies to worry about. I want to evacuate every civilian who wants to leave, and do it swiftly enough to prevent any bombardment of the town itself."

"Are we just going to surrender, then? Because if that's your plan, then I request permission for me and the Buffaloes to ride out of here tonight and take our chances in the wilderness. As you well know, a number of my men are deserters, just as I was. And what about all the runaway slaves in Captain Reubens' company? They may not even be *allowed* to surrender!"

"Calm down, Colonel Fairless! By the time the enemy reaches Shelborne's Point, we will all be long gone and heading for the safety of Fortress Monroe. Our friend and patron, General Butler, foresaw this happening and is sending a convoy of transports to evacuate both the garrison and all the civilians who wish to go with us. Our margin of safety, however, is mighty slim, and the docks are only big enough to handle two of those transports at a time. Barring bad weather, the first transports should arrive around 1:00 A.M. tomorrow night. With any luck, the Unionist civilians and most of our heavy equipment will be gone by ten o'clock on the morning of the twentieth. *If,* that is, that Rebel column isn't able to move any guns into range of the docks before that time. If they do, a lot of helpless people will be killed. Only after all the civilians are safely gone will I start boarding troops. All of this will take *time,* however, and I need to buy a few more hours of it. The Buffaloes have proven they know how to fight a delaying action, so I'm asking you to do it again, to prevent a possible bloodbath. It will be very risky, so I'm not making this a direct order, but . . ."

Fairless leaped to his feet. "By God, sir, we will or die trying!"

"I hoped I could rely on you, Jack!" Hawkins pumped Jack's hand warmly, then unrolled a map on the nearest tabletop.

"Here's how I want it done: This afternoon, I want you to reconnoiter three or four successive defensive lines, so you'll have fallback positions. When the pressure builds up too much on one line, pull back to the next, and so on. The terrain is too rough for the Rebels to outflank you with mounted cavalry, and the road's too narrow for them to bring their artillery forward without wasting a lot of time and causing a lot of disorder. After you engage them at your first line, it will take them at least an hour to work a large number of troops through the woods to positions where they can exert pressure on your flanks. When you sense that is happening, don't wait, don't risk getting cut off, just stage an orderly withdrawal to your next line and wait for them to come into your sights again. Each time you do that, it will take them twenty or thirty minutes to get formed up in column and another half-hour to make contact with your men again. If you can keep them out of artillery range of the docks until, say, ten o'clock, that should give me enough time to get all the civilians safely away. Any time after ten, you are free to break contact and hightail it back to the docks, where the last transports will be waiting to pick you up."

Fairless was very sober-faced, but Hawkins was relieved to see that he was accepting the scenario without argument or objection. He came to attention and saluted. "This is the most important task you've ever entrusted to the Buffaloes, General Hawkins. I speak for all the men when I say 'thank you' for the honor. We will not let you down!"

"Good man. Just knowing you'll be guarding our backs takes a big load off my mind! Now, Jack, I have a hundred chores I must attend to, so I advise you to go back and tell your company commanders what's in the wind. If I were you, I would also advise them not to tell their soldiers—so the men can get a good night's sleep. Sometimes the best medicine for that is . . . ignorance about tomorrow."

Almost as soon as Fairless closed the door, he poked his head back in.

"Yes, Colonel?"

"One more thing, sir. It's about the whores."

"The black ones or the white ones?"

Fairless shrugged eloquently. "Whores is whores. The chocolate-flavored ones, they don't have to wait for us to escort them to the boats, do they?"

"No, no, of course not. They will be taken aboard along with the other civilians."

Fairless nodded happily—he was reportedly very attached to one of the light-skinned wenches out at Captain Reubens' colored bordello.

As soon as Jack left the room, Rush Hawkins muttered to himself: "I am certain Ben Butler can find suitable, um, positions, for the more comely ladies at least."

One of Rush Hawkins' "hundred chores" involved the systematic destruction of every scrap of paper that might yield to investigative eyes any details of the swindle Ben Butler and his consortium of rich but increasingly squeamish investors had set up here at Shelborne's Point. Hawkins had managed, very efficiently, the switching of legitimate, extremely valuable, export cotton for cargos of defective guns and tainted food. Butler's industrialist cronies got their Dixie yarn and the Army of Northern Virginia got the squitters; on the margins of these shady transactions, Rush. C. Hawkins got rich. Thus hummed the dynamo of Free Enterprise. Now, evidently, Butler had decided that the profits-to-be-made no longer justified the risks-to-be-taken. As for Hawkins' private spoils of war—a cellar full of valuables ranging from the late Judge Murdoch's Masonic ring to Hawkins' one-third cut of all the gold, silverware, and antiques Cyrus Bone had extorted from local Confederate sympathizers—those assets were already crated and piled on the cargo wharf, labeled as "Misc. Tools," and would be among the first items loaded into the transports' holds.

While Hawkins burned evidence, he also laved his conscience with copious amounts of Ben Butler's finest wines. Had the matter been left to his discretion, Jack Fairless and his men would have been evacuated along with the Sixth Massachusetts and the Unionist civilians. Asking the Buffaloes to fight a rearguard action and then sailing away without rescuing them . . . well, it was a despicable thing to do; for the white Buffaloes who survived the battle, it meant starving in a Rebel prison camp. For the Negro troopers, it probably meant a much harsher fate. But what choice did Hawkins have? He was following a direct order from his own superior, Ben Butler. The fact that he was counting on Butler to launch his postwar political career was merely a coincidence. As a good soldier, Hawkins did not have the luxury of following only those orders which he found morally palatable.

Damn it, *somebody* had to slow down Hackett's division so there would be enough time for everyone else to escape. That was just a fact of war—always had been—and the "fairness" of it was irrelevant. In fact, the more Hawkins pondered this unsavory situation, the more he was able to convince himself that Butler *did* have a valid point about the Buffs. Fairless and Reubens had whipped them into a crack unit, but they were still "irregulars," best suited for independent guerrilla-style operations. Where would they fit into the ponderous, formal mass of Grant's Army of the Potomac? They obeyed Reubens, Fairless, and Big Red Elliott without question because those men had ascended to command by virtue of grit and natural ability—well, actually, in Jack's case, because he'd had the balls to kill Cyrus Bone, which sort of amounted to the same thing. The rank-and-file Buffaloes would be nothing but trouble for any new officers who could not make allowances for their rough-edged individuality. Send them to the mountains, or out to the Western territories, where bloody partisan ambuscades were more common than set-piece battles, and they could be an asset; but many of them had already deserted from *one* army and would promptly desert the other one, too, if they found the rules and regulations too irksome. Viewed in that light, Hawkins was probably saving some of those men from a court-martial and a firing squad!

By the time he had polished off his second bottle of wine, Hawkins had managed to convince himself that maybe he was actually doing the Buffaloes a big favor by hanging them out to dry; once they recovered from the shock of betrayal, they could easily evade Hackett's patrols and melt back into the wilderness . . . there was a whole lot of wilderness in coastal North Carolina, after all; fish and game were plentiful, sympathetic Unionists would help them out. They could live off the land for a few months. It shouldn't take much longer than Thanksgiving for Grant's human steamroller to capture Richmond, and then the damned war *would* be over! Jack Fairless, Bonaparte Reubens, and whoever had stuck it out with them could emerge and resume their civilian lives . . . Well, the *white* troopers could, at any rate! Yes, Hawkins might very well be doing Jack and his men a favor.

Of course, the surviving Buffaloes might put a different interpretation on the matter. If perchance he ran into one of those men after the war, he could always do what Butler had suggested: "weasel" his way out of a confrontation by claiming good intentions that were foiled by circumstances beyond his control. In a way, that was what had already happened. *Wasn't it?*

Jack Fairless had found a perfect place to initiate the Buffaloes' delaying action against Hackett's division: a steep embankment extending east and west of a culvert beneath the narrow weed-choked road connecting Plymouth to Shelborne's Point. Like a natural breastwork, the embankment gave them both cover and a superb field of fire. Below the embankment, spreading wide on either side of the culvert, a rain-swollen creek formed an effective moat. And beyond the creek stretched a sodden, briar-studded morass that looked impassable to cavalry and was totally unsuited for the deployment of field artillery. Fairless noted a few patches of dry ground where the Rebels *could* emplace 12-pounders, but the strongest team of oxen in China could not drag guns to those hummocks in less than an hour—assuming it was feasible for Hackett to move his guns forward from the rear of his column while Jack's riflemen were throwing heavy fire all across their path.

Even better: behind this first defensive line, at seven-hundred to nine-hundred-yard intervals, Fairless had selected four additional fall-back positions. It was almost a shame General Hawkins only needed the Buffaloes to fend off Hackett until ten o'clock—Jack felt confident the Buffaloes could hold off that division for days!

"Gentlemen," Jack asked Reubens and Elliott, "Does this not look like a good place to mount an ambush?"

"Never seen a better," rumbled Elliott, lofting a gob of tobacco juice into the creek. Well satisfied with the set-up, the Buffaloes ate their last hot meal, doused their fires, and settled in for whatever sleep they could snatch from the local wildlife and their own inner tension.

While none of Shelborne's Point's civilians wished any harm to come to the young men of the Sixth Massachusetts, there were still loyal secessionists in the town whose political views remained as firm as they were secret. Among their number were several friends or relatives of the families Cyrus Bone had robbed, terrorized, and in some cases murdered. To them, the very word "Buffalo" was anathema—never mind that Cyrus was long dead, or that Colonel Fairless had turned the unit into disciplined soldiers. When the rumor flashed around town that Plymouth had fallen to Rebel forces and General Hawkins was preparing to evacuate his garrison, the long-thwarted Secessionists took action.

Just as these white families had remained staunchly loyal to Richmond, so had some of their Negroes remained loyal to them. For two years, these faithful colored folk had been insinuating themselves into the workforce that cleaned and maintained the Buffaloes' quarters, cooked their meals, and washed their laundry. On the very morning Jack Fairless assembled his companies and told them about the rearguard mission Hawkins had entrusted to them, word of their impending departure reached the town's Rebel sympathizers within two hours. A twelve-year-old boy, mounted on the strongest horse available, had been dispatched down the same primitive road the Buffaloes were preparing to block. After riding all day, he reached the pontoon bridge across the confluence of the Roanoke and South Roanoke Rivers, just in time to deliver a report to the detachment Hackett had left to guard the crossing. From there, the message was relayed to General Hackett just as his column was setting out.

It confirmed what Sam Parker had said: the Buffaloes were more numerous and much better led than Hackett's stale information indicated. Five hundred determined riflemen, some of them armed with repeaters, constituted something more than a mere nuisance. Hackett immediately sent cavalry patrols to reconnoiter the trail, ordering them to take note of likely ambush sites and to leave dismounted pickets under cover, near those sites—men who were just as skilled at bushcraft as the Buffaloes but with considerably more experience in the art of patient concealment. These men were not fazed by the dense, half-drowned terrain—they had seen worse in tidewater Virginia, and they could be trusted to give some hours' warning to the main column.

Hackett also made some last-minute changes in his order-of-march: his artillerists broke down into pack loads a trio of their light howitzers—stubby 8-pounders, short of range but capable of lobbing high-angle fire *over* the intervening foliage—and repositioned them near the front of his column. The bushwhackers would expect Hackett's cannon to be at the tail end of the column and would be unpleasantly surprised to come under shell fire at the very start of the battle. His regular cavalrymen were briefed on what to expect and were prepared to deploy as infantry skirmishers at the first shot. Finally, between the advanced cavalry and the mass of his regular infantry, Hackett positioned 300 lightly equipped sharpshooters, the finest marksmen known to each of his brigade commanders, and divided them into a pair of ad hoc companies. While the dismounted cavalry and the three "surprise" howitzers kept the Buffaloes pinned down, these two detachments would strike off into the wilderness on either side of the road and execute wide flanking movements intended to make the Buffaloes think they were being surrounded. Such a sudden, bold, reaction to a well-laid ambush might turn the tables. In effect, Hackett's basic plan was to bushwhack the bushwhackers and rob Jack Fairless of the psychological advantage he was counting on so heavily. If Hackett could rout the Buffaloes quickly, he could still capture Shelborne's Point before sundown.

At first light, the Buffaloes stood to behind their embankment and waited. Sunrise came . . . and they were still waiting. The road where they expected to see a mass of scouting cavalry remained as barren and empty of targets as it had been the previous afternoon. Jack Fairless could feel his men fidgeting as the minutes crawled by. Already it was ten minutes past six, and one hour was gone out of the five Hawkins had asked the Buffaloes to buy him. *Where the hell is that Rebel cavalry?*

A blistering volley of carbine fire gave him the answer: that Rebel cavalry was *right in front of him*, only a hundred yards or so from his carefully chosen line. They had somehow managed to sneak that close without being seen or heard. "Them boys is good!" cried one Buffalo, just before a carbine round pitched him, face-first, into the clay-colored stream. The Buffaloes returned fire vigorously but uncertainly. Their targets were muzzle flashes and darting phantoms, men who knew how to fight this kind of battle as well as they did. These Confederates were veterans—they would not be so stupid as to charge across a flooded creek, however much Jack Fairless wanted them to. Jack figured he would trade shots with them for fifteen minutes, then execute a phased withdrawal to the next ambush site. Very well, this was not the battle Jack had planned to fight, but the Buffaloes were still "buying time," just as Rush Hawkins had asked them to.

Major Manchester's trio of 12-pounders was concealed 150 yards behind the creek, but so far the gunners had seen no firm targets to fire on. Not wanting Manchester to interpret his early withdrawal as a panic, Jack sent a messenger to tell Manchester to limber up and pull back to the second ambush line; once there, he was to reload with canister instead of shells. No sooner had the messenger scuttled off, however, than Jack heard three blunt thumps from behind the nearest bend in the road, followed by the tearing silk noise of shells arcing overhead and then exploding somewhere in the general vicinity of Manchester's battery. Jack looked inquiringly at Bonaparte Reubens. Reubens responded with a looping gesture of his hands and by shouting *"Howitzers!"*

They must have brought those guns up last night, and we didn't hear a thing! Hackett had been tipped off, no doubt, by Rebel sympathizers from Shelborne's Point. So much for his lovely ambush, but as Jack's Pappy used to say: *When the chickens come home to roost, it's too damn late to white wash the coop!* Three more times, that trio of unseen howitzers thumped, and nine more sharp explosions raked the undergrowth around Manchester's guns. *Get out of there fast, Adolphus! They've got your range!*

Just then, Jack's runner came scampering back toward the creek, zigzagging at full speed, disregarding the shower of balls that clipped branches and spewed pine chips all around him. Fighting for breath, the man came to a stop near Jack and shouted: "Colonel Fairless, the guns are all limbered up and pullin' back, but Major Manchester's been hit pretty bad—shell went off right beside him and sliced open his thigh! His men slapped a tourniquet around his leg, but if he don't get back to a surgeon fast, it'll surely come a-loose and he'll bleed to death."

He needs proper medical attention, and fast, thought Jack. *We can't take care of him and fight our way out of this mess at the same time. And we can't leave him for the Rebs, because if they find out he's a deserter . . .*

"Can he still ride?"

"I think he can, Colonel, if somebody helps him into the saddle."

"Have you got enough wind to go back there? If so, tell the gunners I've ordered them to withdraw right now, back to the next defensive line!" The messenger looked pretty dried out, so Jack yelled "Somebody throw this man a canteen full of liquor. Goddamn it, don't look so innocent—I know you're carryin' some!"

Sheepishly, a nearby private dug a flask out of his knapsack, tossing it into the runner's outstretched hands. After a couple of lusty swigs, the man announced he was miraculously restored to full vigor.

"All right, now, you high-tail it back there are and tell Colonel Manchester that this is a direct-fuckin-order from me: He is to ride back to Shelborne's Point, get his wound properly dressed, and place his ass aboard a transport *right now*. If the Rebels capture him, he's as good as hanged, and I've got enough shit on my conscience already, without adding his death to the load! Now scoot!"

No sooner had the runner departed than Fairless heard a sudden wild spatter of fire on *this* side of the creek, in the direction of the Buffaloes' dangling left flank. *Hell and Jesus, they've outflanked us already! Time to fall back while we still can!*

Adolphus Manchester knew his femoral artery had been nicked, if not severed by shrapnel; if the makeshift tourniquet came loose, he was a goner and no mistake, but as long as he could still function minimally as a battery commander, he was determined to stay. From the way his men kept looking at him, he finally realized that by staying with them he was more of a distraction than an inspiration. Jack Fairless's order absolved him from further responsibilities. His men could work their guns with better concentration if they did not also have to nursemaid him too. They helped him onto his horse, wished him Godspeed, and began pulling their guns to safety. Manchester let his horse find a comfortable, steady gait and made good progress, picking up the pace slightly when he reached the well-traveled road leading from Edgecombe Plantation to the waterfront.

As he neared the docks, Manchester was surprised at how smoothly things were going and at how far advanced was the process of evacuation. The only civilians in sight were those standing at a distance, just spectators, apparently. All the other inhabitants had already gone aboard their ships. As temporary protection, Hawkins had ordered four 12-pounders, positioned behind improvised revetments built out of cotton bales and dirt-filled barrels. The battery was supported by two very anxious-looking infantry companies. A third company was drawn up on the docks, in tight formation, awaiting its turn to file aboard the next empty transport. Around the gunners and soldiers milled another hundred or so clerks, quartermasters, teamsters, and sundry administrative types, all swiveling their heads nervously for any sign of the dreaded *Hatteras*. On the periphery of this impromptu rearguard, General Hawkins bustled around nervously; he too paused every thirty seconds to stare fretfully upriver, praying that the great ironclad would not make an early appearance.

Manchester counted three more transports queued up in midstream, just about the right number needed to embark everyone still waiting. Something about the scene troubled him, but he was dizzy from blood loss and fatigue, so he put aside all concerns save his own urgent need for medical attention. Not knowing what else to do, he rode up to the nearest group of blue uniforms and called "Hello?" several times until one of them turned around and saw the blood covering his leg. Fortunately, one surgeon and several teams of stretcher-bearers were still on duty; they carried Manchester quickly into a shed and placed him on an improvised operating table. The doctor snipped off his ragged pants leg and washed the matted gore from his wound.

"That's a nasty one, Major," the doctor remarked, sagely confirming the obvious. "Lucky for you that tourniquet stayed in place."

"No need to amputate, then?"

"Thankfully not. However, I will have to clean out the wound, probe it to make sure you're not carrying any fragments, and then sew it up. Unless you have a greater capacity to bear pain than most men, I suggest you let me chloroform you. By the time you come to, you'll be halfway to Fortress Monroe and a long, quiet rest in a first-rate hospital. Unless the wound mortifies, you should regain full use of that leg."

"I'll gladly accept the chloroform, doc, but promise me you'll not load me on to a transport until the rest of the unit arrives."

The surgeon's expression became quizzical. "Which unit might that be, Major?"

"The Buffaloes, of course—they're fending off the enemy so the rest of the garrison can evacuate safely."

"Are they indeed? Well, I am grateful that somebody's doing so, but those three boats"—he gestured toward the river, where a full ship was casting off, crowded to the gunwales with passengers and equipment—"are the last of the transports—or so I've been told. Once they've taken us aboard, Shelborne's Point is officially out of business as a military post."

Manchester sat up angrily, and a sudden wave of pain kidney-punched him back down. He grasped the startled doctor's coat and bared his teeth in a grimace both furious and incredulous.

"Are you telling me that no provision has been made to evacuate the very troops who are keeping the enemy at bay?"

"Sit down, you damned fool—you're starting to bleed again! I'm only stating what I've been told, which is that those are the last three transports and we're the last passengers. I do not know who planned it that way or why, but unless you want to commit slow suicide, you'd better lie down and let me put you to sleep so I can do my work. General Hawkins is only following his orders, which presumably come from that donkey's ass Ben Butler! If Butler told Hawkins to sacrifice the Buffaloes in order to safeguard the evacuation as a whole, then that's what Hawkins would do. He's Butler's lapdog, you know, and always has been. I understand why that does not sit well on your own conscience, but that's the reality of it and it is much too late for you or anyone else to change things. Now will you behave yourself, so I can save your damned life?"

Gritting his teeth, Manchester grabbed the butt of his revolver, still holding the doctor's lapels with all the strength in his left arm, and jammed the muzzle against the surgeon's forehead, cocking the hammer as he did so.

"Listen carefully, saw-bones, unless you want to lose a jugful of brains! You will seal that wound tightly with bandages, replace the tourniquet, and tell your orderly over there to load a pair of saddlebags with as many medical supplies as they will hold. Then place me back on my horse and go on about your business. I intend to rejoin my comrades, and since it appears that they must now fend for themselves in the heart of Rebel territory, I intend to bring some medical supplies back with me when I report how treacherously we have all been abandoned. And may I say, Doctor, that it is precisely this kind of callous indifference to the common soldier that motivated me to switch my allegiance back to the Union."

"Good lord," the surgeon muttered, "you're the fellow who deserted after Gettysburg! I heard something about you . . ." The surgeon's tone of voice changed and he very gently motioned for Manchester to lower his pistol. In his semidelirium, Manchester took this gesture as a cue to explain himself.

"I never believed in secession, Doctor, much less slavery, which I personally find abhorrent, but I did believe in defending my homeland against armed aggression. I stuck it out faithfully until nearly every man I signed up with had been killed or maimed for life in the service of a government that has proven to be every bit as tyrannical as I once thought Mister Lincoln's to be."

Meanwhile, far from lecturing Manchester for his threatening behavior, the surgeon was bustling around the room, gathering bottles and bandage rolls and an assortment of professional cutlery (probes, scalpels, forceps, bone-saw, necessary but disturbing objects). He dispatched the orderlies to find two large saddlebags.

"I can patch you up temporarily, Major, if you can keep from passing out while I do so, but you must find someone competent to suture your wound; either that or do it yourself, just as soon as you can. I agree that it was despicable to throw the Buffaloes to the wolves, and I understand your first priority is to ride back and warn them. In all frankness, though, I must warn you that if you don't get that leg sewed up pretty damn quick, you're a goner. Speaking professionally, mind you, I would choose bleeding to death over just about any other form of battlefield mortality that is not instantaneous—it's relatively painless, rather like falling asleep.

I suppose that's why so many Roman nobles chose to cut their wrists rather than fall upon their swords. Very rational way to go, if one has any selection about the matter. Clearly, you are determined to warn your comrades or die trying, so the least I can do is send you back with as many medical supplies as you can carry. Here, I'll even throw in my own surgeon's manual, so whoever becomes the Buffaloes' doctor can at least read up on the subject while you boys are running for your lives."

Then, while Adolphus Manchester oozed sweat and tried to stifle the urge to scream, the doctor expertly probed the open flesh of his thigh while simultaneously barking muted orders to his assistants. Satisfied that Manchester's own blood had washed out any shell fragments, the surgeon made a few critical sutures ("All you've given me time to do, Major!"), then wound a great swaddle of tight bandages around the gash, fashioning a much thicker girdle than necessary, so as to give the wounded man some extra support when he regained the saddle. At the conclusion of their brief but very intense acquaintance, the physician ordered Manchester to slug down a few ounces of medicinal brandy, then helped himself to the same bottle.

"I think it's safe to say you'll be my last patient of the day," he said. Manchester's horse, watered and fed and weighed down by twenty-odd pounds of medical kit, was brought around, and the two orderlies, whose expressions demonstrated both surprise and approval at Manchester's decision, hoisted him into the saddle as gently as they could. All three men stood in the doorway as Manchester grasped the reins and tried to thank the surgeon.

"Thank me by staying alive."

"If I do, I shall probably try to murder General Butler."

"You'll have to stand in line," growled the doctor.

Those few people who saw Manchester riding *away* from the succoring transports, rather than toward the impatient throng waiting to board them, had no interest in stopping him. The last sound he heard before he lost sight of the village was the festive toot of steam whistles announcing the departure of the final boatload.

No sooner had that ghoulishly ironic sound faded from his hearing than Manchester was startled by an eruption of gunfire coming from the opposite direction. From the volume, he judged that the noise was emanating from the last and closest ambush site. Jack Fairless had staked out yesterday. Manchester tugged out his watch: 9:53 A.M. Well, Hawkins had asked the Buffaloes to buy him five hours, and given Fairless permission to withdraw at ten o'clock; Fairless and his men had certainly kept their part of the agreement. Manchester urged his horse to a more rapid pace, just as he heard once more the aggravating explosions of those Rebel howitzer shells. But this time, they were answered by the more powerful report of his own 12-pounders. *Good for you, men! But you might as well spike those guns and forget about your comrades at Shelborne's Point, for they are long gone by now, and safe, and you've been left holding the bag!*

Manchester rounded a bend and suddenly saw his gun crews feverishly throwing their remaining ammunition into the nearest pond. He reined up just in time to see one burly gunner sledgehammer a spike into the touch-hole of the last 12-pounder. When they saw that Manchester had returned, Lazarus-like, the gun crews ran joyfully to meet him.

"No time for explanations," he gasped. "Where is Colonel Fairless?"

"About a hundred yards up, sir, behind a big ol' oak tree. He told us to fire one last round from each gun, then spike 'em, throw the ammunition into a bog, pick up a musket, and join him on the firing line. He claimed we still had to fend off the enemy for another ten minutes, then we was 'free to retire,' but I think maybe we'll be pushing our luck if we try to hang on for another five. Shit! I can see some Rebels right now, sneaking around our left flank, 'bout two hundred yards that way!"

Overhead, a sizzling like cold water on hot grease, and then a sharper, heavier bang in the direction of Fairless's line.

"Aw, sheee-it," drawled one ex-gunner. "Sounds like they've brung up a twenty-four-pounder now."

"Yes," agreed Manchester, suddenly possessed by an immense calm, "that was definitely a twenty-four. Listen to me well, now, and if I should faint before I have time to repeat this to Colonel Fairless, you must quote me word for word. Our time in Golgotha is over. I've just come from Shelborne's Point, and the situation there has changed for the worse. It seems that our former commander, General Hawkins, never had any intention of waiting for the Buffaloes. He and his regiment are long gone, and there is not a single boat, barge, or floating log waiting for us at the docks."

In response to a chorus of savage oaths, Manchester raised a calming hand. "Orders from General Butler, apparently, and Hawkins did not have the backbone to stand up on our behalf. There never was any intention of taking us off with the others. So there's not any point in you men picking up a musket and trying to fight a whole Confederate division. Find some good cover down the road a ways and wait there—the rest of us will be along directly. Meanwhile, I'm going to tell Jack Fairless what I've learned."

Catching sight of a hitched-up supply wagon already full of wounded Buffaloes, Manchester asked for someone to untie his saddlebags and told the gunners what was in them. "Any of you who's ever said 'I could do a better job than most of those butchers!' well, now's your chance to prove it!"

His vision momentarily went fuzzy, and there was fresh blood oozing from beneath the doctor's cofferdam of a bandage. Without another word—he did not know how many words he still had in him—Manchester spurred his horse toward the firing line.

He had covered perhaps a third of the distance to Jack Fairless when another one of those damned howitzer shells came dropping out of the sky and burst about four feet behind the horse's tail. Manchester bent low and heard fragments whine as they zoomed past his ears. *"Missed me again, you pukes!"*

But the horse took a red-hot fragment in the rump. The animal reared crazily on his hind legs, more terrified than hurt, and bolted out from under the major. The saddle flew out from under him as though covered with butter and he landed, full force, on his tightly bandaged thigh, which burst on impact like a split seed pod, unleashing such a torrent of pent-up blood that by the time someone reached him, he was already able to verify the anonymous doctor's prediction: *You were right, Doc—bleeding to death is far less distressing than many other battlefield terminations I've witnessed over the years.* As he succumbed to the drowsiness enfolding his mind, he managed a small laugh.

"By God, he was right about this, too . . . it really is like falling asleep."

"Lie still, sir!" cried one of the men who were trying so hard and so pointlessly to get a grip on his blood-slick body.

"Leave me here, boys, and that's an order! Just go tell Jack Fairless what I was going to tell him: I'm sorry, but you're on your own now."

Refugees

GENERAL GRANT DID not really expect Butler's Army of the James to capture Richmond from behind, but it was not unreasonable to hope that, if Butler only paid attention to the expert corps commanders Grant had assigned to "advise" him, his army might seize Petersburg, or at the very least, cut the rail connection between that city and Richmond along so great a length as to knock out Lee's most important supply line.

When the Army of the James began operations, with a large amphibious move from Hampton Roads to the Bermuda Hundred Peninsula, on May 4, 1864 it seemed for once as though Butler might actually be able to capitalize on the good luck that attended the first days of his campaign. Unopposed, Butler landed 32,000 men and 82 guns, only thirty miles from Petersburg. Between him and the most important rail nexus in Virginia, were scattered Confederate cavalry and skirmishers amounting to no more than 4,000 men. Aside from 600 coast artillerymen manning the forts atop Drewry's Bluff, there was not a single organized Confederate unit in Butler's path.

Nevertheless, even though his own cavalry patrols *assured him the way to Petersburg was wide open, Butler advanced timidly and did not capture his first piece of the Richmond-Petersburg RR until May 9. By that time, the situation had changed dramatically.*

Granted emergency powers to organize the defense of Petersburg, General Beauregard arrived in that city on May 5 and with near-demonic energy, set about creating an army to defend it. It was a brilliant, seat-of-the-pants improvisation. Summoning individual companies from back-water outposts as far away as Georgia and Florida, and then forming them into four ad hoc divisions, Beauregard had assembled, by May 14, an army of 22,000 men.

Butler knew what was going on, and despite near-insubordinate out-bursts of "advice" from his corps and division commanders, he dithered hopelessly, unable to decide whether to go all-out for Richmond or for Petersburg. By the time he chose Petersburg as his target, it was too late. Beauregard was already preparing a surprise counterattack.

Among the reinforcements rushed to Petersburg was Beauregard's old friend and prewar drinking companion, Gen. William Chase Whiting, who for two years had begged, argued, and prayed for a second chance at a field command. Beauregard gave him that chance, but alas for Whiting, conditions on the railroads between Wilmington and Petersburg were so chaotic that Whiting did not meet his "new" division staff until thirty-six hours before he was scheduled to lead them into battle, across some of the most confusing terrain in tidewater Virginia—a landscape every bit as strange to 90% of Whiting's men as it was to their new commander.

Beauregard did not expect his four raw, heterogeneous divisions to carry out complex maneuvers, so he crafted a beautifully simple plan for a "rolling" attack that would fix Butler's attention on one part of his line (the right flank, closest to Richmond, and where his maneuvering room was restricted by the fortified heights of Drewry's Bluff), pin down his reserves by pressure against his center, and then finish him off by a sharp surprise thrust against his extreme left (bounded by the Appomattox River).

First to attack would be the division pivoting on Drewry's Bluff (at 5:00 A.M., May 16). Each of Beauregard's other three divisions would subsequently assault at half-hour intervals, until Chase Whiting's small (5,000 men) division went forward at 7:00 A.M. and delivered the coup de grace. *To synchronize the start of each division's attack, Beauregard gave their commanders a very simple instruction: When you hear the division on your left begin firing, wait exactly thirty minutes, then attack straight ahead. Whiting's command and control problems would be made even simpler: all he had to do was keep the unmistakably broad, winding shape of the Appomattox River on his right and he could not help but advance exactly where Beauregard wanted him to.*

To say that Whiting was "excited" was be to cheapen the adjective; the feisty little general was, in the words of one adjutant, "so hopped up on coffee and adrenaline I thought his skin would explode from his head."

But the bad luck which had cost Whiting his first field command (and earned him the enmity of Jefferson Davis) had not deserted him. At 5:00 A.M., Whiting's sector was absolutely snowed in with fog. As dawn drew near, the fog lifted elsewhere *on Beauregard's front, but on Whiting's end of the line, visibility remained approximately fifty feet. As for the impossible-to-miss Appomattox River, no one had the slightest idea where it was, how far away, or in which direction. After sunrise, Whiting sent out four scouts, at ten-minute intervals (each one a native Virginian who swore he was "quite familiar" with this area) to locate the river so Whiting would at least point his division in the right direction when his own attack jumped off at 7:00 A.M.*

Only one of them ever returned, and that was not until 3:30 P.M. Two more blundered into Federal outposts and were captured, and no one ever learned what happened to the fourth man.

Worse: since the ostensible jumping-off time of Beauregard's attack (5:00 A.M.), neither Whiting nor any man in his division had heard so much as a single rifle shot, never mind the roar of pitched battle which was supposed to be their "alarm clock." *As happened numerous times during the Civil War, the bizarre atmospherics, thermal inversions, wind patterns, and large stretches of dense forest—combined with the funky sound-transmission qualities of black powder explosives—had created a major acoustic anomaly. The division to Whiting's left had, in fact, been hotly engaged ever since 6:30 A.M., only three miles to the northwest, but not even a rumble of cannonfire had been heard on Whiting's front.*

Logic suggested that for some reason Beauregard had called off the whole attack, so Whiting desperately sent more scouts and dispatch riders in what he presumed to be the general direction of Richmond. At that same time, Beauregard was sending his own scouts southeast, seeking answers to his most pressing question: Where the hell is Chase Whiting and why isn't he attacking? By now, the reader will not perhaps be shocked to learn that all of these riders managed completely to miss the people and units they were looking for.

When the fog on his sector finally lifted, around noon, Whiting's division got embroiled in a long, sporadic firefight with shadowy bunches of Union troops and acquitted itself very well. But these brisk skirmishes were not contributing to Beauregard's hard-won advances as a whole—and most historians agree that if Whiting had been able to attack when and where he was supposed to, Butler's army would have been shattered, instead of being able to retreat behind the fortifications across the narrowest part of the Bermuda Hundred Peninsula. Not until 8:30 that night did Beauregard and Whiting actually meet each other. When the full story came out, and many of Whiting's officers testified that Whiting had acted prudently and soberly *throughout the day, Beauregard accepted Whiting's version of events. But by then, the Richmond papers were already blaming Whiting for Butler's escape, and all the ancient allegations about his prodigious fondness for good bourbon were back on the front pages.*

—Wilkes, Frazier K. *The Last Full Measure—The Decline of the Army of Northern Virginia from Drewry's Bluff to Appomattox Courthouse. University of Virginia Press, 1980*

By the time the *Hatteras* steamed within sight of Shelborne's Point, the docks were lined with cheering Confederate soldiers. Sam Parker relaxed and ordered his gun crews to stand down. General Hackett welcomed Parker ebulliently and filled him in on the morning's events.

"Your assessment of the Buffaloes was accurate, Captain Parker. They put up a stubborn fight at four roadblocks, withdrawing very professionally as soon as they sensed we were outflanking them. Then they pulled back to a new defensive line and stopped us again. For a bunch of wild bushwhackers led by an amateur colonel it was very skillfully done and we had to work hard to lever them out of their positions. But all of a sudden, in the middle of heavy fighting at their fourth line, they simply melted away. We killed or captured more than two hundred, but do you think they could possibly regroup and raid our supply lines?"

"I doubt it, General. Shelborne's Point was their refuge as well as their base of operations. Now that the Confederacy has reclaimed this region, they will find few civilian accomplices willing to help them. My guess is that they will drift south and hole-up deep inside Gum Swamp until the war ends. Unless they need food or ammunition, they're not likely to venture out again. I suspect you've seen the last of 'em."

Hackett nodded. "I have already dispatched warnings to every Home Guard post within a hundred miles, urging them to keep a lookout. Having done so, I will now proceed to invest New Bern as speedily as possible and give no further heed to the 'Belligerent Bisons.' How soon will the *Hatteras* be able to join us down at New Bern?"

"We could start out today, if need be—our magazines are full and the crew is keen for the job."

"Excellent. Some local Rebel sympathizers have told me that Washington was also evacuated yesterday, so we should enjoy an unopposed march to our main objective. We'll rest here tonight, start at dawn, and I hope to have a proper siege underway by noon on Friday. If all goes well, we shall look for the ironclad again on that day!"

"We'll do our best, sir, although I expect there will be a passel of Union warships between us and New Bern."

Hackett's manner suddenly became more somber. "Don't push your luck, Samuel. By all means do whatever damage you can, but try to withdraw before you suffer major damage. Even if you have to lay up for repairs, the knowledge that the *Hatteras* is still lurking about will discourage Butler from risking his big transports to reinforce the New Bern garrison. But if we lost the ironclad for good, we've lost any chance of regaining coastal North Carolina."

Hackett's confidence was a tonic, but Sam Parker was not quite as optimistic as he would have liked. One of the ironclad's engines had turned cranky after the strain of the April 17 battle and was now prone to sudden, unpredictable, fluctuations in steam pressure. He had no doubts about the *Hatteras*'s ability to take on any two or three Union warships, but he did not know if she was nimble enough to outmaneuver fifteen or twenty gunboats at once, especially if the new enemy naval commander, whoever he was, decided to try ramming attacks as well. How many such blows could the ironclad absorb before something broke? He had already decided to leave Charlie Smith and his Musketeers behind for this engagement. The Federal ships would be packed with sharpshooters, and any man trying to fight them from on top of the ironclad's casemate would not stand a chance.

Parker shook off his misgivings. So what if the odds might be twenty-to-one? The ironclad would just have to knock out as many Yankee ships as possible, as fast as possible. And there was always the psychological factor: the U. S. Navy was *afraid* of his ship, if only because the ironclad had been the instrument of Charles Flusser's death.

At seven-thirty on the morning of April 24, the remaining citizens of Shelborne's Point assembled to watch the *Hatteras* depart for what many feared would be her last cruise. Rip-van-Winkle-like their Confederate passions has been rekindled by the majestic presence of the ironclad. For two years the iron-girt Goliath had been only a rumor; now it was *here* and it was an awesome symbol of resurgent Southern might. But there were no cheers or patriotic songs when the ironclad's grim-faced crew squared-away the mooring lines and the propellers began to ruffle the placid surface of the South Roanoke. Both Parker's crew and the people of Shelborne's Point had heard the rumors: the U.S. Navy was frantically assembling every warship capable of transiting the Outer Banks inlets. Gunboats were said to have arrived from as far away as Norfolk and Charleston; the odds against the *Hatteras,* by the time it confronted the enemy fleet off New Bern, were estimated as high as forty to one.

So when Samuel Parker ordered the Stars-and-Bars run up the ram's small flagstaff, no brass bands played. Instead, acting on communal impulse, the people of Shelborne's Point had brought baskets of flowers and blossoms from their gardens and threw upon the ship a floral blessing: azaleas, pansies, oleander, crepe myrtle, dogwood blossoms, hydrangeas, white-shouldered magnolia blossoms, and roses of every shade. As the ship began to move, the people on shore rained down upon her cold dew-clammy carapace a silent tribute of glorious colors and achingly beautiful fragrances. By the time the *Hatteras* worked up to cruising speed, she was transformed into a floating garden, her brute utilitarian form softened and glowing with constellations of many-hued petals, her somber iron torso sparkling, like a pearl-encrusted brooch, as the morning sunlight danced on dewdrops beyond counting. Bathed in iridescent splendor, the *Hatteras* steamed resolutely into Pamlico Sound, heading into the most one-sided naval battle in history.

Succeeding Charles Flusser as commander of the North Carolina Squadron was a newcomer to the region, Commander Silas T. Meeker. Like Will Cushing, Meeker had known and admired Charles Flusser at Annapolis. Three weeks ago, Flusser had requested Meeker's services because that officer had displayed remarkable courage and resourcefulness in a dangerous and unglamorous job: clearing hundreds of mines and torpedo-booms from the waters around New Orleans and Vicksburg. There were not many officers with Meeker's expertise in that deadly but decidedly unromantic area of naval warfare, and Flusser thought he would have need of such specialized skills. Meeker had been down at the Port Royal base, countersigning his transfer orders, when the stunning news arrived of Flusser's death and the humiliating defeat of two powerful steam frigates by a Rebel ironclad of unprecedented power. Meeker was even more amazed to learn that the panicstricken Navy Department had promoted him to Flusser's job. When he arrived in New Bern, only two days after his promotion, Meeker found the naval base seething with rumors and alarms; the administrative and staff operations were in a state of near-paralysis; new warships were arriving hourly from distant bases; and the town's Unionist sympathizers were packing their belongings and burying their silverware.

Trying to radiate a confidence he did not quite feel, Meeker began to untangle the knots and sort things out. Flusser's shocking death had left a vacuum, and partially to fill it, Meeker's first action was to request Will Cushing for his temporary second-in-command and tactical advisor. Working long hours behind closed doors, the two men began to bring order and method to the previously blind and lurching efforts of the local naval authorities. The first thing Cushing did, was to write a succinct set of professional notes about the battle on Albemarle Sound and a realistic appreciation of the Rebel behemoth's strengths and possible weaknesses. Meeker had this pamphlet printed and distributed to ever ship under his command. The intent of the document was to demythologize the *Hatteras* and to remind everybody that it was, after all, but a single warship, and just as there was no such thing as a truly "impregnable" fortress, there was also no such thing as an "unsinkable" ship. The big ironclad posed a professional challenge, but its coming did not herald the Apocalypse.

As Cushing saw it, there had been two flaws in Flusser's plan: 1) it was too complicated; and, 2) its success depended on the Confederate captain not realizing he was heading into a trap until it was too late. Parker had been too smart, or too sharp-eyed, to fall for it, and once the *Hatteras* gained enough maneuvering room to use her ram, the battle was as good as lost.

With Meeker's endorsement, Cushing designed a small poster, complete with simple diagrams. Printed copies were posted on every Union ship gathered around New Bern:

> We must encircle the Rebel ram in the manner of Indians circling a wagon train. We must shoot early, and without letup, from every

> angle, on every side. Gang up on her, surround her, hammer every square inch of her with every gun you can bring to bear—until SOMETHING breaks or a lucky hit takes out one of her guns.
>
> Our secret weapon is the lowly TUGBOAT! They have the strongest engines for their size of any class of ship in our fleet, and they have reinforced bows, ribs, keels, and bulwarks, to withstand many casual collisions. Turn the tables on the Rebels and use your tugboats as rams! Keep them behind the larger fighting ships until you see an opening, then charge in and smite the ironclad, particularly on her STERN. Dislodge a propeller or bend a shaft, and the *Hatteras* will steer like a pregnant sow.
>
> Keep reminding yourself that NO SHIP IS UNSINKABLE! This vessel is the South's best, last hope to regain naval parity. Destroy her, and you not only avenge the many brave sailors she has killed, but you take away from the enemy every hope of future naval victories!

It was late afternoon, April 24, when the *Hatteras* finally appeared. By that time, General Hackett's artillery had been shelling New Bern's outer ring of fortifications for seven hours and an impetuous bayonet charge by Ransom's brigade had captured two semidetached bastions, possession of which gave Hackett's men an excellent view of the inner defenses. If a formal siege be likened to a game of chess, then Hackett had just taken the first pawn.

When Meeker's lookouts first spotted the *Hatteras*, she was two miles off and bow-on; she looked almost disappointingly tiny. That impression was dispelled when the range closed.

The Rebel captain was not going to oblige Meeker by giving him time to spread out. In fact, Parker figured he was so hugely outnumbered as to render "tactics" irrelevant. His intention was to smash head-on into the nearest enemy ship and try to knock one opponent out of the fight in the first two minutes of the battle. He had no idea what kind of damage the big ram would do in a head-on collision, but he was counting on the enemy skipper to instinctively turn out of his way, thus presenting a more favorable angle for the ram's "bite."

Despite Meeker's order to encircle the ironclad "like Indians attacking a wagon train," his subordinate officers were obviously more concerned about getting out of the ram's way they were in closing with it for battle. All around his flagship, the formation was losing cohesion. Will Cushing took over the megaphone and signal lamp, and his language was not temperate; but his threats and entreaties did serve to chivvy some of the strays back into formation.

Observing these signs of confusion, Samuel Parker smiled and thought: My God, the odds are fifty to one and they're still afraid of us! What difference does it make that they have ten times as many guns, if not one of them can hurt the *Hatteras*? As though to underscore the ironclad's aura of invincibility, a snap shot by the starboard Brooke crew scored a direct hit on one of Meeker's armed transports, setting off the magazine and boiler. Broken in two, ablaze from stern to bow, the auxiliary ship sank in less than thirty seconds. There were no survivors.

One lucky hit from a Brooke, and look how they scatter!

We might just pull this off, after all, thought Parker, ordering Mr. Steeley to set a collision course for the nearest large Yankee ship and shouting down the voice pipe to the engineers: "Brace for ramming impact!"

But just as the *Hatteras* started to gain momentum, the whole ship whipsawed, throwing Parker and Steeley out of their chairs. Parker heard the agonized shriek of metal and smelled overheated bearing-grease.

"Chief engineer, give me a report!"

"It would appear we've been rammed, sir."

"By what?"

"A tugboat, sir. The portside propeller shaft is bent! And the bearings are heating up, and the gauges on that engine are climbing into the red. We have to reduce speed, to no more than two or three knots, or we won't make it back to Plymouth. I'm sorry, Captain."

Parker felt bitter laughter welling up (along with a shameless sense of relief—no fifty to one battle today, thank you Lord!). He was now in command of a 400-ton sitting duck.

"We will have another day, chief. Reduce speed on the port engine to two and a half knots. Helmsman, set course for Plymouth. Gun crews, shift both Brookes to the stern positions, so they can discourage any ship trying to pursue us. Also start some decoy fires on deck—whatever makes the foulest smoke. I want the enemy to think we're retiring due to battle damage and not mechanical problems."

Steering a drunken, wobbling course, the *Hatteras* retreated; judging from the amount of smoke pouring from her, she was badly hit. Cushing longed to chase and finish her off, but he knew Meeker's orders were to take his ships back and assist in the defense of New Bern, "after the Confederate ram has been neutralized, sunk, or chased away," so back they all sailed, to a besieged city.

By the morning of April 26 General Donald Hackett's division was within two days of capturing New Bern. He had taken the outer ring of fortifications, which gave him room to press the siege from the town's inland side, where Meeker's naval gunfire was more a nuisance than a threat. He sent poor dispirited Sam Parker, once more becalmed in Plymouth, a consoling message: By dusk on April 27, New Bern would be in Southern hands again!

But when the sun went down on April 27, Hackett changed that verdict to "*could* have been in Southern hands . . ." Right after breakfast, he received an urgent telegram from Robert E. Lee, ordering him to bring his division back to Virginia "without delay, no matter how favorable the situation is at New Bern." Grant was on the move, with an army reckoned to be 100,000 strong, and the odious Butler was moving his army of 40,000 up the James River, forcing Lee to stretch his resources thin from the start. Hackett knew it was pointless to argue with Marse Robert in this matter; during the earlier lull, Lee had seen the dramatic as well as the strategic value of recapturing North Carolina's coast, but now, with the enemy's boots once more violating the sacred soil of Virginia, Lee was oblivious to any other consideration.

The night after Hackett received Lee's order, all three of his brigade commanders came to his tent and remonstrated forcefully that he should simply not acknowledge Lee's telegram until after New Bern fell—a matter of no more than thirty-six hours. Hackett could always claim the message was delayed in transmission.

But Donald Hackett did not believe that Lee would be fooled, not for one minute, by such a transparent dodge—Virginia was threatened! Every man and musket was needed! As a North Carolinian, Hackett was mightily tempted, but as a loyal professional soldier, he could not bring himself to disobey a direct order from General Lee. So in silence and sadness, he withdrew his men and guns from their siege parallels and from the numerous Federal positions they had already captured, and turned them around toward Virginia.

When the hard-pressed defenders of New Bern looked out the next morning and discovered their nemesis had gone, they could scarcely believe their good luck, for they had planned to launch one do-or-die counterattack that very day, and if it failed, as most of them expected to happen, then they had already drafted terms for the city's surrender.

Rain drummed on the cracked, dusty windows of the passenger coach, painting them with mud; javelins of lightning showed swollen creeks and flooding quagmires; the tracks groaned ominously. The train from Goldsboro was creaking along at five miles an hour, sometimes less, trying not to outrun its own headlight. At this rate, Chase Whiting would not set foot in Wilmington until well after midnight, which was just fine with him. He did not want to slink back in the light of day, disgraced a second and final time. He would never have another field command—even though General Beauregard knew what had happened and still referred publicly to Whiting as "my friend," the Richmond press had pilloried him savagely. The only thing Whiting could do to salvage a crumb of self-respect was to resign before Jefferson Davis sacked him.

So many ways it could have gone differently . . . *Is that not what every beaten commander thinks? But what is the point of torturing yourself? Things happened as they happened . . .*

Although they had only served together for forty-eight hours, Whiting's staff, and many of his men, came by his tent to offer their best wishes and voice their regrets. But when the last of them had gone, Whiting shouldered his bags and boarded the first train to depart in the general direction of Wilmington, a weary and brokenhearted man. Beauregard had given him the second chance he wanted so desperately, and Whiting had failed miserably to justify his patron's confidence. For better or worse, he was back in command of the Cape Fear Military District, and here he would stay until either the war ended or the North finally got around to capturing Wilmington.

When the train finally pulled into to Wilmington, it was 3:30 A.M. and still raining. Whiting had told no one that he was coming back. He planned to find a room in town and return to his old headquarters at Smithville on the morning ferry. But there on the platform stood William Lamb and an honor guard from the fort. They snapped to attention and saluted Chase Whiting as though he were returning from a great triumph.

"Welcome home, General," said Lamb, shaking his hand warmly. "There's a covered carriage waiting for you, and it would be my great honor to offer you the guest room at the Cottage. I suspect it would do you a lot of good to sleep late tomorrow . . ."

"Bless my soul, Lamb, but it is awfully kind of you to arrange such a welcome. And, yes, now that you mention it, I could use a nice long sleep."

"We need you here, Chase," said Lamb quietly. "I think the enemy will attack Fort Fisher before the year is out, and I want you at my side when that happens."

"My last chance at redemption? . . ." Whiting laughed, but his heart was bitter.

"And my only," replied Lamb.

It had not taken long for the Buffaloes' resistance to collapse once the word spread down their line: *Hawkins has sold us out—there are no boats waiting for us at Shelborne's Point.* Many of the Buffaloes were so stunned by the betrayal that they could not even flee, just threw down their rifles, raised their hands, and waited apathetically to be taken prisoner.

Of the Buffaloes who did manage to mount up and keep their weapons, Reubens' colored company retreated in better style than the white troopers, even daring to turn and fire at their pursuers now and again; surrender, for them, was a greater peril than flight—already there had been some shouts of "Faison's Groves!" After twenty minutes, the pursuing Rebel cavalry turned back, presumably to rejoin Hackett's main force as it took possession of Shelborne's Point.

When Fairless estimated the remaining Buffaloes were at least five miles south of the last path leading toward Shelborne's Point, he called a halt. The horses were blown and the men so exhausted they could not summon the energy to dismount, but slumped against their horses' necks in a stupor. When Jack took a head count, he realized that the Buffaloes were finished as a combat unit: when the first shots rang out that morning, he commanded more than five hundred men. Now he counted one hundred fourteen, at least twenty of them wounded and all badly shaken, no fight left in them at all. After counting heads, he summoned his two remaining company commanders to a conference over a spread-out map. There were no contingency plans for situations like this. Obviously, they could not just keep riding south on the same road indefinitely.

Where to go? Jack's mind churned furiously, but so painful was the effort of organizing his thoughts that his brain seemed to be covered with lint and shards of glass. Then Big Red Elliot bent closer to the map, as though the markings on it had suddenly snapped into focus, and thumped a powder-blackened finger on the scabrous squiggle of lines the cartographer had used to delineate the desolate wilderness of Gum Swamp.

"Look here, Jack! I grew up on a 'baccy farm right about here, just outside the market town of Trenton. I spent God knows how many weekends huntin' and pirogue fishin' inside Gum Swamp. So did lots of folks from around those parts. It ain't all quicksand and 'gator pits deep inside, either. There's dry land, and a lot of single-file game trails, if you know where to find 'em. My uncle was a well-off railroad man from Kinston, and he owned a hunting and fishing camp 'way back in there, next to a black-water river that has the best catfish you ever tasted. Uncle Billy used to entertain businessmen out there, too, before the war, so it was *not* downright primitive—you could sleep maybe twenty men in the bunkhouse, and there was a kitchen and a freshwater well. It's been six, maybe eight years since I last saw the place, so it might be in ruins for all I know. But if it isn't, it won't take long for us to turn it into a right cozy hideout. There ain't but one trail in or out, unless you're traveling by boat, so there's no way any regular troops could sneak up on us. There's game and fish, and even 'skeeter nets over the windows! If we get a move on, I reckon we could be there before dark."

"It sounds too good to be true, Red," said Reubens. "It sounds like such a perfect hideout that it may already be occupied."

"It if is," said Jack, "it'll most likely be deserters and fellows hiding out from conscription—in which case, they got no quarrel with us nor we with them. If they're Rebel partisans, we'll surround the place first, then kill 'em. I mean *all of them*. If the word gets around that there's colored soldiers hiding out in Gum Swamp, it'll be 'Remember Faison's Groves' all over again. We'll take possession, one way or the other. If Hackett does capture New Bern, we'll just fortify the place and wait out the rest of the war—can't last much longer, not with one army always growing bigger and the other one always shrinking. If Hackett doesn't take New Bern, we'll wait until he pulls out of the state and rejoin the Union garrisons there. Whoever's in command could probably use some experienced scouts."

"There's some of us think the Union Army's already thrown us out of the ranks, Colonel Jack," said one exhausted colored trooper.

Jack Fairless somehow found the energy to be a colonel again: "I won't hold it against any man who feels that way, but until we learn the outcome of this campaign, soldier, we're sticking together and you *will* continue to follow my orders. Everybody clear about that?"

Nobody else had the energy to grumble. Jack gave them ten more minutes to rest, then they remounted and rode hard in the direction of Gum Swamp, racing the sun. Captain Elliott spotted a familiar pond, one distinguished from hundreds like it by a cluster of cypress stumps that looked like a pipe organ, and after poking around in the underbrush for ten minutes he found the path he was looking for.

Fortune finally smiled on the surviving Buffaloes: the old fishing camp was not only intact, it had been enlarged and repaired and comfortably furnished. It had been the field headquarters, for the past two years, of a small band of Confederate guerrillas, part scouts and part brigands, who preyed on Unionist sympathizers in the surrounding counties and who went after known deserters for the bounty that Richmond's local agents paid for their recovery. In short, they were men very similar to the earliest incarnation of the Buffaloes. They numbered thirty-six, and most of them were already drunk by the time Jack's men surrounded the encampment. The Rebel outliers were getting set for a real banquet: venison roasting on a spit, and catfish already cleaned and ready for the skillet. Most of them died with the Buffaloes' first volley, and those who were not killed instantly were finished off quickly and coldly with pistol balls to the head. Then the Buffaloes lugged the bodies to a bluff downstream from the boathouse and slung them into the water. Even before they had finished disposing of the last ones, three alligators came crashing through the underbrush with astonishing speed and apparently ravenous appetites. Captain Elliott located the pump, joyfully announced that it still worked, and after everyone washed his hands and face, the exhausted Buffaloes sat down and offered up a quick prayer of thanks before helping themselves to the feast laid out for them by the men they had just massacred.

On the cloudy night of June 2, 1864, lookouts attached to the Union signal post at the Cape Hatteras lighthouse were puzzled to spot a modest-sized dark-painted steamer moving at flank speed straight through the treacherous channel of Hatteras Inlet. No flag adorned her mast, no lights showed behind her portholes, and she carried no discernible armament.

She had the general shape and dimensions of an intracoastal freighter; even if she were packed to the gunwales with contraband, there was not really enough cargo space below her decks to make it worth her owners' time to risk her in the runner trade. Since the mysterious vessel clearly presented no threat, the 24-pounders emplaced on the ruins of old Fort Clark did not even fire a warning shot. Whatever the vessel's business, she was soon shrouded in darkness. It was conceivable that she carried Union agents, bent on some secret reconnaissance. A brief report of the incident went out over the submarine cable to New Bern, along with the morning weather and tide reports that were the main reason for the very existence of this dismal outpost.

Eventually this information was copied on up the chain of command, until it reached the new commander of the North Atlantic Blockade Squadron, Admiral David Porter, who had only recently settled in as the successor to Admiral Samuel Philips Lee, who retired in May, after two productive years devoted to strengthening, modernizing, and improving the tactics of the blockade squadrons. By the time Porter read about the silent, swift, enigmatic ship that ran the Hatteras Inlet, the information was two weeks old and nobody had seen hide nor hair of that vessel since. Still, there was something so odd about the incident that it gave the irascible Porter a sensation he described as being akin to "a skeeter bite on the brain."

In point of fact, the blockaders-vs.-runners equation *had* subtly changed in recent weeks. Although the siege of New Bern had failed, strong regional Confederate forces had garrisoned Plymouth, where the fearsome *Hatteras* was still laid up with engine problems, and were industriously fortifying the smaller but strategically located village of Shelborne's Point. In theory, at least, the blockade-runners now had two new havens in addition to Wilmington. The biggest, most outrageously profitable runners could no more pass through Hatteras and Ocracoke Inlets than could the U.S. Navy's mighty high-seas cruisers. But so great was the South's need for imported goods that it struck Porter as entirely reasonable to assume that small, fast runners might dash in and out of these new secondary ports and deliver small cargoes of strategic metals, chemicals, and machine tools.

So on June 28, Porter ordered some new cannon, signal stations, and Marine detachments to take up positions screening even the smallest navigable passages through the Outer Banks. Those chosen to man these desolate outposts were not happy about the assignment, and when sultry June gave way to the torrid scorch of July, the secondary inlets were duly garrisoned, but not a single additional ship was sighted trying to make for Shelborne's Point or Plymouth. Porter's intuition began to seem like an idle fancy, and being wrong always made Porter grumpier. He had hoped to bag at least a few small runners, but none had obliged him.

Maybe he should have followed Admiral Farragut's advice. Farragut had been the Navy Department's first choice to replace Admiral Lee, but Farragut respectfully declined the job. He also advised Porter to shun the assignment. For every hour of runner-chasing excitement, he warned, the blockade fleet endured many days of excruciating tedium, bad food, and repetitive drills (*"Stand by to repel boarders!"*) which no one ever expected to perform for real. But Porter had studied the maps and emerging strategies of the two contending commanders in chief and drawn his own conclusion: so diminished was Confederate naval power, and so few coastal objectives remained in the South that were worth fighting a battle over, that the *only* place left where he might enhance his personal share of Glory was in the waters off Cape Fear. Why no major campaign had been launched to wrest control of Wilmington from the enemy was an oversight that struck him as bordering on negligence. Everyone was obsessed with Richmond, but capturing Richmond only gave you one decrepit iron foundry! Indeed, by liberating General Lee from always having to worry about protecting that stuffy, self-righteous city, the loss of Richmond might actually improve the Confederates' military situation. But capture Wilmington, and you cut off Lee's primary source of everything from tinned food to boot leather. So despite Farragut's advice, David Porter followed his instinct and accepted command of the North Atlantic Fleet, absolutely convinced that the climactic naval battle of the war *would* be fought off the mouth of the Cape Fear River.

Redeploying valuable assets to choke off all the small inlets had been Porter's first major initiative since taking command. When the anticipated rash of miniature runners failed to materialize, Porter's mood grew foul. Farragut was right: the boredom was beyond comprehension to anyone not familiar with the psychological effects of long prison sentences.

But the boredom ended rather dramatically on the evening of June 27, when the CSS *Hatteras* ambushed a routine four-ship convoy steaming from New Bern to Elizabeth City: two gunboats escorting a pair of transports packed with replacements, rations, and sacks of mail. The ironclad had been hiding patiently deep inside a desolate jungly cove on the coast of Pamlico Sound. It had emerged suddenly, with the setting sun behind it. No one in the convoy even spotted the hulking ram until it was only a few hundred yards off their port side. The ironclad closed in fast—much faster than anyone had ever seen the *Hatteras* move before—and her great ram sliced one of the transports in half as though the ship were made of cardboard. With undiminished speed she turned slightly to starboard and stove-in the bow of the second transport, causing it to sink in a matter of minutes. Sam Parker had one Brooke gun on the right side and the other on the left, and he reduced speed as he steamed straight between the two warships so that his gunners would have time to get off several shots with the first pass. The portside gunboat took a hit in her steam-chest and disintegrated in one savage thunderclap, while the starboard escort lost its forward Parrott gun to a shell and had its entire bridge carved away by a solid shot that decapitated the executive officer and demolished the helmsman so thoroughly that the only remnant of him later recovered was his cap. Parker refrained from sinking the starboard gunboat simply because he wanted some witnesses to carry the news back to New Bern: the *Hatteras* was on the loose again! She might be lurking in any of a thousand unnamed inlets, tributaries, and densely shrouded coves! In seven minutes, the ironclad had sunk three ships, two of them carrying about six tons of supplies and a mixture of replacements and men returning from furloughs. Thirty-eight men were known to have perished, and the sole surviving gunboat limped back into New Bern with gore splashed on the sides of her deckhouse, looking as though she had been gnawed on by a giant alligator.

Commander Meeker, Flusser's successor as leader of the suddenly diminished brown-water navy in North Carolina, was aghast at the carnage wrought by the *Hatteras*'s ambush, though he grudgingly admired Captain Parker's audacity. But at a hastily conferred command conference the day after the incident, he publicly acknowledged that Admiral Porter had been right about one thing: the Rebs *had* been up to something, and the "mystery ship of Hatteras Inlet" *had* played a part in resurrecting the ironclad. According to fragmentary reports from well-placed Unionist informants, Governor Vance had been so angry when he learned that Lee had pulled Hackett's division back to Virginia, only a day or two before Hackett would have captured New Bern, that he had intervened personally to get the ironclad back into action as soon as possible. Using his emergency wartime powers, Vance dipped into the state's gold reserves and ordered a brand new steam plant from the Liverpool firm of Trenholm & Bulloch, an engine of the most advanced type that could possibly be fitted into the ironclad's port side. Hobart-Hampden had commanded a high-speed run on the *Ad-Vance* to Liverpool, where he loaded the engine, then went on to Nassau, where he leased the fastest available steamer capable of hauling the engine straight through to Plymouth.

Parker's engineers and metal-fitters had already stripped out the old engine, and removed the aft decking so that when the new steam plant arrived, it could be installed quickly. In his first, very cautious, trial runs, Parker found the new engine almost too powerful—it cranked out 110 more horsepower than the older plant, and all that added thrust made the *Hatteras* steer like a garbage scow. Steeley quickly tamed the propulsion system and reported, to Parker's delight, that the ironclad could now work up a top speed five knots greater than her previous best, which in turn almost doubled the striking power of a ramming attack. With Vance's enthusiastic encouragement, Parker decided to strike a hard, dramatic blow as the first step in mounting a one-ship guerrilla war against the enemy's coastal forces.

During the week after that stunning attack, Admiral Porter collected eyewitness accounts of the *Hatteras*'s depredations and forwarded them by courier straight to Gideon Welles, Lincoln's Secretary of the Navy. In his attached letter, Porter summarized the current situation in the starkest terms: *"At present, there is absolutely nothing to prevent the Rebel ram from going anywhere she pleases and destroying any ship she encounters. Until a solution is found to this emergency, the United States Navy may fairly be said to have lost all control over the inland waters of North Carolina."*

Certainly, no rumors about a naval disaster had reached the USS *Monticello,* which was then stationed on the northern end of the inner blockade run, patrolling a twenty-mile arc due east of the Rebel saltworks at Masonboro Sound. Just for the hell of it, Cushing had submitted a request to Admiral Porter for permission to "jab another pin in the enemy backsides" by steaming close to shore and lobbing a few practice broadsides into the drying pans and their ancillary structures, but Porter had turned him down coldly. By the straitlaced standards of the Old Navy, Cushing struck Porter as a reckless glory hound whose actions had sometimes taken him right to the edge of reprimand, if not a court-martial, and before the *Hatteras* crisis erupted, Porter had planned to ignore Cushing as much as possible.

Cushing suspected as much from the aloof, terse, manner in which Porter had declined his request to mount a nuisance raid on the saltworks. Cushing was therefore greatly surprised, on July 6, when his afternoon nap was interrupted by the news that Admiral Porter's flagship, the *Malvern,* had just anchored alongside and the Admiral had requested Commander Cushing's presence in his quarters to discuss "a matter of grave importance."

"Oh, shit," muttered Cushing, as he hurriedly buttoned his jacket and tried to smooth the wrinkles from his trousers, "What have I done now?"

18 No Braver Thing

JULY 8, 1864

Dear Commander Cushing—

I have never had the pleasure of meeting you, but through letters of my dear friend (I hesitate to say "my fiancée," because we have made no official announcement of betrothal yet) Lt. Comm. James Valentine, I feel that I know you well enough to visualize you standing in my parlor. I trust that you will keep this letter in confidence, for James's pride would be deeply injured if he knew I was writing you on his behalf, but I have read in the newspapers about the recent depredations of the fearsome Rebel ironclad, the Hatteras, *and I have learned from James about your unquenchable desire to exact personal vengeance on that ship because you hold it responsible for the awful death of your friend and mentor, Commodore Charles Flusser. James is convinced that you are planning one of your daring raids against that vessel and he is trying to prepare me, I think, for the news that he will volunteer to accompany you on this perilous undertaking.*

Why it is that men must perform dangerous deeds in order to affirm their courage, I do not understand, but I know that his devotion to you will compel him to volunteer if such a mission is authorized.

In slightly more than one year, James will be eligible for retirement on full pension, and thanks to you he will be able to do so at a higher rank than he would have achieved otherwise. We are not young people anymore, Mr. Cushing, but we still have a chance to enjoy many years of peaceful happiness together. You may scorn that mysterious faculty called "woman's intuition," but I have a very persistent and alarming feeling that, if James joins you in an attack on the Hatteras, *he will not survive. Has he not done enough for his country? Has he not faithfully joined you in many earlier adventures? We both know that the war is entering its final stages and that a Union victory is inevitable. We have postponed our own happiness for the sake of the Navy for many years, and I implore you, if you can manage to convince him not to risk his life yet again, without injuring his pride, please do not allow him to participate in this extremely dangerous undertaking! If I were to lose him now, after so many months of living with fear for his safety, it would mean the end of my hopes, virtually of my life.*

I cannot say this to him without wounding his pride, but ***you can.*** *If God so favors us that we have a son, we plan to name him "Will" and to make you his godfather.*

I implore you, for our sakes, and for the sake of our unborn son, to reject his pleas to accompany you. He will be unhappy, he will probably sulk, but in time he will be grateful to you. James has suffered, professionally, from his unwavering loyalty to you, and has never asked for anything in return. Therefore, I am asking on his behalf. He has served you, and this Nation, unselfishly and with unqualified devotion. Does he not deserve some happiness? Do not I, who have waited almost ten years, for him to complete his years of service to the Navy.

James is too proud to ask to be excused from this expedition, and so I am asking for him. I must close now, else my tears will blur the ink with which I compose this letter. You are young, and fearless, while he is a mature man who has neither your stamina nor your fierce compulsion to seek battle. Surely, his place can be taken by a younger sailor, someone who does not have a loving friend waiting at home, living only for the day her true love returns to her for good.

I only pray that this letter reaches you before you undertake this bold but exceedingly dangerous mission, and that you can find it in your heart to reward James's love and respect by affording him the chance to live through this war and to spend his final years in peace, harmony, and fulfillment.

Yours very sincerely,
Anna Thomas Sullivan, Boston, Mass.

Admiral David Porter did not strain himself to present a picture of hearty welcome when Cushing was piped aboard the *Malvern.* After rendering the salutes required by naval etiquette, the Officer of the Deck simply pointed aft and said, "Admiral Porter's waiting for you there by number four gun, Mister Cushing."

Porter had adopted a pose of studied indifference, leaning his right elbow across the back end of a 6-inch Parrott and pretending to study the condition of the *Monticello*'s upper rigging. Cushing's first impression was one of barely controlled pugnacity: stern black brows, narrow ice-blue eyes, and black beard. Porter's large and powerful hands were knotted into fists, as though he intended to punch Cushing in the jaw rather than salute him. But the nine gold stripes covering the admiral's sleeves attested to a lifetime's hard and scrupulous service. Porter's affected nonchalance, Cushing realized, was a pose intended to put a young headline-seeker in the awkward position of a supplicant approaching the throne of an indifferent monarch. Not until Cushing had approached within handshake range did the admiral slowly turn around to face him. Cushing braced to attention and cracked his sharpest salute, "Reporting for duty!" which Porter returned with no discernible change of expression behind his ursine beard. He did not offer to shake hands but merely growled: "Follow me below, sir, and get your mind up to flank speed. Time is of the essence, and I need to determine very quickly whether or not you're the sort of hero your supporters claim you to be, or just another glory-hound."

It was far from the most cordial welcome Cushing had ever received, but Porter's gruff manner was well known throughout the fleet, and young officers who incurred his displeasure might find themselves suddenly transferred from sea duty to pencil-pushing in the lower intestine of the Navy Department bureaucracy with no idea what had caused their fall from grace. Old salts of Porter's generation did not look favorably on restless mavericks like Cushing, and no doubt Porter would have been happy to discover that Cushing's exploits had been inflated by the journalists who wrote about them. But of course Porter had studied the young officer's dossier and had already concluded that Cushing's heroics were real enough. He also found ample evidence that the Secretary of the Navy Welles considered Cushing to be a valuable asset in terms of public relations. Porter did not doubt that Cushing was brave to a fault, but he was also recklessly insubordinate. His requests to lead daredevil raids seemed mostly predicated by his personal boredom with the tedious but vital duties of the blockade line, and in the margins of the most recent such document, Porter's predecessor, Admiral Lee, had scrawled: "Open complaints like this do nothing good for his colleagues' morale—should be taken down a peg or two, for the sake of general discipline!" Admiral Porter enjoyed taking brash young officers "down a peg or two," but under the circumstances, he was willing to forgo that pleasure.

A crisis was at hand, and every ranking officer who was privy to the details of the *Hatteras*'s latest bloody rampage had emphatically told Porter, "If you want the ironclad sunk at its moorings, put Cushing on the job, for he will either succeed splendidly or die trying."

Two spanking-fresh Marine sentries barred the door to the *Malvern*'s wardroom with crossed bayonets, so Cushing was instantly aware that something big was brewing behind that door. The Marines knew it, too; they snapped to attention and crashed the butt-plates of their Springfields against the deck so hard their bayonets rang, a clash-of-arms exclamation point. When Cushing entered the heart of officer country, he felt adrenaline in the air, like scorched ozone after a lightning bolt. Rising to meet Porter and his guest were several high-ranking officers, only one of whom—Commander Meeker—was familiar. Meeker introduced the others: an aide-de-camp to Gideon Welles, and an Under-Secretary-of-Something who worked with President Lincoln; lastly, he was introduced to a rather scholarly-looking civilian who kept fingering a sheaf of schematic drawings that Cushing could not quite glimpse but which were obviously important and "top secret." Atop the wardroom dining table were charts of the local coastline and a scale model of some kind, its details currently obscured by a dust cloth. Introductions finished, Porter closed and locked the door.

"I'll get right to the point, Cushing. The *Hatteras* has come out again, refitted with powerful new engines, and the resourceful Captain Parker has begun a very dangerous one-ship campaign of guerrilla warfare. So far he has sunk four ships, damaged five, and killed at least two hundred men. We cannot move supplies or reinforcements except in daylight and under heavy escort. It is distinctly possible that this one ship—all by itself—may drive the U.S. Navy completely out of North Carolina waters. I need not elaborate for you the consequences to our cause if he succeeds. Therefore, he must not be allowed to succeed. I've been assured, by everyone from Secretary Welles down to my own sailors, that if anyone can take out that ironclad, it is you . . . and furthermore, there are persistent rumors going around that you have vowed to do exactly that, in revenge for the death of your friend Charles Flusser. Let us bring you up-to-date on things, show you the ironclad's current position, demonstrate the curious new piece of ordnance invented by Professor Thomas Lay"—Porter here indicated the young civilian—"and then ask you pointblank: Can the job be done? And are you the man to undertake it? Weigh your answers carefully, sir, because there are only two likely outcomes to this mission: death and glory, or death and abject failure. The odds of sinking the ram *and* returning safely are too small to calculate."

Cushing had been bent over the map while Porter made these remarks. When he raised his face and turned it toward Porter, the admiral saw beneath the normally sunny blue of Cushing's eyes that core of ice only a few other men had witnessed, and then only when bullets were flying close and hot. In that very instant, David Porter altered his opinion of Will Cushing—the last time he had seen a sailor's eyes look that way was at the moment Admiral Farragut shouted his immortal battle cry "Damn the torpedoes!" Yet when Cushing replied, his voice was mild and businesslike.

"Admiral Porter, Commander Charles Flusser instilled in me every deep and cherished belief I possess regarding honor, courage, and naval tradition. His last words to me were: 'Destroy the *Hatteras* for me, Will!' I swore that I would, because I regarded those final words as a direct order—one I had despaired of ever being able to carry out. I'm indebted to you, Admiral, for giving me a chance to do so. That is all there is to say about the matter."

Now Porter offered his hand to Cushing, and clasped it with intense feeling.

"Here is what we know about the ram's situation:

"Unless she has moved in the past twenty-four hours, the *Hatteras* is moored to a pair of immense riverside oaks just downstream from Plymouth. The Confederates have moved up several batteries of heavy field guns to protect her against any attack, and there are at least four companies of infantry quartered in the town who would turn out at the first alarm. On both sides of the ram's anchorage, a circle of enormous bonfires has been prepared and covered against the elements—accelerants are stored nearby, so the fires may be brought to full blaze very quickly. Anything on the river within five hundred yards of the ironclad's position will be illuminated. To protect the *Hatteras* against ramming attacks, Plymouth's engineers have erected a stout boom that skirts the ram out to a distance of about twelve feet. Between the ironclad's own armor, the shoreline defenses, and the tightly restricted confines of the anchorage itself, the ironclad is safe from anything save a surprise boarding assault by a large and very determined force. But such a raiding party could hardly approach unobserved and would suffer prohibitive casualties before getting close enough to make the attempt."

Cushing's bloodthirsty expression indicated that he was certainly ready to *try* such a forlorn hope, but Porter firmly ruled it out as being "a pointless waste of brave sailors."

"That leaves but one practical means of striking the *Hatteras*: by jamming a spar torpedo under her keel and blowing a big hole in her ass. For an explanation of how that *might* be accomplished, I commend your attention to Professor Thomas Lay, a scientist employed as an ordnance consultant at the Naval Research Laboratory at the Brooklyn Navy Yard. Professor Lay has come up with some innovative ideas and has brought a scale model to illustrate the gist of his scheme. By modifying one of the navy's thirty-foot utility launches, he thinks a small crew in a small boat might be able to do what several very large warships have so far failed utterly to do: knock out the *Hatteras*. Professor Lay, you have our full attention."

Thomas Lay was a scientist, not a warrior, but Cushing liked the forthrightness of his handshake and the keen intelligence that flashed behind his spectacles; and Professor Lay, it turned out, knew a lot more about contemporary naval technology than many career officers Cushing could name.

"One of my many jobs, gentlemen, is to welcome, chaperone, and exchange information with delegations from the naval services of Great Britain, France, Italy, Russia, and several other states. Two topics seem to be of particular concern to all of them: mines and torpedoes. Our Civil

War has become, in effect, a great laboratory for developing these infernal devices and exploring their potential as both offensive and defensive weapons. The Rebels, we must all admit, have been the real pioneers in this new and specialized form of warfare, and for obvious reasons: mines and torpedoes are great *equalizers*, because they enable a poor nation to sink the very expensive warships of a rich one. Like the sling of David, a submerged mine, weeks or months after the men who planted it have left the area, can bring down a Goliath of a warship.

"But they are primarily *defensive* weapons, because until someone invents a reliable miniature propulsion engine, they cannot actually be aimed and fired at a distant target. They can only lie in wait, hoping that the enemy ships obligingly run into them. I and my associates have spent two years *thinking* about such weapons . . . and that preoccupation eventually led me to come up with an idea about how a target such as the *Hatteras* might successfully be attacked, even in a heavily defended anchorage.

"When the *Hatteras* finally did emerge and engage Commander Flusser's ships, she proved her devastating power in a manner so stunning as to move that tactical problem to the top of the U.S. Navy's list of priorities. Secretary Welles sent me a memorandum that stated the urgency quite bluntly. I am paraphrasing, of course, but the essence of it was this: For God's sake, come up with some workable plan to eliminate that ironclad and do it quickly, before she wipes out another flotilla of gunboats! Take a long, hard look at every kind of ship and machine already in active service and see if there is not a way to modify something *we already have on hand,* because we do not have time to invent some totally new contraption!

"I racked my brain, and no inspiration came. Then, about six weeks ago, I was strolling along the boardwalk that surrounds the navy yard, enjoying a postprandial cigar, when I suddenly realized that one possible solution was sitting in the water right in front of me."

With a flourish, Professor Lay removed the dust cloth from the object Cushing had correctly identified as a ship model.

"There it was, floating gently on the swells: one of the navy's all-purpose thirty-foot utility launches, which are scaled-up versions of those wonderfully seaworthy boats Great Britain has been using, for more than a hundred years, to rescue crews and passengers from ships driven aground by high winds and heavy surf. The proportions, the rake and balance of these lifesaving boats, combined with their extremely rugged construction, make them almost impervious to capsizing. The version currently in service is powered by a reliable, hundred-ten-horsepower centerline engine. These boats can ride over the biggest waves or steam through riptides powerful enough to hurl a steam frigate onto the rocks, yet they can still maneuver handily enough in tight spaces to pluck half-drowned men from beneath a capsized hull. In short, a plain but virtually unsinkable craft that has been tested under the most strenuous conditions and has repeatedly proven both versatile and reliable. But then, you are all familiar with this admirable jack-of-all-naval-trades."

"Indeed, Professor, I *thought* I was familiar with these boats," said Cushing, "but what is that . . . combing or covering that you've placed over the engine mount and wrapped like a glove around the smokestack?"

"That, Commander Cushing, is the first of my innovations: a sound-absorbent baffle made of chemically treated cotton stuffing, held in place by such highly advanced scientific equipment as bailing wire, chicken-coop fencing, and carpet staples! When you 'cap' the engine with one of these, you reduce the noise to a mere whisper. Unless the night air is perfectly still, without a breath of wind, a man standing on the riverbank thirty feet away will hear nothing louder than the river's own current as it sighs and gurgles over boulders and through the limbs of fallen trees. And when you attach *this* apparatus"—the scientist picked up a scale model of what looked to be a long barge pole—"you turn a lifeboat into a man-o'-war!"

The "barge pole" snapped into a set of spring-loaded holding clamps in line with the boat's starboard gunwale. The shaft was swivel-mounted amidships, and curiously hinged about five feet from its forward end, where it terminated in a thick, heavy-looking cylinder, tapered to a sharp point—a fixture very similar in appearance to a big-caliber, contact-detonated artillery shell.

Cushing inhaled sharply. "By God, it's a spar torpedo!"

"Correct, sir! A very flexible, double-jointed, telescoping kind of spar torpedo, culminating in a twenty-two-pound warhead of compressed nitrocellulose."

"Of what?" chirped Admiral Porter. "Twenty-two pounds of any kind of powder isn't going to do much damage to the *Hatteras.*"

"Not *powder,* Admiral. Nitrocellulose is a compound that produces three times the blast effect of the same amount of conventional gunpowder. It was invented by an Austrian chemist about eight years ago, but turned out to be much too unstable to use in artillery shells—the Austrians kept blowing up their own guns when they tried it. However, if placed inside a torpedo warhead, it is perfectly safe. And this twenty-two-pound warhead will explode with the same, or even greater, force as a one-hundred-pound shell.

"As long as the shaft is mounted securely to the side of the launch, nothing short of a sledgehammer against the detonator will set it off, not even the sort of jolt you would feel by running hard around. So you needn't worry about it going off when you jump the launch over the log boom. Assuming you've done that and are now resting next to the ironclad—well, I suppose 'resting' isn't . . . um . . . anyway, you're *there!* So now you deploy the spar for action . . . THUS! After detaching the spar from its holding clamps, you unlock it by pulling on *this cable,* which renders it fully movable, while the strongest men in the crew give a good, hearty push from behind, which extends it forward. In effect, the steam launch becomes a charger, and the spar, a lance! At full speed, this thirty-footer should work up enough momentum to simply vault over the log boom, putting the bow just a few feet from the line where the ironclad's casemate is bolted to the main deck. You are then ideally placed to position the explosive head *beneath* the target's keel."

Lay picked up a small black thimble and placed it on the launch's bow. "And THIS represents a 12-pounder boat howitzer, double-charged with grapeshot—and rocks, nails, buckshot, whatever else you want to cram in to fill up the barrel. You will fire the howitzer at the instant the launch grinds across the boom, to force the defenders to take cover and thus give you a few undisturbed seconds so you can adjust the angle and depth of the torpedo. Its effect will be like raking the side of the ironclad with a giant shotgun, and it should buy you a few priceless seconds of diversion—which could mean the difference between success and failure.

"Try to place the charge as close as possible to the ironclad's bottom. When you think you have it positioned just right, pull on THIS cable, and the torpedo will drop into a vertical position. We have encased most of the guncotton in a steel cap, which will focus ninety percent of its explosive force *upward.*

"When you're satisfied that the charge is aligned vertically—you should be able to feel the tension on that line go slack when it does—then pull on THIS cable, which in turn pulls out a thin disk of tin and allows a half-pound ball of lead to smash a glass cylinder, the contents of which will detonate the main charge. Inside the glass are two chemicals, quite harmless and inert as long as they are kept apart, but extremely volatile when mixed together. Once started, the chemical reaction cannot be reversed. Between fifteen and eighteen seconds after you drop the lead ball and break the glass wall separating the two chemicals, the mingled compound *will* produce a small but violent explosion, which, of course, will set off the guncotton, rather like the percussion cap on a rifle sets off the powder cartridge, and BANG! The torpedo blows a big hole in the ironclad's hull."

"How big?" asked Cushing.

"It varied, in our tests, depending on water conditions, humidity, and so forth, but it is always *big enough!* Whatever the initial size, simple hydraulic pressure will enlarge it rapidly. The *Hatteras* is a very heavy ship, and her own weight will cause a powerful jet of water to erupt like a geyser, ripping out every piece of hull planking, every frame member, that was weakened by the initial explosion. The more water that pours in, the heavier she becomes and the faster she goes down."

Professor Lay was sweating now, having worked up considerable intensity as his demonstration reached its climax. He mopped his forehead and polished the steamy lenses of his spectacles. Then he looked up, owl-eyed, at the silent, grim-faced oval of naval officers.

"Rather elegant, isn't it?" he said, beaming with an inventor's pride. "Any questions?"

"Let me see if I have this down correctly, sir," piped Cushing. "To pull this off, I must aim the launch at high speed straight at the log boom, execute a smooth jump over it, unhook and maneuver the spar into just the right spot under the target, and pull four different levers at exactly the right time and in precisely the right sequence, all of this while three hundred infantry, six or seven field guns, and two gigantic Brooke rifles are shooting at me from several directions and at pointblank range . . . Then, after pulling the final lever, I have fifteen seconds to get far enough away from a four-hundred-ton ship before it blows up and sinks, creating enough suction to drown an elephant."

"Um, I think that about covers it, in a nutshell."

"I am very relieved to hear it, Professor! I had expected something much more complicated and dangerous! But this—this should be a snap! Thank you, sir, for a vivid and illuminating presentation. Now, I must go round up some volunteers. I do hope you won't mind going through the drill again, for those who haven't seen it."

Professor Lay beamed happily. "Yes, of course, I would be delighted! You and your crew might want to rehearse the process a few times before launching the raid for real."

Admiral Porter pretended to glare sternly at Cushing, "Yes, Commander, I want you to drill them hard! It's been my experience that the really *simple* battle plans are the ones most likely to go awry. I'll have my carpenters rig a mock-up so you can rehearse while we're waiting for the real launch to be towed here from New York."

"How long will that give us?"

"About three days."

"Ample time, Admiral—all my men are quick studies!"

Somehow the word had already gotten around: "Cushing is going to lead another raid!" He was besieged with volunteers. Fourteen men were needed, so he picked seven from the *Monticello* and solicited the advice of Admiral Porter and the officers of the *Malvern* to select the best-qualified volunteers from that ship, too.

Once the volunteers had been chosen, Cushing addressed them privately in the *Monticello*'s wardroom: "I am deeply moved by your eagerness to serve with me. But before you make an irrevocable commitment, I want you to know that this action will not be a bold, prankish adventure, such as the night we tried to kidnap General Whiting from his own bedroom. That was certainly risky, but it was also one hell of a lot of fun!

"But I want to tell you plainly that this new expedition will not be a lark; even the gentlemen who authorized it don't give it more than one chance in ten of succeeding. It is a desperate venture—much riskier than some of the 'pranks' I've pulled off before, and no sane commander would dream of executing such a plan if there were any other way to knock the *Hatteras* out of the war. I have racked my brain trying to design a simpler, less suicidal plan . . . so has Admiral Porter . . . so have many other fine professional naval officers. And all of us have failed to improve upon this insanely complicated and perilous procedure. Lieutenant Valentine, over there, has taken part in some missions that did have their component of 'fun' . . ."

"Like trying to kidnap General Whiting . . ." suggested one Cushing fan from the *Malvern.*

"Yes. Quite an escapade wasn't it, Jim?" Valentine nodded and held up a two-fisted victory sign. Nervous laughter and applause greeted this reference to an incident that had long since passed into blockade-fleet lore. But when the mood in the room turned boisterous, Cushing lost his temper and slammed his palm on the wardroom table.

"*Enough!* Some of us—perhaps all of us—in this room tonight *will not* return. It is as stark as that. So anyone who chooses to back out now may do so without anyone thinking the less of his character or his courage. You are all brave men, but your oath to the navy does not require you to perform voluntary suicide. On this mission, not only must you not *expect,* but you must not even *hope* to return safely. What waits for us up that river is death or glory. If we are very lucky, perhaps death *and* glory. I have already made out my will and written a final letter to my mother. I strongly suggest the rest of you do the same. Go and think about it, men. If any man decides to back out, he can do so without the slightest reproach from me. I shall be in my cabin tonight, studying my charts, and if any man wishes to speak with me in private, I will open my door to you.

"In any case, we will have two days of intense practice on the mock-up, and on Thursday night, August eleventh, we launch the raid, regardless of the weather. AttenHUT! Dis-MISSED!"

Cushing quickly added: "All except for Lieutenant Valentine. Jim, please remain for a few minutes so we can chat."

The wardroom was empty except for Cushing and the middle-aged lieutenant who had faithfully served as his executive officer for two action-packed years. They had been in, and gotten through, some very tight spots together, but this time Cushing was drawing a line.

"Goddamn it, Jim. I do *not* want you to join me on this one!"

"Am I not qualified, sir?"

"Belay that 'sir' business. Of course you're qualified—no man more so in the whole fleet. Don't you understand, man? Even if by some miracle we do sink that ironclad, we are none of us coming back to a friendly berth. We *will* die, or become prisoners. No third alternative realistically exists. I've recommended you for another stripe and a command of your own—and in two years you can retire on a lieutenant commander's pension, marry that sweetheart in Boston you keep writing to, live to a ripe old age, and have wonderful stories to tell your children. That's one future for James Valentine. The other future: drowning in a cold, black river, being torn apart by Rebel bullets, or slowly dying of starvation or typhus down in that pukehole Andersonville."

"I'm going, Will, and that's all there is to it."

"What if I order you to stay behind?"

"Then you'll have to charge me with mutiny, because I won't obey that order."

Cushing peered sadly at the seaworn, sun-leathered face of his older friend.

"In that case, I can't think of anyone I would rather have at my side when the Rebels finally kill Will Cushing."

A sultry July coastal night: air so heavy with moisture it makes the lung sacks feel sticky; sullen quarter moon just hangs there—won't go up, won't go down, like a panting yellow dog curled up on the sky's front porch; unpleasant fitful breeze feels gritty; hot, pissy little rain showers dimple the sound and river; a landscape streaked with torpid, greasy swipes of cloud . . .

Will Cushing was not in the mood for colorful metaphors as he slung a Spencer over his shoulder, made sure his holster flap was tightly closed against the drizzle, gripped the ratline holding the thirty-footer in fragile tether to the *Monticello.* He counted one by one the thirteen armed and tight-lipped sailors who climbed in behind him. Valentine brought up the rear, tiller man for tonight's Naval Version of the Charge of the Light Brigade—and also the guy responsible for making sure none of those critical cable-release lines got knotted up until it was time for Cushing to slip their braided tips between his fingers and open up the throttle when he had the launch lined up for its high-speed, one-way lunge over the Rebel torpedo boom.

Cushing had practiced his cable-pulling technique like a nervous piano student on the eve of his first public recital; Professor Lay had thoughtfully colored each line differently until Cushing pointed out that the manipulation would take place at *night.* "Ah! Yes, of course—how silly of me!" the scientist had muttered, and gone off to ask the ship's carpenter to locate differently textured wrappings instead, like labels in Braille: oil paper for the first pull, coarse-grit sandpaper for the one that triggered the chemical detonator, etc. Cushing had practiced blindfolded, had asked Valentine to mix up the cables and time him to see how fast he could untangle them, had even asked Valentine to put strange knots and entanglements in them so that—like a man walking four high strung dogs—he could figure out the fastest way to un-do the tangles and snags. Cushing put in hours and hours of practice just so he could *pull four thin cables in the proper order at the proper time while approximately four-hundred-fifty Confederate soldiers and sailors were trying to kill him with everything from revolvers to heavy artillery.* And when Cushing discovered that his lank, cable-webbed body was in such an awkward shape as to prevent the man behind him, Ensign Stokesdale from the *Malvern,* from efficiently aiming and firing the boat howitzer, Cushing added the gun's firing lanyard to his left hand. From behind, when he was performing the curious exercises, Cushing looked like a deranged marionette attempting to manipulate his own strings.

11:30 P.M.: All aboard! The muffled steam engine purred reassuringly, the helmsman obeyed Cushing's command "Starboard fifteen, ahead one-third," the mooring umbilical cords dropped away, and the torpedo launch swung toward the wide, dark, rain-dappled mouth of the Roanoke. Crews lining the railings of both the *Malvern* and the *Monticello* gave three lusty cheers for the departing heroes, and Cushing shouted back over his shoulder, "Another stripe or a coffin!"

11:47 P.M.: Softly churring and steaming vibrationless through gritty streaks of dank mist, the launch passed the foretop, mast, and crumpled stack of the *Smithfield,* the ironclad's first kill, and twenty minutes later crossed the mild, pleated crosscurrents where the Roanoke River lumbered into Albemarle Sound. From here on, they were in the river proper, almost certainly steaming past Confederate lookouts and, for all Cushing knew, maybe straight into the contact detonator of a newly seeded mine. But for a while the river was broad and unobstructed and so quilty-patched with mist and rain spits that they were well hidden, and the engine remained as discreetly quiet as Professor Lay had promised it would be.

12:28 A.M.: "How far you reckon we've come, Mister Cushing?" Ensign Stokesdale whispered at Will's left shoulder, striving hard to keep his youthful voice from betraying the tension Will could feel radiating from him like heat from a woodstove.

"About halfway, I think."

"They tell me the hardest part is the waiting . . ."

"The 'hardest part' of *what*?"

"The hardest part of a battle."

"Then 'they' have never been in one," growled Cushing.

1:02 A.M.: A ghostly light ahead in the murk. All fourteen volunteers are sweating like stevedores from the humidity, and the enforced stillness is starting to cramp their bodies. Now the launch noses, at 10 percent throttle, through the last of the narrows below Plymouth. The town comes into view: a scatter of lights, transient as fireflies in the drizzly mist, a jumble of pilings, jetties, and ramps that mark Plymouth's waterfront. Any minute now.

Where the hell is she? God, don't let them have moved her back to Holman's Ferry! Time for the marionette master to take the reins. The cables, all neatly bundled as a bride's bloomers on their way to the washtub, are passed forward, and Cushing carefully fixes the right cables to the right fingers, making sure all the control lines are straight and free of kinks.

"There she is!" whispers Ensign Stokesdale, and Will's head swivels to the left and *My God, she's HUGE!* The *Hatteras,* blacked out except for a small warning lantern on her stern, resembles a titanic slab of featureless ebonite as the launch glides by and Will realizes they have overshot their target and will have to go upstream and make a U-turn in order to have the necessary angle and room to make their attack. And looking over the bow, he sees, as though the man were tightrope-walking on the mouth of the howitzer, a Rebel sentry only ten feet away, staring at them with openmouthed astonishment, but recovering quickly, sliding his rifle strap over his shoulder, jamming the butt against his shoulder, cocking it—the sound of a mousetrap snapping a pantry rodent's neck—and the inevitable challenge comes very loud: *"Ahoy the boat! Identify yoahrself immediately or Ah will FAHR AT YOU!"* The shout rouses a dozen dogs and alerts every other sentry in North Carolina—a very individualistic babble of challenges: *"Who goes thar?"—"Hawlt or Ah'll shoot!"* and a very confused-sounding *"Advay-yance and be reco'nized!"* and so on until the launch is a quarter mile north of Plymouth and Cushing can order, "Bring her about and ring on emergency speed!" As the bow sweeps the landscape around in a dizzying semicircle, making the fourteen raiders feel like men who have hitched a ride on the second hand of a giant watch, those long-prepared bonfires start to bloom, whooshing coal oil feeding mushrooms of fire, throwing the river and ragged shoreline into stark relief, turning the rain patches into semisolid white scabs. Cushing chances a quick look back, and the crew's faces have the pallor of old piano keys—*Ba-Ka-Da-BAM!*

The first ragged volleys crack from the dock, from atop Wessells' old parapets, even from the church steeple (that one is dead accurate, too, striking the muffled smokestack with a flat *"thunk!"*—angry spikes of water stippling all around the launch as it picks up speed and the distance closes—boot heels pounding on the wooden docks, sergeants commanding volley fire, sheet lightning stabbing out for them, a full octave's worth of minié-ball whines and zooms, close enough to feel the air snap like whip cracks behind them. A field gun fires blindly from a revetment guarding the *Hatteras,* and Cushing loses his sight line behind the cascade of water raised by a 24-pounder ball, but there she is again, much closer!

A dull gray mountain now swarming with armed men and sparking all along the casemate roof and through the flung-open gun ports—splinters flying off the launch, zinging off the metal parts. Someone two benches back takes a ball so hard his reflexive jerk shudders down the length of the whole boat. "Catch me!" he shouts, and the closest sailors try, but too late—big wounded-man splash and a stunned cold-water grunt, fast receding. Somehow, automatically, Cushing has pulled the first cable, and the spar, already lifted from its spring-loaded storage brackets, swings free and some crewmen aft, including Valentine, do a "Heave-ho!" on the butt end, causing the spar to telescope out to its full practical length, now free-swinging and Cushing can aim it like a harpooner—and *Christ A-mighty!* The whole starboard casemate and boat deck of the *Hatteras* are snapping flames at him like a gaggle of hysterical fireflies, men firing at the launch with pistols, Enfields, shotguns, some even chucking sputtering hand grenades, and filling up one of the open gunports is the absolutely HUGE muzzle of a big Brooke rifle, a sinister black eye staring down Cushing's squinted blue ones. *Now!*—he yanks the howitzer lanyard and rakes the ironclad's whole starboard side with 114 tightly packed pistol balls, raising a fearful clanging-banging-pots-and-pans racket and making the armor plates seem to twitch and dance from the blacksmith-sparks of all those lead balls flattening out and zinging off at wild, careening arcs. THAT'll make 'em pull their heads in! And just like Professor Lay predicted, buys the launch a few precious seconds so Cushing can scream "Tilt!" and every other man leans as far aft as he can, causing the bow to rise just enough to permit the whole heavy hammering boat to hit the log boom like a carpenter's plane. Actually rising up, one-quarter airborne, it sails smoothly over the log and crashes down again, throttle yanked back to "emergency stop," but the launch still moving at such a clip that it actually rams the ram and bounces off HARD—which would have been the end of everything except Cushing has the presence of mind to push the spar down into the water before it can smash into the ship, and when all motion ceases, he finds, amazingly, that he has planted the torpedo exactly where it ought to be: three feet protruding under the ironclad's keel and the torpedo somewhere between the bottom of the ram and the bottom of the river . . . so . . .

PULL the third cable, and he feels the torpedo flop loose and heavy like a lead weight on a fishing line, and hopes it has swung to the vertical, as its inventor intended, because now the shooters who cleared the decks when the howitzer went off in their faces are coming back and opening fire. He feels a terrific kick as a pistol ball clips the heel off his left boot, an angry-cat-scratch down his spine as a load of buckshot rips across the back of his jacket, and OH, LORD being run out not more than two feet from his nose is the muzzle of that Brooke rifle again, looking big enough now to drive a stagecoach through—and he can clearly hear the gun crew coolly at their drill and sees a hairy-backed pair of hands raising up a gigantic canister charge and ramming it into the barrel, and another gunner shouts "Prime!" so Cushing knows there's a Rebel at the back end of this enormous piece of plumbing who is sticking a sharp wire into a powder bag, and another who is about to follow the withdrawn wire with a friction igniter . . . calmly reminding himself that another five seconds remain before the Brooke is primed and ready and the gun captain draws taut the firing lanyard, so Cushing pulls the last, most crucial cable, hopefully priming the torpedo with two chemicals so angry at the touch of each other's molecules that they fight, generate a passel of heat really, really fast, and annihilate each other. *You have about three seconds to do something, Cushing, so jump or dive or levitate as you choose, but do it NOW!* But wait, what's this? The Brooke crew is pausing for what seems, under the circumstances, to be a positively silly gesture of chivalry: a Rebel gunner's head poking around the muzzle and shouting, "Surrender now and we won't shoot. Hands up by the time I count three or we'll blow you to bits!"

"I'll see you in hell, Johnny Reb, before Will Cushing raises his hands to the likes of you!"

The gunner's head pops back inside—"Can you believe it, men, that's *Will Cushing* in front of our gun!" And another gunner responding, "Long as it ain't Jesus, I'm firing, now GET OUT OF THE WAY!" Cushing knows the Brooke will fire, so he shouts, "Save yourselves men, and good luck," then leaps over the side just as two things happen: (1) The guncotton torpedo charge explodes, and (2) the 9.5-inch Brooke goes off, both explosions joining into one super-blast and throwing out such a vacuum that several cubic tons of the Roanoke River come boiling up, crushing the front of the launch like so much pasteboard and causing all four hundred tons of the *Hatteras* to recoil backward. Cushing feels his ears pop and for an instant thinks his eyeballs are going to be sucked out of their sockets, and has just enough time to draw a deep breath before those same cubic tons of water fall down again, smashing the log boom, washing about thirty Rebel musketeers overboard, and crushing the rest of the launch into an accordion-pleated wad of wood pulp.

Cushing is buffeted aimlessly by the boiling, heaving masses of water, dragged by current in one direction, pushed by water pressure in another, he is about one second away from a drowning man's last involuntary and fatal submarine gasp when, *Hallelujah!*—his head breaks the surface and he sucks in air, not river. All around him things are on fire and ships are listing and a lot of guns are still firing, mad chaos, too much for his stunned, overtaxed senses to sort out just now, thank you, although he does hear some of his men shouting for help and some of the enemy's men demanding their surrender, and since these dialogues are not punctuated by rifle shots, he assumes that at least some of his brave fellows survived and are being allowed to give themselves up. That two-for-the-price-of-one explosion next to and underneath the ironclad was sure enough spectacular, but he has a hunch that it was mostly foam and fury, not the backbreaking mortal blow he had hoped to deliver . . . but still, that ironclad wasn't going back into action any time soon, so the volunteers who died tonight did not die in vain—and he assumes, accepts, and can live with the notion that at least a third of them must have perished.

Okay, Will Cushing, now that your mind's working again, let's take inventory! Arms and legs all present, although he either sprained or broke an ankle when the muzzle blast of that Brooke picked him up and slammed him around before the returning water volcano broke the vacuum and drove him, like a nail made of flesh, so far underwater that he can feel bottom-slime caked under his fingernails. His hearing is pretty much gone, but that's to be expected and may be temporary . . . his whole body aches and throbs but there's no jetting spurts of arterial blood and no compound fracture splinters poking through his skin. Water temperature is so pleasant it's well-neigh amniotic . . . current's moving him downstream at about half a knot . . . he's okay to drift for a while but not okay if he passes out again. He decides to put another mile between himself and the still-lively ruckus lighting up the sky behind him. The banks are steep here, but he knows he'll find a shallow climb somewhere ahead, where the river starts to widen. He'll crawl out there, then walk to the river's mouth and signal for rescue. Yes, this is a good and reasonable plan. So comfortable is he with his chosen strategy that he immediately passes out again.

But only briefly, because a familiar voice is calling his name, and calling it in conjunction with the words "Help me!" At first Cushing can see nothing new: river; weeds; stumpy, granulated clouds; hot nasty summery things bereft of all poetry. "Cushing! Over here—help!" Now he spies a low, sodden shape bumped up against a fallen tree like the corpse of a drowned muskrat, only this muskrat is waving feebly to attract his attention. Not much distance separates them, but Cushing is already level with the supplicant and so must swim across the current and against it, an effort that uses up his last reserves of strength. For a great naval hero, he really is just a rather frail twenty-three-year-old, much afflicted by sniffles, sore throats, and long spells of Byronic melancholy. Whoever this half-drowned sailor is, he had better not need or expect to receive heroic physical exertions, because Will Cushing is fresh out of those.

"My God, Valentine! It's you!"

"Well, it's some of me, Will. The explosions knocked me into something real hard. Couple of broken ribs, at least. It's hard to breathe, too. I'm afraid I punctured a lung with the end of a rib bone. I gave up trying to swim . . . hurts so bad when I do, I get woozy, start feeling blood way down in my throat."

Valentine raised an arm and wrapped it around Cushing's torso. A secondary explosion, back in Plymouth, faintly cast light on their part of the river, enabling Cushing to see his friend's face. Will's eyes filled with tears, for he had seen that look on badly injured men before—Valentine had seen it, too, and he knew perfectly well how he must have appeared: the glazed eyes, the slack gray flesh tones, the worn-out, overloaded, near indifference of his nerve endings to additional pain—a man on the verge of relinquishment.

Cushing probed gently under the surface until he found Valentine's injured side, then drew his hand back as though he had touched live coals. The right side of Valentine's body felt like it was just plain stove-in, like a small boat dashed against a cliff. Where the firm ladder of ribs ought to be, there was a massive indentation and a lot of sharp, ragged, sheared-off bones. That lung might as well have pitchfork tines stabbing into it, and God knows what other internal organs had been crushed, torn, or rearranged in unnatural configurations. It was a wonder he had lasted this long.

"Feels pretty awful doesn't it, Will?"

"I won't lie to you, old friend—you've felt it yourself, so you know how grave your injuries are. If you can stand the pain, I will try to move you onto dry land, make you as comfortable as I can. Maybe when daylight comes we can get a Rebel surgeon to patch you up."

"I thought you weren't going to lie to me," Valentine chided, trying desperately to smile. "My kind of damage is beyond 'patching up,' and we both know it. And please, Will, don't try to move me! Just keep your arm around me and I'll drift off soon enough."

"Damn it, Jim. I begged you not to come!"

"Oh hell, you knew I couldn't stay behind and miss *this one!* Your finest moment, and a fitting occasion for my last. Shake my hand one more time, Commander. It has been my great honor and pleasure to fight beside you, Will. Men follow you into the craziest, most hopeless fights, you know, because when you lead them into the flying lead, there's this weird kind of light that shimmers around you—and men cannot help but think, I'll get through this if I just stick with Mister Cushing. The bullet hasn't been cast that can kill him! Sometimes the rest of us feel a touch of it, just by being around you, that amazing craziness . . . Never met any other officer who had that kind of magic. Thanks to you, I've had adventures I never would have had, done braver things than I ever knew I was capable of . . . Even now, I do not regret one minute of it!"

Valentine's body shuddered, and inside his shattered rib cage, organs sloshed in blood that had not yet found an exit. His face contorted and he made a series of dreadful *"Uh-uh-uh!"* sounds that Cushing realized were coughs. When the spasm passed, blood began to well up at last through Valentine's lips. He cried out in sudden pain and clutched fiercely at Cushing.

"Will! Will, just hold me for a minute, until it's over!"

Those were his last words. Cushing wrapped the dying man in his arms and wept, while he felt the last vitality gutter and fail in Valentine's body.

When the sun rose, the heat of its first slanted rays woke Cushing from a black, deathlike sleep. He was wrinkled as a prune, but refreshed enough to push Valentine's stiff, cold body to the nearest low shore, and strong enough to haul him out into the harsh glare of morning. He took off his jacket—amazed to count four bullet holes in the fabric, along with more punctures—shotgun pellets he assumes—than the front of a Dutch pie-safe—and then sat down with Valentine's body to wait for whatever came next—either a Rebel patrol, or one of Admiral Porter's boats, searching for survivors.

But instead, the growing heat made him drowsy again, and when he woke, it was not Admiral Porter standing over him, but a Confederate naval officer, gravely sad of face, eyes ringed with exhaustion, uniform sooty and torn.

"I suppose I am your prisoner, sir," Cushing managed to stammer through cracked lips.

"I do not care to take your surrender, Will Cushing. I saw you blown overboard last night, and hoped you would survive by drifting downstream and finding shelter. I rode out at first light so I could find you before any of the patrols who are out rounding up the survivors of your crew. If it's within my power, I intend to return you to your people. If someone else had found you, you would end up in that hellhole down at Andersonville. To my surprise, you're not a very robust young man, Cushing, and I do not think you would long survive in that dreadful place. By the way, I had some of my crew follow me in a steam launch—by now, they should be conversing with David Porter under a flag of truce, telling him where to find you. I will remain here with you until your comrades come to take you home."

Cushing stared at the officer with a curious objectivity. "By doing this, you might be setting yourself up for a court-martial . . . but then, you already know that, I expect."

"Well, yes, our navy did copy its regulations from your navy, after all. But what I'm doing is saving a very brave man from a fate he does not deserve."

"I am truly in your debt, sir. May I ask who you are and why you have done this honorable favor for me? I do not think we've met before."

"Yes, we have, in a manner of speaking. My name is Samuel Parker, and I am . . . well, I *was* . . . the captain of the *Hatteras*. And we encountered each other on the day my ship sank the *Smithfield*. I was told you were with Commander Flusser . . . his death is the only thing I regret. I had also heard that you had vowed to avenge him by destroying the *Hatteras,* so I was not entirely surprised to learn it was you who . . ."

"Did we . . . I mean, the *Hatteras*—is she?"

Parker sighed and knelt to offer Cushing a drink of whiskey from his canteen.

"I'm afraid you did sink her, sir. I was not onboard when you attacked, but I went to the ship just moments after the explosion. There was a hole in her bottom you could drive a wagon through. She's sunk and no mistake, nothing left above water but the smokestack. We will try to salvage the guns, of course, but the ship cannot be raised. The import of all this has not really sunk in yet, but when it does, I will grieve for my ship as I would for a dead child. Did you know, Cushing, that when I first took command of the project, there was nothing but a stack of drawings and an empty cornfield? You cannot conceive of the struggles, the obstructions, the delays we had to overcome to finish the *Hatteras* or the elation I felt when I took her into battle for the first time and realized that, in spite of it all, we had built one of the strongest warships in history. And after all that struggle, I got to command her in battle exactly four times—and a lucky thing for your side, too!"

"Captain Parker . . . what we achieved tonight—that was sheer good luck, and we both know it."

"Oh, good Lord, Cushing! Men like you *draw* good luck, like a magnet draws iron filings! But this exploit was more than good luck—I know, because I was not aboard the ironclad when you struck, so I was able to observe the whole attack from start to finish. May I say, as one naval officer to another, that no braver thing has been done in the whole course of the ghastly war? *No braver thing has been done in all the annals of naval history!* Ah, look yonder! Here comes a Union boat flying an admiral's pennant. It would seem that Admiral Porter himself has come to collect you in person. I suppose it is time for me to ride back to Plymouth and see to cleaning up the place—with the *Hatteras* out of the way, your side can recapture the town any time you want to."

"Have you any word for me about casualties among my crew?"

"Only two killed, so far as I know—this poor lieutenant and one other. Seven have been captured, four of them slightly injured. How many were there altogether?"

"Fourteen, counting me."

"So four are still missing—they will turn up by the end of the day, I imagine. I will do my best to have them incarcerated down in Wilmington, rather than shipped on to a prison camp. If Flag Officer Branch cooperates, and he does owe me a favor or two—your comrades stand a good chance of surviving. We both know the war won't last much beyond next Christmas . . ."

"When it is over, can we be friends, do you think?"

"Why not? I may even stay in the navy. And you?"

"If the navy will still have me!" Cushing stood up and waved to Porter's launch. Parker remounted his horse.

"Good luck, Parker. And thank you for the consideration you've shown for my crew. They are all brave men, and deserve to return safely to their families. And you, Captain, what next for you?"

Parker shrugged. "I imagine I will end up commanding a gun crew down at Fort Fisher. That *is* where the final act will be played out, of course. So perhaps we shall confront each other one last time—you from the deck of a frigate, and I from behind the walls of Colonel Lamb's great sand castle. Send up a rocket, and I'll try to aim at some other ship."

"No, sir! You must fire at me and I must shoot back at you, and we will both take our chances. That is what we vowed to do when we donned our respective uniforms, is it not?"

"It is indeed. And no one ever said that 'duty' is an easy thing."

The Short, Sad, Sortie of the CSS Raleigh

FLAG OFFICER BRANCH might have felt less frustrated if he had known the real reason why the Raleigh *broke in half so quickly: her keel had been eaten to pieces by colonies of teredos, a tiny, insignificant-looking sea worm which happens to have a ravenous appetite for wooden hulls. Earlier that year, the Confederate government ordered Branch to tow the ironclad downstream to a secluded inlet just south of Smithville, so the slipway in Cassidey's yard could be used to affect emergency repairs on the giant, government-owned runner* Hanseatic Prince. *Predictably, the repairs took many weeks longer than expected, giving the sea worms ample time to burrow into the ironclad's bottom, excavate nests, and lay thousands of eggs—which proved equally voracious when they hatched. If the* Raleigh *had been towed upstream into freshwater once every ten days, all the adult sea worms and their larvae would have been killed, and the ship's hull would have been strong enough to withstand the pressures exerted on it when the tide ran out around that sandbar.*

The existence of this tiny menace was not exactly a secret—mariners had known for two hundred years where it was safe to park their ships in the Cape Fear delta and where it was not. All that was required to purge a ship of these tiny menaces was to rotate the hull into freshwater at regular intervals. But nobody had the presence of mind to inform poor Branch, so he assumed it was safe to leave her anchored below Smithville indefinitely. No wonder the Confederate rear admiral (the Union equivalent of flag officer rank) was such a bitter man by the closing days of his tenure in Wilmington.

Farewell, Christopher. *The Wilmington Campaign.*
Broadfoot Press, 1997

When Flag Officer Branch learned about Cushing's raid on the *Hatteras,* he was dismayed. Yet he was also consoled by the fact that the *Raleigh* might be perceived, by the public at least, as the *"Successor to . . ."* and *"the Avenger of . . ."* and *he* would be its captain. When Samuel Parker and his forlorn crew showed up in Wilmington, eight days after the raid, humbly requesting to serve on either the *Raleigh* or the *Chickamauga,* Branch rather nastily said that all berths on both ships had long ago been promised to other navy personnel who had not yet been given their turn to play heroes. If Parker heard the spite in his old friend's voice, he gave no sign of it. Perhaps, he suggested, they might instead be sent to Fort Fisher—which was the logical place for Richmond to send the 9.5-inch Brookes, if Richmond got around to salvaging them before the Yankees got around to recapturing Plymouth. Branch had no objection—in fact, the sooner Parker and his dispirited sailors removed themselves from his office, the better. So Parker and his men dutifully packed their sea bags, took the first ferry down to Confederate Point, and were welcomed effusively by Colonel Lamb, who promptly gave Parker command of the existing guns atop Battery Buchanan "until the bigger-caliber weapons are shipped down from the *Hatteras,* and permanently if they are not."

According to reports from Wilmington, the *Chickamauga* was nearing completion. It was long past time for Matthew to apprise his wife of the Faustian bargain he had made with Flag Officer Branch. Naturally he had put off doing so. When he *did* broach the subject, he acted from that remarkably obtuse male delusion that a sexually replete woman, drifting into the sleep-of-many-climaxes, is less apt to become angry when her partner whispers bad news than that same woman would be after a good night's sleep and two cups of coffee. All Matthew had to say were the magic words: "I suppose I should have mentioned it before now, but . . ." and the soft, drowsy lady beside him turned into a fully alert harpy tensed to strike.

Mary Harper waited until the words ". . . so it really is best, for all of us, if I return to sea . . ." before she sprang up, eyes flaring and claws fully extended.

"Not six months back on dry land and you're already bored with our marriage bed? We are rich, our children are healthy, our plantation is in good order, our Negroes are loyal and productive, so OF COURSE it's time for you to go gallivanting off on the high seas again! My God, how can you *endure* the stifling boredom of our company for so much as another minute?" And off they went!

By 3:00 A.M., Matthew's attitude had changed from one of simpering regret (mostly at the stupidity of his timing!) to one of truculent defiance. Mary Harper's attitude had gone from bitter sarcasm to one of venomous retaliation. They were right on the edge of that demarcation between a domestic argument and a real *fight,* the sort of acrimonious verbal brawl that would not end until one of them had drawn blood from the raw heart of their intimacy. A rhetorical dagger lay on the bed between them, and when Matthew tried a bit too hard to convince her of how miserably lonely his life would be if he were coerced back into a seafaring life, Mary Harper picked it up first and slashed him, flinging into his face the one verbal thrust she had vowed never to use, no matter how angry she was.

"As I recall, Matthew, the last time you were suffering from such 'loneliness' you managed to find consolation close at hand. How long, d'you think, before you encounter another femme fatale as exciting as Belle O'Neal?"

For a frozen moment, Matthew looked to be on the verge of striking her across the face. For the duration of that moment, he *wanted to.* Instead, he wrested the verbal dagger from her and reposted with acidic cruelty.

"As 'exciting as Belle O'Neal?' The answer to that, my dear, is *never!*"

Round One then terminated with Matthew slamming the bedroom door and retreating to the library, where he indulged in a mighty sulk and half a bottle of bourbon.

The next morning, they both knew they had gone too far, and Mary Harper had come to terms with the reality of Matthew's situation: Branch did have him over a barrel, and that was a fact. Whether or not Matthew was *glad* to be in that position, was irrelevant. Without any training in land warfare, Matthew would probably not last six weeks on the frontlines in Virginia; but he *did* know seamanship now, and Branch had promised him subordinate officers who were experienced advisors in naval tactics. By assuming the role of "figurehead hero" on the *Chickamauga*'s bridge, he *did* stand a better chance of surviving the war and coming back in one piece.

"But isn't this what they call 'impressment,' Matthew? Isn't this what we went to war with Great Britain about back in eighteen-twelve?"

"I think we went to war so we could grab Canada. But yes, that was one of the justifications the newspapers fed to the public. By the way, it's called 'impressment' when a foreign navy does it. When your own navy does it, it's called 'getting drafted'."

"Whatever you call it, I won't agree to it unless Mister Branch negotiates a few concessions to us first!"

What a relief to hear a reasonable tone in her voice again. Now Mary Harper was coming to terms with the situation, just as he had been forced to do. This kind of rational, if slightly chilly discussion, was infinitely preferable to savaging each other with recriminations. All the same,

Matthew knew it would be a cold day in hell before they ever made love again with the sort of newlywed relish they had enjoyed before the subject ever came up.

When the Sloanes suggested that certain conditions be attached to Matthew's commission, Branch was willing to oblige them. Now that the children were in residence year-round, security was again Mary Harper's foremost worry. Branch offered her a permanent garrison—a Marine squad comprising ten riflemen and a sergeant—to be rotated periodically with a fresh squad from Wilmington. The men would arrive as soon as one of Pine Haven's outbuildings could be converted into a barracks. Together with the Pine Haven Militia (and the firepower of their Spencers), the Marines should be enough to deter any likely band of marauders.

When Mary Harper expressed fears that they might be menaced by a force too large for both Marines and Militia to repulse, Branch offered to install a trunk line from the boathouse to the busy telegraph relay post adjacent to the Wilmington-Goldsboro railroad bridge. "If you detect the approach of such a force, just send an emergency wire to my headquarters, and in ninety minutes I'll have two hundred Marines here, aboard patrol boats armed with twenty-four-pounders."

These were not small favors, so Mary Harper thanked him and pretended to be happy with the arrangements. When the day finally arrived for Matthew's swearing-in, she put on a brave, patriotic performance. Branch's marines, pleased with the prospect of home-cooked meals and leisurely duty far away from the sharp tongue of the flag officer, made a dramatic show of marching through the plantation to their new "barracks," a large utility building that had formerly been used for rice-threshing, but was now comfortably outfitted with bunks, furniture, and a woodstove.

After the Marines stowed their gear, they lined up ceremoniously on either side of the veranda staircase while Matthew Sloane, ruggedly handsome in his new captain's uniform of dove's-wing Confederate gray, descended the steps arm in arm with his wife. At the foot of the stairs, he handed her off to a very proud-looking Francis Marion and walked on, alone, to the shaded patio where Branch duly administered the oath of service. The Marines and the assembled crews of Branch's little auxiliary ships, gave three cheers, fired a volley into the air, and Matthew persuaded Branch to let Francis Marion pull the lanyard of a 24-pounder and blow a tree in half on the far side of the river. Still fully in command of her emotions, Mary Harper stood with the children and waved farewell as the tiny armada chugged back down the Uhwarrie, bearing her husband toward new adventures on far-off exotic seas . . . and once again, leaving her to run the plantation while he was having them.

* * *

Moonrise on the night of August 10 was not until 1:40 A.M. Full dark would descend over the Cape Fear delta at nine fifty-five. Colonel Lamb promised to have all the sea-face guns manned and loaded by that time. Flag Officer William Branch had positioned the CSS *Raleigh* approximately five hundred yards north of the hulking landmark of Battery Buchanan. Steam was up and all her guns run out and loaded. One mile behind the ironclad, the sleek, swift *Chickamauga* strained at an invisible leash. At precisely 10:00 P.M., a red signal lamp hanging from the ironclad's stern would be exchanged for a green one, and Branch would take his proud new ship into hostile waters for the first time. If he got the chance to ram and sink a Yankee ship, he would surely take it, but the main purpose of this sortie was to cause as much confusion as possible in order to cover the blacked-out *Chickamauga*'s dash for the open sea. His plan: to steer the *Raleigh* in wild, unpredictable loops and circles, his gunners firing only when they had a high probability of scoring a hit, trying to generate the maximum confusion possible for at least ninety minutes, hoping to draw Union ships away from New Inlet and into range of Fort Fisher's big guns. After generating ninety minutes of mayhem, he could retire to the safety of the Cape Fear River again—the commerce raider, by that time, would be fast and free upon the vast Atlantic.

Although the *Raleigh* was of conventional design—incorporating neither Reilly's ingenious "rolling" system of gun mounts nor his layered "composite" armor protection—she was formidable enough to take on any two or three Yankee ships at a time. Her 6.4-inch Brookes had neither the power nor the range of the *Hatteras*'s prototype monsters, but they were equal to most of the enemy's armament. And Branch's crew were in a high fever of readiness, determined that after tonight the blockade ships' crews would never again feel so complacent.

Only one aspect of the *Raleigh*'s construction worried Branch: the best engines Richmond had been able to send him were elderly and just barely adequate to haul the *Raleigh*'s great weight at slightly more than five knots. Theoretically, Branch's chief engineer informed him, he might be able to coax another knot and a half from them for short periods of time—the run-up to a ramming attack, for example—but neither the engineer nor Branch had dared to test that hypothesis. "Best not to tempt fate," was the engineer's phlegmatic attitude. "But if we get a clear shot at ramming one of the bastards, I will *find* you a couple of extra knots!"

10:58 P.M.: Signal from the Mound Battery, relayed to Branch from the top of Buchanan: An old side-wheeler had been spotted eight hundred yards off Zeke's Island, bearing thirty degrees southeast of the channel marker at the Mouth of New Inlet. Branch had his first target! Such an elderly ship ought to be a sitting duck. A couple of Brooke rounds through her paddle box would stop her cold, and then Branch would bore in for a slashing ram attack. The resulting tumult would provide the perfect distraction for the *Chickamauga*'s high-speed run through the inlet.

When the *Raleigh* crossed the bar at the mouth of New Inlet at approximately ten-fourteen, a shielded signal lamp from the back side of the Mound flashed a quick *"Good hunting!"* Then Branch was through the swirling narrows and out on the broad, ink-black Atlantic. Keeping the throttle pegged at five knots, he steered a course straight for the paddle wheeler's last reported position. Fortunately, the sea was calm, just a few light swells, and he had nothing to fear from an accidental collision. Indeed, he would have welcomed one if he could arrange for a ramming attack!

Was that a silhouette ahead? Was that tiny firefly glow a binnacle lamp? Should he ring on full speed now or wait for a better look?

Suddenly he got more than a "better look": signal rockets scorched fiery trails along the horizon, ships' whistles shrieked, and calcium flares exploded between the inner and outer blockade rings. A runner had been spotted coming in, and ships of the outer ring were giving chase. This was even better than Branch had dared to hope for! Confusion compounded! The *Chickamauga* charging out, a runner zigzagging in, and the *Raleigh* in the middle, with stirred-up Union ships steaming in hot pursuit from several directions!

Although he was expecting it, he still jumped when one of his port-side Brookes fired the first shot. Turning his head, he traced the faint arc of a shell and was enormously pleased when it appeared to explode against a blockader's port bow. Instantly he ordered a course change—he could always pick off the old paddle wheeler later. . . . A solid six-inch shell hit ought to carve a few knots off his new target's speed, and as slow as she was, the *Raleigh* might overhaul a more modern, more valuable ship. But other ships' outlines crisscrossed in the night, and he lost sight of his target. None of the vessels he could see were on fire, so maybe that flash was a near miss, or had struck an armor panel. Well, there was no shortage of other targets.

BANG! His bow chaser fired, but at which target? *KRANG!!* A lightning bolt flashed, acrid smoke filled the command cupola; both Branch and his helmsman were knocked sprawling by the impact, he supposed, of a hundred-pounder solid bolt. The *Raleigh* seemed intact, but spun in slow circles, shuddering from two shell-strikes, and the helmsman was gesturing frantically at the wheel which was spinning like a top. *Damn!* Concussion had damaged the linkage between wheel and rudder, leaving Branch unable to order any course changes except by shouting into the voice pipe. But every time a gun discharged or a shell exploded, his orders were drowned out. The ironclad was now zigzagging wildly, her gunners taking potshots at any target which caught their fancy.

Now the waters off New Inlet became a theater of pandemonium as some Union ships chased the incoming runner, and others started curving in Branch's direction, obviously to investigate the mystery ship that was firing from shoreward. Flares, rockets, shell-flashes—the night was ablaze, yet still as black as squid-ink; the outlines of scores of ships jerked, jittered, seemingly hopped-about like rabbits. No sooner had Branch gotten a fix on a likely target, than that target disappeared or multiplied into two or three additional targets. For a mile straight ahead of New Inlet the scene was sheer chaos as ships darted briefly within range of Lamb's Sea Face guns, which bracketed them with furious salvos, throwing up whole forests of water spouts, and Yankee skippers, made bold by the excitement, tarried long enough to catch a good roll of the tide and reply with taunting broadsides of their own.

Branch could feel things slipping out-of-control; all his carefully thought-out tactics were reduced to jagged shards rattling around in his aching, deafened skull. Finally, the helmsman got his attention by waggling his pocket watch in front of Branch's nose. *Astonishing! This violent game of blind-man's-bluff had now lasted almost two hours!* And the helmsman, who clearly thought they were pressing their luck way too far, shouted: "Any time you're ready, Captain, we are free to retire!"

Branch snapped out of his funk and bellowed into another voice pipe: "How's our ammo holding up?"

"One hundred four rounds left, sir."

My God—we've fired off three-quarters of our magazine! Despite the steady *ping!-zang!* of shrapnel on the casemate, Branch simply *had* to go topside and risk a thorough, methodical look around, hoping he could make some sense out of the enveloping chaos, hoping to see signs of damage inflicted on the enemy before he gave the order to retire to the safety of the Cape Fear River. But as he swept full circle with his glasses, the only flames he saw were the stabbing darts of enemy muzzle blasts; the only smoke was that which poured from their stacks. Was it conceivable that with thirty-odd warships swarming around in less than ten square miles of ocean, his gunners had failed to hit *anything*? Out of three-hundred-sixteen rounds, surely, if only by the law of averages, the *Raleigh* MUST have landed a shell on some enemy vessel! Oh, yes, there! He saw a nice tattered hole in the auxiliary jib-sail of an elderly sloop! Oh God, it was intolerable!

It was also very unsafe to remain where he was—about two miles farther north than he had previously thought, and far outside the range of Fort Fisher's largest weapons. He ordered all guns to cease firing, so the enemy could not get another fix on his position, and set an arrow-straight course for the inlet. It was imperative to get across the bar before low tide—unlike the *Hatteras,* this ironclad drew so much water that he would have only a few inches of clearance, and the sandbars were always shifting.

Another twenty minutes passed without the *Raleigh* taking additional hits. Branch was not far, now, from the protective umbrella of Colonel Lamb's cannon, a fact his pursuers knew as well as he did, so he doubted there would be any more attempts to overhaul the ironclad, despite its slow speed.

He was wrong. One very aggressive Union cruiser shot in front of him, fired a calcium light to fix the *Raleigh*'s course and position, then doubled back. Was that damn fool captain trying to ram *him* . . . board *him*? Any second now, the fort would . . .

Zeeeee-oooooo—Ka-whoosh! The 10-inch columbiad atop the Mound Battery put a solid shot right in the charging cruiser's path, only a hundred yards from her bow. If that skipper had any sense, he would veer away instantly. But whoever he was, he ignored the fort's firepower and continued to close on the *Raleigh* at high speed. Branch held his breath for the next shot from the Mound gunners, who had the range perfect and the deflection almost as dead-on. Their second shot was a gunner's dream, putting a 10-inch shell smack into the Yankee's bow gun and setting off every powder bag in its ready-ammo locker. The big bottle-shaped Dahlgren flew off its mount and carried a sizable chunk of the ship's bow with it, leaving a raging bonfire of splintered wood where the gun mount had been. *Now* the cruiser veered to starboard, and as she did, Branch saw that the airborne Dahlgren had smashed into the cruiser's foremast, cracking it in two and dropping an enormous wad of spars and rigging across the port side. Having nailed the target perfectly, the Mound gunners dropped a solid shot dead amidships, decapitating the smokestack and cutting the cruiser's speed by two-thirds.

"She's a sitting duck," he muttered. *We can ram her and still make it through New Inlet before low tide!* He ordered the signal light to blink to the Mound Battery: *Great shooting! Please hold fire while I ram!*

By God, he was going to sink one after all! Feverish with excitement—he had dreamed of such a moment for so many, many months—Branch ignored the warnings of his chief engineer and rang "Full speed." The *Raleigh* accelerated only two more knots, but after cruising sedately at five and a fraction, the change to seven knots felt positively racy. Two minutes, that was all he asked for, two minutes until he crushed that ship like an eggshell. Surely the fucking engines could put out two measly additional knots for just two minutes!

The starboard engine tolerated the added strain for exactly seventy-one seconds before seizing up. By that time, the *Raleigh* was so close to its intended prey that Branch could hear the catcalls and jeers of its crew when they saw what had happened. He froze. It was unbelievable, really it was. So close to the one victory he had prayed for: *Just let me sink one, please God, and I will be content, my shame erased, my honor washed clean of all that presently tarnished it!*

Realizing that Branch was in some kind of fugue state, his executive officer took command and did exactly the right things to save the ironclad: draw down the starboard engine—emergency reverse on the port engine—swing the bow around until it's pointed back at the inlet—resume original course at five knots—wrestle the helm to compensate for one-engine steering—the fort's guns would protect her now. "Mr.Branch, sir, *will you for Chrissakes snap out of it!*"

"You're doing fine, Lieutenant . . . you take her in." Branch stumbled, dazed, down to the gun deck, ignoring the accusatory stares of his crew, went into his tiny cabin, locked the door, and pulled a pint of whiskey from his personal locker.

At Annapolis, they fill your head with John Paul Jones and Lord Nelson, and the lesson is plain—a naval hero does not hesitate when closing with the enemy—his single thought is to sink his opponent—if he flinches from that objective, he is unworthy of the heritage he is heir to. But John Paul Jones's government didn't equip the Bon Homme Richard with cheesecloth sails and cardboard guns—while Richmond made me wait two years to finish a ship that a Yankee yard could turn out in ninety days—then sends me a worn-out tugboat engine and another one pulled from a sunken steamboat in the Mississippi that still had rust and river shit caked inside the boiler when we unloaded her—and with that one ship asks me to defend the most vital port in Confederate hands against the might of the North Atlantic Fleet! I see a chance to finish off a disabled enemy cruiser, so I do the correct thing, the Annapolis Thing, *and close with the enemy—all I ask is that the goddamned engines hold up for two fucking minutes—and now I can hear those enemy sailors jeering, "Look at that laughable excuse for an ironclad, running away with a broken wing!"—will I thus be mocked until this obscenely stupid war is over?*

He was halfway through the bottle and full fathom five in self-pity when he was knocked out of his bunk by a hideous, grinding screech. Unable to steer nimbly enough, or even turn out of the way, the *Raleigh* had run hard aground on a monstrous sandbar, halfway through New Inlet.

There was plenty of time for an orderly evacuation, and Branch did not protest when his crew helped him into the longboat, rowed him to the beach behind the Mound Battery, and gratefully accepted the blankets and hot rum brought to them by some of Lamb's soldiers. Just as the sun came up and revealed the beached ironclad in merciless clarity, the tide finished going out, exposing most of her keel, and with a pitiable moan, like a beast in terminal pain, the CSS *Raleigh* began to sag at both ends, inexorably bending into the shape of a bow as the water ran out and her own titanic weight obeyed the laws of gravity, until mere iron could stand no more. With a thunderous crash like locomotives colliding at full speed, the ship broke in two symmetrical halves, each of which slid ponderously down the slope of the exposed sandbar then disappeared from sight, leaving above water only the stern-mounted flagstaff and a sopping-dishrag mockery of a Confederate flag.

Utopian Notions

WHEN WE SEIZED the Gum Swamp encampment from those Rebel guerrillas, we killed them to the last man, and given our desperate circumstances, I have never felt the slightest pang of conscience. If that sounds callous, let the reader imagine what they would have done to us coloreds had the situation been reverse! Since they had been using the place as their headquarters for two years, and had collected abundant supplies from Confederate loyalists in the five counties bordering Gum Swamp, they had abundant stocks of food, liquor, furniture, even a small library. At first, we thought it was Eden.

Col. Fairless gave us two months to rest and regain our spirits, for our morale was shattered by Gnl. Hawkins' treachery and by the loss of so many comrades. We ate and slept, played cards, went swimming, read books, and I began taking down the notes that would form the basis for this memoir. The only "serpents" in our Eden were the local alligators, which somnolent beasts were far more interested in the piles of edible (to alligators) garbage generated by 104 men they were in pursuing us as delicacies. True to racial stereotype, however, Negroes and alligators do not mix very well, and the white troopers got awfully tired of hearing full-grown, battle-hardened Negro soldiers yelping with terror whenever they so much as glimpsed one of those reclusive beasts!

In fact, after two months, we had all grown bored with the limited amenities, the heat and insects, the monotonous diet . . . and each other. Fairless sensed that it was time for the Remnant-Buffaloes to move on. Each man had to decide, according to his conscience and private inclinations, whether to rejoin the Army, or to join the "Bonapartists"—the faithful disciples who wanted to attach their fate to Capt. Reubens compelling but still nebulous vision of the "New South," which he planned to nurture on the (to him!) mystical ground of Pine Haven plantation.

First off, though, we needed to learn what the local military situation was, so on June 21, Colonel Fairless detached Red Elliott and four white troopers to make a cautious reconnaissance in the direction of New Bern . . .

—Sgt. Washington Pierce, "Adventures of a Black 'Buffalo.'"
Unpublished manuscript. State Archives, Raleigh.

Captain Elliott brought back good news from New Bern. Hackett's division, he said, had been *this* close to capturing the town when, for some inexplicable reason, he broke camp and marched back to Virginia. The *Hatteras* had been sunk and Plymouth was once more in Union hands. Rebel activity on this part of the coast had dropped off to almost nothing—and the surviving Buffaloes had been welcomed back with surprise and real joy—most folks figured the unit had been annihilated. "They buried about eight bodies, on the road to Shelborne's Point, and assumed the rest of us was taken prisoner. So ain't nobody lookin' for us as 'deserters,' and nobody was rude enough to ask where we'd been hiding out these past two months."

Jack Fairless thought that made the final breakup of the unit somewhat easier: those who wanted to serve out their enlistments could do that, no questions asked, while those who wanted to follow Reubens and his "vision" were perfectly at liberty to do so. So after discussing the matter with Bonaparte, Jack selected Sunday, August 7, as the Buffaloes' last assembly as a military entity. After all they had been through together, some kind of closing-down ceremony was appropriate; oratory was called for, and each man would be free to make a parting speech or to bear witness in silence.

Approximately one-third of the surviving Buffaloes had chosen to go back to the Army, and Big Red Elliott rose to speak for them:

"Colonel Jack, Bonaparte, even though the Buffaloes are splitting up, and each bunch is going in very different directions, we'll always ride together in our memories. I never expect to serve with better officers, or command braver men. And by the example of your friendship, you made something work in this outfit that's never worked anywhere else in the U.S. Army: white soldiers and black soldiers, living, as well as fighting, side by side. We became true brothers-in-arms, and we gained both honor and pride from that experience.

"Hell, even now, on the day the unit's splittin' up. I have some black soldiers riding with me, and some of the white troopers want to cast their lot in with Bonaparte's vision-thing, so the spirit of this outfit will ride with all of us.

"The boys who've chosen to ride with me, are doing it because this war ain't over yet and they aim to finish what they started. Now I'm all for that, don't get me wrong. But I've got a personal mission, too, and I want y'all to know about it so in case you read about me bein' court-martialed and shot, you'll know why. It has to do with why I shaved my beard—so I'd be harder to recognize by anyone who knew me only during the years I wore it.

"You see, I'm going back to the Army so I can track down and kill that lying son of a bitch, Rush Hawkins! At night, boys, I am visited in dreams by the ghosts of all the men who died because he ordered us to fight his rearguard, and then after he pulled everybody *else* out of Shelborne's Point, he left us for buzzard bait. Them dead Buffaloes call out to me: *Avenge us, or our souls will not rest in peace.* So that's what I will do. And that's why I'm going back to New Bern and back into the Army—so I can pick up that polecat's trail and track him down."

Elliott's oration was like red meat to hungry wolves, and his vow was greeted with a general murmur of approval. Having just made the longest and most eloquent speech of his life, Big Red Elliott waved for silence.

"Now, for those of you who haven't yet made up your minds as to which road you want to travel, I hereby turn this meeting over to the Buffaloes very own resident prophet, Captain Bonaparte Reubens!"

When Reubens rose to speak he seemed already to have shed the persona that went with his blue uniform, but he also seemed unsure of what he had traded it for. The robes of a prophet, the bells of a jester, or the thorny crown of a martyr? There was an endearing hesitancy in his voice, as compelling in its way as the thunder of his battlefield commands.

"Many of the first recruits to join my colored company were runaway slaves. They, more than any other class of men, have the greatest reason to hate Southern whites, to gloat over their imminent downfall, to pay them back for the insults and scars they suffered, from behind the protection of occupying Federal bayonets. And yet those same men were the first and most passionate converts to my philosophy! To those men, I extend my thanks for your faith and your wisdom; you understand what I mean when I say: the beaten South is fallow ground where the seeds of a bright future can be planted and tended by men of all colors and creeds . . ."

Bonaparte's speeches were definitely becoming more preacherly in tone lately, just as his solitary walks through the depths of Gum Swamp had grown longer. For the past four or five weeks, he had been trying out his Man of Destiny themes on individual Buffaloes whenever there was a conversational opening. And he had thereby gained new followers, just as he had gained Jack Fairless (whom the skeptics now referred to as "St. Peter"). But this was his first and only chance to address all the remaining Buffaloes at once, to sway the undecided, to cement the faith of the hesitant. So Jack figured it would be a real stem-winder. He sat down under a tree to watch, if only to learn just how seriously his friend was starting to take himself.

Reubens claimed his long "communions with nature" had helped bring his "vision" into sharper focus, but to Jack's way of thinking, he had only succeeded in more enticingly articulating some pretty vague notions, so that he stirred powerful emotions without overtaxing his listeners' intellects. Reubens seemed to view the prostrate, beaten down, postwar South as part laboratory, part public theater, and part personal fiefdom, and there was no doubt that his confidence had grown enormously. If you were a man obsessed with moral and historical questions, Bonaparte had answers . . . or at least the *outlines* of answers.

Those who heard his rambling discourses and suddenly "got it," tended to report that his talk had given them a powerful flood of illumination, but when pressed for specific details, seldom could provide them.

Jack was reminded of the time when he was eleven and his granddaddy had taken him to hear a famous traveling preacher who could "speak in tongues"—a skill which young Jack found hard to visualize, but which certainly piqued his interest. But once the actual service got to the speaking in tongues part, it sounded like a roomful of deranged turkeys (*"Gobballa-Kabballa-Wobballa!"*) and not a thing like the Bible. Still, he was impressed by the way the phenomenon spread from one preacher to the whole sweaty crowd, as more and more people "got it." Grandpa *really* got it—by the end of the service, the old coot was not only "Obballa-Gabball-ing," he was dancing, spinning in circles, and ready to graduate to snake-handling. Such was that preacher's hold over them, that even though the experience did not make any of the congregation smarter, healthier, or less impoverished, they all agreed that it had been a mighty encounter with "the Holy Spurt."

Reubens had acquired a touch of that preacher's spellbinding aura, no question about it. He had disciples, and he even had a Promised Land he was going to lead them to. It was called—as Jack already knew—Pine Haven, and once Bonaparte had established a community there, he was going to make everybody rich—provided the Sloane family invested a shit pot full of money in his schemes, which he was sure they would gladly do.

Jack Fairless certainly had no objection to being rich, but his main reason for tagging along was to look out for his friend, just in case things didn't work out as Bonaparte thought they would. If the Sloanes met him with shotguns instead of open pockets and hosannas or if a bunch of nightriders showed up waving torches and screaming "Faison's Groves!" Jack was ready to cold-cock Reubens with his pistol butt and drag him out of harm's way.

Jack sat up and took notice: here was a new wrinkle! Bonaparte was taking questions!

A Negro sergeant, a runaway from a plantation whose owners were as cruel and backward in their thinking as the Sloanes were compassionate and progressive, expressed skepticism. "Cap'n Reubens, what makes you think that after three hundred years of treating black folks like livestock, you're going to change former slave-owners' minds about our race without grinding their necks under your boot *first*?"

"Why do I believe this? Because, sergeant, it's very simple human psychology! When the Confederacy falls apart, every tradition, every certainty, by which the white aristocrats have lived, will simply vanish. For a long time to come, after the Rebels surrender, there will be not just a political vacuum, but an aimlessness of the soul, an enormous *void* where the old ways once existed. My plans, my projects, will provide something *tangible* to fill that void. All people are unhappy living with chaos; all souls shun the void, sir! While other Yankees may flood this state in order to carve up the spoils and steal from the survivors what little they have left, *my plans* will result in *real things*; things like structure and order and prosperity where there was only—"

He had lost Jack at the second "void," but he had not lost any potential followers. About half of the previously "undecided" Buffaloes were drawing closer, hanging on every change of cadence. The rest were saddling up and joining Red Elliott's faction. Jack sauntered over to say good-bye.

After they shook hands, Elliott gestured in Reubens' direction. "Colonel Jack, you don't really take all that horse shit seriously, do you?"

"Well, Bonaparte does. And he's got a gift for swaying others. I'm going along mainly to see he don't get lynched for saying the wrong thing in the wrong place. And besides, having been turned into 'a student of human nature,' I'm damn curious to see how this turns out!"

"If it turns out the way I think it will, I reckon we'll see your ass in New Bern in about a month. I'd be happy to serve with you again, Jack Fairless."

"Don't you think Bobbie Lee's going to surrender before Christmas?"

"About as much as I believe in fairies. What do you think?"

"I'm a hillbilly, Red. Up there, we *do* believe in fairies! I'll see you around, brother."

Pine Haven was the land on which Bonaparte Reubens had been standing when the God of Creation smote him with that long ago predicted call to Destiny. As he remembered the old Jesuit's translation, the "rules of the game" (so to speak) required that a man so honored *must* begin his great work upon the *very same ground* where he was standing when the revelation came to him. The problem for Reubens was that Pine Haven was also a place from which he had been forcibly expelled. He was fairly certain that neither Matthew Sloane, if he was in residence, nor his overseer, Mister Something-hyphenated-Bright, would not be pleased to see him return, especially not at the head of armed Negro soldiers. And it was inconceivable that either of those men would accept Bonaparte's explanation as to why he had behaved so violently. If he tried to tell them about Africa . . . well, ever since Faison's Groves, even the most liberal-minded white man in these parts would be inclined to shoot first and ask questions later.

The key to a peaceful entry into Pine Haven, he suspected, was to convince at least one member of the household to prepare the others for his arrival, convince them it was worth their while to give him a chance to present his case. According to what Elias had told him, the person most likely to do that was *Missus Sloane,* whose strength of character had grown exponentially as the challenges of managing Pine Haven single-handedly had grown more daunting. But what were the chances of arranging such a meeting? More than likely, he would meet a blast of buckshot if he even tried.

Before he did anything, however, he needed more information about the current state of affairs on the plantation. After locating a sheltered but comfortable site for his men to encamp—a mile north of the route taken by the Pine Haven militia's mounted patrols—Reubens and Jack Fairless went on a two-day reconnaissance mission. They examined Pine Haven from every angle, crept close enough at night to overhear scraps of conversation, and then compared notes at night when they returned to the Bonapartists' hideout.

While he quietly observed the plantation, and the activities of those who lived and worked there, Bonaparte Reubens' thoughts and emotions crystallized. The more he scrutinized Pine Haven, the more he examined the bizarre and circular pattern of events that had brought him here twice, the more certain he was that his destiny was connected to this place. By returning to Pine Haven, he was squaring the circles of irony that comprised his earlier life. He was also exposing his soul to a degree of spiritual risk commensurate with the worst danger his body had ever faced on the battlefield. His return to the site of his original—anointing? selection? or whatever it had been—might also act like a beacon, attracting the interest of the Chaos God, whose role in History was to thwart men of destiny, to abort or destroy their works. And *both* deities could work through human surrogates, so Reubens would perforce have to rely on the protective, forewarning powers of the wooden fetish he still wore next to his heart. When the God of Creation and the God of Chaos fought to elevate or destroy a mortal man, not only his potential achievements but also his very sanity might be forfeited. A deeper courage might be required of him than he had ever displayed as a leader of soldiers.

On the third morning of his encampment near Pine Haven, Reubens awoke with an inspiration. He already *had* an ally within the Sloane household—Agrippa, the boss nigger of the big house! With the passing of time, Reubens had come to believe that the manifestation of the Creation God's voice from Agrippa's mouth might well have been a hallucination. Nevertheless, it was Agrippa who had understood both the power and the significance of the fetish-necklace, and it was Agrippa's knife that had cut him free.

Reubens therefore sent two of his best infiltrators to kidnap the old retainer, using chloroform to subdue him without force. Child's play, they reported, when asked if the Marine sentries had been a problem.

Agrippa regained consciousness inside Bonaparte's forest lean-to. When he raised his eyes and saw the man sitting across from him, he was one surprised darkie.

"Oh, Lord, what *you* doin' back here, you black debbil?"

Reubens leaned around the fire and handed him a cup of strong coffee, sweetened with a bit of honeycomb. Agrippa hesitated, then warily accepted the beverage. When Reubens spoke, his tone was all reason and reassurance,

"I mean you no harm, old man. Far from it. Please, enjoy your coffee and let's talk a while. I promise, you'll be back at Pine Haven well before sunrise."

"Dat so? Why you drag me out here, den?"

"Just to have a conversation, that's all. One black man to another"

"You talk while Ah drink dis coffee," muttered Agrippa. "Maybe Ah'll tell Cap'n Sloane not to horsewhip yo' black ass."

Reubens smiled affably. "Now, old man, don't lie to me. Matthew Sloane's never whipped a black man in his life, and even if he had, he couldn't whip my ass when he's a thousand miles away on a Rebel commerce raider, could he."

"Somebody been sneakin' around and eavesdroppin'. You so smart, what else you know?"

"I know your mistress, Missus Sloane, is not very happy about that, but is carrying on bravely as Pine Haven's manager. I know the Rebel navy sent a truly pathetic squad of bored young Marines to 'guard' the plantation in his absence. I know where the Pole, the Chinaman, and the Portuguese sleep and where the guns are kept. I know the South is losing the war, a lot faster than you probably realize. And I know what happened to the rebellious young Elias."

"What did happen?"

"He died in my arms, Agrippa, after fighting very bravely at my side. He got blood poisoning from a contaminated Rebel bullet, and I wept when he died, because I had come to care for him during the time he served in my company."

"You not quite the same man you was the last time I saw you."

"No, and that is what I brought you here to talk about."

Agrippa now began to fidget and sip his coffee nervously, his eyes darting every which way except straight into Reubens' penetrating gaze.

"You not gon' go crazy again, are you?"

"I'm not talking about what happened when I had my . . . spell that afternoon. I'm talking about what happened that night, when you came into the barn and cut me loose. Something very strange happened to you that night, didn't it, Agrippa? You probably don't remember much, but you *do* remember that something came over you, and you spoke to me in a voice that was not your own."

Agrippa's hands began to tremble. He remembered *something*, all right.

"Ah got taken over by a *haunt!* I could still feel my body, but I didn't have no powers over it."

"I know. I saw it clearly. But can you remember what you said to me before that 'haunt' came over you? Think hard, now."

He doesn't want to remember. One cannot blame him . . .

To further gain Agrippa's trust, Reubens reached into his pack and held out a half a pint of whiskey.

"Hold out your cup, Agrippa. I know you're fond of a nip now and then. I won't tell anybody."

"How you know dat 'bout me?" Agrippa's voice became suspicious again, but he did extend his cup.

"I know a few other things about you, too. Perhaps the most interesting thing is that your ancestors came from a part of Africa that is near the Valley of Diamonds."

"Oh, Lawd . . ." If Agrippa could have turned pale, he would have.

"Now do you remember? What you said to me, what you saw in my eyes, before the 'haunt' came over you? You said: 'I know you been 'touched' in a special way, Boss! I got no choice but to let you go, because you done been *chosen!* You must try to build something new and noble *here, in the South . . .*" And Reubens was astonished when Agrippa's voice joined his in unison, not the voice of a spirit possessed automaton, but the plain careworn voice of an old black man, whose hands reached out to grip his, and whose eyes glittered in the lamplight:

"because it will become fallow ground, and its old ways will be smashed forever when the conquerors put their heel upon its neck. You are charged with showing men a new way, a vision of what can be done by the power of brotherhood . . ."

"Ah thought it was a dream and Ah was scared for days afterward that you would go crazy again, and maybe come back one night and do harm to the Sloanes!"

Reubens held the old man's hands, and this time Agrippa met his gaze directly, bravely. Reubens could feel a surge of power arcing through his body and running from his hands into Agrippa's.

"I, too, thought it must have been a dream. But the freedom you gave me that night was very real, and I've had a long time to think about what 'freedom' really means. The prophecy that came from your mouth has come true, Agrippa! I *have* had a vision of how blacks and whites can work together to build a new South on the ruins of the old. And I am certain as the sunrise that my work should begin here, at Pine Haven. I brought you here tonight to tell you about that vision and to see if you will join me in turning it into a reality."

"How you gon' convince people to believe in an *African* god's commandment?"

"I shan't even try! I shall convince them that my plan will lead to the one thing all Americans desire from their lives and labors: *a damned good profit!* If I can convince my listeners that moral progress goes hand in hand with greater *prosperity*—if only they can forget about *race and color* long enough to work together, then I may succeed. For now, all I ask is that you hear me out, make up your own mind, then decide *of your own free will* whether you want to help me."

"I will listen as long as you keep puttin' some more of that fine whiskey in my cup."

Reubens laughed. Perhaps this was going to work, after all.

When Mr. Bright returned from his routine supply run to Wilmington on August 20, inside the mailbag was the first letter Mary Harper Sloane had received from Matthew since the *Chickamauga*'s getaway. It was posted from the Canary Islands to Nassau and had been brought to Wilmington only one week ago, aboard a blockade-runner. So far, Matthew assured her, the *Chickamauga*'s maiden voyage had been successful and blessed with good weather. He had taken three Yankee merchantmen, and had just deposited them in care of the U.S. embassy in Tenerife; he was planning to hit the main trade routes in the Indian Ocean next; two days ago he had seen an immense flock of glitter-winged flying fish. His health was good. Love to her and the children, etc., etc.

A perfectly innocuous letter, but Mary Harper could tell that Matthew was enjoying himself immensely. She tried not to feel envious or resentful, and absolutely refused to speculate on what the women in Tenerife might look like. Surely the war would be over by next summer and Matthew would be back, a twice-retired sea rover, magically transformed once again into dutiful husband and father. Would he go back to rice-farming? Change over to another primary crop? Or just sell Pine Haven and use their blockade-running fortune to set up in some totally new place?

Never mind what *he* wanted! What did *Mrs. Sloane want*?

The future was one enormous question mark. Did she want to remain in North Carolina? Would the Negroes stay and help keep the place running, even if there were better opportunities elsewhere? Would their old way of life still be viable—even with new crops, new technologies, and salaried labor instead of slaves? Cataclysmic change was coming on the heels of military defeat, and her greatest frustration was her impotence to plan for it. The worst thing that could happen to them, as a family and as the owners of a big plantation, was for them to drift helplessly on the tides of those changes. All she was doing now, all anyone was doing at Pine Haven, was marking time. The only certainty was Confederate defeat; everything beyond that was occluded and ominous. She wanted to present Matthew, upon his return, with a *plan* for the future, but she had no inkling of what to plan *for*.

Aurelia brought the children in for a good-night kiss. After their footsteps on the stairs came blessed silence. Well, it was nine-thirty at night, so she thought there would be no harm in taking a drink or two before retiring. What did she have to look forward to in the morning but more of the same?

Mary Harper was on her second drink and unsuccessfully trying to browse through some scientific journals that had come in the same mailbag as Matthew's letter—he had never let his subscriptions lapse, and usually there was a pile of magazines waiting in Nassau whenever one of their ships was preparing for a run back to Wilmington. Ordinarily she would have been quite interested in reading about "Electricity—The Steam Power of the Future," but she was having a hard time following the explanations of how galvanic current might be generated and used in the year 1885. The trick, she thought, was to *get* to 1885.

The knock on the library door was that of Agrippa, making his final, ritualistic inquiry as to whether there was anything she wanted him to do before he retired. There seldom was, but the old fellow seemed to need her blessing before he considered his daily work complete.

But instead of his usual perfunctory question, Agrippa surprised her by saying, "May I have a word with you, ma'am? It's important."

Curious, she placed a bookmark in Matthew's *Abstracts of the Proceedings of the Royal Academy of Science,* moved the whiskey bottle discreetly out of sight, and motioned for Agrippa to take a seat. From the seriousness of his expression, she thought he was about to tell her that someone had taken sick or been in an accident.

"Missus Sloane . . . dey's somethin' you need to know."

Such gravity in his voice—her stomach fluttered. As tedious as most of her days were, she did not want that tedium to be interrupted by a crisis.

"Then I suppose you'd better tell me."

"Dere's a man who wants to come here an' speak with you. He's with some friends who used to be Yankee soldiers. Don't think that's what they is now, but the point is that he don't want you or the chillun to be frightened when he shows up."

"You say 'used to be Yankee soldiers.' Are they a band of deserters?"

"Not 'zactly. But they ain't fightin' the war no more, neither."

"I'm too tired for riddles, Agrippa. Just tell me plainly: Who is this man, and why does he want to talk with me so urgently?"

"It's somebody you met before, but he be a deeply changed man now. You 'member the rice harvest of '62?"

"How could I forget it? When that black foreman went crazy in the fields? Oh, what was his name . . . Caesar or Bismarck or—"

"Bonaparte. His name was Bonaparte."

Comprehension swept over Mary Harper, and she sat stiffly upright in her chair.

"You don't mean to tell me that . . . not that man! He cannot set foot on this plantation again, I don't care how hungry or poor he is!"

When Agrippa continued, he was no longer speaking as an old darkie making supplication to the mistress of the Big House, but as a man announcing a fait accompli.

"Dis how it is, Missus Sloane: If Bonaparte wants to come onto the grounds of Pine Haven, he gon' do it, wid yo' permission or not, don' make no nevermind, 'cause he's a captain now and he's got about forty armed men behind him. 'Less you want this house turned into a battleground, you'd best listen to my explanation. What I'm gon' tell you just might change yo' mind—just like it changed the minds of Sonny Chiang, Stepan, and Fernando, and if dere's any three men in the world who got good reason to shoot Bonaparte Reubens on sight, it be them three, 'cause of how bad he used to treat 'em. Last night I took dem out to meet Bonaparte and talk wid him at his camp, and when dey heard him out, dey kinda said to each other, 'Dis man ain't crazy no more—dis man *grown wise!*' So dey *not* gonna shoot him; dey gon' give him a chance to set some things in motion. If'n you still need convincin', after I tell you de story, I'll bring dem in and dey vouch for what I say."

Mary Harper Sloane was flabbergasted. Was *this* Pine Haven's equivalent of a slave revolt? And if so, why was Agrippa acting more like John the Baptist than John Brown? Agrippa had run the Big House loyally and faithfully since Matthew was a child; if Agrippa swore this man meant no harm, then she probably had nothing to fear.

Her mind churning, she poured another inch of whiskey in her glass, and reminded herself that there was a loaded pistol in the desk drawer and eleven well-armed Confederate Marines within shouting distance. Agrippa was watching her patiently, sympathetically, as though he understood her conflicting emotions and was content to wait while she made up her mind whether to trust him, as she always had. Finally she realized that she was more curious than afraid. She tried to relax, leaned back in her chair, and cautiously encouraged Agrippa to continue.

"All right, Agrippa, I'm willing to listen, but this had better be good!"

Agrippa chuckled, and his laughter was disarming.

"He tol' me you would say somethin' like dat! And he tol' me to tell you: 'Nothing is guaranteed, Missus Sloane, but it *could* be very *profitable* without in any way being un-Christian.' "

Mary Harper took a big, shivery gulp of her husband's best whiskey and said, "Take it very slowly, Agrippa. I have a feeling my imagination is about to get stretched every which way."

"Yessum!" He beamed. "Dat's jus' de point!"

When Agrippa became excited, his dialect tended to thicken until Mary Harper was deciphering two or three sentences behind him, but the old man's enthusiasm was palpable and quite beyond his usually phlegmatic manner. She lost him when he tried to explain something labyrinthine about African metaphysics, but after he spoke breathlessly for thirty-five minutes, Mary Harper conceded that there must be something extraordinary about Captain Reubens and his "vision fo' de future." At that point, she held up her hand to shush Agrippa's monologue.

"Agrippa, please—I shall get a headache from listening to you. It's obvious that this man has made a great impression on you, despite the terrible way he treated you on his previous visit. If a safe but private meeting could be arranged, I am certainly willing to hear what he has to say. But I will judge his character for myself, so you may as well stop banging the drums for him. You say he and his . . . 'company'? 'followers'? . . . have an encampment near Pine Haven? Perhaps, if you and the militia escort me, we could ride over there tomorrow, so I can at least take his measure."

"Ain't no need to ride, Missus Sloane! He been out on de sun porch all dis time, right through yonder door! He figured a private meeting'd be best, too, so why wait 'til tomorrow?"

"Why indeed?" muttered Mary Harper, suddenly tense again. She poured another inch of whiskey into her tumbler. "Just let me get a little Dutch courage here. . . ." Agrippa was already opening the door to the glassed-in veranda that was Matthew's favorite reading spot when the weather was just so.

"Do you think Mister . . . Captain . . . Well, whatever he wants to be called, do you think he would like a drink?"

"Yes, as a matter of fact, he would. Whiskey with a splash of branchwater, please." The low but penetrating baritone voice drifted in from the porch. "It's very gracious of you to offer, Missus Sloane, considering my abominable behavior the last time I accepted drinks from you."

Mary Harper poured another drink, took a deep breath, then followed Agrippa out to the porch. The broad-shouldered man who rose from the rope hammock to greet her bore little resemblance to the foul-tempered dandy she remembered from the dinner he had shared with her the night before he had a seizure in the rice fields. Older, much calmer—of course—with an officer's posture and glossy, light-brown skin. Gone was the furtive, almost hunted look she remembered. It was not easy to rise gracefully from a rope hammock, but he managed it, almost elegantly, then he bowed and extended his hand for either the drink or a handshake. She handed him the drink.

"Please, sir, come inside before those Rebel sentries spot you."

He smiled, revealing very white, even teeth and attractive smile lines. "Frankly, Missus Sloane, it's a good thing I'm *not* still commanding Unionist guerrillas—those boys couldn't spot a herd of yellow elephants. Still, you're right—privacy is desirable."

Not until she had closed and relocked the porch door did Mary Harper realize that Agrippa had vanished. Strangely, she was not uncomfortable being alone with Reubens—she just did not know how to begin this conversation with him. Reubens sensed as much, and while she was uncorking a new bottle, he quietly took a seat at the upright piano near Matthew's big glass-enclosed bookcases and began to play, rather exquisitely, something she vaguely recognized but that was far beyond her modest technique.

"I know that piece, I think. Mister Haydn, isn't it?"

"A good guess, but actually it's the larghetto from Mozart's C-minor piano concerto, number . . . oh, number twenty-something. This is a good German upright, but in this humidity, you really should have it tuned every six months."

"Are you trying to impress me, Captain Reubens?"

"As hard as I can, Missus Sloane. I need a treasurer for my new . . . venture, let's call it. And I know you have quite a fortune in easily disposed-of gold buried in various spots around Pine Haven."

"Am I supposed to infer from that remark, that if you had come here to rob me of it, you would already know where to start digging?"

"Precisely." He spun out the end of a dreamy melodic phrase with an improvised cadence. "There is one chest buried under the butter churn, another inside the water tank, etc. And if I *were* a brigand, I could learn the location of the other hiding places very quickly."

"*If* you were a thief. Well, since you're not a thief, and no longer an active soldier, what exactly are you?"

"Hard to say, really. Like this nation, I am in a period of profound transition. As far as our personal dealings go, however, you can think of me as a businessman—one who has some exciting ideas, but who desperately needs both capital and a secure base of operations. I know, I know: you and Captain Sloane are already rich. But I'm getting way ahead of myself. Let's start with some basic understandings."

"No," she said firmly. "Let's start with you telling *me* why you've come to Pine Haven. Technically, you are trespassing on my land. Why should I offer to share it with you?"

"That's what I'm going to tell you, madam. Some of it—particularly the parts dealing with African mythology, I don't expect you to accept easily. Frankly, it isn't necessary that you *believe* that part of it, but when I was struck, as though by lightning, with the insight that it was true, that I did have a great work to perform, I knew that it must begin *here,* on the earth of Pine Haven. If my faith in that insight were not absolute, why would I have returned, so openly, to a place where both your overseer and your husband would probably kill me at first sight? . . ."

Before this encounter, Mary Harper Sloane had cringed before the onrushing future, which loomed before her configured as a mass of unanswerable questions. Bonaparte Reubens sketched a "vision" which seemed almost a perfect antidote to her growing phobias: a vision that began at a single bright reference point of personal experience (or private mythology, a black aristocrats fantasy of Mother Africa; what difference did it make?) and expanded, in a smooth ever-wider parabolic curve into truly sweeping vistas of social, economic, political and technological achievements (their concrete visible presence on the coast of North Carolina spreading like a golden ink-spot from the tiny dot that was Pine Haven!). Mary Harper had been cowed by *questions*; Reubens came armed with *answers.* His plans were synergistic—he was the first man who had ever used that esoteric word in her hearing—and that made them bold in the aggregate, yet less risky in each discrete step. His imagination made breathtaking leaps into half-glimpsed futures, yet he was also pragmatic, clear-eyed, and flexible enough to react to sudden contingencies. Perhaps he *was* a little bit crazy, but it was the right kind of crazy for the latter half of the nineteenth century, for it made him ravenous for new invention, receptive to new ideas, unbounded in his allegiance to science (yet inspired, or so he claimed, by the mumbo-jumbo of a wizened African witch doctor, or something like that), and Mary Harper hung on for every hairpin twist in his rhetoric, down to the last resounding flourish:

". . . open-ended opportunities; interlocking ventures; goods *and* services, organic to each other, not compartmentalized as they are today—products and projects, from merchandise you can hold in your hand, to beachfront resorts where families of modest means, black and white alike, can enjoy a rich man's holiday, because technological innovation in our hotels and lodges will cut down the overhead to a fraction of what it was previously. We shall track the course of *every new invention*, seeking possible applications for it that its own designer had never thought of—"

"Stop, please, Captain Reubens! I need no more convincing! You have put into words a comprehensive strategy for dealing with the future, while I have been moping around this house, scared to death of what the future would do to Pine Haven, but damned if I was going to stand here and let the future roll over us! I mean, sir, to confront it head-on, face-to-face, and stare it down. You, in a brilliant and half-mad way, are getting ready to wage war on the future, to conquer it, to make it beg for mercy, and put it to work for us! Everything you have just said has put some steel into my backbone and purged the salts of dread from my liver!"

She was almost shouting now, pacing, restless as a tigress, and it was Reubens' turn to gape at this creature: a woman-on-fire. Tonight, surely, there had occurred a meeting-of-minds that could only be ascribed to destiny. But in midstride, she turned around and jabbed a finger at him.

"But before I commit my heart, my land, and a damned big portion of my personal fortune to your schemes, Mister Reubens, I want to administer a practical, small-scale, test. As a way of coming back down to earth, so to speak. Are you willing to take such a spontaneous test?"

"If I am not, then everything I've just told you is humbug."

"Very well. You have been observing Pine Haven every closely for several days, scrutinizing it in fine detail. Pine Haven *as it is today, sir,* not as it might be in some idyllic utopian future. I want you to find for me, tonight, right now, an example of a product, or an idea based on what you know of our natural and human resources, from which we can generate a profit in less than six months. I want to see how adroit you are at turning theory into reality."

Rising, he threw her a sharp, foxy grin. "I assume *rice* doesn't count . . ."

"Get moving, Bonaparte! Idle dreamers are ten dollars a trainload. But a man who can forge dream-stuff into a useful kitchen appliance is the man who will inherit the future. Such men are rarer than black pearls . . . if you'll pardon my play on words."

"Never apologize for coming up with le mot juste!"

Reubens paced warily around the library, as intent and alive to vibrational nuance as a human dowsing rod. Suddenly, he "got it," and strode to the door leading to the sun porch. Opening it, he pointed into the darkness.

"I must say, that hammock out there is one of the most comfortable pieces of recreational furniture I've ever encountered! Light and breezy and nap-inducing . . . and unlike a conventional fabric or canvas hammock, you don't leave a pool of sweat behind you when you get up from it. Tell me about it."

"Tell? . . . Oh. I think I see. Well, those are simply called 'rope hammocks' because . . . because that's *what they are.* One of the older slave families, people who've been here for three generations, brought that skill here when Matthew's great-grandfather first settled this land. We used to give them out as presents, and people were always happy to get them. They *are* very comfortable, but time-consuming to produce, as there are only two women who know the craft now. They collect strips of fabric, twine, scraps of real rope, weave them all together to form the hammock lining, then they soak and bend the wood for the curved braces and drill holes for attaching the handmade ropes. Working in their spare time, it takes the two women eight to ten weeks to fashion a single hammock."

"A jealously guarded trade secret?"

"No, not really—just a family tradition, one the two ladies are proud of. I suppose if they had a stock of regular store-bought rope and precut frames, they could make one in a couple of days."

"You know, Missus Sloane, a novel yet practical piece of leisure furniture like that . . . well, they don't have anything like that up North. Nor have I seen them anywhere else along the coast other than here at Pine Haven. Looking at that hammock with the eyes of someone who is *not* Southern, my feeling is that it evokes a sense of warm, drowsy summer afternoons, a shady porch, a pitcher of lemonade—the soft, sensual, slow-paced aspect of Southern life."

"The good stuff, in other words? Not Simon Legree and lynch mobs?"

"No, indeed! Magnolias, moonlight, mint juleps—all that sort of thing. There is nothing about that hammock that anyone could associate with secession, racism, or this Civil War. It practically oozes charm—makes you want to take off your shoes, pick up a good book, and loaf away the whole summer afternoon! It has the appeal of something handmade, crafted with love-of-tradition, and in more practical terms, it's lightweight, easy to roll up for storage in the winter, easy to pack in a carton for shipping, and it never needs oiling, repairing, or expensive spare parts!"

"Do you think we could . . . *sell* these? I mean, in large volume?"

"You never had any trouble *giving* them away, I presume?"

"God, no. We had people on a waiting list every year. But the Benson sisters—those are the Negro ladies who make them—only worked on them when they had gathered enough material to do a complete hammock, and only one at a time, and only when they felt like it—so we usually only had six or seven a year."

Reubens was taking notes energetically. "Just guessing here, but I'd say if you bought the rope in bulk, and ordered the supporting staves predrilled by the gross, and compensated the, um, Benson sisters generously for their labor, say a gold dollar for each of them per unit, you could make one hammock for between three and four dollars, then easily sell them for ten . . . maybe more, if they caught on in a big way."

Mary Harper thought the profit margin was impressive. "But who would you sell them to? After the war, I mean. People around here will not have ten dollars to spend on a luxury item! Damn few people, anyway. Why are you grinning like that?"

"Ah, here's where the entrepreneurial aspect of my 'vision' comes into play. Think, Mary Harper, *think!* For at least three years, possibly more, Wilmington is going to be occupied by several thousand Union soldiers. Do not think of them as 'conquerors' but as *customers!* And many of them are going to want souvenirs of the South that they can send home to their friends and loved ones. They can't send seafood! They can't send a quart of sand! But one of these 'Pine Haven rope hammocks'? It is the perfect gift! Redolent of coastal Carolina! Untainted by political associations! Something that adults will enjoy as much as children! Practical, actually rather sophisticated, yet *certifiably quaint* in the bargain! I can see the word-burned label now: *"Hand Made with Love and Pride by the Freed Slaves of Pine Haven Plantation."* Abolitionists will go wild for them—they'll become symbols of status!"

Mary Harper jumped in, as the flow of ideas heated up. "We might even turn 'Pine Haven' into a trademark. There are other things, too, that are made here, such as those lightweight, floppy-brimmed reed hats, which are perfect for gardening in hot weather. There's one old fellow who lacquers and carves intricate designs on to crab shells, like scrimshaw! And, oh God, wait till you taste this!" She ran to the mantel and opened a covered dish. "Aurelia and her daughters specialize in these. They're called 'pralines,' and we have three acres of pecan trees right here. Go on, take a nibble!"

Reubens almost swooned. "Mon Dieu, this is decadent. We could never export these to Paris—too many chefs would commit suicide because someone else thought up the recipe."

"And I almost forgot! Did you know we already have a store, a retail outlet? Well, my close friend Largo owns a store, and she would happily let us use one corner of it to display and sell our wares. And another thing, so we don't have to depend on the Yankee occupation army too heavily, is our connection with England! Ninety percent of our blockade trade was done with Great Britain. And every Englishman I know is absolutely fascinated by the South—we could run advertisements in the London papers! Our pralines would have . . . *reverse snob appeal!* The way everybody pretends that Cadbury's tea biscuits taste ever so much better than plain ol' sugar cookies, when the fact is they taste like pasteboard. And—"

"Slow down, please, ma'am—I can't write the ideas down fast enough!"

Utopia Denied

THE SOUTHERN LANDSCAPE of 1880 bore the signs of the preceding twenty years. Symmetrical rows of slave cabins had been knocked into a jumble of tenant shacks. Fields grew wild because it did not pay to farm them. Children came upon bones and rusting weapons when they played in the woods. Former slave-owners and their sons decided which tenants would farm the best land and which would have to move on. Confederate veterans at the courthouse or the general store bore empty sleeves and blank stares. Black people bitterly recalled the broken promises of land from the Yankees and broken promises of help from their former masters . . .

Ayers, Edward L. *The Promise of the New South.*
Oxford University Press, 1992

The Pine Haven *coup d'etat* was entirely bloodless and more than a bit odd, as though drifting pieces of the war's wreckage had clumped together to form, in embryo, something clearly born from the same causes as the conflict itself, but beholden to neither side that was still fighting it. The Marines did not know anything unusual was happening until one private woke up well after sunrise, looked at his watch, and realized that their sergeant had not rousted them out of their beds for the usual 6:00 A.M. roll call. In fact, the sergeant was nowhere to be seen. Neither were the Marines' firearms, which had mysteriously vanished during the night. Figuring *somebody* was in trouble—somebody almost *had* to be if he and the other eight men in the makeshift barracks were still snoring peacefully at a quarter to ten—he went to the nearest window and threw open the curtains, flooding the old threshing shed with sunlight. Only after he did that, and turned around to make a head count, did he see Jack Fairless and two of Reubens' white followers sitting calmly at the all-purpose eating/card-playing/letter writing table. All three men wore belted Colts and had repeaters either resting on their laps or leaning against the table in easy reach. When Fairless met the astonished private's gaze, he nodded affably, and pointed to the coffeepot, biscuits, and fresh churned butter set out for breakfast.

"Morning, gents! Y'all sleep good? There's coffee and ovenfresh biscuits here. Why not come help yourselves?"

"Who in tarnation are you? And where's Sergeant Petrie? And them other two men on sentry duty?"

"Whoa, son, too many questions! I could've let the sergeant wake you up at the crack o' dawn, but seein' as how today's schedule is a mite different from the usual, I thought you boys would appreciate some extra shut-eye. That way, you'll have 'fresh minds,' as Bonaparte is fond of saying, for absorbing the news I have to impart. Well, come on up and get some breakfast, or can't you eat and think at the same time?"

The private looked around at his barracks mates and shrugged. That coffee did smell mighty inviting and the three strangers were relaxed and hospitable, like men who had brought their guns just for insurance, not because they planned on shooting anybody. Besides, the blue-eyed man had spoken with a gen-you-wine Southern accent. All three were dressed in civilian work clothes, but kept glancing down at their shirts and trousers, expecting to see a uniform instead.

Yawning and scratching, the Marines shrugged and shambled to the table. After helping themselves, they adjusted their chairs, instinctively forming a classroom arc around Jack and his two comrades, waiting to see what Jack might say next.

"First, let me assure you that Sergeant Petrie and the two sentries who pulled the graveyard shift last night are all fine and have just finished their own breakfasts. I thought it best to keep them separate for a while, so we could get acquainted without the constraints of military discipline getting' in the way of a frank, manly discussion. Anyhow, my name is Jack Fairless, and for what it's worth, I'm a colonel."

"In which army?" piped one Marine.

"Well, we've kind of formed our own, here at Pine Haven. And it's not strictly an army, although let me assure you that we're fully able to defend ourselves. But one reason why we've set up camp here at Pine Haven is so we can get on with the important experiment we're embarked on, without much chance of any outsiders barging in. Later on, after we all become friends—as I hope will be the case—we can exchange personal information, but for right now, here is what you need to know:

"All the men in my outfit have seceded from the war. We ain't your garden-variety deserters—any of my men who want to, are free to go back to New Bern, or down to Wilmington, any time they wish, and serve out the remaining months of the war under whichever flag they're partial to. I'm afraid that privilege does not extend to you gentlemen, however. See, it's really important that nobody knows about what's going on out here until we've had time to get things organized and started making a profit on our first business ventures. Long as you respect our wishes in this matter, no harm will come to you. When everybody's learned to trust everybody else, y'all can have the run of the place, just as long as you help out with the chores and with our production work."

"Production?" snorted another Marine. "Of what, for God's sake?"

"Oh, anything that seems likely to turn a profit. We ain't really got a handle on that yet."

"Hey, 'Colonel Jack' or whatever the fuck your name is, stop playin' word games with us and tell us what's going on!" Several other Rebels muttered assent.

"Sorry, I guess we are feelin' a mite cocky this mornin'. See, we originally thought we might have to shoot our way into the plantation, but once the colored folks met our leader and heard him speak, well, they threw in with us. They're the ones who snuck in here last night and removed your guns, by the way. We figured, if you boys looked up and saw a sharp-lookin' company of Negro troopers ridin' down the carriage way, you might jump to the conclusion that we were hostile and do somethin' dumb, like firin' at us."

Now that they were fed and full of coffee, the Marines were alert and bristly—after all, they had been taken in their sleep. Some of their questions were a bit testy.

"Just what would you have done if somebody *had* shot at you?"

Jack shrugged, and for just an instant—quite deliberately—he dropped the mask of affability and showed them the *other* set of blue eyes, and the steel-cold light in them that had been the last thing some men had ever seen.

"We'd have made very short work of you, boy, and that's a fact. You ever heard tell of a regiment of mounted rifles called the 'Buffaloes'?"

"Holy shit! You ain't *them,* are you, Colonel?"

"Well, we *was* them until recently, but we're somethin' different now, and nobody's quite figured out the word for what that is yet. We're kind of making this up as we go along."

Another Marine, timid and rather queasy of face, waved his hand for recognition. Jack nodded to him, all smiles and sparkling blue eyes once more.

"Did I hear you right, when you said 'a company of nigger troopers?' "

Jack's eyes went flat again and his voice even flatter. "No, you heard me say 'a company of *Negro* troopers.' Rule number one: You may refer to my dark-skinned comrades as 'blacks,' 'Negroes,' or hopefully, just by their Christian names, once you get used to the idea that they're every bit the men you are and ten times the soldiers. But racial insults can be unlearned as easy as you learned 'em, and if you call one of Bonaparte's men a 'nigger,' well, that could earn you anything from a nasty look to a busted head. You would all do well to remember one thing: not one of you fancy-pants storefront Marines has ever been in a battle, have you?" Heads reluctantly shook. "Well, me and every other former Buffalo on this plantation have been fightin' for as long as three hard years, black soldiers and white soldiers side by side, and by now we'd just as soon kill a man as spit tobacco juice, so we ain't impressed by tough talk and uncooperative attitudes. Got it?"

They certainly seemed to.

"As I was sayin', once we get to trustin' each other, you boys can join in with us and be free to come and go as you wish. Now, we ain't got time or inclination to put a guard on each and every one of you, and nobody's goin' to chain you up at night, so for those of you who are thinkin' about how easy it would be to bust out of this shed and run off to raise the alarm—and I know exactly who you are, just by lookin' at you—the rules are like this: there will be sentries in abundance every night, and while Bonaparte's given orders to shoot any fugitives in the leg, not to kill but to stop 'em from *bein'* fugitives, well, it might be kinda hard to aim when you're shootin' at some fool runnin' zigzag through the pines and in the dark. But the thing that's really goin' to stop you from trying that is that telegraph set down by the river. Anybody who runs away, why one of our signalmen'll put his fist on that key and warn Confederate navy headquarters about a deserter who might be headin' their way, followed by a description of said fugitive. You come all soggy and breathless out of the river with a crazy tale about niggers takin' over Pine Haven, and the men you're telling' it to have a description of a deserter that just came in on the wire, and you would likely as not be starin' at a firing squad before sundown."

"I thought you said we wasn't supposed to say the word 'nigger'?"

"*You* aren't. But some of our niggers call each other niggers, and that's different."

"That's not very logical . . ." mumbled the questioner.

"It's just a way they have of talkin'. You'll get used to it."

"When do we get to meet this here 'Bonaparte'? And why is he your leader? He a general?"

"Not unless he got promoted since breakfast!" Again, Jack and his two companions guffawed.

"No disrespect intended, Colonel, but none of this makes a goddamn lick of sense!"

"I can surely understand why you might say that, mister. Basically, the idea is that the war can't last much longer, and all of us—Rebels and Yanks, whites and blacks—we need a *plan* for makin' it through the troubled times that are sure to follow. After you meet him, shake his hand, hear what he has to say, you'll understand why we threw in with the man. It's bad enough to lose a war, gentlemen, but what's worse is to lose any hope of a decent future because of the dumb-ass way the Confederate government fought this war. Don't glare at me, son—I've got men in my outfit who fought for Jeff Davis for three years, and they can tell you the truth if you don't trust me for it. Bonaparte's got ideas to burn, ideas for turnin' this part of the South, at any rate, into a happy, prosperous place. You want to live like a sharecropper the rest of your days, that's fine by us. But if you want something better for yourself and your loved ones, then my friends you are in the right place at the right time. All you need is a willingness to work hard, and enough sense to get shut of the idea that God gave all the brains to White People.

"We Buffaloes were never beaten in a stand-up battle, gentlemen, and there's a reason: because we purged all racism from our hearts—and I know that is no easy thing to do, but once you've done it, you'll wonder what all the fuss was about. It makes you a superior warrior. Not one outfit in the Union Army had better morale than we did. Now that we're businessmen instead of soldiers, that same *esprit de corps* will make our products more profitable, our services more dependable, and when we make our move into politics, it'll make our candidates more electable!

"Y'all are welcome to join up and get rich while the rest of the South gets sent to the poorhouse. Once you really think about it, it don't make any more sense to believe in white supremacy than it does to put all your money into Confederate war bonds.

"Well, I reckon I've confused you enough for one mornin'. Y'all need to use the pump or the crapper, we'll take you out by twos. Bonaparte and the other ex-Buffaloes will be stagin' a grand dress-parade entrance at noon—mostly to make a big impression on the Negroes, you understand—and after a while, he'll want to talk to each of you, man to man. Just listen to what the captain has to say and I guaran-damn-tee you'll be impressed."

Mary Harper was very concerned about how Francis Marion would react when he saw a column of Yankees riding down the carriage path to his ancestral home. They would appear dignified rather than belligerent—Reubens had promised her that—but somehow her son had found equilibrium between the horrors of the gunfight at Sparkling Rock and his still-fervid sense of Confederate patriotism. True, he no longer decked himself out in Rebel Hero uniforms, but from his few oblique references to the day Stepney's mansion had been invaded, it was clear to her that he had fixed those wretched outliers with the label: "Unionist Bushwhackers." Perhaps that was the mechanism which enabled him to rationalize killing two men. Reubens had a more subtle view of the boy's thinking: "On that day, he learned what soldiers really do, other than strut around in dashing uniforms and posture on their horses before cheering civilians. Part of his mind longs for the innocent pleasures of dressing up and playing soldier—

the more grown-up part now understands that when you put on a uniform, it signals that you are ready to kill other men who wear uniforms of a different color. This is not an easy thing for grown men to reconcile, so think what convolutions must be raging in the mind of a boy! You know him as only a mother can, so you must prepare him for our appearance. As long as he does not reach for a gun and start shooting at us, I think I can defuse the moment in a suitable way, for I already have an unspoken bond with your son: we have both taken men's lives, and that makes us akin in ways that can't be put into words. I have a feeling it will work out all right, but it is up to you to lay the groundwork so that he will not instantly perceive us as a threat to his home and family."

"Thanks for giving me the easy part of the job," she said, tight-lipped.

"Mary Harper, there is no 'easy' part to it. Your son killed men at so close a range he could see the stains on their teeth. Whether he can articulate it or not, he *has* tasted the copper of blood upon his tongue, and yet he still sleeps well at night? I would say he is handling the matter better than many veteran soldiers I have known."

On the night before the Buffaloes had scheduled their dramatic but peaceful entrance, Mary Harper formulated a pretext that she thought might put Francis Marion in the right frame of mind to accept, calmly, the appearance of Union soldiers at Pine Haven.

"Did you know that there are bands of outlaws who live in the swamps north of here that are just like those men who killed your grandfather?"

"Yes. They're called outliers, and I'm very grateful the Marines are here, so I don't have to fight them again."

"Yes, of course, but some of those outlier bands are very numerous—if they were to attack Pine Haven, our Marines might not be able to beat them. So I have made an arrangement with the Yankee high command in New Bern, because the outliers sometimes attack Yankee outposts too. Flag Officer Branch cannot spare any more Marines, but there is a very brave Yankee officer who has offered to reinforce our Marines, because the outliers are the enemies of both sides. And tomorrow, that Yankee officer, whose name is Captain Reubens, is bringing a company of mounted riflemen to protect us. His men and the Confederate Marines will work together, instead of fighting each other. That way, no one would dare attack Pine Haven. I think we are very lucky, don't you? That both sides are cooperating to defend our home, I mean. At noon tomorrow they will stage a grand parade up our carriage path, with flags waving and horses prancing. It should be something to see!"

Francis Marion's eyes lit up. He may have lost his boyish enthusiasm for being a soldier, now that he had learned what soldiers really did, but he was still a twelve-year-old boy, and the idea of Pine Haven becoming a veritable fortress, of a whole company of veteran soldiers making the plantation into their headquarters, was irresistibly exciting.

"Will I like this Captain Reubens? Have you met him?"

"Yes, I have. I think you'll find him very interesting to talk to. And there is something else you should know about him and his troops: most of them are Negroes."

"But, Mother, won't *our* Negroes think *those* Negroes have come to abolish them?"

"I think you mean 'abolition,' dear. Well, just remember what I've told you before: after the war is over, Pine Haven will not have slaves any more, only 'employees.' I cannot tell what the future will bring, Francis Marion, but I am fairly certain there won't *be* a Confederacy for very much longer, and I know that our Negroes are glad that Captain Reubens will be here to guard their homes as well as ours. Sooner or later, we will all be part of the same country again—for us, it will just happen a bit sooner than it will for people living in other parts of the South."

The boy tried hard to digest a lot of new and surprising information.

"Well, I guess it was bound to happen—General Lee hasn't won a battle in a long time, has he?"

Bonaparte had promised that the ex-Buffaloes would make a memorable entrance, and they did. It was probably just as well they no longer had a Union flag, but they did have their "Fighting Bison" banner, and that added a splash of dramatic color when the horsemen rode up the carriage path. As best they could, they had washed the dust from their tattered uniforms and the mud from their horses, and Company A's bugler still had the lips of Gabriel, so when they rode in—thirty-three blacks and eleven whites, in a column of twos to make the formation look bigger than its numbers, with sabers drawn and faces proud—they made a grand impression.

All of Pine Haven had turned out, lining both sides of the carriage path. Mary Harper had declared a holiday, and the slaves—if that's what they still were—had spent all morning gathering flowers in baskets, so the Buffaloes were treated to the one and only victory parade they would ever know, riding proudly through cascades of blossoms and the appreciative squeals of comely black girls.

When the column halted in front of the great white columns and the wide, gracious veranda, Francis Marion suddenly stepped forward, dressed in his fanciest "Little Confederate" uniform. His appearance startled everyone and brought down apprehensive silence. With precise parade-ground pacing, he marched to the top of the stairs and saluted Bonaparte Reubens, before extending to him, with the utmost solemnity, his favorite wooden sword. Reubens was clearly taken aback, but recovered with magnificent noblesse oblige. He returned Francis Marion's salute and said:

"Word has reached me, sir, of the outstanding courage you displayed at the Battle of Sparkling Rock. I cannot accept the sword of so brave a man, and therefore I return it to you as a symbol of honor. You are hereby paroled, Francis Marion Sloane, with one condition: that you climb up here and ride with me on my horse!"

Agrippa sidled up to Mary Harper and muttered: "Ah tol' you, dat man got *class*! He just made dat boy his friend for life!"

Gracefully balancing Francis Marion, Bonaparte Reubens turned to address his troops.

"Men of the First North Carolina Mounted Unionist Volunteers! My Buffalo comrades! Today we bid farewell to our old life, and turn our eyes toward the future. Care for this plantation as you would for your own home; treat Missus Sloane and her children with as much respect as you would want shown to your own wives and children. The same goes for those three ruffians standing by the rocking chairs—Mister Chiang, Fernando, Stepan—they were once my brothers in adversity and they have forgiven me for treating them badly and paying them a dog's wages, so honor them as *my* brothers. And these good black people who have welcomed us today with flowers and cheers, they *are* your brothers and sisters, so set an example for them worthy of their faith in you. Now it is time to stack our rifles and trade them for hammers and saws, so that we can build our own living quarters and not impose on our hosts one day longer than is necessary. Until those quarters are built, each of you will sleep with a family that has volunteered its hospitality. Go with those people now, and exchange your uniforms for the honest clothes of working men. Tonight, Missus Sloane has arranged a picnic supper in our honor, and tomorrow, our real work begins. Color sergeant: Furl and cover the Buffalo flag, and preserve it for History. Let no dishonor ever stain this banner!"

"Change that name, Bonaparte, for God's sake! 'Produced by the Free People of Pine Haven' sounds like a charity foundation or a political party." Mary Harper sounded a touch exasperated, as she always did when one of the twice-weekly "executive meetings" went on past ten o'clock and her attention grew less focused on the agenda than on the contents of the library's bar. The "open meetings," held once a week in the same setting, usually finished earlier, even though there were more people in attendance—every "citizen" of Pine Haven could voice an idea, lodge a complaint, make a suggestion for improvement, and often these could be dealt with more expeditiously than the long-winded debates the administrators bogged down in.

"It is not carved in marble, Mary," retorted Bonaparte Reubens. "I just made it up on the spur of the moment. I'm more than eager to hear any suggestions for a new corporate identity, as long as it truly reflects what we're doing here."

"Since we are still in the process of *finding out* 'what we do here,'" interjected Jack Fairless, "Mary Harper and I were kicking around some ideas this afternoon, in the kitchen, when Aurelia suggested something that struck us as perfect. Aurelia, please tell everyone your idea."

First cousin to Agrippa, she had run the domestic affairs of the Big House for twenty-one years, and Mary Harper had arranged to have her tutored long before she started holding literacy classes for the other slaves, so that Aurelia could handle some of the paperwork, maintain accurate inventories, and sign for shipments of goods when her mistress was absent. But today, encouraged by the new and vibrant mood on the plantation, this fifty-two-year-old black woman had found her true voice for the first time.

"I been thinking that the name should reflect the idea that this venture has no limits, hasn't got any racial or political axes to grind, and is not bound to this moment in time—God willing, it will still prosper a hundred years from now! Our title should cover the things we grow and make, the services we perform for clients—when we get any—the real estate developments y'all been daydreaming about—all of it. So I came up with this: 'Pine Haven Products and Services—The Future is What We Are About.'"

Simple. Dignified. Farsighted. The room went contemplatively silent for thirty seconds, and then Aurelia received the first ovation of her life.

Everybody agreed that rice-farming was deader than John Brown's body. But if all those laboriously constructed and irrigated acres were plowed up, what should Pine Haven grow instead of rice? Cotton was not going to be king in the postwar South. Great Britain had paid top dollar for every bale the runners could smuggle out, and after three years of being price-gouged, Her Majesty's government had concluded that it would be far cheaper, in the long run, to greatly expand cotton production in Egypt and India than to import it from nations outside the boundaries of the Empire. What postwar demand there might be for Dixie cotton, could easily be met by small and medium-sized farms; without slave labor, the vast dinosaur plantations such as Limerick were no longer economically viable.

So what *could* be grown at Pine Haven?

The answer was found in a presentation given at an "open meeting" by three men who had put their minds to it. One was the Pine Haven groundskeeper, a gardener so expert Matthew Sloane liked to say he could make orchids bloom in the Sahara; the second was a black Buffalo who had worked tobacco farms in Georgia and Alabama. Their reasoning was tight, logical, and succinct:

(1) Between four and six million young men would leave their respective armies with a keen fondness for tobacco—its pungency, its stress-reducing medicinal effect, its value as a symbol of manliness and adulthood.

(2) Pipes are too inconvenient; cigars too expensive and for many young smokers, too harsh—besides, nobody could finish a whole cigar at one smoke, not unless he wanted to get sick. What's more, if our hypothetical discharged tobacco addict lives in some backwoods flyspeck like Spillcorn Creek, it's a long, long way to a store that stocks cheap cigars—which makes it hard to enjoy a spontaneous smoke whenever you feel like it.

(3) The future of smoking, therefore, lies in the humble cigarette. According to the ex-Buffalo member of the "project team":

"It's cheap, it's convenient, it's milder than cigar or pipe tobacco, and you could sell 'em *factory-rolled* in *packs*—say a dozen, maybe twenty if it's practical. Right now, on both sides of the lines in Virginia, if a fellow wants a cigarette, why he has to roll newspaper around a mess of coarse leaf, and you got to be *desperate for a smoke* to suck up that hot, stinky newsprint. Mister Groves, it's your turn now."

The Pine Haven gardener unwrapped a tray full of tender green tobacco sprouts and cleared his throat. "Gentlemen and Missus Sloane, too—My experiments indicate that with careful grafting and selection, the soil in eastern North Carolina could easily produce the softest, finest-grained tobacco in the world. Leaf that would roll easily into a cylinder, burn slow and even, and be much easier to pack inside porous, lightweight paper than the coarse shag tobacco folks use when they roll their own nowadays. If my numbers are right, and we started converting the rice fields into proper tobacco beds this autumn, we could be producing enough prime tobacco to manufacture *twenty million cigarettes* by eighteen sixty eight, sixty nine at the latest. Now as for developing the right sort of wrapper for Pine Haven Golden Leaf Cigarettes—ahem, that's just my suggestion, of course, for the brand name—I'd like to bring out the third member of our team, Corporal Albert T. Walker, of the Confederate Marines!"

Applause and whistles! The agricultural future of Pine Haven was no longer in jeopardy! Everybody in the room could feel it: *This was going to work!*

"Thank you, friends, thank you. I know little of agriculture, but I believe my colleague's estimates of the future cigarette market are far too conservative! Just think how big that market will be when *women* take up smoking! Well, that's a ways off, I admit, but I do know that you sell a lot more of anything if it's attractively packaged, and that people will buy the Pine Haven brand in preference to other brands if they can be confident that when they get that pack home and open it, they won't find half the cigarettes broken or crushed. Now it so happens that my first cousin, Wilbur Duncan, owns a paper mill just outside of Savannah. I got a letter from him just before we shipped out of Wilmington, and Sherman never even passed close, so he's still in business. If I send him specifications for both the package and the prerolled cigarette papers, I believe he can devise just the kind of light, strong, paper stocks we need for each. And I happen to know that he'll be looking for a new line of work fairly soon, so he will probably give us a very attractive bid for the job."

"I'm curious," asked Jack Fairless, "but why would your cousin be needing a new 'line of work' in the near future? What does his paper mill produce now?"

"Confederate money . . ."

Fitz-John Bright began having bad dreams, accompanied by severe headaches, not long after Mary Harper threw a party to celebrate Francis Marion's thirteenth birthday. Initially, Bright had been appalled to see Bonaparte Reubens again, and only the direct orders of Mary Harper, together with Reubens' sincere apologies, had kept him from jumping into the steam launch and heading down to Wilmington to raise the alarm. But soon, even Bright was won over by Reubens' charisma and eloquence. He, too, had worried about what might happen to his beloved Pine Haven after the Yankees captured Wilmington, and Reubens had laid a foundation for the continued survival, at least, of the grand old plantation. He finally embraced Reubens' "New South" philosophy because he had seen the genuine affection growing between the Sloane children and their new black friend, "Uncle Bonaparte." As he expressed it to Mary Harper, "You can't argue with happiness."

But as the weather turned cooler, Bright's nightmares attained the intensity of hallucinations. He woke, some mornings, bathed in malarial sweat and so utterly disoriented that he felt disembodied, and had to crawl back into his own flesh in order to wake up at all. Night after night, a low, insidious voice spoke to his mind: *Reubens is not what he seems! He will bring fire and ruin down on Pine Haven! Unless someone stops him . . .*

When two ex-Buffaloes took the first wagonload of "Pine Haven Rope Hammocks" up to New Bern, the Union garrison bought out the whole supply in two days, and the drivers came back home with advance orders for 46 more. The profit margin was almost 200 percent, and the shy, retiring Benson sisters, who suddenly found themselves with more money than they had ever dreamed of having before, started training six new apprentices.

When Mary Harper told Largo about what was going on out at Pine

Haven, Largo not only offered a quarter of her retail space for Pine Haven Products, she also convinced Mary Harper to consider investing in beachfront property, a great deal of which was now for sale at rock-bottom prices, with an eye toward opening a chain of comfortable but inexpensive resorts. "When the Yankees see how beautiful our beaches are, they'll want to come back with their families—provided they know they can find clean, affordable rooms."

Hobart-Hampden thought so much of that idea that he brought Mary Harper a magazine article about a German inventor who was seeking financial backing to produce the prototype of a new machine he called "the refrigerator."

"Your establishments will be the only ones on any beach in North America where patrons can eat *fresh* seafood five days after it was caught!"

On Sunday night, October 27, Bonaparte Reubens was relaxing in his very own rope hammock—a present from the Benson sisters, which he had mounted on the support columns that held up the back-porch roof of the small private house Jack Fairless and some of the old Buffalo gang had built for him on the banks of the Uhwarrie River, a hundred yards north of the very spot where Agrippa had hidden the boat in which he had escaped from Pine Haven back in sixty-two.

He was satisfied with the way things were going. Whether or not he was creating a Great Work, remained open to question, but he had brought hope and racial harmony to this small part of the South, and every day the roots of it were growing stronger, the tender shoots closer to bearing real fruit. Now if only that stiff-necked fool Jefferson Davis would sue for peace while he still had an army to bargain with, Pine Haven's enterprises could move into the open.

Yes, and if wishes were horses, then beggars would ride!

Well, there was nothing he could do about Jefferson Davis's pig-headedness, but in the meantime, he could rock in his hammock, watch the gentle Uhwarrie flow by, and savor this most excellent mint julep.

Tap-tap!

Oh, Lord, who could be knocking at this time of night? "I'm on the back porch, whoever you are! Come around and have a drink!"

Surprisingly, he had two guests: Francis Marion and "Sunny" Chiang, of all people.

"Evening, Boss," said the Chinaman, in his flutey singsong voice. "We need to talk to you, okay?"

"Ssshhh! Don't disturb the moon!"

"Moon velly pretty tonight, for sure. But other things not so pretty."

"What on earth are you talking about, Mister Chiang?"

"The Chaos God—your success has made him *notice* you again. God of Creation, God of Destruction, there is much strife between them.

Chaos God is ascendant at the moment. This shit goes back and forth, you know . . ."

"All the way from the Valley of Diamonds!" echoed Francis Marion.

"I have felt nothing, seen nothing, heard nothing—there hasn't even been a warning twitch from this thing around my neck. And what does a Chinaman know about West African metaphysics, anyway?"

Chiang shrugged, glancing around uneasily. "Same two gods contend everywhere, Boss, all through Time. Different names, maybe, but always same idea, always same struggle." Chiang gave a nervous little titter that scratched Reubens' nerve endings like a hangnail.

Francis Marion had matured greatly in the past year, but adolescent vocal cords could not explain the deeper, more resonant voice that rode piggy-backed on the words coming from the boy's mouth. "You carry strong protection, Captain. The Chaos God cannot hurt you, not while you stand on the very earth where the God of Creation charged you with your Destiny. But He can use a surrogate, another who is even more deeply tied to this land."

"You mean Mary . . . your mother? Nonsense! I had tea with her just this afternoon."

"Wrong, Boss," sighed Chiang. "There is one other, who was deeply rooted in this place long before Missus Sloane set eyes on it: Mistah Bright. He been overseer here since eighteen twenty nine. His father, before him. We just looked, and he's gone. So is steam launch. Don't know how long, but chances are you ain't got much time until things start turning ugly around here."

"This is hard to accept. I know old Bright was skeptical at first, and in his place, I would be too. But lately, he's been very cooperative, even friendly."

Not-Quite-Francis Marion shrugged. "A bad god can be a good actor. I knew something was wrong when he came up to me in the garden this morning and asked if I knew anything about a place called 'Fearsome Cove,' or something like that. I said I'd never heard of it. He made a very nasty laugh and said: 'That man Reubens—he was there, he saw the killing! He heard the white women scream while the bucks lined up to rape them! He was there, yet he did *nothing!*'"

"He is wrong! Damn it, Francis Marion—if you're still inside there listening to me—I *did* do something about it. I drew my gun on that son of a bitch DeWitt, I ended the suffering of a man he was torturing to death, and I testified at his court-martial! Neither I nor any of my men took part in those atrocities!"

Chiang began to speak, very sternly, and not-quite-like-Chiang either: "The point, I think, is that while you *were* there and while your gun was drawn, maybe you were supposed to USE that gun, not just make threats with it. You did *something,* yes, you made a gesture—of which you are both proud and ashamed—but you did not shoot, because then there would have been a battle between his men and yours and Jack's men, and you *did not want any Buffaloes to die from black men's bullets!* Chaos God, he paints all the horrors of Faison's Groves inside Bright's head, but over DeWitt's face, he pastes a picture of *yours*. You are protected; he cannot kill you; but he can put into Bright's mouth the words that will make other white men *want* to kill you. Pretty soon, maybe even now, those white men be saddling their horses or loading into boats. Boss—maybc someday you come back here and finish the Great Work you began, but right now, you got to ride the hell away, and you got to do it fast!"

Mister Chiang might have become wholly Mister Chiang again, but his figure remained still and silent, eyes fixed on the cold stark moon.

Bonaparte Reubens leaped up and ran, kicking over his mint julep.

Jack Fairless's bushwhacker instincts had not entirely atrophied. At the sound of running boots and urgent whispers, Jack came instantly awake, his hand closing around the stock of his Spencer before his eyes popped open. Clad only in his nightshirt, he ran outside and halted, amazed, at the sight of Bonaparte's black troopers girding for battle, buttoning their blue jackets, pulling saddles from the railings near the stable, buckling on their gunbelts and scabbards. Sleepy-eyed Pine Haven Negroes emerged from their cabins, took one look around, and darted back inside, bolting the doors behind them. Jack hailed the nearest black soldier.

"What the hell's going on? Where's Captain Reubens?"

"Right behind you, Jack."

When Jack had last seen Bonaparte, he was laughing and relaxed, content and proud; proud of himself, proud of the Sloanes, proud of the work being accomplished and the fecundity of ideas now percolating and maturing, under the lofty trees that inspired Pine Haven's sonorous name. Now, Fairless beheld an altogether changed man: eyes hard and furtive, mouth a downturned bitter slash.

"Captain Reubens, what in God's name is going on?"

"Long story short, Jack—the furies of Faison's Groves are loose again, and there are a lot of vengeful white men heading this way. My boys and I are going to make a run for it to New Bern. Maybe we can still make it. If we do, you will hear from me. If we don't, at least we can draw them away from Pine Haven. They're after black men in blue uniforms, and we're the only people around here who fit that description. If we can get them to chase us, they won't bother the Sloanes, or these other good black folks." Reubens embraced his friend and smiled sourly. "I'll see you later, Jack, in this world or in Hell."

"Goddamn it, Bonaparte, wait till I get my fucking boots on and I'll come with you!"

"No, you're not. You are staying here with the white soldiers, to protect what we've started to build here and the people in the Big House who gave us their blessing and the use of their land. If another lynch mob shows up, it will be up to your white troopers and those Rebel Marines to protect Pine Haven, and I think the sight of Rebel uniforms and repeating rifles will deter them from mischief. The mobs are looking for *black soldiers,* Jack, and if you go with us into the night, they might not notice your white skin or hold their fire if it comes into their sights. Any man who rides with me tonight is fair game! Now get your ugly redneck face out of my sight!"

Jack only shook his head and ducked back inside long enough to sling his boots over one shoulder and a cartridge belt over the other.

"Maybe you've forgotten I outrank you, Bonaparte, but I am ordering you to wait up long enough for me to get my damn boots on. I will not stay here while some posse chases you all over hell and half of Carolina!" Jack bent over to tug his boots over his shanks.

Reubens clouted him on the head with the butt of his Spencer.

"I'm sorry, my friend, but tonight we ride on different roads . . ."

Fitz-John Bright drifted silently down the Uhwarrie for two miles before he started the boat's engine. He had to get somewhere as fast as he could, although the exact motive for his urgency kept sliding in and out of focus, harder to grasp than a bar of soap in a bathtub. When he saw the big railroad bridge ahead, that same vague but painfully insistent sense of direction—or of *being directed*—made him turn the launch hard to the right. That illuminated shed was his goal, commanded the voice in his head, because there was a telegraph inside. *Spread the alarm! Quickly!*

A few moments later, he was inside a sentry post, a wild, hysterical tale pouring from his lips: *"Remember that terrible massacre at the village named Faison's Groves?"* he babbled. "Well, those black heathen savages who plundered Faison's Groves have seized Pine Haven plantation! Stop 'em before they do awful things to Missus Sloane and her children!"

Once the telegraph key began to stutter, the alarm spread with the speed of light. Within minutes, answering telegraphs reported the mobilization of a large posse, preparing to converge on the railroad bridge; and in Wilmington, Flag Officer Branch was loading one hundred Marines into boats. The dreadful nigger barbarians would be trapped between the two forces. And Mister Bright was to lead that posse. Men were coming with bloodlust engorging the chambers of their hearts; they were coming with torches and lynching ropes and skinning knives. And if any darkies managed to run into the swamps, there would be hunting dogs here by morning. In so far as it could mimic human emotions, the God of Chaos smiled within the meat of Fitz-John Bright's no-longer sentient brain.

For a time, Bonaparte thought they might make it. But he halted, prudently, just before the rutted, seldom-used track entered the worst patch of swampland between Pine Haven and Plymouth, a narrow mile-long defile hemmed-in by terrain that was mostly quicksand and briar thickets. He sent two of his best men forward to reconnoiter. They returned quickly.

"Roadblock, Cap'n, crude one, but there's 70, maybe 80 Home Guard from Tarboro working on it. Ain't no way to outflank it."

Reubens felt the walls closing around them. Until that moment, he had clung to the hope that the strain of possession might prove too much for Mr. Bright's 62 year-old body, but he was one tough old bird—somewhere deep inside, his consciousness was probably still fighting the takeover, and that alone would add enormous strain to his physical shell. Reubens and his men could not go forward—they were not strong enough to take that roadblock; they could not return to Pine Haven, or Jack and the white Buffaloes would be discovered; and as soon as the posse was gathered in sufficient numbers, the thing that was-not-Bright would lead them up this road.

Bonaparte saw one chance only. If his small force could get the drop on *that* bunch, ambush them while they were riding pell-mell toward Pine Haven, the firepower of his Spencers could administer such a lethal shock that, in the confusion following the first volleys, he might be able to lead his men back across to road and through the woods to the Uhwarre River. It *was* possible to follow that stream halfway to New Bern; he knew, because he had done it once before. On that trek he had noted several shallow fording places, the first one maybe three miles north of Pine Haven. Once they reached the eastern side of the Uhwarrie, they would be safe from tracking dogs. Not every man would survive the initial skirmish, or the brutal march that would come after, but he was still their leader, and he owed them a chance to survive, no matter how slim.

He explained the plan; the men were ready to give it their all . . . one last time. They rode back to a bend in the road that seemed to offer an excellent field of fire, secured the horses out of sight, and took up positions.

Bonaparte could hear the posse—whooping and shouting curses at their intended prey—long before they came into sight. Half of them were already drunk, and that was helpful; they had no scouts out in front, which was even more helpful; and they would be no more than fifty yards away when the Buffaloes opened a withering fire on their disorganized column. Bonaparte began to feel a stirring of hope—he could see the vigilante column now, and they numbered no more than 70. The Spencers at his command could throw out 180 rounds in the first six seconds. Whoever survived that fusillade would be awestruck, dazed, and slow to react. He gave the orders: empty your magazines as fast as you can work the levers, then remount and charge across the road. "Keep going until you reach the river. We'll regroup there—I know the way out!"

Just as the vigilantes were about to enter the killing zone however, an authoritative stony voice called out for them to halt, and they did so instantly, responding to the icy force of that command. No more jokes and Rebel yells, just the nervous wickering of their horses and the metallic jangle of equipment. A lone rider emerged from the column and slowly advanced up the road, obviously sensing danger. When the horseman rose into a patch of moonlight, Bonaparte saw that it was Fitz-John Bright, or at least the mortal shell of him. But there was no trace of Mister Bright in those eyes —baleful and almost too intensely bright to look upon, they were no longer human organs, but coals from the slag heaps of Hell. If those eyes were searching for you, no earthly darkness could hide you.

Gaunt, wraithlike, the unholy scout that was not-Bright rode forward another three feet, then stopped once more and began to swivel its head methodically, probing every possible shadow where a sniper might be concealed. At first, those searing eyes swept the arc of terrain quickly, then they repeated the survey more slowly, zeroing in. Once, twice, the probing gaze swept past the Buffaloes' hiding place, and each time Reubens and his companions felt an icy breath caress their skin.

Then the scout sat up in his saddle, rigid as stone, raised the stiff left arm of Bright's usurped body, pointed directly at the Buffaloes' location, and opened a black cavern that had once been a human mouth. From that abyss, rose a deafening, bestial roar so alien that the very air felt violated by its vibrations:

"THEEYYY ARRRE THERE THERE THERE THERE!!"

From the entity's eyes a meteoric ray streaked across the road and illuminated their hiding place. Leaves withered and sap bubbled in pine bark. But the energy released in that outcry drained the last vitality from the Chaos God's host. The flesh of Fitz-John Bright could no longer sustain the burden imposed upon it and his stout old heart exploded like a torpedo, with such force that his chest blew open. Like a writhing, vaporous tentacle, the God of Destruction took form and substance in order to escape the withered husk it had manipulated, and lunged toward the stars, returning to the unholy dimensions whence it came.

Though shaken by what they had seen, the vigilantes began to shake off their paralysis and reach for their weapons. After all, they had come here to kill some niggers, and now they knew where to find them.

One of Reubens' troopers grabbed his shoulder urgently.

"Time for you to run, Captain! Me and the boys will buy you as much time as we can." Spencers began to bark—white men fell, but the others recovered quickly and began finding cover.

"He's right, Captain! You all that's left of the regiment now—it's your duty to survive! Don't feel guilty about us, either—we doin' this because we want to. And they won't take any of us alive. We each already vowed that."

Reubens did not know what to say. He tried to thank them, tried to find the words to express the love he felt for them.

"Stop trying to make a fuckin' speech, goddamn it, and get yo' black ass across that road while you can!"

Crouching low, half-blinded by tears, Bonaparte Reubens sprinted across the road and into the wilderness. Flopping against his chest, the fetish-object felt weightless, drained of power; its work was done. Reubens drew his knife and severed the cord that had tied it to his neck for forty years, and threw the totem into a stagnant pond. Then he ran for the river. If necessary, he felt strong enough to run all the way to New Bern.

The old bull alligator lived a serenely uncomplicated life. His rudimentary saurian brain recognized only a few states of being; HUNGRY/NOT HUNGRY was by far the most important. When he was hungry he did something about it, and when he was no longer hungry, he slept. But Beauregard did have the capacity to dream. In random rotation, his minuscule consciousness played and replayed two dreams, and since he was incapable of feeling boredom, that was an ample repertory. One dream was quite pleasant: for a while ("a while" being his only measurement of time), a human named "Mister Bright" had assiduously trained him to attack "Yankees." At regular intervals, each afternoon, for a long "while," Mister Bright lowered a "Yankee" into Beauregard's cage and patiently repeated the words "Yankee, Beauregard! Yankee!" until the alligator worked up enough energy to lunge at the offering. After "a while," he began to do this with increasing gusto, because "Yankees" were good eating. They consisted of a big slab of delicious fly-covered horsemeat wrapped in a distinctive blue covering. Beauregard always ate the blue part, but only so he could get to the Yankee-stuff inside, which to him was a true delicacy. Alligators did not, as a rule, get many chances to sample horsemeat, and Beauregard thought its yielding, gristly texture, robust bouquet, and full-bodied sickly-sweet flavor were far superior to his usual diet of cold scaly fish and annoyingly crunchy turtles. Insofar as he was capable of anticipating anything, Beauregard began to look forward to his daily Yankee. Then one day, another human told Mister Bright that alligators were not allowed on ships and other humans might strenuously object to the practice of feeding Yankees to large prehistoric-looking reptiles, so Mister Bright unceremoniously dumped him back into the Cape Fear River, and for a long "while" he did not taste any more of them.

But a year or so later, he spotted some rather scrawny-looking Yankees trying to get across the river that ran in front of Mister Bright's home, and instinct took over at once. Instead of a culinary treat, however, one of these Yankees turned out to be a savage predator who lashed out with a shiny thing called a "cutlass" and lopped off one of Beauregard's front paws.

That was the subject of Beauregard's *other* dream: Pain. In all his ponderous armor-plated life, Beauregard had never felt pain, and he did not like it one bit. Although the pain eventually went away, the lack of a paw caused him to miss catching a lot of lesser snacks, food items which he used to obtain easily, back before that traumatic amputation. So when he was not sleeping or feeding, Beauregard brooded over the injustice of Existence and vowed that the next time he saw a Yankee, he would not lunge at it with reckless abandon, but would approach with patience and stealth.

Patience was one quality alligators had in abundance, and Beauregard's patience was rewarded on this brisk October night, when he was awakened from a tranquil (dreamless) slumber by the sound of some large, obviously distraught creature stumbling through a shallow part of the river. He could scarcely credit his good fortune when the gasping, fleeing Yankee ran straight for the log behind which Beauregard was lurking.

But this Yankee was running so hard that Beauregard knew he would only have time for one lunge. He dug his hind legs into the river bottom and coiled every cable-thick muscle in his twelve-foot body into a powerful spring. In the end, one lunge was more than enough. At the very last instant before he would have trodden on Beauregard's snout, the Yankee looked down, saw an immense cave-like maw, filled with glittering teeth as big as railroad spikes, opening to receive him, and let out the beginning of a very loud scream.

Beauregard took his time with this meal, savoring every dark-meat morsel. It might be a long time before another "Yankee" crossed his path, so he made this one last as long as possible. Certainty had returned to his world.

Yankees tasted even better than he remembered.

Wanted: One Volunteer for Hazardous Duty!

WE UNDERSTAND THAT General Bragg has been sent to take command of Wilmington. Good-bye, Wilmington!
—The Richmond Enquirer, October 10, 1864

General Braxton Bragg always wore the look of a man perpetually aggrieved. Tintypes of him from the Mexican War period revealed a stern but ruggedly handsome young West Pointer; the intervening years had not been kind to his physiognomy. Like a soft-skulled newborn forced to wear an anvil instead of a lace cap, the weight of his responsibilities, and the calumnies heaped upon him by the general public's perception of his signal military failures, had given his forehead a "squashed" appearance, a flattened ovoid, which in turn made his squinty gimlet eyes seem squeezed unnaturally close together; his nose jutted belligerently, as though grossly overstuffed with too much cartilage; his once-manly mouth had retreated into a bitter, downturned slit; and his close-cropped beard was a woe to behold—like a poorly threshed stack of hay, it resisted shaping by scissors, comb, or soothing emollients. A surgeon's hacksaw appeared to have been the last implement to take a whack at it, but at least it drew attention away from Bragg's most unappetizing feature: the boar's-bristles comprising his simian pelt of conjoined eyebrow, a wild thicket of coarse scraggly weeds that overhung the rest of his face like a perpetual thundercloud.

Debating the riddle of Bragg's personality had become a national obsession to the Confederate people, just as the enigmas of his generalship were the subject of endless campfire debates among his fellow officers. Some of the issues were petty and personal: how could a man as fastidious in his personal habits as Jefferson Davis stand to be closeted with Bragg in the airless chambers of the Richmond bureaucracy? Others were of historical magnitude: Excluding the motive of treason, how had one general (as editorial writers never tired of saying) managed so consistently to snatch defeat from the jaws of victory? The latest, most spectacular example was when Bragg absolutely smashed Rosencrans' right wing on the opening day of the Chickamauga campaign, and he had frittered away that triumph with such breathtaking ineptitude that five weeks later, he had managed to lose Chattanooga—along with every other Confederate stronghold in eastern Tennessee—through a series of tactical blunders so egregious that his earlier victory had to be judged a fluke. Even the world's worst poker player gets dealt a sweet hand on rare occasions.

Far better strategists—Joe Johnston came foremost to mind—had been sacked *permanently* for lesser defeats, yet even when public outrage demanded Bragg's resignation, Davis had merely recalled him from Tennessee, without rebuke, and then installed him close at hand as supreme "military advisor" to the Confederate government! Bragg mistook Davis's personal loyalty for vindication of his generalship, and continued blithely meddling in the business of better officers. Not being a man given to deep introspection, Bragg never felt compelled to exercise self-criticism; indeed, he thought there was something suspect, even effete, about officers who made a habit of that practice. It smacked of professional and spiritual onanism, a practice Bragg found deeply abhorrent—any soldier, he had once averred (in a West Point dormitory bull-session that had become a Corps-of-Cadets' legend) who habitually flung his seed into the void, was using up his God-given fund of innate valor and was destined not only for blindness but for a coward's death to boot.

Such dour humorless eccentricities did not endear Bragg to his comrades, but the root cause of Bragg's baffling performance as a battlefield leader was very simple: with the exception of his one close friend and powerful patron, Jefferson Davis, Braxton Bragg simply *did not like* people very much. Had it been possible, Bragg would have never left his office or his tent, but would have conveyed his orders entirely through written memoranda. This aloofness worked both ways, of course, and his relations with subordinate officers were characterized by a more or less constant state of friction and animosity; when tempers flared, strategy conferences degenerated into shouting matches, for Bragg was constitutionally incapable of quelling dissent by means of tactful debate. When faced with defiance, he tended to sulk, to retreat behind the parapets of rank and snarl self-righteously at those who disagreed with him. By the autumn of 1864, there were many senior Confederate officers who flatly refused to be in the same room with him.

This was not a new state of affairs. During the Mexican War, on the eve of the Battle of Cerro Gordo, parties unknown had rolled a live sputtering 12-pounder shell under Bragg's cot while the future general was sound asleep. Fortunately or not for the Confederacy, the fuse was a dud, but ever since that incident, Bragg had been distracted by trying to watch his back almost as closely as he watched the nominative enemy in front.

He was not without valuable ability, of course, otherwise he would never have lasted long in the small professional army of the 1850s. Even his most hostile critics admitted his skills as an administrator, an organizer, a logistician. He was more comfortable with paperwork than with other soldiers. He grew calm and focused when working the maps, trainload tonnage, *numbers*. Dependable things, numbers. Two and two always equaled four; numbers had no agendas, no emotions, no axes to grind. Most importantly, numbers were nonjudgmental. Bragg had served under, and been served by, men whose characters were confusing amalgams of the petty and the exalted, the gross and the subtle; men who were simultaneously obedient and insubordinate, loyal and spiteful. By the start of 1864, Braxton Bragg was fed up with all of them. He knew that other men took no pleasure from his company, but his innate lack of social grace, his imperviousness to a well-told joke, were defects he had been born with, like a clubfoot or Ben Butler's rolling squid-eye; he inhabited the personality God gave him, not necessarily the one he had chosen.

No man had worked harder for the Confederacy, yet no man had been so vilified by its newspapers. In the face of chronic shortages, Bragg had displayed a genius for organizing, transporting, and supplying armies in the field—and then *with those same armies,* other generals far more glamorous and popular had won their most acclaimed victories. Bragg's successes, those triumphs of logistics and scheduling, had not captured the public's attention because, compared to the high drama of combat and maneuver, they made for very dull reading. Only President Davis seemed truly to appreciate Bragg's gifts, to understand how stoically Bragg had borne the cross of scorn and sarcasm.

At least by giving him command of the Cape Fear District, President Davis had liberated him from having to endure, on an almost daily basis, the insufferable saintliness of Robert E. Lee, whose "genius" had finally been exposed for the myth it had always been by his fumbling performance at Gettysburg—a debacle that had squandered ten times more Southern blood than Bragg's defeat in Tennessee.

Bragg did not honestly know if he or any other commander could save Wilmington, given the paucity of Confederate resources and the enormous amount of force at the enemy's disposal. But he *was* confident that he had the power to smooth over some of the irritants that had been continually poking splinters into Richmond's all-important sense of propriety. He could establish a coherent firm-hand command over the whole unruly region; he could communicate, emphatically but impartially, President Davis's intolerance of Whiting's bantamweight defiance, soften the jagged edges of Whiting's pickled self-righteousness, and above all, curb his incessant *whining*; he could exert a calming maturity over the boyish underconfidence of Whiting's naïve acolyte, the handsome *beau chevalier* William Lamb (beloved by his puny garrison as no soldiers had ever loved Braxton Bragg!). Ever since the sinking of the *Hatteras*, Lamb and Whiting had been feeding off of each other's anxieties, sending forth weekly, now almost daily, shrieks of imminent disaster; apocalyptic and, as far as Bragg could see, groundless predictions that served to justify their incessant pleas for more men, more guns, more shells. President Davis had told Bragg that the mere sight of another molten harangue from Whiting, when deposited on his desk by an aide, bestowed upon the president's overworked brain a murderous headache—and if there was anything Bragg knew well, it was the toll such headaches could take on a man's equilibrium. Bragg's primary job in Wilmington was to be the president's headache remedy.

Didn't Lamb and Whiting realize there was not a company or battery to spare, not anywhere in what remained of the Confederacy? *Of course,* the Yankees would move against Wilmington! After Mobile Bay, the only other significant port left in Confederate hands, had fallen to Admiral Farragut on August 5, and "Crazy Billy" Sherman had torched most of Atlanta on September 2, there simply weren't any other big strategic targets left in the whole Confederacy. Savannah had already been written off as indefensible, and had never been a major blockade-running port to begin with, so that left only Wilmington. Prophetic powers were not required to reach that conclusion—just a grim process of elimination. So *of course*, Admiral David Porter was gathering a gigantic fleet in Hampton Roads for the purpose of capturing Fort Fisher, but when Bragg arrived in Wilmington, on October 22, armed with the rank and authority needed to calm the feverish distemper of Whiting and Lamb, he brought with him a mandate to restore the faith of those gentlemen in Richmond's ability to succor them in their hour of need. Rebel agents were watching Porter's fleet, and there would be plenty of warning before it sailed. Grant was still bogged down in the siege of Petersburg, but Lee had assured Davis, who in turn assured Bragg, that he would be willing and able to dispatch Donald Hackett's elite 8,000-strong division in ample time to entrench that unit where it could best support Fort Fisher *and* protect the city of Wilmington itself: on the dominating elevation of Sugar Loaf Ridge, five miles north of the Bastion.

Despite Whiting's liquored-up hysterics and Lamb's more gentlemanly but no less aggravating cries of alarm, Bragg believed that, relative to the crises elsewhere in the South, things were reasonably under control here in the Cape Fear District. Well, things *would be,* after Bragg consolidated his power and laid down the law to these two malcontents. His job was to bring coolness and clarity, method and orderliness, the reassuring solidity of overriding authority, into a scene where passion and panic were balanced on the edge of the sword.

As Bragg saw the situation, his first task was to convey simple reassurance. To that end, he paid perfunctory courtesy calls on Whiting at Smithville, and afterward, with gritted teeth, had endured, under the guidance of Colonel Lamb, a brief tour of the dank confines of Fort Fisher. The young colonel had showed off his various engineering feats like a child shows off his Christmas presents to a visiting uncle. At the end of those meetings, Bragg handed each man a written order summoning him to a formal strategy conference at his headquarters in the DeRossett House, on the corner of Second and Dock streets. The meeting was an obligatory exercise in correct procedure, a necessary formality of military courtesy, but merciful God!—the toll it had taken on him!

All the roiling symptoms that turned a portion of Bragg's every day into an internal crucifixion, had started doing their worst upon his mind and flesh within minutes of the frigid exchange of salutes which opened their discussion.

"I understand your need for more men, Colonel Lamb, and will endorse your requests, and lend my authority to round up whatever odds and ends of troops there may be in this region, and order them to join the men already inside the walls."

The cynicism and disdain on Lamb's handsome, Roman-coin face caused the first vipers to wriggle in Bragg's digestive tract. Tiny shoots of pain and gnawing muscular cramps—bound to get worse, and fast!—began to distract him, making his manner even stiffer and colder than usual.

"No, General Whiting, I do not intend to usurp your tactical authority in the least, Rest assured I will monitor every development which might affect the situation on the Cape Fear. You will find me sensitive to your concerns, and fully cognizant of the strategic importance of this district. Please accept the realities of the situation, sir: an urgent request from me will move President Davis, and through him, General Lee, to send significant veteran reinforcements to Confederate Point much more expeditiously than additional importuning, and if I may say so, intemperate, telegrams from you."

Whiting's pride was so wounded that the tightly wound little general made no effort to hide the contempt in his gaze, or the sarcasm in his voice. Why did these men not take Bragg at his word? (*Oh, Christ, not again, not now!*) The inflammation in Bragg's stomach triggered a scalding geyser of acidic fluction, razor-cuts of gorge that seared his gullet and made his breath go shallow and gaspy, so that his tone of voice changed pitch in midsyllable from a commanding baritone to a high-pitched squeak, and then his vocal cords failed altogether, while he tried, through spasms of coughing and shrill intakes of air, to forestall and beat down a growing urge to lean over a wastebasket and discharge a sour-vinegar dribble of puke. The effort it took to suppress this, true to form, caused the formation of angry gastric bubbles in the pitted, unstable caverns of his gut. Lacking any other means of escape, the gas bubbles crawled further down the digestive tract—Bragg felt as though someone were drawing through his lower intestines a line of scratchy manila rope, with knots as big as fists tied every couple of inches along its length. Gamely, he continued to speak.

"According to my preliminary study, there are several companies, presently detached on nonessential duties, which can be transferred to augment the garrison, and some companies of new conscripts in training near Goldsboro and Raleigh, which can be brought down as well—naturally it would be best if they completed another few week's instruction—but I think I can safely promise another 300 men for you by the end of November."

Now the knotted rope was wedged hard against Bragg's anus, building up a pressure so intolerable that he simply *must* allow some of the poisonous vapors to siphon out. This was a common and particularly vexatious symptom, and Bragg had learned to master the art of silent, incremental gas-release. It was very demanding to exercise this fine degree of sphincter control and still carry on a conversation, but one lapse of concentration and instead of an inaudible hiss, Bragg would unleash a raucous *Brrr-aaa-ppp!* Another problem was that even the quietest, most discreet expulsions brought into the room a whiff of sulfurous corruption, a villainous old-man-stuffed-with-cabbage kind of fart that built up in the atmosphere, puff by puff, until a man with the worst head cold in Iceland could not possibly ignore it. Could there be anyone more pathetic than a man who cannot stand the smell of his *own* wind?

"General Bragg, you look peaked, sir. Can I fetch you some water?"

"Thank you, Lamb, but it's merely a bit of dyspepsia and will soon pass."

(Well, *something* was going to pass, because the pressure was building faster than Bragg's ability to safety-valve it silently.) In acute distress now, he tugged on the bell rope hidden under his desk, which rang a soft chime in the anteroom, summoning his new aide-de-camp, a Georgia brigadier named Alfred Colquitt. Almost instantly, the office door burst open.

"General? Forgive the intrusion, but there's an 'urgent' telegram for you from Richmond. President Davis wants an immediate reply."

"Damn the inconvenience! Your pardon, gentlemen, but I will be back as soon as I've carried out my master's wishes."

Bragg all but dashed through the door, down the hall, and into the backyard. Deep inside a winter-brown grove of boxwoods, already verified as being a safe place, invisible and inaudible to anyone on the street, Bragg let 'er rip, a long, serpentine blast reminiscent of a phlegm-clogged trombone. If the nearby foliage were not already wilted by the season, it would surely have shriveled and died on-the-spot from the toxic cloud issuing from the seat of his pants. Bragg waited until equilibrium returned to his colon, brushed off his uniform, and reentered his office.

"Well, that didn't take long, anyhow. Where were we? Oh, yes: could each of you give me your appreciation of the tactics the enemy might use, other than a long, conventional siege, which would be too hazardous for them this far away from a major source of supply? Could they, for instance, pass a few companies through the inlet and support the naval attack by sniping at the fort from the rear?"

First Lamb, then Whiting, launched into pedantic, exhaustive, well-thought-out lectures on topography, tides, sandbars, fields of fire, electrical mines, and—over and over, the same tiresome song of woe!—their pressing need for infantry reinforcements. Bragg had read most of this before, in these two officers' unending stream of written reports and appreciations. He frankly did not want to hear one more word from Chase Whiting, and Lamb's focus was too narrowly bound by the walls of his precious fort and the confined acreage of Confederate Point. Bragg was merely going through the motions, as President Davis had instructed him to, of showing "courteous consideration" for the feelings of both men. Abstractly, Bragg understood why these men were so overwrought: Fort Fisher had been their obsession for so long that neither was capable of seeing beyond its ramparts. He expected them to react, when the Yankee fleet finally *did* appear, with something close to dementia. So did President Davis, who had sent Bragg here so that Bragg might exert a cool, objective, steadying influence. Bragg knew he was not an "inspired" commander, but sometimes what was needed was a dispassionate and steady hand, acting from a dignified distance, to counterbalance the passions of those on the firing line.

He nodded at the right places, pretended to take notes, rubbed his porcupine-quill beard thoughtfully, but his mind was drifting and he hoped this conference could be terminated before . . .

Oh, God—too late!

Today, the headache had decided to manifest itself earlier than its usual two o'clock starting time. Changes of environment, the necessity of spending too much time in confined spaces with disagreeable people, something unwisely eaten or badly cooked on last night's menu—these were the things that triggered the headache early, or made it reach peak intensity more rapidly. It had been Bragg's daily and thoroughly evil companion since late 1862, and a sporadic affliction as far back as his West Point days. Its cumulative effect on his mood, temper, and clarity of thought could become every bit as debilitating as a bullet wound. It was as though a Yankee saboteur had sneaked into his tent one night, more than two years ago, and dropped through the portals of his hearing some kind of malevolent, carnivorous earwig, a tiny thing composed of needle-teeth, a long tunnel of gullet, and an insatiable appetite not just for the meat of his brain, but for the most delicate and sensitive pain-conducting nerve fibers. Every day, so close to two o'clock he could set his watch by it, this hideous parasite awakened, ravenous with hunger, and took its first tiny canapé-bite on one of Braxton Bragg's nerve-conduits. He knew the cursed thing was awake when he felt that first tiny spark of discomfort. *Hello, Braxton! Did that get your attention? Good! I'm going to tuck in, now, so brace yourself!* And from that tiny first nip, the headache began to feast on his most delicate and sensitive channels of sensation, gradually taking bigger and bigger bites. There was an unvarying and sadistic pattern to the affliction: the pain grew in a slow crescendo, expanding gradually until it filled one-third of his brain-mass with remorseless drumbeats of agony, until it interrupted Nature's fine-spun web connecting sensation to cogitation and its victim became incapable of cogent reasoning, unable to carry on the most mundane of conversations; until Bragg was ready to smash his head against a wall or beat on his own skull with a hammer; until his vision became jangled and electric—lightning storms exploding through his optic nerves, so that he could not bear to look at anything brighter than a candle flame; until the words of someone across the table punished his eardrums like the blast of a hundred-pounder firing inches from his head. He would scream and writhe like a madman *if that would make the gnawing worm stop its cruel feast,* but only one thing would do that, and Bragg could not start chugging from a bottle of laudanum in front of the two most important officers he had been sent here to command. No use ringing for Colquitt again—not even his aide-de-camp could be allowed to witness the ritual of medication that was Bragg's only salvation. If Jeff Davis could so readily sack Chase Whiting for even the rumor of drunkenness-on-duty, how deeply would it damage his faith in Bragg to get eyewitness reports of the amount of narcotic distillate Bragg must consume in order to find blessed relief, regain composure, and restore his mental equilibrium? Davis, whose personal habits were so abstemious that no one had seen him consume more than two glasses of wine at the longest of state banquets, would be shocked. But, goddamn the man's stiff-necked pride and deluded obstinacy, it was not *Davis* who must suffer these daily excruciations!

Thankfully, in this case, neither Whiting nor Lamb wanted to spend any more time in Bragg's company than absolutely necessary and they ran out of rhetorical points after only sixty-five interminable minutes. Bragg escorted them to the door, mouthed some reassuring platitudes about how much faith he had in them and how certain he was that their mighty fortress could withstand whatever the U.S. Navy threw at it, then left it to Colquitt to show them out, escort them back to their launch, and block anyone else from access to Bragg for the next two hours.

When solitude enfolded him once more, Bragg retired for his regular "afternoon nap," locked his bedroom door, and savagely pulled the cork from the first bottle of laudanum. He might have been in time to beat down the headache before he literally went blind, and thought this might be a three-bottle day instead of one of those dreaded four or five-bottle episodes, which did leave him pain-free and tranquil, but also in a state of dazed euphoric inertia. After two bottles, the pain began to retreat, and relief washed through his raw, rat-chewed nerve endings, bathing his tormented brain like the tears of Jesus. He was safe once more, encased in a cocoon of sweet buzzing tranquility. He felt time dilate exquisitely, and self-confidence return. In this particular state, his personality altered: he became placid, utterly sure of his ability to handle any shock or surprise, immune from panic, unbeatable, capable of the most crystalline analyses and the most subtle solutions to any problem that might jump out from behind a closed door and try to take him unawares. He was calm; there was plenty of time for taking any needed action; his scarred and pummeled ego became whole again. He knew now that he was wiser and more perceptive of the larger strategic picture than any of those *little men* who pecked on him like scavenger crows. When the full story of this war came to be written, the spiteful accusations of his critics would be seen for the petty jealousies they really were. Yes, the men of posterity would say, it was Bragg, even more than the sainted Lee, who was the granite heart of the Confederacy!

Bragg was determined to lay the foundation for history's reassessment by the way he performed his duties here in Wilmington: He would be as steely in resolve as a great cannon; he would be as sagacious in his strategies and as canny in his tactical dispositions as Caesar or Napoleon, and infinitely less wasteful of his soldiers' blood than that aristocratic iceberg of Virginian arrogance, that overrated butcher, Bobby Lee!

When Bragg finished savoring the last bitter drop of the third bottle, he was an island of dispassionate resolve amidst the chaos and confusions and opaque sudden fogs of battle. He knew, now that the pain was banished and his body vibrated within the glow of well-being that replaced his agonized confusion, that it was destiny, even more than Jefferson Davis, that had brought him here to defend the South's last port. On this sandy ground would he redeem his honor as a soldier and a man, and win on the dunes of the Cape Fear, the last great Rebel victory, even while the aristocratic Lee presided over the penultimate defeat that would surely be the outcome of his desperate stand at Petersburg. Lee would be stretched until his line finally broke, but when the enemy marched at long last through the muddy shell-pocked streets of Richmond, Bragg would still be defiant, a veritable granite cliff, the savior of Wilmington, the redeemer of mighty Fort Fisher. He would not even have to be present when the enemy went all-out against those ramparts of sand—if he could maintain this utterly lucid mood, he need only stretch out his arm and bid the shell-lashed waters: "Be still!"

"Breathtaking, isn't it, General Hawkins?"

Rush Hawkins was, in fact, so mesmerized by the sight that he jumped in surprise when Admiral David Porter clapped a big, meaty hand on his shoulder. Hawkins and Butler had arrived in Hampton Roads very late on the evening of December 10— or very early on the morning of December 11; Hawkins had no idea which, as both he and Ben Butler were roaring drunk by the time they climbed into Admiral Porter's coach for the clattery half-hour ride from Butler's headquarters to the admiral's flagship, where Hawkins had passed out minutes after the officer of the deck had showed him to the visitors' stateroom. In the captain's cabin next door, however, Butler and Porter must have ushered in the sunrise together, for when Hawkins woke up briefly, at 3:35 A.M. to visit the chamber pot, he heard the two men guffawing and proposing thick-tongued toasts. This struck Hawkins as passing strange, because Porter ostensibly despised Butler and on the two previous occasions Hawkins had seen them together, their remarks to one another had been frigidly correct, nothing more.

Now, in the promise of morning light, Hawkins quickly recovered his composure and came to attention, observing as he did so that Porter looked remarkably fresh and was obviously in a high good humor.

"I came topside to get some air and finish this excellent coffee your steward brought me, but when I actually *saw* this spectacle, I was so nailed in place with awe that the coffee grew cold before I remembered I was holding it. Admiral, this surely must be . . ."

". . . the greatest fleet ever assembled under the American flag," Porter finished. "I must admit, I sometimes have to pinch myself to verify that it's real and remind myself that I command it. Sixty-four warships, mounting six hundred and twenty-four guns! And on the far side of the bay, forty-seven transports and auxiliary vessels. Nothing like it since the Spanish Armada. And you, sir, get to play a role in this drama that should not only be the most exciting of your military career, but may very well earn you a niche in the pantheon of great heroes!"

Hawkins felt his stomach flip over. He had no idea what Porter was talking about, and was not at all sure he liked the implications of "exciting" when conjoined with "pantheon of heroes." The words conjured an image of dignified but very silent sarcophagi, embossed with Homeric motifs and Latin phrases, each tomb containing one dead "hero" who had undoubtedly *been* "excited" in the final moments of his mortal existence. Hoping for enlightenment, Hawkins nudged forward a conversational pawn:

"Ah, yes. That must have been what you and General Butler were celebrating, around three or four in the morning . . ."

"Indeed, indeed! That, and the prospect of a swift, history-changing victory. I confess, Hawkins, that until I heard Ben's proposals and ideas last night, I shared the general low opinion of him, but when he got wound-up and started talking about the very latest military inventions and theories, I suddenly beheld a brilliant mind unfortunately imprisoned within a gross vestment of flesh. Why, that man knows more about futuristic military theories and machines than any Annapolis scholar I've ever met. Using hot-air balloon ships, driven by screw propellers, to drop giant shells and flammable liquids on the enemy's factories and shipyards—it's brilliant! And because this war has swept away the old mossbacks and their aversion to new ideas, men who can harness steam and electricity to machines capable of devastating this nation's enemies, well, their day is coming! Mark my words, we shall hear much more about our mutual friend and his creative notions."

"Did he, um, give you an idea of how far along *my* project is? We were too busy entertaining some ladies last night for me to think of inquiring."

Porter cocked his head in puzzlement. "He must have been enjoying himself, if he forgot to bring you up-to-date . . . Well, the coastal survey scientists have confirmed that the shoals and currents off that portion of Fort Fisher are suitable for you to approach within a hundred-fifty feet, and the engineers have worked out a truly ingenious fuse which should detonate all three hundred tons of powder instantaneously. I was going to station my ships ten miles offshore that night, but now I'm thinking it might be prudent to move them twice that distance—the shock wave could rupture some boilers if we don't err on the side of caution. But you should have one hell of a view of the fireworks! Well, I must be off to make sure all the charts are laid out before the big strategy conference, so I'll see you and Butler in about, oh, forty-five minutes?"

With those cryptic remarks and a jaunty wave, Porter slid down the brass-railed stairs to the *Malvern*'s main deck and was piped over the side into his personal launch.

Instantaneous fuse? One hundred-fifty feet from Fort Fisher?? Shock waves and bursting boilers??? *THREE HUNDRED TONS OF GUNPOWDER????* None of these cryptic but dangerous-sounding phrases meant a thing to Rush Hawkins, but when he mixed them together with "pantheon of heroes," the chilling but logical implication was that Ben Butler had "volunteered" him to demolish some critical part of Fort Fisher, a mission which sounded only slightly less dangerous than poking your head into the mouth of a 32-pounder at the same time someone was yanking the firing cord. Hawkins went hurriedly to Butler's cabin and pounded on the door. No answer! A seaman nearby looked up from his deck-mopping assignment and said: "Gen'ral Butler's already gone ta shore, sir. 'Bout an hour ago. Slid a note under your cabin door a-fore he left, though."

Note? NOTE?? Hawkins had seen no note! He flung open the door to his own cabin and, sure enough, there was a folded message lodged against the washstand, evidently whisked there by the draft when he exited to drink his coffee:

> *Top o' the morning, Hawkins! Big thrills coming our way! There will be a steamer coming around at eleven o'clock, collecting skippers for the big powwow—suggest you hitch a ride. I wouldn't want you to miss the surprise I have planned!*
> *Cordially, & c.,*
> *B. F. Butler P.S.: Didn't you think the blonde had abominable taste in perfumes?*

Back in mid-October, when Butler confirmed the rumors that Admiral Porter had finally wheedled enough soldiers from Grant to mount the Fort Fisher attack, Hawkins had naively commented: "Whatever took them so long to make up their minds about it? Even a numbskull like Grant can see the benefit of shutting down Wilmington. If we had done it two years ago, the war might be over by now."

To which Butler had given the rather acerbic reply: "Two years ago you and I were making huge amounts of money out of the fact that Wilmington was *not* shut down. And so were a number of highly placed gentlemen who made a point of downplaying that city's strategic importance and exaggerating the strength of Fort Fisher, which really is nowhere near as impregnable as the enemy deludes himself into believing. Once our profits started shrinking, our anonymous colleagues stopped trying to divert attention from Wilmington, and after Farragut captured Mobile Bay, there was no point in postponing the inevitable. Still, the troops assigned to take Fort Fisher will be drawn from my command, so I might still mine the gold of glory from those sandy beaches, and so might you, my gallant fellow, if I can sell one of my schemes to Admiral Porter . . . and you have the kidney for making it successful."

Now, apparently, Hawkins was about to find out what lay behind that cryptic exchange, and Butler's note made it clear that the general was tickled at the thought of surprising his protégé with a "choice" new assignment. (*THREE HUNDRED TONS OF GUNPOWDER???*).

So many ship captains and infantry commanders were involved in the operation that the only suitable place to reveal the plans to all of them at once, was an old lecture hall near the parade ground of Fortress Monroe, a twenty-minute boat ride from the *Malvern*. On a table near the lectern, several of Porter's aides were piling up stacks of secret orders, still warm from the printing press, which he intended to pass out at the end of his presentation, but he began by moving a bright yellow pointer around a very large sketch-map of Confederate Point and its defenses. The fort was a bull's eye, and Porter's ships were the semicircles surrounding it. With the relish of a man who revels in detail, the admiral described his plan and the ships he had assigned to various aspects of the attack.

Porter intended to form his armada in three concentric lines, each column staggered in echelon so all of the ships could fire on Fort Fisher without getting in each other's way. The best-protected ships in his fleet were five of the newest class of monitors, two of them mounting a pair of turrets, the others a single turret amidships; these he planned to station closest to the target, only 500-600 yards from the North-East Bastion. They were shallow-draft, and so low in the water that the Rebel gunners could only aim at their turrets, which were very small targets even at that range. More to the point, the monitors carried the heaviest guns in the U.S. Navy: 11-inch Dahlgrens and 15-inch Rodmans, capable of firing 178-pound shells or 260-pound solid bolts. Those projectiles would be his "battering rams." Next to the main gate, facing the riverside road to Wilmington, the North-East Bastion was the most critical feature in the whole Rebel fortress, and the monitors' giant guns would dismantle it the same way the Rebels had constructed it: one chunk of sand at a time.

Firing *over* the monitors, from a range of 680-700 yards, would be Line One, comprising the biggest and most powerfully armed cruisers and steam frigates, typified by the flagship of that line, the *Colorado,* a majestic vessel displacing 3500 tons and carrying 52 big guns. Line Two, also firing from a northeasterly arc, was stationed at a range of 1,000 yards, and contained the heavier types of oceangoing gunboats; Line Three, positioned 1300-1500 yards out, comprised the slower, older warships—mounting fewer guns but potent ones: 100-pounder Parrotts, 120-pounder Blakelys, 10-inch Dahlgrens, and dozens of 12- and 15-inch mortars, whose high-arcing shells were expected to wreak havoc among the wooden buildings and open-faced shelters scattered around the fort's interior. Each line was assigned priority targets: Line Two, for example, would systematically concentrate on individual Land Face batteries and on chopping down the palisade of sharpened logs that made up the defenders' first line of obstacles. As for the ships in Line Three, they would sharpshoot individual Sea-Face batteries, massing fire against one until it was silenced, then moving on to the next, while using their older, less accurate weapons to silence the dangerous Rebel guns atop the Mound Battery.

"I plan to bombard the fort heavily and continuously for an entire day before the arrival of General Butler's transports; weather permitting, the complete landing force should be unloaded during a single night. A dawn, the fleet will reopen its bombardment until such time as the fort's guns have all been silenced, or significant breeches ripped through the walls. When the infantry attack begins, the ships will shift their fire so as to prevent the enemy from maneuvering troops at will against the most threatened sectors. General Weitzel, please take your turn at the map, now, and show everyone the planned disposition of your infantry."

Major General Godfrey Weitzel was one of those stolid, get-on-with-the-job, officers that was not likely to achieve real excellence as long as he was stuck in Butler's Army of the James, but who seemed perfectly content not to have an occasion to rise to. On Confederate Point, there was no room for brilliant maneuvers, and if the fort were sufficiently pulverized by Porter's six hundred cannon, not real need for a desperate do-or-die charge—a steady, unflinching walk would do the job, and Weitzel was capable of sustaining that kind of advance until someone of higher rank told him to stop. To prevent the Rebels from relieving the fort by means of a counterattack from the direction of Wilmington, Butler had detached two brigades from his all-Negro Third Division. Their job would be to construct a line of earthworks across the whole peninsula, between the sea and the Cape Fear River and thereby block any move Bragg might order against the Union beachhead. Provided most of the fort's Land Face guns were knocked out by the fleet, the infantry operations would not last long and were not expected to involve sustained, heavy combat. Weitzel was not an inspiring orator and the plan was so simple as to require no detailed explanation, so he covered the basics in ten minutes and sat down. The assembled officers folded their notebooks and stirred restlessly, waiting for either Porter or Butler to dismiss them. Those two gentlemen exchanged sly glances for a moment—just enjoying themselves by teasing their underlings—and then Butler went back to the speaker's lectern and made a dramatic gesture for attention.

"Before you all return to your respective commands, Admiral Porter and I want to mention one more thing: none of the actions we have just outlined may turn out to be necessary at all!" *That* caught everyone's attention, as it was intended to, and caused Rush Hawkins to lean forward with painfully tense shoulders. Butler smiled at him, just a little too much like a cat contemplating a caged bird.

"Approximately two months ago, I happened to be glancing through some recent issues of the *London Times* that had been found aboard a captured blockade-runner, and I was struck by that newspaper's account of a dramatic and tragic accident that occurred last July on the river Thames. Due to some cause never determined by the authorities, two Royal Navy barges loaded with vast quantities of gunpowder caught fire and exploded in a single combined blast. The shock wave generated so much kinetic energy that it completely flattened every waterfront building within a hundred yards of the river, severely damaged structures several blocks farther away, and killed more than two hundred people. The London journalists coined a new term for this kind of destruction: the *shock wave effect!*

"Now when I contemplated the destruction wrought by those gunpowder barges on large, stoutly constructed urban buildings, many of them made of brick and iron girders, I indulged in the idle fantasy of what might happen if an explosion of similar magnitude were to be set off, intentionally, near to the walls of a fortress built entirely of . . . SAND! Those of you who live near the sea, or who have enjoyed holidays at the shore, are quite familiar with the way a perfectly ordinary brisk wind can eroded a sand dune, grain by grain. Imagine, if you will, the effect upon Fort Fisher's walls of the kind of shock wave described in that London newspaper. Take into account, as well, the weight of the numerous giant cannon emplaced on the very top of those sand ramparts. While Admiral Porter's ships can, and if necessary will, batter down the North-East Bastion by the cumulative effect of hundreds of hits, what advantage would be gained if we could simply obliterate the whole position in a flash, sweeping it away like a great tidal wave? With one violent blow, we not only create a yawning breach through which General Weitzel's infantry could pour into the fort, but we also stun the majority of its defenders into such a stupor that those who are not killed outright, will not be able to defend themselves.

"I put this idea to Admiral Porter, and his reaction was thoroughly sensible: *What have we got to lose by trying it*? All we need is 300 tons of powder bags, packed tightly inside the hull of an old vessel that's already fit for nothing but the scrap yard, and a reliable clockwork fuse that will insure the simultaneous detonation of the entire charge, *and* someone brave enough and resourceful enough to steer that floating bomb as close to the northeast corner of the fort as it will go.

"With very little effort, we found the ideal ship—the old revenue cutter *Tuscarora,* which formed part of the first blockade squadron sent to the Cape Fear region back in the spring of '61, and which was quietly rotting away in a creek near the repair docks at Beaufort. The gunpowder we obtained through, um, the usual channels. An ingenious clockwork fuse was designed, in great secrecy, by the ordnance laboratory of the Brooklyn Navy Yard, and successfully tested several times, though naturally on smaller boats and with much smaller loads of powder. And last but far from least, we found an officer of proven resourcefulness and courage who was willing to volunteer to be towed to the edge of the surf-line and then to run the bomb ship into the shallows as near to the foundations of the Confederate bastion as possible, activate the fuse, and be winched back to safety aboard the towing vessel. I already had a man with those requisite qualities on my very staff, and I am proud to introduce him to you now. If he succeeds in this hazardous enterprise, he will blast a gateway for you into the heart of the Rebel stronghold, and obviate the need for a long and perhaps costly battle between Admiral Porter's ships and the Confederate batteries, allowing us to win a great victory without also having to fight a great battle. Gentlemen, I give you my good friend and valiant comrade, Brigadier-General Rush C. Hawkins!

"General Hawkins? Ah, there you are! Don't be modest, man, stand up and take a well-deserved bow!"

THREE HUNDRED TONS OF GUNPOWDER???

BUTLER, YOU FAT, SADISTIC, CORRUPT INGRATE!

More than one incredulous officer correctly interpreted the rapid flush of color on Hawkins' face and understood that it was not caused by the natural reticence of a would-be hero.

Part Three

December 12, 1864—January 15, 1865

There's a Fizzle . . .

THE ORIGIN OF the mysterious explosion was finally confirmed by accounts in the Northern press; the main response among Confederates everywhere was envy for an opponent who could afford to waste so much gunpowder. Perhaps the last word on the powder boat fiasco came from a Confederate deserter who was questioned by Admiral Porter himself a few days after the incident. Be perfectly frank, Porter encouraged the fellow, and tell me what effect the explosion really had on the garrison. With a straight face, the Rebel replied, "Why Admiral, it was truly dreadful —it woke us all up!"

—William R. Trotter. *Ironclads and Colombiads. John F. Blair, 1991*

From the moment he first set eyes on the isolated, demoralized handful of batteries guarding New Inlet—on July 5, 1862—the Young Soldier of the Lord had *known*: his engagement with Destiny would take place on these barren, windswept sands; had *known* that one of the war's most fateful battles would eventually be waged here; had *known* that when it came, the contention would be mighty and desperately fought; had *seen,* with the searing clarity of an Old Testament prophet's vision, the phantom shape of the great fortress he must construct here if that battle were to be won for the Confederacy. Like a smoky *Arabian Nights* mirage of a caliph's gilded palace, conjured by djinns, William Lamb saw a grainy daguerreotype image of Fort Fisher as it *would* be, after he linked the pathetic isolated scribbles of earthworks into a coherent functional shape and then raised and broadened the modest preliminary walls into massive ramparts, punctuated by the black exclamation points of powerful cannon.

And now, in the waning days of the Confederacy's grimmest year, Lamb's vision was vindicated. All the elements needed to decide the issue *were* converging on Confederate Point, and history would pivot on Fort

Fisher. William Lamb knew he had done everything one mere colonel could do, and that Chase Whiting had supported him at every turn, scrutinizing Lamb's ideas, and finding them not only sound, but sometimes inspired. By dint of unceasing petition, argument, and patient waiting upon the pleasure of Richmond, Lamb had found the big guns and refined each massive gun-traverse, each bombproof shelter, laboriously sawed the palisade logs and excavated the ditch that girded the Land Face from the high-tide line of the Atlantic to the marshy all-but-impassible bogs and watery defiles on the river's edge. More than two years of daily toil had reshaped a half-million cubic tons of sand and sod. Incessant drills and skirmishes with the blockade fleet had turned his amateur gun crews into crack professionals. But despite two years of closely reasoned argument and outright servile begging, he had not received so much as a single company of infantry reinforcements—only one tiny band of forgotten men comprising Samuel Parker and the crew of the sunken *Hatteras.*

Not one company of infantry! Not one new artillery piece! Not even one additional boxcar of ammunition. Lambs entire stock of ammunition, for all calibers and makes of cannon, totaled a mere 3,681 rounds!

Instead of these critical items, Richmond had sent, for unfathomable reasons, Braxton Bragg. And from the moment Lamb sets eyes on that notoriously unpopular general he understood why nobody, except the president of the Confederacy, liked or trusted the man. Bragg moved and spoke and, most alarming of all, appeared to *think* like a man who lived within a separate sphere of time, wafting like a dry gray dandelion-puff on the shifting winds of mood; sunk in morose brooding one moment, frantic with unfocused scattergun energy the next, always slightly out of synch with the collective reality of everyone around him, dwelling, part of the time, in a private, inscrutable, continuum where strange geometries and even stranger chronologies held sway.

While the whole Yankee world could see the great armada assembling in Hampton Roads and deduce instantly what its destination and purpose must be, only in the second week of December did small increments of trained manpower begin to trickle into Fort Fisher—and these were sent by Governor Zeb Vance, not by General Bragg: small companies of the North Carolina Junior Reserves (sketchily trained teenagers who sometimes began to tremble and on occasion wet their trousers at their first sight of Lamb's big guns, which conveyed, by their brute size and aura of latent power, that *this was serious business).* Pathetic as they were, these youths were the best and only help Governor Vance could send, for even his third-rate Home Guard companies were all committed now, tied down guarding bridges and depots and preserving at least symbolic pockets of law and order in the mountain towns, where sedition, anarchy, and undisguised banditry now seethed unchecked in every county.

Both Whiting and Lamb sent letters and telegrams to General Bragg, reminding him of his promise to beg Lee for the loan of Hackett's division, should Fort Fisher be threatened by imminent attack. With maddening equanimity, Bragg had wired back: *Am convinced reports of both the size and readiness of Porter's fleet are greatly exaggerated. If compelling evidence alters this impression, I will ask Lee for Hackett's div. But believe such a request both premature and an imposition on Lee, who will be highly irritated if this is a false alarm. Situation will no doubt be clearer in another week or two. Meanwhile suggest you make best use of reinforcements already sent to you.*

When Lamb read this, he was flabbergasted. Bragg had sent *no* reinforcements at all. That he seemed to believe he *had,* was inexplicable by any standard.

All the elements of a climactic showdown *were* converging on Fort Fisher. And one of those elements was Braxton Bragg—Lamb found *that* more alarming than the rumored size of the enemy's fleet.

December 12: Admiral Porter's armada departs from Hampton Roads, a hard-to-miss event which draws the attention of congeries of Confederate spies who have had plenty of time to make accurate counts of each type of vessel in the fleet, and to extrapolate from the capacity and number of Porter's transports some very accurate estimates of the infantry committed to the operation: approximately twelve times as many men as Fort Fisher's defenders, even counting their dogs. These reports are expeditiously forwarded to General Lee's headquarters behind the siege lines at Petersburg, where Lee weighs them in one hand against his reluctance to lose eight thousand veteran soldiers, especially when General Bragg sends him solemn assurances that Fort Fisher has already been "substantially reinforced." Furthermore, Bragg believes Porter might actually be setting off to mount a land attack on stubborn Charleston, and the accepted notion that Porter's objective is Wilmington may well be a clever ruse. Lee draws the inference that Bragg must have his own secret agents deep inside Porter's camp. Otherwise, why would Bragg put so much credence in the Charleston hypothesis? Charleston may not literally have been conquered yet, but it has been shut down utterly as a blockade-runners' port and even a bungler like Butler would see the pointlessness of fighting a costly battle for possession of a city that had already been, militarily speaking, neutered. But the very irrationality of Bragg's suggestion makes Lee hesitate—it could only be based on some private sources of information Bragg considers more reliable than some of Richmond's most experienced spies.

But Bragg has no private network of spies. The whole notion of Charleston came flashing into his head during the preternatural clarity bestowed by four bottles of laudanum and at the time Bragg penned his confidential report to Lee, he had thought it such a fascinating and creative interpretation of the facts that he would impress Lee just by offering it as a hypothesis. Then when he retracted it two days later (*My sources now confirm that Charleston was the diversion and the fleet is, in fact, heading for the waters off the Cape Fear . . .*) Lee would think: Bragg has finally learned to be decisive and admit his own misjudgments—perhaps President Davis was correct in sending him to Wilmington. Hackett's division could still be sent in time, but meanwhile Bragg's inspired bit of chicanery will have raised Lee's estimation of him. No harm done; actually a rather clever manipulation!

Except that Bragg forgets to send the corrective telegram until *four* days later, not two, and when Hackett's division finally boards a series of hastily assembled trains, it encounters so many stretches of broken track and so many defective locomotives, that in raging frustration, Hackett decides it will be faster to *march* from Goldsboro to Wilmington than to ride. Actually, it works out to be about the same, except that his regiments get strung out over a distance of twenty miles, suffer great discomfort from freezing temperatures and a freak snowstorm, and thus arrive in Wilmington fragmented, hungry, chilled to the marrow, and dog-tired.

December 15: Butler's transports arrive in the waters off Confederate Point and anchor, just over the horizon, about fifteen miles offshore and northeast of Fort Fisher. Everyone aboard is greatly cheered by a sudden and most unseasonable moderation of the weather. Men crowd the decks to escape the funk and cramped conditions below, basking in the sun, thanking God for such calm seas, fervently hoping this balmy interlude lasts until they land on hostile shores.

December 18: It does last, for exactly three days, during two of which, Porter's warships anchor placidly a few miles south of the transports. Weitzel's infantry grow restless. What are Porter and Butler waiting for? Such calm seas promise easy landings —the troops might even hit the beach with dry feet! What's the hold up? What are they waiting for?

"They" are waiting for the outcome of Butler's daring "powder boat" scheme, which cannot of course be known until the *Tuscarora* shows up and self-destructs at the foot of the Northeast Bastion. But the *Tuscarora,* as Rush Hawkins quickly learned when he reached Beaufort to take command of her on December 16, is so beat up from years on the blockade line that she cannot be loaded with 300 tons of gunpowder until repair crews finish caulking the warped, leaky, and barnacle-scarred hull.

Delay and vexation are compounded by the fact that Butler had received $16,000 from the army for the purchase of his gunpowder, but was finally able to convince a former associate in the bogus blockade-runner scheme to sell him 300 tons for $9,500, enabling Butler to pocket a tidy personal profit after first doctoring the bill of sale to reflect the authorized price. The powder seller had the last laugh, however (as he thought, on Butler, but rather more acutely on Rush Hawkins), by not only shorting the quantity (250 tons) but also by foisting off on Butler 250-pound canvas sacks that had been rejected by the army as being too shoddily made to preserve the powder in prime condition. Some bags had slow leaks and were only partly full by the time they reached Beaufort, others split open while being winched into the *Tuscarora*'s cargo hold. Using his own funds, Hawkins hired a gang of local urchins to scrape up the spilled powder and some impoverished widows to restitch the bags after the urchins fluffed them out again with buckets of soiled powder, intermixed with dockside grit, coal dust, and a wide variety of tiny contaminants. Examining a few of these reconstructed sacksful, Hawkins thinks that *most* of them ought to explode, but others are more apt to smolder like cheap pipe tobacco.

Equal vexation was visited upon the scientist who had devised the elaborate clockwork fuse needed to ensure uniform, simultaneous detonation. The apparatus, which resembled an octopus with 30-foot arms and a gigantic alarm clock mechanism in place of its bulbous head, had been *precisely* calibrated to work with 300 tons' worth of tightly packed sacks, not 250 tons of sacks indifferently piled on top of each other; no matter what the dockworkers did, the cargo load always ended up lopsided and unbalanced, which virtually guaranteed that either the mechanism would not work at all, or it would detonate the powder bags unevenly and in ragged sequence, dissipating at least half of the calculated blast and shock wave. By this time, Hawkins no longer cares whether the bags blow en masse or not, just as long as they blow up in some fashion or other. The blame for failure would land on his head instead of the swindler who sold Butler the inferior powder to start with. The fuse-inventing scientist, likewise, could have cared less about Ben Butler's opinion of his skills: "I thought the whole idea was harebrained from the start. I have a full professorship waiting for me at Harvard when the war's over, and Ben Butler's influence on that institution is as insignificant as his reputation is unsavory. Look, Hawkins, just take a ten-minute length of slow-match primer cord and jab one end of it into a powder bag, then string the rest out all over the place. Nothing is more guaranteed to set off gunpowder than a good old-fashioned fire, right? You could set a slow-burning trash fire as a last resort. So one way or the other, the damn ship will blow up more or less when it's supposed to, and you'll still come out a hero. If it destroys the fort, then Butler's a hero, too; if it doesn't, he's the same old buffoon he ever was, but as long as it *does* blow up, you'll come out smelling like a rose."

"What if the Rebels spot the boat and open fire?"

"Well, a minié ball won't normally set off a powder bag, but if they lob a shell or a hand grenade down the hatch, take consolation from the fact that you will be vaporized instantly. No better way to go! In any case, I've done all I can here, considering the way Butler got snookered and the variable condition of the powder. I do wish you luck, as you seem to be the innocent man-in-the-middle here, but I'm not going to accept your invitation to witness the fireworks from aboard the tugboat. After all, I could be completely wrong and the blast might generate a ten-foot tidal wave! Oh, one more thing: be a good fellow and countersign this contract right below General Butler's signature, so I can pick up my fee before catching the first steamer out of here."

By twilight on December 18 the urchins have finished scraping, and the widow-ladies are resewing the powder bags as fast as their cramped old fingers will allow, but Hawkins realizes it's going to take another twenty-four hours for the wary stevedores to finish arranging the layers of sacks on *top* of the spiderweb of fuse cords, so he dictates a message to Butler, explaining the delay purely in terms of unanticipated repairs to the *Tuscarora* and the fact that the cans of gray paint needed to disguise the ship as an errant blockade-runner have only just been uncrated. *Extremely unfortunate these delays, but entirely beyond my control. Expect to rendezvous with the fleet sometime in next 48 hours. Pray God the weather holds fair—* Using powers temporarily loaned to him by Butler, Hawkins appropriates a fast picket-launch to deliver the message to Butler's flagship, the USS *Malvern.*

December 19: Weitzel's men are growing restive and claustrophobic, and wondering why their illustrious commanders have neither started bombarding the fort nor commenced the amphibious landing. Being cooped up like sardines for three days of perfect small-boat weather is starting to wear down their patience. More and more, they are starting to realize just how irritating are the personal habits and smells of the men in the canvas hammocks nearest to their own. Restricted to Navy rations only, the monotonous diet of salted pork and hardtack is beginning to affect 8,000 digestive systems in various unpleasant ways. Admiral Porter enjoys a much better menu than his seamen, but is no less impatient to *get on with it*; he knows that when you commit thousands of men to a hazardous operation, you need to *commence operating* or they will rapidly start to lose that pumped-up "edge" that lends vital impetus to the opening hours of battle. At noon, his lookouts report there's a fast picket steamer making a bee line for the *Malvern.* Porter assumes that this signifies a dispatch for Butler, presumably informing him of the status of the *Tuscarora.* He waits a decent interval—gentlemen should give other gentlemen time to read their mail before making inquiries as to its contents—then detaches the *Malvern* and steams over to the gaggle of transports. He wants to question Butler through a megaphone rather than by the impersonal medium of a signal lamp. When the two flagships are within hailing distance, Porter bellows that he needs to speak with Butler in person.

Naturally, Butler takes his own sweet time donning his dress uniform and climbing topside; he has a pretty good idea what Porter's going to ask him about, and he wants to look as dignified as possible when he gives the Admiral answers the Admiral is not going to like.

The two commanders' megaphone-conversation is stuttery—the wind is picking up and some portions of sentences are carried away by gusts—but in essence goes something like:

PORTER: *Where the hell is your powder boat?*
BUTLER: *Unavoidably detained due to last-minute repairs!*
PORTER: *I've got 624 guns whose crews are anxious to open fire on Fort Fisher; how much longer must they wait?*
BUTLER: *Well, I've got 8,000 infantry who are asking the same question, and I've sent word to all the ships that if the powder boat succeeds, they can walk into the fort without getting shot at. When the matter was explained to them in those terms, they agreed to be patient a while longer. Suggest you tell your gun crews the same.*
PORTER: *How long, exactly, is "a while longer"?*
BUTLER: *General Hawkins expects to depart Beaufort tomorrow at dawn and explode the boat tomorrow night.*
PORTER: *This excellent weather will not last much longer, I guarantee it!*
BUTLER: *I suggest our chaplains combine forces and beseech the Almighty for another day of fair skies; can you think of anything further we might do?*
PORTER: *I know what* I *intend to do—I intend to commence a general bombardment on the morning of the Twentieth, regardless of powder boat.*
BUTLER: *Hawkins will be here if he says he will; his word is his bond!*
PORTER: *Not everyone who has served with him shares your estimate of his character; nevertheless, I will tell the fleet to be patient for another twenty-four hours.*

Being a literal-minded man, Porter *does* in fact order all the fleet's chaplains to pray for continued fair weather. But with that inscrutable sense of irony for which He is famous, God evidently decides that three days of springlike weather off the most notoriously stormy coastline in North America is enough of a lucky break, and by four o'clock in the afternoon, the wind is rising, white caps are tumbling, and the transports are starting to wallow in the sort of long, slow, premonitory swells that usually indicate an approaching gale.

After four o'clock the weather deteriorates alarmingly, and the rails of Butler's transports are crowded with soldiers who just keep vomiting, contractions uncountable, long after their stomachs are cleaned out. The sky had closed down like a coffin lid, an ominous, iron-colored ceiling that sucks up shadows and renders every man's skin, be he sick or healthy, the same putrid, washed-out shade of ashen, fungal green. All that remains of the beautiful clear morning skies is a sad thin strip of yellow on the eastern horizon. While there is still some visibility, Porter orders Butler to run for shelter at Beaufort, eighty miles to the north, replenish his supplies, and bring back with him the goddamned powder boat as soon as the weather moderates. The warships will ride out the gale at anchor where they are. Butler relays the news to all his ships, and there are a few feeble cheers at the sound of anchor chains rumbling upward. Fearing the worst from the moment he felt the wind pick up, Butler has wisely retained the picket launch from Beaufort, which he now dispatches back to that port with a message for Rush Hawkins: *Stay where you are! Expecting gale-force conditions by morning. I am bringing the transports in for replenishment and you can follow us back out when the weather moderates.*

Even before the smoke from Butler's transports fades, Admiral David Porter changes his mind. A lifetime at sea has honed his instincts, and by four-thirty those instincts are sending him a message he would be foolish to ignore: this is shaping up to be not merely a "bad" storm, but one of those truly evil ship-killers that have given this coast its folkloric nickname, "Graveyard of the Atlantic." There is already a hint of malevolent green in the brawny shoulders of the biggest waves, and if just one of his sixty-four vessels breaks an anchor chain, there's enough power in such a wave to lift a four-thousand-ton frigate as though it were a child's bath toy, and hurl it into another ship, with more destructive force than all Fort Fisher's guns combined. There is still enough ambient light to shepherd the most vulnerable class—his five massive monitors—into a protective windbreak formed by the frigates, cruisers, and gunboats. Such is the palpable, growing, malevolence of this gale that Porter quickly decides to head for the sheltered waters between Beaufort and Morehead City. This monster might not blow itself out for *days*.

December 20: Daisy Lamb has been digging in her stubborn New England heels for several days—she wants to stay behind, as close to her husband as possible, and is convinced the Cottage is safe from enemy bombardment. The Negroes and the children can take refuge at Orton plantation, safely remote from the fighting and on the west side of the river, but she will not go! By the time William Lamb has a chance to ride back home, arriving just after midnight, Confederate Point is being scourged by intermittent blasts of cold, hard rain, and the stunted groves of yaupon pines are moaning from the force of strong, contradictory winds. Lamb has just spent four hours frantically and futilely seeking reinforcements by telegraphing to places as distant as Charlotte; he is both agitated and marrow-tired. Not to put too fine a point on the matter, he is in no mood to put up with any melodrama from his wife. Daisy's assertions that she will be "perfectly safe" in the Cottage, are born of her complete ignorance of two things: the destructive power of heavy naval ordnance and the dependable percentage of even well-aimed shots that will sail completely over the fort and land anywhere between the river and Sugar Loaf simply because the ship firing them takes an unpredictable roll at the instant it fires a broadside.

There is an awning-covered excursion boat chugging impatiently at the dock, and several slaves from Orton, along with Cassius and Aunt Charity from the Lamb household, pass in and out through the kitchen door, shouldering travel bags, hatboxes, crates full of toys, and assorted containers of personal effects. Dick and Maria run out into the rain, heedless of Daisy's admonitions, to hug their father as he dismounts. Lamb kneels to soak up the precious warmth and substance of his children—quite possibly for the last time—but refuses to stretch the moment out. He must remain in full emotional battle armor now, until this crisis is over, and it will weaken him, literally drain strength from his body, if he draws out these farewell hugs. He disengages himself rather brusquely from the children and herds them back under the front porch awning. Daisy stands defiantly in the hall, apparently dug in for another round of argument. In his most forceful command voice, Lamb restrains Aunt Charity from carrying a rocking horse toward the back door.

"There are already enough children's things in the launch, Auntie C. I want you and Cassius to finish packing Missus Lamb's belongings and I want every member of this household on that launch and heading for Orton in thirty minutes or less. Is that clear?"

Aunt Charity looks anxiously from one white person to the next. "But Cuh-nul Lamb, Miss Daisy said . . ."

"I *know* what she said. I ought to, because I've had to listen to it for three damned days! Daisy Lamb, I'm at the end of my patience: it is *not* safe for you to remain in this house or any other place on Confederate Point, and I have far too many things to worry about as it is without also wondering, every time I see a Yankee shell sailing over the fort in this direction, whether or not it's going to blow you to pieces! Either you herd the children on to that launch and take your seat beside them, or I will have a detachment of soldiers carry you onboard. We are finished with 'discussions' and through with 'arguments.' As commander of this place, I have the power to eject any civilian whom I deem to be either a nuisance or a hindrance to the performance of my duties, and that includes you. I need all my concentration and all my energies to defend this place against the most powerful fleet ever assembled by the United States Navy, and I simply cannot do that if I am also worrying about *you!*"

William Lamb is babbling now, his emotions so confused there's no vocabulary to describe them. But one thing is certain: never has his wife looked lovelier, more desirable, than she seems at this moment, which might be the last shared moment of their lives.

Then he notices how full her eyes are, and how much effort she's expending to control the trembling of her lips. With a self-righteous flourish she picks up a folded umbrella and wags it at him like a switch.

"All my things are already on the boat, William. Don't you think I have enough sense to realize what a burden I would be imposing on you by staying? I simply could not accept the fact that this day has finally come, and so I fought it, rebelled against it, because I had to lodge some kind of *protest* to *someone*. And because—" Daisy Lamb breaks down, finally, and cannot stop the tears or throttle-back the sobs that distort the rest of her words "—because I love you with all my heart and I wanted to postpone this moment as long as I could."

They hold each other, fiercely seeking to confirm how absolutely *right* they are for each other. So momentous is the looming prospect of battle, that mere words can't survive contact with the brute, cold *fact* of it. Lamb kisses away his wife's tears, which have run their course now, and then seals the moment with one last, ceremonially tender kiss on her lips. Coming up for air, Daisy squares her shoulders and forces a business-as-usual tone of voice: "We had best get started before the river grows any rougher. William, please take this list I've drawn up—it describes where we've buried the silverware and several caches of food and liquor. If you have to make a run for it back to Wilmington, at least you can pause here and fortify yourself."

"We used to joke about how God had reserved a special destiny for me. Well, I must meet that destiny with all my courage. The soldiers must not see me waver, nor hear from my lips one word of despair. This will be war to the last extremity, so you can expect to hear many dire rumors. Pay no attention! Comfort the children! Whatever the outcome, God will give you the strength to bear it—and it wouldn't hurt if you asked Him to send me a regiment or two of good soldiers as well. Now please go! Go and don't look back!"

At the threshold of the kitchen door, she hesitates, wanting to run back and embrace him one last time, but she feels his gaze following her; knows she must not. The sooner she and the children are safe across the river, the sooner he can barricade his heart against his emotions.

Outside, she discovers that the storm has grown markedly more violent even in the short time they stole from history to say good-bye.

December 20–22: By the time Admiral Porter's lookouts spot the two signal lights marking the sanctuary of Bogue Inlet, the gale has reached maximum power, and Porter knows it has been a very close-run thing. Dawn comes sickly and slow, but it reveals how truly monstrous the seas have become and how incredibly lucky he is not to have lost any ships during the long, wild, passage up the coast. Several times he thought he would lose the monitors, when those low, flat, barely seaworthy vessels vanished beneath gigantic green-water mountains, only to see their black, foam-streaked turrets slowly emerge once more. He cannot imagine how terrifying the voyage must have been for their crews, thrown violently from side to side in their cramped coffin-tight quarters, trapped in vessels that would sink like an anvil if so much as one hatch got torn off by the power of a single rogue wave.

Conditions must have been even more appalling in the transports, for as the light grows and the warships pass into the calmer waters of Bogue Sound, they steam past scores of swollen, broken-legged horses who had been shot and thrown overboard both as a mercy and to keep them from driving the uninjured animals mad with fear. Already the sharks have ripped great chunks from the carcasses, and Porter makes no objection when some of his Marines ask permission to hold target practice on the slashing predators. No doubt sharks had some role to play in God's greater scheme, muses David Porter, but he has always hated the sight of them, and just to release his own tension, he draws a Spencer from the ship's armory and plugs a six-foot brute right in the head. The shark doesn't even stop chewing, so Porter puts five more slugs into his body, again without noticeable deterrence. When Porter loses sight of him, he's was still tearing off enormous bites of horseflesh despite the long cloud of blood trailing from his punctured skull.

Goddamned things don't even feel pain! How could anything that ferocious have such utterly *dead* eyes?

Both fleets remain in the sheltered waters of Bogue Sound for two days, while repairs are effected, supplies replenished, and Rush Hawkins supervises a paint job that might successfully disguise the *Tuscarora* as a typical blockade-runner. He dreads an inspection by Butler, but the General contents himself with a sightseeing tour of the port's colonial-era graveyard and a quick visit to one of the local brothels.

As for the pale, starving soldiers crammed inside Butler's battered transports, they are not permitted even a few hours' liberty to stretch their legs and breathe some fresh air. Butler keeps them locked belowdecks, as a "security precaution." It is a churlish and petty exercise of power, because if the Fort Fisher Expedition ever *was* a "secret" it surely isn't now—even the newspapers in Richmond are openly speculating on the day and hour of the impending attack.

Butler finally sends a message to Hawkins on the afternoon of December 22, after the worst of the storm has passed and the sky's appearance suggests that tomorrow might be tolerable, if not ideal, for the return of both fleets to the vicinity of their target. Butler doesn't even ask if everything is ready; he merely informs Hawkins that the powder boat *will* be towed by the oceangoing tug USS *City of Pembroke* at a distance of three miles behind the rest of the armada and that he expects Hawkins to take his floating bomb into Rebel waters by midnight sharp. The "Good luck" added at the bottom seems decidedly perfunctory. By this stage of his "mission," Hawkins thinks he could do more damage to the Northeast Bastion by shooting feathers out of a blunderbuss than by detonating this badly loaded, leaky, piece-of-shit derelict in the surf adjacent to that formidable work.

December 23: Lieutenant Zachary Wright can barely control his excitement. A team of Admiral Porter's ordnance specialists is converting his 60-foot tug into a gunboat, by mounting 24-pounder howitzers fore and aft and girding them with sandbagged revetments. *The City of Pembroke* was chosen to shepherd the *Tuscarora* on its one-way voyage because she carries the most powerful propulsion plant that could be fitted into a ship of her size—if necessary, she could pull a steam frigate off a reef—and is therefore ideal for towing the powder boat at high speed, whipping around suddenly, and imparting to Hawkins' ship enough "slingshot" momentum to carry it aground near Fort Fisher. All Hawkins has to do is steer.

The reason for arming the tug, explains Lieutenant Wright as he shows Hawkins around, "Is so that if the Rebs try to rush the powder boat before you've given us the signal to pull you out, we can dash in and sweep the beach with grapeshot. In theory we'll be so close to the fort that none of their big guns can depress far enough to hit us."

"That *is* comforting. But what's to prevent the Rebs from swarming aboard her and putting out the fire I plan to set in the galley?"

Lieutenant Wright mumbles, "Nothing was said to me about a fire, sir—"

"In case that fancy clockwork fuse device doesn't work, there has to be some alternative way of setting off the powder. I've installed *two*: one is a ten-minute coil of slow-match cord, and the second is the old-fashioned fire-in-the-galley technique. I suppose you could throw grapeshot into the surf to discourage boarders, but then you also would be dangerously close to the ship when she blows up."

"Hmmm. I was told the clockwork fuse was guaranteed—extensively tested and all that—the work of a brilliant scientist."

"Not to disillusion you, Lieutenant, but it is the work of a *skeptical* scientist, and the gunpowder is not loaded on the ship in the manner prescribed and tested for, nor is it powder of uniform, superior quality. I have no idea in hell whether it will all blow up simultaneously, or one bag at a time, but it *must* go off or Butler will think I funked out at the last minute and ran off without setting any kind of fuse at all. And as you are charged with the success of this half-baked plan almost as much as I, it would behoove both of us to come up with another idea. Something no boarding party is likely to discover in time to prevent the boat from blowing up under their very noses."

"What if we can discourage them from boarding the ship at all?"

"That might work, too."

"Just stack a few ordinary twenty-pound kegs of powder in plain sight, on the fo'c'sle. Would *you* board a grounded, burning ship carrying a cargo of powder kegs?"

"Capital idea, Lieutenant! We'll make a good team."

December 23: By dawn it is clear that the gale has either blown itself out or moved into the mid-Atlantic. Moderate chop still makes for a bumpy trip, and the wind has regained the full bite of winter, but Porter's ships are fully replenished, and the admiral is hopping about the bridge of the *Malvern,* rarin' to go. His warships assume an orderly formation in the roomy calm of Bogue Sound, and a final exchange of signals with Butler leaves Porter with a promise that the transports will be on station by nightfall, ready to conduct a full-scale landing on Christmas Eve Day, should there still be enough left of Fort Fisher to warrant it.

Mooring lines are cast off at eleven o'clock, and a volunteer helmsman and two assistants take the wheel of the *Tuscarora,* just to keep the powder boat from yawing and possibly breaking the five-hundred-foot line tethering her to the tug. Rush Hawkins shares a surprisingly ample bacon-and-eggs meal with the tugboat's officers, then retires, ostensibly for a long nap, in Lieutenant Wright's small cabin. Hawkins is much too anxious to sleep, however, so he relaxes by drinking half a bottle of Butler's good whiskey, and spends the afternoon writing a full account of the ways Butler has been cheated by the contractor who supplied the powder. He will leave this with Wright just before embarking on his perilous solo voyage, telling the enthusiastic young officer that it contains his will and earnestly imploring him to make sure it is delivered to Butler "in case I do not return." Hawkins is resolved that if he does get blown to bits on this errand, at least Butler will know about the gunpowder swindle and can avenge him later on.

Hawkins is shaken awake at 10:30 P.M. and the sudden wash of adrenaline, when he remembers the reason *why* he is being awakened at this uncivilized hour, surely minimizes the hangover he would otherwise be suffering from.

"We're in great luck!" exclaims Lieutenant Wright as Hawkins struggles to a sitting position. "There's a blockade-runner sneaking in ahead of us, about a thousand yards. We're going to tail along in his wake—might confuse the Rebel lookouts!"

Hawkins doubts that by this stage of the war, Fort Fisher's lookouts are easily confused by much, but he likes young Wright's enthusiasm. The cockpit of the *Tuscarora* is open to the elements and there's a sputtering but icy wind blowing from the southwest, so Hawkins pulls a Cape Cod fisherman's sweater over his uniform jacket and a thick wool cap over his head. Lastly he dons a standard army-issue overcoat and a scarf, then tucks a pair of gloves into the coat pockets. He'll need to take them off, of course, to set the clockwork mechanism and light the secondary fuse, but until then he wants warm hands.

While he is dressing for what promises to be a miserably cold as well as nerve-rasping night, the tugboat's powerful stern-mounted winch reels the powder boat in like a huge gray marlin. Wright keeps urging him to hurry, lest they lose sight of the blockade-runner's wake, but Hawkins resists the urge to rebuke the young man. This is probably the most excitement he's had in his whole naval career. All during breakfast he was prattling about "helping to write a page in naval history" with such witless enthusiasm that Hawkins wanted to smack him across the chops. But at this moment, for all his fear and cynicism, Hawkins shakes the lieutenant's hand warmly—he doesn't want any ill feelings between them now, not when he is depending on Wright to haul his ass back from the powder boat to the tug just as soon as the various fuses are ticking, sputtering, or burning.

Wallowing about thirty feet behind the tug, the *Tuscarora* looks old, tired, and forlorn. If ships really did have spirits, Hawkins reflects, that one is ready to meet its end in a blaze of useful glory. Helped by a pair of strong-armed sailors, Hawkins carefully climbs down a short ladder to the tiny skiff attached to the tow rope with a cable and a sliding eyehook. *Christ, feel that wind!*

Despite his layered clothing, he's worked up a good shiver by the time he reaches the *Tuscarora*. He climbs aboard and uses a hand-cranked winch to raise the skiff into a slotted ramp cut into the larger ship's port side. Once on deck, he stows the little lifeboat away, then flashes a shaded lantern at the tug and it pulls ahead until the tow snaps taut, then begins to pick up speed smoothly. All Hawkins has to do for the moment is nudge the helm and keep the powder boat moving straight and true, building up speed nicely. He cannot yet see anything of the shore except a low, sullen darkness; it's just as well for his peace of mind that he cannot yet see the fort itself. He's really zipping along now, at least ten knots, and when he detaches from the tug, this momentum, aided by an incoming tide and the fact that the wind is blowing from a neutral angle, ought to propel him the remaining distance to his target. A signal winks from the tug's fantail: "Stand by!" Hawkins jumps from the wheelhouse, scurries forward, and pulls the lever that detaches him from the tugboat just as that vessel makes its hard-left turn away from the shore, and suddenly—*Oh, my God!*

There is Fort Fisher, the Northeast Bastion positively looming, all it is cracked up to be and more! He can feel the tide helping him drift, but he's losing momentum awfully fast and judging from the dim white bustle of the surf and what he assumes is the base of the Northeast Bastion, he is still two hundred yards from the beach when he feels the "slingshot" momentum fade entirely, leaving him adrift on the incoming tide. Each swell pushes him a few feet closer, but—*What's this*—the wind is shifting and pushing on the port side, so instead of closing at a perpendicular angle to the beach, the powder boat is drifting closer to the shore but also moving *away* from the fort. If he continues on this course until he runs aground, he's going to be a quarter mile north of where he's supposed to be. A quick rationalization: If all the powder goes off at once, seawater will transmit the predicted shock wave better than wet sand. How much braver, really, does he have to be, especially when he doesn't have much faith in the short-changed powder load anyhow?

This will have to do! He ropes the helm in place so the ship won't turn broadside to the incoming waves and broach helplessly, then lifts the hatch leading into the hold, opening the shutter on his lantern as he descends.

Arrayed in deep, orderly piles, the powder bags look like nothing so much as hundreds of dead sailors stitched into weighted sacks for a burial at sea. Jittery shadows make him twitch anxiously. As he kneels before the controls of the clockwork fuse, a stowaway rat suddenly squeaks and darts past him, inducing a heart-stopping bolt of panic that leaves him bathed in sweat and trembling worse than he did the first time he was under fire.

Forcing himself to take deep breaths, he calmly observes that the rat is peering at him curiously from behind a mound of powder sacks.

"Did Butler send you to spy on me, you filthy little bastard? Probably not the only specimen of vermin he has on retainer! Well, my furry friend, you're about to receive the biggest surprise of your life."

The dials, wind-up springs, and clock hands on the primary detonator all work as they're supposed to. He now has exactly thirty minutes to set the back up fuses and get far enough away to escape the blast effects. Not the fifteen ludicrous miles at which Porter has deployed his fleet, but two or three miles would be nice.

He lights the primer cord as his secondary fuse, then scuttles aft to what was once the *Tuscarora*'s galley and strikes an ordinary match, touching it to a wad of old newspapers buried under small wedges of dry kindling, which will eventually spread, if the fire thrives and is not stamped out by boarders, to a big pile of cabinetry and furniture pieces.

All three fuse arrangements are now triggered. Incredibly, no one has raised an alarm from Fort Fisher. *I'm going to make it out of here!*

Indeed he is, as fast as he can scurry. He tips his cap to the rat in parting and the rat crouches tensely, alert to a sudden, disturbing sense of danger that its tiny brain cannot identify. It glares at Hawkins with pure malevolence, and in return Hawkins makes damned sure the hatch is dogged tight so the little monster can't possibly crawl out before being either roasted or vaporized. In too much haste now for his customary caution, Hawkins drops the little skiff hard enough to make a splash that must surely be audible above the surf. He cannot actually see the *City of Pembroke,* but he has faith in Lieutenant Wright, so he unshutters the lantern and makes the "Reel me in!" signal twice. No light shows in reply, of course, due to the proximity of the fort, but the skiff begins to move so vigorously it's all he can do to keep from toppling overboard.

Just as the tugboat's shape materializes out of the spume-clouded darkness he hears an indistinct shout from the direction of the Northeast Bastion. God knows what the proper countersign is—whoever's spotted him wouldn't be able to hear it, anyway. The sentry's minié ball smacks the water, alarmingly close to the skiff, before the report of his rifle reaches Hawkins' ears, and in response, that fire-breathing maniac Wright, who simply *cannot resist* shooting a load of lightweight canister at a fortress wall that's got to be at least twenty feet thick, cuts loose with his forward gun. From Hawkins' position, it appears as though the howitzer is pointed straight at him, so he ducks and screams: "Cease fire, you imbecile! Do you *want* to get sunk??"

"No, sir!" replies Wright cheerfully, and Hawkins is astonished to find his skiff already bumping up against the tugboat's bow. Lifelines drop into his grasping hands and he grabs hold fiercely while two crewmen roughly haul him aboard, dropping him to the deck like a gaffed marlin.

Whang! Smash! Bullets from atop the Bastion gouge holes in the deckhouse and smash a nearby porthole. Wright gleefully replies with another blast from his howitzer. Hawkins has visions of the tug disintegrating under a rain of pointblank cannon fire.

"Mounted patrol on the beach, General Hawkins, approaching the powder ship! I am aiming to discourage them!"

Standing up, Hawkins can now see that the *Tuscarora* is at least one hundred yards from the actual beach. How, exactly, that "mounted patrol" was going to leap their horses over the intervening heavy surf is not immediately clear. At least he hears Wright shouting for flank speed and calling out a zigzag course of retreat, and feels the powerful little ship accelerate rapidly. They are five hundred yards farther out before the first cannon fires from the ramparts, and since the shot-plume erupts fifty yards behind the tug it's clear the fort's gunners are just guessing. Evidently Colonel Lamb concurs, for after a few more desultory rounds, the fire stops. Realizing they have twitted the Rebels at close range, planted a gigantic time bomb close to their walls, and managed to escape without anything worse than a damaged porthole, the crew breaks into wild cheers. Hawkins gets hugged, clapped on the back, and handed—ambrosial reward!—a mug of hot buttered rum.

"How far out should we be when she blows?"

"Don't get your hopes up, Lieutenant. *Something* is going to happen, but I do not think the walls of Jericho are going to tumble down. I'd say a mile and a half, two if it makes you feel safer."

"But Porter's pulled his ships out to fifteen miles!"

"Admiral Porter's been sold a bill of goods by one of the slickest crooks in the business. I do not think he and General Butler's recent spate of mutual regard is destined to survive the night."

This young officer knows the tang of good gossip when he catches a whiff, his ears all but prick up like a German shepherd's.

"Tell me more . . . while we wait for the explosion, that is."

Hawkins wishes he could, for he would love to see this naïve young patriot's response to some of the juicier anecdotes, but finally decides that might not be wise.

"Sorry, but I can't. Oath of Official Secrets, don't you know?"

As far as Hawkins knows, there is no such thing, but Wright immediately nods in a very knowing and thoughtful way. "Of course, of course—I did not mean to pry into matters far beyond my rank."

"I'm sure your rank will advance rapidly, son, and I'm sure your service has been exemplary. This is far enough, I think."

12:12 A.M.: The officers and crew of the *City of Pembroke* crowd forward. Any second now.

12:17 A.M.: Any second now.

12:28 A.M.: "Try your telescope, lieutenant. Surely we ought to be able to see *something* . . ."

But there's no need for a spyglass after all. The galley fire, at least, has taken hold, and a few tongues of flame have reached the outside air. Now that his objectivity has returned, Hawkins finds himself rather hoping the rat found an exit in time.

Now, a rather pretty phosphorescent glow begins to expand from that initial flicker of light—like a fat, drunken, Fourth-of-July rocket, a single powder bag heaves into the sky, trailing grains of saffron-colored fire, reaching a height of perhaps fifty feet, then exploding in a dull smear of yellow-white—a rippling wave of blasts follows, some full-throated and powerful, some as disappointing as a failed erection. Big chunks of the old ship are ripped apart by sequential explosions, but no titanic devastation sunders the night—just a lot of thumps and bangs and rat-a-tat spurts, along with a few single bags still arcing forth like popcorn spitting from hot oil. A slow growling thunder reaches their ears, swelling like a pipe-organ's pedal notes—and at last there rises a great pillar of smoke, spreading into a mushroom cap two hundred feet above its own reflection. And, yes, there it comes—*finally* they can feel a faint strumming vibration in the water, neither "wave" nor "shock" ever manifests itself—if this bronchial coughing-fit is doing anything more lethal than stunning a few Confederate fish, the damage is certainly not visible, even though most of Fort Fisher's Sea-Face clearly is—and its parapets, Hawkins wryly observes, are lined with incredulous but hugely entertained spectators, many of whom appear to be cheering and applauding. The pyrotechnic display goes on for ten lively minutes, and when the last soggy *whumph* dies away; what remains of the *Tuscarora*'s hull burns slowly down to the water, as homely and unthreatening as a campfire in the woods.

"There's a fizzle if ever I saw one," mutters Lieutenant Wright.

Christmas Eve in Hell

WHAT THE SHERMAN TANK was to World War Two, the Parrott rifle was to the Civil War era. Both were fielded in response to mass conscript armies and those armies' need for unprecedentedly large numbers of supporting heavy weapons that would "do the job," rather than small numbers of finely crafted weapons that would last forever. A Parrott gunner knew that after his cannon got really hot—say, after firing fifty rounds—there was a very real chance it would explode. The longer it maintained continuous fire, the higher the chances of self-destruction; after 200 rounds, it was only a matter of time (unless the order to "Cease-fire!" came down first). Similarly, Sherman tank crews knew their vehicles were helpless against Tigers and Panthers (unless they greatly outnumbered the German vehicles and were able to shoot at them from behind), and were so prone to burst into flames that the crews bestowed upon them the macabre nickname "Ronsons" (after a popular brand of cigarette lighter). However, both Parrotts and Shermans shared numerous virtues: they were cheap to make; mechanically robust; easy to operate by inexperienced crews; and rugged under field conditions (if a Rebel solid-shot knocked off the front five inches off a Parrott's barrel, you could keep right on shooting it—at least, until it overheated and blew up). Neither weapon was "the best" of its genre, but in wars where quantity was more useful than quality, both were considered "good enough."

Sir Ian Hogg. *The Lore of the Big Guns.* Scribners and Sons, 1972

DECEMBER 24, 1864

6:28 A.M.: The sun cleaves the horizon, lemon-white, rising into a scrubbed-clean winter sky, throwing a blinding sheen across smooth, glossy water, bestowing a balmy fifty-two degree morning. "Hard to believe what this same patch of ocean looked like two days ago," comments the handsome, smooth-shaven, green-eyed young skipper of the *Malvern*, whose name happens to be Lieutenant Benjamin H. Porter.

"That's the Outer Banks for you," growls the burly, scowling admiral of the fleet, who happens to be Lieutenant Porter's father. Admiral David Porter is scowling not because he prefers vicious gales to this benign, unseasonable calm, but because General Butler's transports are late . . . again. Ever since the powder boat scheme turned into such an embarrassing fiasco, Porter has been cursing himself for a fool (something he does not do often or with good grace). The expedition had already lost three days of excellent weather waiting for the *Tuscarora*, then took a beating from a snarling gale while Butler's "secret weapon" was being patched for leaks, and now here's perfect weather again, so where the hell is Butler? Porter's cursing Butler for flimflamming him; can't even bear to speak his name—just refers to him as "that man." Basically, he's cursing Butler for being, well, *Butler,* and for not showing up with his transports when he solemnly assured Porter he would. Porter suspects that Butler's infantry, who have now been cooped up in their cramped, stinking quarters for more than a week, are doing the most powerful cursing of all; it's a dead-sure bet those troops are not going to be in good shape when they finally do execute the amphibious landing.

"To hell with him!" Porter finally says, snapping shut his old-fashioned Nelsonian spyglass and nodding decisively at his son. "It's time to start blowing the bejesus out of that fort, with or without Butler's seasick soldiers. Copy this signal to all ships . . ." And Porter barks out a series of orders that will set in motion the most colossal naval bombardment in history.

The signal for action galvanizes the fleet: the "Beat to Quarters!" rattle of snare drums stirs captains and crews alike into frantic but well-orchestrated activity. First to come through the hatches are the eager gun crews, a mob of shouting, cheering tars who quickly separate into disciplined teams and lay out the tools of their craft; unfastening the covers over their lockers of powder and pyramids of shot, they begin the touchy process of screwing fuses into shells. Deep belowdecks, in the lazarets, surgeons wash down their tables with buckets of cold water and lay out their grisly tools: gleaming probes, bone saws, rolls of bandages, and brass-handled tourniquets. On each gun deck and around the base of each pivot mount, other sailors move about with buckets of ash and coke from the engine rooms, spreading a layer of absorbent grit on the polished wooden decks to prevent men from slipping on the puddled blood of the wounded. Engineers fiddle with the knobs and levers of bleeder valves so there will be adequate steam for maneuver but not so much that a lucky Rebel shot through the boilers will set off scalding eruptions; and in the galleys, the cooks extinguish all fires and don their coveralls in case they are needed as stretcher-bearers. Porter darts here and there, spot-checking his ships' battle-readiness aboard the fast but relatively small *Malvern*, which he has chosen for his flagship instead of a bigger, more comfortable frigate, precisely because she is so nimble. He does not expect to do any major damage with her six medium-sized guns, but he does want to keep a keen eye on the lines of larger ships that will be fully engaged.

10:25 A.M.: "Porter certainly knows how to make a grand entrance," remarks Major Frederick Reilly, commander of Fort Fisher's Land Face artillery. Lamb is too awestruck to respond. It is one thing to have a realistic intellectual conception of what a fleet of sixty-four warships might look like, but quite a different thing to watch as it unfolds into four orderly columns and bears down upon you with majestic disdain, sunlight winking off a forest of run-out gun barrels and innumerable fittings of polished brass. With deliberation born of high professional skill, maintaining exactly their prescribed intervals, each of the Union battle lines steams to the range Porter has assigned them and anchors, while the smaller reserve line brings up the rear, forming a backdrop two miles offshore. Lamb picks out one splendid blue-water cruiser, the USS *Colorado,* largest of the second line vessels, and ponders the significance of certain statistics: the *Colorado* has a crew of 468 officers and men, virtually the same as the number of reliable infantry Lamb presently could deploy without stripping men from the gun crews, and she carries 52 heavy cannon, more than the fort's entire complement. First to drop anchor are Porter's 5 hulking monitors, only 500 to 600 yards from the corner of the Northeast Bastion, two of them packing the biggest class of gun carried by the U.S. Navy: 15-inch Dahlgrens. While the conventional warships steam past the monitors, or fill in the first line behind them, the monitors' turrets begin to crank and rumble as the tars inside throw their muscles on the rotating gears, and soon the defenders in the Bastion are face-to-face with the enormous dark pits of muzzles protruding from gunports surrounded by iron so thick that Lamb doubts he could drive a single monitor off the firing line without expending fully half his ammunition on that one turret. At such close range, the turreted 15- and 11-inchers will gnaw into the Bastion like beavers chomping birch logs. Just how much kinetic energy can all that sand absorb before it crumbles? Neither Lamb nor any other architect of fortifications in the world has any idea, but a baseline measurement is about to be established, one that will be closely studied by an entire generation of engineers and ammunition crafters.

10:46 A.M.: Major Reilly walks the length of the Sea Face, from gun chamber to humped traverse to gun chamber, pausing to engage each crew in conversation, quietly reminding them that although they're outnumbered, they have the high ground, and better protection, and probably much more skill than their navy adversaries. At each gun chamber he makes sure the crews know the tactics he and Lamb have worked out, to preserve both men and ammunition: make every shot count; fire only when you think you have a 90 percent probability of scoring a hit; ration your fire to one round every half hour. Between firings, just hunker inside the bombproofs carved into the traverses. Ignore the noise and the sheer weight of metal being thrown at you, because there aren't enough shells in North America to batter down these walls. While the most efficient way to defend the fort is to damage as many ships as possible, forcing Porter to thin out his lines to make temporary repairs, it will do wonders for the garrison's morale if at least one Yankee vessel could be sunk outright, in view of the many witnesses on both sides.

When Reilly finishes his pep talks and pats on the back, the crews in each gun chamber respond with determined smiles and rousing cheers (*"We'll show 'em, Major!" "Five dollars says Battery Purdie sinks a ship before Battery Roland!" "Shoe 'em what that Armstrong gun can do, Major Reilly!"),* all the proper signs of grit and spirited defiance; but he can see in their eyes that most of them are scared shitless. He probably should be, too, but for the moment his overriding emotion is one of curiosity: Just how formidable will the Armstrong gun prove to be? He will soon find out, for as Land Face commander, he has reserved the privilege of firing it for the first time as the signal for all the fort's cannon to commence fire. The Armstrong is the only gun they have that is equal or perhaps superior in its throw weight and accuracy to Admiral Porter's huge Dahlgrens, but Reilly has only thirty-one rounds for it, so he prays that the gleaming, arrogant weapon will prove to be a ship-killer. One thing gives him hope: a fort cannot be sunk. The massive Land Face will suck up solid shot by the hundreds, and a significant number of Porter's shells will bury themselves in the sand ramparts before exploding, minimizing the damage they can inflict. Of the shells fired high, timed to go off inside the walls or in midair over the gun chambers, he can do nothing but hope for rougher seas to spoil the Union gunners' aim.

It is almost noon by the time Reilly finishes visiting every battery on the Sea Face, so when he returns to the Armstrong position, located exactly halfway between the Mound and the Northeast Bastion, he takes time to eat lunch and refresh his already jangled nerves with a few more cups of strong, bitter coffee. Line three of the enemy fleet is just finishing its deployment, extending a crescent of ships down to the mouth of New Inlet, where it can enfilade the Mound Battery from a range of 1¼ miles. *Won't be long now.* When they observe Reilly replacing his coffee cup on a shelf inside their traverse, the Armstrong crew snaps to attention. Already waiting inside the barrel is a 150-pound elongated tapering shell with a contact fuse screwed tightly into its point.

"Well, boys, have you selected our first target?"

"Yes, sir, Major Reilly. See that semiarmored sloop midway down the second line? Since we don't know if these newfangled fuses will work on wood as well as metal, we've drawn a bead on the iron panel between the last starboard gunport and the fantail. Might be there to protect the engine or even the aft magazine. With good luck, we can knock out a broadside gun and destroy whatever she has behind that plate. Also, she's a beam-on, zero-deflection target, riding at anchor in calm water. Once everybody starts shooting, there'll be a passel of smoke hanging over everything, but right now she is dead in our sights." Reilly peers through his field glasses: 2,000 tons, 6 broadside guns, big Parrotts bow and stern, plus she's hard to miss.

"I concur, gentlemen. We are about to smite the USS *Susquehanna*, and may God have mercy on her skipper and crew!"

11:40 A.M.: So many ships were vying for the honor of firing the opening broadside that Admiral Porter had to hold a lottery to make that historic determination. Winner: the USS *New Ironsides,* in line number one, sixth in formation behind the five monitors. Porter makes a final scrutinizing pass in the *Malvern,* cleaving the water between lines two and three, decides that his sailors are as ready as they'll ever be and the weather as close to perfect as a mariner might wish, and orders the hoisting of an appropriate flag and the firing of a green rocket.

Ka-blam!

"Note the time," says William Lamb as all eyes turn to follow this first projectile. Clearly visible against the taut, cloudless sky, it's got to be a shell aimed at the flammable buildings clustered around the parade ground. With a sinister whoosh, it sails over the ramparts and drops in perfect trajectory . . . right on top of William Lamb's headquarters. A sharp cotton ball of white smoke, followed by a geyser of roof tiles, gutter spouts, and bricks, half the roof and most of one wall shattering before his eyes.

"They got yer bed, Colonel!" shouts a gunner in the Pulpit Battery.

"For that, take THIS!" Lamb raises a red signal flag and drops it toward the enemy fleet.

Reilly pulls the lanyard, the firing pin slams home inside the Armstrong's reinforced rear chamber, and the great, gleaming British behemoth lurches against its mounting, producing a sharper, spikier muzzle flash than he's ever seen before. With incredible velocity, the Armstrong shell scores a dead-center hit on Reilly's aiming point, the impact so sharp that the iron crumples like wadded paper even before the contact-fuse detonates, causing the entire vessel to rock violently, vomiting chunks of wood and interior paneling as big as beer barrels, ripping open the gunport adjacent to point of impact, and setting off a ready ammo locker. The secondary explosion dwarfs the shell burst, smashing the gun mount, flinging the entire weapon, a 3½-ton Dahlgren, up through the main deck like a massive battering ram, tearing apart a lifeboat, three cross-tree spars for the aft mast, the fantail ensign and flagpole, and expelling a big cloud of infernal *things,* including some crimson streamers of body parts. Rising out of the last reverberation comes the ear-splitting shriek of a ruptured steam chest, and the sudden yellow-red pennants of multiple internal fires. The *Susquehanna*, pouring smoke and lurching drunkenly as she tries to maneuver with only one engine, reels out of formation—if not sinking, at least grievously wounded.

One thing, at least, has now been proven: Sir George Armstrong manufactures the finest brand of coast artillery money can buy. A tremendous cheer rises along the whole length of the Sea Face, but is quickly drowned out by the stupendous roar of approximately seven hundred Union and Confederate cannon firing at will. Like an anxious shepherd, the *Malvern* whips around and charges toward the stricken vessel. In truth, Admiral Porter is *very* impressed by Fort Fisher's opening shot. He is, in fact, seriously concerned about the possibility that Lamb has more of those Armstrongs. When the *Malvern* pulls alongside the limping, shaken *Susquehanna*, Porter screams into his megaphone, "How bad is the damage?"

"One starboard gun and crew destroyed, aft mast badly damaged, starboard engine holed and unusable, three men killed, and at least twenty wounded!" shouts the distraught skipper. "I am retiring to make repairs!"

"Any damage to your port side?" bellows Porter.

"Don't think so, Admiral."

"Then turn that fucking ship around and start shooting with your portside guns! If you don't, I'll sink you myself!"

11:50 A.M.: The congregation and choir of St. James Episcopal Church in Wilmington has just finished singing number 113 in their hymnals ("A Mighty Fortress Is Our God"—how could Rev. Dane resist?) and returned to a seating position amid a three-minute crinkling of petticoats and hoop skirts. With his customary patience, Dane waits for silence, then stands up to begin his prepared sermon. Gradually, everyone realizes that the stained glass windows are rattling in their leaded frames and the floor beneath their feet has started to vibrate gently but steadily. Then a shift in wind direction brings the dull summer-lightning mutter of a massive cannonade, almost twenty miles away down at Confederate Point. Occasionally, when the wind is strong, they can hear individual detonations above the generalized tumult. The great clash has begun; sounds no one has ever heard before lap at the windows and stimulate their sharp Protestant ears. A number of Confederate officers, tightly gripping their scabbards so as not to fill the church with saber rattles, rise grim-faced, exchange nods, and make their way up the aisles; there are duty-stations to which they must report. Rev. Dane puts aside his prepared sermon and improvises on the theme of God's protection bestowed on those who must walk through the Valley of the Shadow of Death. It's quite the most inspired oration Dane has made in a coon's age, and some of the congregation begin quietly to weep—because the muted thunder just doesn't stop, doesn't even ebb and rise, just stays full-throated, constant, hinting of a power as prodigious as God's, and far more immediately threatening.

12:38 P.M.: A Parrott gun aboard the USS *Kansas*, line number one, overheats and blows up, killing one sailor and wounding five others.

12:56 P.M.: The captain of the USS *Powhatan*, 24 guns in the second line, can't see for shit or sour apples because there's not enough breeze to move the powder smoke aside, so everything from the fort's parade ground inside the walls to the space between the third and reserve lines is one huge, impenetrable curd of thickening dirty cream, pierced by muzzle flashes beyond counting. His ship is supposed to be concentrating its broadsides on the battery between the Northeast Bastion and the Pulpit, but his gunners are firing blind. He turns to Able Seaman Francis Evans, normally assigned to the galley or the laundry room but now just standing around, waiting for someone to give him something useful to do. Finally the skipper states: "Take these binoculars, Evans, climb up to the crosstree on the mainmast, and see if our broadsides are landing where they're supposed to."

Evans doesn't bother asking how he's supposed to recognize the *Powhatan*'s shots from all the others, but as long as that part of the fort's getting pasted, he can tell the captain what the captain wants to hear. He scampers off, happy to be doing something even slightly bellicose. Now that he's momentarily undistracted by the spectacle, he remembers he forgot to eat breakfast, so he detours through the seamen's galley to stuff some hardtack into his blouse pockets before climbing to the fragile-looking iron cage forty-nine feet above the bridge, wondering why there's not already an observer up their in the crow's nest. Halfway up the mast, he realizes that there was someone up there, but from the streaks of blood on the varnished wood, and the hammered-in dings and dents on the metal ribs of the lookout's cage, whoever it was caught some shell fragments and went below to seek medical attention. Evans is not frightened; this insight only adds a welcome frisson of excitement to the job: What are the odds, after all, of a second Rebel shell bursting over this very same spot?

He settles in, ignoring the scars on the mast and the lookout's cage, and crams a big piece of hardtack into his mouth. From this height, far above the clinging webs of smoke, he is offered a breathtaking view of both the fleet and its target. He clamps the binoculars to his eyes and adjusts the focus, his jaws slowly and automatically working on the hardtack. The *Powhatan*'s target is easy enough to spot: the Northeast Bastion is unmistakable, despite the fountains of sand heaving up all around it from the concentrated fire of Porter's monitors; and despite the hundreds of rounds aimed at it, the flagstaff on top is still intact and still beflagged. Evans need only move his glasses slightly to the left to bring the target battery into focus.

Although hc knows, rationally, that it is not possible for the Rebels to see him individually, or sensible of them to waste a shot on him even if they can, his field of vision suddenly comes to rest on a single enemy gun crew, fearless despite the sand raining down on them from near-misses and the puffs of exploding shells twenty feet above their heads, coolly elevating the muzzle of a ten-inch columbiad. Evans and the cannon's mouth are now eyeball to muzzle, seemingly staring directly at each other. Boiling flame fills his vision when the 10-incher fires. He lowers the glasses and observes with absolute amazement a dark, blurry shape coming straight at him, as straight as though it were gliding down invisible rails. Nowhere to duck, no time to run; if he jumps from this height, he's more likely to smash himself to jelly on the deck than land in the sea, which is not so tempting, either, given the number of shell spouts popping up all around, so he hunkers into a ball with his hands over his face and starts to pray.

A hammer blow cracks against the mast, just below him, and splinters zing all around him, some of them stabbing him in the legs and the buttocks. The crow's nest lurches alarmingly; then, as the shattered mainmast breaks off with a drawn-out groan of rending wood, he topples into space, buggy-whipped by snapped rigging and blinded by torn patches of sail cloth that flap all around him like the wings of huge demented birds. He gropes blindly for something that is not torn and falling—to hell with the skipper's binoculars!—and finally manages to arrest his fall by grasping a tangle of shroud lines still attached to something undamaged.

Thank you, Jesus! Momentarily safe, Evans takes a quick inventory of his arms and legs and tries to laugh with relief—except for a few splinters, he is just fine! But he can't manage to draw breath for a shout of joy. No air goes in. His throat and windpipe are completely blocked by the big chunk of hardtack, which he has apparently swallowed whole. He tries frantically to dislodge it, but the raw powder-reeking air has dried up all the saliva in his mouth. He tries to cough out the blockage, but he can't draw enough air for a cough, and there's no one nearby to whack him on the back. Twisting inside the web of lines that saved him from falling to certain doom, Able Seaman Francis Evans bucks and thrashes like a madman, high above the great battle, and slowly chokes to death, perhaps the only combatant of the whole war, on either side, who has been killed by a piece of friendly biscuit.

1:35 P.M.: Because the Armstrong gun must be loaded, block and tackle, through the muzzle, and because the shells are so ponderous, Reilly's crew has to accomplish their drill in several stages. Whenever there seems to be a lull in the fire directed toward their part of the Sea Face, they dash from the bombproofs and go through as many steps as they can before they're spotted and driven back under cover by the angry whip of shrapnel slashing the sandbags and kicking up little sprays of sand all around. After three tries in forty minutes, the piece is finally ready to fire its second shot, and Reilly's picked out the gunboat *Montgomery*, next ship in line behind Cushing's *Monticello*, not for any tactical reason, but because it offers another excellent beam-on target and it's an unarmored, medium-sized vessel that might be sinkable with a single hit. The moment there's another lull in the shelling, Reilly leaps out; rechecks his aim, which looks to be perfect; and fires. Again, the results are a tribute to British science: the 150-pound elongated Armstrong shell blows the starboard paddle box apart, passes on at a downward slant, and explodes below the waterline, punching a four-foot hole in the gunboat's bottom and igniting a sizable fire. Shuddering with structural ague, the *Montgomery* takes on a twelve-degree list almost immediately. This time even Admiral Porter realizes he's going to lose a ship if the gunboat isn't pulled out of line promptly, so he signals the reserve line, and an armed tug peels off and attaches a towline to the wallowing, helpless gunboat. Other Rebel guns begin concentrating on this pair of targets, and Reilly's crew cheers at their handiwork until the major snaps out of it and orders them to take cover, for retribution is surely heading their way. Angrily bracketing the Armstrong position, half a dozen warships concentrate 38 guns against that one small segment of the Sea Face, a cyclone of iron. Crouched under a rain of grit, buffeted by concussion, Reilly has a cold premonition that this time there won't *be* another lull—the Armstrong has fired only two shells and both of them have effectively knocked two ships out of action. It's even money that the *Montgomery* won't last an hour, even though it's now been towed out of effective range. Admiral Porter doesn't like surprises and that Armstrong gun is a nasty one; thank the Lord the Rebels have only one such weapon! Reilly braces for the inevitable, and then it comes: a titanic gong stroke of metal striking metal, followed by another glancing hit that sounds like a blacksmith's hammer coming down full force on a red-hot anvil, followed instantly by another tearing, rending, grinding sound. He peeks quickly from the dugout, and the sight confirms his worst fears: the first strike has cracked a broken-teacup piece from the Armstrong's muzzle; the second has dismounted it. While he watches, a third hit, from a 100-pound Parrott bolt, carries away the last iron integuments holding the gun in place, and the entire piece staggers from the shock, teetering for an instant on the lip of the gun chamber. Then it slides like a fallen monument, massive and unstoppable, down the slippery inner wall, coming to rest only when it strikes the interior plane, rolls over three times, and finally lies still, small swirls of smoke rising from the fractured, bitten-off edge of the muzzle. The pride of the sea-face, the greatest of all Fort Fisher's guns, now looks like nothing so much as an abandoned section of sewer pipe, and is every bit as useless. Inside their shelters, two of its gunners bury their faces in their hands and weep.

1:59 P.M.: Aboard the USS *Wabash*, 44 guns in line two, an overheated *Parrott* bursts, wounding six.

2:10 P.M.: A cluster of shells brackets the fort's stable, blowing down one wall and setting fire to the straw inside. A herd of terrified horses bursts out of the flaming building, only to emerge into a hail of bouncing cannonballs and crackling shell fragments. Wild-eyed, rearing, convulsing like rabid dogs, the animals gallop desperately in all directions, seeking escape, succor, another stable, just a kind word and a pat on the muzzle, but the parade ground's being lashed by so much iron and fire that no living thing can long survive in the open. One by one the horses crumple, legs shot away. Disemboweled by shrapnel, they roll and hobble and stagger in frenzied circles, their intestines spooling like long, purple snakes from gaping belly wounds. Their plight is unbearable to see and to hear, for their screams are audible all over the fort, cutting through the din of explosions. As fast as they can draw a bead, sharpshooters put them down, but when the last mangled animal falls silent, the parade ground is strewn with mangled horse anatomy, a sight that does nothing to improve morale. Eventually the rain of projectiles chops the carcasses into unrecognizable pulp, but the stink lingers for days.

2:37 P.M.: Everything is under control aboard the *Monticello*, of course, and by now, the fort's return fire has grown sporadic and much less effective. Aside from a few holes in her auxiliary sails, the ship is undamaged. Will Cushing can't see much through his glasses, but when the smoke parts enough to let him study things, it appears to him that at least half of the Sea Face batteries have been silenced, if not destroyed, and the fort itself looks as though wild beasts have been clawing at it all day. Things seem to be going so well, he decides he can relax and let the crew carry on without his supervision. Now he can do what he's wanted to do for the past hour: climb up to the crow's nest and *spectate,* soaking up a memory picture of the whole panorama.

From the *Monticello*'s place in the third line, and from his sturdy perch high above the obscuring murk, the entire battle lies spread out for Will Cushing's delectation, and his first thought: *God, how I wish Charles Flusser could be here to see this!* Rummaging through his knowledge of naval history, he can think of very few battles comparable in scale and spectacle. Trafalgar, maybe, or that enormous, history-changing slaughter of Greek and Persian galleys at Salamis . . . but this engagement off Cape Fear is unique, pitting the greatest steam-powered fleet ever assembled against the most formidable fortress ever built in this hemisphere. Being privileged to witness such a thing is reward enough for all his years of service; its scope, power, and dreadful majesty are beyond any poet's powers of description. Cushing is spellbound, almost levitated by rapture.

Three concentric rings of warships, anchored fearlessly in place—inviting the Rebels to do their worst, in trade for stable firing platforms and precision aim—are wreathed in continuous, self-renewing billows of smoke, pierced by sharp dagger-points of fire lancing out from their hulls, or throwing big singular lightning bolts from the pivot-mounted heavies on bow and stern; there's an almost hypnotic rhythm to the oscillating pattern of broadside, two-gun salvo, and bass-drum exclamation points from the monitors' stupendous Rodmans—to Cushing's ears, a grand symphony indeed! Acting independently, clusters of ships are ganging up on whatever enemy gun had been impudent enough to attract their attention, turning an impersonal barrage into a duel. What a glorious, pellucid sky for a backdrop! Stark and three dimensional, each detonation as unique and subtly different from the others as snowflakes, the sky seethes with whistling, shrieking, whirring projectiles, flocked with the sharp flash-bang of time-fused shells, starfish flashes that imprint the pale blue silk of sky with cotton balls of startlingly white smoke that linger long after the flash, dissipating languidly in the slow, wispy breeze, drifting slowly toward the masts of Porter's ships until they melt into the vast tapestry of general smoke, or moving off, like spectral veils, across the river, westward, losing shape until they bring to some distant farmer a sinister hint of brimstone over his fields. From Cushing's vantage point, the great traverses between Fort Fisher's battery sites resemble giant upturned soup bowls, or perhaps those outsized mounds of earth between the freshly dug graves of a pharaonic dynasty. By now, every combustible thing within the walls is burning—huts and stables, sheds and offices, barracks and kitchens, packing crates and a wide variety of shithouse designs—each one ablaze, their small fires converging like a root system to form the trunk of a gigantic smoke-tree reaching five hundred feet straight up, a thick, brown twist curling slowly into promontories, mesas, ridges as solid-looking as stone, rising column-straight until it reaches a high strong thermal wind and suddenly bends to the southwest, casting an immense, menacing shadow over Cape Fear, the fishing shacks south of Smithville, the walls and barracks of Fort Caswell, and out across the ship-killing reefs of Frying Pan Shoals. It must be visible from Bermuda, thinks Cushing. Skip-shots from the fort kick up evenly spaced lines of waterspouts as they smack the calm Atlantic like flat stones thrown by boys across a pond, occasionally taking their final bounce into a gunboat's hull. Observing the frantic movements of the *Malvern,* Cushing is reminded of those tireless, pond-skimming waterbugs that never seem to touch the surface. The *Malvern* scoots tirelessly from line to line, carrying the furiously agitated Porter wherever he wants to go.

Evidently Porter thinks the bombardment's pace is growing slack, so he orders a ten-minute free-fire crescendo by every gun still in working condition. After he deciphers the admiral's signal, Cushing reflects on the peculiarity of such a command; Porter had fully expected Fort Fisher to be torn apart by now, and evidently he regards its stubborn refusal to collapse as a personal affront. But who knows how much more the fort can take? Maybe this hammer-of-God barrage will accomplish what Porter desires—the sudden collapse of some portion of the ramparts and/or the final smothering of two or three pesky cannon that just keep popping back to life no matter how many tons of iron the ships bring down on their positions. Cushing knows the tactic will certainly accomplish one thing: it will totally exhaust Porter's already weary gun crews, and it probably will cause a few more overworked Parrotts to blow up. But, sweet Lord, what a sight it is when the "rapid fire" sequence begins: the ramparts, humps, and pockmarked outer wall of the Sea Face seems to turn liquid, like boiling mud, as hundreds of projectiles gouge and rake and pile-drive into it, throwing up rooster tails of sand and sod twenty feet high and causing a fine rain of acrid, stinking, shit-brown dust to drift across the decks and sweating bodies of all the gunners in line one and even some as distant as line two. Even at this distance, perched high above the hammering fury of it, Cushing smells the powder char and feels a subtle thickening in the air, enough to irritate his eyes and make him wheeze. At the end of Porter's ten-minute free-for-all, the admiral has expended another two thousand rounds, brought most of its gunners to the verge of physical collapse, and rucked up the Sea Face like a giant laundry mangle. But it still hasn't torn a breach in the walls! When the din subsides, the ships' fire drops to a sullen, desultory rumble while the gasping, bone-weary gunners pour endless streams of water down their sandpapered gullets and lave their swollen tongues. Porter's had his fun now, and the drama reaches intermission time so that more ammunition can be hoisted from the magazines. With exquisite timing, during a short interval when the entire Federal fleet has fallen silent, a lone Confederate columbiad bangs in defiance, hurling its solid-shot round all the way out to line three, where it neatly clips in half the smokestack of the USS *Aries.* The message from Colonel Lamb is clear: *Is that the worst you can throw at us? Too bad, because we're still in business!*

2:54 P.M.: Daisy Lamb drove a buggy down from Orton to a bluff just north of Smithville and has been watching for the last three hours, rigid with anxiety but also unable to avert her eyes from a sight so awe-inspiring, so end-of-the-world spectacular. When Porter's ten-minute saturation commences, the roll of thunder across the river reaches such an unprecedented, earth-shaking volume that Daisy assumes it is the prelude to a grand, climactic ground assault. She has left Maria back at Orton—this is not a thing her daughter should see or remember—but cannot rationalize forcing Dick to stay behind. If this is the day when his father is fated to die, she wants his son to remember the stupendous arena where it happened, and the tremendous pillar of smoke that signified the defiance and courage of William Lamb and the men who gave their all for him. But the crescendo of firing finally breaks little Dick's facade of nonchalance and he runs to his mother, quaking, grabs her leg tightly, and cries: "Momma, if I pray real hard to God, will he spare Papa's life?"

Wishing there was some way she could honestly answer "Yes," Daisy scoops the boy up into the buggy seat and hugs him fiercely; giving him the only answer she can think of: "By all means, Dick, pray to God for your father, for it may be that God pays more attention to the prayers of a child. . . ."

He has certainly paid no attention to the prayers of half a million other wives and mothers, not so anyone might notice. So go ahead, boy, and try your luck . . . how could it hurt?

3:36 P.M.: A Parrott gun on the USS *Juanita* cooks off with a fresh shell in the tube, decapitating one gunner, blinding another, and tearing the right arm off a third.

3:52 P.M.: A Parrott gun explodes aboard the USS *Seneca*, killing two men and wounding four.

4:04 P.M.: Two of Porter's monitors report that their ammunition is completely exhausted. For four hours they've been hurling 15- and 11-inch rounds into the Northeast Bastion, and there are now so many huge cannonballs overlapping in the sand that the walls look like loaves of bread covered with poppy seeds. The navy gunners have tried to collapse the work by sheer brute battering, they have tried "bowling" their shots by skipping them across the water so they will bounce high and dig great furrows in the walls, and they have tried every fuse setting available, exploding rounds on the surface, and timing them to explode only after the projectiles have tunneled as deep as they can go. From time to time, sizable cascades of sand slither down on to the beach or erupt like pricked skinblisters, but the imperturbable Bastion just eats round after round, and the monitors cannot elevate their giant guns high enough to touch the Rebel battery on top. Grumpily—or at least as grumpily as semaphore signals can be made to appear—Porter gives the two shagged-out ironclads permission to withdraw from line one and orders the big conventional frigates to close up the column and try to silence the 8-inch Blakeley and the 8-inch columbiad mounted on the top. From the big frigate *Brooklyn* comes a flashed inquiry: *Guns on top have not fired in two hours; one appears dismounted, the other buried in sand. Can we shoot down their damn flag instead?* Porter ruminates. He, too, has not seen any fire from the guns on the Northeast Bastion in quite a while, and he, too, is irritated by the fact that not one of the hundreds of shells aimed at that big Stars and Bars has brought it down, and now, with the waning sun and cooler afternoon temperatures bringing a stronger wind, that flag is unfurling defiantly. Every sailor in his fleet can see it, so Porter wants it *gone* and no longer cares how much ammunition it takes to do the job. Despite Porter's earlier order not to waste ammunition on a flagpole, every ship in all three lines has taken a crack at the target at some point during the day, and it is almost mathematically impossible that not *one* round has scored a hit! To sail away now and leave it intact, streaming arrogantly in the wind—*intolerable!* Porter knows his gunners are turning into zombies, stumbling through their drills with numb fingers, eyes bloodshot, stone-deaf, many of them wiping at nosebleeds from the effect of sustained concussion, and—*BOOM! Goddamn it, there goes another one!*—more and more Parrotts are reaching their limit from heat and metal fatigue. By rough count, he figures he's now lost as many men from exploding Parrott guns as he has to enemy hits. He's going to have to wind things up soon anyhow, so why not finish off the day by shooting down that mocking banner?

Ships in line one, concentrate remaining ammunition on enemy flagpole.

One minute later, the summit of the Northeast Bastion burbles like a volcano as a torrent of projectiles rains down on the area near the flagstaff. In reality, only one of the two cannon mounted on top has been damaged, and their crews have been sheltering in nearby dugouts, planning to pop up and man the Blakeley as soon as Porter starts to withdraw, hoping to score a few hits on fantails and stern-mounted heavy guns—a last-minute gesture that might take the enemy by surprise. That plan no longer seems feasible. In fact, the topside portion of the Bastion feels like it's going to collapse any second, if only because so many tons of inert iron are piling up inside such a small area. So the gun crews scatter like mice, some sprinting south toward the Pulpit, other scuttling down the long ladders to the base of the Sea Face, then ducking into the deep, bombproof galleries where Lamb's infantry reserves have been sitting out the barrage all day.

4:17 P.M.: The concentrated naval fire finally brings results: shell fragments sever the halyards holding the flag to the staff, and like a wounded game bird, the banner crumples and flutters down, landing on the battered columbiad mount. Raising his head above the sandbagged bunker he has not left all day, William Lamb groans at the sight. It is galling to realize that Porter will have the last word, after all that Fort Fisher has endured this day. Even more galling are the cheers of the Yankee sailors, carried over the surf by the freshening twilight breeze. As soon as they see the Rebel flag spiraling down, Porter's gunners cease their fire, secure their weapons, and stretch their aching muscles. Time to pack it in for the day; time for chow; time for rest. The Federal fleet retires; a massive and amazing stillness descends on Lamb's smoldering fortress. What a melancholy end to a violent but not terribly destructive day. . . .

What's that? Sudden movement swivels Lamb's head. From a bombproof near the Bastion appears a very determined-looking and *very small* Confederate soldier, scaling the ladder to the topside gun chamber, a coil of tent rope looped over his shoulder. Many of Lamb's men have started to emerge now, and the colonel draws their attention instantly when he points to the climbing rope carrier and shouts, "Look over there, boys! God bless me if it isn't Corporal Conver!"

All eyes turn to where the colonel points. Sure enough, there goes the shortest soldier in the Confederate army, the man known by all and loved by many for having a heart as large as his body is small, the legendary Corporal Ezekiel Jeremiah Prosper-for-Me deVonell Conver, who finishes climbing into the columbiad position and walks calmly through the mass of overlapping craters and jagged shell fragments, and hops nonchalantly over steaming solid-shot and blistered iron bolts. Upon reaching the columbiad mount, Conver kneels down, reverently enfolds the fallen banner in his skinny arms, then loops it twice around his shoulders like a bed roll, tying the ends together around his waist, and without so much as pausing for a deep breath, starts to shinny up the flagpole. At first, no one on Porter's receding ships pays much attention, but inevitably the lookouts catch on to what Conver's doing, and word goes out to man the guns once more. By the time Conver reaches the top, shells start to speckle the sky above his head. Porter orders two of the ships nearest Fort Fisher—the *Kansas* and the *Huron*—to turn back and pull into rifle range. Marine sharpshooters, responding to a blunt order flaring from the *Malvern*'s bridge *(Stop that man!)*, take positions in the rigging and open a brisk fire at their diminutive target. These are some of the best marksmen in the fleet, and it doesn't take long before their bullets find the range. Lamb can see bits of flagpole snapping off just below Conver's feet and close to his steadily climbing hands. But Lord be praised, he's reached the top! Conver chooses to milk the moment, so he acknowledges the cheers of his comrades by giving a jaunty wave. Then he gets to work, trying to put the Confederate flag back where it belongs. The bottom bracket goes on . . . the top one, too . . . the wind puffs up (Is God applauding and lending a hand? Many a Confederate is ready to suppose that He is, and high time, too!), and with a lusty whip-crack, the Stars and Bars snaps taut and proud in the offshore wind! Corporal Conver tosses a salute toward the rejuvenated banner and another courteous but brazen salute to the enemy ships. It's such a crazy-brave theatrical gesture that it wins approval from the Marine snipers—a real *Semper Fi* thing for the little Rebel to do! Killing him now would not be fair or honorable; instead, the Marines wave their caps and hail Corporal Conver with cheers and shouted tributes: *Go to it, little Rebel! Hold your fire, men, that there's one brave little monkey!*

Others are not so sporting. Just as Conver finishes his descent and plants his feet once more on terra firma, another cannonball hits the flagpole, snapping it off just below the lower flag-bracket. Once more the banner falls, attached to the top four feet of the pole, and lands, perversely, right on top of the same battered columbiad mount. By now, Fort Fisher's ramparts are lined with spectators, and a roar of disappointment rises from five hundred throats. Incredulous, shaking his head in disbelief, Corporal Conver surveys the negation of all his heroism and disappears once more into an internal passageway. The men on the walls start to disperse, and Porter's ships resume their unhurried retirement. William Lamb, crestfallen but very proud of his smallest warrior, puts his foot on the ladder leading down from the Pulpit. The curtain has come down on today's drama.

Or maybe not. Halfway down, Lamb hears a chorus of amazed shouts: *Thar he is again, by God! That's the stuff, Corporal!*

Lamb climbs back to his observation post and is astonished to see Corporal Conver climbing back toward the flag, brandishing a Bowie knife almost as long as his arm. He looks bound and determined to get it right, to remount that flag no matter how many times the Yankees shoot it down. There's no way he can reattach the broken top of the pole, so he cuts the banner free of its mounts, spreads it flat, pulls out a pistol, and blows two holes in the mounting corners. So the onlookers will know his intentions, he waves some precut lengths of rope and mimes the act of threading the cord through the bulletholes, then simply tying the flag as high up as he can on the bottom half of the truncated mast. That will make the point well enough. Just as long as he gets that banner up again, high enough for the sea breeze to fluff it out; then Fort Fisher's defenders, not Admiral Porter's gun crews, will have the last laugh. Lamb says a prayer for the little man's safety—somehow, to Lamb as much as to the lowliest private, it has become very important to put that flag back up.

This time Conver doesn't have such a long climb; it's only seven feet, give or take, from the base to the splintered upper end, and hardly any of Porter's ships are throwing shells at him now, despite renewed fuming on Porter's part. Independent of high command, the captains and crews have decided that it's no longer morally acceptable to kill that tiny Rebel on the flagpole. Relieved not to be under heavy fire, Conver takes his time trying to rig the top end of the flag, a process that calls for some tricky balancework and a degree of deftness that would not be possible for a normal-size man.

The last of Porter's ships to turn their line toward the horizon are his monitors, and the last one in formation, the USS *Mahopac*, has been positioned at such an angle and distance that none of her crew had witnessed the flag-raising drama from the start. As the monitor swings its bow due east and pulls away from the fort, the exhausted gunners inside its reeking turret note that someone on top of the Bastion is securing the enemy flag. The *Mahopac*'s crew has just one round left for their huge 15-inch Rodman, a solid-shot. It seems a pity to leave the battle without firing that round at *something.* Since they already know it won't damage the Bastion's walls, and since they now have enough room to elevate the Rodman, that flagpole is the only logical target. There's nothing vindictive about it—nobody's paying much attention to the Rebel on top, and surely the man will jump off as soon as he sees the gun turret rotating in his direction. But Corporal Conver is so obsessed with securing the flag that he doesn't even know there's a monitor down below, taking aim at his flagpole with the biggest cannon in the U.S. Navy's inventory.

If that last round of solid shot had struck Conver, he would simply have vanished in a gruesome red puff. But something much more astonishing happens. The gigantic round passes so close to Conver and the rumpled wad of a flag he's clutching to his heart, that the powerful vacuum formed just behind the projectile sucks the little man into its slipstream and almost rips the flag from his grasp. But the flag unfurls, and before the incredulous stares of every Confederate on the Sea Face, and several hundred Yankee sailors who just happen to be looking in the right direction, Corporal Ezekiel Jeremiah Prosper-for-Me deVonell Conver, grasping the Stars and Bars with both fists so that the flag streams behind him gloriously taut and defiant, sails through the air, dragged along by the suction of a gigantic Rodman round as though by a speeding locomotive, and as he arcs across the sky, above the surf line, down the entire length of Fort Fisher, he's not screaming in fright, but giving full-throated vent to the wildest, most hair-raising Rebel yell ever heard on the coast of North Carolina. His battle cry reverberates in the air for long seconds after the cannonball, Corporal Conver, and the bravely streaming flag disappear into the thickening afternoon haze above the seething turbulence and fanged reefs of Frying Pan Shoals. Like the prophet Ezekiel, who ascended to heaven in a fiery chariot, Corporal Conver's earthly remains will never be discovered; and his death, like Ezekiel's, can only be an eternal presumption, never a case-closed verity. Even as Major Reilly watches, openmouthed with wonderment, when the little man and his flag streak past the ruined Armstrong position, roaring his battle cry, Reilly knows he is witnessing the birth of a legend; knows that two hundred years from now, versions of this incident will be recounted to cynical tourists like a homegrown variation of the Flying Dutchman. *Let it be so that on every Christmas Eve from now to the end of time, there will be some who swear on the Bible that they stood on these worn old ramparts and heard the last Rebel yell of Corporal Conver soar across the sky, eternally bearing the flag of a lost cause. Sail on, my brave but tiny comrade—may we drink together soon from Valhalla's golden cups!*

Such a battle as this, Reilly believes, ought to produce at least *one* good ghost.

4:32 P.M.: Message to Colonel Lamb from Captain Samuel Parker, in the observation post atop Battery Buchanan: *Here comes the answer to your prayers: yet another company of Junior Reserves!* Lamb reads the dispatch and groans. Bragg is beating the bushes for infantry reinforcements, all right, but sending more Junior Reserve companies to Fort Fisher is like offering new clothes to a starving man instead of solid food!

The North Carolina Junior Reserves had been one of Zeb Vance's not-so-bright ideas, even though the governor's intentions were laudable. Two months ago, the Richmond government began drafting 15½-year-olds en masse, and permitting the enlistment of boys as young as 13, provided they had written permission from one parent—and one parent was all that many North Carolina boys still had. Vance thought that the new draft laws were criminal—any nation so desperate for troops as to draft 15½-year-old boys might just as well sue for peace. To prevent a slaughter of the innocents, Vance came up with the idea of a new kind of state-controlled militia, the Junior Reserves, and sold Richmond on the idea by billing the boys as "the seed-corn of the Confederacy." The state would recruit and train these companies, thus saving Richmond a lot of trouble and money, and make them available for combat service after eighteen months' militia duty. During that time, any boy enrolled in the Junior Reserves was exempt from forced conscription, and Vance had no doubt that the war would be over long before eighteen months had passed. His intent was to scatter the Juniors throughout the state, assigning them to guard useful but nonessential facilities, handle routine clerical jobs, serve as guards for prisoner-of-war camps, and perform manual labor on fortifications—thus freeing older, more experienced men for front-line service. He never intended for them to get anywhere near a battlefield. But Bragg's emergency powers overrode those of the governor, and Bragg was funneling Junior Reserves toward Wilmington wherever he could locate them. Companies of Juniors had been trickling in to Fort Fisher for the past week, but after inspecting the first few, Lamb put the boys to work filling sandbags and tried to forget about them.

Although, technically speaking, Bragg could now claim he had sent "three hundred or more fresh infantry" to bolster the garrison, the Junior Reserves were without doubt the worst excuse for soldiers Lamb had ever seen: beardless boys aged 14 to 16, poorly armed, raggedly dressed—quite often in uniforms taken from the dead—and so indifferently trained that most of them barely knew which end of a musket to point at the enemy. Of infantry tactics, they knew just enough to endanger themselves. Major Reilly had suggested, only partly in jest, that if Lamb sent them to attack a Yankee invasion force, perhaps the Yankees would laugh themselves to death.

And now, at the height of Porter's prodigious bombardment, another boatful of them was about to arrive.

4:38 P.M.: When General Bragg wired the commander of Fort Holmes "requesting" (not "ordering") him to send reinforcements to Fort Fisher, the choice fell upon Company 28, North Carolina Junior Reserves, a superfluous outfit that was draining Fort Holmes' food reserves while adding nothing to its strength. The boys barely had time to pack and draw their weapons before being crammed onto a big, slow barge and told they would receive specific orders after disembarking at the wharf behind Battery Buchanan. At first they were too bewildered to be scared. They had been sent to Fort Holmes for eight weeks' basic training, but were treated there with scalding contempt and open derision. So far they've been given four weeks' training, and been armed with old muskets rebored with crude rifling and jury-rigged to accept percussion caps. They've had exactly one hour of target practice, five rounds each, and uniformed in patched-up, mismatched shirts and trousers rumored to have been taken from dead men—scrubbed clean but showing a lot of hastily stitched-up holes. Half of them are barefoot, or wearing footgear so rotted out they may as well be. There's one canteen for every two or three boys, maybe fifteen rounds in their cartridge boxes; eight dull, rusty bayonets to go around; and nothing more. They'd been told they would be guarding railroad bridges, prison camps, warehouses, and such. "Governor Vance will not send you into combat," they were told when they signed up, so there must be some mistake! What's going on over at Fort Fisher certainly looks like combat from where they're sitting!

They're being ferried across the Cape Fear River straight for what looks like an exhaust vent from hell—the roiling, shell-flashed murk above Fort Fisher—and every so often on their voyage, big black whirring objects arch down and throw up huge fountains of water. Nobody's in command except for a nasty-tempered, acne-scourged lout named Gaskins, who was named "sergeant in charge" because he got the highest score at target practice, and now even he is mighty quiet for a natural-born bully, but none of the boys feels like teasing him at the moment, because a big white-puffing shell went off twenty feet over his head in midriver and a piece of it clipped off the bill of his cap and burned a hole in the boat rail where he'd just been resting his hand, and now Gaskins is puking his guts over the side, so terrified they can see pee-pee dribbling from his britches. Then all of a sudden, bang, they're hard against this beat-up, heavy-duty dock and the grown-up pilot from Fort Holmes—the Charon to their Styx—figures he's been under fire as much as he cares for, so he kicks and shoves them out of the boat, screaming at them to get the hell into the fort so they can earn their goddamn keep for once, and then he's gone, backing away so fast some of his passengers fall into the river and have to be rescued by their friends. Now that the boat's gone and everybody's together on the dock, Gaskins orders them into marching formation and they tromp raggedly around a big mound of packing crates and get their first look at the parade ground—littered with hundreds of jagged black shell fragments, steamy-hot cannonballs, and strewn with mushy lumps that look as though they were once part of a horse, a coverless expanse ripped by flashes and violent upthrows of torn earth. "I ain't crossing that," says one boy, speaking for all. The only visible cover are the half-finished entrenchments around the base of Battery Buchanan, so that's where they run to, and there they huddle, paralyzed with fear and indecision.

After a while, someone in the topside gun batteries notices them and starts to tease them pitilessly. "Lookee here, men, we got some more of North Carolina's pets, and this bunch looks even more bloodthirsty than the last. It sure is comforting to know General Bragg wants to send us the best!" Another sweat-glazed, powder-blackened face peers down at them and deliberately squirts a wad of tobacco juice in their direction. "It's goddamned *pitiful* when a place this important is under attack by the whole U.S. Navy and all the Confederate gov-mint can send to help us out is a kindergarten class. I dunno whether to laugh or cry." Then a door at the base of the huge mound pops open and Captain Sam Parker darts out and kneels beside them in the trench, speaking in a more kindly voice: "Boys, y'all can't stay down here, because the Yankee fleet keeps throwin' shells at this rather prominent target, and every four-five minutes one blows up right over where you're hunkerin'. Up on top, we've got bombproof holes we can dive into, but you boys got no protection but the hair on your heads, so sooner or later some of you are goin' to get your brains scrambled. Look where I'm pointin'—straight across the parade ground, there's a big bombproof cave where another bunch of Junior Reserve kids are holed up. They'll make room for you. It's a half-mile run, and I know that open space looks pretty scary, but that's the fastest way to reach safety. Those shell bursts aren't nearly as dangerous as they look, so just haul ass, try not to trip over those roundshots, don't stop to stare at anything dead, and you'll be all right. My advice is to start moving right now, before you have time to get any more scared than you are—believe me, the longer you put it off, the harder it gets to take that first step. Good luck to all of you!"

But the cringing, hopelessly confused boys don't want to move. Big cannonballs are still bouncing around out there, and shells are still popping overhead, and not one of them wants to be the first to stand up and make the commitment. Finally, wiping the snot and upchuck from his shirt, Gaskins the bully heaves himself upright, even though he's shaking so hard the others can hear his teeth clacking. But he's just realized that something else came to him with those stupid sergeant's stripes, something besides the right to torment the boys with only one stripe, and he doesn't have a word for it, but he knows it requires him to pick up his weapon and shout in his unsettled adolescent voice: "You heard what the officer said, boys. We stay here, somebody's liable to get kilt, so suck up a lot of air and follow me!" He's in the open, now, and loping along at a fair pace, but not so fast the others can't keep up with him, and one by one, the boys stand, tuck their heads down, and move out. A hundred yards from the bombproof, they hear other pack of J.R. boys cheering them on, telling them "You kin make it now! Just keep runnin!"

Glory be, they've made it! Next thing most of them know, there's another company of boys whompin' them on the back and making room for them. Gaskins makes a rough head count as they stumble through the entrance, then looks back to make sure there's no one still out there in that horrible open space. "Oh, for shit's sake!" There's a straggler, this one skinny crybaby kid has tripped and turned his ankle and is squatting fifty yards away from safety, shrieking in terror, so Sergeant Gaskins, 16, from Lumberton, runs out to pick the kid up and carry him in, but halfway there, a grotesquely slow-looking round shot from a 10-inch Dahlgren smoothbore takes a quirky bounce and there's this weird "Sssshhh-klak" noise and for a good four seconds, the wide-eyed boys inside the dugout can see just a pair of legs and hips still running, and absolutely nothing attached to them except some stringy ligaments and six inches of knobby white backbone, sharp as a fishhook where the ball snapped it off. After a few steps, the bottom half of Gaskins' body gets the message that there's nothing up top controlling its movements anymore, and it falls forward, the legs still twitching. The crybaby straggler doesn't need another rescue, either, because a big-bore shell lands right on top of him and turns him into a cascade of small, wet chunks no larger than cubes of stew meat. And every boy inside the shelter just sits there with his mouth gaping, unable to accept the reality of what he's just seen, until one small voice declares: "I don't care if they shoot me, I ain't ever comin' out of here until I grow old and die." Chorus of "Amens."

4:45 P.M.: Not until William Lamb followed the Munchhausenesque ascendancy of Corporal Conver had he taken a long, scrutinizing look southward, down the chopped-up, shell-rumpled axis of the Sea Face. Since it fired its first devastating shot, he has lost track of the vaunted

Armstrong gun amid the welter of explosions, but now that it was safe to stand upright and take a careful look around, he is distressed to see Reilly's pride and joy lying cracked and impotent at the base of the wall. Reilly himself also appears, now that the shelling is tapering off. Looking weary and sad, the major's making his way toward the Pulpit, pausing at each gun chamber to inspect the damage and to say some encouraging words to the uninjured crewmen. Reilly plays the role of comforter well; Lamb wonders if he can do the same for Reilly.

Lamb jumps in surprise when a runner taps his shoulder and hands him a smoke-stained dispatch. Numb-fingered, Lamb unfolds it, already knowing, from the messenger's dull-eyed expression, that it contains more bad news. It seems that a parting shot from one of Porter's monitors has deprived him of the best weapon on the Land Face, the 7-inch Brooke rifle that had been sharpshooting all day at the monitors' gunports, suppressing their fire very effectively. A hundred-to-one direct hit, late in the day, when the enemy gunners weren't even trying. The Brooke is a total loss. Only one of its crew was injured, but that was a man Lamb can ill afford to lose: Colonel Malcolm Sutton, Reilly's counterpart for the Land Face artillery . . . one arm hanging by a thread, severe facial lacerations, possible skull fractures. . . . Dr. Reece gives Sutton a 50–50 chance of living through the night, but a 100 percent chance of being blind and brain-damaged for the rest of his life, however long that might be. Foul luck indeed! Lamb wads up the message and throws it toward the sea. An aide climbs the Pulpit ladder and hands the colonel a bucket of clean water. What luxury to wash the grit from his face and hands!

Now, only the back half of Porter's first line is still pumping out broadsides, while its captains wait for their turn to join the eastward wheel of ships. Their big stern pivot mounts are trying to "bowl" their round shot up the beach and into the log palisade screening the Land Face. One round takes an abortive flight path thanks to a defective powder charge; it sails high over the palisade and drops two hundred yards beyond, into Lamb's galvanic minefield, where it lands atop one of those buried spheroids and detonates it, pushing up a very impressive mushroom of sand. Lamb remembers how excited he was about planting those deadly seeds and wonders how many of their detonating cables have survived today's nonstop concussion. His ordnance men have struggled all year long to keep the mines active, despite storm surges, erosion, and the fact that sand crabs keep nibbling on the waterproofing stuff that's supposed to keep the circuits functioning at all times. Perhaps, when the Yankees land, they will oblige Lamb by charging right through the torpedo field. He makes a note to send an ordnance team out to check on the cables' condition, but at the moment that seems a low priority.

Reilly finally makes his way from the Pulpit Battery to the Pulpit itself, crawling part of the way on hands and knees because much of the connecting walkway has collapsed. Tersely, he describes the ruination of the Armstrong gun and boasts about the terrific damage it caused with the second and last shell it ever fired.

"If Richmond had given us three more of those, and ample ammunition, we might have sunk a dozen ships today," mumbles Reilly. Then, forcing an optimistic but shallow smile, "So, how did we do, Colonel? As a whole, I mean."

Lamb shrugs and sags against the split pods of fallen sandbags, finding they made a surprisingly comfortable lounge. "The reports are still coming in, Major. And by the way, you are hereby promoted to brevet colonel and placed in sole command of all Fort Fisher's surviving artillery. The seven-inch Brooke got smashed to pieces at about four o'clock and unfortunately Colonel Sutton was gravely wounded. Reece thinks he may not last the night, so like it or not, you are his successor. And while I'm thinking happy thoughts, I'm naming you my second-in-command. Of everything. If I should fall tomorrow, I will at least feel secure in the knowledge that you will make a hard fight of it after I'm gone. Unless some miracle brings General Bragg to his senses, we will probably be outnumbered by at least ten to one when the Yankees launch their assault. Even if you are pushed back all the way to Battery Buchanan, resist as long as humanly possible. Every hour we hold out improves our chance of being rescued by Hackett's division. Ideally, Fort Fisher will grab the enemy by the nose, then Hackett will come down from Sugar Loaf and crush them from behind."

"Thank you for your confidence, Colonel. I will do my best. Hell of a way to get promoted, though."

"I know you will, and yes, it surely is."

The last of Porter's battle lines had passed beyond effective range. The ear-cracking, all-enveloping roar, which had been constant and oppressive for five hours, is over. It is possible, once again, to hear the rush of waves and the cry of birds. As the ringing in their ears subsides, they also can distinguish individual voices, as more than three hundred men, who have spent most of their day buried alive in cramped dugouts, begin to emerge, blinking in the light like moles, jubilant to find themselves alive, and giving thanks to God for the simple pleasure of drawing a deep breath untainted by falling sand and the brimstone reek of powder smoke.

"Somebody's hailing you, Colonel. Down there." Reilly points to the terraced stairs leading from the parade ground to the Pulpit. Yes, a familiar voice, but distorted, dry and cracked in pitch, its owner quite out of breath but gamely shouting his name. Lamb rises with great effort and peers over the railing at the back of his command post. "As I live and breathe, Chase Whiting! Reilly, look there—it's General Whiting! And he looks like he could use a hand."

Whiting gratefully allows the two stronger men to boost him up the final steps. The general is no longer a robust man—if, indeed, he ever was—and he's about to fold from sheer exhaustion; his uniform's black with sweat and crusted top to bottom with sand. Lamb helps Whiting to recline against the sandbag lounge, hails a nearby soldier, and orders a fresh canteen brought up for the general. That request is passed along from one shouting man to another, and in remarkably quick time, a flying canteen sails up from below, which Reilly neatly catches and passes to the panting, woefully begrimed Whiting. Eyes shut with pleasure, Whiting drains half the water in one long guzzle.

"General, you look like you've just run a mile."

"More or less, Major Reilly. If I remember the survey data, the distance from the apex of the Northeast Bastion to the wharf behind Battery Buchanan is about sixty-two hundred feet. I landed at the dock about twenty minutes after I heard the start of the bombardment, and it's taken me this long to cross that distance on foot. Of course, I was forced to take cover numerous times. Do you know, gentlemen, there's enough iron strewn around that parade ground so that a sprightly man might cross that same distance, leaping from fragment to fragment, and never once put his feet on solid earth? So, although my intentions were to join you as soon as I heard the firing commence in earnest, it has taken me much longer to get here than I planned."

Lamb comes to attention and salutes. "Now that you are here, General, I relinquish command of Fort Fisher into your capable hands!"

Whiting peers up at Lamb as though the colonel has been knocked senseless by concussion.

"Christ, William, you can't be serious! I came over to lend moral support, offer the benefit of advice, based on my infinite military wisdom, remove from your shoulders the burdensome task of dictating needling telegrams to that human cipher, Bragg, and if necessary, add one more rifleman to your infantry reserves. Besides, wild horses could not have kept me from witnessing this battle—although Admiral Porter's rain of shells apparently kept me from seeing most of it. Not least of all, though, I came to bring good news."

"A commodity that's been in very short supply recently. I am all ears."

"Reinforcements are supposedly on their way, by barge and ferry, from Fort Caswell. Only two companies, not a tenth of what you need, but at least it's a start, and they're grown-up regulars, not those pathetic scared-rabbit 'Junior Reserves' that Bragg keeps digging up. Even better: you will not have received a telegram about this yet, because the line to Wilmington's been cut by the naval barrage, but a picket launch arrived from upriver just as I was climbing onto the wharf, and it seems that the lead element of Hackett's division has finally arrived in town—General Kirkland's brigade. By now they should be deploying into the earthworks on Sugar Loaf. If the enemy attempts a landing tonight, Kirkland's men might wreak havoc while the Yankees are still jammed in their landing boats. Hackett's other two brigades will straggle in later tonight or tomorrow morning—the rail lines between here and Petersburg are shot to hell, as usual. Speaking of shot to hell, has there been any sign yet of Butler and his transports?"

"None whatever. I suspect Admiral Porter is asking the same question right about now."

5:26 P.M.: Indeed, Admiral Porter is. Pacing like an angry bear on the *Malvern*'s bridge, he vents an ursine roar when Butler's armada finally appears on the horizon. At first, the two commanders in chief exchange salvos by signal lamp, but Morse code is a poor medium for expressing umbrage, rancor, and mutual recriminations of a highly unprofessional nature, so the two flagships drift dangerously close, so Butler and Porter may rant at one another through megaphones, much to the amusement of their nearby subordinates. Butler knows he's late—very late—arriving at the rendezvous, and so attempts to gain advantage by launching the first rhetorical broadside:

> BUTLER: *Why was the powder boat detonated without my being here? You had no right to do that!*
> PORTER: *"Detonate" is hardly the word—the experiment was a farce, a flop, a very pretty fireworks display that entertained the Rebels greatly but did no more harm to their fort than I would have accomplished by ordering every man in the fleet to turn his arse toward the walls and all break wind simultaneously. Had you been on station when you were supposed to be, you could have given the order to start the action, if that's what it can be called. You were not, and as I am in command of everything that floats, I proceeded.*
> BUTLER: *I explicitly told General Hawkins not to start his assignment until I was on hand to give the order! I never dreamed he would be insubordinate!*
> PORTER: *He was not insubordinate—he simply assumed you were there, which you should have been. You made him your sacrificial goat, but General Hawkins made a very brave attempt to carry out your orders, and I am happy to say we rescued him after the great fizzle.*
> BUTLER: *Where is Hawkins now? I demand you return him to my ship immediately!*
> PORTER: *He is recuperating from wounds and fatigue. You'll get him back when I judge him to be recovered, and not before.*
> BUTLER: *He's a valuable member of my staff, Porter! I need him close at hand when we launch our amphibious landing!*

> PORTER: *If you value him that highly, why were you so eager to put his life at risk by ordering him to carry out a suicidal assignment?*

The two commanders continue in this vein until both are reduced to hurling the rudest personal epithets. Porter finally announces that he's too tired to continue such a "pointless argument" after supervising the "greatest bombardment in naval history" and informs everyone in earshot that he expects the two "most important" ground force commanders, Generals Weitzel and Curtis, to attend a last-minute strategy conference in the *Malvern*'s wardroom tomorrow at ten o'clock sharp. He very pointedly does not invite Butler. Butler protests the implied insult. Porter tells Butler he can attend only if he plans to take personal command of the land battle, a task even Butler knows is ludicrously beyond his competence. Butler knows when he's been outharangued, and stomps off the bridge of his new flagship, the *Chamberlain*, in such high dudgeon that men clear a path for him lest some drop of venom fly off his quivering jowls and contaminate their skin.

6:52 P.M.: Porter commands that every gun crew in his fleet be treated to a double ration of rum, and excused from duty until tomorrow morning. As for the sailors who more or less spent their day as spectators, Porter puts them to work restocking ammunition from a supply convoy that arrived from Beaufort just after dark. Once these two final orders are promulgated, Admiral Porter considers his duties complete and retires, as usual, to enjoy his supper in the privacy and comfort of his cabin. After the colored stewards clear the table, Porter writes a note to Rush Hawkins, inviting him to join the admiral for brandy and cigars. When Hawkins reads this summons, he immediately senses that something is in the wind; he just hopes he won't become a pawn in the new, rapidly burgeoning power struggle between Porter and Butler. Hawkins has seen Butler crush too many foes, political and bureaucratic, to relish the idea of being in the line of fire. But he finds the normally garrulous Porter in an expansive mood.

"I have informed General Butler that you're recovering from unspecified injuries and extreme fatigue. Which means, my dear Hawkins, that unless you have a burning desire to bask in his company again, you're free to stay aboard my flagship as long as you wish. It's the least I can do for a man who showed such courage in trying to accomplish an impossible task, one that was almost certain to get you killed or captured."

"Just doing my duty, Admiral."

Porter regards him skeptically but not unkindly. "You didn't really volunteer for that job, did you? I saw your face when Butler made the announcement. He sprung that on you like a bear trap, and in such a public setting that you could hardly refuse without appearing to be a rank coward."

Hawkins fidgets uneasily and drains his brandy glass, hoping Porter will offer a refill. Porter obliges, then leans forward to light Hawkins' cigar.

"You have something on him, don't you?"

"I beg your pardon, Admiral?"

"On Butler. You know where that rancorous little toad has buried some of the bodies, or hidden the loot, or . . . whatever it might be. Nothing is too outrageous to surprise me where that man is concerned, but I wouldn't *dream* of putting you on the spot by asking why, exactly, Butler 'volunteered' a general to carry out a mission that could just as easily have been given to a private. Had the powder boat scheme succeeded, you would have been a national hero and most unlikely to spill the beans. My hunch is that Butler somehow corraled you into some kind of shady operation that may have left you compromised, vulnerable to being tarred with the same brush as Butler. But if you'd come back as a hero, you'd be far less inclined to work against Butler than for him. If, on the other hand, the powder boat was a dismal failure, and you got an arm blown off for your efforts, your anger at Butler might have provoked you to reveal . . . who knows? Something that he preferred to keep well hidden might be thrust into the light of journalistic and political scrutiny, so if the powder boat was sunk by enemy action, or blew up prematurely, it was to Butler's advantage that you go down with your ship. Whichever way the affair turned out, Butler gained an advantage, either by ensuring your continued discretion and loyalty, or guaranteeing your permanent silence. He did not expect that the powder boat would be a flop *and* that you would not only survive, but also come back as a hero."

Hawkins is clearly flustered, so Porter adopts his most soothing tone of voice. "Your pardon, sir, I didn't invite you here to give offense or cause distress! Again, let me assure you that I'm not trying to pump the specifics out of you—I know you only as a brave man who did his best to carry out a crazy assignment. But you might at least tell me if I'm getting warm."

"Much to my discomfort, sir, you are. My thoughts are too jumbled to know whether I should tell you more than that."

Porter chuckled appreciatively. "In other words, having been manipulated shamelessly by a general, you naturally don't want to be snared by an admiral as well! Don't worry, Hawkins—if I had any personal political ambitions, *then* you would be doing exactly the right thing. But I am much too blunt-spoken to succeed in politics, and I wear my ambitions on my sleeve, for all to see. Unless I'm greatly mistaken, however, you *do* harbor postwar political ambitions. Things may well turn out, as a consequence of this last great naval campaign, that Butler's stock will fall and my prestige will soar. You are free to return to Butler's service if you like, and with my sincerest wishes for good fortune; or you can remain informally attached to my command, as a special liaison officer. There may be congressional inquiries into Butler's affairs; I assure you, there will be none with regard to my own. Serve me well for the duration of this campaign, Hawkins, and you may find that the endorsement of a popular naval hero could be worth more votes than the patronage of a politician whose best days are behind him and who has made far more enemies than friends during the past four years. And now, if you'll excuse me, I have some paperwork to wade through before I can retire. Please, take the bottle and a few more cigars with you. If you like, you may join me on the bridge to watch tomorrow's bombardment. Best seat in the house!"

This comment is an obvious cue that his tête-à-tête with Porter is over, but Hawkins remains standing, fidgeting uneasily, like a man holding an internal debate. Curious, Porter leans forward with an encouraging but subtly impatient expression: Why-don't-you-tell-the-vicar-what's-troubling-you-my-son? With a sigh hinting at a grave struggle of conscience, Hawkins takes a sealed envelope from his jacket and holds it like a poker player who can't decide whether to fold or raise the ante.

"To keep my mind distracted from my fears, I spent the last hours before the powder boat tug composing this document. It details the means by which General Butler obtained the powder for the *Tuscarora.* He made a deal with one of his profiteering cronies, using funds provided by the army. The supplier sold the powder to Butler at below cost. Butler pocketed the difference and jiggered the paperwork to cover the difference. But the gunpowder was substandard—in fact, it came from a production run that had already been rejected by army purchasing agents. As a result—well, you already know what happened—or *didn't* happen. I don't think Butler knew the powder was inferior but I can produce the original bill of sale as well as the altered one Butler submitted to the government accountants. The name of the industrialist who swindled Butler is recorded in this envelope, and the trademark of his company appears on several documents. Any attorney worth his salt—and I *was* one before I joined the Army—can backtrack from these documents and bring to justice a man who knowingly sold substandard powder and thereby compromised a top-secret military operation. The name is a prominent one, and the firm in question has made millions by doing contract work for the Army. It seems obvious from the crookedness of the gunpowder deal that this gentleman no longer holds General Butler in very high regard.

"My hunch is that if a team of Federal investigators suddenly showed up at his office, confronted him with proof that he has defrauded the U.S. Army, and offered to go easy on him in exchange for everything he knows about Butler's *other* shady dealings, along with information about the various cartels that did business with Butler on a regular basis, lining his pockets and theirs at the expense of the war effort as a whole. In other words, I've laid a trail of bread crumbs that could lead to major scandals in which General Butler was either a participant, or the guiding mastermind behind the schemes.

"If you find this information sufficiently thought-provoking, Admiral Porter, I'll hand this over to you, in return for your promise to lock it up in that wall safe yonder. What, if anything, you choose to do with the information later is a matter for your own discretion. I'm sure you would only make use of it for the good of the American people."

Porter's eyebrows furrow, his eyes reveal a complex parade of emotions, but he does reach out and take the packet.

"Why are you entrusting this to me, General Hawkins?"

"Because I believe you to be a man of integrity, and also because I look on these documents as a kind of life insurance policy. There's another copy, by the way, on file with my personal attorney. If anything unusual, not to say suspicious, happens to me during the coming campaign, or if Butler later attempts to discredit me personally, I trust you to do the right thing. You've shown a gratifying interest in me, and reposed no small amount of trust in me as well. This is my way of reciprocating."

Porter rises, walks to the other side of his cabin, twirls a combination lock, and places the packet inside his safe, next to the cipher codes and other sensitive documents already hidden within. Then he takes his seat again and pours another round.

"There are two qualities I value in a man above all others, Hawkins: courage and frankness. The former is what wins battles, the latter is what binds men in honorable friendship. Tell me: How does the title 'chief coordinator of joint Army-Navy operations' sound to you?"

"Far more impressive than 'errand boy'!"

"Then I shall draw up papers confirming your new status, and once I sign them, Butler can rant and rave all he wants to, but he shall never get you back under his thumb. Welcome aboard, sir! Let's clink glasses one more time, to seal our arrangement, and then I really must shoo you out of here so I can finish this damned paperwork."

9:27 P.M.: After Hawkins leaves, a Marine aide brings Porter the last batch of reports, so for the first time the Admiral has a chance to read summations from the skippers of all sixty-four ships, enabling him to tally up the salient facts about this action-packed day, the raw material from which he will fashion his own formal report to the Navy Department. Every ship captain agrees: Fort Fisher took a serious drubbing, its structural integrity must surely be weakened, and apparently most of its big guns have been silenced. On this single day, his warships fired 8,102 projectiles, weighing almost a 500,000 pounds, while sustaining casualties of 22 killed and 69 wounded, fully half of them inflicted by exploding "friendly" ordnance. The auguries are entirely favorable: this operation will be a resounding Union triumph, and to the public at large, the U.S. Navy is going to get credit for making it possible.

9:30 P.M.: William Lamb no longer has a house to use as his headquarters—just a pile of smoldering wood and pulverized bricks—so he's set up a cot, a desk, and a camp table inside one of the bombproofs. Fort Fisher, on this day, suffered 4 men killed and 19 wounded. He defiantly put the name of Corporal Conver in the column labeled "Missing"; let his name remain there always. The fort has expended a third of its ammunition, and a third of the cannon and/or their mounts sustained damage. But amazingly, only two—the Armstrong gun, and the Land Face Brooke—were permanently knocked out of action. Even more amazing is the fact that after absorbing an estimated 9,000 rounds, including some of the heaviest shells ever fired from naval ships, Fort Fisher suffered no significant damage! Lamb feels a quiet glow of pride that his design has been so vindicated, but also regards this as confirmation of his other main contention: the mortal threat to the fort will be from a *land* attack, and despite Whiting's unflagging exertions to find reinforcements, Lamb still commands only 871 infantry, 336 of whom are raw, scared, unreliable Junior Reserve boys. The consolation that finally brings sleep on this most uncommon Christmas Eve, is Lamb's knowledge that Hackett's division is at last on its way. The corollary to that fact, which disturbs him enough to bring on indigestion, is that Hackett's tough, experienced soldiers will find themselves under the tactical command of an officer whom Hackett once famously described as "a pustule on the ass of the Confederacy," General Braxton Bragg. This arrangement is a severe example of what the army euphemistically calls "a bifurcated command," the military equivalent of oil and water. Don Hackett cannot stand Braxton Bragg, and Bragg cannot abide . . . well, just about anyone other than Jefferson Davis.

9:35 P.M.: There's not a man in Fort Fisher who's still bright-eyed and bushy-tailed. The artillery crews are too tuckered out to lift anything heavier than a forkful of beans, so Lamb gives them as much food as they care to eat, distributes a double ration of whiskey, and sends them all to bed. The comparatively well-rested infantry—if one defines "rest" as spending the day huddled like moles in tunnels, caves, and dank bombproof shelters—are the only repair crews Lamb has, and so must work through the night on the most critical sectors of the fort. Lamb sets up a tight rotating schedule: two hours on, two hours off. To fuel their exertions, Lamb's ordered the cooks to set up a temporary field kitchen between the hospital entrance and the big half-moon earthwork constructed in front of the operating theater, which is intended to let fresh air in and keep shell splinters out. The mess table is stocked with ten-gallon pots of coffee and piled high with all the leftover cookies, tea biscuits, cheeses, and expensive canned meats, luxuries previously kept in the storerooms of the Cottage, the accumulated tributes of blockade-runner captains who owed their successes to the shield provided by Lamb's big guns. So far, this work-sleep-eat arrangement seems to be working. Guns are being remounted, ruined sandbags replaced, and sagging bombproof ceilings shored up with additional timbers.

9:45 P.M.: After taking care of these high priority matters, Lamb leaves his makeshift headquarters and walks the length of the parade ground to have an important discussion with Major Reilly, one that Lamb hopes will lead to an acceptable solution to the "Junior Reserves" conundrum. All told, Lamb now has 336 of the poorly trained, wretchedly equipped boys huddled within his walls. The last few days have been so hectic for him and Reilly, that they haven't had time to keep track of how many different "companies" and "partial companies" are represented. For the past ninety minutes, Reilly's been carrying out the only practical scheme he can think of for dealing with the issue. He and two assistants have been combing the fort's caves, tunnels, and bombproof chambers, rounding up the lot of them and assembling them in a relatively uncluttered wedge of parade ground between the Mound and Battery Buchanan and cordoning off an "examination area," ringed with bonfires and dozens of lanterns—enough light to permit Reilly and his aides to take a close look at each Junior and draw conclusions from that individual's face, eyes, equipage, and overall demeanor. One by one, the boys have been inspected, questioned, and subtly tested by engaging the youths in brief dialogues that reveal more about their character than they can possibly imagine. The winnowing-out process isn't as formidable a task as Lamb feared it would be. Given Reilly's many years of service, and his innate ability to take stock of an individual soldier's present state of mind, as well as his potential, most of his choices are easily made.

First to be culled from the herd were those so young, so shaken, so hopelessly bewildered by their situation (made worse by catcalls of "Crybaby!," "Chickenshit!," and "Go home to Momma!"), that no possible use could be made of such pathetic material. Reilly had them shepherded away quickly, deprived of weapons, ammunition, and any other useful military belongings, then packed into one of the fort's little steamboats and taken over to Smithville, where Chase Whiting intended to give them all honorable discharges and send them home.

By the time Lamb joins him, Reilly has divided the remaining 236 Juniors into two groups. The larger by far—184 lads—are not openly quaking in their boots (those who even *have* boots), but Reilly thinks they are weak reeds anyhow. He extends that judgment to include the braggarts and chest-beaters who profess their bloodthirsty eagerness to "Kill me a passel o' Yankees!" As Lamb approaches, some of these boys call out to him ("Hey, Colonel, can we take some Yankee scalps?" etc., etc.), and Reilly mutters out the corner of his mouth: "Mark my words—those are the sorts who'll shit their pants and throw up their hands at their first sight of a Yankee bayonet." Lamb concurs, but surely, within a population of 184 males, one can expect a huge variation in behavior. Reilly agrees. "Oh, sure, some percentage of them will fight, and a few may fight steadfastly. On the other hand, there's also a certain number, maybe fifteen percent of those we interviewed, who haven't got the intelligence of a cannonball—the end products of ten consecutive marriages between first cousins. Do you really want our men standing beside morons?"

Lamb sighs; to ask that question is to answer it. He cannot plausibly justify shipping all 184 of these lads back to the mainland, but, like Reilly, he considers their presence inside the fort to be a liability. They take up space, consume valuable rations, and by virtue of their mere presence are a distracting irritant to his old-time regulars.

But Reilly has also separated a third group of Junior Reserves—a varied mix of 43 boys ranging in age from fourteen to seventeen. What they all have in common is a certain calm, somber, resignation. They're quietly talking among themselves, but he hears no bragging, no whining, no piddling complaints. When questioned, they respond in terse but respectful language. They hold themselves erect, they know their manual of arms, and each one has kept his weapon scrupulously clean.

"What's the story with this lot?" Lamb asks.

"Those are the 'keepers,' Colonel. They may not be very well trained, but I think if you put them in line with the regulars, behind the parapets, they *will* fight. Some potentially good soldiers, here, and they'll learn the necessary stuff pretty quick. Given our shortage of infantry, forty-three more riflemen will come in handy. I took each one aside and asked him privately if he was willing to pitch in, despite the horrors of that bombardment, and each one said 'Yes.' "

"All right, then—see to it at once. Try to match them up with company commanders who won't belittle them, then put them to work like all the others. Just for the symbolism of it, go ahead and have them sign up, take the oath, and draw some clean uniforms that don't already have bulletholes in them! One thing we do have is plenty of spare muskets, so make sure anybody who's carrying a rebored flintlock gets to pick up a new Enfield."

Reilly calls the chosen 43 to attention, marches them out of earshot of their comrades, and explains that they are now officially transferred to the Fort Fisher garrison. While one of Reilly's assistants marches the new recruits off to finish enlistment formalities, Reilly rejoins Lamb, who is still wrinkling his brow at the remaining 174 Junior Reserves.

"Okay, Frederick, I'm waiting for an inspired suggestion as to what we do with this remaining bunch. I don't want them inside the fort, I can't send them back to where they came from, and I can't just drive them out at bayonet point. . . ."

"I'm fresh out of bright ideas, Colonel. I guess, for now, just put 'em to work with everybody else. Maybe something will come to us. . . ."

Hardly are the words out of Reilly's mouth before something does. Or, at least, some*one,* a hard-riding courier who is admitted through the main gate on the riverbank road. The rider brings good news: the first element of Hackett's division has reached Wilmington, and its commander, Brigadier General Rutherford Kirkland, wants to establish contact with Lamb as promptly as possible. Hackett himself, along with his other two brigades, stores, and three-fourths of his field artillery, won't start straggling into Wilmington for at least another twenty-four hours, Kirkland had written, "so my three regiments and five Napoleons are at present all that stand between the town and the enemy landing force that is expected at any hour. There are fairly complete earthworks on the eastern half of Sugar Loaf Ridge, but I intend to extend that line all the way to the river. I am in a quandary as to what I should do about the two isolated batteries covering the presumed landing beaches south of Sugar Loaf, and as I assume you were the officer who ordered their construction, please inform my dispatch rider as to your intentions with regard to those positions. I have no cavalry as such, just few score of mounted scouts, and therefore cannot keep an eye on them with any degree of effect. Nor can I spare a single man or gun to augment those works, not when my line is already stretched to the limit. If such was your desire, I must disappoint you—perhaps you can spare a company or two to bolster these outposts, as General Bragg informs me he has recently dispatched about 400 additional men to your aid. . . ."

Lamb looked at Kirkland's rider in utter bewilderment.

"I did not construct two batteries between here and Sugar Loaf; in fact this is the first I've heard of them. Please, sir, come to my headquarters and show me where these curious emplacements are located. I can offer you a decent meal and some strong refreshment for your obvious thirst."

"If you mean something stronger than coffee, Colonel, I would gladly ride clear to Raleigh for such refreshment! Lead on."

The messenger pointed and Lamb penciled in two U-shaped symbols representing the detached, isolated artillery batteries. They were well sited to cover the best landing beaches on Confederate Point, but that was the only discernible logic behind their existence.

"Major Reilly, the distance between these works cannot be less than 800 yards—they cannot even mutually support each other!"

"Not only that, sir," muttered the courier, between bites of food and gulps of whiskey, "but they're out in the open, just *beyond* the tree cover instead of just *behind* it. I detoured over to this one, closest to Sugar Loaf, and asked the gun crews what perverse reasoning was behind their location. They rather forlornly answered that they had no idea of anything, except someone higher up had named their position Battery Gatlin, and their neighbors to the south Battery Anderson. All the men could tell me was that they were supposed to 'wreak great execution' on the Yankee landing boats, but Colonel Lamb, they won't get off more than two or three shots before the supporting gunboats blow them all to hell! They don't even know who ordered them here. Three days ago they were guarding the bridges at Tarboro and Goldsboro; then they got 'urgent' orders to entrain for Wilmington. No sooner had they unloaded their guns than an officer named Codpiece or Coldcuts or something like that—"

"Colquitt!" exclaimed Lamb. "General Bragg's long-suffering adjutant. So it was Bragg's brilliant idea to emplace those guns where they are. What in God's name does he hope to accomplish with them?"

"You heard the courier, Colonel: 'the wreaking of great execution,' " Reilly says, chuckling mirthlessly. "Please inform General Kirkland that until tonight, we had no idea those batteries even existed. I suppose Bragg expected that either your men or ours would provide infantry protection—in which case it would have been considerate of him to let us know."

"Yes, sir, Major, those gunners are surely hoping *somebody* will send some troops to reinforce them. They've made a halfhearted attempt to dig some rifle trenches on both flanks, but with Butler's eight thousand men expected at any moment, they're mighty skittish about being all alone out there. Unless they get some help, the only thing those boys will 'wreak' is the fastest retreat on record. I suggested they either pull back and join us up on Sugar Loaf, or head south and add their guns to yours. But just this afternoon, a rider came up and handed them written orders, signed by this Colquitt fella, forbidding them to retire without doing 'all the damage in their power' to the landing force. Their position is not enviable. If they stay and open fire on the boats, they'll get buried alive by gunboat fire, and if they pull out without written permission, they'll get court-martialed."

"The whole farcical business has Bragg's fingerprints all over it," says Reilly.

Lamb is busily scratching a reply to Kirkland, avowing his ignorance of Batteries Gatlin and Anderson, and asking Kirkland if he could obtain Bragg's permission to abandon those two useless positions. The courier drains the last of his whiskey, tucks the letter into his dispatch case, and asks for his horse.

"You are welcome to stay and rest a while."

"Thanks, Colonel, but just in case the Yankees sneak some reconnaissance patrols ashore tonight, I'd rather get on back to Sugar Loaf than chance getting caught in an ambush. Perhaps General Bragg would listen to reason if you telegraphed him."

"I doubt it, and in any case, Porter's barrage cut the line between here and Wilmington. I'll try to relay a message through Smithville, but I fear it would be just another exercise in futility. Have a safe trip back!"

Lamb watches the courier gallop off, then turns and stares in slack-jawed astonishment at the map. "Of all the harebrained—"

"William—don't be too hasty! An inspiration just popped into my head."

"I'm all ears, Major."

"Those Junior Reserves we can't figure out what to do with? Why don't we divide them into two companies, put them in charge of two dependable but—well, kind of 'fatherly' sergeants—and have them march up there to reinforce those two batteries? Now, wait, hear me out before you start laughing!

"We have plenty of picks and shovels to hand out—put those boys to work digging entrenchments on both sides of the gun emplacements. When the gun crews see they haven't been forgotten, it will raise their spirits greatly. Between now and daybreak there will be time to throw up some decent earthworks. With infantry protecting their flanks, the gunners might be more inclined to stand and fight, and with artillery next to them, even the Juniors might fire at the landing force too. There will be an interval when the gunboats must cease firing for fear of hitting their own men, and during that time, the defenders at both batteries might be able to hit Butler's men while they're still helplessly crammed into their boats. Sink four of five landing craft, that's a hundred, a hundred and fifty Yankees lost right there!"

"Yes, but once the landing force hits the beach, those Junior Reserves are going to run like rabbits and you know it."

"So what? The ones who want to fight can hide out in the woods and snipe, the ones who want to run can run, and the ones who're inclined to surrender can do so honorably."

"There will be a heavy bombardment before those landing boats go in. . . ."

"If the defenders stay in their trenches, they can ride it out. The dunes up there are pretty flat—my guess is that half the gunboat shells will sail right over their heads. The point is, this enables us to get those boys out of our hair, it gives them something useful to do, it gives those who want to fight a chance to kill some Yankees, and it gives those who want no part of it a perfect chance to run off during the confusion."

"I grant you all those points, Major, but what if the Yankees come ashore north or south of that section of the coast, hit those positions from behind, or on both flanks? Half those boys would die before they had time to put their hands up. And what if the gunboats *don't* shoot high? I know I'm too tired to think straight, but I can't help feeling like I'd be ordering some of those boys to their deaths!"

"You think they'd have a brighter future if they stayed here? Some of them may get killed, sure, but a lot more of them will live if they're up there in the wilderness where they can hide or run away, than would be the case if they were locked inside these walls. Let those who want to test their manhood go up there and do it! And those who just want to get quit of the whole mess can surrender to the first Yankee that comes along. We had a problem, and now it's been solved. There's an end to it."

Lamb needed to hear some words along those lines, and does not mind Reilly lecturing him. Reilly, of all men, has earned the right to speak his mind.

"Of course you're right. Well, go pick out a couple of sergeants to chaperon them and tell the boys that we expect prodigies of valor from them! Don't forget to tell the sergeants that they're free to return here just as soon as they deliver their charges safely to . . . what are they called, again? Yes: Batteries Anderson and Gatlin."

"I wonder who Anderson and Gatlin were?"

"Probably the only two West Point cadets who ever said 'Good morning' to Braxton Bragg. . . ."

Reilly turns and starts to walk away, then pokes his head back inside Lamb's little cave and laughs sarcastically: "Leave it to Bragg to conceive that two isolated, unsupported batteries of field artillery would be able to intimidate a dozen gunboats and eight thousand veteran Yankee soldiers! What's your honest opinion, William? Is Bragg mentally defective, perpetually drunk, or simply the dumbest son of a bitch ever to make the rank of general?"

"Every man I've ever spoken to who's served under Bragg has asked those same questions. Perhaps, now that our turn has come to serve under him, we shall be the first to discover the answers!"

Lamb empties his coffee and draws a curtain across the mouth of his cave. In view of the sort of day he's put in, he thinks it's permissible to crack the seal on one of the last bottles of ten-year-old Scotch he salvaged from the cottage. His final chore of the day is done: he's gotten rid of the Junior Reserves, or at least all of them except that last batch that came over from Fort Holmes so late in the day. Reilly had tried everything to get them to come out of their cave, but nothing worked: gentle entreaties, cajolery, gruff commands—nothing had worked. Like terrified puppies, the boys huddled together in their dank chamber, whimpering, praying, calling softly for their mothers; too massively stunned by the horror they had seen even to ask for food. *("Gaskins was dead, sir! His whole top half was gone, but his legs kept trying to move!")*

What a way to go through your baptism of fire! Yes, it was a horrible, freakish way to die, but at least it was instantaneous—his damn legs didn't feel any pain! Lamb had ordered food and water brought to the cringing boys, and then washed his hands of them. He has no more pity to spare. If they won't fight when the times comes, to hell with them!

William Lamb throws back a big-bore round of Scotch, and the simple physical release bestowed by the liquor plunges him halfway into sleep. He lifts the glass one more time, however.

"Here's to the memory of Corporal Ezekiel-Make-a-Profit-for-Me Conver! May you fly as far as heaven, my comrade, may Elijah share his chariot with you as you drive out to take a look at Mars or Jupiter. . . ." And suddenly, without any preamble, he begins quietly to weep. Not for himself, for he is the Young Soldier of the Lord and this is the place God brought him to, but for Daisy and Corporal Conver, for Junior Reservist Gaskins and for dear, drunken Chase Whiting, who had showed more faith in Lamb than Lamb knew he deserved. Could he not have taken on the Richmond authorities with more courage and less deference, so that his fort might now be home to a thousand more infantry, and its walls bear the steely gleam of twenty more Armstrong guns instead of the grab-bag collection of obsolescent mongrel guns he had scraped together? Could he not have gone to the public press and formally announced that he would resign his commission rather than serve under Braxton Bragg? Too late now. While others praised the magnitude of what he had achieved on these windswept sands, Lamb could only lament the things he *hadn't* accomplished.

For on this very morning, when he finally looked out from the Pulpit and saw the armada he had dreamed of seeing, the nemesis he had known would one day come to test his creation and pass history's verdict on his achievement; when at long last Admiral Porter's stupendous armada had emerged from the blinding fireball of the rising son, William Lamb understood at last the truth of things: no power on Earth could save his fort.

From the day he took command and saw the first shovelful of sand thrown down on the spot where the great Mound Battery would one day rise, everything he had accomplished was futility hiding beneath the mask of heroism. Even to stand a chance, the Cape Fear District needed every man, gun, and shell the Confederacy could send, and yet, for no greater reason than the fact that Chase Whiting's drinking offends the milk-fed sensibilities of Jefferson Davis, the Confederate government had hung around their collective necks an anvil named Braxton Bragg.

One more drink—*My God, where did it all go?*—shifts Lamb's mood from the tragic to the manic. So numerous and grotesque are the ironies converging on this spot, on the circumstances that will shape this fateful battle, that he begins to giggle silently on his cot. Major Reilly, who has returned to tell Lamb that the Junior Reserves were formed up for their own march into destiny and were so full of beans at the prospect that they might actually end up killing some Yankees after all, hears this weird tittering behind Lamb's tent flap and very discreetly pokes his head inside, to see if Lamb might be choking on something. But Lamb is merely exhausted to the marrow of his bones and reeling drunk from throwing down a whole lot of expensive Scotch in a really short time. He waves cheerfully at Reilly and keeps on giggling, even while he's falling asleep—a phenomenon Reilly has never witnessed until this night and one he would have thought, on the face of things, to be physically impossible.

"Hi there, Fred! All our young heroes ready to gorge on their portion of glory pie? Excellent, splendid—then victory is assured. You know what strikes me as funny, Fred? Aside from the fact that I am usually such a cautious, moderate drinker, I mean. It's just that between our walls and Don Hackett's division, we *ought* to be able to crush Ben Butler's balls in a butter churn, y'know? Given the importance of this place, at this time, we should have as our commander in chief a general who combines the steadfastness of Bobby Lee, the tactical audacity of Stonewall Jackson, and the bloodthirsty ruthlessness of Attila the Hun! So, as natural as night follows day, they send us Braxton-fucking-Bragg! As Aunt Charity loves to say, '*Ain't that just like life*?' "

"Which Part of the Turkey Will You Have?"

"CURSES ENOUGH HAVE been heaped on Butler's head to sink him to the deepest hole of the bottomless pit! Everybody is disgusted. Both officers and men express their conviction that the fort was theirs for the taking and that nobody but Butler prevented them from taking it. He is either a black-hearted traitor or an arrant coward."

—Lt. Jonathon Enwright, 117 New York, to his brother, Dec. 28, 1864

DECEMBER 25, 1864

6:30 A.M.: Generals Weitzel, Curtis, and Ames are being rowed to their morning conference with Admiral Porter. General Butler's presence was pointedly not requested, so instead of "seeing them off" he "glares them off." All three generals can feel the mortified rage of Butler's glowering as he skulks from one wing of the *Chamberlain*'s bridge to the other. As titular commander of the Army of the James, Butler should be included, if only as a matter of routine military protocol. But Porter's snub is a calculated gesture of military *contempt*, and Porter knows that Ulysses Grant—who did not want Butler anywhere near this expedition from the start—will back him up. As far as Grant is concerned, Porter can make Butler walk the plank with a cutlass up his ass. So all Butler can do is sputter indignantly as he watches his three subordinate commanders being piped aboard the *Malvern* like visiting heads of state.

They are a study in contrasts, these three Union generals, although they are each coincidentally twenty-nine years old. Until this assignment, General Godfrey Weitzel has not been known as an infantry tactician, but primarily as the best engineer in Butler's army—that he finds himself leading a high-stakes amphibious operation against the biggest fort ever built in North America is a leap in status that can only be explained by his close friendship with Grant. Stolid but reliable, Weitzel is cautious in battle, always more interested in conserving his men's lives than in personal glory. His men, of course, prize him for that, but to the other gentlemen in the boat, Weitzel seems a just a bit, well, *thick*. General Adelbert Ames, commanding Butler's 2nd Division, is slim, wiry, elegant, and considered "Frenchy-fied" thanks to his long, pointed goatee, needle-sharp mustache points, and his irritating habit of incessantly quoting Napoleon's maxims, whether or not the occasion is suitable. Ames is a combat leader of the aggressive, follow-my-sword variety; but he's also generally successful and considering the risks he loves to take, very lucky. Lucky enough to make brigadier general at twenty-seven.

Looming taller than his colleagues and looking, in profile, not unlike a uniformed stork, is General Martin Curtis, commanding the 1st Brigade of Ames' division. Curtis is a hair under six-foot-six and seems incapable of sedate movement—he does not "walk" so much as bound and lope, mantis like. Gravely wounded early in the Peninsula Campaign, Curtis has spent the past two years recuperating at a succession of desk jobs. He knows that this campaign will not only be unique, but will probably be the last big military operation to be fought outside Virginia. The *scale* of the thing appeals to Curtis, too, for it will certainly be judged a "big" battle, yet it is not so huge that one bright, ambitious young general cannot find an opportunity to distinguish himself amid a host of equally bright, but far better known, young generals. Curtis always knows where he is and where he wants to go and he has a knack for spotting the shortest route between those two points. Right now, what he most wants is to be the first Union officer to set foot inside the walls of Fort Fisher. Most of his colleagues are perfectly willing to yield that honor to him.

Admiral Porter greets his three army visitors cordially. He's feeling very optimistic about today's prospects. He is absolutely convinced that yesterday's punishing barrage has weakened the fort considerably and either destroyed or damaged most of its artillery. If the Rebels were able to repair some ordnance overnight, and are impudent enough to challenge the fleet again, Porter intends to detach "hunting parties" of vessels to crush each defiant battery in turn. By midafternoon, he calculates, Fort Fisher will be defenseless. He wants his army colleagues to be able to walk into Fort Fisher virtually unopposed, singing the navy's praises. Porter's been sending ships back and forth all night in front of the landing beaches, provocatively close, hoping to draw enemy fire. The Confederates were playing possum, he tells the three generals, but those patrols netted some useful information. He leads them to a map and proudly points out the newly located Batteries Anderson and Gatlin, in which are housed four 24-pounders, one 6-pounder, and one 32-pounder of unknown provenance. The very existence of Batteries Anderson and Gatlin is news to the army.

"From the look of them, very hasty work, gentlemen, but they are perfectly placed to pour a nasty crossfire into your boats. To eliminate them for you, and to prevent the Rebs from springing any more such surprises on you, I've decided to give you your own private navy: a squadron of fourteen gunboats. To coordinate their actions with the army's needs, I'm also sending a team of expert signalmen who can call down heavy, accurate fire on any part of the landing zone you ask them to hit. The three generals nod approvingly—such massive, flexible artillery support will do wonders for their soldiers' confidence. General Curtis taps his finger on the large, irregularly shaped patches of maritime forest that carpet much of the peninsula, all the way down the edge of Fort Fisher's "dead zone," the 100- to 150-yard-wide strip of bare ground in front of the Land Face. "Lots of good places for bushwhackers to find cover in that scrub-forest," observes Weitzel. "Did your patrol boats see anything suspicious?"

"Well, let's say that there *are* 'bears in the woods,' gentlemen, for we spotted a number of campfires. My gunboat skippers recorded the coordinates of those locations, and we're using the same maps you are, so if a sniper fires on you from *this* sand dune, just flash the coordinates to the nearest gunboat, tell them how many rounds you want fired on that spot, then watch the feathers fly. I've tried to think of every possible way the navy can assist—seeing as how General Butler does not appear to have given the matter of fire support much, if any, thought."

Porter's little jab at Butler is rewarded with nods, suppressed sniggers, and exaggerated eye-rolling. Porter wants them to know he, too, thinks Butler an incompetent ass, but he doesn't want to overplay his hand. Butler *is,* after all, an army man, and so are his guests . . .

"Now, while we enjoy this excellent breakfast, pray enlighten me as to the army's plans for this undertaking. For instance, which one of your units will be the first to go ashore?"

Weitzel clears his throat, and his expression suddenly changes from sleepy to sly. "Well, naturally, we all coveted that honor, sir. A number of coin tosses finally narrowed it down to General Curtis's brigade, and from that brigade, the hundred twenty seventh New York. As long as the sea remains calm, we have sufficient small boats to land about five hundred men in each wave—*after* your gunboats have silenced those two batteries, of course! The first companies of the hundred twenty seventh will charge ashore, set up a defensive perimeter, and signal 'All clear!' even as their landing boats are returning for the next wave. We'll shuttle back and forth until the entire expeditionary force has landed, regrouped, and our patrols have ascertained whether there are significant Rebel forces in the vicinity. I expect we can land two regiments tonight, and the remainder, along with the bulk of our supplies, by noon tomorrow. I myself plan to come ashore in the second wave, comprising the hundred seventeenth New York."

Porter thoughtfully strokes his belligerent spade-shaped beard. "What supplies are going ashore tonight?"

"The usual light marching-order stuff: a hundred rounds per man, field rations for two days, some entrenching tools, a few kegs of water. General Butler's in charge of bringing the heavy loads ashore." A shadow of consternation crosses Porter's face.

"I assume he packed the supply vessels in regulation amphibious order."

"Hell, Admiral, none of us has ever made a shore landing before—I don't even know what 'regulation amphibious order' is," says Weitzel.

"It's a pretty simple concept, General Weitzel, one even Butler should have no trouble grasping. That simply means you load the supplies in reverse order, so that the things you're likely to need first are the last items packed in the holds."

The three generals look at him blankly. Not wishing to cast a shadow over this bright and auspicious morning, Porter decides to drop the subject. He does feel duty bound to press the larger issue on his mind.

"If you don't mind some advice from an old sailor . . . I would make every effort to land the entire expeditionary force, along with as many supplies as you can manage, tonight. I did not care for the look of the sky this morning, and I fear we may be in for some more nasty weather."

"I could not agree more, Admiral," pipes Adelbert Ames in a startlingly shrill voice. "We should not dally, but press ahead with the utmost vigor. As Napoleon said, '*Audace! Audace! Tujours l'audace!*' " Porter notices the other two generals hiding a smirk and gets the notion that Ames may have a tendency to quote the emperor a bit more often than his colleagues care to hear.

"And what of General Butler's subsequent plans, after the first phase of the landing has been completed?"

Blank faces. Obviously the three generals thought they *were* describing Butler's plan, but if the admiral is *really asking:* "When will Butler move his own fat ass ashore?" they don't have a clue.

There's a knock on Porter's door, and the admiral calls out with unexpected jollity, "Enter, o bearers of the Yuletide feast!" A spick-and-span Marine guard flings wide the cabin door, and in stroll three almost ridiculously jolly sailors clad in festive holiday costumes, right down to green stocking caps with annoying little bells sewn into their tassels, bearing large trays full of tarts, cakes, fruit-filled pastries, and bowls full of hard candies that are so true to their designation that General Ames chips a molar biting into one. Bringing up the rear are two extremely self-conscious Negro stewards bearing two large vats of well-fortified eggnog. Porter scoops the first cup and raises it in salute.

"Gentlemen, as ludicrous as it may sound, given where we are and what we're about to do, I truly wish you all a merry Christmas! Dig in, gentlemen, dig in! Indulge yourselves for twenty minutes or so, and then I have to weigh anchor, so that I can give the order for my fleet to open fire and completely ruin the enemy's Christmas!"

"My word, Admiral," exclaims General Curtis, "I do believe there's a great deal more 'nog' in this recipe that my mother uses in hers!" Evidently Curtis prefers this recipe to Mom's, for he drains three cups with hardly a pause for breath. The other two generals follow suit, and before long, the wardroom is awash in conviviality. Porter beams—nothing props up a man's spirits more than good, strong Cuban rum! Had Porter another hour to spare he would order up the flagship's little band and teach these tight-assed West Pointers how to dance a hornpipe—by the time they've being rowed back to Butler's flagship, they'll be singing sea chanteys. Porter lets the party roll on for another twenty minutes before diplomatically showing his army friends to the door. As he's shaking hands with them, he remembers to make a subtle and ambiguous gesture that all three generals, now fairly well lubricated, regard as wonderfully magnanimous: he places in General Weitzel's hands a quart jar full of eggnog, wrapped in gaily festive red and green ribbons, to which is affixed a card inscribed: "To General Butler! You've been a good boy, Benjamin, so here's a present to brighten your Christmas spirit, from old Saint Nick!" Weitzel takes one look at the card and begins to laugh so hard Ames has to pound him on the back.

On the boat ride back to the *Chamberlain* the three generals are in boisterously high spirits. General Butler is, of course, watching them from the port bridge wing, like a one-eyed fox outside a chicken coop, but his pique at their rollicking mood is at least somewhat mollified by his Christmas present, especially after he drinks the first cup.

7:45 A.M.: Between 3:30 A.M. and dawn, William Lamb found a slice of time when he honestly could not think of anyone or anything that still laid claim on his attention. He therefore steals from history two hours and eleven minutes of sweet restorative sleep. But now, in accordance with his final mumbled order, he's awakened by a sentry, who brings news that the enemy fleet has just popped over the horizon. This time Lamb feels no sense of urgency—amazing how quickly one gets used to certain extreme situations! Having paid rapt attention yesterday when the U.S. Navy performed its battle-line ballet, he has no great interest in watching the spectacle again; he knows that another seventy minutes must elapse before Porter orders firing to commence. Lamb therefore prepares for today's encounter in a leisurely fashion, taking time for a hot-water shave, a pancakes-and-ham breakfast, and a quick perusal of the telegrams that have piled up during his slumber. There's no mention of "reinforcements," although Bragg exhorts him to "punish the enemy's squadrons even more severely than you did yesterday!" This last remark is a bit of a head-scratcher.

Considering the enemy has 624 guns and Fort Fisher only 38, Lamb's artillerists made a brave showing yesterday. Early in the fight they *did* damage two Union ships so badly they were forced to haul away for major repairs, but that still left Porter with 62 ships and these put out such an avalanche of fire that Lamb's gunners were forced to spend much of their day cringing in their dugouts. Whenever there was a lull, they emerged gamely to return fire and did so to good effect. All told, Lamb's gunners probably tagged another fifteen Union ships, but the damage inflicted ranged from trifling to moderate. "Punishment" was not the right word for it; the hard headed and thoroughly practical Admiral Porter probably would have described the cumulative damage sustained by his ships as "annoying" rather than threatening. And how the hell did Bragg know any details of the Christmas Eve engagement? He had never left his headquarters in downtown Wilmington—which in itself was rather puzzling. Bragg might be aggravating, erratic, grumpy, and fully capable of taking vindictive action against someone who had played a joke on him forty years earlier, but he is not a coward. Most generals would have been curious enough to hop on a steamer and make the twenty-seven-minute trip downstream to see with their own eyes how things were going at the fort.

To hell with Bragg! Lamb prefers instead to relish the thought that on this second day of battle, Fort Fisher has a surprise in store for David Porter. When the Admiral sailed away, his last glimpse of the fort must have given him the impression that his barrage had mauled the place, for there was still an immense pillar of smoke rising from the interior and none of its guns had not fired for more than an hour. But Lamb's basic theories had been validated beyond question: fortifications built out of sand proved remarkably easy to repair. His garrison has worked like Trojans to rebuild parapets, breastworks, duck board pathways, and broken gun mounts. Porter doubtless thinks today's action will be more or less a mop-up; figures he can finish demolishing the place in time to enjoy an early supper. Lamb smiles at the thought of how furious Porter will be when he focuses his old-fashioned Nelsonian spyglass on the Sea Face and sees the fort looking virtually untouched despite the hundreds of hits his ships scored yesterday. Doubtless, too, Porter must have felt certain he had shattered or dismounted all but a handful of Lamb's big guns. In point of fact, Lamb has lost only two pieces. Thanks to the all-night efforts of his work crews, Fort Fisher *still* has twenty functioning cannon on the Sea Face alone. Assuming the Rebels have not already evacuated the fort as a doomed relic, the most opposition Porter expects to face is the occasion brave, defiant, but mostly symbolic shot flung at him by a few die-hards.

As Lamb watches the Union ships for their battlelines with a deliberation and lack of vigilance that borders on smugness, he gnashes his teeth in frustration. How simple it would be to order nine or ten guns to track a single target, then, at his jubilant signal, catch that vessel in a devastating cone-of-fire ambush, hammering it from bow to fantail with a couple of massive, devastating salvos! Any ship smaller than the *Colorado* would be ripped apart instantly. What a shock would surge through the entire armada! What a *message!* What a temptation! There was a world of difference between damaging a warship and totally obliterating one with a single concentrated blast. The obvious problem with this trick is that you could play that card only once, because doing so would reveal the location of all the operable Sea Face armament. Porter's response would be to mass groups of ships against each of the gun positions thus unmasked, and take them out one by one. So Lamb has to reject that tactic, although it galls him terribly. His task is to preserve as much of the fort's powers of resistance as he can for the longest possible time. Reluctantly, therefore, his orders to Major Reilly remain the same as yesterday: one shot, fired by different weapons every half-hour, to drag out the contest as long as he can, so as to deny Porter the satisfaction of easy demolition, to buy time for the whole of Hackett's division to assemble on Sugar Loaf. He can do nothing to prevent the Union Army from landing, but he doubts they will launch an all-out assault until the fort's guns really *are* knocked out of commission. So Lamb must forgo the joy of scoring a clean, decisive sinking in favor of landing a blow here, another one there, throughout another long, noisy, exhausting day. If only Lamb had a few more Armstrongs, a fresh regiment of reserve infantry, a few hundred more shells! But he does not. He must husband ever shot until the ground attack, at which point there's no reason not to expend every shot in his magazine if by doing so he can slaughter enough Yankee soldiers to halt the attack in its tracks.

8:19 A.M.: Porter's fire is more methodical today, too, and his second and third lines are each three hundred to four hundred yards closer to the shoreline. Lamb had read his opponent's mind accurately: Porter is chagrined and angry when he realizes that his "smothering" Christmas Eve bombardment had generated more smoke and fireworks than actual danage to the fort and its armament. So today, Porter's rules of engagement call for shorter ranges and more precise aiming—tactics predicated on destroying Lamb's guns, not knocking down his walls, a goal that appears beyond the Navy's ability to achieve even with 624 guns. If Porter's ships have to endure a few more hits in exchange for more accurate targeting, then so be it. And so it proves to be, for even at the rate of one shot every thirty minutes, Lamb's gunners score eight thumping-good hits that morning, inflicting more damage and casualties than they did during the whole Christmas Eve bombardment.

8:26 A.M.: Lamb is blown off his feet when a 10-inch columbiad in the Pulpit Battery rears up, muzzle digging into sandbags, after a red-hot splinter from an air burst penetrates the barrel and explodes the powder bag just rammed home by the crew. The columbiad is a total loss.

8:32 A.M.: Porter is especially eager to silence the Mound Battery and detaches three ships with orders to fire only at that target. Not long after those three vessels open fire, they score simultaneous hits on *both* sides of a 6.5-inch Brooke rifle, sundering the reinforcing bands and splitting the barrel like a peeled banana, decapitating one gunner, transfixing another with a 4-foot piece of iron that spears through his belly and nails him to a revetment; a third member of the gun crew suffers an even novel injury when the massive powder flash incinerates his clothing and peppers his flesh with thousands of grains of blazing gunpowder. For a few seconds, he spins around and around like sparkling, shrieking top, until one of Porter's Marine sharpshooters takes pity and drops him with a remarkably accurate head shot.

On the *Malvern*'s bridge, Lieutenant Benjamin Porter congratulates his crotchety father by remarking on how much improved the fleet's shooting is today. "One by one, we are pulling out their teeth!" he exclaims. But Admiral Porter is unhappy with the slow, ponderous progress his gunners are making in their systematic reduction of Fort Fisher's aggregate firepower, and it really chaffs his sense of fairness that even if he does "pull the teeth" of every battery on the Sea Face, not even the combined efforts of every ship at his command will be sufficient to blow one good breach in those walls of sand. His gruff response to the lieutenant's intended compliment: "Yes, that is all well and good, but I would be much happier if I could break the whole jaw instead."

11:04 A.M.: Porter has placed one of his most experienced officers, Lieutenant Commander Oliver Glisson, in charge of the fourteen gunboats he's loaned to Butler to support the amphibious landing. Glisson's primary job is to silence Batteries Anderson and Gatlin. But it turns that out these batteries really don't need much "silencing"—not a single one of their cannon fires a shot at the gunboat squadron. Despite the frantic entreaties, curses, and appeals to patriotism made by a few veteran sergeants and one foolishly brave lieutenant who is standing upright on Battery Anderson's sandbagged revetment, trying to demonstrate to his raw, poorly trained gunners that this kind of barrage "ain't half as dangerous as it looks" when a Parrott bolt slices off his left arm between elbow and shoulder, leaving the limb attached by an inch-thick strand of muscle and skin. His young, inexperienced artillerists are flat-out paralyzed with terror and refuse to budge from their log-roofed shelters, even for the time it would take to pull a firing lanyard. All they can see of their fallen lieutenant is a pain-knotted fist dangling over the lip of their trench, and in their well-intentioned haste to drag him to safety, they lunge for the hand and start pulling on it.

"Not THAT one, you fools!" howls the wounded man, but too late—the lieutenant's arm tears off in their hands and that's the last they see of him, for he leaps to his feet, screaming in mingled pain and indignation, and runs into the woods, making a beeline for Sugar Loaf so he can find a surgeon, leaving the gun crews of Battery Anderson, and the Junior Reserve infantry hiding in rifle pits on either flank to fend for themselves, which they do by leaping up right into the gunboats' barrage and scattering pell-mell into the forested maze of dunes behind the now-abandoned strongpoint.

Things are no better eight hundred yards to the north, at Battery Gatlin, where an exasperated sergeant is trying to get *his* gun crews to at least shoot back at the gunboats, only to run into a brick wall of logic when one crewman retorts: "What the hell for? We'll only make 'em mad at us!" Minutes later, these gunners too, along with their half of the Junior Reserves, simply abandon the position *en masse.* Out of pity, the naval gunners hold their fire—there is no fight left in those refugees, and continuing to lob shells at them while they're running away smacks too much of outright murder. Shortly after 11:30 A.M., the lookouts in their crow's nest perches can't see any more life at all in Anderson and Gatlin.

With no more Rebel cannon to shoot at, the gunboats form a single column and steam slowly up and down a five-mile loop from the seaward rump of Sugar Loaf to the edge of the cleared "dead zone," 150 yards north of the Land Face. In a leisurely but thorough fashion, they drop concentrations of fire onto every sand dune and patch of woods that looks as though it might shelter a band of bushwhackers. Even though the gunboats are within easy rifle range, nobody fires a single shot at them. Glisson suspects there's a good reason for the lack of resistance: except for the boys who ran away earlier, there just *aren't* any Confederate troops between the top of Sugar Loaf and the Land Face of Fort Fisher. No scouts, no wily bushwhackers playing possum—*nobody.* Glisson orders his flotilla to stop wasting ammunition. It's quite obvious to him that Butler's landing boats can go ashore wherever and whenever Butler tells them to. Leaving the other thirteen ships slowly patrolling up and down the coastline, he anchors his vessel close to the general's flagship so that he can deliver this good news personally to Butler. After coming alongside the *Chamberlain*, Glisson signals his intention to come aboard and convey "important information" directly to General Butler. Ordinary military courtesy requires someone on Butler's flagship to acknowledge this message promptly, but after ten minutes of truculent silence, Glisson orders his own boat lowered and is "welcomed" aboard by a nervous, insecure-looking ensign.

"Has General Butler been informed of my visit?" Glisson snaps at the uneasy young man.

"I believe so, sir."

"And? . . ."

"None of the ship's officers has been told what to do. It may be that General Butler is ill . . . or something."

"If I have to report to Admiral Porter that Butler refuses to see me, the general's condition will surely worsen. Just point me toward his stateroom, son, and I'll take it from there."

Glisson finds Butler behaving strangely, oscillating between slump shouldered inertia and brief spurts of manic activity. When Glisson states unequivocally that both Rebel batteries have been destroyed and that neither the cannon nor the infantry supporting them fired a single shot at his gunboats, the information seems to irritate Butler more than please him. His bulbous, nerve-dead right eye keeps rolling as if it were not properly attached and the unafflicted left eye twitches in such a regular, repetitive manner that Glisson imagines there's a tiny, gnome-like entity imprisoned within Butler's skull, frantically sending a coded message: *Help me, kind stranger, to escape from this vile cavity!* After Butler digests the news that Batteries Anderson and Gatlin are no more, he makes a very cryptic observation:

"Well now, sir, that might be good news or it might be the bait that sets us up for a cunningly laid trap!"

"If there were some Confederates lurking about, why would they sit by passively and allow us to demolish two well-entrenched and perfectly good batteries of field artillery?"

"Ah-HAH!" Butler exclaims, wagging a stern finger at Glisson. "Exactly my point!"

Glisson is frantically trying to think of some way to bring this bizarre dialogue back down to earth—for God's sake, there's a major military operation scheduled to begin . . . well, in about fifteen minutes from now. He tries to mollify Butler by sounding as unctuous and fawning as he can.

"General Butler, every time we saw a possible Rebel hiding place, we shelled it vigorously. I assure you, there *was no resistance whatever*, nor any sign of enemy troops attempting to move away from our salvoes, not even when I took the risk of moving my ships so close to shore the enemy could have thrown rocks at them. Aside from those two pathetic batteries, we saw no entrenchments, no scouts, no movement of troops from either the fort or the direction of Wilmington. We could have rowed ashore and had a picnic, it was so peaceful along those beaches."

"Mmmm. Yes, but then, it *would be*, wouldn't it?"

"I'm not sure I understand the general's meaning."

Instantly, Butler's mood changes and he becomes decisive, jittering with energy. Glisson can't wait to get back to the navy, where any officer who behaved in this manner would soon be facing a board of inquiry.

"Five hundred men! I shall commit only five hundred to start with, and leave the boats drawn up for a quick evacuation if the Rebels ambush us."

"Begging your pardon, General, but I *am* an experienced sailor and I would bet my brass buttons against your gold watch that we're in for bad weather tomorrow. Wouldn't it be smarter to land as many men and supplies as possible while the surf is still favorable? My guns will be covering you all the way in, and if my lookouts spot so much as a single skirmisher creeping up on you, we'll bring down the wrath of God on his head with all of the one hundred and eighteen guns at our disposal. I give you my word on it."

Maybe *that's* the reassurance Butler's been waiting to hear, because his mood and manner suddenly improve. He sounds quite rational now.

"Very well, then, very well, we shall see what we shall see, after the first wave goes ashore. My God, look at the time! We'd better get cracking, eh?"

2:00 P.M.–3:00 P.M.: It takes longer than expected to lower all the gigs and lifeboats and to load them, but not overload them, with troops. Despite their many rehearsals of the procedures involved, the New Yorkers are on edge—expecting to be fired on at any moment—and they get tangled footed performing even the simplest actions. When the boat-line—bearing 500 men from the 127nd New York regiment—finally gets moving, General Curtis orders his oarsmen to double their stroke, so he can have the honor of being the first Union soldier to set foot on Confederate Point, a historic achievement that takes place at approximately 2:50 P.M. The remaining boats land in good order, General Weitzel arriving with the second wave. With commendable energy, Curtis throws out a half-moon line of skirmishers. Weitzel is surprised at how smoothly things are going, and he knows it would be foolish not to take advantage of the amazing lack of resistance, so he sends Butler an upbeat report: *Landing area secure. No shots fired. No sign of enemy activity whatsoever. Suggest you land the 114th New York in its entirety as rapidly as possible. I am organizing a reconnaissance in force toward Fort Fisher*

3:50 P.M.: General Adelbert Ames comes ashore with the last installment of the 117th New York, 420 men, and a random assortment of supplies piled in to fill any leftover spaces in the boats. Just as Ames steps ashore, there's a ruckus among the skirmishers posted on the southern end of the landing zone: they've spotted a white flag waving above the battered remains of Battery Anderson, about 350 yards away. Ames rounds up two companies from the 117th and marches off to investigate; General Curtis—who doesn't want to miss any moment of high drama—tags along. At a prudent distance, Ames deploys his men in a skirmish line, ready to fire if this turns out to be a trap. He commands the white-flag-waver to show himself, hands raised high. A trembling, very youthful voice wafts out in response: "We-all want to surrender, but we're scairt you might shoot us!"

"Don't be ridiculous—nobody's going to shoot you. You have my word."

The response to this is somewhat bizarre: a rustling, sniffling, conclave that sounds like a debate among elves. Then, slowly, the white flag rises, clutched by a sand-covered boy, not more than sixteen, whose nose is running like a spigot. Hesitantly, another disheveled head pops up, then another, then twenty . . . thirty . . . the faces of frightened, shivering kids.

Before Ames can coax them forward, there's a veritable children's choir of echoes from other nearby locations: "Hey, mister, we want to give up, too!"—"Us, too, gen'ral, just please don't hurt us none!"—and like families of rabbits, out from behind nearby dunes and from deep inside brushy thickets, rise more and more boys, hands raised as high as they can reach. They are beyond question the most wretched-looking assortment of teenaged conscripts any of the Union soldiers have ever seen. All identify themselves as belonging to a previously unknown organization called "The North Carolina Junior Reserves." Once they realize that the Yankees really don't intend to murder them, their relief is so palpable that some of Ames' veterans can't help but become emotional.

"If Jeff Davis is reduced to sending children like these to do his fighting," growls one grizzled sergeant, "he deserves nothing but contempt from his own people."

"I'd vote for a good tar-and-feathering," says a nearby private.

When all the prisoners are assembled into a ragged column, their captors start marching them back to the beachhead. Almost immediately the prisoners start asking so many naïve questions that they sound almost like schoolboys let out early for an excursion.

"Will you feed us three times a day?"

"Yes, we will, and it will be better grub, I'll wager, than what your own army's been feeding you."

"Sure can't be any worse," declares one slightly older lad, incongruously sporting a sergeant's stripes. "We ain't ever been paid a penny, neither, not in all the time since we joined up! And them recruiting officers, they *promised* us we wasn't going to be shipped up to the fightin' in Virginia! *Now* look where they've sent us!"

"Stop bellyachin', Billy," chides the Junior Reservist marching beside him. "You ain't IN Virginia, are you?"

"Maybe not, but it sure looks to me like there's a passel of fightin' about to break out right around here."

General Curtis walks over and tries his best to sound reassuring.

"Well, boys, I can't promise there won't be a battle—I mean, that's what all these rifles are for, after all, but we will try to find a safe place to put all of you until we can make arrangements to put you aboard a transport heading north. It may take a while, because there are more important things going on, as you can see, so just stay together, don't cause any trouble, and keep your heads down in case anybody starts shooting. Everybody clear on that?"

"We'll be good as gold, your excellency."

When he realized the Yankees were finally landing troops, General Kirkland decided there was a reasonable chance of hitting the invaders with a surprise counterattack while they were still milling around on the beach. He set off with two of his three regiments, about thirteen hundred men, taking a long detour down the southern side of Sugar Loaf. It might be possible to cut down part of the landing force with a surprise volley, a vigorous bayonet charge, and enough loud Rebel yells to make his modest force sound like an entire brigade. He's counting on the Yankee gunboat captains being reluctant to fire when both sides are so close to each other. If his men can pull this off swiftly, there's a good chance of bagging a few hundred prisoners before the enemy can react with a big enough force to surround his two regiments. The engagement won't decide the campaign, of course, but if it works it will raise Confederate spirits to the sky and greatly discomfit the Union commander in chief, who is rumored to be none other than "Beast Butler," an officer not famous for his ability to react quickly to an unexpected crisis.

At the place where the River Road bends around the western slope of Sugar Loaf, he halts long enough to deploy in battle formation. Before he can resume his approach, however, a couple of mounted scouts ride up and apprise him of bad news: There are now three full strength Union regiments on the beach, and intermingled with them are large numbers of Confederate prisoners. This reduces Kirkland's chances of success to just about zero, so he has no alternative but to cancel the raid and retrace his path back to the fortifications atop Sugar Loaf. Given the number of transports anchored offshore, Butler still might have another full brigade at his disposal, and sufficient daylight left to land it if he chooses. Should Butler decide to march on Wilmington, Kirkland's three regiments are the only Rebel troops available to stop him. Kirkland is also concerned that he's heard nothing from Hackett all afternoon—and it's not like Don Hackett to stay out of touch for this long. There really is nothing the defenders on Sugar Loaf can do now except wait for orders, information, or both. Kirkland prays the next order he received will come from Hackett, not Braxton Bragg.

3:00 P.M.–5:00 P.M.: In point of fact, the rest of Hackett's division *has* detrained in Wilmington, after almost five interminable, wretched days of stop-and-go travel from Petersburg. They're crabby and worn-out from rattling along at a snail's pace in drafty box cars for a few hours, then climbing out and marching on foot while the broken tracks are repaired and the broken-down rolling stock can catch up with them again. Some of Hackett's companies have boarded, disembarked from, and reboarded the same filthy boxcars ten different times. Hackett wants to make damned sure *all* his companies are finally regrouped in the same place at the same time before marching to Sugar Loaf, and when he discovers that the rations gathered at the rail yard by local Confederate authorities are sufficient to feed only half his men, he explodes with frustration. Fortunately, the citizens of Wilmington, who have been anticipating his arrival with near-evangelical fervor, mobilize their own resources to help. From the blockade-runners' storehouses, from the merchants who are still well stocked, and from the cellars, pantries, and smokehouses of private citizens, a cornucopia of food and drink rolls into Hackett's assembly area, conveyed in everything from picnic baskets to freight wagons, and passed out by grateful citizens into the eager hands of their half-starved saviors. Hackett is deeply moved by this spontaneous demonstration of Wilmington's affection and he marvels, not for the first time in his military career, at how quickly a warm meal and a kind word can revive the spirits of demoralized soldiers. Once his men have been fed and hugged and cheered, they form up in high spirits, anxious to reach Sugar Loaf and tear into Butler's expeditionary force while its component regiments are still disorganized and unloading their supplies.

But wait! Here comes the one man Donald Hackett wanted to avoid more than any other person in the Confederacy: Braxton Bragg. Already heavily medicated, Bragg is in a rare mood of benevolence, and after exchanging salutes with Hackett and his staff, Bragg gestures expansively to the crowd of citizens gathered to witness the newly arrived regiments marching off to thrash the legions of that scurrilous rogue, Ben Butler. Wouldn't it be a capital idea, Bragg suggests, for Hackett to stage an inspiring "dress review" through downtown Wilmington? Such a display of Confederate power would raise the citizens' spirits to the sky! And after all, such a parade would only take Hackett "slightly" out of his planned route of march.

Hackett is too dumbfounded to speak. He had planned to march around the city, precisely to avoid its narrow, run-down streets, now clogged with unruly, festive inhabitants, all anxious to get a glimpse of his legendary warriors. The sort of parade Bragg has in mind will add at least two hours to the time required to get his men deployed behind the prepared defenses on Sugar Loaf. At first, he tries politely to demur, suggesting to Bragg that instead of wasting time holding a "dress review" today, it might be even more uplifting to stage a "victory parade" instead, right after he's whipped the Yankees. Right now, every minute of lost time diminishes his chance of attacking the landing force before it has time to dig in. This is not the response Bragg wants to hear, and the general's bristling brows contract in a scowl of distemper. The more Hackett tries to reason with him, the more Bragg pouts and cajoles. Bragg *does*, the general reminds him, have the authority to detain Hackett and his men right there at the railroad station until Hackett accedes to his wishes; Bragg also mentions that he is quite prepared to fire off a petulant telegram to Richmond, the tone of which Hackett can easily imagine: *how much this ceremonial match will mean to the demoralized citizens, how unreasonable and obstructionist Hackett's attitude is, how helpful it would be if the president tactfully reminds Hackett that Bragg's suggestion is an excellent one and, like most "suggestions" made by commanders in chief, can also be rephrased as a direct order—if General Hackett insists on forcing the issue . . .*

A countercomplaint from Hackett to Davis will only serve to further aggravate the Confederate president and accomplish nothing beyond additional delay. Seething with resentment, Hackett finally gives in, reorganizes his men into a long, thin column suitable for moving through the city, while dryly observing to Bragg that it is hardly possible to mount a "dress review" with raw-boned troops clad in ragged, sooty, threadbare uniforms; that in fact, allowing the good people of Wilmington a chance to observe at close hand just how gaunt and travel-worn his men really are, might well have an opposite effect from the one Bragg envisions. Putting in bluntly, his division may be one of Lee's elite frontline outfits, but at the moment they look more like filthy vagabonds and moreover, after being cooped up in boxcars for five days, they *stink.* None of this fazes Bragg, whose opiate-saturated brain has dictated its own agenda and will continue to soothe Bragg's disposition, subdue his physical discomforts, and reinforce his sense of omniscience only if conflicting realities remain at least nominally in harmony with its chemistry. The grinding resentment in Hackett's voice and the eye-rolling incredulity of his staff simply do not register, because Bragg *wants* to see a parade; *needs* to see one; anyone who does not understand the necessity for this thoroughly reasonable request is not to be trusted.

So off they march, to the grudging, pissed-off, music of the division's band, whose snare-drummer stays fractionally off beat, the cornets sour as lemons, and with normally excellent piccolo player emitting a sound that makes stray dogs whimper and slink away. Wilmingtonians lining the curb cringe and grit their teeth; Bragg soaks up every note with a beatific smile, toes tapping to a rhythm only he can parse.

4:34 P.M.: Generals Curtis and Weitzel waste no time in organizing a reconnaissance in force toward Fort Fisher, comprising 240 men of the 127th New York and a score of sharpshooters. As they probe down the River Road, they pay scant attention to the modest brick house that was until just days ago, the home of William and Daisy Lamb. At a prudent distance of one mile from the fort, the two generals leave their main force under good cover, ready to intercept or ambush any Confederates who might show up on the road. Curtis and Weitzel proceed, with their aides and an escort of twenty marksmen, to a low-lying hillock just at the edge of the cleared "dead zone" north of the Land Face. From this well-chosen vantage point, Weitzel steadies his binoculars and makes a very careful inspection of the fort's Land Face, which is still taking sporadic fire from the Navy. Weitzel has seen masses of infantry attack forts before, and his baseline for comparison is the gruesome slaughter attending the failed assault on Fort Wagner near Charleston. In contrast to that modest stronghold, the sheer mass of Colonel Lamb's masterpiece is blood-chilling. Fort Fisher dwarfs Fort Wagner; it's the difference between a modest tombstone and Nelson's Column in Trafalgar Square—the conceptual distance between something merely practical and something truly monumental. He observes that although Porter's barrage has chopped a few narrow gaps in the log palisade, the ramparts behind it look to be virtually unharmed. Positioned to sweep the artificial plain Lamb's men have cleared out to create their "dead zone," Weitzel counts seventeen big guns, apparently untouched by the naval bombardment. Beneath those gun chambers, the walls are so massive, so steeply angled, that scaling them in peacetime would tax the stamina of the strongest infantryman—climbing them *under fire* is not something he wants to think about, much less order his men to attempt. As an engineer, Weitzel knows that the weakest point of any fort, is its gate, but Fort Fisher has no "gate" per se—the Land Face is pierced by a narrow arch, to admit the River Road, and then tapers off to ground level about ten feet on the other side. There is no gate because Lamb could never figure out a way to attach one. But that arched portal is definitely sealed, by a 7-foot-high barricade cut with firing slits, like crenellations on a castle wall; and in front of that barrier, a deep ditch lined with sharpened stakes and tree branches, clumps of vines prickly with briars the size of horseshoe nails; and in front of the ditch, a six-foot strip of tent pegs strung with ankle snapping webs of telegraph wire. From Weitzel's viewpoint as a combat engineer, that barricaded arch is a nastier proposition than a real gate would be. Moreover, the arch is flanked by a pair of stoutly fortified gun emplacements, each housing a 24-pounder. The only way to storm the gateway would be to send a mass of infantry up a narrow causeway and then straight across a slender plank bridge that's almost certainly rigged for instant demolition. To go around this murderous bottleneck, his men would have to wade through a briar-choked wilderness of bogs and black water ponds—the kind of boot-sucking, wading-through-molasses terrain that drains a soldier's resolve no less than his physical strength. Once the troops finally got across this obstacle, they will face yet another: a wide tidal creek that looks forbiddingly deep. Now Weitzel understands why the garrison did not extend the outer wall all the way to the banks of the Cape Fear River—the ground would not support its weight, and it isn't really needed. In the heat of battle, an attacking formation would instinctively drift westward, because in that direction there *was* no massive wall extending toward the river. And by doing so, it would be caught on flypaper. The terrain is so inhospitable, that 50 determined men could stalemate a thousand, once the attackers became ensnared in all that muck and water and saw-toothed weed thickets. Weitzel no longer finds it strange that he can't see a single Rebel soldier keeping watch. To avoid decimating friendly troops, Porter's ships will have to cease fire long *before* a ground attack begins, not *when* it begins, thus giving the defenders a clear warning and ample time to emerge from their shelters and swarm up to their assigned firing positions. Weitzel can't help being impressed by what this fellow Lamb has accomplished simply by having a brilliant eye for terrain—given its location and primary function, Fort Fisher is a masterpiece of military engineering. Even its traditional "weak point" is a death trap. If the defenders have even a single regiment held in reserve, the capture of this target is going to be a slow and bloody proposition, assuming it can be captured at all. As a rough guess, Weitzel figures he will lose one man in three just to get through the gate or across the ramparts and the rest of them, by that stage of the battle, will be exhausted, disorganized, and very reluctant to keep advancing.

So Weitzel tells the men with him that unless Porter's fleet can smash a lot more of the palisade and silence at least two-thirds of the heavy guns mounted atop the Land Face, the proposed assault will be "sheer, pointless butchery." He tells General Curtis that he's going to recommend to Butler that the attack be cancelled.

"General Weitzel, I respect your opinion," replies Curtis, "But I have a very different impression. Those walls, that barricade across the open gate, they are not manned; nor are those big guns on top even trying to fire back at the fleet. I think Fort Fisher may be mostly a gigantic *bluff.* With your permission, I'd like to take a couple of volunteers up to the palisade, so we can get a closer look."

"Help yourself if you must, but don't do anything to get the Rebels riled up—we are utterly unprepared for a general engagement! Personally, I've seen enough for now. I'm returning to the beach to see how many more men have landed."

The way Martin Curtis reads the situation, Weitzel is being too cautious by half. After all, *someone* inside the fort must have seen the New Yorkers' approach, but not one shot has been fired at them. In short rushes, Curtis advances to within fifty yards of the palisade; he notes that the logs are more badly damaged than Weitzel could see from his more distant, oblique inspection. Many of them are so chewed up by shellfire, so loose in their sockets, that a few strong men could yank them out or chop a lane through them with axes. The ramparts and gun chambers don't merely look unmanned, they look downright *abandoned.* Where Weitzel sees latent menace, Curtis smells a whiff of Rebel desperation. He wonders how much closer he could really get . . . then he feels a tap on his shoulder. It's one of the two aides who was adventurous enough to come with him, and the lieutenant is pointing, first, to a man-sized hole in the palisade, and second, to a knocked-down Rebel flag lying about fifteen feet below one of the gun chambers. Curtis understands that this time he might be pushing his luck too damned far (after all, Porter's shells are still landing nearby, although the fleet is concentrating most of its fire on the Northeast Bastion), but he just cannot resist. He slithers through the broken palisade, crab-scuttles up the rampart, snatches the flag, rolls it into a ball, and slip-slides back down the wall, trailed by a plume of cascading sand. From under the very guns of the men to whom it belonged, Martin Curtis has just stolen the flag of the 3rd North Carolina Heavy Artillery.

The aide-de-camp, grinning like a schoolboy, fingers the banner as though it were cut from the Robe of Calvary. "Godamighty, General! If you can talk Weitzel into trying it, I believe we can capture that fort with just the men we've already landed!"

Curtis feels a tingle of excitement. Oh, God, the temptation! From everything he has seen, not to mention the prank he just pulled off, the defenders of this supposedly impregnable fort appear to be utterly cowed by Porter's stupendous bombardment. Butler's probably landed more troops by now, but Curtis thinks that if Weitzel will just hurry forward the regiments already setting up camp on the beach, Fort Fisher is theirs for the taking! He scribbles a note to Weitzel: *Have made extremely close inspection. Damage to fort much greater than you realized. Garrison appears totally demoralized. Land face guns not even manned. Hurry forward with every man you can muster, and we will seize this place before dark!*

But Weitzel is no longer on the beach to receive this startling report. He's already been rowed out to the *Chamberlain*, where he's doing a splendid job of reviving Butler's earlier hesitations. No question, by four o'clock, that the weather's worsening and the barometer is falling fast. Butler knows he has about ninety minutes of reliable daylight left in which to do . . . *whatever*. But he also knows that General Grant told him, in a frigidly worded private letter, that if Butler *does* land his entire force, he had better capture Fort Fisher without dallying or begging for additional troops, or Grant would remove him from command, this time *permanently.* Technically, Butler has some leeway because half of his Second Brigade and his entire Third are still packed in the transports—altogether, he has so far landed approximately three thousand men. Weitzel's gloomy prediction about "sheer pointless butchery" strikes Butler as excessively hyperbolic, but at least Weitzel can testify that Butler's caution was prudent and justified. Butler decides he ought to take a closer look at the fort for himself, before *making a decision*, so he orders the *Malvern* to make a quick run south. Porter's bombardment is certainly a spectacle, and has done a lot more damage to the eastern end of the palisade than to the part Weitzel inspected, but Butler thinks about half the Land Face cannon aren't disabled so much as buried under sand. Attacking that wall is going to be a costly proposition, even if it doesn't quite meet Weitzel's sanguine expectation of "butchery."

But even Ulysses Grant would not want Butler to attack without committing his entire force, and if the weather turns so bad that the entire force cannot *be* landed, then Butler's off the hook, at least temporarily. As the *Malvern* sails back to the landing site, Butler begins praying for bad weather, and the sooner the better.

5:15 P.M.: So near, yet so far! Too agitated to just lie there staring at Fort Fisher's unmanned walls, Martin Curtis storms back to the beachhead and collars Colonel Galusha Pennypacker, the able commander of the 3rd New York, which has just arrived on the strand, demanding to know why his regiment is not already marching to join the other two regiments assembled near Fort Fisher. "We were eager to do just that, General Curtis," insists Pennypacker, "but no sooner had my men disembarked from their boats than a courier arrived from General Butler and handed me this order, which clearly supercedes your own." Curtis grabs the paper and reads Butler's astonishing directive: *No more troops will be landed; prepare to evacuate those who have.* Curtis can see the weather's getting worse, but it isn't *that bad* yet. Well, all right, it's bad enough for the ships' crews to start battening the hatches for a nasty blow, but they're moving around methodically, not scampering up and down the ladders in a state of panic. Worse, though, is the sight of launches and gigs already ferrying men *away* from the beach, one boatload at a time, under lowering clouds that impart a sad, heavy quality to the scene. There is still time, if Butler and Weitzel can summon the energy and nerve, for the Union expeditionary force to grab a once-in-a-lifetime opportunity. He orders a signal flashed to the *Malvern: I am holding your order in abeyance so that you may learn the true condition of the fort. I personally advanced to within fifty yards of the main gate without drawing fire, and climbed to the top of the east-west rampart and captured an enemy flag. I have 250 skirmishers excellently placed to storm the gate at this very moment—the guns emplaced to protect it are not manned, and I can hold the gate with those men alone until the rest of my brigade comes up to reinforce, after which we can sweep the rest of the work without serious opposition. Is my meaning not clear enough? THE GATE TO FORT FISHER IS NOT DEFENDED. IT IS OURS FOR THE TAKING, AND ONCE WE GAIN A FOOTHOLD, THE REBELS HAVE NOT GOT THE NUMBERS OR THE SPIRIT TO EJECT US! If you act quickly, we still have time to achieve a stunning victory!*

Curtis is absolutely sure that Butler—even Butler!—will rescind his order to withdraw as soon as he learns the facts. Unable to just stand there and wait for Butler's response, Curtis lopes off to find Adelbert Ames and plead his case with the division's commander. Ames spots him coming and pauses expectantly—from the Mad Prophet fever glazing Curtis's face, the pending conversation is bound to be interesting. Actually, Ames finds it *very* interesting—if Fort Fisher really is as "takeable" as Curtis says it is, Ames is willing to gamble, but he's not betting all his chips on Martin Curtis's babbling enthusiasm. He tells Curtis to go back and prepare the 127th N.Y. for an assault, and he will personally bring up four companies from the 117th New York to lend a hand—but only if Curtis will take sole responsibility if this shoestring assault turns into a massacre.

"And, Martin, I mean 'take sole responsibility' *in writing*. It's taken me two years to earn command of this division, and I'm not going to throw that away just because you're jumping out of your skin with enthusiasm. I will, however, come along to watch the show, and if I order you to pull back, you'd damned well better obey that order. Do we understand each other?"

"Yes sir, and thank you!" and off goes Martin Curtis, in full-throttle pursuit of Glory. Ames picks four companies from the 117th and orders them to fall in. To avoid argument, if not outright mutiny, he decides not to tell them, until the last possible moment, that they're about to try storming Fort Fisher with less than a thousand men.

As soon as the four companies catch up with Curtis's men, who are already deployed in attack formation on the River Road. Curtis practically drags Ames up to the vantage point Curtis had earlier used when he surveyed the fort. Ames is agreeably surprised: the damned place looks completely deserted! Yes, by thunder, it *is* tempting, and since Porter is still half-heartedly shelling the walls, it might really be possible to cross the "dead zone" without being endangered by anything except the odd "over" round from the naval guns. If they advance at the double-quick until they reach the causeway leading to the gate, and then charge right over that wooden bridge, they can capture that barricade, along with two field guns, which can be turned against their former owners in a matter of seconds. Ames decides to go with his gut on this one. "Okay, Martin, we'll give it a try. But if you suddenly come under heavy fire, I want you to pull back as fast as you can—and that's another direct order."

Ames tells the captains in charge of the four newly arrived companies that they are now under Curtis's temporary command, then goes back to the brush-covered hillock and settles down to watch the drama about to unfold. Martin Curtis moves to the head of the attacking columns and draws his sword. Very dramatic—that blade is the only bright object in a cloud-darkened bruise-colored landscape. No sooner have the two New York regiments cleared their tree cover, and started double-quick through the dead zone . . . and then an unnerving silence descends like a guillotine blade: Porter's fleet has stopped firing, and his timing could not be worse. Ames tenses. If there still *are* Confederates behind those burial-mound traverses who are not as "demoralized" as Curtis thinks they are, it won't take long for some of them to come out of their bombproofs and see what the Yankees are up to. When Curtis and his shining sword reach the halfway point in the Dead Zone, Ames hears the first Confederate shouts of alarms. *Don't wait any longer, man, order the charge NOW!*

But on this occasion, Curtis chooses to follow his orders to the letter. There's still a good chance he can pull it off—so far, nobody's emerged to man those cannon flanking the gate. Another sixty seconds and the New Yorkers will reach the causeway, another forty-five and they'll be pounding across the bridge. The attack obviously has taken the garrison by surprise, otherwise that plank bridge would have been set on fire or blown up, but it's still intact, so maybe . . . Yes, yes, now Curtis is shouting "Charge! Charge!" and his troops break formation, swarming up the causeway as though passing into the wide end of a funnel.

Too late! Too late! Ames spots Rebel heads bobbing up along the Land Face parapet, and the muzzle of the hulking 10-inch columbiad nearest the gate is beginning to turn. *Call it off, man!* Curtis probably doesn't see how quickly the defenses are filling up. Ames feels sick to his stomach—so close, so damned, grab-the-Glory close! Well, there is nothing for it. Time for Ames to act like a division commander. He stands upright, cups his hands, and screams at Curtis to retreat. No doubt Curtis does hear him, for he falters in confusion, all the cockiness goes out of his gait, and he turns around to see Ames standing out in the open, frantically waving for him to pull back.

All day long, the Fort Fisher garrison has been taking it, and now they're eager to dish it out. A ragged, spattering-grease volley flickers atop the Land Face, maybe twenty rifles, hastily fired, and four of Curtis's men go down. Even worse: just as Curtis hesitates at the northern end of the plank bridge, he sees the field artillery crews pouring through the gate and manning their 24-pounders, which are almost certainly crammed with canister. Curtis is brave to the point of recklessness, but he's not going to lead his men into a crossfire of grapeshot delivered by a pair of guns only fifty yards in front of him. He spins around and yells something unheard above the increasing volume of musketry, but Ames can guess it must be something on the lines of "Run for your lives!" and the New York regiments respond with alacrity, sprinting back for the tree line as fast as they can go, slowing down just long enough to pick up their dead and wounded, chased all the way back through the dead zone by swirling dust-devils of spurting sand. Thank God the Rebels' aim is more affected by enthusiasm than accuracy, and only a few more New Yorkers get tagged before they plunge back into the trees. Once under cover, Curtis's men don't even pause to get their wind back—they just keep on running.

"Well, *shit!*" yells Ames, and then he back-crawls down from his sand dune seat and rejoins the others. Behind them, the Rebels are blazing away wildly, throwing out prodigious volleys, whooping and jeering, and cutting down a lot of foliage, but like most overexcited and inexperienced troops, they're shooting way too high and Curtis is able to shepherd his men back to the beachhead without additional casualties.

6:00 P.M.–10:00 P.M.: In all, Butler has landed twenty eight hundred men this day, out of the approximately eight thousand men Grant had authorized for this expedition. By the time Ames and Curtis straggle back to the beachhead, Butler's order to evacuate has been in effect for an hour and ten minutes, but the boatloads of troops are having a much harder time getting through the surf than was the case just thirty minutes earlier. Two boats have already capsized. The wind has turned from chilly to frigid, and from gusty to excoriating—sheets of stinging gray sand sweep down the length of the beach. Just as Ames and Curtis reach the shore again, another boat gets hit broadside by a long thundering comber, plunging thirty-two soldiers and four brawny oarsmen into paralyzing cold and dangerously powerful surf. With commendable courage, their comrades rush out to affect a rescue. All but two of the men thrown out of the capsized boat are hauled to shore, some of them vomiting sea-water and all of them shivering uncontrollably. General Ames curses himself for sneaking off to watch Curtis's long-shot attack when he should have been here, helping to organize the pull out. He climbs up on a dune and makes a quick eyeball estimate, one that turns out to be pretty accurate. About half of the men landed earlier have been taken back to the transports, but the pace of things has greatly slowed. It's not safe to load more than twenty passengers per boat, the oarsmen are dog-tired now, and each leg of their trip takes twice as long. After checking with his officers, he estimates there are still thirteen hundred of his men waiting to be evacuated, and some boat crews are now refusing to take more than a dozen passengers per trip, so only forty or fifty men are being pulled off every half-hour. As soon as the gloomy twilight gives way to full dark . . . well, no point in worrying about that until it happens.

Using whatever tools they've found in the ruins of Battery Anderson, along with flat pieces of driftwood, the young Rebel prisoners are expanding the sketchy existing trenches and rifle pits. "The Juniors", as everyone in Ames' division has taken to calling them, are well aware that they will be the last people evacuated, if they're taken off at all, but they aren't complaining. They're cleaning the debris out of the ruins of Battery Anderson and patiently building a big communal windbreak out of sandbags and empty supply crates, and very skillfully bracing the structure with unfired cannonballs. Big kids are sheltering the littler ones, stoic boys are hugging the frightened ones. Before the eyes of their captors, they're turning into soldiers, in spirit if not in fact.

Meanwhile, the Union regulars remain gathered in the open, afraid to seek shelter for fear of losing their places in line. They try, again and again, to construct bonfires out of soggy driftwood, using torn-open powder cartridges to prime the process. But between intermittent blasts of rain and sadistically unpredictable high winds, they're not having much luck. "Welcome to sunny North Carolina!" grumbles more than one man.

8:20 P.M.: The storm turns worse so suddenly and to such an extreme degree that the surf turns from merely violent to downright murderous, throwing up white-fanged breakers that capsize two more loaded boats as easily as a cook turning flapjacks. Three sailors and five soldiers vanish under mountainous breakers. The survivors have to be pulled out by one of the empty incoming boats, which turns around and heads for the nearest ship. Now there is only a single empty boat struggling toward the beach—which means that out of the nine hundred-odd men still stranded there, only twenty can be taken off. As conditions worsen, the number of sailors volunteering for a turn at the oars has dwindled. When word gets around that three oarsmen have just drowned, that will be the end of tonight's volunteering.

Although as division commander, General Ames is legitimately entitled to preferential treatment, he's been a good sport about letting his men escape first. But now he decides he's had enough. Turning to Martin Curtis, he shouts above the roaring wind: "We're not all getting off tonight—you realize that, don't you?"

"Thought had crossed my mind, yes," mutters Curtis through clenched teeth.

"You know, somewhere on those transports are boxes containing eight thousand blankets."

"I know. Not to mention paraffin and matches, food and water, sheets of water-repellent tenting—a great many useful things, none of which General Butler has thought about loading into those empty boats."

"Hell, he probably doesn't have a clue as to which ship is carrying which stuff."

Curtis knows how to pick up on a hint. "But you do, General Ames, or at least you could find out. There's no point in your staying here and being miserable—take a seat on that boat and go to Butler's flagship. That might be the last boat that makes it in tonight, but in case they try to send some more, you know what supplies we need. Butler will listen to you. He'll need all the sympathetic witnesses he can round up, after today's fiasco. Go on—everybody appreciates your sticking with the troops, but you can help them a lot more by lighting a fire under Butler's ass than you can by staying here."

"Well, perhaps you do have a point. Why don't you come, too, Martin? You managed to capture a Rebel flag, so you're the only hero we've got."

"No. I intend to stay here until every one of these men is taken off. And that includes those poor Rebel sprouts we captured. Damned if I don't somehow feel responsible for their safety, too."

General Ames motions for the incoming boat to hit the beach near his location, then shakes General Curtis's hand. "You did a great job today, Martin. I truly think we came within a cock-hair of pulling it off. I'll see if I can't at least get those blankets ashore before this operation shuts down. Don't worry about being abandoned—there will be gunboats watching over you, and the minute the weather abates, you'll be plucked off in no time."

Because the oarsmen are so worn out, they accept only six more passengers before shoving off, followed by a chorus of curses. Martin Curtis observes how perilous the outward trip is, even when the launch is only carrying one-third its normal complement of passengers. That's the last of them, for certain. It's now pitch-dark, the surf is impossibly rough, and the rain squalls are so thick, he sometimes cannot see the running lights on the transports, even though some of them are anchored only three hundred yards offshore. Ames is a man of good intentions, but he has absolutely no chance of sending back a load of blankets. But the men who've been standing in line for almost three hours do not want to accept the idea that it's all been for naught. They continue to stand in the rain, waiting for the miracle that every one of them thinks he deserves.

Curtis would like to give them a morale-boosting speech, but he can't think of a single phrase. On this beach, at this moment, there is no morale to boost.

We came so close today, I could smell it! If Butler had landed when he should have, and we had stormed Fort Fisher an hour earlier than we tried to, this whole campaign would already be over.

Having told his commanding officer that he feels "responsible" for those wretched Junior Reservists, Curtis now feels obligated to go check on them, at least say a kind word to the most wretched-looking tykes. When he draws near the entrenchments where the Juniors are being held, he is alarmed to see that the three guards assigned to watch them have vanished! No—actually, they've gone down inside the ditch *with* the boys. While the grown-up soldiers were bemoaning their luck and stamping their feet to stay warm, the Juniors have patiently been improving things. They've widened, deepened, and cleaned out the trench. At three evenly spaced intervals, they've excavated fireplace chambers along the side of the trench, which get a nice flow of circulating air but not those killer gusts that have ruined every other driftwood fire, and behold: fireplaces! For starting fuel, they have filled some old ration crates with small dry branches from beneath the gnarled copses of the maritime forest—barely damp! By dismembering a "knapsack Bible" someone's mother gave him, and continuously burning the thin, silky pages in small wads, they've been able to dry out a pile of shards, splinters, and twigs. Once they got a tiny core fire going with those, they stacked slightly bigger pieces of wood against the radius of heat until they're ready to burn, too, and so on, very painstakingly. Now they've got three robust fires blazing, so hot and so impervious to the elements that they can throw any old piece of wood onto the pyre and it will dry out quickly, then combust. So the three "guards" are hunkered down with their captives, toasting themselves on one side, then another. The entire setup is really inviting and Curtis feels a bit like an intruder when he coughs to get their attention.

"Say, fellas, I have some men who got thrown overboard by a giant wave, and they're liable to catch pneumonia and die if they don't get thawed out. Is there maybe enough room to squeeze them in around those fires?"

From their expressions, it's clear to Curtis that some of these boys are enjoying the ironies implicit in the situation. One of the sixteen-year-olds responds with a solemn dignity Curtis finds oddly moving: "Seems to me, we're all in this mess together. Our army lied in every promise they made to us, and your navy's gone off and left you stranded. Boys? Okay if those poor Yankee souls scrunch in among us and get the chill out of their bones?" From the Juniors, a chorus of downright hospitable agreement. Several of the boys even drag blankets and sweaters out of the knapsacks piled above their part of the trench and hand them up to the *general* so he can pass them to the neediest and pretty soon the home-made hearths are ringed with teenage Rebels and grateful Yankees. All the boys want in return for their hospitality is to hear some good, gruesome war stories, which the freezing refugees are only too happy to recount.

Martin Curtis shakes his head in wonder. Those boys were ten, eleven years old when this war started, and here they are tucking blankets around these hardened *enemy* veterans, giving up their places near the fires, and asking questions like: "Have they really got buildings in New Yawk that go up higher'n ten stories?"

This nation will heal. It may be that we had to fight this awful war now, or else fight a worse one in ten years, with even more horrible weapons, but my freezing soldiers and those curious, ignorant, ill-used boys will all remember the night they played "Robinson Crusoe" in this godforsaken place.

There's goes a rocket from the *Malvern* . . . gets the attention of those not too miserable even to look up . . . signal from Butler: *Conditions too dangerous to permit further evacuation efforts. You will be taken off soon as weather moderates. Good luck.*

What a surprise. Other soldiers drift over to observe this memorable vignette and pretty soon they're pitching in, too, rounding up more firewood from the underbrush. Another ten minutes go by and there are now *four* big cheery fires. From his flagship, Butler flashes a petulant reminder: *Extinguish all fires immediately. Do you want enemy to learn your position?*

Scrounging around in heaps of miscellaneous abandoned supplies—none of them food or water, of course—Curtis finds one small signal lamp and flashes a reply that will surely earn him a court-martial if Butler ever finds out who's responsible: *Enemy already knows our fucking position, better than you know your ass from your elbow. Six hundred abandoned and very hungry men of the 2nd Division send their fondest wish that you die of the pox and then roast in hell forever, basted by all that grease on your hair.*

Will Butler up the ante? If he does, will Curtis call his bluff?

"Yes" to both questions! From the ship: *Extinguish those fires at once or I will fire on them with a Parrott gun!*

From the beach: *Try it and we will fire on your ship with six hundred rifles plus this 24-pounder we've remounted.*

Dawn, December 26: Not much sleep for William Lamb and his seven-hundred-man garrison. For all Lamb knows, there are still thousands of Union soldiers hunkering down in the woods north of the fort. At first light, Lamb descries a sizable group of Union uniforms milling around on the beach in the general vicinity of Battery Anderson. He is tempted to launch a sortie and capture them, but there still are a few gunboats hanging around, and besides, when the sun comes up and Lamb gets a better look at those men, every one of them looks cold and hungry. Of course, they might be bait, and he cannot take the chance of losing even one man to an ambush. Besides, as bone weary as his garrison is, there is much work to be done, for Porter's second all-day barrage has done much more damage than the Christmas Eve pounding. For the time being, however, Porter's pulling out, ships vanishing over the bright line of the horizon. Surely the admiral must be low on ammunition. Once Porter's magazines are restocked and the landing force reorganized, the fight will resume. If this day is without violence, Lamb knows it will only be a brief intermission. He prays that, however long the respite, his own government will use it to send him the men, ammunition, and weapons he must have if Fort Fisher is to survive another hammering, much less withstands a better organized land attack than the puzzlingly inept one attempted last night.

6:50 A.M.: Up on Sugar Loaf, General Don Hackett is planning to march down and capture those six hundred stranded Yankees. He knows that, after a night's exposure to the kind of weather those men have endured, they won't put up much of a fight. He's also pretty certain, from General Kirkland's account of yesterday's events, that those poor bastards are the only Yankees left on Confederate Point. It'll be a quick, cheap victory that will give both his division and the people of Wilmington a tremendous boost in confidence.

Unfortunately, Braxton Bragg rides up just as Hackett's about to send Kirkland's brigade down to round up the marooned enemy leftovers. Bragg listens to Hackett's proposal, then irritably shakes his head and growls "Absolutely not, sir! That's clearly a trap! The enemy would like nothing better than for you to divide your command and fall into an ambush."

Hackett explains once again, thinking (praying!) that Bragg has either misunderstood or just wasn't paying attention. He ticks off the salient points on his fingers: There *are* no other enemy soldiers—General Kirkland's scouts saw Butler land about three thousand, and then, apparently changing his mind, evacuated two-thirds of that number last night. This is an action involving zero risk, and it will yield tremendous benefits! Even as he pleads, Hackett sees Bragg's expression turning hard and remote, his perceptions withdrawing beyond the reach of logic and reasonable argument. *What strange world does this man inhabit?* It's incredible, but Bragg seems to be canceling the plan precisely because he knows it *will* work, and if it does, that Donald Hackett, not Braxton Bragg, will get credit for its success. The more passionately Hackett argues his points, the more perversely obstinate Bragg becomes in his refusal. Finally Hackett blurts out: "General Bragg, if you can furnish me with a reasonable explanation for your objections, I am more than willing to hear it."

Bragg takes several long seconds to reply, giving Hackett lots of time to observe the scrofulous flakes of dandruff in Bragg's eyebrows, the repulsive tufts of hair poking out of his ears, and to contemplate how remote Bragg's "truth" seems to be from other men's. *Bragg is not hearing the words being addressed to him!* Hackett might just as well be asking for permission to let his men go swimming naked in the polar-cold ocean or march en masse to Paddy's Hollow for a quick tumble with the whores. Finally, Bragg cuts him off in midsentence by muttering: "Improve your fortifications here, sir, and await further orders." Then the commander in chief of the Cape Fear District turns his horse around and rides back toward Wilmington.

General Kirkland is openmouthed, incredulous. "Maybe if all of the officers signed a petition to President Davis, attesting to the fact that General Bragg has clearly lost his wits and is incapable of exercising rational command—"

"Forget it, Bill!" Hackett snaps, kicking the ground in disgust. "It's been tried before, by far more esteemed generals than I. Davis thinks Bragg's turds smell like rosewater and the only thing that would happen as a result of such a petition is that Davis would simply order us back to Virginia, and replace me with someone more compliant or just someone totally ignorant of what's at stake here. You know the Yankees will make another try, and if necessary another one after that. And at least we are *here.* If we get pulled out, there may be *nobody* else sent to replace us before Grant sends another expedition. As long as we are on the spot, we may be able to work around Bragg, or he may snap out of his trance long enough to make a rational decision or two. Meanwhile, we're stuck with him, so let's do what he just ordered us to do: 'improve our fortifications.' Which I interpret very loosely as meaning: give the men as much rest as you can. I'm off to Wilmington, then down to the fort, to see what Lamb's most pressing needs are. We must do what we can, and time is short."

10:00 A.M.: Benjamin F. Butler knows the seas are still too rough to send more boats in for Curtis and his shivering flock. For an indecisive hour, he storms furiously about the decks of his flagship, trying to figure a way to wriggle out of this mess. But *everything* has conspired against him: the damnable weather, the failure of Porter's bombardment to demolish Fort Fisher, the humiliating flop of the powder boat, General Grant's transparent determination to see Butler fail, the congressional vultures circling around a number of potential scandals, most notably the bogus blockade-runner scheme that operated out of Shelborne's Point—even his crafty plans either to turn Rush Hawkins into his abject political flunky, or to arrange for his heroic death aboard the powder boat—just in case Hawkins decides to testify on behalf of Butler's enemies—things just haven't been going smoothly! Butler wonders if he's losing his touch. All those who want to gnaw his bones and cast him down into obscurity, or into the shameful glare of obloquy, those who gave him military tasks which they knew in advance he was not trained to perform; the conspiracy against him seems to be gaining momentum. But other powerful men have lived to regret the day they plotted against Ben Butler—and one strategy remains open to him: A host of very rich, very influential, and variously corrupted men owe him many favors. If he can get hold of them before they realize how disgraced he will be when word gets out about the failure of this expedition, he might still be able to dodge and weave his way out of the snares of his enemies. And let's not forget the niggers! They love him, at least, and their stock is going to rise rapidly once this war is over. Butler needs to get back on to his home turf and start calling in the debts, mobilizing the constituencies, pulling levers and twisting arms. If he reaches Washington even a few days ahead of the news about this current fiasco, he can draw on a lot more power than his enemies suspect.

At least he does remember to leave orders that Curtis's men should be rescued just as soon as conditions permit. Then, without any word of explanation to the rest of his command or the captains of his transport fleet, he orders the *Chamberlain* to hoist anchor and steam north at full speed.

1:05 P.M.: Admiral Porter doesn't learn about the *Chamberlain*'s departure until his son, Lt. Benjamin Porter, arrives somewhat late to join the postponed Christmas banquet Porter has arranged for the officers of the *Malvern* and for his new disciple, General Rush Hawkins, to whom Porter has taken a genuine liking. Benjamin bursts into the wardroom ten minutes after the jolly feast has begun, and pauses to survey the diners with a quizzical expression.

"I must say, Father, you're looking remarkably calm in view of the news."

Admiral Porter lowers his fork, sips champagne, and returns his son's agitated expression with one of studied equanimity.

"I haven't a clue as to what you're referring to, Benjamin. What's in the wind?"

"It's that man Butler! This morning he suddenly pulled up anchor and sailed north at full speed. He's even left five or six hundred of his men stranded on the beach! He swears that Fort Fisher simply cannot be taken and anyone who tries is doomed to inglorious failure!"

Admiral Porter reinserts his forkload of meat and dressing, a sly, immensely satisfied smile glowing beneath his beard.

"He has? He does? My word, what eccentric behavior! Well, we shall just have to take the fort ourselves, shan't we? Do sit down, Benjamin, and dig in. Which part of the turkey will you have?"

If at First You Don't Succeed . . .

I WAS AGREEABLY surprised to receive a telegram this morning from General Grant, who promises that he will find a man who is "the antithesis of Butler" to lead the second landing force. I gather, from Grant's tone, that something has happened to make him take a more intensely personal interest in the capture of Ft. Fisher than was the case when he gave grudging permission for the first expedition. Pray enlighten me, if you can, as to the reasons behind this most welcome change of attitude . . .

—Admiral David Porter to Asst. Secretary of the Navy, Gustavus Fox, Dec. 30, 1864

DECEMBER 27, 1864—JANUARY 13, 1865

The last boatload of evacuees, including General Ames, just barely made it off the beach at 10:00 P.M. Christmas night.

Despite hopes, prayers, and a welcome slackening of rain just before sunrise, General Curtis and his castaways are not extracted on December 26. From their vantage point on the beach, surf conditions seem to have moderated, but to the crews on Butler's transports, the waves look every bit as lethal as they did when the evacuation shut down the night before. The best they can manage is cobbling together a big, clunky raft, lash some crates of food and water to it, and set it adrift, hoping the current will carry it ashore to their stranded comrades. But once launched, the vehicle stubbornly refuses to move more than a few feet toward shore. After a lengthy exchange of signals, the transport with the shallowest draft inches slowly toward the surf line and tries to nudge the raft gently enough to push it into the landward current. This proves very tricky, as the bottom is constantly shelving and dropping. By the time the ship's bow does find a spot where it can whack the raft without running aground, the hastily constructed vehicle is so soggy and unbalanced that it breaks apart, spilling its precious cargo into the breakers. Some of the men ashore, who haven't had anything to eat for twenty-four hours and nothing to drink except rainwater, begin to cry.

So Curtis and Company spend a second, even more abysmal night stranded on a hostile shore, this time without even raindrops to slake their tormenting thirst. Night comes and brings near-freezing temperatures and the usual merciless wind; they stare enviously at the campfires on distant Sugar Loaf. For the Junior Reserve boys, their first forty-eight hours in "captivity" had seemed rather more of an adventure than an ordeal; being able to share their craftily built hearths with cyanotic and deeply grateful Yankee soldiers had been fun, too. Now, however, everybody's tired of war stories, and the fun diminished when it became necessary to go farther and scrounge harder for firewood. The Juniors have become grumpy, hungry, and are starting to bicker among themselves. Their ostensible captors aren't paying much attention to them anyhow, so a group of 36 boys—as much from boredom as any other reason—decides to make a break for it. Around two in the morning, they simply vault out of the trench and start running. A shivering, half-conscious sentry on the northern perimeter suddenly spots a pack of furtive shadowy figures running through the dunes. Mistaking the mass escape for a sneak attack by Confederate raiders, he fires. This, in turn, causes the other sentries to fire reflexively. Soon there's a lot of wild shouting and helter-skelter firing, not always aimed at anything in particular. One of Curtis's signalmen lofts a yellow rocket, which tells the offshore gunboats to saturate the Yankees' right flank with a ten-minute barrage. The gun crews, being pretty bored themselves, oblige with a fifteen-minute saturation bombardment, walking their shells back and forth in a 200-yard arc until they spot the "All Clear" signal.

After this incident, all the sentinels are so jumpy that they raise three more alarms during the night, and each time the gunboats dutifully respond with another blistering barrage. So in addition to being hungry, thirsty, and chilled to the marrow, nobody gets much sleep. In the morning, General Curtis sends out a patrol, which finds the mangled bodies of eight teenage boys, caught in the barrage as they tried to make their way to Rebel lines on Sugar Loaf. Curtis is now fed up with having to nurse these unpredictable kids, so he hands one of the older boys a piece of white cloth and tells all the remaining Juniors that they are free to go. In fact, if they don't get the hell out of his sight in ten minutes, he's liable to start shooting them himself.

At daybreak, December 27, Admiral Porter steams over to appraise the situation. He's disgusted beyond words to learn that Butler took Generals Ames and Weitzel with him and that the only senior Federal officer left is poor Curtis, who has now been marooned for three days. Porter is equally enraged by the fact that the transport crews haven't made another attempt to rescue the castaways, claiming that the surf is still too dangerous for their boats. "Not for navy oars, it isn't," Porter signals, and then proceeds to give the army crews a demonstration of professional seamanship. *His* boat crews have no trouble getting through the breakers, but no one is greatly impressed because in the hours since sunrise, the wind has mellowed to a gentle breeze and the waves have moderated so drastically that a canoe full of grandmothers probably could make it to shore and back without undue effort. In any case, by 1:00 P.M., all the castaways are wrapped in clean blankets, sipping hot coffee, and channeling their revived energy into fantasies of what they would like to do to Ben Butler.

Once the life-saving mission is accomplished, Porter orders the transports back to Hampton Roads and then leads his armada up to Beaufort for repairs, restocking, and two days of shore leave for his sailors—who have earned it many times over. Porter, however, remains on the *Malvern* in order to compose his official report. Although such dispatches must perforce be written in an objective and dispassionate style, Porter is so good at penning these documents that he can stay within those guidelines and still include scathing accounts of the bungled decisions that contributed to the expedition's humiliating failure. His conclusion is typically blunt: every bumbling mistake and botched opportunity can be traced directly to the dithering incompetence of General Butler. To Secretary of the Navy Gideon Welles, Porter attaches a private letter that is even more explicit than he can get away with in a formal report:

> *I am ashamed that men calling themselves soldiers should have left this place so ingloriously. It was, however, nothing more than I should have expected when General Butler got himself mixed up in this operation. If this temporary failure succeeds in sending Butler back into private life, then it is not to be excessively regretted. Aside from the men who drowned, we suffered no casualties; the biggest cost was all the ammunition, and my gun crews needed the target practice anyway.*

With Assistant Navy Secretary Gustavus Fox, Porter enjoys a much more personal relationship, so in another private letter, the admiral makes clear how determined he is to take another crack at Fort Fisher, and soon:

> *It is strange but true, that the desire to kill and destroy grows on a man, the oftener he hears shot whistle and shells roar, and I must confess that I and all hands are itching to go to work again on Ft. Fisher. In two days of the most intense duel yet fought—in this war and perhaps in any other as well—between fort and fleet, and despite the generally good shooting of Colonel Lamb's artillerists, only two of my ships sustained damage so severe as to keep them out of action for an extended period. By the end of this week, all the damaged vessels will be fully repaired and ready to engage the Rebels in another test of arms.*

> *You know full well how "modest" is my character, but a professional officer must be able to reflect coolly on the mistakes he made in the last battle, and be prepared to correct them in the next. I positioned my battle lines closer on Christmas Day than on the first day, but in the next go-round I intend to throw caution to the wind. I may take a few more hits as a result, but am willing to do so if by engaging the fort from even closer range, I can methodically destroy the fort's guns, one by one, instead of merely silencing them temporarily or knocking them off their mounts. It is clear that no amount of bombardment, from now till Doomsday, is going to break down those massive sand ramparts, but repeated and accurate hits to the guns themselves will greatly facilitate the infantry's task of storming the work.*

Indeed, General Grant's attitude *has* changed, and his enthusiasm for a prompt return to Fort Fisher, followed by a swift and decisive land attack that ends with an unequivocal victory, is prompted by two salient factors.

First, of course, is his rage at Butler, who snookered him by grabbing operational command from the hands of Godfrey Weitzel, who was Grant's first choice to lead the expedition. Grant is still convinced that if Butler hadn't been breathing down Weitzel's neck, the entire landing force would have been put ashore before lunch, and Fort Fisher would have been captured that same afternoon, while its garrison was still pinned down by Porter's fire. It would not have been a flashy victory—that was not Weitzel's style—but it would have gotten the job done in a thoroughly professional manner and at a low cost in blood. Weitzel knows he has let Grant down by allowing Butler to browbeat him and chooses not to petition Grant for a second chance.

Second, Grant wants to do everything in his power to expedite the success of Billy Sherman's bold decision to cut loose of his supply base at Savannah and strike directly at the heart of the rebellion by cutting a swath of devastation through South Carolina, and then North Carolina, with the ultimate objective of linking his army with Grant's somewhere between Petersburg and Raleigh—the greatest double envelopment in military history if they can pull it off, and a deadly noose around the shrunken remnant of Lee's army.

Sherman's chances of success will be greatly enhanced if he has a forward base of supply already in place to support him by the time he crosses into North Carolina. Beaufort has been developed into a good naval base, but its rail and river connections with the interior are too limited to support an army the size of Sherman's. Wilmington, however, is ideal, because the Cape Fear River is navigable all the way to Fayetteville, and if Grant can seize Wilmington quickly, he can have a mountain of supplies already in place when Sherman reaches North Carolina.

Grant sees no reason to replace the troops already allocated for the Fort Fisher attack—members of his staff report that those men feel cheated of a victory that was well within their grasp. Since reaching Hampton Roads, they've read the newspapers, too, and are quite properly outraged at being associated with Butler in any way. They're eager to go back and show what they can do, and Grant thinks they should get that chance. All they need is a new commander, one who has all the qualities so markedly absent in his predecessor.

Grant makes inquiries to some of the generals for whom he has the most respect: you all know what happened and why, now give me some recommendations as to the best available man to replace "you-know-who." The same name appears on several lists: Major General Alfred H. Terry, a thirty-eight-year-old "volunteer" officer whose steady rise up the ladder of rank has impressed even the crustiest West Pointers with whom he has worked. So what if he was an attorney before the war, writes one of Grant's most staunchly chauvinistic West Point classmates? "A case can be made that Yale Law School is to that profession what West Point is to ours," a remark that piques Grant's curiosity even more.

General Terry's record is impeccable. He has that rare gift of leadership which commands respect from his superiors and unswerving loyalty from his troops. He is honest and mild-spoken. In offensive actions, he has demonstrated initiative and determination, and in defensive actions he is always calm, steady, and resolute. Terry also has another especially valuable qualification: he has worked with the navy in combined operations at Port Royal, Fort Pulaski, Charleston, and in several of the river campaigns out west. Even the Annapolis zealots credit him with being "uncommonly up-to-date on issues of naval doctrine, tactics, and technology." Grant forwards these accolades to David Porter, who grudgingly agrees to meet with General Terry, but makes no promises.

Remarkable! The two men get on famously from the moment of their first handshake. Terry somehow manages to suggest improvements in Porter's plans for the second attack on Fort Fisher, but does so in such a subtle, tactful way that Porter thinks they are his own ideas and Terry is merely endorsing them with exceptional perception. "This man is all right," wires Porter to Grant. "I anticipate a harmonious atmosphere in every phase of the coming operation."

One last-minute addition to the roster of infantry units: the two-thousand-man all-Negro 2nd Brigade from Butler's 3rd Division. Both Porter and Terry agree that the most dangerous threat would be an attack from the rear by Hackett's division on Sugar Loaf. It will be the 2nd Brigade's job to throw a line of breastworks across the whole length of Confederate Point to discourage Hackett from attempting such a maneuver. Because the brigade has limited combat experience, Grant allocates six 12-pounders to strengthen their powers of resistance and Porter details four gunboats to remain on station close to their line, to provide heavy fire support if Hackett does try to storm south from Sugar Loaf.

Now that Grant has given the second expedition his full support, the enterprise takes shape with unprecedented speed and efficiency. Two days before its scheduled departure, Admiral Porter summons his new protégé, Rush Hawkins, to the wardroom for a private chat.

"Good news!" Porter booms, pumping Hawkins' hand with the kind of exaggerated "manly" grip that makes knuckles crack and tendons wince. "Sit down, sir, and join me in a proper 'navy' toast!"

Rum is not Hawkins' favorite potion, especially the 150-proof rust remover Porter regards as mother's milk for the true Old Salt, but he understands this midday libation is Porter's way of showing favor.

"What are we drinking to, Admiral?'

"Oh, just the news that Ben Butler has been permanently sacked—not just removed from command of the Army of the James, but booted out of the army forever. This is not only manifest justice, it also has some delightful ramifications. For one thing, it means that Butler has fallen into such a pit of disgrace that he will never run for president, which was his ultimate ambition! Viewed in that light, the failure of our first expedition may literally have saved the Republic! For another, it means you are no longer beholden to him, and whatever shenanigans he forced you to take part in are now forgotten, forgiven, and expunged from your record. Which is distinguished, I might add, by your early victory at Cape Hatteras, your bold attack in the battle for Roanoke Island, and your singular heroism in trying to carry out Butler's ludicrous powder-boat scheme.

"By the way, I've recommended you for a second star. I've also requested you as my chief aide-de-camp for the duration of any operation requiring army/navy cooperation. Butler's successor—one General Ord, I believe—doesn't know you from Adam, has already approved the appointment. So welcome aboard, Brevet Major-General Hawkins! I have a very special assignment in mind for you during the coming attack on Fort Fisher, one that should be, as the saying goes, 'right up your alley.'"

Hawkins feels his stomach knot, the same way it did when Butler told a roomful of officers that Hawkins had "volunteered" to sail the powder boat. But then he relaxes—unlike Butler, Porter has no motive for wanting Hawkins dead. Whatever this 'special role' might be, it can't possibly be as suicidal as the job Butler gave him.

"But, alas, security is so tight for this operation that I cannot reveal the nature of the job until just before the land attack commences. Trust me, though: you'll never have a better chance to earn a medal!"

Hawkins doesn't like the sound of that, either, but thanks the admiral for his trust and assures him of absolute loyalty. Who knows? Porter is the only high-ranking officer to emerge from the Christmas fiasco with his reputation not only intact but greater enhanced. If the navy acquits itself superbly in the new offensive, Porter might become an even more valuable patron than Butler. *Rush, my boy, you have found a cushy berth for yourself!*

Alone among the Confederate authorities involved in December's action, Braxton Bragg is unshakably convinced that the enemy cannot possibly make another attempt to seize the Cape Fear region until late spring, if ever. His report to Jefferson Davis, besides exaggerating the importance of his sagacity, planning, and inspirational leadership, contains euphoric assurances that the immediate danger to Wilmington is over. Were it not for General Lee's insistence that Hackett's division remain in the Cape Fear District for another couple of weeks, Bragg would already have sent those regiments back to Virginia. When Whiting sends Bragg a closely reasoned memorandum, arguing that the important lesson to be learned from the December attack is the absolute necessity to strike an amphibious invasion *at the water's edge*, where its troops are virtually defenseless, Bragg finds it an insultingly fussy and pessimistic document and doesn't even bother to send Whiting a reply. As far as rounding up more cannon, more infantry, and more construction materials for rebuilding the fort to its original strength, Bragg does absolutely nothing. *Why go to so much bother when there won't* be *another attack?*

So Whiting, Lamb, and the already understrength garrison must make what preparations they can. Night and day, the work goes on feverishly. A new, submerged telegraph cable connects the fort with a relay station at Smithville; tons of sand are moved to restore the battered traverses, shattered gun mounts are rebuilt and damaged cannon repaired. Whiting makes a personal visit to the other Cape Fear forts, relying on old friendships and such titular powers as he still can wield as Bragg's second-in-command to appropriate one or two spare guns from each post—reminding their commanders that if Fort Fisher falls, Bragg will surely order them to retreat and blow up everything too heavy to carry away. Most of the pieces he acquires are not equal to Fort Fisher's best (banded 32-pounders and rifled columbiads of elderly vintage and uncertain reliability, but enough of them to bring the fort's artillery back to pre-Christmas numbers). He also pays a few calls on Flag Officer Branch, who had never been one of Whiting's admirers, and finds they have a new common cause: Braxton Bragg, whose chronic inertia and hermetic personality Branch finds acutely disturbing. "Every time I leave the room after speaking to that man, I feel an overwhelming desire to take a hot bath!" grumbles Branch. Sunk in depression after watching the *Raleigh* break in half without a single victory to show for all the time and labor invested in her, Branch has taken up the opium pipe again and doesn't give a damn who knows it. But he does confide in Whiting his strong suspicion that one reason for Bragg's sudden swings from sullen lethargy to manic but unproductive energy, may be attributed to a secret dependency on narcotic medication. These discussions between Branch and Whiting don't produce any warm personal affection—it's far too late for that—but they do agree to cooperate behind Bragg's back. There is still one unfinished warship on the ways in Beery's shipyard, a semi-armored gunboat named the *Asheville*. It's not fit for sea duty yet, having received only one engine instead of the two Richmond has authorized, but it *can* move on the river, and it does mount four 32-pounders and a 6.5–inch Brooke rifle on the bow, so Branch promises to dispatch it down to New Inlet, along with his motley little squadron of armed tugboats and converted coastal steamers, when the enemy fleet returns. The ships will be firing at extreme range, and maximum elevation, so as not to hit the Sea Face by mistake, but Samuel Parker can adjust their fire from his perch atop Battery Buchanan, and at the very least, their combined firepower will give the Yankees something else to worry about. Bragg has issued specific orders that no Marines are to be sent to the fort without his written authorization, but since Bragg has never bothered to find out exactly how many Marines Branch has in Wilmington, he surely won't notice the absence of a boatload or two.

Sam Parker's been pestering Branch about the mighty Brookes still aboard the sunken *Hatteras*, but just as Parker feared, Richmond never sent the equipment needed to raise them and Plymouth fell into Yankee hands only two weeks after the ironclad went down. In lieu of those potent weapons, Parker and Chapman have been training their crews to place accurate long-range fire on the ground in front of the main gate, where the River Road crosses the swamp, and have also prepared firing data for every fifty-yard interval between Battery Buchanan and the interior wall of the Land Face, so that if the enemy does breach the gate, they will be forced to advance through at least a modest sprinkling of heavy shells. Major Reilly thinks this is a wise precaution and orders the Mound Battery crews to start drilling for the same contingency. Of the Sea Face guns, only three of the four comprising the Colombiad Battery can traverse in that direction, but Reilly orders their crews, too, to start zeroing in and has aiming stakes driven into the ground at suitable points, even though there's not much chance they'll remain standing for very long once the naval barrage starts.

But the most onerous job of all is the removal of all the scrap iron Porter left inside the walls, and for that Whiting has to requisition two hundred slaves—the white soldiers won't touch this assignment because there are too many unexploded shells hidden among the general clutter. Lamb's engineers defuse as many as they can, and have the Negroes cart away the live ones that look too touchy to mess with, so they can be dropped into the river. Casualties among the slaves are, fortunately, light, but the knowledge that an apparently harmless piece of junk might explode without warning, does nothing to improve their enthusiasm for the task. It takes a full week to clear all the metal from the parade ground, and when the job is finally complete, Reilly brings to Col. Lamb some very interesting statistics: by his careful calculations, Porter's fleet had fired approximately 20,300 rounds, or roughly 1.3 million pounds of iron. Fort Fisher's entire supply of ammunition, for all types of guns, now amounts to a mere 3,105 rounds. Porter's ships will fire that many rounds every three hours.

If neither Bragg nor the Davis administration feels any urgency about renewed danger to Wilmington, Robert E. Lee is beginning to feel anxious. Confederate agents have gotten word to him that a great armada, the very same that had attacked Confederate Point on Christmas Eve, and this time augmented by several more transports, was observed leaving Hampton Roads on the morning of January 6. Lee has no doubt whatever of the destination and while he cannot spare another division, he's heard enough reports about Fort Fisher's chronic shortage of ammunition to offer Bragg not one but two trainloads of shells suitable for most of the fort's artillery. Bragg thanks him, but assures Lee that the fort is in no immediate danger of another attack—Porter's ships, Bragg assures Lee, are instead headed for Charleston, to affect the long-delayed capture of that city. He gives Lee no hint of the reasons why he's reached this fantastic conclusion—Charleston is so closely invested that there simply is no motive, consistent with common sense, for committing so many resources just for the sake of physically occupying the city itself. Lee finds this suggestion a real head-scratcher for another reason—doesn't Bragg remember having advanced the same peculiar notion back in December? By the time Bragg realizes the truth, it's much too late for those ammunition trains to reach Wilmington in time. Just as well for Lamb's peace of mind that he never learns about it. Resigned once again to making the most of what he does have, Lamb instructs Reilly to adopt the same pinch-penny tactics as before: one round per gun, every half-hour.

Knowing their time together will be brief and bittersweet, Daisy Lamb insists on bringing the children back from Orton and setting up house in the Cottage—which miraculously escaped damage during the Christmas attack. Being able to go there, at the end of each brutally strenuous day, does more to restore William Lamb's spirits than anything short of a fresh division of good infantry. But Daisy and the children do not unpack all of their luggage, for when the time comes for them to flee the impending second attack, they might not have as much warning as they did before.

As it happens, they don't. They send the children back to Orton on the afternoon of January 13, secretly planning to spend one last night alone in the Cottage, refreshing their memories of how very fine it is to lie naked together, a man and woman who know God intended them to be thus, else the contours of their bodies would not *fit* so superbly, so satisfyingly, even after many years of marriage. Daisy is unusually passionate, desperately intent of branding her husband's mind with an erotic icon fit to bring a smile to him even in the hour of his death. William's spirit is attuned, and his heart overwhelmed with tender gratitude, but his nerves are so tight-strung for battle that it takes two hours of patient womanly ministrations before he can rise to the occasion, but by eleven o'clock he is primed for virile duty! And sure enough, at the most promising stage of things, a courier pounds on the door, crying excitedly that Colonel Lamb must return at once, for the lights of the enemy's fleet are coming into view. There's nothing for it but a promise and another kiss. Lamb goes limp again and stumbles out of bed and into uniform. He tells Daisy to pack quickly—he will telegraph Smithfield, and from there a message will be sent to Orton for the plantation's launch to come pick her up. He wants her off the Point before daybreak. "And remember where we were when we left off!"

"I will," she says, rising naked from the bed to enfold his shrinking manhood in a valedictory caress. "I will remember it forever." She will also remember the harsh finality of one certain sound: the metallic slap of scabbard against hip as he strides unhesitatingly down the stairs, to keep an engagement with Destiny that has only been postponed for two weeks, not rescinded or abrogated, as she had prayed it might be, by the mercy of the same God who brought them together so long ago and so perfectly.

One Hundred Thirty Shells Per Minute

WE ARE ALL trustfully looking forward to your operations; may Divine Favor crown your efforts.

—President Jefferson Davis to Gen. Braxton Bragg, Jan. 14, 1865

JANUARY 13, 1865

12:40 A.M.: Somehow, it's more menacing at night: no sound except the omnipresent shuffling of the waves, the undulant wind making its endless sculptures of sand, the running lights of Porter's fleet multiply against the black wall of horizon—an armada so powerful and secure it can announce its presence to the enemy with all lights blazing. One by one, more constellations pop into sight, forming a new galaxy due east of the fort. Lamb, Reilly, and a handful of sentries silently observe their doom taking form. And to the north, dimmer but no less numerous, a second dusting of lights, which can only be the transports. How badly Grant and Porter must want to eradicate the stain of December's repulse, to have remobilized, on such a scale, in only two weeks!

"Wonder who's taken ol' Butler's place?" muses Reilly.

"Does it matter? They don't need to send Napoleon. There is no shortage of perfectly competent generals in the Federal Army." Lamb is grinding his teeth, and it isn't altogether because he's freezing in the wind. "The departure of this fleet could not have gone unnoticed, nor could there be any doubt of its destination, and yet we have heard no word about it from General Bragg! Does he even *read* his mail?"

Reilly tries to sound reassuring, but he, too, is mesmerized with foreboding as more and more lights wink on. Is the entire U.S. Navy committed to leveling this one fort?

"Colonel Lamb—William—the men have been working night and day to repair the damage and General Whiting's been doing everything in his power to find reinforcements. As long as everything has to be routed through Bragg, the most we could expect were half measures taken much too late, by a man gripped in a perpetual stupor. Now, at least, the situation is stark and clear: there comes the invasion, and even Bragg cannot pretend otherwise. He *must* take action—this is his last chance to redeem his reputation, and for that reason alone, he *will* send us help."

Lord, that sounds feeble!

But Bragg already knows the sea is spangled with menacing stars. He's just flummoxed by the unfairness of it all! He has assured Richmond that the fleet in Hampton Roads was "in all likelihood" intending to bring supplies to Sherman at Savannah. Lee's acerbic reply: *"Last week you assured me the fleet was intended to capture Charleston. Just in case it* is *bound for Wilmington, please send exact account of steps you've taken to reinforce Col. Lamb."* How can Bragg now confess the magnitude of his confusions? To make matters worse, Bragg's once-loyal but now barely tolerable aide-de-camp, young Colquitt-from-Georgia, pointedly showed Bragg a stack of Bragg's own earlier dispatches, many of which asserted that Fort Fisher has "already received perfectly adequate reinforcements." Scanning them in private Bragg was astonished—he had apparently alerted dozens of small out-of-the-way detachments, as far away as Charlotte, yet he had forgotten to follow up those alerts with orders that would set those troops in motion toward Wilmington! At this moment, Bragg *honestly* cannot remember which units he has sent down to Lamb, or when. But they *must* be "adequate," because he's assured Davis, Lee, Zeb Vance, and everyone else who's been needling him that they *are.* What's still out there that he can call on at this eleventh hour? How can he word the appeals without sounding completely addled? While all these loose-cannon thoughts are rattling through his brain, Bragg is pouring libation after libation on the vicious tapeworm gnawing on the meat of his cortex. Only after three bottles does the headache finally recede.

Alone in his locked room, Bragg hears the anxious pacing and muted urgency of whispered consultations among his underlings. Soon, he hopes, the laudanum will bestow its blessed sense of clarity and omniscience. When it does, he will take decisive action. He will!

Chase Whiting has been hanging around Bragg's headquarters all afternoon, pretending to process paperwork, organize files, but all the time waiting for his outflank Bragg in Whiting's surreptitious efforts to find reinforcements. It was worth three hours of tedious pretense just to watch Bragg's face crumple when he read confirmation that Admiral Porter was bearing down on Confederate Point, shepherding an even stronger landing force than Butler had brought in December. Naturally, instead of immediately springing into action and firing off telegrams for emergency reinforcements, Bragg balled up the offending dispatch about Porter's fleet, threw it on the floor in disgust, and disappeared into his private chambers. That was the last anyone had seen of him in almost an hour. "How long is he usually, um, secluded?" Whiting asks the hapless but well-intentioned Colquitt. "On the average, about three hours," Colquitt replies with a smirk.

"That gives me time to do take some very insubordinate actions," says Whiting. "If perchance the general inquires after me, just tell him I'm on my launch, heading down to the fort. Technically, you cannot be implicated as my accomplice." Colquitt smiles grimly. "General Whiting, this conversation absolutely never happened."

So Whiting takes the liberty of sending urgently worded appeals to every possible source of help, affixing Bragg's name at the bottom. If Bragg ever discovers that Whiting has done this, of course, it means a court-martial. But Whiting doesn't think he has any more long-term career prospects to worry about, not after the sun comes up tomorrow. His last telegram goes out to William Lamb, over Whiting's own name: *The enemy transports are off Masonboro Sound and a landing appears imminent. Be on your guard. I will be with you soon, either inside the walls or out, leading to your aid whatever troops I can scrape together!*

Having done all he can for the moment, he takes his launch back to Smithville, calmly writes out his will, guiltlessly throws down five shots of bourbon, and lays out his finest dress uniform. He tells an orderly to awaken him at 5:00 A.M., then lies down on a cot in his office for a nap. He's read, and heard from other old soldiers, that there's often a strange kind of peace which descends upon a man who has learned, if not the exact hour, then at least the general circumstances of his demise. So far, that seems to be the case. He falls asleep quickly, and feels surprisingly refreshed when the orderly shakes him awake in the first gray wash of winter dawn.

He enjoys a full breakfast, a few cups of real blockade-run coffee, then performs a ritual as solemn and meaningful as an old matador donning the Suit of Lights for the last time, preparing to face a bull so terrifying and powerful that it would turn the spine to water of many a younger, stronger, more glamorous rival. He adorns his uniform with a racy sash of yellow silk, buckles on his sword belt and pistol. Then he tiptoes into the bedroom and takes one last, loving look at his dear Kate, deep in peaceful sleep. To waken her at this moment would be cruel, so he forgoes any melodramatic "parting words" or overwrought embrace. Instead, he simply leans down to inhale her warm, milky scent and soundlessly mouths the words *I love you*.

Then he walks briskly downstairs, shakes hands with the telegraphist and sentries on duty, and goes down to the dock, where his launch has steamed up and his pilot avoids eye contact and seems rendered mute by the circumstances of this trip. Whiting is agreeable to silence. On this particular voyage over to Confederate Point, Whiting wants only to savor the vistas of the mighty old Cape Fear River, spreading its vast arms toward the sea, smooth as glass, a restful, smoky gray this morning. Halfway to the wharf below Battery Buchanan, the sun comes up and throws the shadow of Fort Fisher across the waters it has guarded so faithfully. The day promises to be fair and brisk, invigorating, and he exchanges a profound glance with a big old pelican who's spent the night on top of a channel marker and is just now stretching its magnificent wings, no doubt contemplating the day's first fish and thankful for the clarity of sky and water, which will make breakfast easy to find. Then the launch enters the dark massive shadow of the fort, and the temperature drops five degrees. The chill of a waiting grave, thinks Whiting, but also the cold purity of honor redeemed. However the battle goes, however long he and Lamb can postpone the inevitable, Chase Whiting knows it will not be *his* name that posterity will revile when the record of this catastrophe is finally untangled. Upon this ground will he purge all ambiguities from his record; after what happens at Fort Fisher, nobody will remember that day in Virginia when everything went wrong for Chase Whiting. Many things *will* go wrong in the coming struggle—such is the very nature of battle—but his conduct will not be one of them.

8:00 A.M.: After studying the maps and interviewing the officers who went ashore in Butler's abortive invasion, General Terry has chosen a different landing site, about one mile north of the beach where Weitzel, poor dunderhead, disembarked his men: a broad sand spit on the southern end of Masonboro Sound, where a long finger of water conveniently guards his right flank from the Rebel forces entrenched on Sugar Loaf. In this calm sea, his men can come ashore dry-footed. Hackett might try to harass the landing with field artillery, but he would be foolish do to so, because revealing the locations of his guns will give Porter's escorting warships a chance to demonstrate that they mount almost fifty times the firepower at Hackett's disposal.

Nevertheless, Hackett's gun crews are itching to sink a few landing boats, and his sharpshooters are confident, even at this long range, that they can throw the landing into confusion. Hackett would like nothing better. He's not afraid of the gunboats, either, because his men can fire, then dive into strong bombproofs before the navy gets their range. But he wants to wait until there are so many Yankees ashore on that wide-open beach, a mass of blue stark against an eggshell-white plain, that he can do the maximum hurt to them in the thirty seconds or so he will have before the navy reacts. He figures he can drop fifty men in that time, and lose only a few in exchange. But just as he's about to give the order, here comes the ultimate spoil sport, General Bragg, who takes one quick look at the mass of blue uniforms streaming ashore and absolutely forbids one shot to be fired at them.

"General Bragg, we can throw them into severe disorder with a single volley, then take cover before the ships return fire. It is worth the risk, sir, if only because it will shatter their confidence!"

"No, sir, I forbid it! I am concerned that they mean to push across the peninsula and attack Wilmington itself, along the River Road, and your division is the only thing blocking them if they do."

Bragg has that glassy-eyed mask of imperturbable calm that signifies his mind is made up and Socrates himself could not marshal enough logic to budge the general's muddled intentions. Hackett gives it a try, though: "General Bragg, why in God's name would they march on Wilmington and leave Fort Fisher untaken in their rear? Whoever their commander may be, he is surely not an imbecile! That strategy would put them practically at our mercy, because the only possible route for such an advance—*as you yourself just pointed out*—would be along the River Road, where the gunboats could not support them and where they would run straight into my strongest fortifications!"

A sudden nasty glint in Bragg's eyes shows he is not so far gone in delusion that he missed the little barb Hackett planted in the word "imbecile." Stone-faced, he turns his horse around and growls: "You have your orders, General. When I have different instructions for you, I will communicate them. The enemy may well choose to strike at Wilmington first, precisely because we do not expect it! I must return to my headquarters now, and compose an urgent message to General Lee. Keep me informed."

General Kirkland's mouth opens in amazement. "*Urgent message to General Lee?* Does he expect Marse Robert to hop on a train and come down here to hold his hand?"

8:45 A.M.: From General Braxton Bragg to General Robert E. Lee:

The enemy has come ashore, in strength greater than one division, near Masonboro Sound, with a large bay screening his landing beach and numerous gunboats in support. While the lay of the land makes it impossible to disturb his landing operations, I do not see that he gains any significant advantage by this choice of location. I retain full confidence in my ability to thwart his intentions, but will not act rashly until those intentions become clear.

9:04 A.M.: This time, Admiral Porter forms his battle lines much closer to shore, as close as the ships can go without running aground. Lamb gives Reilly permission to fire at will while the warships are maneuvering, since this is the fort's best chance to inflict damage. And by God, the gunners load and fire in record time, shredding smokestacks, snapping off a monitor's gun port, perforating hulls, dismounting a couple of pivot guns, cheering as they load and fire and swab and reload, releasing all their pent-up frustration and rage in every blast, knowing these are the best shots each cannon's going to get all day. Lamb counts fourteen direct hits and some near-misses that cut up rigging and injure some sailors, but there are no secondary explosions, no ruptured boilers, and only trifling fires that are quickly extinguished. Porter's ships just shake it off, lurch a little bit from the impact, then resume forming their columns, maddeningly undisturbed. The message is clear: *Do your worst while you can—it makes no difference whatever, in the end.*

Reilly's sense of timing in these matters is now honed to the millisecond—he hoists the "Take cover!" flag exactly eight seconds before Porter's first titanic broadside.

Colliding planets could not rend the air with greater violence than Porter's initial broadside; Porter has 656 guns this time, a 4 percent increase over December. The admiral is demonstrating his Jovian power; it is clear to Lamb and his staff that this first broadside is louder, more puissant, and delivered with much greater accuracy than the heaviest fire these ships put out in December. Fort Fisher's entire Sea Face is hidden from view by a vast rolling gush of sod, shattered timbers, and ruptured sandbags. Porter has positioned all of his monitors, along with his deadliest ships of the line, behemoths such as the *New Ironsides* and the 26-gun *Brooklyn*, where they can rake the Land Face lengthwise, bowling their shots straight down its axis like gigantic plows. The medium-caliber guns of his smaller ships he concentrates on the log palisade, hammering it inside the narrow end of a cone, so that each hit will damage as many logs as possible. Another refinement over December: half a dozen wide-decked ships, mounting large bore mortars and loaded with hardened case-shot for their conventional guns, concentrate on the acreage where Lamb is thought to have planted a large minefield—the case-shot rakes away the protective cover, exposing those dangerous black pods, and the mortar shells set off their detonators and sunder the cables connecting the bombs to the fort. Porter has seen what torpedoes and mines can do, down at New Orleans, and he wants to neutralize this threat before the infantry has to cross that ground. Slowly but steadily, that's what happens. Every time Reilly dares a peek over the Pulpit in that direction, he sees another mine blow up harmlessly. He's not surprised; he's never shared Lamb's faith in the efficacy of galvanic mines—they're just too touchy to survive this kind of pounding. More worrisome is the cumulative damage to the palisade. A few more hours of this barrage, and all those fallen logs will be more of a protection than an obstacle to any infantry mounting an attack on the Land Face.

Another change of tactics is that Porter has ordered his gunners to *maintain* at a steady blistering rate, the volume of fire established by their first titanic broadside. Today, there will be no lulls, no letups that might induce the fort's gunners to spring out and get off a shot or two. Those who bravely try, suffer heavy losses in exchange for a few lucky hits that don't amount to much. Lamb notes the discrepancy between the gunners' courage and the paucity of results they're achieving; notes also their alarming casualties, and has no choice but to order all his gun crews to stay under cover and not even try to return Porter's fire. He will need those men later, as infantry, to help repel the ground attack. There is so much smoke and debris, Lamb can't see how many guns he's lost in the first two hours of this renewed contest, but by eleven o'clock—just from counting the visible corpses and the number of stretcher cases streaming into the fort's subterranean hospital—Lamb thinks it likely the garrison has already suffered, in just two hours, as many casualties as it sustained during the entire Christmas engagement.

Reilly scuttles over to Lamb's side and holds out a pocket notebook covered with calculations and stopwatch numbers. Bending close to Lamb's ear so he can be heard over the smothering thunder, Reilly shouts, "This is all academic, I suppose, but I thought you might find it interesting. Porter is breaking records today." Wiping sand from his eyelids, Lamb slowly focuses on the notepad. Just for the hell of it, Reilly's been keeping track of the numbers, and Lamb has to admit they are pretty damned impressive: *Average number of shots per minute: 130 to 143!! How long can they sustain this?* Taking out his own pencil, Lamb writes:

More apt is the question: how long can we endure it? Where in Christ's name are the reinforcements Bragg promised?

But just after Reilly reads this and reacts with a fatalistic shrug, at least one of their questions is answered. Like a specter from an open grave, slathered head to toe with sweat-plastered sand, one epaulet streaming smoke from a nick of burning shrapnel, face as black as a minstrel's, Chase Whiting has suddenly appeared. Actually, he had landed near Battery Buchanan at 6:30, but it has taken this long to reach Lamb's command post because he's had to spend so much time taking cover in craters and detouring to check things out along the way—a pep-talk to Parker and his men atop Battery Buchanan, assuring them that help *is* on the way, and a couple of turns as a stretcher-bearer when fragments cut down the men assigned to this harrowing job, then another half-hour helping the overwhelmed Doctor Reece and his staff perform triage, saying prayers for the dying men who took comfort from the notion that a benediction offered up from a major general might carry more weight with God than their own humble entreaties—and helping doomed men raise their parched mouths high enough for one last good drink of whiskey. There are already at least forty wounded men crammed into the hospital, Whiting reports, and the only comforting thing about the situation is that, compared to other battlefield hospitals Whiting has seen, Fort Fisher's is relatively *quiet*: the generosity of blockade-runner captains has provided Doctor Reece with an abundance of anesthetics, and if you cannot save a man's life by doping him with morphine, you can at least detach his flickering consciousness from the agony that would otherwise turn his last hours of earthly existence into a foretaste of hell. Whiting's fine dress uniform is now stained with the blood of dying men, and the smutty mask of his face shows clear channels where his tears have flowed while taking down their last messages to loved ones. But now, finally, Whiting has reached his destination and when Lamb helps him up the ladder and into the relative safety of the Pulpit, the two men embrace for a long moment. While his mouth is close to Lamb's ear, Whiting declares himself:

"William, my boy, I have come to share your fate. We are to be sacrificed, and should be prepared for it."

"Don't say so, General! We can lick 'em yet, once they try to storm the walls. Surely, help is on the way."

"That may be true, but it will arrive in typical Bragg fashion: too little, too late, and in the wrong place. I was in Wilmington for much of last night, and saw with my own eyes that Bragg has already begun preparations to withdraw from the city. Wagons full of documents and such are being loaded into boxcars, and his engineers are laying demolitions and preparing to fire the shipyards, the warehouses, every structure that might be of use to an occupying force. The man has already written us off. His comprehension of the situation here is totally at odds with reality."

"But for the love of God, if he wants to know what's going on, all he has to do is get on a boat and sail down the river to see things with his own eyes!"

"Indeed—most commanders would avail themselves of such a simple path to knowledge, but I don't think the idea's even crossed his mind. I don't think he *wants to know the truth*, because if he did, he would be compelled to act on that knowledge. He prefers to stay insulated, so that later on he can blame poor communications or bad staff work for keeping him in the dark. If he is seen actively investigating our plight, he loses that excuse. In any case, our sometime-friend, Flag Officer Branch, is mobilizing his Marines and his collection of toy boats, and I think we can count on him, at least. After the ignominious failure of the *Raleigh*, he wants to redeem his honor. In practical terms, it won't make the slightest difference, but I salute him for making the gesture."

Lamb suddenly understands that Chase Whiting is also making a reference to his own presence. Whiting has come here to die at his side, nothing less. He has come because Bragg will not; he has come because that's the only way he can erase from history the botched record of his two brief field commands; he has come in order to show Jefferson Davis—whose fathomless faith in Braxton Bragg has imperiled Fort Fisher, indeed the very continued existence of the Confederacy—exactly what kind of soldier William Chase Whiting really is. Out of profound respect, Lamb once again offers to yield command to Whiting; again, Whiting waves it away. He does however suggest that when the Federal ground attack begins, he may be of some use by taking command of the troops assigned to defend the Land Face, and for that Lamb is grateful, because *his* place truly is here in the Pulpit, where he can view every part of the fort and make informed decisions about when and where to deploy his slight reserves.

2:00 P.M.:–8:00 P.M.: General Terry, having completed the landing of 9,200 men and several batteries of field artillery in a manner more orderly and expeditious than most training exercises, forms his brigades into textbook marching order, extending skirmishers 200 yards in front across the entire width of the peninsula, cautiously heading south, delayed only by the unstable, water logged terrain, whose configuration bear only the vaguest resemblance to what is shown on his maps. Periodically, the advance comes to a halt, while his engineers fan out, searching for some place on the peninsula that offers a continuous band of dry land from seashore to riverbank, where they can sketch-out the defensive line for the Negro troops who are tasked with blocking any attack from Sugar Loaf.

The Last Sortie of the Confederate Navy

NOT FAR IN advance towered the frowning Fortress, and, though none saw, all knew, that above, in imperial majesty, sat the Angel of Death,

Surgeon J. A. Mowris, 117th New York

January 14, 1865

2:00 A.M.–8:00 A.M.: Not until 2:00 A.M. do the engineers locate what they're looking for: a belt of relatively open dry terrain extending from the ruins of Battery Anderson all the way to the edge of the Cape Fear River. It's the best ground they can find for deploying the two-thousand-man 2nd Brigade, United States Colored Troops, in a continuous fortified line suitable for securing Terry's main force from a surprise attack in the rear. Eight hundred shovels and thousands of empty sandbags are passed out and the Negro soldiers begin industriously to dig. By eight o'clock in the morning, Generals Terry, Ames, and Curtis are all satisfied that the line is strong enough for them to resume their advance on Fort Fisher without having to worry constantly about a surprise attack from Sugar Loaf.

9:00 A.M.: Hackett's minuscule cavalry assets had ridden out again at first light and have now returned with the disturbing news that overnight, the enemy has secured his rear by throwing up a strong, continuous line midway between Sugar Loaf and the fort. Hackett's first question: *Is it vulnerable to an attack?* Actually, the cavalrymen can't say whether it is or not, but the presence of eight field guns suggests that this line cannot be broken without a stiff fight. General Bragg nods sagely, as though this were *good* news, and pedantically lists the dangerous consequences of such an action: it will deplete Hackett's strength, burn up much of his ammunition, and leave his men too bushed to do anything else that day. Hackett thinks his veterans can punch through "one thin line of half-trained niggers" in three minutes. Bragg turns away in apparent distaste, either at Hackett's language or his attitude. Furious, Hackett throws his hat to the ground and berates Bragg in front of several dozen witnesses.

"Goddamn it, General, I told you we *had to* offer battle either at the water's edge, or soon after the enemy started marching south! If we had struck them while they were on the march, we could have broken up their whole plan, thrown them into disorder, in terrain where their gunboats could not support them without equal risk to their own men! Now they've been allowed to do as they please, without any interference, and they've thrown a line across the peninsula in open ground, so the gunboats could enfilade the hell out of us before we got close enough to launch a charge! Is the Yankee commander to dictate the terms of this campaign in every detail? Have we handed him the initiative without firing a shot?"

Bragg, too, is nonplussed by the news of Terry's rearguard line. During the night, Bragg had hoped that Terry would oblige him by dividing his forces and sending at least some part of them along the River Road, where he would have to fight without the benefit of naval support. Bragg has been trained to shun nighttime operations as being uncontrollable, chaotic, and almost never successful. It never occurred to him that an aggressive harassment under cover of darkness might have reaped advantages disproportionate to the risks involved.

Hackett sees things differently: his men have had all the advantage in a nocturnal skirmish because they can hardly get lost if they keep the campfires on Sugar Loaf *behind* them, and the hard-to-miss river on their right, as points of orientation. There was no reason his men couldn't have sniped at Terry's columns all night long and, while they might not have inflicted serious losses, they would certainly have spread confusion and fear, and maybe prevented the Federals from building that new line of breastworks. At the very least, such harassment would have upset the enemy's timetable and given Bragg more time to gather reinforcements for Lamb.

"What's done is done," is Bragg's feeble riposte. "If they have detached two thousand men to guard their rear, that means they have two thousand *fewer* men to commit against the fort. Once they have been thinned out by Lamb's artillery, and their rearguard line softened up by fire from our ships on the river, we may have a splendid opportunity to crush them in a vise. Do not, General Hackett, fret over such things before there is sufficient reason to. My orders remain the same: hold the Sugar Loaf line resolutely until they dash themselves to pieces against the fort. Now I must repair to my headquarters and see what can be done to increase Lamb's powers of resistance."

There's no point in Hackett stating the obvious: that Bragg has already had ample time to do just that and has not bestirred himself to issue the necessary orders. Neither has he gone downriver to appraise the condition of Fort Fisher with his own eyes. It is already too late for Terry's attacks to "dash against Lamb's heavy guns" because by noon on the fourteenth, Lamb's firepower has been drastically reduced—except for the field pieces guarding the gate, he has only two big Land Face guns still in commission. Porter kept his monitors on line all night, maintaining such a heavy fire against that portion of the fort that Lamb's men could not venture out of their shelters to repair the growing damage.

10:25 A.M.: Having to listen to that gloomy update on Sugar Loaf has Bragg's myriad dyspepsias and neural torments reporting for work very early on this day; his coffee-and-oatmeal breakfast is already bubbling in his stomach like a mud geyser, and the first tiny diamond-tipped drill bit of a headache is already probing the base of his skull by the time he mumbles "Good day!" to Colquitt and retreats behind the locked door of his bedroom. Two bottles ought to be enough, if he catches the afflictions at the earliest stages. His body cells know what they need, all right, and reward him quickly by coating his digestive tract with warm, soothing wax and by spreading the blessed unguents of calm along the coating of his crackling neurons. Very soon he is composed and utterly lucid, filled with a slow, syrupy kind of energy; the pressure's off, the pain's gone; time has dilated in that marvelously reassuring way that whispers *What's the hurry, Braxton? Just take each day's aggravations one at a time, and things will work out.*

Bragg comes back into his war room radiating such exaggerated good-will and confidence that his staff exchanges uneasy private glances. In their experience, it's a toss-up as to which Bragg is more likely to fuck things up: the morose, wrinkle-browed, profoundly "misunderstood" and bafflingly lethargic incarnation, or the "other" Bragg, who radiates the hermetic confidence of Caesar's marble bust. First, the ritual they have nicknamed "Braxton's Morning Prayers"—his daily report to Robert E. Lee, the first of the general's daily Stations of the Cross:

11:56 A.M.: From Braxton Bragg to Robert E. Lee:

> *After studying the information brought in by my cavalry patrols and other reliable sources, I do not feel the slightest apprehension for the fort. I am perfectly confident that the enemy has assumed a most precarious position, from which he will not escape without great difficulty and severe punishment. Wholly adequate supplies and reinforcements are on their way, which should render the Bastion invulnerable to assault and also provide Colonel Lamb with sufficient forces to play his part in the double-envelopment counterattack I plan to launch, simultaneously from Fort Fisher and from Hackett's formidable works on Sugar Loaf, the very instant I deem the Federal expedition to be so weakened by losses*

and declining spirits as to allow us to crush them between the two forces. Porter's naval barrage is more annoying that lethal, and once we close upon the trapped enemy with the bayonet, Porter will be unable to fire without inflicting terrible slaughter on his own side. This day or tomorrow, we may well execute devastation upon the invaders equal in its decisiveness to Hannibal's victory at Cannae.

Of course, this dodges the fact that *after* winning at Cannae, Hannibal went on to lose the war, and Carthage was ground to dust beneath salted earth. Bragg's staff has a hard time keeping straight faces as they read this fantastic presumption of a victory Bragg has done nothing to lay the groundwork for, and the telegraphist appends an editorial comment to his anonymous pal in the relay station in Goldsboro: "Ever read such a load of horse poop in your life?" Quickly, in the familiar "fist" of the Goldsboro key clicker's style, comes the response: "One does not know whether to laugh, cry, or upchuck . . ."

1:30 P.M.: Deafened and punch drunk from Porter's remorseless deluge of shot and shell, Chase Whiting sends Bragg yet another realistic appraisal of the *real* situation, not from any hope that Bragg will take his words at face value, but simply to establish so much documentation that, when the whole catastrophe is finally played out, Bragg cannot possibly hide behind the excuse that his subordinates failed to provide accurate and timely information:

The sooner you attack the better. The Colored Troops manning the line between Hackett and the fort number only two thousand and they are a raw, unbloodied outfit that has never experienced a serious battle before and who are likely to be so terrified by the sight of cold steel rushing at them, that they will break like glass. Naval gunfire will, to be sure, inflict some rough punishment on Hackett's left flank when he makes the assault, but the open terrain he must cross is nowhere wider than 150 yards, so his men will not be exposed to the gunboats' fire for longer than a few minutes. The enemy's game is very plain to see, and the strategy required to lay it in ruins is blindingly obvious. That they were permitted to land—on an open beach within easy range of Hackett's rifles as well as cannon—without a shot fired against them, admits of no rational justification. Now that they have thrown up that defensive line, you must not hesitate to break it, for if it is not swept away, the reduction of this fort is only a matter of time. The reinforcements repeatedly promised by you have so far failed to materialize, and the unprecedented, unremitting weight of the naval bombardment has destroyed at least three-quarters of our artillery. Both Lamb and I have sworn we will defend this place to the last extremity, but unless you strike our besiegers from behind, and furnish us with adequate numbers of fresh infantry, no amount of courage will suffice to offset the enemy's advantage in numbers and the crushing effectiveness of his naval support. This, sir, is the plain truth of the situation, and I do not know how I could portray the gravity of things more clearly. Take action! Take it now! If you do, a great victory will be yours and your place in the history of this war will be one of honor and you will earn the sweet satisfaction of confounding your enemies and critics. If you do not, all that remains of Fort Fisher will be a tale of squandered heroism and needless sacrifice!

4:10 P.M.: True to his word, Flag Officer William Branch has spent this day feverishly massing his pathetic naval assets: the lightly armed tugs and patrol cutters and motorized barges that, in their aggregate, comprise an armada just slightly more dangerous than the old Mosquito Fleet he commanded in 1861. His greatest shock comes from discovering that the unfinished, partly armored gunboat *Asheville*, the only ship in his farcically small "fleet" carrying big enough guns to do more than chip the paint off Porter's ships, has never received the full complement of ammunition Richmond promised to send. For its most potent weapon, the bow-mounted Brooke, there are only 41 bolts and shells. But at least her aging 32-pounders can discomfit the Union ground troops. There's room enough to load 120 Marines, about half of his total force, so they will have to be delivered to the fort in two trips. But at least they are keen, and so are the crews of his motley little armada. For three days he's been pleading with Bragg: You have promised the fort reinforcements, well *here are some*, but Bragg has never authorized the Marines' release. Branch does it on his own responsibility. *If Bragg wants them back, he can fucking well come down and get them.*

The *Asheville*'s sole engine, a rusty, patched-up relic more fit for a transportation museum than for active duty, proves balky and slow, giving every sign of sudden, total breakdown if asked to produce more than two knots, so Branch's vessels don't arrive until much later than he'd planned. From the bridge of the *Asheville* he sees clearly the new line of fieldworks carved across the peninsula, and the colored soldiers manning the riverside flank react to the gunboat's appearance with gratifying, comical panic. All of Branch's guns fire simultaneously, scattering them wildly in all directions and leaving a few bodies. Visibility is ideal, and Branch suddenly spots the target of a lifetime: a lumbering supply ship either just coming or just going from delivering its cargo to the Negro soldiers. The Brooke gunners are right on it, even though it's a small target and their view is narrow and compromised by sand dunes and underbrush. After three shots, they find the range, although by that time the transport's rung on flank speed and is already moving beyond their arc of fire. There's just time enough for three more shots before the target pulls out of danger, but Branch has the enormous satisfaction of seeing all three impact on the aft section, blowing apart a deckhouse and cargo boom, smashing the fantail to kindling, and the final one exploding somewhere inside the hull, evidently starting a major fire, because even after the ship itself disappears, they can follow its course north by a thick ribbon of smoke.

For a while, Branch's ships fight a spirited duel with the land-based 12-pounders protecting the Negroes' left flank. The soldiers themselves have vanished, but Branch's collection of small craft manage to do a lot of damage to their earthworks and throw a few dozen shots into the presumed location of their shelters. Sharp shooting with the Brooke, his gunners also smash the wheels under one 12-pounder and blow up an ammunition caisson; in exchange, the Union gunners return fire with commendable vigor and score a dozen hits on Branch's ships, damaging one armed tug so badly that it turns out of the fight and limps back toward Wilmington.

Suddenly a cluster of really *big* waterspouts brackets the river squadron and a pair of big steam frigates join the fray from the Atlantic side. One or two hits from their guns will sink any ship Branch commands, and he prudently orders his flotilla to disengage and continue toward the fort, so he can at least deliver the Marines. About a mile farther downstream, Branch sees Craig's Landing, the big commercial dock that used to be the peninsula's main contact with the outside world. There's a team of Yankee officers on the main dock, apparently studying his ships with great concern. One of the larger tugs fires a canister load at the Yankee spotters, who dive into the water to escape, pursued by a big cloud of splinters torn from the planks they were just standing on. Not far downriver from Craig's Landing, Branch sees what used to be the Cottage of Colonel and Mrs. Lamb, and the sight of a Union flag flying from the chimney makes him furious. Obviously the place has been commandeered by some Yankee officers as their headquarters. More than ample reason to stop the *Asheville*, only 200 yards from the little house, and methodically blow it into brickbats and red dust. When a blue uniformed body, or portions thereof, flies out from an upstairs window, Branch cheers as lustily as the crew. By God, he might not be leading the Spanish Armada, but it's awfully satisfying to know that whoever the men were that had helped themselves to the Lamb's home, they would be sleeping in tents tonight (or in the arms of their Maker) instead of William and Daisy's feather bed. Enough fun, though—now it's time to deliver the Marines, and a bargeload of 32-pounder ammunition to the wharf at Battery Buchanan. Just as well Branch doesn't know that Lamb *has* no more functioning 32-pounders. Branch orders the anchor raised and voice pipes to the engine room: "All ahead, slow; maintain two knots."

The *Asheville* slowly begins to move south, covers a distance of about eight hundred yards, then something goes *"Krang!"* down in the engine compartment and she loses all power. She's also drifting toward the enemy's side of the river, so Branch has the anchor dropped again and waits resignedly for the engineer's report.

"She's packed it in, sir. Jesus Christ couldn't bring that piece of junk back to life."

He'd been halfway expecting it. Nothing for it now but to order the Marines to keep going down to the fort in the smaller boats. When the boats return, Branch will hitch a ride to the fort, too, along with any volunteers who want to join him. The Confederate Navy in Wilmington has fought its last—and come to think of it—*only* fleet action so the only contribution it can make is to offer Lamb a paltry but well-trained group of fighting men.

5:20 P.M.: Just before the tugboats return to pick him up, Branch witnesses an astounding event, one that confirms to him just how out-of-touch Bragg truly is. A fair-sized cargo steamer, the *Isaac Wells* has been loading all day, with food, mail, and small-arms ammunition bound for the fort. It's the first sensible action Bragg has ordered since the Federal fleet reappeared. But in stupefying ignorance, her skipper is turning in to Craig's Landing, which has been in enemy hands for at least twenty-four hours. How could Bragg not know this? Maybe he *did* know and just forgot to update that skipper's instructions. Several tons of desperately needed supplies and morale-boosting mail are about to land in enemy hands! Branch orders a warning shot fired across the *Isaac Wells'* bow, but her captain, probably assuming the water-splash is just a random "over" from Porter's barrage, boldly keeps on going, and is greeted by a cheering, jeering gang of Yankee soldiers who run out on the dock and happily secure the ship for their own use.

Roaring a string of oaths so venomous they actually cause some of his sailors to blush, Branch clears the Yankees from Craig's Landing with a broadside of grapeshot, killing several of them, then holds his fire while the steamer's captain and crew, confused, scared, and probably covered by a field gun that Branch cannot see, march off the *Isaac Wells* under a white flag. Once the sailors are clear, Branch sees no alternative but to sink the freighter at her moorings, so he orders the Brooke crew to punch holes below her waterline with their remaining shells. By the time the steamer goes under, not completely sunk of course, but deep enough to ruin her cargo, Branch has exactly four rounds of Brooke ammunition left in his magazine.

6:10 P.M.: Flag Officer William Branch and the entire crew of the *Asheville*, after transferring all their food, small arms, medical stores, blankets, and other personal gear, board a tug and steam downriver, to add their minuscule number to Lamb's hard-pressed garrison. After opening the sea cocks to scuttle her, Branch makes a last-minute choice. Instead of reverently bringing her Confederate ensign with him, he's going to leave it on the mast, as a gesture of respect for a ship that never had a chance, but still managed to raise a lot of hell during her one and only combat sortie.

6:24 *P.M.:* Generals Alfred Terry, Martin Curtis, and Adelbert Ames halt their columns and order their forces to encamp for the night five hundred yards from the Land Face. Then Curtis leads the generals on a close-up reconnaissance of the forts main gate, so he can check on the current state of the defenses covering the River Road. Curtis follows the same path he used in December, even finds the exact sand dune, and all three commanders lie prone and study every detail through their binoculars—which sometimes isn't much, because Porter's been replenishing his ships' ammunition all day, a few at a time from the supply vessels anchored far out to sea, and thus has been able to maintain the tempo of his barrage against the Land Face. Even now, as darkness enshrouds Confederate Point, huge shells continue to burst steadily all the way from a point uncomfortably close to the scouting generals up to the Northeast Bastion, which is taking such a beating that it resembles a big, smouldering torch. Gone now is the rude grandeur Fort Fisher once projected: the Land Face looks as though a horde of giant wolverines has been gnawing on it for thirty-six hours. So many tons of iron have been driven into the sand ramparts that portions of them are now just shapeless heaps, and the run off from all that pounding has very nearly filled up the moat between palisade and wall. As for the palisade itself, only a few sections of stakes are still standing and the uprooted, shattered ones will provide good cover for Terry's sharpshooters. Other piles of stakes have been pounded by so hard they've been reduced to forlorn mounds of wood pulp. Gun chamber revetments have been reduced to lumpy cavities, their protective timbers and massive sandbag walls broken, broken again, then smashed yet again as though a deranged giant had rained blows on them with a ball-peen hammer. And of those dangerous heavy guns, not one of them appears still to be in firing condition. Through the intermittent eruptions of flame-cored earth and drifting smoke, General Terry can see four dented or dismounted cannon either blown onto the front of the rampart, or tossed like toothpicks onto the pockmarked domes of traverses. General Ames calls the others' attention to half of an eight-inch columbiad barrel standing upright in a furrowed dune only a hundred yards to their left, looking like some kind of monumental spittoon. It is logical to extrapolate: if they can easily see five utterly destroyed cannon on the western extremity of the Land Face, how many guns could possibly still be operable along the more distant part of the wall, where Porter's been whacking at them from closer range and with much better visibility?

No, the three scouting generals conclude, there is no longer any danger of their attacking columns being raked by enfilade fire from the Land Face cannon. Turning to their right, they observe that the field gun emplacements and barricade sealing-off the gate are still intact, as is the plank bridge across the wide creek that affords such strong natural protection to Lamb's dangling left flank. West of the bridge, the ground is just too mushy to bear the weight of heavy walls, so from the gate to the riverbank there's a gap of about 120 yards fortified primarily with sandbag breastworks, a pointy-stick abatis, densely interlocked snarls of briar-patch vines, and hundreds of yards of ship's cable and spare telegraph wires threaded into ankle-snapping entanglements. Add to these formidably nasty obstructions the wide expanse of semiliquid, boot-sucking quagmires flanking the creek, *and* as for the fifteen-foot-wide creek itself? God knows how deep it is or what fiendish barbs and spikes the Rebels have seeded on its bottom, but the tidal current appears strong enough to carry away the heavily encumbered body of any infantryman who falls in. No, indeed; one cannot accuse Lamb of leaving his riverside flank unprotected. It is, in fact, an expanse of ground far more difficult to cross than the iron-littered plain in front of the gun chambers and traverses. General Curtis also observes that *because* there is no tall rampart on this flank, any force attempting to enter the fort via this gap would be subject to punishing long-range bombardment from the heavy guns of the Mound Battery and Battery Buchanan, assuming both positions are able to shoot. No, the generals conclude: the assault *must* punch through the main gate, supported by flanking troops clawing up the ramparts to the left of the archway and slogging painfully through the bogs and barriers to the right. The Union troops will be forced into a dense narrow wedge as they charge over the bridge (assuming the bridge is still there tomorrow), and heavy casualties are inevitable until significant numbers of them squeeze through the gate and redeploy on the open parade ground beyond. It *can* be done, though, if the assault is furious enough and the Navy keeps putting down heavy fire until the last instant before the troops go forward. Those 24-pounders flanking the gate can do wicked execution with canister, but how long will their crews survive with hundreds of riflemen shooting at them?

Now the decision is General Terry's to make. "General Curtis, if your division can withstand a certain amount of heavy fire without losing cohesion, and if the navy keeps the Rebels suppressed until the very moment you launch your attack, can you and your men storm that gate and hold it open for the regiments massed behind you?"

"General, we could have done that with three thousand men in

December, even with the big guns firing on our flank. Yes, we can force that gate and probably thrust a good way into the work's interior. As soon as 2nd Brigade joins us, we shall sweep the length of Fort Fisher like a steel broom. This 'impregnable' work is a hollow sham, and that gate, its feet of clay."

"'Foot,'" mumbles Ames; "*foot* of clay . . ." Curtis glares at him, then realizes Ames is attempting a smidgen of levity.

"Then we are all agreed?" says General Terry. "This is the point of attack, and that attack must be pressed home with the utmost resolution. If it is, the enemy will not be able to break our momentum. Very well, then, inform your subordinates and deploy your steadiest commanders in the forefront. I will row out to Admiral Porter's flagship and make known our intentions. I'm confident that the navy will cooperate to the fullest extent. The admiral and I have even worked out a tactic that might take the enemy by surprise, and that will certainly force him to divide his forces and divert his attention."

"A secret arrangement between you and the admiral?" Ames sounds a little miffed. "Well, there's no reason to keep it secret now, and it would help us if we knew what to expect."

Terry motions for the other officers to slide down to the base of their sandy observation post. There's just enough light left for him to make a quick sketch in the sand.

"Here is the Northeast Bastion . . . and here is the river and the gate at this end of the Land Face. When we launch our attack here, Admiral Porter plans to assault the Northeast Bastion with an improvised brigade of two thousand Marines and sailors, who will swarm up the Bastion just as though they were boarding a pirate ship! Because the Rebels will see that attack forming up, their attention will be riveted on it. *Our* attack will be formed under cover—they will not know our strength, or even if we plan to attack at all. If Porter's 'boarding party' storms the Bastion at the same time our men emerge from the woods and rush across the dead zone, funneling our best troops toward the gate, the Rebels will have massed *their* best troops to stop Porter's column. By the time they realize *we* are the main threat, it will be too late for them to redirect any reserves to this end of the fortress. And since we outnumber the entire garrison by at least three to one, we will have the initiative from the start, forcing them to react to our movements and spread their resources dangerously thin."

General Ames points at the arrows Terry has drawn, converging on the Northeast Bastion. "That's a bold plan, all right, and might well distract the Rebs, but even if they don't have much artillery left, they'll cut up those sailors pretty bad. Look: they will be advancing completely in the open, and with the sea hemming them in, greatly restricting their movements. Does Porter not realize the kind of casualties his men are likely to suffer?"

General Terry wipes the sand sketch clean with his boot. "He wants the navy to have its share of glory in capturing the fort and has got it in his head that the Rebels will shit themselves in terror at the sight of two thousand blue jackets charging at them with fire in their eyes. If we capture this supposedly 'impregnable' fortress in a single day, there will be plenty of glory to spread around. I don't mind letting Porter grab his little slice. And his recklessness may save a lot of our men's lives. Don't fret about it, Adelbert—just be thankful the man sees little difference between storming a pirate ship at sea and launching a frontal attack against a formidable earthwork. Just focus on our job and don't worry about the navy."

8:10 P.M.: With the coming of full dark, 250 sailors disembark at a point 200 yards north of what's left of the fort's palisade. Nobody inside the fort can hear them, due to the undiminished bombardment, and those few men on the walls who do glimpse them, by the staccato flash of shell bursts, don't find the sight alarming—probably just a resupply mission. What can 250 sailors do by way of offensive action? Not a thing, unless their fleet suddenly stops firing, in which case Lamb can bring at least 300 riflemen to that corner of the fort in a matter of minutes. So no one pays much attention to those flickering shadows milling around on the strand, other than the idle speculation about how gratifying it would be to throw a big wad of grapeshot at them. Lamb rules that out—if he fires one of his surviving guns at night, he might as well shine a light on it and invite the ships to do their worst.

What the sailors are doing, however, is not without its threatening aspects. Each man is wielding a shovel as hard as he can, excavating a rifle trench across the dunes, starting as close to the shore as the water table permits then extending it in a crescent at least 120 yards wide. While they did, they pile up the displaced sand as high as it will go. They are not digging for clams, these iron-thewed tars, but erecting a firing position for 150 Marines who will be landing early the next day.

Not long after the ditchdiggers start to move sand, Admiral David Porter mounts an upturned box on the *Malvern*'s fantail and gestures for silence. His audience is composed of 65 ship captains, from every vessel in his fleet, and all afternoon they've been congregating on the flagship, responding to Porter's summons. Rumors abound, but something big is clearly in the offing. Will Cushing tends to believe one of the stronger rumors: Fort Fisher's capacity to resist has been so grievously reduced that Porter's going to send his shallow-draft ships straight through New Inlet, in order that they may support the ground assault with a crossfire.

When Porter, rather theatrically, tells them of his *real* plan, every man who's made a bet loses. Porter works up to his climactic remarks with the controlled intensity of a great conductor tearing into Beethoven. "Your performance today," he assures the captains, "has been superb; your gunnery unequaled since the Battle of Trafalgar; the newspaper accounts of the first day's bombardment, already flashed northward via submerged cable from Beaufort, have caused great excitement among the general populace!" Porter pauses for dramatic effect . . .

"Just wait until they read about what you'll accomplish tomorrow!"

Porter explains the gist of the plan in purely navy terms: He does not want the U. S. Navy to play second fiddle in the coming land battle, not after doing all the dirty, dangerous work of preparing for it. After extensive and very cordial discussions with Major General Terry, the navy has accepted a critical role to play in the storming of Fort Fisher. Porter's description of the tactics is verbose and meandering—the terminology of land warfare does not fall trippingly from his tongue—but the point of the scheme is easily summarized: "We will grab them by the nose, while the army kicks them in the ass!" (Cheers and *Huzzahs.*) An audience of ship captains gets the point! As for how Porter wants this joint operation prepared for—that's the cue for his captains to pull out their notepads and pencils.

The admiral wants every captain to return to his ship, explain the plan, and ask for volunteers to represent *his* ship in the landing party. From those who volunteer, each skipper will pick at least thirty-five of his strongest, bravest, most experienced men, and convey them to the beach no later than 1:30 P.M. When all eighteen-hundred sailors are assembled, Porter wants his second-in-command, Fleet Captain Randolph Breese, to organize them into three "divisions" of roughly six hundred men each. When the time comes to attack, the signal will be a sustained blast by every steam whistle in the fleet. The naval divisions will advance along the firm sand between dunes and surf, and when they reach the mangled log palisade at the foot of the Bastion, they will fan out, left-right-center, and storm the position as though it were an enemy ship and they were an old-time boarding party.

To keep the enemy's riflemen pinned down, Porter boasts that he is at that very moment erecting a stout breastwork just 200 yards north of the target, with room enough to accommodate 150 Marine sharpshooters armed with Spencer repeaters. The rapid, accurate fire from those Marines ought to discourage the Rebels from showing themselves to fire down on the beach, and once the boarding party ascends to the parapets, who could withstand their impetuous valor?

Porter has designated the rendezvous point on a broad level strand, which will be clearly marked with—what else?—the banner of the Naval Academy, and once the volunteers are formed into their respective divisions, "appropriate weapons" will be issued.

By now, the audience is aflame with enthusiasm! A real scrap! On dry land! Not merely "supporting" the army, the navy's usual second fiddle role, but fighting as an equal partner; one might even say—and Porter hopes the assembled journalists *will*—that the navy's role will be critical in bringing about the swift capitulation of the last great Confederate stronghold save for Richmond itself! Are there any questions, gentlemen?

Just one, it seems: all the ship captains want to join the fun, too! Is that permitted?

"It is *encouraged!*" laughs Porter. "But you'll have to endure the pouting of your executive officers!"

Cushing is whooping and cheering with the other skippers. Once the initial spectacle lost its novelty, Cushing has found round-the-clock bombardment almost as tedious a duty as blockade patrols, especially now that the enemy isn't shooting back. He's been suffering from a headache (the noise and perpetual shaking of his ship), congestion of the sinuses (too much gunpowder dust in the air), and is growing heartily sick of having to wear big wads of cotton in his ears. Admiral Porter could not have planned a more stirring, invigorating, excursion if he had used as his sole criteria the entertainment of Will Cushing! In fact, as he described how the doughty tars would climb the walls of the Bastion, just like Nelson's lads boarding a French three-decker, Porter managed to throw a sly wink right at Cushing.

Before sending all these fired-up young heroes back to their ships, Porter introduces the three officers he's chosen to lead the naval divisions (no need to introduce Breese, for every officer in the navy knows him if not personally then by his impeccable reputation for courage and loyalty). Each man receives his due ovation. By now, even the crusty, crab-shelled Porter is showing unprecedented emotion, On impulse, he points to a young lieutenant with striking green eyes and the finely sculpted features of a Greek paladin: "Gentlemen, for those who have not made his acquaintance, I take the greatest pride in introducing a young man who will one day, I am certain, be one of the finest naval officers of his generation: the skipper of the *Malvern* and my own dearest son, Lieutenant Benjamin Porter! Wait, wait, please hold your cheers! When General Terry and I devised this plan, I offered Ben command of one of the naval divisions. But he declined, saying, 'Admiral, such a distinction would make me very proud, but for the larger good of this historic engagement, you must give command to someone who is older, wiser, and more experienced in battle than I. With your permission, I shall join the contingent of sailors from the *Malvern* and fight at their side. That will be honor enough for me!' "

Here, Admiral Porter becomes too emotional to speak, so he just throws an arm around the slender shoulders of his dashing, handsome son. What a remarkably mawkish display! This is a side of David Porter that no one has witnessed before, and his willingness to peel away, for a few moments, the needful but hard-as-flint visage of high command, and appear before them in the plain aspect of a proud father, generates a surge of devotion among the assembled captains. Even those who have felt the lash of Porter's displeasure are now prepared—if Porter so orders—to storm the gates of hell.

Just before he dismisses the conference, Porter remembers one more detail.

"I almost forgot to introduce you to an army officer whom fate cast into my care after the despicable Ben Butler abandoned him. This is the man who had the cold-blooded courage to sail Butler's ridiculous powder boat right up to the walls of the fort, performing the task with great skill and coolness, even though he must have known his chances of coming back alive were one in a thousand. Well, the powder boat may have been a grotesque failure, but this man is still very much among the living, and General Butler is skulking in the disgrace he so richly earned. May I present my new friend and a very brave soldier indeed, General Rush C. Hawkins?"

Hawkins steps forward and salutes the forest of gold braid that's applauding him. He knows that skill and courage had nothing to do with his survival—what saved him from being transformed into a cloud of red mist was the crappy powder some swindler unloaded on Butler. If he's stumbled into the role of Porter's favored protégé, the army-officer-even-crusty-sailors-can-like, he figures he paid for the ticket and he's going to milk it for all it's worth. Porter's favored him with an assignment that will allow Hawkins to share credit for taking part in the naval assault, but does not require him to *join* the assault, which, frankly, sounds to him like a very bad idea.

"General Hawkins will be my liaison officer, responsible for making certain the landing force and General Terry's columns launch their attacks simultaneously—he'll be facing great danger . . . from saddle-sores! . . . by riding continually back and forth across the peninsula. If one force or the other encounters a delay, he will swiftly convey that information, so that army and navy may synchronize their movements to a nicety. General Terry and I have set three o'clock as our mutual starting time, but General Hawkins is the man responsible for giving the order to advance, because he will know when both forces are in place and set to go.

"I shan't keep you any longer, gentlemen. Return to your respective ships and select your best volunteers. Don't be late tomorrow, or the party will start without you!"

The tone may be jocular, but Porter's eyes sweep the assembled captains with a sharp penetrating glance, so none can mistake the unspoken message: *You had all better have your asses on that beach at the right time, or I shall remember the names of those who dallied, and woe betide you when it comes time for me to initial your next evaluation report!*

Appropriate Weapons

SUCH A HELL of noise I never hope to hear again. Hundreds of shells cleaving the air at once, all shrieking in a grand martial discourse that was a fitting backdrop to the macabre dance-of-death in which hundreds of brave but hopelessly unprepared sailors were about to fall.

—Commander William B. Cushing,
in a letter to his mother, dated January 19, 1865

JANUARY 15, 1865

1:30 P.M.: From every ship in Porter's fleet, longboats full of volunteers converge on the assembly area, a wide, dry oval of beach about 1 and 1/2 miles north of Fort Fisher. To facilitate the boats' passage, Porter has grouped all his ships in one dense line, no more than a half-mile from the silent, smoldering Gibraltar of the South. The volunteers' longboats can therefore row safely behind the bombardment arc, and their slow undisturbed passage affords them a stunning view of the whole panorama. The sea trembles when the big guns fire; the air turns raw and brittle from the shock waves dashed against it. From his vantage point in the bow of the *Monticello*'s longboat, Cushing can see the big monitor shells in mid trajectory, great dark blobs trailing ribbons of white fuse smoke, and brace himself for the impact when they land. Some sail over the walls and detonate unseen, others land on the already-mauled ramparts, exploding in a morning-star corona of yellow-white surrounded by a dense coiling wreath of smoke as wide as a barn. Porter is no longer aiming at individual gun chambers, for there hasn't been a return shot from the fort since mid-afternoon yesterday. Cushing's close enough to see with his unaided eyes the bent, split, overturned barrels, the smashed mounts, the collapsed revetments and caved-in sandbags. Fort Fisher appears to have been utterly disarmed—all Porter's doing with this morning's barrage is making sure Lamb's infantry stays huddled in their bombproofs, deafened and exhausted and scared to venture out into the rippling, flashing, shrapnel-lashed open air.

Near the end of the monitors' line, the converging longboats are close enough for Cushing to feel the festive, innocent mood of the chosen sailors. They're yelling jokes at each other, timing their oar strokes to classic sea chanteys, and loudly boasting to the Northeast Bastion, as they row past it. "We'll carve you up like Blackbeard!" and "Nobody can stop a navy boarding party, Rebels, so you may as well give up now!" The contrast between the landing party's high good spirits and the frowning, plowed-up verge-of-collapse appearance of their objective could not be greater. Cushing positively basks in the lemon-white sunshine, the calm sea, the incredibly puissant thunder of the bombardment—it is grand and beautiful, perhaps the greatest sheer spectacle in all naval history—an unbeatable demonstration of American sea power and the professionalism of the officers to whom that power is entrusted. Never has he felt prouder of his chosen service! Oh, he doesn't doubt that there will be a few rough moments during the actual assault, but the lads' spirits are so passionate that they're treating the whole thing as a lark, maybe a bit more dangerous than a prize fight or a bear hunt, but that's part of the excitement. By God, it feels marvelous to stretch your limbs in an open boat, on your way to a glorious escapade on terra firma! Cushing has never seen a group of men so *happy* at the prospect of going into battle.

Crunching into each other at the landing sight, as if the oarsmen were in some kind of competitive regatta, the longboats grind ashore and disgorge their quota of volunteers. All of the officers, apparently, share Cushing's taste in combat uniforms, for they have come ashore in their finest, flashiest outfits: blindingly bright buttons and insignia, trousers pressed and steam-cleaned, tricorn hats bold with cockade and plume, boots as impossibly shiny as they are utterly impractical for the sort of terrain they'll be advancing through. Off to his left and a mile or so down the beach, he sees the breastworks thrown up overnight and the Marine marksmen are already marching to occupy their firing line. Bosun's mates with penetratingly loud voices shout orders to each new boatload of volunteers: "Form a line, single file, and draw your weapons! Then choose which division you want to march with by forming up under the appropriate flag! Don't matter which one you choose, because by the time we blast through the palisade, everybody'll be jumbled together anyhow!"

Cushing and his contingent join the nearest line and make fair progress advancing to the piles of weapons crates stacked up under a purple silk awning with gold fringe. Where on earth did *that* come from? What was it Admiral Porter said last night? We will be issued "*appropriate* weapons . . ." Cushing is curious to learn what Porter considers "appropriate weapons." As he edges closer to the front of the line, Cushing hears the same kind of groaning complaints he could hear in the mess line aboard a ship when the food's running low and the men have been given the same, rancid slop for five nights in a row. Something is amiss and that makes Cushing uneasy. Even though he can't name or see the problem, he knows there is one. Just at that moment, a loud roar from a 15-inch Rodman turret near the end of the monitor line snaps his mind into focus. Where are Porter's boat howitzers? Every ship in the fleet has at least one, and the big Kansas-class frigates have two or three—lightweight, mounted on special wide wheels to make them maneuverable in sand, those compact, handy 12-pounders would be invaluable in forcing the Rebels to keep their heads down—far more so than the Marine sharpshooters. Why did Porter not land a few of those guns?

Suddenly Cushing's at the head of the line and someone brusquely hands him a big, heavy cutlass and a Remingtom revolver with a belt and a cartridge pouch containing two extra preloaded cylinders.

"Where's the rest of it?" Cushing responds incredulously. Porter must, *must* have arranged to equip at least half the landing force with Spencers or even those new sleek lever-action Henry rifles with tubular magazines holding nine cartridges. He would really enjoy carrying a Henry into this fracas!

"I'm afraid that's all you get, sir. Admiral Porter's orders. 'Traditional' boarding party weapons only! He wants the journalists to see a classic navy attack. The Marines are the only ones with rifles."

"But . . . but . . ." Cushing sputters.

"Can't be helped, sir. Now move along, please, so the next fella can draw his 'appropriate weapons.' "

Dear God, the phrase has already become notorious! But as he wanders over to where the "divisions" are forming, Cushing observes that none of the ordinary seamen seem worried about their equipage. In fact, they're jolly well delighted to play Blackbeard on this lovely morning. Many of them are taking ferocious cuts at the air, practicing blood-curdling battle cries, or staging mock duels with one another. He can see what's in their minds, and it does not bode well: this is the sort of swashbuckling adventure they joined the Navy to experience, and they feel ten feet tall, invincible, the true and mighty heirs of John Paul Jones. In the high drama of the moment they're finding release from all the boredom of blockade patrols, from the powder stink, sweat, and concussion of the three-day bombardment and the suspense of wondering when the next Parrott gun's going to cook off and kill them or one of their mates. They are coiled springs, these blue jackets, and they think cutlasses and pistols are perfectly suitable for the occasion. Cushing understands their excitement, and until *he* was handed a sword and a revolver, he had shared it; but now he realizes the sailors' let-me-at-them enthusiasm, like Admiral Porter's tactical concept, is based on dubious assumptions. First, the notion that Fort Fisher's guns are all smashed and useless, and the garrison punch-drunk and terrified by the pounding they've endured; and second—well, if the truth be told, they don't have the *slightest idea* of just how brave and determined a foe is waiting for them behind those frowning ramparts.

Cushing does, and he knows that even if Colonel Lamb has only a hundred soldiers fit to man the walls, those hundred men will fight like tigers. As for the demise of Lamb's big guns, Cushing's not too confident about that assumption, either. Just because the fort stopped shooting back doesn't mean it has no operable cannon left. Brave as they were, those Rebel gunners who emerged to fire back at the fleet did no significant damage to any of its ships and suffered heavy casualties every time they came out of their bombproofs. If he were Colonel Lamb he, too, would have ordered the guns to fall silent, husbanding whatever he has left for just the sort of target this naval column is going to present.

Cushing has a *bad* feeling about this one; for the first time, he feels no trace of the battle fire that has led him into and out of so many dangerous scraps. It feels like there's a stone-cold, rock-hard loaf of stale bread filling his stomach. This is not a familiar sensation. He's *never* felt it before when going in harm's way. It's *very* unpleasant. Is he ill? Reluctantly, comprehension dawns: *This must be what men call "fear"!* Fear as other men have felt it but Will Cushing—for whatever biological, chemical, or neurasthenic reasons—has always been immune to. Good Lord, how can a man feel this way and still *fight*? His hands are actually trembling, and the foremost thought in his mind is: *Get me out of here!* Most of these brave, innocent young sailors are going to die or lose some major body parts, and they think this is going to be FUN? Like swinging through the cannon-smoke and landing on the enemy's deck, slashing picturesquely with your cutlass like a fearless sea-dog—that's what they actually think is going to happen? Oh, sure, some of them will fall, but not one sailor believes it can happen to *him.*

Cushing knows it bloody well *can* happen to him or any other man. And no amount of blustery courage is going to stop a burst of grapeshot. At this point, quite simply, he does not want to go! If it were not for the presence of all these comrades, Will Cushing would turn around and hide behind the nearest sand dune. Then comes a blinding insight: *Hundreds of thousands of men have felt exactly this way and yet they have gone forward, fought bravely, seen their friends blown apart, and done it again and again.* This is why everyone thinks he's a little crazy! Because he's never felt this kind of dread before—it just wasn't in his makeup. Christ, if he *had* felt this way before, he would never have performed any of the crazy stunts that have made him a legend in the fleet.

Like a somnambulist, he's wandered into the 2nd Division and taken a place in the fourth rank. These tars don't know him from Adam, but they welcome him, shake his hand, "Glad to have you with us, sir! Going to be one hell of a thing, ain't it?"

"Yes," mumbles Cushing, his consciousness floating somewhere above his body. "Yes, it surely will be . . ."

Then someone politely taps him on the shoulder. Cushing turns around and there is none other than the admiral's son, Lieutenant Ben Porter. He grasps Cushing's hand warmly. "It's a great honor to meet you, sir! If I may say so, your exploits have been an inspiration to me!"

Such a handsome young man, with a smile as charming as his father's scowls are intimidating. In time, he'll make a fine officer; right now, though, he has a rough row to hoe, having to serve under his father's unforgiving gaze, always having to live in the old man's shadow. How he must have prayed for a chance to distinguish himself! And how profound is the dread he must feel at the possibility that today's fight will not present him with a chance to rise above the ordinary! Ben Porter, sparkling in his finest uniform, is the very embodiment of the navy's self-image: manly, confident, proud of his service, and no doubt held in great esteem by his crew. But Cushing takes one close look into Ben Porter's beautiful green eyes and sees that he, too, is terrified. They are, on the instant, good friends, and distract each other by talking about anything but the battle they're about to initiate. Finally the officers assigned to command each division blow their whistles and shout "Fall in!" and the jabbering conversations stop, the men snap to attention, their revolvers and utterly useless cutlasses held at shoulder arms. The sudden silence that envelops the landing force is a shared, communal vibration. The thud and bass-drumming of broadsides seems far away and muted. The clear hard sky above Fort Fisher still boils with cotton-ball explosions, and five seconds later comes the faint, firecracker patter of the shell bursts. But inside this vault of silence it's possible to hear the seagulls squawk . . . and impossible not to think about what some of them will be eating for dinner.

"Mister Cushing, sir?"

"Yes, Ben?"

"Is it all right with you if we march together? I should like to tell my children that I once fought at the side of the bravest man in the navy!"

The young lieutenant's words strike Cushing like a series of kidney punches. It takes every bit of his self-control not to turn aside and vomit. But somehow he manages to keep his voice calm and his gestures fraudulently confident. He offers his hand to the admiral's son and replies: "I would not have it any other way, Ben."

1:45 P.M.: In the dank cave that's become his headquarters, William Lamb and Frederick Reilly stare, for the hundredth time, at a big map of Fort Fisher and its surroundings. A report has just come down that the naval landing force has assumed formation. Soon, Reilly and Lamb must go in opposite directions, and this is their last chance to coordinate their plans before the ground attack begins.

Lamb has exactly one big gun still in firing condition on the Land Face: an 8-inch columbiad in the Northeast Bastion—its survival is miraculous, considering the thousands of rounds aimed at that strongpoint—but during the night, his men have built a ramp up to a devastated gun chamber smack in the middle of the Land Face and the instant Porter's bombardment ceases, a detachment of volunteers is prepared to manhandle a 12-pounder up to that site, where it can fire on the naval force from a perfect enfilade angle. And this morning, Lamb learned he has a new piece of artillery! Late last night, one of Flag Officer Branch's auxiliary vessels brought a 3.5-inch Parrott rifle and two hundred rounds, both gun and ammunition simply stolen from a Confederate army warehouse. Branch and his little Navy contingent are feverishly filling sandbags around that gun, which is positioned ideally to engage any attack formation approaching down the River Road. This new emplacement, in effect, gives Lamb one-third more firepower on that critical flank than he had yesterday. The two 24-pounders already posted by the gate are preloaded with double-canister and can be run-out in a matter of seconds. Lamb feels more confident, now, about the strength of his defenses athwart the River Road.

Reilly is in command of the Land Face today; in addition to the three cannon, he has 250 regular infantry. Lamb commands the columbiad and 350 regulars. It's a calculated risk, dividing his forces like this, because he estimates the Federal army has at least four times as many men hidden in the scrub-pines as the navy does in that dense column on the beach. The Yankees' strategy is obvious: simultaneous attacks to pin down all the surviving defenders. Lamb thinks, and both Reilly and Whiting concur, that if he can smash the naval column quickly enough, he'll be able to concentrate all his resources around the gate. Reilly thinks he can hold there with what he's got for at least an hour. If the enemy presses so hard that Reilly cannot hold them back, he can call on the general reserve: two-hundred-odd artillerists now outfitted as infantry and sheltering in the cave-like bombproofs dug into the Land Face traverses. That's all Lamb has to repel eight thousand infantry and two thousand sailors.

The question on both men's minds, of course, concerns the "significant" reinforcements Bragg has promised, mainly the thirteen-hundred fresh and experienced infantry of General Johnson Hagood's South Carolina brigade, along with "numerous" smaller detachments—although Bragg's never specified exactly *where* those small detachments are coming from. Not one additional reinforcement has landed since Branch led his small force of sailors ashore from the sinking *Asheville.* Bragg knows the accepted military wisdom: to capture a strong defensive position, the attacking force must have a superiority of at least three to one. Right now the Yankees' advantage is more like ten to one, but if

Lamb receives just two thousand fresh reinforcements, he thinks he can hold the place until doomsday.

While Lamb and Reilly are coordinating last-minute plans, Chase Whiting is firing another blast of venom in Bragg's direction:

> *General Whiting to General Bragg:*
> *Where are the reinforcements promised? Not one boatload has appeared. I do not wish to bore you by repeating the facts, but the situation in this fort is very grave. After almost three days of naval bombardment, on a scale without precedent in history, all our heavy artillery has been destroyed, many defensive works battered down, and our losses heavy. The enemy is massing in great strength seven hundred yards north of the fort and in front of the main gate—we have nothing we can fire that will disturb his preparations. A determined attack from Sugar Loaf, in conjunction with a sortie by every man we have under arms, will catch the enemy by surprise and might even rout him. We will charge as soon as we know Hackett's troops are also attacking. Either that, or send us enough reinforcements to at least defend ourselves. In any case, for God's sake take action! Otherwise, all is lost. That is the plain and simple truth of it!*

2:00 P.M.: Braxton Bragg is a man of his word . . . after a fashion. When a member of his staff hands him yet another telegram from Whiting, he refuses to read it. He *has* dispatched Hagood's South Carolinians, in two large steamers, and they should be arriving at any moment. And he has no intention of releasing Hackett's division—the only force standing between Wilmington and the enemy.

Bragg *could*, however, have dispatched Hagood's brigade during the preceding night, when it could have unloaded without being seen by the Federal fleet. But Bragg's instinctive reluctance to countenance any sort of nighttime operation caused him to wait, inexplicably, until after he and General Hagood enjoyed a very civilized lunch together. Bragg's become so irritated by Whiting's alarmist reports that he automatically subtracts half of their urgency and discounts half of the damage reports. He's never fought against a fleet before and so has no realistic conception of the sort of overwhelming fire Fort Fisher's been under for 2½ days. His mind cannot summon images of it. A few bursting shells, of course, but Hagood's men are veterans and should be able to take a little shelling in stride.

Hagood and his troops may be experienced veterans, but the steamboat crews hired to ferry them downriver are not. Only one mile into the trip, they can smell the gunpowder; another twenty minutes enable them to see the air bursts over the fort, splatters of white like snowballs thrown against an invisible dome of glass. What *really* gets their wind up, about a mile from the wharf beside Battery Buchanan, is a random "over" round that raises a big, threatening splash between the steamboats.

When both crews finally haul around the last bend and actually see what's going on at Fort Fisher, their nerves freeze. It looks like fifty volcanoes are erupting under Confederate Point. Civilian sailors that they are, and all of them well past conscription age, the sight seems unbelievable, the thunder ear-stunning. The continuous rippling explosions, from the far northern wall to New Inlet, make them feel as though they're peering through a window into the anteroom of hell. How can men survive such punishment? Determined to fulfill his contract, the skipper of the first steamboat pulls up to the wharf; Sam Parker and a few of his men run down to help with the gangplanks—two absurdly narrow walkways. Hagood's men funnel down them fast as they can, and strike out for the best cover in sight, the entrenchments surrounding the massive base of Battery Buchanan.

When they spot those two big, white, slow targets, obviously full of reinforcements, Porter's lookouts can't believe anyone would be stupid enough to risk doing this in broad daylight. Although it seems more like murder than honest combat, the ships off New Inlet start ranging on the steamboats. It's good shooting—by now, Porter's gun crews are the best in the navy—and the second steamer is bracketed by half-a-dozen shell plumes. That's the end of the contract, as far as its captain is concerned; there isn't enough money in Wilmington to keep him there one second longer. He orders "full reverse" and backs away until he's no longer visible to any Federal ships. Then he turns the boat around and heads back for Wilmington. His soldier-passengers feel a little bit ashamed at leaving the fort's garrison to its fate, but after seeing the holocaust up close, they don't see how they can cross the open ground from the landing site to the ramparts without losing half their number.

At least the captain of the first steamboat sticks it out a little longer, but when a big Yankee Parrott bolt shears off the top of one smokestack, he, too, loses his nerve. *Why in Jesus' name couldn't we have done this last night?* He orders his crew to sever the mooring lines, and backs up with the gangplanks still full of disembarking soldiers, most of whom end up having to be fished out of the river by their comrades already ashore.

William Lamb at last has the reinforcements Bragg had promised him: 368 scared, disorganized men, fragments of four different regiments, supplied only with what they were carrying. In other words, Bragg has sent Lamb approximately the same number of men as he has already lost. And it will take two or three hours for the South Carolinians to make it into bomb proofs and recover from the harrowing one-mile run across the shell-torn plain that was once the parade ground.

2:28 P.M.: Major Reilly arrives at the command post he's chosen near the place where the River Road enters the gate. His 250 men and their supporting gunners are surprisingly steady; their main complaint is the redundant length of the enemy's barrage, and they're ready to come out and fight. After checking on the men, Reilly climbs to his observation post and takes stock. Only sporadic shells and bolts are landing in the vicinity; except for a few stretches of palisade logs, there's just nothing left to shoot at. Reilly turns binoculars on the tree line 200 to 250 yards away, and there they are, forming up for their attack, dressing their ranks, screwing bayonets into sockets, unfurling regimental flags. Reilly's guess is that Porter will continue firing until two-thirty, then those regulars in the woods and that sitting-duck naval force will advance simultaneously. It would be highly desirable to prevent that, to force the enemy to make a sequential instead of a simultaneous assault.

Frederick Reilly has one—but only one—ace up his sleeve. After seeing how poorly Lamb's buried mines weathered the December bombardment, Reilly suggested it might be better not to use their small stock of reserve mines to replace the ones damaged in December, but to extend a supplementary minefield into the tree line, using the ravines and bogs to hide the waterproof detonating cables instead of more sand, which would only get blown off a second time. So during the brief intermission between battles, Reilly supervised the planting of eleven torpedo mines, on both sides of the River Road, 250 to 300 feet from the dead zone; he figures that's where any Federal commander would form his troops for an assault—not so far that they'll wear themselves out closing with the fort, but far enough to hide their numbers and deployment. Rebel spotters have a general idea of where Terry's columns are massing, because the maritime forest is not uniformly dense or tall, but they don't see more than brief, flickering targets, hardly worth a sharpshooter's bullet. As the scheduled hour of the attack draws closer, the Yankees are rarin' to go. Not a single cannon shot from the fort has been fired at them. After the pasting Porter's given them, however many men remain in the garrison, they have to be demoralized and shaken. Generals Curtis and Ames both expect to suffer some casualties from the field guns guarding the gate, but once those emplacements are overrun, they intend to sweep away any Rebels who try to make a stand. They figure it shouldn't take more than an hour or two before Colonel Lamb, if he is still alive, runs up the white flag.

Nothing to do now but watch the minute hands go 'round. General Terry makes his final report to Admiral Porter's courier, a young New York general named Hawkins, who's spent the past several hours galloping back and forth between the army and the navy contingents, seemingly doing a good job of helping coordinate the two attacks.

"General Hawkins, I think it is safe now for you to take your final report to Admiral Porter: 'Our brigades are formed up, the men are eager to come to grips with the enemy, and resistance is expected to be relatively feeble. We *will* advance the moment we hear his signal.' "

"Very good, General Terry. Excellent. May I wish you and your men the best of luck? Now, I should be off—I don't want to miss my chance to participate in the assault!"

Hawkins spurs his horse to a canter, detouring in a wide northerly loop as he has all morning, to avoid being seen from the enemy's ramparts. As soon as he's out of sight of Terry's columns, he slows the horse to a lazy walking pace. Rush Hawkins has no intention of taking part in Porter's lamebrained "boarding" attack. He delivers General Terry's confident note to Fleet Captain Breese, overall commander of the landing party, then announces that that he wants to join Terry's assault—some old comrades will be taking part, etc., etc. Breese sees no reason to deny this perfectly reasonable request, so Hawkins rides west with a look of fierce determination on his face, and when he gets halfway between the two attacking formations, he plans to dismount, find a comfortable and well-hidden vantage point, and watch the show unfold.

But no sooner does he slow his horse than he's startled by two extremely powerful explosions in the direction of the River Road. His personal indulgence will have to wait, because this sounds like a major kink in the timetable. Indeed, when he gallops back to the Union staging area, he finds, instead of order and discipline, a state of panic and confusion. Reilly's just tried to set off the entire minefield, and is disappointed to learn that only two of the connecting cables haven't been cut by shellfire. Nevertheless, the two mines that *do* explode, make one hell of an impression on General Terry and his men. Neither blast inflicted heavy casualties—the flash and loudness of the powder charge was much more powerful than the fragments were deadly—but both explosions left very impressive craters and engendered panic far out of proportion to the losses they inflicted. Terry's regiments now realize they've been forming up for an attack right in the middle of a Rebel minefield. God knows how many more there are, and they could go off at any second. General Terry thinks this is nonsense; if the Rebels *could* have set off more mines, they would have. Nevertheless, he's going to have to probe the sand with bayonets and send men dangerously forward to find the detonating wires, cut them, and bring back samples, so the nervous infantry will realize they have nothing more to fear.

Ah, good—here comes Hawkins! This little setback will take some time to resolve. He scribbles a note to Porter, explaining the incident, and the need to regroup his men and calm them down before launching the attack. He requests a new starting time of three-thirty, and will assault at Porter's signal, even if some of his men are still shaky. This is the most urgent message Hawkins has been asked to carry, so he puts the spurs to his mount and rides for the beach as fast as the slippery terrain will permit.

He's just about halfway when he hears a shockingly loud rifle shot, followed by the bumble bee sound of a minié ball zipping past his ear so close he can feel the wind of it. Jesus Christ, somebody is shooting at him! And it can't possibly be a Confederate sniper, not this far from the fort. Hawkins draws his pistol and spins around, trying to spot his assailant. There! Behind a thick bunch of sea oats, fifty yards away, a flash of blue, and the pumping motions of someone reloading a Springfield.

"Who the hell are you?" Hawkins shouts. "I'm on your side, you idiot, so why did you take a shot at me?" Hawkins gets a fleeting, partial look at the man's face. Both his countenance and his voice are vaguely familiar, but Hawkins could not put a name to them to save his soul—which this man, apparently, thinks is already destined for damnation.

"Because you're a lyin', yellow-bellied, back-stabbin' son of a whore!" snarls the enigmatic would-be assassin. Now the man pops up and takes a snap shot at Hawkins while Hawkins empties his revolver. A loud "godDAMN IT!" indicates that Hawkins at least winged the gunman, but the man's second shot unluckily strikes the horse smack between the eyes, causing the animal to drop like a sack of coal, carrying Rush Hawkins down and cracking his head against a large piece of driftwood. Hawkins swoons and passes out.

3:00 P.M.: Admiral David Porter was immensely relieved when Breese signaled from the beach that General Terry was all set to go; Porter had been worried about some last-minute delay by the army, and even he can tell, through his binoculars, that his three "divisions" are tired of standing in ranks on the beach and are anxious to get on with it. This, actually, is Admiral Porter's interpretation of their demeanor. In fact, more and more of the sailors are starting to exchange their early bravado for darker, more pessimistic thoughts. It is an awfully long way to the base of that Northeast Bastion, and every foot of it is wide open. No doubt the Marine marksmen will do their best, but their skirmish line and their little sandcastle breastwork look mighty skimpy in comparison to the mass and sheer, brooding *presence* of Fort Fisher.

Admiral Porter orders the "cease-fire" flag run up his halyards, and shoots off three red rockets just to make sure every ship gets the message. For the first time in fifty-six hours, the overheated guns of his fleet fall silent. It is a moment of memorable drama, and Porter savors it for a while before walking over to the steam whistle cable and giving it a good, hard yank. The flagship's shriek is instantly picked up by all the other vessels, creating a banshee wail that sends a thrill down the spine of every man.

"Well, there it is," remarks Will Cushing, astonished at the banality of the remark. The 1st Naval Division steps off smartly ahead of the 2nd. Their turn will come as soon as a fifty-yard interval has been established.

"It's a relief, isn't it? They say the hardest part of any battle is the waiting before it starts!" Benjamin Porter chirps this hoary cliché as though it were a demonstrable and universal truth. "Has that been your experience, Commander Cushing?"

Poor, decent, brave, hopelessly father-dominated young lieutenant! What else can Cushing say but "In general, yes. Once the actual shooting starts, you're far too busy to stay frightened." Until this particular operation, that's been very true for Will Cushing. Now Will Cushing suspects it's just another self-protective delusion that most ordinary men are scared shitless every minute they're under fire. Well, he is about to find out . . .

3:02 P.M.: After hearing that eerie, heart-stopping scream of the steam whistles Lamb and Whiting toss back a couple of robust shots, almost the last of that classy Scotch Lamb brought in from the Cottage. Footsteps pounding on duckboards, the long roll rattling on a snare drum—the riflemen are coming out of their shelters and climbing to the ramparts. Somewhat redundantly, a hyperventilating corporal pokes his head into Lamb's little cave and shouts "Colonel, sir, the enemy is preparing to charge!"

"Thank you, Corporal," replies Whiting, savoring each drop of the Scotch. "We assumed that was the case and we'll join you momentarily."

Lamb and Whiting shake hands, then spontaneously embrace. "This is our day, William. Let us meet it together, as befits true soldiers." With steady, inspiringly calm steps, they mount the stairs to the Pulpit, uncase their field glasses, and turn to watch the segmented, brass and steel-flashing blue worm inching its way down the beach. Puffs of sand spurt all around, and a ricochet whangs off the barrel of the Bastion's sole functioning cannon. The Marines are banging away with their repeaters, and Lamb finds it very annoying, so he authorizes the 8-incher to throw a couple of canister loads at them.

3:12 P.M.–5:00 P.M.: Those two blasts of canister macerate about fifteen Marines and pry the rest out of their trench in panic. While the columbiad crew cheers, the leathernecks spill down toward the beach and intermingle with the advancing naval divisions. At 250 yards, Lamb orders his best marksmen to kill as many officers as they can; the mass of his troops are enjoined to hold their fire until the enemy is jammed up against the palisade's remnants and the base of the Bastion itself. Chase Whiting is still coolly studying the oncoming mass of bluejackets.

"Well, now, here's a truly marvelous thing! Take a look, William! I do believe that except for the Marines, that entire force is armed with nothing but pistols and cutlasses!" Lamb takes another close look. Whiting is right!

"Does Admiral Porter think Fort Fisher is a corsair's ship? Those poor men are defenseless! Even their pistols won't do them any good until they're right in front of us."

"At which point we will slaughter them like sheep in a pen." Chase Whiting is so eager to punish these men that he's hopping up and down. At two hundred yards, the leading ranks of the navy column see a small ridge of sand fringed with grass—just high enough to shield them from the artillery rounds that have been tearing holes in their ranks, so instinctively the head of the column veers to the left, putting that sand dune between themselves and the fort. Just as instinctively, the rest of the landing force follows. But the route narrows to a strip of wet sand ten to twelve feet wide: a natural funnel wide enough for five or six men to pass through abreast, no more. The 2nd and 3rd divisions collide with the 1st, everybody in one ungainly mob, shoving and gasping for breath. Fleet Commander Breese has lost all control of the situation; officers are dropping steadily all around him—splendidly distinct targets in their gold braid and shiny buttons—and the men at the rear of the stalled column are starting to waver. *They're* not protected by any sand dune, and the Rebels have somehow contrived to haul a Napoleon up the wall and into a ruined gun chamber, so now there are two cannon raking them with canister. Already the beach behind them is dotted with gruesomely mangled men, some lying still amid their own entrails, the gulls already descending for a grisly snack, and others crawling pitifully up the beach. The sailors' earlier bravado is quite gone now. They're winded and plastered with sweat and they're starting to look at their cutlasses incredulously: *What are we supposed to do with these things? Throw them at the Rebels?* Whenever a Marine falls, there's a rush to snatch his Spencer.

Finally the column heaves like a giant inchworm—hundreds of men have decided that it's safer to charge *over* the sand ridge and get to their objective swiftly than it is to take the long way around, through that narrow bottleneck.

On comes a wild blue wave, breasting the sand dune, waving those silly cutlasses, wasting ammunition by firing their pistols on the run, cheering each other on. Chase Whiting has been dreaming about such a target for four years, and here it is! He climbs up to the parapet, cups his hands, and shouts defiance:

"Come on, you Yankee bastards! Come on and get a taste! We'll kill every last one of you!" Lamb's riflemen, straining at the leash, point at Whiting and cheer him on. There's a *real* general, taunting the enemy and waving his sword aloft, even though a fair number of Marines have noticed this tempting target and puffs of sand are starting to erupt around Whiting's boots.

Then a Spencer bullet clips off one of the stars from Whiting's epaulettes and Lamb decides his friend has had enough fun. He grabs Whiting by the ankles and shouts: "Goddamn it, Chase, that's enough! They're almost close enough to hit you with a rock!" Giggling like a schoolboy, Whiting tumbles back into the command post and brushes the sand from his clothes, blows a few specks off the cylinder of his Colt, and turns to the defenders on both sides of the Pulpit, shouting encouragement.

You have to hand it to those sailors, thinks William Lamb; they keep on coming even though they know they're heading into a slaughter pen, they're streaming through the gaps in the palisade and trying to climb the crumbling sand at the base of the Bastion. Lamb estimates there are at least four hundred men crowded together within fifty yards of where he's standing. The time is right. He raises his sword and screams "Volley fire!"

In one continuous rippling line of flame, 350 rifles discharge as one, straight down into the faces of the men swarming toward the Bastion but not finding any way to climb it. More and more sailors and Marines crash through the palisades and only add to the density and helplessness of the mob. Lamb calls for rapid, independent fire, and his men load and shoot as fast as humanly possible, howling like demons at their victims. The front of the navy column simply melts away, like a candle pressed against a hot frying pan. Some of Lamb's men start dropping crude hand grenades down into the roiling mass, raising the level of havoc. Now and then, one of the defenders staggers and falls, hit in the head or upper chest by a pistol shot, but mostly the killing is one-sided and absolutely merciless. For 2½ days the garrison's been crouching like moles inside their bombproofs, while the earth quaked and heaved beneath them—now at last they can strike back at their tormentors.

Incredibly, one naval officer *has* managed to claw his way up the wall, shouting in vain for others to follow him. It seems a pity to kill him, really, after such a demonstration of grit, so there are shouts of "Surrender, you idiot! Nobody's following you!" With one arm hooked over the Pulpit's rampart, the young ensign turns around and sees that he is, indeed, all alone, and those of his comrades who can shove their way out are already starting to flee. The ensign turns around now, his eyes wide, just a few feet away from some whiskey-breathed Confederate general. As soon as he can figure out how to raise his hands without falling back into the abattoir, the ensign plans to surrender. Chase Whiting steps up to him and says: "Very bravely done, sir!" and then thrusts his pistol against the young man's forehead and blows off the back of his skull.

"They're running!" shouts Lamb, emptying his own pistol over the parapet. There must be 150 bodies piled up against the root of the Bastion, and a carpet of dead and wounded leading to the palisade. This is something no one has ever witnessed: hundreds of U.S. sailors and Marines running for their lives, sometimes trampling on their own wounded. Lamb's men pick their targets individually now, and the retreating mob drops a trail of bodies in its wake until the last stragglers pass out of rifle range.

Lamb's two cannon, however, keep firing for a while longer. Will

Cushing and Ben Porter never got closer to the fort than two hundred yards and when the landing party's morale snapped, they were swept along in the rout. Young Porter did what officers are expected to do in such extreme circumstances: he stood in the path of wild-eyed, terrified, broken-souled men, arms out wide, calling on them to "Stop and regroup, men! Reform on me! We must give covering fire to those storming the fort!"

"With what?" shouts one sailor, rudely knocking Porter's arm aside.

Cushing watches the debacle without much emotion—it is no less than he expected. There's still a lot of shooting and yelling around the Bastion, but no one moving in their vicinity except a few wounded. Cushing knows that all he has to do is give the word, and Porter will follow him toward the fort, no matter how petrified he is—he'll do it for "the honor of the navy" or some such rot. Instead, Cushing puts his arm around the young lieutenant and counsels prudence instead of sacrifice. "Benjamin, there is nothing we two men can do to salvage the battle or to redeem the navy's honor. And by the way, we're the only two men standing up on this stretch of the beach, so the best thing we can do is try to assist some of the wounded to safety, then try to find a bit of safety ourselves."

"The admiral may be watching us at this moment, sir. I cannot retreat in front of his gaze."

"It's the admiral's fault these men got slaughtered! It will not improve his mood to learn that you were among the dead. Come on, now, be a sensible fellow—let's pick up that man down there, before he drowns. He looks to be salvageable. Ben—Damn it, Ben, don't do that!"

But Porter's drawn his sword and his chest is heaving as he steels himself. Cushing tries to physically restrain him before he charges—prepared, if necessary, to knock him out with a pistol butt—but he's a second too late and grabs only the waft of young Porter's sprint. Ben Porter runs toward the enemy steadily, not wildly, and not zigzagging. Cushing finds a bit of cover behind a dune and watches his new friend valiantly and senselessly "redeeming the navy's honor." Cushing waits for the inevitable. It comes after Porter's gone maybe forty yards. That 12-pounder coughs, a dark blur streaks across the dunes, and the canister balls simply erase Ben Porter in a gush of wet sand. After the debris cloud settles, all Cushing can see that's identifiable is one boot, a severed hand, and the lieutenant's sword, its point driven into the sand, slowly oscillating back and forth, a grave marker of steel. He wonders, for just a few seconds, if there is any point in retrieving the young man's sword—a memento for the admiral and a brand on his heart forever—but the Rebel gun already has that spot zeroed-in. Besides, the lieutenant's sword is identical to the hundreds of others now strewn along the shoreline. Wearily, Cushing gets up and forces himself to start walking north. Along the way, he finds one wounded man who's not too heavy for him to carry and who might survive if a surgeon finishes cutting off the remnants of his left leg. No one fires at Cushing as he carries this stunned, half-delirious stranger out of danger, and behind him, around the Bastion, there is no more firing now.

Only cheering! At trifling cost to themselves, Fort Fisher's defenders have routed utterly two thousand sailors and Marines, killing or wounding hundreds. Chase Whiting is so elated he dances a little jig atop the Pulpit.

"I told you we could lick 'em, Billy Lamb! And by God, we licked 'em good and proper!"

Then Whiting realizes that the cheering is dying off for some reason, and troopers on the Land Face parapet are shouting, trying to get his and Lamb's attention.

The men are pointing urgently toward the Cape Fear River. Squinting in disbelief, Whiting's jaw drops. Lamb raises his binoculars, gasps—there's no mistaking it: there are Union flags already waving over the traverse nearest the gate. The Yankees are inside the walls!

“Attack! Attack! That is All I Can Say . . .”

THE ENEMY HAS broken through despite heroic resistance. We are greatly outnumbered and have received wholly inadequate reinforcements from you. Now, while the enemy is pinned down inside the walls, is the time for you to unleash General Hackett's division. Attack! Attack! That is all I can say and all that you can do!

General Chase Whiting to General Braxton Bragg, 6:22 P.M.

General Terry's engineers don't find any more "live" mines—Porter's barrage has sliced all the detonator cables to shreds. The two that did explode comprised the whole extent of this particular threat, and their effect was more shocking than lethal. Once the soldiers realize there won't be any more nasty surprises, they shake off their panic and re-form with commendable discipline. But they're not ready to attack when Porter's steam whistles rend the air. Could something have happened to the courier, young General Hawkins? Well, it cannot be helped—the two assaults will not go in simultaneously, as he and Porter planned, which means the sailors will catch hell. Terry wants to get going, so while his regiments finish re-forming, he assembles his three brigade commanders—Martin Curtis (1st Brigade), Galusha Pennypacker (2nd Brigade) and Louis Bell (3rd Brigade, bringing up the rear)—for a final reprise of his plan. Curtis will start the assault, but without the usual preparatory sequence of commands. He will give just one signal, then his men will then rise up from the shallow cover they've been resting in and rush the fort. There's one stretch of palisade, in front of Shepherd's Battery, that has somehow escaped destruction, and Curtis plans to send thirty brawny men, swinging big timber axes, to chop it down, enlarging the gap for the 2nd Brigade, whenever Terry orders it forward. This means Curtis's men will have to advance somewhat obliquely to the right to get around that obstacle. He wants his two right-flank regiments to charge for the gate, and his two left-flank regiments to storm the section of parapet adjacent to it. Dirt simple stuff. Speed and violence, not fancy maneuvers, are the keys.

"When will you be ready to start?"

"As soon as I take my post at the head of my men. I will, of course, yell *CHARGE!*" Curtis makes a wry smile, and Terry grasps his hand.

"When I see your men on top of that wall, I'll know this attack is going to succeed. Good luck!"

Major Reilly has set up his command post in Shepherd's Battery, the largest gun chamber on the Land Face. Roughly shaped like the numeral 8, both of its original weapons have been conveniently ejected by 15-inch Rodman shots from the monitors; from here, Reilly can see the whole landscape. He's done what he can to prepare. Last night, a squad of his men went out and removed all the planks from the bridge in front of the gate, leaving only the wooden stringers. More importantly, he's worked out signals and coordination with every remaining gun that can fire on this bearing, including, more than a mile to the south, the giant coast artillery pieces on Battery Buchanan, preregistered to "walk" their rounds up and down at 50-yard increments. Periodically, they've lobbed a round or two in the general direction of Terry's presumed location, but they must be sparing of their ammunition until the ground attack actually begins. And only a little while ago came unexpected good news: despite the unbelievably hammering it has sustained during sixty hours of non-stop bombardment, the Mound Battery is back in business, its gunners having repaired a 10-incher, and they, too, are ready to support Reilly. Seven pieces of artillery, given the level of punishment the fort's taken, will go a fair ways toward compensating for the fact that Reilly has just three hundred men to repel an attack by six thousand.

General Terry hates those huge freight train rounds that occasionally plunge into his assembly area—only one or two land per hour, but they spook his men badly and they've cost him three killed and nineteen wounded. They probably won't be a problem once his men are inside the walls, however, and the attack that will carry them inside is about to start. Terry settles down in the lee of the same brushy sand knoll he's used before, and focuses his binoculars on the tree line from which Curtis's men will momentarily emerge. Well, by damn, there he is now, looking absolutely calm. Curtis steps into the open, looking even taller than his normal six feet, six inches, raises his sword, sweeps it down in the direction of Shepherd's Battery, and yells *"Chaaarrge!"* so loudly they can probably hear him up on Sugar Loaf. Four veteran regiments come pouring out of the woods, bayonets sparkling, moving as fast as the sand will permit.

At that moment, all of Reilly's direct fire guns cut loose with canister, raking the flanks of Curtis's formations, slashing deep gashes in their ranks. From atop the ramparts, Reilly's riflemen rise up as one and deliver a murderous volley. As planned, Curtis's main force takes a slightly oblique path toward the gate, which makes them even better targets. Meanwhile, his "lumberjacks" start chopping down that bothersome stretch of palisade logs.

The charge has great momentum, the Yankees are steady and determined, but before they can approach the gate, they run headlong into the combination of wide tidal creek and gooey, tangled morass that used to be the raison d'être for the plank bridge. All mixed together, portions of the 117th and 3rd New York suddenly find themselves stuck in glue, advancing in slow motion with tenacious muck sucking on their feet and a rain of lead sweeping down on them from above. A few exceptionally brave men try to get across on the bridge stringers, by moving hand over hand and upside down, like a family of monkeys. Flag Officer Branch orders his gun crew to swivel right ten degrees and fires a canister round directly at the bridge supports. Both beams disintegrate, and all the men trying to cross on them are swept away. The swift black-water creek pouring into the Cape Fear River turns oily with blood, a sinister demarcation that all but shouts to Curtis's men: *This far and no farther!* Lashed by cannon fire and anxious to get out of the bog as fast as they can, the largest part of the 1st Brigade drifts eastward, toward the big new gap Terry's ax men have cleared for them, flailed all the way by brisk and accurate fire from Reilly's men.

There is dead ground ahead, though, and as they flood through the palisade stumps, every sensible man heads for it—a wide, uneven ditch left over from the original construction of the Land Face. Three years of erosion have carved an overhang that screens them from Confederate fire. Curtis allows the men a couple of minutes to catch their breath. It is twenty-four feet to the top, straight up a 35 to 40 degree slope, with absolutely no cover. But they've tried to breach the gate, and the terrain made that impossible—this is the only way inside, and every regimental color guard wants to plant the first Union flag atop Fort Fisher. So when Curtis yells "Charge!" again, they do.

But the height and angle won't allow anything like a "charge." Instead, the men claw and gouge and hump forward, sometimes crawling, sometimes walking on their knees, none of them able to fire back, some of them losing purchase and tumbling back into the ditch, knocking down others in their path. Overall, Curtis and his men ascend inch by fire-swept inch, appallingly slow and vulnerable.

Reilly's first indication of an assault coming straight up the wall is the sight of several flags bobbing up and down, followed by more and more heads. Leaning over the sandbagged wall, he sees hundreds of Yankees climbing toward him like blue spiders.

"They're climbing the wall, boys! Lean over and stop 'em!"

By now there are fifty to sixty Confederates crammed into Shepherd's Battery, more than the place can comfortably hold, so only about forty of them manage to find room on the parapet, poke their rifles over the edge, and witness a remarkable sight: the whole forward slope carpeted with creeping, struggling Yankees, and the nearest ones are only five or six feet away. There's time for two volleys—one big, then a smaller one as those who have fired step aside to make room for those who haven't—and both do dreadful execution, knocking over Union soldiers like ninepins. Reilly watches in awe as the flag-bearer of the 3rd New York, blood pouring from three holes in his chest and shoulders, calmly rises to a kneeling position and with great final dignity passes the flag to a comrade's outstretched hand, then nods his head as if to say, *My earthly work is done, carry on for me!* then falls back dead.

Reilly also sees that there are just too many of them pressing up from the base; for every one his men kill, three take his place, and you have only to look into their eyes to know that these Yankees *will not stop coming* until they are all killed or they reach the top. Reilly grips his revolver two-handed, rests the butt on a sandbag, and pops off all six rounds, the last two only a foot away from their targets, and all six balls smack flesh with an audible thud and skulls with a brittle, breaking-teacup sound, blood and brains and puffs of uniform cloth scalding on his face. Six shots, six dead but that isn't nearly enough. Now that they can actually see and reach out for the parapet, Curtis's men feel a renewed surge of energy—*they're going to make it, they're going to be the first Northern soldiers to breach these "impregnable" walls!*—and they swarm up the last few feet with knees churning, using rifle butts like alpine stocks.

"Brace yourselves, men—here they come!"

No time to reload now, and Reilly forgets he's wearing a sword, picks up instead a big shell-bent cast iron aiming spike. Swinging it like a club, he brains two Yankees, but suddenly there's a flood of others who pour over the rim, a cresting blue wave, heralded by breathless shouts of triumph. There's no room even to swing an iron bar, much less to reload and so many men are struggling hand to hand that few Confederates in nearby positions dare risk a shot. For five minutes, Shepherd's Battery seethes and boils like a kicked-over anthill. Men curse and scream and grapple savagely, rifle butts and bayonets, Bowie knives and clubs, rocks and bare hands, fists and teeth. Reilly's matted with gore and someone's torn the iron bar out of his slippery hands, so he backs up to draw his sword. He's never seen a fight like this, not even conceived it. These are no longer trained soldiers, they're barbarians, wild beasts—if you tied together one hundred starving wolverines and threw them into a dry well then dropped in a single piece of food, this is the kind of chaos you might see. By reflex, Reilly slashes down and lays open some poor man's cheek. A pall of mutual exhaustion slows the piston strokes of blows, mutes the decibel level of the screams—the oaths and cries of rage are diminished now, and somewhat feeble. For a while, at least, both armies have hit their limits, drained dry the wellsprings of their resolve. The floor of the Shepherd's Battery is choked with bodies, the living trampling the dead and the helpless writhing toward escape, if they can find it. Friend and foe grind each other's bones indiscriminately, for there is no visible way out, and withdrawal back down the wall is impossible because there are still so many men lined up on the edge of this arena, waiting to join the madness; as soon as there's enough room, another surge of Yankees pours over the parapet. Reilly's hacked his way to the side of the first traverse mound, where he can get a touch of perspective. There's no more stopping them because they can't be killed fast enough; not enough gray uniforms, far too many blue. His men have done all they can in Shepherd's Battery—either he pulls them back and re-forms, or they'll be drowned in Yankees. Reilly shouts and waves and makes it clear: *Fall back over the traverse! Regroup in the next gun chamber! There's just too many of them!*

3:50 P.M.: General Alfred Terry's never seen anything like it, either, and by his rough estimate Curtis has already a third of his entire brigade, but by God, they've breached the wall, and there goes the first Union flag ever planted on this fort: the banner of the 117th New York. It's a triumph, but Terry knows that Curtis's men have shot their bolt; it'll be all they can do to hang on to that first gun pit; the traverse between Shepherd's Battery and the next gun chamber might as well be the Rocky Mountains. He orders the 2nd Brigade to advance, reinforce, and exploit.

If the capture of one foothold has reduced the amount of lead coming at them from above, the men of the 2nd Brigade can't tell the difference. Four lieutenants, two captains, and three colonels go down before the line reaches the bog in front of the gate, and those damned 24-pounders are still peeling off men's faces. Terry's ordered the 2nd Brigade to bifurcate: two regiments swarm up the wall to reinforce Curtis's hard-won salient, the other two press on for the gate. They don't bog down as badly as Curtis's men, because some of the latter have been hiding in depressions and bushes on the northern side of the creek and every chance they get, they're been rolling stones and tree limbs into the water as fast as they can. By now they've built up a rough causeway, broad enough for a few men to cross without getting stuck in deep mud, ripped by briars, or breaking their ankles in webs of interlaced telegraph wires. Some of the 2nd Brigade is making progress—Flag Officer Branch retargets his Parrott to smash them back into the muck. But, unheard above the general tumult, another of those huge 11-inch Brooke shells comes sailing in from far-off Battery Buchanan. If it had landed in the creek at that moment, the 2nd Brigade's advance might have collapsed. But it doesn't. It's a "short," and it falls down like a groaning meteorite on top of Branch's Parrott rifle.

Branch hears it coming, knows what it is, and has time to yell "Take cover!" before the huge shell crashes into his cannon and blows it into perdition. Ears ringing, eyes wide with disbelief at the sheer bad luck that's just eliminated a third of the artillery defending the gate, Branch and his gunners rise slowly to their feet, all except for one poor sailor who's been decapitated by a big iron wedge.

"Mister Branch, sir—they're storming the gate!"

"Pick up your rifles, men, and let's go lend a hand. That's what Marines are supposed to excel at, isn't it?"

"First time we've ever had a chance to excel at any damn thing," grumbles one leatherneck.

"I would not mind dying so much," gripes another, "if I could ram this here bayonet up Braxton Bragg's ass first."

Branch laughs bitterly. "I outrank you, Corporal Garnett, so I get first crack at the bastard, but you're welcomed to take the second poke!"

There's nothing holding the Yankees back now except for the pair of gateside 24-pounders and about thirty-five men firing over the sandbagged barricade plugging the archway. Even as Branch hustles his men forward, they lose the 24-pounders—the Yankees got quite a lift from seeing Branch's cannon get blown up by a friendly shell, so they're pushing on hard. And they must be close, because now Branch can see the gun crews frantically spiking the weapons and emptying their revolvers. Then a steel-tipped blue wave crashes over the gun emplacements, and Branch never sees the artillerymen again. At the barricade, the defenders are loading and firing as fast as they can, but when Branch's men join the line, they're startled to see a great wedge of Union infantry surging up from the creek bed, pouring onto the causeway, no more than thirty yards away. *God bless you, Braxton Bragg, for placing fifty brave men behind a sandbag wall and expecting us to stop the charge of fifteen hundred equally brave foes! This will not take long, at least . . .*

Branch has a Spencer and two Colts, so he figures he can kill a dozen men at least before someone shoves a bayonet into his breast. At least his body will be identifiable, and perhaps some Yankee survivor will say of him: "That Rebel naval officer, he went down fighting like a real lion." *Okay, Mister Branch, start counting . . . That's . . . one . . . two . . . three . . ."*

He only gets to eight.

For a disjointed, outside-of-time moment, Lamb and Whiting are transfixed, paralyzed, by the sight of Yankee flags on the walls of Fort Fisher. Two minutes ago, they were cheering at the total repulse of Porter's naval force, upon which they had inflicted more casualties than the number of Lamb's entire command. And now, *this*? No time to wonder how it happened—it just *has,* and only prompt, resolute action can make it un-happen. While Whiting rounds up men for a counterattack, Lamb quickly determines that the gate cannot hold much longer, that the enemy's going to burst through and start flooding across the parade ground. He needs, quickly, to improvise a line across their path. Every man within earshot, he orders down from the wall, pointing to an imaginary line at right angles to the direction the Yankees will likely follow after piercing the gate. "Throw up a breastwork from *there* to *there!* Take tools from the abandoned gun chambers! Use sand, bricks, trash, anything that will stop a rifle ball! And do it fast! I'll dig up as many men as I can find along the Sea Face and reinforce you."

Lamb heads south, scouring every tunnel and dugout and cranny in the Sea Face, gathering punch-drunk artillerists, the walking wounded, a handful of shamed shirkers, and imploring Hagood's demoralized South Carolinians—his only fresh and uncommitted troops—to by God stop skulking like dogs, come out, and start fighting like men! By persuasion, by the rawest emotional appeals to patriotism and honor, by entreaties and commands and threats, Lamb motivates twenty-eight men to rise up and shamble off with him; the rest of Hagood's men simply refuse to budge, and when Lamb tries pulling rank on them, a stony-eyed sergeant actually cocks his Colt and tells Lamb to back off or die.

Lamb leads this rag tag company back along the Sea Face to his rough, improvised defense line. The men from the Bastion are feverishly carving rifle pits to define the position, dragging charred timbers, rain barrels, sacks of cornmeal, anything that *might* stop a bullet, and throwing up a crude barricade. It was a snap decision, this improvised line, but as the situation around the River Road becomes clearer, Lamb realizes he's made a good choice—from this line, he can enfilade the Yankees on top of the Land Face and he also can bring a fair amount of fire to bear on the Federal troops now cautiously advancing through the gate, who seem confused, winded, leaderless—twenty-eight officers killed or wounded so far—and who are shocked to find themselves in a desert of iron fragments, overlapping craters, and rotting corpses. They're still taking some fire from the riverbank as well, where a few Confederate holdouts are sniping from thick weedy cover, Parker's men are firing heavy ordnance from the top of Buchanan, and now the intruders are stung by a ragged volley from Lamb's ad hoc skirmish line. Seems like every time they score what looks to be a decisive breakthrough, more Confederates materialize, each man fighting like ten, and stop them cold again. Until somebody important comes up and tells them to get the hell up and keep going, the Union gate crashers go prone and start scraping up their own personal mounds of sand, rubble, and cold scrap iron. For the time being, at least, Lamb has stalled the enemy's advance across the pitted wasteland where he once reviewed his troops. He looks to his right and sees that, down around the fourth or fifth traverse, Chase Whiting and one hundred relatively fresh men from the Northeast Bastion are counterattacking like a battering ram of flesh.

"Tear down those goddamned flags!" was Whiting's rallying cry as he moved off from the northeast corner and collected every man he could find. None of Whiting's detachment has any idea how outnumbered they are, nor can they afford to be slowed down by the sight of more than a thousand blue uniforms carpeting the parade ground. It's those fucking Yankee flags, pulling them westward on a wild waterfall of hate and defiance. Those flags are going down; neither Whiting nor the men following him have the slightest doubt about it. By the time they drive across the sixth traverse and can actually see the Yankees' faces, the counterattack has worked up a furious head of steam.

Not a moment too soon, either. Reilly's command is now reduced to about eighty five, and they're holding on to the fifth traverse by their fingernails. The two sides are firing into each other's faces now, but for each traverse they've wrested from Reilly, the attackers have paid a heavy purse of blood. There are so many trodden-on bodies clogging Shepherd's Battery that the newly arrived men of Terry's 3rd Brigade have to pick their way single-file around that charnel pit, dying men snatching at their trousers as they pass, begging for water or bandages or their mother's good-night kiss. At the fourth traverse, Terry's men have run out of momentum even as Reilly's men, a mere eighteen feet away on the other side of the traverse, have run out of endurance. Until enough fresh troops collect at the fourth traverse, there aren't enough Yankees to tackle Reilly's men hand to hand. On such a narrow battlefield, the Federals' numerical advantage counts for little. Moment by moment, however, Reilly's burned out command is shrinking, the dead falling where they were struck or punched by impact off the wall and breaking their necks when they hit the iron-studded plain below; the wounded fight on if they can, lie in quiet agony if they cannot—Reilly can't spare anyone to lug them to the hospital. A few, too badly hurt to fight but still able to move, crawl out of the fifth traverse and stumble as best they can in the direction of the overflowing hospital.

"Major Reilly, look! It's Whiting and some reinforcements!"

God bless that bantamweight alcoholic screw-up! Whiting's got the contorted get-out-of-my-way-or-I'll-fucking-kill-you visage of a true berserker, and his followers are infected with the same sense of invulnerable fury. Reilly's men cheer hoarsely as Whiting and his boys pile in beside them.

"How many men have you got left?" gasps Whiting, waving his pistol at the next gun chamber.

"I've been too busy to count. Maybe fifty able-bodied and a couple dozen wounded. But the Yanks are getting reinforcements all the time.

We will support you with fire from here, but I don't think my men have anything left for a charge."

"From the bodies I saw piled up between here and the gate, it's a wonder you still have any men at all, Reilly. Don't worry—we will seize the place and roll 'em back or die trying." Whiting pops his head up, ignoring the angry hornet buzz of minié balls, and sees some fresh reinforcements dribbling into the enemy position even now, led by a tall, barrel-chested color sergeant proudly waving the regimental silk of the 14th Indiana. Whiting *wants that flag*, wants to rip it out of that Yankee's hands and cast it down into the mud. All of his men are ready, their bayonets trembling in the afternoon sun, their bodies like coiled springs. No need for Whiting to shout a command; he simply vaults onto the dome-shaped traverse and throws his body at the enemy. Howling like demons, one hundred Confederate desperadoes are right beside him, and their sudden appearance on top of the traverse takes the hard-breathing Federals by surprise. Every man stuffed into that claustrophobic arena meets his enemy in a state of atavistic frenzy, bellowing curses, growling like animals. Whiting's men drive home their steel, yank out the dripping blades, firing from the hip, stomping fallen men in the face and balls. Inside the cyclone of gun smoke it appears to Lamb like cannibals run amok inside a pit full of deranged rattlesnakes. When the wind clears away some smoke, those Yankees still able to do so are scrambling madly out of the gun chamber and up the hump of the third traverse.

"They're running, boys!" shouts Whiting. "Reload and keep going!"

So sudden and powerful is the shock of this unexpected counterattack that Terry's men recoil all along their end of the rampart, the panicked survivors spreading the infection of fear, disorder, and confusion, upsetting the certainties of what had been a simple, one-sided situation. How many more crazed Confederates are back there? Inside the third traverse there's a mixed batch of Yankees from all three brigades, and no officers still standing, so that tall fierce color sergeant from Indiana takes command, because *somebody's* got to or this position will fall. Indeed, the Rebels might recapture the whole wall, and the color sergeant isn't going to allow that. He has the kind of booming drill-field voice that could cut through plate glass and easily overrides the roar of musketry. While the defenders form a line in Whiting's path, the Indiana sergeant stabs his flagstaff into the ground, signaling to friend and foe: the panic stops *here*. Whiting and his men reach the top of the traverse and leap, slide, stagger, or simply *fall* into their opponents—few have reloaded, there's no room for fancy bayonet work, so the weapons of choice are entrenching tools, the rifle butt, and the stock of the weapon swung like a club—and those British Enfields are strongly made rifles. The Indiana sergeant bares his teeth and tries to shoot Chase Whiting, but in the excitement he's forgotten to shove a cap onto the percussion nipple, *snap* instead of *BANG!*

Whiting hacks wildly with his sword and slashes with the barrel of his empty Colt, but the sergeant keeps blocking the little general's blows with his flagstaff. Snarling like two starving dogs after the same bone, Whiting and the Indiana sergeant struggle for possession of the flag while all around them men are strangling, stomping, biting, slashing, and throwing sand into each other's eyes. Finally Whiting sees an opening, feints with his sword, and doubles with a pistol-whip that breaks the sergeant's nose and demolishes most of his front teeth. Of course the man reacts, screams, spits out bits of tooth and thick gobs of blood, mucus, and a small sliver of tongue. *Goddamn it, let go of that flag!* Through all his pain and shock, the Yankee's grip never falters. Whiting simply chops off three of his fingers, and that does the trick. Roaring his triumph, Whiting wrests the banner and shakes it aloft, so all the Rebels around him can see, and the color sergeant, who feels as though his manhood, pride, and honor have just been stolen by this howler-money of a scrawny Rebel general, crawls up the slope, dribbling blood, snarling and also weeping. Whiting swats at him in annoyance. The sergeant just keeps coming, his right hand now wrapped around a big rock.

"Give me back our flag!"

Whiting's incredulous—won't this fool ever stop?—and Whiting is *impatient!* He needs to press on, while the enemy is still recoiling from the demented fury of the first collision. So Whiting kicks the man in his ruined face, feeling cartilage compress like a sponge, then rains sword blows on his head, loping off an ear, shearing off a big flap of scalp . . . But the man keeps crawling after his stolen banner, blubbering and drooling blood, carved-up like a ham. This is ridiculous, thinks Whiting, who can feel the momentum starting to ebb from his men and the resistance blocking them starting to thicken.

"Go to hell, you Yankee bastard!"

Whiting takes aim and prepares a mighty guillotine stroke—*Let's see how far you can crawl without a head, you maniac!*—but when he tries to bring his arm down a sledgehammer crashes into his right shoulder and he can no longer control the muscles. The sword falls from numb fingers and bounces comically off the groveling sergeant's head.

"I think I'm hit," says Whiting, to no one in particular.

No sledgehammer this time, but a red-hot poker somewhere below his waist—then another impact, like the flat of an ax. Whiting cannot tell exactly where he's hit, or how many times; the overlapping blows spread paralysis through his entire body, his left leg won't hold him up anymore, he cannot hold the captured Yankee flag—no longer cares about it very much, really, and when he looks down at his own body, with eyes that seem detached and floating high above it, there's so much blood he utters a bewildered little bark of amazement, and a great mouth of vertigo opens and swallows him whole. He spins around on the failing stalk of his one good leg, buffeted by waves of dizzying pain. It seems to take forever before he hits the ground.

5:06 P.M.: Generals Terry and Ames pass through the body-clogged gate, excited by the moment of entry and thrilled by the elan their men have shown today; they're also astounded at how thin was the crust of Confederate resistance and yet how fierce! Another five or six hundred men, thinks Ames, and we would never have gotten farther than the first gun chamber! But now it appears the whole Federal attack has run out of steam. A curiously intimate kind of communal paralysis has descended on both sides: There's still a firm line of Rebel resistance midway down the length of the Land Face, and there are at least two thousand Union soldiers lying prone on the parade ground, pinned there by what appears to be a pathetically weak line of enemy riflemen. And Terry's men are still dying, one every twenty-eight seconds; another big shell drops in their midst from the seemingly impregnable Mound Battery and from that big, squat earthwork at the verge of the river and the mouth of New Inlet; the Bastion with an Irish-sounding name that Ames can't quite recall. Each shell throws up a big geyser of debris and stirs a whirlwind of old, cold, Union shrapnel. Christ, he's losing men to parts of rounds that Porter fired three days ago!

It's not far from twilight now, and when darkness falls, if the fort is not entirely subdued, surely General Bragg will execute the maneuver Terry dreads the most: a desperate attack down the peninsula. That Negro brigade, he fears, will not long stand up to Don Hackett's tough, battle-wise veterans, and if his men are suddenly struck from behind by a fresh Confederate division, the day's apparent triumph could quickly turn into a bloody shambles. Terry and Ames agree: something dramatic needs to be done to break this stalemate and it must be done quickly. There is one expedient that might shake things loose again, and it's a desperate measure, one Terry knows is going to kill as many of his men as it does Confederates. But he has men to spare, and Lamb does not.

5:21 P.M.: Eight of Porter's larger warships form an arc around the Northeast Bastion, and another ten form a line of battle across the throat of New Inlet. There is no fire whatever from the fort and Porter's gun crews already have the range and deflection for any part of the crumbling structure they wish to hit. They start with the fifth traverse, which vanishes in a volcanic upheaval, the heavy shells killing indiscriminately, but finally driving Reilly's battered and shrunken band of stalwarts out of position. All it requires is a signal rocket to Porter and his gunners recalibrate and start pounding the next Rebel position in line. It's a brutal tactic, and General Terry's men are so closely engaged that they suffer almost as many losses as Reilly's. One of them is the gallant Martin

Curtis, knocked cold by a chunk of iron the size of a grapefruit, which causes the right side of his head to swell up like a purple balloon; the men bearing him off to the surgeons half-expect his brains to squirt out, but he's still breathing when they deposit him on a table already gummed with blood.

Terry orders the men stalled on the parade ground to resume their advance. But the naval bombardment is so intimidating that those pinned-down soldiers will not rouse themselves to charge through it. Colonel Lamb's scratched-up skirmish line, never more than 130 men, has successfully halted the advance of 2,000—the stalemate has lasted almost an hour. What an incredible foe that man is, thinks General Terry. Most of Porter's shells are plowing up debris in the space between the two sides, and whichever commander can stir his men to charge through it will gain a huge bonus of momentum. Both Lamb and Terry understand that this deadly equilibrium cannot last much longer.

Lamb has only one card left to play: if he can rally enough men, and lead them through the curtain of bursting shells, a sudden bayonet charge might be enough to break the Yankees' will. All he need accomplish is to cause a few dozen men to flee for their lives, and the whole Union salient will collapse. On the face of it, the very idea is absurd: that 200 men can drive 2,000 into headlong flight , but it's been known to happen in battles as hard-fought as this one.

Lamb sprints back to the dank galleries and tunnels where Hagood's recalcitrant South Carolinians are still holed up. There's no time for an oration. He snarls at them with contempt: there is still one chance to win this fight, he says; and you are it. You are the last fresh men in this fort, and the parade ground is carpeted with scared, worn-out Yankees. *One charge! We'll be through the naval barrage in less than thirty seconds, and hit them like a thunderbolt! For God's sake, men, you've been cringing down here all day while others have fought the battle for you. Either make this one supreme effort, or live forever with the shame of cowardice. I and my men will charge in exactly seven minutes. Either join us, or wait here for the enemy to round you up like whipped dogs.*

5:36 P.M.: Lamb's contempt has roused most of the South Carolinians from their caves. Like condemned men moving toward a firing squad, they rise and follow him in sullen, bitter silence. But when they join with the men already at the barricade, Lamb has a force of 236 men. He'll lose some when he leads them through that fearsome scrim of explosions, but there may still be enough bayonets emerging on the far side to trigger a panic and break the enemy's will! Like the jeweler's tap that shapes a diamond, all it will take is one hard jab at one brittle edge, and the Yankees will break, run, pour back out through the hard-won gate, splash mindlessly back through the bogs . . . and General Terry won't be able to reorganize for another attack before dawn. By that time, Lamb continues to believe, even Bragg will scent that a tremendous upset victory is within his grasp.

William Lamb draws his sword and stands atop the rubble of his improvised barricade, against a backdrop of spurting flames, searing iron, fountains of sand, choking coils of smoke, and he steels himself to hurl his body through that wall of fire. Win or lose, he knows this gamble is his final act as the commander of Fort Fisher. His men rise up and crouch tensely for their death-defying rush through a searing blizzard of burning iron.

"Charge!"

He does not look back, but he senses they're right behind him, heads down, eyes closed, bayonets leveled, lunging into that furnace mouth of explosions, and suddenly he's *through* it, into cold clean twilight air, and—*Yes!*—the enemy ranks in front of him recoil in shock and terror, as though one of Porter's shells had torn a new exit through the walls of hell and a horde of demons is pouring through. The Yankees before him waver—no, no—*They are breaking!*

"Come on, men! We've got them on the run!"

And then the angle of Lamb's vision tilts wildly, he is slammed brutally hard, knocked sprawling, sword flying from his grasp—a single minié ball, with the force of a Parrott bolt, has broken his hip, and no amount of courage or willpower will enable him to stand.

When they see Lamb struck down, the men behind him lose all heart. Most simply run for their lives or throw up their hands and surrender, but a few are resolved not to leave the Young Soldier of the Lord where he has fallen. Strong hands grab his limbs and bear him away into deepening shadows, away from the thunder that has battered his ears for three interminable days. Lamb closes his eyes, and figuring it would be best to sleep, now, before the numbness wears off and the pain comes shrieking up his spine.

A Proclamation to the Citizens of Wilmington
From Headquarters, the Cape Fear District, January 15, 1865

The sensational and defeatist reports circulating through this city, about the situation at Fort Fisher, are greatly exaggerated and entirely unfounded. This headquarters has received numerous official reports from General W. H. C. Whiting, throughout the afternoon, indicating that the enemy's attack was unsuccessful and costly. The fort remains securely in our hands, and active measures are being taken to reinforce the garrison. Everyone should remain calm.

General Braxton Bragg, Commander in Chief

7:28 P.M.: At sunset, General Donald Hackett sends cavalry patrols down the peninsula. Their reports, being transcribed verbatim by a stenographer, as part of the documentation Hackett is gathering to support the charges he intends to bring against Bragg, are both ominous and exhilarating. Until moonrise, at 9:34 P.M., the Federal fleet will not be able to fire on any moving troops with the slightest degree of accuracy; the enemy has indeed taken a large part of Fort Fisher, but there is still heavy resistance around the northeast angle, and shells are still plunging down from the Mound Battery and from Battery Buchanan. As for that line of breastworks manned by the Negro brigade, it is a hasty affair rather than a serious obstacle—most of those soldiers are watching the spectacle behind them and do not appear either alert to the danger of a sudden attack, or fit to withstand one. A silent approach down the River Road axis, a thunderclap bayonet charge, and they *will* break. Their only line of retreat will carry them into Terry's command, spreading alarm as the two forces collide. After dispersing the Negroes, Hackett can redress his line, and continue south to hit the disorganized Union brigades from the rear, at the moment they are most vulnerable.

It is all so clear to Hackett, and to his men, who've been expecting the appropriate order from Bragg all afternoon and are eager to redeem the battle. In one hour, two at the most, Hackett can turn a catastrophic defeat into a stunning Confederate victory. After dismissing the cavalrymen, he gathers up his notes and rides down to Bragg's headquarters, intent on a showdown.

8:00 P.M.: Bragg has been trying all day to damp down what must surely be the worst headache in the history of human suffering. Five bottles of "medicine" have finally quelled it; they've also put a cork in the maelstrom of gas he's been straining to suppress since breakfast. Now, instead of worrying about Colquitt and the rest of his staff holding their noses when he walks past them, Bragg can feel a tightening in his sphincter that promises days of iron-clad constipation. He just can't win; has not known one moment of peace since waking up. Telegrams have been landing on his desk like hand grenades all afternoon. He refuses to read any more from Whiting—the man is obviously raving drunk, and his mounting tone of hysteria, not to mention his coarse, insulting language, have had the opposite effect on Bragg from the one intended. He's simply put wax in his ears to muffle the irritating mosquito whine of Whiting's complaints. Late in the afternoon, came two increasingly venomous wires from Governor Vance, demanding "action of the greatest urgency"—as if Vance, in far-off Raleigh, has better knowledge than the commander on the scene! Worse was yet to come: a very testy inquiry from Lee himself—Bragg's not sure how to answer that one yet. Next came a delegation of the rich and influential clan from Orton Plantation, imploring Bragg to come down the river and view the situation for himself; they will gladly provide a boat. General Hagood was the most recent sliver thrust under Bragg's fingernails. It seems Bragg has forgotten, or willfully misunderstood, Hagood's earlier report: Hagood's entire brigade did *not* land at Fort Fisher—only a tiny fraction of it. As soon as darkness hides the river, the steamboat captains are ready to make another run and try to land the rest of Hagood's troops. Bragg doesn't think that's necessary, not at this point; he brushes Hagood off with a vague promise to make a decision "in plenty of time," but refuses to specify what that amount of time might be. So Hagood's gone over Bragg's head and wired Lee for permission to act independently, assuming full responsibility in advance, for any problems that may arise. Lee, evidently, wanted to vet this unorthodox proposition past Jefferson Davis, who bristled at the insubordinate tone of Hagood's request and quashed the idea with his own frigid telegram: Any such action, Davis declares, undertaken without proper authorization from General Bragg, will be treated as tantamount to mutiny.

And now here comes Don Hackett, eyes blazing, nostrils flaring, waving a bunch of notes in Colquitt's face and demanding to speak to Bragg in person, immediately. In the wooden tones of an automaton, Colquitt replies, "General Bragg is indisposed at the moment, sir—if you care to leave a message with me, I will convey it to him." Hackett's glare, drenched in contempt, makes Colquitt feel like a servile lackey. He turns his head away and points down the hall toward Bragg's bedroom. Hackett's boots make the floor shake as he storms toward the general's inner sanctum. He does not so much knock on Bragg's door as assault it like a battering ram. No response from within, except a dismal exhalation like the moan of a malaria victim. Hackett's brawny fist pounds on the door again.

"I left orders not to be disturbed, Colquitt!" Bragg's voice has the pitch and scratch of an old woman complaining of her bunions.

"This is General Hackett, not your lap dog, Colquitt! I have urgent new information that requires a swift decision! You have a chance to turn a disaster into a great victory!" *Always be careful about your choice of pronouns when talking to deranged superior officers!*

Jesus, thinks Hackett, if *anything* will stir Bragg, it should be the chance to redeem his military reputation on the cheap. Hackett's willing to let Bragg claim all the credit; all Hackett wants to do is save his fellow soldiers in the fort before they're wiped out. Ponderously, come the sounds of Bragg rising from a chair, followed by the crash of breaking glass and a muttered *"Shit!"* After what seems like hours, Bragg finally opens the door. He's red-eyed, there's some sort of eczematious crust flaking off his eyebrows, and his breath would knock a buzzard off a shit wagon. With exaggerated patience, Hackett explains the situation reported by his cavalry patrols. All Bragg need do is nod his head, and the sun will rise on a brilliant Confederate victory.

"So . . . you are proposing a full-scale *night* attack?" Bragg rumbles, as though the concept was just too complicated to wrap his mind around.

"As I explained, General, the situation demands it—and I guarantee success!"

"No commander can 'guarantee' success, sir. A night attack is the most hazardous maneuver imaginable. Troops will get lost . . . friend and foe become all mixed up . . . impossible to keep formation . . . recipe for disaster, if ever there was one."

Hackett is on the verge of weeping. He tries one more time, marveling again at Bragg's ability to detach himself from reality and then blame others for "not keeping him informed." How many times has Jeff Davis bought that lame excuse? Hackett even takes a pencil and draws a sketch on the wall. Bragg squints at it as though it were an esoteric calculus theorem.

"Look: Here is the Cape Fear River! Here is the Atlantic Ocean! There is Fort Fisher! It is not necessary for my men to advance in strict formation—only that they *advance*. As long as they keep the *ocean* on their left side, and the *river* on their right, *how in God's name can they get 'lost'?"*

Bragg just stares at him. Hackett can barely discern sentience in the man's eyes. What is so complicated about this? He can imagine how Lamb's battered remnants must feel—they're still fighting because they know it's not too late. And General Terry's probably frantic to clean out the last pockets of resistance, because *he* knows it's not too late, and his victory could be overturned at any moment.

"Too risky . . ." mumbles Bragg. "Perhaps in the morning . . ."

"In the morning, sir, the goddamned Union fleet will be able to *see us*! Right now, it is *dark*, so they cannot see us!" Hackett has observed keener perception in the eyes of newborn kittens.

"If you insist, General Hackett, I will send someone *whom I trust* down to the fort to take a look. If I am satisfied that the situation warrants an attack, I will authorize it."

Exactly what does this statement mean? Even Bragg probably doesn't know. But at least it's some kind of vague opening in the closed window of the general's mind. And the entire bizarre conversation has been clearly heard by General Colquitt and several other shame-faced aides. Hackett knows that if he presses for more—for a "definite maybe," even—Bragg is likely to retreat into his shell again. So he salutes and withdraws down the hall, dropping his tactical notes on the desk of the long-suffering Colquitt. As Hackett leaves the building, he hears Bragg's querulous bark: "Colquitt? I have a job for you!"

When Hackett hears that, he knows there is no more hope.

9:15 P.M.: Brigadier General Albert Colquitt does not have the most distinguished military record in the world, but neither is he a fool or a coward. The eight weeks he's spent as Braxton Bragg's aide-de-camp have been a purgatorial punishment for some sin he cannot remember committing. And now, *this*? He heard that surreal conversation between Bragg and Hackett—and was determined, on the instant, to steam down for a quick look around, then telegraph Bragg that he agrees completely with Hackett: launch an attack at once! But instead of authorizing that, Bragg has scribbled an order naming Colquitt as the successor to Chase Whiting! Is he supposed to place Whiting under arrest if Whiting refuses to comply with this lunacy? Is Whiting still alive, for that matter?

There is still a lot of firing down near the wharf—a last stand, perhaps, around Battery Buchanan? Colquitt and his five assistants hardly amount to reinforcements, and if they try to land at the wharf, they'll be shot to pieces. So he puts the boat aground in the tangled marshes near the western terminus of the Land Face and proposes to continue south under cover of the riverbank, making notes as he goes. If there's a chance to make contact with Whiting, or whoever is still in charge, he will try. What he plans to do next, he cannot imagine.

By now, there's a glaring moon ascendant in the east, and the darkness covering the fort's interior rises like a slow curtain, revealing more and more. Colquitt and his staff can't quite believe the scene that crystallizes before their eyes, tinted bone-white by the moonlight. Aside from stretcher parties and small bunches of stragglers and souvenir hunters, many of them reeling drunk, Fort Fisher is a necropolis, an abomination to the earth on which it stands—clotted on the ramparts, piled in heaps near the gate, strewn randomly across the parade ground, are approximately eleven hundred hideously mangled bodies. Fires gutter fitfully in subterranean galleries and tunnels; scavengers exploring those passages cast the distorted shadows of goblins. Enormous cannon barrels have been flung great distances by scarcely imaginable force, like discarded Cyclopean toothpicks. Acres and acres of shell fragments and enigmatic iron bolts—objects forged on the anvils of mythic titans; the cumulative weight of metal thrown at this place is beyond computation. Colquitt now understands the crescendo of anxiety in Whiting's telegrams. It is a wonder that these men were not driven mad by concussion alone.

The last five hundred yards, Colquitt and his aides have to crawl past exhausted-looking Federal skirmishers, still trading volleys with the garrison's remnants, stubbornly clinging to their trenches at the base of Battery Buchanan. Holdout snipers still fire occasionally from behind the crenellations on top, although the big guns on the walls have fallen silent. Colquitt tells his men to wait and to stay under cover; he will proceed alone, by crawling under the sagging wharf, and try to make contact with whoever is in command. When he gets close enough for the defenders to hear him, he calls out: "Hold your fire, men! I have a message for General Whiting from General Bragg!"

"From Bragg? It's about time! Run for it and we'll cover you!"

Colquitt's pulled into the rifle pits by Frederick Reilly, who looks like a cross between a chimney sweep and a ravenous ghoul, a strong-bodied man now shivering from fatigue. Yet, when he looks at Colquitt, Reilly's eyes are still animated by a spark of hope. The gaunt survivors manning this last-ditch perimeter stare at Colquitt as though he had just arrived from Mars, but Colquitt sees that same feeble prayer guttering in their sunken eyes, too. He would give anything to say what they want him to say, but when he does not, when he won't even meet their gaze, they slump back behind their revetments and mechanically reload their blistering rifles for one more pointless volley.

Reilly leads Colquitt to a narrow passageway and holds aside a leather curtain. By the smoky orange light of two lanterns, he sees a tunnel-eyed surgeon, matted with blood from head to foot, bending over a pair of dying men—there's nothing Dr. Reece can do for the newly wounded except dose them with morphine and hope they survive until the fighting stops. Side by side, on two blood-black stretchers, lie Colonel William Lamb and General Chase Whiting. Both of them look quite dead, but when Major Reilly whispers in their ears, their eyes snap open and stab Colquitt with that same accusatory plea.

"What news from General Bragg?" croaks Whiting, struggling up on one elbow.

Colquitt wishes the earth would swallow him whole before he has to answer. "I realize how . . . grotesque, this must sound, but the only thing I have from Bragg is this note, authorizing me to take command."

Lamb begins to laugh, his eyes rolling toward heaven.

" 'Take command'? *Of what?*"

"Since three o'clock this afternoon," growls Whiting, "we have held off a force ten times our number, killed them in droves, and repeatedly driven them back with the most desperate counterattacks, sustained only by our pride and by the belief that even a conniving weasel like Braxton Bragg *would not sacrifice us without at least trying to come to our aid!*"

"Gentlemen, I understand. All day, Bragg . . . well, even by Braggian standards, he's been like a man under a spell. He still does not realize what's happened here! I saw for myself the windrows of dead Yankees piled up around your works. The fight you put up! It may not yet be too late, however. If I can wire Bragg that I *have* 'taken command' and the enemy is wide open to an attack from Sugar Loaf, he will have to comply or be held solely responsible for a defeat that may very well signal the end of the Confederacy itself! Is the telegraph still working?"

"Not since about five-thirty, when my men were forced to retreat from that part of the fort. We smashed the apparatus first, of course. The nearest working line is in Smithville. Have you a boat?"

"Yes, but we had to beach it just below the gate and come the rest of the way on foot. I'm afraid it will take another thirty or forty minutes to retrace our path—assuming we don't get caught. Then another thirty minutes to Smithville."

Lamb's voice is papery and faint with pain—he's refused any morphine as long as he remains capable of command, just as he has spurned no less than four increasingly vehement appeals from General Terry to surrender and terminate the "useless effusion of more blood."

"So the earliest Bragg can possibly get your message will be . . . something over one hour from now, and there's still no guarantee he will act on it, is there, Colquitt?"

"I have no earthly idea, sir."

Lamb turns to Reilly.

"Fred, how many of our men are still fighting?"

Reilly can't give an accurate count anymore. All he knows is that every few minutes, he loses another man.

"Best of my knowledge, Colonel, no more than fifty, and many of them already wounded."

"Can you repel another assault?"

"No. Not a determined effort . . . and I think the enemy's about ready to launch one. They're as tired as we are and want to get this over with, *before* there's an attack from Sugar Loaf."

"And how far away are their nearest positions?"

"No more than fifty yards, sir. We would have time for one volley. None of my men have the strength for a hand-to-hand fight, but it isn't that we've run out of courage!"

Very gently, Lamb reaches out and takes Reilly's hand. "I know it isn't, Fred. What we've run out of is hope. I was determined to hold out to the end, as long as there was even the slightest chance of help. Now I know there is not."

With an effort that costs him so much pain he almost faints, Lamb manages to unbuckle his sword belt. Tears running down his filthy cheeks, he holds it out to Reilly.

"I do not want this to become some Yankee officer's trophy!"

"I can bury it . . . perhaps, after the war . . ."

"No. Just throw it into the river." Chase Whiting has fallen unconscious, for which small mercy Lamb thanks the Lord. He points to Colquitt. "Now, sir, you had better leave, while you can. To put the matter bluntly, I do not want anyone to witness our surrender except the northern soldiers who fought us so gallantly today."

Colquitt salutes. "I will tell the Southern people what I saw here tonight, and who is responsible."

"Fred?"

"Sir?"

"Have someone take the bedsheet up to Captain Parker and his sailors, assuming they're still alive. The flag will be most visible from up there. Then, please dispose of my sword. I would perform both of those unpleasant duties if I could. Please get on with it, Major Reilly—I don't want one more man, on either side, to die in this awful place. And now, Doctor Reece, I believe I will take a couple of those morphine tablets. I want to be composed when I meet the enemy commanders face-to-face, and I've put up with this pain about as long as I care to."

Albert Colquitt and his party have just begun to retrace their soggy path toward the boat when the crackle of musketry subsides. There's a man in a Confederate navy uniform, one arm in a sling, waving a soiled bedsheet on top of Fort Fisher's last redoubt. The sudden silence is a vast suspended breath. The last thing Colquitt hears, before the Union soldiers start cheering, is a faint splash in the waters of the Cape Fear River.

10:56 p.m.:
From General Braxton Bragg to President Jefferson Davis and General Robert E. Lee:

I am mortified to have to report the unexpected capitulation of Fort Fisher. As late as 7 P.M., a dispatch from General Whiting assured me that the enemy assault had been checked and much lost ground recaptured. This message was in great contrast to some of Whiting's previous communications, which disturbed me greatly by their panicky tone and insubordinate phraseology. I retained, of course, the option of launching a relief attack from the heights occupied by General Hackett, but reliable information indicated that the enemy had moved another entire brigade into their blocking line between Hackett and the fort. The inevitable chaos of a night attack might well have resulted in my best division being held up until daylight, at which time the enemy's fleet would have decimated them. When darkness fell, my mind was easy. I had dispatched more than 1500 reinforcements, and considerable quantities of food and munitions, bringing the garrison's strength to approximately 2,400 men—a force which, combined with the formidable earthworks and numerous heavy cannon at Col. Lamb's disposal, should have been more than sufficient to repel any attack.

After receiving a series of alarming and seemingly exaggerated reports, I dispatched down the river a very reliable man, Gen. Alfred Colquitt, together with yet another boatload of reinforcements. Colquitt found a situation bordering on anarchy, completely beyond the control of General Whiting and Col. Lamb, who had been seriously wounded earlier. Among the sights he described were hundreds of Confederate soldiers cowering in subterranean shelters, or wandering without weapons through protected galleries and behind earthworks, making no attempt whatever to fire the operable guns, the great majority of them quite obviously drunk, as was Whiting, in his usual manner.

More particulars will be sent as I learn of them. You will recall that when I was appointed to this thankless task, I expressed my concern that Lamb's garrison, and Whiting's command in general, had been rendered soft, lazy, and ineffectual by years of gorging themselves on luxurious foods and potent Foreign Liquors; that both officers should be removed and their men replaced with reliable, seasoned veterans who would be immunized against the moral turpitude that was inevitably the most evil side effect of living cheek-by-jowl with the sensualists and unprincipled adventurers who owned and captained so many of the blockade-runners. Despite monumental inertia and resistance, and subjected constantly to personal calumnies, vile insinuations, and the most egregious sorts of denunciations, I struggled to bring new coherence and discipline to a command that was already rotten from within. Had fate given me but a few more months to complete my reorganization, I have no doubt whatever that today's humiliating and shockingly unexpected collapse would never have occurred.

I am, however, resolved to defend this city, and the Cape Fear River itself, most tenaciously—had I listened to those who demanded that I launch a desperate nighttime attack with General Hackett's division, I would now be facing the enemy without my best and most experienced troops. If there is a "silver lining" to this dark cloud, perhaps it lies in the fact that now, at least, I will not have to worry anymore about rebellious drunks, or coddled garrisons who, when the time came for them to make a supreme effort, proved conclusively that they had degenerated into little more than an armed rabble.

I still retain some excellent troops, and the enemy cannot reach this city without first conquering a whole chain of very strong forts, batteries, and torpedo fields. Many will say that the loss of the blockade-running trade is a serious setback. I believe, on the contrary, that it may have a bracing, salutary effect—for now we must defend ourselves with our own resources, and without the morally debilitating stimulation of French Champagne *and* English Cheeses!

The hour is late, and there is much to be done in the coming days. I am confident that, when the true story of this dismal battle has been told, it will become clear that I did everything possible to avert this disaster, that I provided Fort Fisher with timely and adequate reinforcements, and that the real cause of its fall lay not with the enemy's superior numbers and naval power, but with the moral and spiritual decay of the men charged with that fort's defense.

In sorrow but with undiminished honor, I remain, etc., etc.,
Major General Braxton Bragg

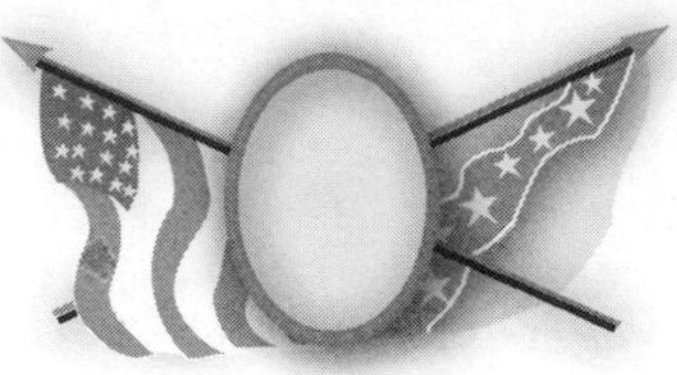

Epilogue: The Kings Depart

Rush Hawkins regained consciousness at about nine o'clock; when the body of the horse he was pinned under grew cold, so did he. He was finally roused by the chattering of his own teeth and the recollection of a wool navy blanket tucked inside his saddlebag. By the time he dug free of the horse, and retrieved the blanket, he was shivering violently. Thank God for the navy—their blankets were about twice as thick as Army-issue, after he located a good windbreak and huddled inside the blanket for a half hour, he was comfortable enough to travel.

His memory of preceding events was rather jumbled: some wild man taking pot shots at him and cursing him and shooting his horse between the eyes . . . By the time he took inventory of his bones and discovered none were broken, he realized that the grand assault on Fort Fisher was over—he could still hear some shooting, but it was coming from deep inside the walls. Porter's armada was still hovering offshore, but its guns were silent. Since he had no idea of the battle's outcome, he reloaded his pistol before investigating the situation more closely.

Stretcher bearers were still coming out of the fort; a field hospital near the River Road was overflowing with wounded Union soldiers, and the dead, from both sides, were being buried, by sullen Rebel prisoners, in large, temporary graves. The guards did not look much happier than their charges, which indicated to him that the fighting had been bitter. Hawkins did not linger near the hospital; the sights and sounds were disturbing, and he felt somewhat obligated to locate General Terry, so he could explain the reasons why he was not able to deliver Terry's last dispatch to Admiral Porter's signalmen on the beach.

A few hundred yards south of the hospital, he encountered some artillerymen setting up a battery of 12-pounders on a bluff overlooking the river. The lieutenant in charge looked vaguely familiar, so Hawkins went over and introduced himself.

"General Hawkins, sir, I'm glad to see you! General Terry was asking after you earlier. Say, that's quite a bruise—shell fragment?"

"Nothing so dramatic. A dead horse fell on top of me. Somebody shot the animal while I was taking Terry's last dispatch over to the navy. Apparently, I was knocked out when the horse threw me off."

"So you missed all the excitement?"

"Every bit of it, I'm afraid. I assume we took the fort."

"Most of it, yes. The Rebs are still putting up a fight down at the inlet. Damnedest battle I've ever seen, or ever want to see again. It was . . ." The young officer struggled for words. "Well, just you keep walking down that road and you'll see. I haven't words to describe it, but if you want a good idea of what hell might look like, you will find it inside those walls."

"If the fort's been taken, or nearly so, why are you setting up a battery in this place?"

"Just in case that division up on Sugar Loaf tries to attack before the last holdouts surrender. The only reason those men are still fighting is because they still hope to be rescued. God's truth, General, I cannot imagine why they didn't strike us from that direction when the battle was at its height. We were so disorganized, and had lost so many men, we were wide open to a counterattack. They could still try it—that's why we're setting up this battery."

"I wonder why they didn't attack?"

"Nobody can figure that out. They missed one hell of an opportunity, though.

"Any idea where I might find General Terry at the moment?"

"Down there where the shooting is, I suppose. He's been trying to persuade the diehards to surrender. If you'd care for a pick-me-up along the way, there are some small boats anchored just off shore, just north of the fort—some opportunistic merchants down from Wilmington with cases of blockade-run whiskey to dispose of. It did not take long for the law of supply and demand to start functioning again."

Thus it was that Rush Hawkins came to observe the capitulation of Fort Fisher with two outrageously overpriced, but extremely therapeutic, pints of Irish whiskey tucked into his overcoat pockets. He had bought three, but so horrific were the sights inside the fort that he had already drained one by the time he heard wild cheering and saw the sky erupt gloriously as all of Porter's ships fired off their rockets and flares to celebrate the news.

He never did find General Terry, but he did run into a captain from the 117th New York, who he knew slightly from civilian life and who in turn led Hawkins into an abandoned Rebel bombproof where a large number of weary but jubilant Federal officers had already set up a marathon poker game, one that had started long before the last Rebels surrendered and looked as though it might go on at least until sunrise. Through a happenstance chain of events, these gentlemen had been among the first customers to patronize the "bar boats" on the river. By pooling their money, they had, in fact, bought out most of one entrepreneur's stock. Hawkins was heartily welcomed once his identity became known. He had, it seemed, acquired considerable fame as "Powder Boat Hawkins."

The night passed most agreeably for Rush Hawkins. He was now reputed to be hero, his new patron was the most popular admiral in America, Ben Butler was no longer in a position to pull Hawkins' strings, a great though bloody victory had been won, and Hawkins had slept peacefully through the most dangerous hours of the struggle while still managing to acquire a very impressive set of bruises that caused everyone to *assume* he had been in the thick of the fighting. A permanent posting as Porter's army liaison officer was his for the asking, and his quarters aboard the flagship were certainly more commodious than a field tent. It now seemed entirely likely that he was going to ride out the closing months of this interminable war in a position of respect, comfort, and safety; ideally positioned, in fact, to begin laying the groundwork for a rewarding political career, financed—*Oh, this was the sweetest part!*—by the fortune he had made while managing Butler's profiteering operation at Shelborne's Point!

Life was good. And, through a marvelously strange and convoluted series of events, he was well situated to enjoy it to the fullest!

The poker marathon went on until everyone was too drunk, too broke, or too exhausted from the battle to shuffle the cards one more time. Hawkins poked around in some storage areas adjacent to the big bombproof, located a bag of corn meal that looked mighty comfortable, and prepared to get some shut-eye. First, though, he absolutely *had* to empty his bladder. Doing so indoors, of course, would have been unacceptably vulgar, so he struggled back into his coat, picked up a lantern, and went outside to find an appropriate spot. He was, by now, very drunk indeed, so he was extremely careful about where he put his feet—the parade ground was carpeted with things that were either hazardous or very unpleasant to step on, so he followed his lantern very gingerly, trying to avoid anything that looked sharp, unexploded, or recently alive. Ah, there was a likely-looking spot—reasonably private, out of the cold wind, the entrance to another storage chamber of some kind, even a convenient hook on which to hand his lantern. He unbuttoned his fly and unlimbered with a deep sigh of contentment.

Somewhere in the shadows nearby, he heard a faint scrabbling. Probably another rat. Damned place was probably crawling with them. His stream began to flow—a near ecstatic easing of pressure. But there was a second, rather less ratlike sound from behind his left shoulder, and there was something so stealthy about that rasp of . . . not a rodent's skittering little claws, certainly . . . more like a sneaky footstep dislodging a bit of rubble.

If Hawkins had not hung the lantern exactly where he did, he would never have seen the fleet shadow of an upraised arm, with a bayonet apparently growing from the fist on one end, poised to stab him between the shoulder blades.

"This is for all the dead Buffaloes!" growled a burly, obviously intoxicated man.

It was the man who had tried to shoot him on the dunes!

Having no other means of self-defense, Hawkins whirled around, just as his bladder went to full speed and aimed the urine jet at the face of his mysterious assailant.

He scored a direct hit on one bloodshot eye, and his piss must have burned like acid because the erstwhile assassin reeled back, cutting nothing but air with his bayonet, pawing at his face with his free hand. Hawkins, still spraying a fine golden arc, had enough presence of mind to knee the man squarely in the balls, and now, almost too late, Hawkins finally recognized this lunatic.

"Captain Elliott?"

"Big Red" Elliott regained his balance against the side of the passageway, fumbling to renew his grip on his bayonet, but still rubbing furiously at the eye Hawkins had hosed down.

"Sent us all off to die, you did! After all the service those men gave you, you left us all to die or rot in some stinkin' Rebel prison camp! I swore I'd track you down and pay you back, you son of a bitch, and now I will!"

Hawkins rejected the idea of trying to reason with this man. "I was forced to follow Butler's orders!" was an excuse Elliot was not going to buy. If he had managed to track Hawkins all the way from Shelborne's Point to this godforsaken place, he was not going to be reasoned with. He was going to kill Rush Hawkins. And he was big enough and tough enough to do it—the fact that both men were half-stupefied with drink only gave Elliott a better edge. Barroom brawls were one of "Big Red's" favorite forms of cheap entertainment. Hawkins did manage to kick the bayonet out of Elliott's hand while he was still trying to regain a killing grip on the haft, but Hawkins' primary weapon—the pressure in his bladder—was out of ammunition. Clearly, the best option was flight and loud calls for help, but Elliott was blocking the entrance. So Hawkins ran in the opposite direction, hoping to find an alternative exit, a hiding place, or something that he could use as a weapon.

Unfortunately, Elliott now had the lantern. And he had located the bayonet. Hawkins stumbled away from him as fast as he could move, pursued by wild gyrations of lantern light that were disorienting to both men. The passageway led downward—not a good sign. But one quick swath of illumination showed some discarded tools ahead, piled at the base of what appeared to be a very large stack of flour barrels. It was not until Hawkins lunged for an iron pry bar that another oscillation of lamplight revealed a placard in bright red letters: NO SMOKING!

"I got you now, you bastard! Cornered like a stinking rat, and you're gonna die like one, too!"

Hawkins grabbed the iron bar—Elliott came in for the kill—the circle of lantern light expanded—and Rush Hawkins' blood froze.

"You maniac! Don't you realize where we are?"

"I know where you're *gonna be* in about ten seconds!"

"We're inside the main-fucking-POWDER MAGAZINE!"

Elliott might or might not have understood what Hawkins was yelling at him, but if he did, it was too late to stop. Elliott was already in midair, aiming the bayonet straight at Hawkins' stomach. Hawkins' reaction was automatic. He swung the pry bar full force at Elliott's stabbing arm, and broke the bone. Happily, this disarmed his assailant. Unhappily, it also caused Elliott to lose his grip on the lantern, which shot through the air and shattered against the wall.

"Oh, shit . . ."

Fort Fisher's central magazine had been designed to withstand any external blow, and it had weathered more than two hundred direct hits during the battle. It was not designed to withstand a fire from a broken lantern. Although the man-made cavern contained only 27 tons of explosives, compared to the 250 tons crammed inside Ben Butler's powder boat, its mysterious accidental detonation, in the predawn hour of January 16th, fulfilled every one of Butler's predictions regarding "shock waves" and "massive structural damage." Exactly how many men died in that apocalyptic blast would always be a matter of speculation. The accepted, though probably conservative, estimate was "approximately 230."

Close enough.

On the night of January 16, 1865, the blockade runner *Banshee*, having completed its seventy-eighth successful voyage, under the command of Captain Standish Pendleton (R.N., on extended leave), arrived at the mouth of New Inlet, exchanged appropriate signals with the Mound Battery, and proceeded to anchor in Smithville for the usual customs inspection. Captain Pendleton broached a keg of excellent French brandy and proposed a toast.

"Gentlemen, the *Banshee* has done it again, and we are now safe in the waters of dear old Dixie! Hip-hip, huzzah!"

As the first drinks went down, there was a brusque knock on the cabin door.

"That will be the customs inspector, I presume. Have we enough to offer him a drink, too?"

"As many as he likes!"

"Very well, then. Come right in, my dear chap, and help yourself to the best-tasting bribe you've ever been offered!"

Instead of one of the usual sour-faced customs officials, however, the man who entered was a lieutenant in the U.S. Navy, in splendid dress uniform, flanked by two armed Marines. The young officer doffed his cap and said:

"Gentlemen, your ship is now a prize of war belonging to Admiral David Porter's fleet. I will be happy to consider your parole, if you give your words of honor that you will not resist, or attempt to scuttle this vessel."

"Perish the thought, sir! You have our pledge—we're as peaceful as lambs, and also, incidentally, subjects of the British Empire."

"Excellent. Now that that's out of the way, and as paroled foreign nationals, or whatever the devil your real status may be, you are at liberty to finish your repast."

"Would you and your men care to join us, Lieutenant?"

"Very tempting, Captain, but we are, as you can see, on duty."

"In point of maritime law, sir, as soon as you set foot inside this cabin, you will also be on British soil, and therefore no longer subject to naval regulations. There's roast duck, Irish potatoes, some first-rate Stilton cheese, a plate of Cadbury's tea biscuits, and plenty of four-star brandy. Able Seaman Tilletson, please bring in three more chairs for our guests."

The lieutenant looked at the Marines, the Marines shrugged, and all three entered, seduced by the smell of rich food and the hearty good manners of their new captives.

"Welcome to Great Britain, lads. Take a seat, pass your plates, then bring us up-to-date on the rather dramatic changes that have seemed to have occurred during our absence."

"I can't believe this is the old *Banshee,*" said the lieutenant, smacking his lips at the first kiss of brandy. "You have no idea how frustrating it was that we were never able to catch her. We did come close, though, didn't we? A time or two, at least."

"Oh, yes," sighed Pendleton. "More times than that, I can assure you."

"I guess she's just one of those naturally lucky ships."

"Indeed, sir, she led a charmed career. One knew, of course, that this day was bound to come, eventually . . . But by God, it was ripping good fun while it lasted!"

On the day after the fall of Fort Fisher was confirmed, Largo Landau drove to the Yellow House, where she was supposed to have lunch with Hobart-Hampton, newly back in town from a fairly long and very secretive mission abroad. She was excited and fearful and very anxious to hear what he would make of the news, and what he planned to do next, now that the door had at last been slammed on the runner trade.

Most of the inhabitants were already packing, and why not? Without the runner trade, Wilmington was going to seem awfully dull and provincial, and a British passport would enable them to hitch a ride on the first commercial ships that followed in the wake of the victorious Union navy. But already, the interior of the place had acquired a faint mustiness, from long-stored dust sheets brought out to shroud the furniture and perhaps dissuade some Yankee officer from stubbing out his cigars on an antique table. The young sailors greeted her warmly, but the carefree lilt was gone from their voices, and already the echoes of laughter and music were fading. This might one day be deemed a "haunted house," but the ghosts would be awfully jolly and flirtatious. Largo passed through familiar corridors and patted her hair and clothes when she came to Hobart-Hampden's suite. This promised to be a fairly emotional occasion, but exactly which emotions would predominate, she had not a clue. She rapped her private knock on his door, and it swung open as though one of those ghosts had already taken up residence.

The rooms were empty, the bed stripped and its mattress folded up. There was a hint of his cigars and scents lingering, but flat and unevocative. Even the floor had been swept clean. The wall safe, with its cipher books and piles of hundred-pound notes and sweet little bricks of hashish, stood open, cleaned out to the last tuppence.

But not quite. There was a small envelope propped up on the bottom shelf, and on it was her name. The wording would be elegant, wry, tenderly ironic—he would not let her down brutally; but all the same, she felt certain of the basic message: *Ta-ta, luv! Great fun while it lasted, wasn't it? I'm off for new adventures and, after giving the matter due consideration, I simply can't be weighed down by a female companion. I'm sure you'll understand. Someday, when we're old and limping, we'll get together in some nice London pub and have a lovely chat about the Good Old Days. Best of luck and all that—H.H.*

For a moment, she was tempted not to open it. Perhaps he meant no harm, but some of those words would sting, and the abruptness of his departure was already a bruise on her heart. *Have I already gone so soft that I cannot read his final message? If so, then I've been deluding myself all along.*

So she did take the envelope, which was not sealed, and read what he had penned, below the stuffy little heraldic crest of the earls of Buckinghamshire:

> *Dearest Largo,*
> *Please forgive my sudden and very rude-seeming departure. As you no doubt have surmised long ago, not all my time and energies during the past four years have been focused on the blockade-running business,*

although that was certainly the most enjoyable and profitable activity. Without going into unnecessary detail, it has suddenly been made known to me that certain rather rough gentlemen are on their way here from Washington, with the intention of asking me some questions that I am strictly enjoined, by various binding oaths and promises, from divulging. They will be very frustrated to learn that I have flown the coop, and it is not impossible that, when they discover the nature of our private relationship, they might also wish to interrogate you. To spare us all some unpleasantness, it is therefore best that I temporarily vanish. By showing them this letter, you can establish proof that you have no earthly idea where I have got to. This will render you of no possible interest to them. Make no effort to track me down—you already now it would be futile. I shan't communicate with you again for a long time. That may sound harsh, but it is the way of the world I've chosen to live in.

Think of me fondly from time to time, as I shall think of you.

H.H.

Well, that was certainly blunt enough . . . the arrogant bugger! But there was a second page, this one on plain paper, scrawled much more hastily.

Largo, my sweet—
That first, rather dastardly, letter was for "public consumption." If those government thugs do pester you, whip it out, start dabbing your eyes like the jilted lover, and curse me ripely for a cad. Just to be on the safe side, you had better either lock this note up or burn it, but this is the one written with my heart holding the pen. I really can't *tell you exactly where I'm going, or how, or when I can next communicate with you. Your ignorance is also your innocence, if you see my point.*

However, with regard to our sometimes ambiguous discussions of the future, I've given the matter a great deal of thought. I do not know if you and I are truly "in love," and I don't think it really matters all that much. We both know people who are "in love" and who are intermittently made wretched by that condition. What I do know is that I find a great delight in your company (in bed and out), and I think we can have some great fun together, for . . . for however long we still have fun together. I make no promises, nor ask any from you. We shall be two free spirits who've chosen each other in preference to many other possible partners. There will be times when I'll be away, doing things I cannot discuss, in places I cannot show you on a map. I can do a much better job, on those occasions, if I know my lady-faire is not moping and lonely and pining in my absence, but is off somewhere having a gay time and soaking up all the color and richness and incomparable variety the world has to offer!

You may very well change your mind, you know. I'm not such a great "catch," and at this point you are much richer than the somewhat shabby aristocrat you've shared your favors with! You can go anywhere, do anything, attach yourself to anyone you fancy, and take your leave whenever it suits you.

But if you'd still like to see something of the wild places and strange cultures, I can tell you where to find me anytime after October 1st. As outlandish as it sounds, Her Majesty has decided that my next official posting shall be as vice admiral of the Turkish navy! When you finally stop laughing and pick yourself up off the floor, all you need to do is head for Constantinople and inquire at the British embassy about the address of "Hobart Pasha." *Delicious, isn't it? HM government believes there's a war brewing between the Turks and the Russians (there usually is, after all, but this one promises to be an ideal testing ground for some of the weapons and ideas engendered by your own Civil War, so my experiences in the South have brought me up to speed!), and England is always looking for a way to discomfit the Tsar without actually crossing swords with him. The "Great Game" between the two empires is entering a new and interesting stage!*

So that is where I'll be, and I can promise you there is no more fascinating city in all the East. If, one day, I am told there is a young lady with incomparable dark eyes waiting in the anteroom, I shall assume it is you. If you think better of it, or find a more attractive prospect, I shall try to carry on, hiding my broken heart behind a stoic face. Or better still, distracting myself at one of the Grand Vizir's seraglios!

Until then, or later, or whenever . . .
A rain of hot kisses on your sweet little love bud!

After the presumed death of Bonaparte Reubens, the surviving Buffaloes went their separate ways. Mary Harper Sloane's indignant protestations had made the naval force from Wilmington slink away without landing a single Marine, so the white Buffs, and the handful of black ones who had chosen not to follow Reubens, decided to stay on as her employees, partly out of gratitude and partly because Mrs. Sloane's fascination with Reubens' grandiose socioeconomic schemes did not fade after he was gone. Many of his ideas would surely prove impractical, and most of them promised large returns only after heavy investment and a long period of nurturing, but Mary Harper was certain Reubens had been dead right about one thing: anybody who wanted to get rich (or in her case, stay rich) in the post-war South was going to have to forget about labor-intensive agriculture. The Sloanes had enough of a financial cushion to afford some failures, and Mary Harper did not think she or her husband were going to be content to cultivate rice for the rest of their lives, even if there was any chance of the market for it rebounding. There was something fundamentally stimulating about taking risks with your money—it focused your intelligence, it compelled you to make smart, educated guesses about the machines and processes of the future. Very discreetly, after throwing a lavish riverside pig-pickin' feast for some of the more cultured Union officers in occupied Wilmington, and richly entertaining them with stories of Matthew's daring exploits (the repulse of the Secret Service gang on the high seas was always a crowd-pleaser), Mary Harper began acquiring "distressed" real estate along the coast—often acting on tips sent her way by her new Yankee friends.

Jack Fairless stayed on until the news of Lee's surrender. Initially, Jack was motivated by loyalty to the memory of his black friend and mentor, and he effortlessly took on some of the responsibilities of Fitz-John Bright. Nobody gave him any lip; he still possessed that compelling aura of command and he was still, after all, a full colonel in the U.S. Army. He worked hard, he treated the children with respect and gradually won their affection. Sometime in February, he and Mary Harper began a discreet, superficial, but physically very gratifying sexual relationship, which lasted almost exactly as long as the war. Two days after the news of Appomattox, he packed his saddlebags, put on his uniform and insignia of rank, and quietly announced that it was time for him to move on.

"Won't be long now until your husband returns. You need some time to get ready for that, I reckon. And these business ventures you're movin' into, those are things I don't have the head for. Bonaparte passed along his vision, and you might actually do well at makin' it come true. But I've got no head for commerce, and frankly don't see any excitement in it."

"So, then, Jack, where will you go? What will you do? Pick up your medal and your pension and go to the mountains?"

He laughed. She would miss the bright smile and the remarkable tow-headed charm that was somehow all the more attractive if you knew he also could be a cold-blooded killer. She could easily picture him in a mountaineer's overalls, rocking on the porch of a cabin, picking tunes on a banjo, and dandling his grandchildren.

"Honestly, Mary, I don't see any excitement in *that,* either. I don't even know if my parents are alive or dead, and I had three younger brothers, two sisters, and thirty-odd cousins, and I'm damned if I can remember what a single one of 'em even looks like. I do know one thing, though, for sure: if times are going to be tough all over the South, they'll be ten times as tough in the mountains. I was raised pig-ignorant, didn't learn how to read until Bonaparte taught me, and I don't think I could fit back into that world. Sure, it's beautiful country up there, but there's a lot of beautiful country out West, too, where a man with some brains and some guts can make somethin' of himself."

"Yes—I can see you as a pioneer, or a gunslinger, or a cattle rancher."

"Can you see me as a general?"

"Ah. You're thinking about staying in the army, then? Make a career out of soldiering?"

"Why not? I'm already a colonel, and I ain't but twenty-six. Most men, all they want is to get out of the uniform as fast as they can. But this country's goin' to need a right-smart standing army, and a fella with my experience can start off where it would take a man twenty years to get to in peacetime. Hell, we'll be fighting Indians for the next thirty years, and *somebody* else after we finish peace-a-fyin' them! I might be chief of staff by the time the century rolls over. I've learned how to lead men in a fight and bring most of 'em back safe when it's over. The pay may not be much, and the food neither, but I've heard it said I cut a pretty sharp figure in a uniform."

She squeezed his hand affectionately. "That you do, Jack. And that's how I will remember you: sitting here in the morning sun, in a blue uniform that makes your eyes sparkle. Don't get yourself scalped, now."

"I will do my best." He rose and adjusted his hat.

"The children will be awake soon—don't you want to say good-bye to them?"

"You give them a hug for me. Best I ride on now, though. It's time they started looking forward to their father's return, and it might be best if they didn't chatter on too much about missing 'Uncle Jack.' Might give Captain Sloane the wrong idea."

"Captain Sloane, I promise you, will never know a thing, or say a word even if he suspects. Nor will I give him any cause to doubt my love for him, which is stronger than ever. Shake my hand, Jack, and go find your destiny as a soldier. It is strange, though, how this war has ruined so many men, but also set other men on a path they would never have considered, but which turned out to be the right one. I expect to read about you in the newspapers . . ."

"Anywhere but the obituaries!"

Five minutes later he rode past the kitchen window and down the carriage path. He did not look back, and she had not expected him to.

Matthew Sloane learned that the war was over on May 21, when the *Chickamauga*, which had sunk or captured twenty-three Union ships and caused a huge spike in the maritime insurance rates, was overhauled by a Brazilian frigate on its way to the South Atlantic, where Matthew planned to tear a big hole in the New England whaling industry. The Brazilian captain flashed the raider a simple message: "Confederacy surrendered in April. Go home to your wives and children!"

As the bold, swashbuckling captain of a commerce raider, Matthew Sloane had enjoyed the greatest adventure of his life, and at first it cost him a lot of effort to pretend to Mary Harper that he had been lonely, miserable, and pining for her during the whole episode. She knew he was lying, but she appreciated his thoughtfulness. And when she showed him the plans she had made for their future, and the calculated risks she had already taken with a sizeable portion of their fortune, he was startled by the way each venture interlocked with the others, by her coherent vision of the future, and very proud of her for making it absolutely impossible for him to go back into the business of planting and harvesting rice.

He had always hated the stuff, anyway.

Historical Postlude

Let us leave the purely fictional characters in freeze-frame status at this point. You are free to imagine the Sloanes as founding a commercial dynasty or going belly-up in the great depression of the 1870s. Or Largo voyaging to Constantinople. Or Jack Fairless becoming chief of staff during the Spanish-American War (or dying bravely in a fight with Apaches in New Mexico) . . .

But as for the characters based on real historical persons, I thought it might be interesting for you, Dear Reader, to learn what *did* happen to them after the war.

The real **Rush C. Hawkins** survived the war and realized his political ambitions on a local and state level. He was a curious man: never married, left no permanent record of distinction, but served honestly and well. He also enjoyed a long vigorous life, and was still in excellent health on the day he was run down by an automobile in 1920. He left his entire fortune to the A.S.P.C.A.

Although both **Chase Whiting** and **William Lamb** initially survived their wounds, and were treated with the greatest courtesy by their captors, Whiting suddenly took a turn for the worse in early March. He died on March 10, 1865—not from his wounds, which were well on their way to healing, but from a sudden and virulent attack of dysentery. This disease probably killed more soldiers than all the minié balls fired by both sides, and it was especially rampant in prison camps.

Before his death, Whiting painstakingly documented the failures and lassitudes of Braxton Bragg, and made sure his letters reached men in a position to add to the calumny heaped on Bragg's grizzled head.

Although Whiting's death took everyone by surprise, the prison chaplain recounted that he met his end calmly and with immense dignity (in his own mind, Chase Whiting had already "died" at Fort Fisher): "I have seldom stood by a deathbed where there was so gratifying a manifestation of humble Christian faith . . . He took Holy Communion at his own request, on the day before his death . . . it was a Christian's death, the death of a truthful, hopeful soul."

Colonel Lamb was treated honorably by his captors and was sent to a hospital at Fortress Monroe, not far from his hometown of Norfolk, Virginia. He was discharged, a free man, on May 1; promptly swore allegiance to the United States; then he went to Rhode Island with Daisy and recuperated fully (although a second operation was required to remove the minié ball in his hip), after seven months on crutches.

He was modestly successful in business, more so in politics. Three times elected to Mayor of Norfolk, he became a staunch Republican and served as a delegate to the Republican National Convention of 1888. It was there that he met, for the first time, **Martin Curtis.** These two aging warriors—who had tried so savagely to kill each other in 1865—became the closest of friends for the rest of their lives. Each was fond of introducing the other, to third parties, as "my friend, the enemy."

Daisy Lamb died of pneumonia in 1892; William died, of complications from a fall, in 1909, at the age of 72. Theirs was one of the great, enduring marriages—neither ever loved another, and cherished each other throughout all their days.

Astonishingly, **Braxton Bragg** remained high in Jefferson Davis's favor even after his inexcusable failures at Wilmington. Indeed, Bragg was among the Davis loyalists who escaped Richmond and fled south, until finally captured in Georgia.

After the war, Bragg moved to Galveston, Texas, and became chief engineer for the Gulf, Colorado and Santa Fe Railroad. Controversy followed him, of course, and he spent an inordinate amount of time writing lengthy and rather pathetic defenses of his actions at Wilmington. He blamed everyone and everything for the fall of Fort Fisher except his own monumental failures as a commander. Perhaps his most egregious slander against Lamb and his men was the assertion that the "entire garrison was drunk" and therefore incapable of resistance. There surely was some amount of contraband hooch inside the walls—as there has been in every military base since the beginning of recorded history—but not enough to stupefy 600 men!

Bragg died of a heart attack on September 27, 1876. For a general so vilified by his contemporaries, he had the last laugh: the largest army base in the eastern United States bears his name—Fort Bragg, in Fayetteville, North Carolina.

Ben Butler remained a cocky and unrepentant scoundrel to the end of his days. He returned to Congress, as a Radical Democrat, in 1866; tried *seven times* to get elected Governor of Massachusetts and finally made it in 1882. He never backed down from a fight, either verbal or political: when a heckler hung a bunch of spoons on a branch over the podium where Butler was giving a speech, Butler didn't miss a beat, but pointed to the silverware and gleefully said to the crowd: "My goodness, there's a few spoons I overlooked in New Orleans!"

He could afford to be eccentric, and was. In his later years, he purchased the championship yacht *America*, sailed her every chance he got, and after failing in his one bid for the presidency (1884, as the candidate of the Anti-Monopoly Party, of all things!), he reentered the judicial life—always showing up in court wearing a strange broad-brimmed hat and carrying his lunch: a sandwich and a bottle of beer. He remained in excellent health until felled by a heart attack in 1893.

Spiteful, vicious to his enemies and sometimes treacherous to his friends, Butler somehow managed to charm even his worst enemies by openly playing the roles everyone attributed to him anyhow. In a speech the year before he died, he expressed the hope that he would be remembered as "the general who saved countless soldiers lives by *never commanding the Army of the Potomac!*"

One has to admire a rogue who can have the last laugh . . .

Augustus Hobart-Hampden did in fact become Vice Admiral of the Turkish Navy and was known as "Hobart Pasha." His blockade-running experience helped him arrange for several Turkish divisions to be equipped with new American Winchesters, during the Russo-Turkish War of 1877, which gave the Turks an enormous advantage over the Tsarist troops, who still carried muzzle loaders.

About the Author

William R. Trotter was born and raised in Charlotte, North Carolina and is a graduate of Davidson College. Since 1980, he has supported himself entirely by his freelance writing. In 1987, he became a Senior Writer for Imagine Media. His monthly column on war and strategy games, "The Desktop General (in *PC Gamer*), has run continuously for 13 years, and is read by approximately 1.2 million people, in 13 languages. Trotter's journalistic work has appeared in more than thirty magazines and newspapers—approximately 1,400 by-lined pieces.

Trotter's concept for *The Sands of Pride* and *The Fires of Pride* grew out of the research he did for his highly successful non-fiction trilogy *The Civil War in North Carolina* (John F. Blair, Publishers), which has been in print continuously for eleven years. One volume of that trilogy, *Bushwhackers!*, was cited by *Cold Mountain* author Charles Frazier as an inspiration for his own best-selling novel. Trotter's other books include *A Frozen Hell: The Russo-Finnish War of 1939-40* (winner of the 1992 Finlandia Foundation Arts and Letters Award), *Priest of Music: The Life of Dimitri Mitropoulos*, and three previous novels—*Honeysuckle*, *Winter Fire: A Novel of Music and War* (currently being developed into a motion picture), and *The Sands of Pride*. His short fiction, primarily in the fantasy and horror genres, has been widely praised, and two of his stories have been nominated for the prestigious Bram Stoker Award.

Trotter lives in Greensboro, N.C., with his wife, fantasy writer Elizabeth A. Lustig, and their three sons. When not busy writing or parenting, he spends lots of time trying to figure out how to organize and store his 7,000-piece classical music collection.